TEMERAIRE:
THE THRONE OF JADE

NAOMI NOVIK

Temeraire: The Throne of Jade

BCA

This edition published 2006
by BCA
by arrangement with *Voyager*
An imprint of HarperCollins*Publishers*

CN 145200

Published by *Voyager* 2006

Typeset in Sabon by
Palimpsest Book Production Limited,
Polmont, Stirlingshire

Printed and bound in Great Britain by
Mackays of Chatham plc, Chatham, Kent

I

Chapter One

The day was unseasonably warm for November, but in some misguided deference to the Chinese embassy, the fire in the Admiralty boardroom had been heaped excessively high, and Laurence was standing directly before it. He had dressed with especial care, in his best uniform, and all throughout the long and unbearable interview, the lining of his thick bottle-green broadcloth coat had been growing steadily more sodden with sweat.

Over the doorway, behind Lord Barham, the official indicator with its compass arrow showed the direction of the wind over the Channel: in the north-northeast today, fair for France; very likely even now some ships of the Channel fleet were standing in to have a look at Napoleon's harbours. His shoulders held at attention, Laurence fixed his eyes upon the broad metal disk and tried to keep himself distracted with such speculation; he did not trust himself to meet the cold, unfriendly gaze fixed upon him.

Barham stopped speaking and coughed again into his fist; the elaborate phrases he had prepared sat not at all in his sailor's mouth, and at the end of every awkward, halting line, he stopped and darted a look over at the Chinese with a nervous agitation that approached obsequiousness. It was not a very creditable performance, but under ordinary circumstances, Laurence would have felt a degree of sympathy for Barham's position: some sort of formal message had been anticipated, even perhaps an envoy, but no one had ever imagined that the Emperor of China would send his own brother halfway around the world.

Prince Yongxing could, with a word, set their two nations at war; and there was besides something inherently awful in his presence: the impervious silence with which he met Barham's every remark; the overwhelming splendour of his dark yellow robes, embroidered thickly with dragons; the slow and relentless tapping of his long, jewel-encrusted fingernail against the arm of his chair. He did not even look at Barham: he only stared directly across the table at Laurence, grim and thin-lipped.

His retinue was so large they filled the boardroom to the corners, a dozen guards all sweltering and dazed in their quilted armour and as many servants besides, most with nothing to do, only attendants of one sort or another, all of them standing along the far wall of the room and trying to stir the air with broad-panelled fans. One man, evidently a translator, stood behind the prince, murmuring when Yongxing lifted a hand, generally after one of Barham's more involved periods.

Two other official envoys sat to Yongxing's either side. These men had been presented to Laurence only perfunctorily, and they had neither of them said a word, though the younger, called Sun Kai, had been watching all the proceedings, impassively, and following the translator's words with quiet attention. The elder, a big, round-bellied man with a tufted grey beard, had gradually been overcome by the heat: his head had sunk forward onto his chest, mouth half-open for air, and his hand was barely even moving his fan towards his face. They were robed in dark blue silk, almost as elaborately as the prince himself, and together they made an imposing façade: certainly no such embassy had ever been seen in the West.

A far more practised diplomat than Barham might have been pardoned for succumbing to some degree of servility, but Laurence was scarcely in any mood to be forgiving; though he was nearly more furious with himself, at having hoped for anything better. He had come expecting to plead his case, and privately in his heart he had even imagined a reprieve; instead he had been scolded in terms he would have scrupled to use to a raw lieutenant, and all in front of a foreign prince and his retinue, assembled like a tribunal to hear his crimes. Still he held his tongue as long as he could manage, but when Barham at last came about to saying, with an air of great condescension, 'Naturally, Captain, we have it in mind that you shall be put to another hatchling, afterwards,' Laurence had reached his limit.

'No, sir,' he said, breaking in. 'I am sorry, but no: I will not do it, and as for another post, I must beg to be excused.'

Sitting beside Barham, Admiral Powys of the Aerial Corps had remained quite silent through the course of the meeting; now he only shook his head, without any appearance of surprise, and folded his hands together over his ample belly. Barham gave him a furious look and said to Laurence, 'Perhaps I am not clear, Captain; this is not a request. You have been given your orders, you will carry them out.'

'I will be hanged first,' Laurence said flatly, past caring that he was speaking in such terms to the First Lord of the Admiralty: the death of his career if he had still been a naval officer, and it could scarcely do him any good even as an aviator. Yet if they meant to send Temeraire away, back to China, his career as an aviator was finished: he would never accept a position with any other dragon. None other would ever compare, to Laurence's mind, and he would not subject a hatchling to being second-best when there were men in the Corps lined up six-deep for the chance.

Yongxing did not say anything, but his lips tightened; his attendants shifted and murmured amongst themselves in their

5

own language. Laurence did not think he was imagining the hint of disdain in their tone, directed less at himself than at Barham; and the First Lord evidently shared the impression, his face growing mottled and choleric with the effort of preserving the appearance of calm. 'By God, Laurence; if you imagine you can stand here in the middle of Whitehall and mutiny, you are wrong; I think perhaps you are forgetting that your first duty is to your country and your King; not to this dragon of yours.'

'No, sir; it is you who are forgetting. It was for duty I put Temeraire into harness, sacrificing my naval rank, with no knowledge then that he was any breed truly out of the ordinary, much less a Celestial,' Laurence said. 'And for duty I took him through a difficult training and into a hard and dangerous service; for duty I have taken him into battle, and asked him to hazard his life and happiness. I will not answer such loyal service with lies and deceit.'

'Enough noise, there,' Barham said. 'Anyone would think you were being asked to hand over your firstborn. I am sorry if you have made such a pet of the creature you cannot bear to lose him—'

'Temeraire is neither my pet nor my property, sir,' Laurence snapped. 'He has served England and the King as much as I have, or you yourself, and now, because he does not choose to go back to China, you stand there and ask me to lie to him. I cannot imagine what claim to honour I should have if I agreed to it. Indeed,' he added, unable to restrain himself, 'I wonder that you should even have made the proposal; I wonder at it greatly.'

'Oh, your soul to the devil, Laurence,' Barham said, losing his last veneer of formality; he had been a serving sea-officer for years before joining the Government, and he was still very little a politician when his temper was up. 'He is a Chinese dragon, it stands to reason he will like China better; in any case, he belongs to them, and there is an end to it. The name of thief is a very unpleasant one, and His Majesty's Government does not propose to invite it.'

'I know how I am to take that, I suppose.' If Laurence had not already been half-broiled, he would have flushed. 'And I utterly reject the accusation, sir. These gentlemen do not deny they had given the egg to France; we seized it from a French man-of-war; the ship and the egg were condemned as lawful prize out of hand in the Admiralty courts, as you very well know. By no possible understanding does Temeraire belong to them; if they were so anxious about letting a Celestial out of their hands, they ought not have given him away in the shell.'

Yongxing snorted and broke into their shouting-match. '*That* is correct,' he said; his English was thickly-accented, formal and slow, but the measured cadences only lent all the more effect to his words. 'From the first it was folly to let the second-born egg of Lung Tien Qian pass over sea. *That*, no one can now dispute.'

It silenced them both, and for a moment no one spoke, save the translator quietly rendering Yongxing's words for the rest of the Chinese. Then Sun Kai unexpectedly said something in their tongue which made Yongxing look around at him sharply. Sun kept his head inclined deferentially, and did not look up, but still it was the first suggestion Laurence had seen that their embassy might perhaps not speak with a single voice. But Yongxing snapped a reply, in a tone which did not allow of any further comment, and Sun did not venture to make one. Satisfied that he had quelled his subordinate, Yongxing turned back to them and added, 'Yet regardless of the evil chance that brought him into your hands, Lung Tien Xiang was meant to go to the French Emperor, not to be made beast of burden for a common soldier.'

Laurence stiffened; *common soldier* rankled, and for the first time he turned to look directly at the prince, meeting that cold, contemptuous gaze with an equally steady one. 'We are at war with France, sir; if you choose to ally yourself with our enemies and send them material assistance, you can hardly complain when we take it in fair fight.'

'Nonsense!' Barham broke in, at once and loudly. 'China is by no means an ally of France, by no means at all; we certainly do not view China as a French ally. You are not here to speak to His Imperial Highness, Laurence; control yourself,' he added, in a savage undertone.

But Yongxing ignored the attempt at interruption. 'And now you make piracy your defence?' he said, contemptuous. 'We do not concern ourselves with the customs of barbaric nations. How merchants and thieves agree to pillage one another is not of interest to the Celestial Throne, except when they choose to insult the Emperor as you have.'

'No, Your Highness, no such thing, not in the least,' Barham said hurriedly, even while he looked pure venom at Laurence. 'His Majesty and his Government have nothing but the deepest affection for the Emperor; no insult would ever willingly be offered, I assure you. If we had only known of the extraordinary nature of the egg, of your objections, this situation would never have arisen—'

'Now, however, you are well aware,' Yongxing said, 'and the insult remains: Lung Tien Xiang is still in harness, treated little better than a horse, expected to carry burdens and exposed to all the brutalities of war, and all this, with a mere captain as his companion. Better had his egg sunk to the bottom of the ocean!'

Appalled, Laurence was glad to see this callousness left Barham and Powys as staring and speechless as himself. Even among Yongxing's own retinue, the translator flinched, shifting uneasily, and for once did not translate the prince's words back into Chinese.

'Sir, I assure you, since we learned of your objections, he has not been under harness at all, not a stitch of it,' Barham said, recovering. 'We have been at the greatest of pains to see to Temeraire's – that is, to Lung Tien Xiang's – comfort, and to make redress for any inadequacy in his treatment. He is no longer assigned to Captain Laurence, that I can assure you: they have not spoken these last two weeks.'

The reminder was a bitter one, and Laurence felt what little remained of his temper fraying away. 'If either of you had any real concern for his comfort, you would consult his feelings, not your own desires,' he said, his voice rising, a voice that had been trained to bellow orders through a gale. 'You complain of having him under harness, and in the same breath ask me to trick him into chains, so you might drag him away against his will. I will not do it; I will never do it, and be damned to you all.'

Judging by his expression, Barham would have been glad to have Laurence himself dragged away in chains: eyes almost bulging, hands flat on the table, on the verge of rising; for the first time, Admiral Powys spoke, breaking in, and fore-stalled him. 'Enough, Laurence, hold your tongue. Barham, nothing further can be served by keeping him. Out, Laurence; out at once: you are dismissed.'

The long habit of obedience held: Laurence flung himself out of the room. The intervention likely saved him from an arrest for insubordination, but he went with no sense of grat-itude; a thousand things were pent up in his throat, and even as the door swung heavily shut behind him, he turned back. But the Marines stationed to either side were gazing at him with thoughtlessly rude interest, as if he were a curiosity exhibited for their entertainment. Under their open, inquisi-tive looks he mastered his temper a little, and turned away before he could betray himself more badly.

Barham's words were swallowed by the heavy wood, but the inarticulate rumble of his still-raised voice followed Laurence down the corridor. He felt almost drunk with anger, his breath coming in short abrupt spurts and his vision obscured, not by tears, not at all by tears, except of rage. The

9

antechamber of the Admiralty was full of sea-officers, clerks, political officials, even a green-coated aviator rushing through with dispatches. Laurence shouldered his way roughly to the doors, his shaking hands thrust deep into his coat pockets to conceal them from view.

He struck out into the crashing din of late afternoon London, Whitehall full of workingmen going home for their suppers, and the bawling of the hackney drivers and chair-men over all, crying, 'Make a lane, there,' through the crowds. His feelings were as disordered as his surroundings, and he was only navigating the street by instinct; he had to be called three times before he recognized his own name.

He turned only reluctantly: he had no desire to be forced to return a civil word or gesture from a former colleague. But with a measure of relief he saw it was Captain Roland, not an ignorant acquaintance. He was surprised to see her; very surprised, for her dragon, Excidium, was a formation-leader at the Dover covert. She could not easily have been spared from her duties, and in any case she could not come to the Admiralty openly, being a female officer, one of those whose existence was made necessary by the insistence of Longwings on female captains. The secret was but barely known outside the ranks of the aviators, and jealously kept against certain public disapproval; Laurence himself had found it difficult to accept the notion, at first, but he had now grown so used to the idea that now Roland looked very odd to him out of uniform: she had put on skirts and a heavy cloak by way of concealment, neither of which suited her.

'I have been puffing after you for the last five minutes,' she said, taking his arm as she reached him. 'I was wandering about that great cavern of a building, waiting for you to come out, and then you went straight past me in such a ferocious hurry I could scarcely catch you. These clothes are a damned nuisance; I hope you appreciate the trouble I am taking for you, Laurence. But never mind,' she said, her voice gentling.

'I can see from your face that it did not go well: let us go and have some dinner, and you shall tell me everything.'

'Thank you, Jane; I am glad to see you,' he said, and let her turn him in the direction of her inn, though he did not think he could swallow. 'How do you come to be here, though? Surely there is nothing wrong with Excidium?'

'Nothing in the least, unless he has given himself indigestion,' she said. 'No; but Lily and Captain Harcourt are coming along splendidly, and so Lenton was able to assign them a double patrol and give me a few days of liberty. Excidium took it as excuse to eat three fat cows at once, the wretched greedy thing; he barely cracked an eyelid when I proposed my leaving him with Sanders – that is my new first lieutenant – and coming to bear you company. So I put together a street-going rig and came up with the courier. Oh hell: wait a minute, will you?' She stopped and kicked vigorously, shaking her skirts loose: they were too long, and had caught on her heels.

He held her by the elbow so she did not topple over, and afterwards they continued on through the London streets at a slower pace. Roland's mannish stride and her scarred face drew enough rude stares that Laurence began to glare at the passers-by who looked too long, though she herself paid them no mind; she noticed his behaviour, however, and said, 'You are ferocious out of temper; do not frighten those poor girls. What did those fellows say to you at the Admiralty?'

'You have heard, I suppose, that an embassy has come from China; they mean to take Temeraire back with them, and Government does not care to object. But evidently he will have none of it: tells them all to go hang themselves, though they have been at him for weeks now to go,' Laurence said. As he spoke, a sharp sensation of pain, like a constriction just under his breastbone, made itself felt. He could picture quite clearly Temeraire kept nearly all alone in the old, worn-down London covert, scarcely used in the last hundred years, with neither Laurence nor his crew to keep him company, no one to read to him, and of his own kind, only a few small courier-beasts flying through on dispatch service.

'Of course he will not go,' Roland said. 'I cannot believe they imagined they could persuade him to leave you. Surely they ought to know better; I have always heard the Chinese cried up as the very pinnacle of dragon-handlers.'

'Their prince has made no secret he thinks very little of me; likely they expected Temeraire to share much the same opinion, and to be pleased to go back,' Laurence said. 'In any case, they grow tired of trying to persuade him; so that villain Barham ordered I should lie to him and say we were assigned to Gibraltar, all to get him aboard a transport and out to sea, too far for him to fly back to land, before he knew what they were about.'

'Oh, infamous.' Her hand tightened almost painfully on his arm. 'Did Powys have nothing to say to it? I cannot believe he let them suggest such a thing to you; one cannot expect a naval officer to understand these things, but Powys should have explained matters to him.'

'I dare say he can do nothing; he is only a serving officer, and Barham is appointed by the Ministry,' Laurence said. 'Powys at least saved me from putting my neck in a noose: I was too angry to control myself, and he sent me away.'

They had reached the Strand; the increase in traffic made conversation difficult, and they had to pay attention to avoid being splashed by the questionable grey slush heaped in the gutters, thrown up onto the pavement by the lumbering carts and hackney wheels. His anger ebbing away, Laurence was increasingly low in his spirits.

From the moment of separation, he had consoled himself with the daily expectation that it would soon end: the Chinese would soon see Temeraire did not wish to go, or the Admiralty would give up the attempt to placate them. It had seemed a cruel sentence even so; they had not been parted a full day's time in the months since Temeraire's hatching, and Laurence had scarcely known what to do with himself, or how to fill the hours. But even the two long weeks were nothing to this, the dreadful certainty that he had ruined all his chances. The Chinese would not yield, and the Ministry would find some way of getting Temeraire sent off to China in the end: they plainly had no objection to telling him a pack of lies for the purpose. Likely enough Barham would never consent to his seeing Temeraire now even for a last farewell.

Laurence had not even allowed himself to consider what his own life might be with Temeraire gone. Another dragon was of course an impossibility, and the Navy would not have him back now. He supposed he could take on a ship in the merchant fleet, or a privateer; but he did not think he would have the heart for it, and he had done well enough out of prize-money to live on. He could even marry and set up as a country gentleman; but that prospect, once so idyllic in his imagination, now seemed drab and colourless.

Worse yet, he could hardly look for sympathy: all his former acquaintance would call it a lucky escape, his family would rejoice, and the world would think nothing of his loss. By any measure, there was something ridiculous in his being so adrift: he had become an aviator quite unwillingly, only from the strongest sense of duty, and less than a year had passed since his change in station; yet already he could hardly consider the possibility. Only another aviator, perhaps indeed only another captain, would truly be able to understand his sentiments, and with Temeraire gone, he would be as severed from their company as aviators themselves were from the rest of the world.

The front room at the Crown and Anchor was not quiet, though it was still early for dinner by town standards. The place was not a fashionable establishment, nor even genteel, its custom mostly consisting of country-men used to a more reasonable hour for their food and drink. It was not the sort of place a respectable woman would have come, nor indeed the kind of place Laurence himself would have ever voluntarily frequented in earlier days. Roland drew some insolent stares, others only curious, but no one attempted any greater liberty: Laurence made an imposing figure beside her with his broad shoulders and his dress sword slung at his hip.

Roland led Laurence up to her rooms, sat him in an ugly armchair and gave him a glass of wine. He drank deeply, hiding behind the bowl of the glass from her sympathetic look: he was afraid he might easily be unmanned. 'You must be faint with hunger, Laurence,' she said. 'That is half the trouble.' She rang for the maid; shortly a couple of manservants climbed up with a very good sort of plain single-course dinner: a roasted fowl, with greens and beef gravy sauce; some small cheese-cakes made with jam, calf's feet pie, a dish of red cabbage stewed, and a small biscuit pudding for relish. She had them place all the food on the table at once, rather than going through removes, and sent them away.

Laurence did not think he would eat, but once the food was before him he found he was hungry after all. He had been eating very indifferently, thanks to irregular hours and the low table of his cheap boarding-house, chosen for its proximity to the covert where Temeraire was kept; now he ate steadily, Roland carrying the conversation nearly alone and distracting him with service gossip and trivialities.

'I was sorry to lose Lloyd, of course – they mean to put him to the Anglewing egg that is hardening at Kinloch Laggan,' she said, speaking of her first lieutenant.

'I think I saw it there,' Laurence said, rousing a little and lifting his head from his plate. 'Obversaria's egg?'

'Yes, and we have great hopes of the issue,' she said. 'Lloyd was over the moon, of course, and I am very happy for him; still, it is no easy thing to break in a new premier after five years, with all the crew and Excidium himself murmuring about how Lloyd used to do things. But Sanders is a good-hearted, dependable fellow; they sent him up from Gibraltar, after Granby refused the post.'

'What? Refused it?' Laurence cried, in great dismay: Granby was his own first lieutenant. 'Not for my sake, I hope.'

'Oh Lord, you did not know?' Roland said, in equal dismay. 'Granby spoke to me very pretty; said he was obliged, but he did not choose to shift his position. I was quite sure he had consulted you about the matter; I thought perhaps you had been given some reason to hope.'

'No,' Laurence said, very low. 'He is more likely to end up with no position at all; I am very sorry to hear he should have passed up so good a place.' The refusal could have done Granby no good with the Corps; a man who had turned down one offer could not soon expect another, and Laurence would shortly have no power at all to help him along.

'Well, I am damned sorry to have given you any more cause for concern,' Roland said, after a moment. 'Admiral Lenton has not broken up your crew, you know, for the most part: only gave a few fellows to Berkley out of desperation, he being so short-handed now. We were all so sure that Maximus had reached his final growth; shortly after you were called here, he began to prove us wrong, and so far he has put on fifteen feet in length.' She added this last in an attempt to recover the lighter tone of the conversation, but it was impossible: Laurence found that his stomach had closed, and he set down his knife and fork with the plate still half-full.

Roland drew the curtains; it was already growing dark outside. 'Do you care for a concert?'

'I am happy to accompany you,' he said, mechanically, and she shook her head.

'No, never mind; I see it will not do. Come to bed then, my dear fellow; there is no sense in sitting about and moping.'

They put out the candles and lay down together. 'I have not the least notion what to do,' he said quietly: the cover of

15

dark made the confession a little easier. 'I called Barham a villain, and I cannot forgive him asking me to lie; very ungentlemanlike. But he is not a scrub; he would not be at such shifts if he had any other choice.'

'It makes me quite ill to hear about him bowing and scraping to this foreign prince.' Roland propped herself upon her elbow on the pillows. 'I was in Canton harbour once, as a mid, on a transport coming back the long way from India; those junks of theirs do not look like they could stand a mild shower, much less a gale. They cannot fly their dragons across the ocean without a pause, even if they cared to go to war with us.'

'I thought as much myself, when I first heard,' Laurence said. 'But they do not need to fly across the ocean to end the China trade, and wreck our shipping to India also, if they liked; besides they share a border with Russia. It would mean the end of the coalition against Bonaparte, if the Tsar were attacked on his eastern borders.'

'I do not see the Russians have done us very much good so far, in the war, and money is a low pitiful excuse for behaving like a bounder, in a man or a nation,' Roland said. 'The State has been short of funds before, and somehow we have scraped by and still blacked Bonaparte's eye for him. In any case, I cannot forgive them for keeping you from Temeraire. Barham still has not let you see him at all, I suppose?'

'No, not for two weeks now. There is a decent fellow at the covert who has taken him messages for me, and lets me know that he is eating, but I cannot ask him to let me in: it would be a court-martial for us both. Though for my own part, I hardly know if I would let it stop me now.'

He could scarcely have imagined even saying such a thing, a year ago; he did not like to think it now, but honesty put the words into his mouth. Roland did not cry out against it, but then she was an aviator herself. She reached out to stroke his cheek, and drew him down to such comfort as might be found in her arms.

Laurence started up in the dark room, sleep broken: Roland was already out of bed. A yawning housemaid was standing in the doorway, holding up a candle, the yellow light spilling into the room. She handed Roland a sealed dispatch and stayed there, staring with open prurient interest at Laurence; he felt a guilty flush rise in his cheeks, and glanced down to be sure he was quite covered beneath the bedclothes.

Roland had already cracked the seal; now she reached out and took the candlestick straight out of the girl's hand. 'There's for you; go along now,' she said, giving the maid a shilling; she shut the door in the girl's face without further ceremony. 'Laurence, I must go at once,' she said, coming to the bed to light the other candles, speaking very low. 'This is word from Dover: a French convoy is making a run for Le Havre under dragon guard. The Channel fleet is going after them, but there is a Flamme-de-Gloire present, and the fleet cannot engage without aerial support.'

'How many ships in the French convoy, does it say?' He was already out of the bed and pulling on his breeches: a fire-breather was nearly the worst danger a ship could face, desperately risky even with a good deal of support from the air.

'Thirty or more, packed no doubt to the gills with war materiel,' she said, whipping her hair into a tight braid. 'Do you see my coat over there?'

Outside the window, the sky was thinning to a paler blue; soon the candles would be unnecessary. Laurence found the coat and helped her into it; some part of his thoughts already occupied in calculating the likely strength of the merchant ships, what proportion of the fleet would be detached to go after them, how many might yet slip through to safe harbour: the guns at Le Havre were nasty. If the wind had not shifted since yesterday, they had favourable conditions for their run.

Thirty ships' worth of iron, copper, quicksilver, gunpowder; Bonaparte might no longer be a danger at sea after Trafalgar, but on land he was still master of Europe, and such a haul might easily meet his supply needs for months.

'And just give me that cloak, will you?' Roland asked, breaking into his train of thought. The voluminous folds concealed her male dress, and she pulled the hood up over her head. 'There, that will do.'

'Hold a moment; I am coming with you,' Laurence said, struggling into his own coat. 'I hope I can be some use. If Berkley is short-handed on Maximus, I can at least pull on a strap or help shove off boarders. Leave the luggage and ring for the maid: we will have them send the rest of your things over to my boarding-house.'

They hurried through the streets, still mostly empty: night-soil men rattling past with their fetid carts, day labourers beginning on their rounds to look for work, maids in their clinking pattens going to market, and the herds of animals with their lowing breath white in the air. A clammy, bitter fog had descended in the night, like a prickling of ice on the skin. At least the absence of crowds meant Roland did not have to pay much mind to her cloak, and they could go at something approaching a run.

The London covert was situated not far from the Admiralty offices, along the western side of the Thames; despite the location, so eminently convenient, the buildings immediately around it were shabby, in disrepair: where those lived who could afford nothing farther away from dragons; some of the houses even abandoned, except for a few skinny children who peered out suspiciously at the sound of strangers passing. A sludge of liquid refuse ran along the gutters of the streets; as Laurence and Roland ran, their boots broke the thin skim of ice on top, letting the stench up to follow them.

Here the streets were truly empty; but even so as they hurried a heavy cart sprang almost as if by malicious intent from the fog: Roland hauled Laurence aside and up onto the pavement just quick enough he was not clipped and dragged under the wheels. The drover never even paused in his careening progress, but vanished around the next corner without apology.

Laurence gazed down at his best dress trousers in dismay: spattered black with filth. 'Never mind,' Roland said consolingly. 'No one will mind in the air, and maybe it will brush off.' This was more optimism than he could muster, but there was certainly no time to do anything about them now, and so they resumed their hurried progress.

The covert gates stood out shining against the dingy streets and the equally dingy morning: ironwork freshly painted black, with polished brass locks and unexpectedly, a pair of young Marines in their red uniforms were lounging nearby, muskets leaned against the wall. The gatekeeper on duty touched his hat to Roland as he came to let them in, while the Marines squinted at her in some confusion: her cloak was well back off her shoulders for the moment, revealing both her triple gold bars and her by no means shabby endowment.

Laurence stepped into their line of sight to block their view of her, frowning. 'Thank you, Patson; the Dover courier?' he said to the gatekeeper, as soon as they had come through.

'Believe he's waiting for you, sir,' Patson said, jerking his thumb over his shoulder as he pulled the gates to again. 'Just at the first clearing, if you please. Don't you worry about them none,' he added, scowling at the Marines, who looked properly abashed: they were barely more than boys, and Patson was a big man, a former armourer, made only more awful by an eyepatch and the seared red skin about it. 'I'll learn them properly, never fret.'

'Thank you, Patson; carry on,' Roland said, and on they went. 'Whatever are those lobsters doing here? Not officers, at least, we may be grateful. I still recall twelve years ago, some Army officer found out Captain St. Germain when she got wounded at Toulon; he made a wretched to-do over the whole thing, and it nearly got into the papers: idiotic affair.'

There was only a narrow border of trees and buildings around the perimeter of the covert to shield it from the air and noise of the city; they almost at once reached the first clearing, a small space barely large enough for a middling-sized dragon to spread its wings. The courier was indeed waiting: a young Winchester, her purple wings not yet quite darkened to adult colour, but fully harnessed and fidgeting to be off.

'Why, Hollin,' Laurence said, shaking the captain's hand gladly: it was a great pleasure to see his former ground-crew master again, now in an officer's coat. 'Is this your dragon?'

'Yes, sir, indeed it is; this is Elsie,' Hollin said, beaming at him. 'Elsie, this is Captain Laurence: which I have told you about him, he helped me to you.'

The Winchester turned her head around and looked at Laurence with bright, interested eyes: not yet three months out of the shell, she was still small, even for her breed, but her hide was almost glossy-clean, and she looked very well-tended indeed. 'So you are Temeraire's captain? Thank you; I like my Hollin very much,' she said, in a light chirping voice, and gave Hollin a nudge with enough affection in it to nearly knock him over.

'I am happy to have been of service, and to make your acquaintance,' Laurence said, mustering some enthusiasm, although not without an internal pang at the reminder. Temeraire was here, not five hundred yards distant, and he could not so much as exchange a greeting with him. He did look, but buildings stood in the line of his sight: no glimpse of black hide was to be seen.

Roland asked Hollin, 'Is everything ready? We must be off at once.'

'Yes, sir, indeed; we are only waiting for the dispatches,' Hollin said. 'Five minutes perhaps, if you should care to stretch your legs before the flight.'

The temptation was very strong; Laurence swallowed hard. But discipline held: openly refusing a dishonourable order was one thing, sneaking about to disobey a merely unpleasant one something else; and to do so now might well reflect badly on Hollin, and Roland herself. 'I will just step into the barracks here, and speak to Jervis,' he said instead, and went to find the man who was overseeing Temeraire's care.

Jervis was an older man, the better part of both his left limbs lost to a wicked raking stroke across the side of the dragon on which he had served as harness-master; on recovering against all reasonable expectations, he had been assigned to the slow duty of the London covert, so rarely used. He had an odd, lopsided appearance with his wooden leg and metal hook on one side, and he had grown a little lazy and contrary with his idleness, but Laurence had provided him with a willing ear often enough to now find a warm welcome.

'Would you be so kind as to take a word for me?' Laurence asked, after he had refused a cup of tea. 'I am going to Dover to see if I can be of use; I should not like Temeraire to fret at my silence.'

'That I will, and read it to him; he will need it, poor fellow,' Jervis said, stumping over to fetch his inkwell and pen one-handed; Laurence turned over a scrap of paper to write the note. 'That fat fellow from the Admiralty came over again not half an hour ago with a full passel of Marines and those fancy Chinamen, and there they are still, prating away at the dear. If they don't go soon, I shan't answer for his taking any food today, so I won't. Ugly sea-going bugger; I don't know what he is about, thinking he knows aught about dragons; that is, begging your pardon, sir,' Jervis added hastily.

Laurence found his hand shook over the paper, so he spattered his first few lines and the table. He answered somehow, meaninglessly, and struggled to continue the note; words would not come. He stood there locked in mid-sentence, until suddenly he was nearly thrown off his feet, ink spreading across the floor as the table fell over; outside a terrible shattering noise, like the worst violence of a storm, a full North Sea winter's gale.

The pen was still ludicrously in his hand; he dropped it and flung open the door, Jervis stumbling out behind him. The echoes still hung in the air, and Elsie was sitting up on her hind legs, wings half-opening and closing in anxiety while Hollin and Roland tried to reassure her; the few other dragons at the covert had their heads up as well, peering over the trees and hissing in alarm.

'Laurence,' Roland called, but he ignored her: he was already halfway down the path, running, his hand unconsciously gone to the hilt of his sword. He came to the clearing and found his way barred by the collapsed ruins of a barracks building and several fallen trees.

For a thousand years before the Romans first tamed the Western dragon breeds, the Chinese had already been masters of the art. They prized beauty and intelligence more than martial prowess, and looked with a little superior disdain at the fire-breathers and acid-spitters valued so highly in the West; their aerial legions were so numerous they had no need of what they regarded as so much showy flash. But they did not scorn all such unusual gifts; and in the Celestials they had reached the pinnacle of their achievement: the union of all the other graces with the subtle and deadly power which the Chinese called the *divine wind*, the roar with a force greater than cannon-fire.

Laurence had seen the devastation the divine wind wrought only once before, at the battle of Dover, where Temeraire had used it against Napoleon's airborne transports to potent effect. But here the poor trees had suffered the impact at point-blank range: they lay like flung matchsticks, trunks burst into flinders. The whole rough structure of the barracks, too, had smashed to the ground, the coarse mortar crumbled away entirely and the bricks scattered and broken. A hurricane might have caused such wreckage, or an earthquake, and the once-poetic name seemed suddenly far more apt.

The escort of Marines were nearly all of them backed up against the undergrowth surrounding the clearing, faces white and blank with terror; Barham alone of them had stood his ground. The Chinese also had not retreated, but they were one and all prostrated upon the ground in formal genuflection, except for Prince Yongxing himself, who remained unflinching at their head.

The wreck of one tremendous oak lay penning them all against the edge of the clearing, dirt still clinging to its roots, and Temeraire stood behind it, one foreleg resting on the trunk and his sinuous length towering over them.

'You will not say such things to me,' he said, his head lowering towards Barham: his teeth were bared, and the spiked ruff around his head was raised up and trembling with anger. 'I do not believe you for an instant, and I will not hear such lies; Laurence would never take another dragon. If you have sent him away, I will go after him, and if you have hurt him—'

He began to gather his breath for another roar, his chest belling out like a sail in high wind, and this time the hapless men lay directly in his path.

'Temeraire,' Laurence called, scrambling ungracefully over the wreckage, sliding down the heap into the clearing in disregard of the splinters that caught at his clothing and skin. 'Temeraire, I am well, I am here—'

Temeraire's head had whipped around at the first word, and he at once took the two paces needed to bring him across the clearing. Laurence held still, his heart beating very quickly, not at all with fear: the forelegs with their terrible claws landed to either side of him, and the sleek length of Temeraire's body coiled protectively about him, the great scaled sides rising up around him like shining black walls and the angled head coming to rest by him.

23

He rested his hands on Temeraire's snout and for a moment laid his cheek against the soft muzzle; Temeraire made a low wordless murmur of unhappiness. 'Laurence, Laurence, do not leave me again.'

Laurence swallowed. 'My dear,' he said, and stopped; no answer was possible.

They stood with their heads together in silence, the rest of the world shut out: but only for a moment. 'Laurence,' Roland called from beyond the encircling coils: she sounded out of breath, and her voice was urgent. 'Temeraire, do move aside, there is a good fellow.' Temeraire lifted up his head and reluctantly uncurled himself a little so they could speak; but all the while he kept himself between Laurence and Barham's party.

Roland ducked under Temeraire's foreleg and joined Laurence. 'You had to go to Temeraire, of course, but it will look very bad to someone who does not understand dragons. For pity's sake do not let Barham push you into anything further: answer him as meek as mother-may-I, do anything he tells you.' She shook her head. 'By God, Laurence; I hate to leave you in such straits, but the dispatches have come, and minutes may make the difference here.'

'Of course you cannot stay,' he said. 'They are likely waiting for you at Dover even now to launch the attack; we will manage, never fear.'

'An attack? There is to be a battle?' Temeraire said, over-hearing; he flexed his talons and looked away to the east, as if he might see the formations rising into the air even from here.

'Go at once, and pray take care,' Laurence said hastily to Roland. 'Give my apologies to Hollin.'

She nodded. 'Try and stay easy in your mind. I will speak with Lenton even before we launch. The Corps will not sit still for this; bad enough to separate you, but now this outrageous pressure, stirring up all the dragons like this: it cannot

24

be allowed to continue, and no one can possibly hold you to blame.'

'Do not worry or wait another instant: the attack is more important,' he said, very heartily: counterfeit, as much as her assurances; they both knew that the situation was black. Laurence could not for a moment regret having gone to Temeraire's side, but he had openly disobeyed orders. No court-martial could find him innocent; there was Barham himself to lay the charges, and if questioned Laurence could hardly deny the act. He did not think they would hang him: this was not a battlefield offence, and the circumstances offered some excuse, but he would certainly have been dismissed the service if he had still been in the Navy. There was nothing to be done but face the consequences; he forced a smile, Roland gave his arm a quick squeeze, and she was gone.

The Chinese had risen and collected themselves, making a better show of it than the ragged Marines, who looked ready to bolt at any moment's notice. They all together were now picking their way over the fallen oak. The younger official, Sun Kai, more deftly scrambled over, and with one of the attendants offered a hand to the prince to help him down. Yongxing was hampered by his heavy embroidered gown, leaving trailers of bright silk like gaily coloured cobwebs upon the broken branches, but if he felt any of the same terror writ large on the faces of the British soldiers, it did not show in his face: he seemed unshaken.

Temeraire kept a savage, brooding eye upon them all. 'I am not going to sit here while everyone else goes and fights, no matter what those people want.'

Laurence stroked Temeraire's neck comfortingly. 'Do not let them upset you. Pray stay quite calm, my dear; losing our tempers will not improve matters.' Temeraire only snorted, and his eye remained fixed and glittering, the ruff still standing upright with all the points very stiff: in no mood to be soothed.

Himself quite ashen, Barham made no haste to approach

any closer to Temeraire, but Yongxing addressed him sharply, repeating demands both urgent and angry, judging by his gestures towards Temeraire; Sun Kai however stood apart, and regarded Laurence and Temeraire more thoughtfully. At last Barham came towards them scowling, evidently taking refuge from fear in anger; Laurence had seen it often enough in men on the eve of battle.

'This is the discipline of the Corps, I gather,' Barham began: petty and spiteful, since his life had very likely been saved by the disobedience. He himself seemed to perceive as much; he grew even angrier. 'Well, it will not stand with me, Laurence, not for an instant; I will see you broken for this. Sergeant, take him under arrest—'

The end of the sentence was inaudible; Barham was sinking, growing small, his shouting red mouth flashing open and shut like a gasping fish, the words becoming indistinct as the ground fell away beneath Laurence's feet. Temeraire's talons were carefully cupped around him and the great black wings were beating in broad sweeps, up, up, up through the dingy London air, soot dulling Temeraire's hide and speckling Laurence's hands.

Laurence settled himself in the cupped claws and rode in silence; the damage was done, and Laurence knew better than to ask Temeraire to return to the ground at once: there was a sense of true violence in the force behind his wing-strokes, rage barely checked. They were going very fast. He peered downward in some anxiety as they sped over the city walls: Temeraire was flying without harness or signals, and Laurence feared the guns might be turned on them. But the guns stayed silent: Temeraire was distinctive, with his hide and wings of unbroken black, save for the deep blue and pearlescent grey markings along the edges, and he had been recognized.

Or perhaps their passage was simply too swift for a response: they left the city behind them fifteen minutes after leaving the ground, and were soon beyond the range even of the long-barrelled pepper guns. Roads branched away through the countryside beneath them, dusted with snow, and the smell of the air already much cleaner. Temeraire paused and hovered for a moment, shook his head free of dust and sneezed loudly, jouncing Laurence about a little; but afterwards he flew on at a less frantic pace, and after another minute or two he curled his head down to speak. 'Are you well, Laurence? You are not uncomfortable?'

He sounded more anxious than the subject deserved. Laurence patted his foreleg where he could reach it. 'No, I am very well.'

'I am very sorry to have snatched you away so,' Temeraire said, some tension gone at the warmth in Laurence's voice. 'Pray do not be angry; I could not let that man take you.'

'No, I am not angry,' Laurence said; indeed, so far as his heart was concerned there was only a great, swelling joy to be once again aloft, to feel the living current of power running through Temeraire's body, even if his more rational part knew this state could not last. 'And I do not blame you for going, not in the least, but I am afraid we must turn back now.'

'No; I am not taking you back to that man,' Temeraire said obstinately, and Laurence understood with a sinking feeling that he had run up against Temeraire's protective instincts. 'He lied to me, and kept you away, and then he wanted to arrest you: he may count himself lucky I did not squash him.'

'My dear, we cannot just run wild,' Laurence said. 'We would be truly beyond the pale if we did such a thing; how do you imagine we would eat, except by theft? And we would be abandoning all our friends.'

'I am no more use to them in London, sitting in a covert,' Temeraire said, with perfect truth, and left Laurence at a loss for how to answer him. 'But I do not mean to run wild; although,' a little wistfully, 'to be sure, it would be pleasant to do as we liked, and I do not think anyone would miss a

27

few sheep here and there. But not while there is a battle to be fought.'

'Oh dear,' Laurence said, as he squinted towards the sun and realized their course was southeast, directly for their former covert at Dover. 'Temeraire, they cannot let us fight; Lenton will have to order me back, and if I disobey he will arrest me just as quick as Barham, I assure you.'

'I do not believe Obversaria's admiral will arrest you,' Temeraire said. 'She is very nice, and has always spoken to me kindly, even though she is so much older, and the flag-dragon. Besides, if he tries, Maximus and Lily are there, and they will help me; and if that man from London tries to come and take you away again, I will kill him,' he added, with an alarming degree of bloodthirsty eagerness.

Chapter Two

They landed in the Dover covert amid the clamour and bustle of preparation: the harness-masters bellowing orders to the ground crews, the clatter of buckles and the deeper metallic ringing of the bombs being handed up in sacks to the bell-men; riflemen loading their weapons, the sharp high-pitched shriek of whetstones grinding away on sword-edges. A dozen interested dragons had followed their progress, many calling out greetings to Temeraire as he made his descent. He called back, full of excitement, his spirits rising all the while Laurence felt his own sinking.

Temeraire brought them to earth in Obversaria's clearing; it was one of the largest in the covert, as befitted her standing as flag-dragon, though as an Anglewing she was only slightly more than middling in size, and there was easily room for Temeraire to join her. She was rigged out already, her crew boarding; Admiral Lenton himself was standing beside her in full riding gear, only waiting for his officers to be aboard: minutes away from going aloft.

'Well, and what have you done?' Lenton asked, before Laurence had even managed to unfold himself out of Temeraire's claw. 'Roland spoke to me, but she said she had told you to stay quiet; there is going to be the devil to pay for this.'

'Sir, I am very sorry to put you in so untenable a position,' Laurence said awkwardly, trying to think how he could explain Temeraire's refusal to return to London without seeming to make excuses for himself.

'No, it is my fault,' Temeraire added, ducking his head and trying to look ashamed, without much success; there was too distinct a gleam of satisfaction in his eye. 'I took Laurence away; that man was going to arrest him.'

He sounded plainly smug, and Obversaria abruptly leaned over and batted him on the side of the head, hard enough to make him wobble even though he was half again her size. He flinched and stared at her, with a surprised and wounded expression; she only snorted at him and said, 'You are too old to be flying with your eyes closed. Lenton, we are ready, I think.'

'Yes,' Lenton said, squinting up against the sun to examine her harness. 'I have no time to deal with you now, Laurence; this will have to wait.'

'Of course, sir; I beg your pardon,' Laurence said quietly. 'Pray do not let us delay you; with your permission, we will stay in Temeraire's clearing until you return.' Even cowed by Obversaria's reproof, Temeraire made a small noise of protest at this.

'No, no; don't speak like a groundling,' Lenton said impatiently. 'A young male like that will not stay behind when he sees his formation go, not uninjured. The same bloody mistake this fellow Barham and all the others at the Admiralty make, every time a new one is shuffled in by Government. If we ever manage to get it into their heads that dragons are not brute beasts, they start to imagine that they are just like men, and can be put under regular military discipline.'

Laurence opened his mouth to deny that Temeraire would disobey, then shut it again after glancing round; Temeraire was ploughing the ground restlessly with his great talons, his wings partly fanned out, and he would not meet Laurence's gaze.

'Yes, just so,' Lenton said dryly, when he saw Laurence

silenced. He sighed, unbending a little, and brushed his sparse grey hair back off his forehead. 'If those Chinamen want him back, it can only make matters worse if he gets himself injured fighting without armour or crew,' he said. 'Go on and get him ready; we will speak after.'

Laurence could scarcely find words to express his gratitude, but they were unnecessary in any case; Lenton was already turning back to Obversaria. There was indeed no time to waste; Laurence waved Temeraire on and ran for their usual clearing on foot, careless of his dignity. A scattered, intensely excited rush of thoughts, all fragmentary: great relief; of course Temeraire would never have stayed behind; how wretched they would have looked, jumping into a battle against orders; in a moment they would be aloft, yet nothing had truly changed in their circumstances: this might be the last time.

Many of his crewmen were sitting outside in the open, polishing equipment and oiling harness unnecessarily, pretending not to be watching the sky; they were silent and downcast; and at first they only stared when Laurence came running into the clearing. 'Where is Granby?' he demanded. 'Full muster, gentlemen; heavy combat rig, at once.'

By then Temeraire was overhead and descending, and the rest of the crew came spilling out of the barracks, cheering him; a general stampede towards small-arms and gear ensued, that rush that had once looked like chaos to Laurence, used as he was to naval order, but which accomplished the tremendous affair of getting a dragon equipped in a frantic hurry.

Granby came out of the barracks amid the cavalcade: a tall young officer dark-haired and lanky, his fair skin, ordinarily burnt and peeling from daily flying, but for once unmarred thanks to the weeks of being grounded. He was an aviator born and bred, as Laurence was not, and their acquaintance had not been without early friction: like many other aviators, he had resented so prime a dragon as Temeraire being claimed by a naval officer. But that resentment had not survived a

31

shared action, and Laurence had never yet regretted taking him on as first lieutenant, despite the wide divergence in their characters. Granby had made an initial attempt out of respect to imitate the formalities which were to Laurence, raised a gentleman, as natural as breathing; but they had not taken root. Like most aviators, raised from the age of seven far from polite society, he was by nature given to a sort of easy liberty that looked a great deal like licence to a censorious eye.

'Laurence, it is damned good to see you,' he said now, coming to seize Laurence's hand: quite unconscious of any impropriety in addressing his commanding officer so, and making no salute; indeed he was at the same time trying to hook his sword onto his belt one-handed. 'Have they changed their minds, then? I hadn't looked for anything like such good sense, but I will be the first to beg their Lordships' pardon if they have given up this notion of sending him to China.'

For his part, Laurence had long since accepted that no disrespect was intended; at present he scarcely even noticed the informality; he was too bitterly sorry to disappoint Granby, especially now knowing that he had refused a prime position out of loyalty. 'I am afraid not, John, but there is no time now to explain: we must get Temeraire aloft at once. Half the usual armaments, and leave the bombs; the Navy will not thank us for sinking the ships, and if it becomes really necessary Temeraire can do more damage roaring away at them.'

'Right you are,' Granby said, and dashed away at once to the other side of the clearing, calling out orders all around. The great leather harness was already being carried out in double-quick time, and Temeraire was doing his best to help matters along, crouching low to the ground to make it easier for the men to adjust the broad weight-bearing straps across his back.

The panels of chainmail for his breast and belly were heaved out almost as quickly. 'No ceremony,' Laurence said, and so the aerial crew scrambled aboard pell-mell as soon as their positions were clear, disregarding the usual order.

'We are ten short, I am sorry to say,' Granby said, coming back to his side. 'I sent six men to Maximus's crew at the Admiral's request; the others—' He hesitated.

'Yes,' Laurence said, sparing him; the men had naturally been unhappy at having no part of the action, and the missing four had undoubtedly slipped away to seek better or at least more thorough consolation in a bottle or a woman than could be found in busywork. He was pleased it was so few, and he did not mean to come the tyrant over them afterwards: he felt at present he had no moral ground on which to stand. 'We will manage; but if there are any fellows on the ground crew who are handy with pistol or sword, and not prone to height-sickness, let us get them hooked on if they choose to volunteer.'

He himself had already shifted his coat for the long heavy one of leather used in combat, and was now strapping his carabiner belt over. A low many-voiced roar began, not very far away; Laurence looked up: the smaller dragons were going aloft, and he recognized Dulcia and the grey-blue Nitidus, the end-wing members of their formation, flying in circles as they waited for the others to rise.

'Laurence, are you not ready? Do hurry, please, the others are going up,' Temeraire said, anxiously, craning his head about to look; above them the middle-weight dragons were coming into view also.

Granby swung himself aboard, along with a couple of tall young harness-men, Willoughby and Porter; Laurence waited until he saw them latched onto the rings of the harness and secure, then said, 'All is ready; try away.'

This was one ritual that could not in safety be set aside: Temeraire rose up onto his hind legs and shook himself, making certain that the harness was secure and all the men properly hooked on. 'Harder,' Laurence called sharply: Temeraire was not being particularly vigorous, in his anxiety to be away.

Temeraire snorted but obeyed, and still nothing pulled loose or fell off. 'All lies well; please come aboard now,' he said, thumping to the ground and holding out his foreleg at once; Laurence stepped into the claw and was rather quickly tossed up to his usual place at the base of Temeraire's neck. He did not mind at all: he was pleased, exhilarated by everything: the deeply satisfying sound as his carabiner rings locked into place, the buttery feel of the oiled, double-stitched leather straps of the harness; and beneath him Temeraire's muscles were already gathering for the leap aloft.

Maximus suddenly erupted out of the trees to the north of them, his great red-and-gold body even larger than before, as Roland had reported. He was still the only Regal Copper stationed at the Channel, and he dwarfed every other creature in sight, blotting out an enormous swath of the sun. Temeraire roared joyfully at the sight and leaped up after him, black wings beating a little too quickly with over-excitement.

'Gently,' Laurence called; Temeraire bobbed his head in acknowledgement, but they still overshot the slower dragon.

'Maximus, Maximus; look, I am back,' Temeraire called out, circling back down to take his position alongside the big dragon, and they began beating up together to the formation's flying height. 'I took Laurence away from London,' he added triumphantly, in what he likely thought a confidential whisper. 'They were trying to arrest him.'

'Did he kill someone?' Maximus asked with interest in his deep echoing voice, not at all disapproving. 'I am glad you are back; they have been making me fly in the middle while you were gone, and all the manoeuvres are different,' he added.

'No,' said Temeraire, 'he only came and talked to me when some fat old man said he should not, which does not seem like any reason to me.'

'You had better shut up that Jacobin of a dragon of yours,' Berkley shouted across from Maximus's back, while Laurence shook his head in despair, trying to ignore the inquisitive looks from his young ensigns.

'Pray remember we are on business, Temeraire,' Laurence

called, trying to be severe; but after all there was no sense in trying to keep it a secret; the news would surely be all over in a week. They would be forced to confront the gravity of their situation soon enough; little enough harm in letting Temeraire indulge in high spirits so long as he might.

'Laurence,' Granby said at his shoulder, 'in the hurry, the ammunition was all laid in its usual place on the left, though we are not carrying the bombs to balance it out; we ought to restow.'

'Can you have it done before we engage? Oh, good Lord,' Laurence said, realizing. 'I do not even know the position of the convoy; do you?' Granby shook his head, embarrassed, and Laurence swallowed his pride and shouted, 'Berkley, where are we going?'

A general explosion of mirth ran among the men on Maximus's back. Berkley called back, 'Straight to hell, ha ha!' More laughter, nearly drowning out the coordinates that he bellowed over.

'Fifteen minutes' flight, then.' Laurence was mentally running the calculation through in his head. 'And we ought to save at least five of those minutes for grace.'

Granby nodded. 'We can manage it,' he said, and clambered down at once to organize the operation, unhooking and rehooking the carabiners with practised skill from the evenly spaced rings leading down Temeraire's side to the storage nets slung beneath his belly.

The rest of the formation was already in place as Temeraire and Maximus rose to take their defensive positions at the rear. Laurence noticed the formation-leader flag streaming out from Lily's back; that meant that during their absence, Captain Harcourt had at last been given the command. He was glad to see the change: it was hard on the signal-ensign to have to watch a wing dragon as well as keep an eye forward, and the dragons would always instinctively follow the lead regardless of formal precedence.

Still, he could not help feeling how strange that he should find himself taking orders from a twenty-year-old girl: Harcourt was still a very young officer, promoted over-quick due to Lily's unexpectedly early hatching. But command in the Corps had to follow the capabilities of the dragons, and a rare acid-spitter like one of the Longwings was too valuable to place anywhere but the centre of a formation, even if they would only accept female handlers.

'Signal from the Admiral: *proceed to meeting*,' called the signal-ensign, Turner; a moment later the signal *formation keep together* broke out on Lily's signal-yard, and the dragons were pressing on, shortly reaching their cruising speed of a steady seventeen knots: an easy pace for Temeraire, but all that the Yellow Reapers and the enormous Maximus could manage comfortably for any length of time.

There was time to loosen his sword in the sheath, and load his pistols fresh; below, Granby was shouting orders over the wind: he did not sound frantic, and Laurence had every confidence in his power to get the work completed in time. The dragons of the covert made an impressive spread, even though this was not so large a force in numbers as had been assembled for the battle of Dover in October, which had fended off Napoleon's invasion attempt.

But in that battle, they had been forced to send up every available dragon, even the little couriers: most of the fighting-dragons had been away south at Trafalgar. Today Excidium and Captain Roland's formation was back in the lead, ten dragons strong, the smallest of them a middle-weight Yellow Reaper, and all of them flying in perfect formation, not a wingbeat out of place: the skill born of many long years in formation together.

Lily's formation was nothing so imposing, as yet: only six dragons flying behind her, with her flank and end-wing positions held by smaller and more manoeuvrable beasts with older officers, who could more easily compensate for any errors made from inexperience by Lily herself, or by Maximus and Temeraire in the back line. Even as they drew closer, Laurence saw Sutton, the captain of their mid-wing Messoria, stand up on her back and turn to look over at them, making sure all was well with the younger dragons. Laurence raised a hand in acknowledgment, and saw Berkley doing the same.

The sails of the French convoy and the Channel fleet were visible long before the dragons came into range. There was a stately quality to the scene below: chessboard pieces moving into place, with the British ships advancing in eager haste towards the great crowd of smaller French merchantmen; a glorious spread of white sail to be seen on every ship, and the British colours streaming among them. Granby came clambering back up along the shoulder strap to Laurence's side. 'We'll do nicely now, I think.' .

'Very good,' Laurence said absently, his attention all on what he could see of the British fleet, peering down over Temeraire's shoulder through his glass. Mostly fast-sailing frigates, with a motley collection of smaller sloops, and a handful of sixty-four- and seventy-four-gun ships. The Navy would not risk the largest first- and second-rate ships against the fire-breather; too easy for one lucky attack to send a three-decker packed full of powder up like a light, taking half a dozen smaller ships along with her.

'All hands to their stations, Mr. Harley,' Laurence said, straightening up, and the young ensign hurried to set the signal-strap embedded in the harness to red. The riflemen stationed along Temeraire's back let themselves partly down his sides, readying their guns, while the rest of the topmen all crouched low, pistols in their hands.

Excidium and the rest of the larger formation dropped low over the British warships, taking up the more important defensive position and leaving the field to them. As Lily increased their speed, Temeraire gave a low growling rumble, the tremor palpable through his hide. Laurence spared a moment to lean over and put his bare hand on the side of Temeraire's neck: no words necessary, and he felt a slight easing of the nervous tension before he straightened and pulled his leather riding glove back on.

'Enemy in sight,' came faint but audible in the shrill high voice of Lily's forward lookout, carrying back to them on the wind, echoed a moment later by young Allen, stationed near the joint of Temeraire's wing. A general murmur went around the men, and Laurence snapped out his glass again for a look.

'La Crabe Grande, I think,' he said, handing the telescope over to Granby, hoping privately that he had not mangled the pronunciation too badly. He was quite sure that he had identified the formation style correctly, despite his lack of experience in aerial actions; there were few composed of fourteen dragons, and the shape was highly distinct, with the two pincer-like rows of smaller dragons stretched out to either side of the cluster of big ones in the centre.

The Flamme-de-Gloire was not easy to spot, with several decoy dragons of similar colouring shifting about: a pair of Papillon Noirs with yellow markings painted over their natural blue and green stripes to make them confusingly alike from a distance. 'Hah, I have made her: it is Accendare. There she is, the wicked thing,' Granby said, handing back the glass and pointing. 'She has a talon missing from her left rear leg, and she is blind in the right eye: we gave her a good dose of pepper back in the battle of the Glorious First.'

'I see her. Mr. Harley, pass the word to all the lookouts. Temeraire,' he called, bringing up the speaking trumpet, 'do you see the Flamme-de-Gloire? She is the one low and to the right, with the missing talon; she is weak in the right eye.'

'I see her,' Temeraire said eagerly, turning his head just slightly. 'Are we to attack her?'

'Our first duty is to keep her fire away from the Navy's ships; have an eye on her as best you can,' Laurence said,

38

and Temeraire bobbed his head once in quick answer, straightening out again.

He tucked away the glass in the small pouch hooked onto
the harness: no more need for it, very soon. 'You had better
get below, John,' Laurence said. 'I expect they will try a
boarding with a few of those light fellows on their edges.'

All this while they had been rapidly closing the distance:
suddenly there was no more time, and the French were
wheeling about in perfect unison, not one dragon falling out
of formation, graceful as a flock of birds. A low whistle came
behind him; admittedly it was an impressive sight, but Laurence
frowned though his own heart was speeding involuntarily.
'Belay that noise.'

One of the Papillons was directly ahead of them, jaws
spreading wide as if to breathe flames it could not produce;
Laurence felt an odd, detached amusement to see a dragon
play-acting. Temeraire could not roar from his position in the
rear, not with Messoria and Lily both in the way, but he did
not duck away at all; instead he raised his claws, and as the
two formations swept together and intermingled, he and the
Papillon pulled up and collided with a force that jarred all of
their crews loose.

Laurence grappled for the harness and got his feet back
underneath him. 'Clap on there, Allen,' he said, reaching; the
boy was dangling by his carabiner straps with his arms and
legs waving about wildly like an overturned tortoise. Allen
managed to get himself braced and clung, his face pale and
shading to green; like the other lookouts, he was only a new
ensign, barely twelve years old, and he had not quite learned
to manage himself aboard during the stops and starts of
battle.

Temeraire was clawing and biting, his wings beating madly
as he tried to keep hold of the Papillon: the French dragon
was lighter-weight, and plainly all he now wanted was to get
free and back to his formation. 'Hold position,' Laurence

shouted: more important to keep the formation together for the moment. Temeraire reluctantly let the Papillon go and levelled out.

Below, distantly, came the first sound of cannon-fire: bow-chasers on the British ships, hoping to knock away some of the French merchantmen's spars with a lucky shot or two. Not likely, but it would put the men in the right frame of mind. A steady rattle and clang behind him as the riflemen reloaded; all the harness he could see looked still in good order; no sign of dripping blood, and Temeraire was flying well. No time to ask how he was; they were coming about, Lily taking them straight for the enemy formation again.

But this time the French offered no resistance: instead the dragons scattered; wildly, Laurence thought at first, then he perceived how well they had distributed themselves around. Four of the smaller dragons darted upwards; the rest dropped perhaps a hundred feet in height, and Accendare was once again hard to tell from the decoys.

No clear target anymore, and with the dragons above the formation itself was dangerously vulnerable: *engage the enemy more closely* went up the yard on Lily's back, signalling that they might disperse and fight separately. Temeraire could read the flags as well as any signal-officer: he instantly dived for the decoy with bleeding scratches, a little too eager to complete his own handiwork. 'No, Temeraire,' Laurence called, meaning to direct him after Accendare herself, but too late: two of the smaller dragons, both of the common Pêcheur-Rayé breed, were coming at them from either side.

'Prepare to repel boarders,' Lieutenant Ferris, captain of the topmen, shouted from behind him. Two of the sturdiest midwingmen took up stations just behind Laurence's position; he glanced over his shoulder at them, his mouth tightening: it still rankled him to be so shielded, too much like cowardly hiding behind others; but no dragon would fight with a sword laid at its captain's throat, and so he had to bear it.

40

Temeraire contented himself with one more slash across the fleeing decoy's shoulders and writhed away, almost doubling back on himself. The pursuers overshot and had to turn back: a clear gain of a minute, worth more than gold at present. Laurence cast an eye over the field: the quick light-combat dragons were dashing about to fend off the British dragons, but the larger ones were forming back into a cluster and keeping pace with their convoy.

A powder-flash below caught his eye; an instant later came the thin whistling of a pepper-ball, flying up from the French ships. Another of their formation members, Immortalis, had dived just a hair too low in pursuit of one of the other dragons. Fortunately their aim was off: the ball struck his shoulder instead of his face, and the best part of the pepper scattered down harmlessly into the sea; even the remainder was enough to set the poor fellow sneezing, blowing himself ten lengths back at a time.

'Digby, cast and mark that height,' Laurence said; it was the starboard forward lookout's duty to warn when they entered the range of the guns below.

Digby took the small round-shot, bored through and tied to the height-line, and tossed it over Temeraire's shoulder, the thin silk cord paying out with the knotted marks for every fifty yards flying through his fingers. 'Six at the mark, seventeen at the water,' he said, counting from Immortalis's height, and cut the cord. 'Range five hundred fifty yards on the pepper guns, sir.' He was already whipping the cord through another ball, to be ready when the next measure should be called for.

A shorter range than usual; were they holding back, trying to tempt the more dangerous dragons lower, or was the wind checking their shot? 'Keep to six hundred yards' elevation, Temeraire,' Laurence called; best to be cautious for the moment.

'Sir, lead signal to us, *fall in on left flank Maximus*,' Turner said.

No immediate way to get over to him: the two Pêcheurs were back, trying to flank Temeraire and get men aboard, although they were flying somewhat strangely, not in a straight line. 'What are they about?' Martin said, and the question answered itself readily in Laurence's mind.

'They fear giving him a target for his roar,' Laurence said, making it loud for Temeraire's benefit. Temeraire snorted in disdain, abruptly halted in mid-air and whipped himself about, hovering to face the pair with his ruff standing high: the smaller dragons, clearly alarmed by the presentation, backwinged out of instinct, giving them room.

'Hah!' Temeraire stopped and hovered, pleased with himself at seeing the others so afraid of his prowess; Laurence had to tug on the harness to draw his attention around to the signal, which he had not yet seen. 'Oh, I see!' he said, and dashed forward to take up position to Maximus's left; Lily was already on his right.

Harcourt's intention was clear. 'All hands low,' Laurence said, and crouched against Temeraire's neck even as he gave the order. Instantly they were in place, Berkley sent Maximus ahead at the big dragon's top speed, right at the clustered French dragons.

Temeraire was swelling with breath, his ruff coming up; they were going so quickly the wind was beating tears from Laurence's eyes, but he could see Lily's head drawing back in similar preparation. Maximus put his head down and drove straight into the French dragons, simply bulling through their ranks with his enormous advantage in weight: the dragons fell off to his either side, only to meet Temeraire roaring and Lily spraying her corrosive acid.

Shrieks of pain in their wake, and the first dead crewmen being cut loose from harness and sent falling into the ocean, rag-doll limp. The French dragons' forward motion had nearly halted, many of them panicking and scattering, this time with no thought to the pattern. Then Maximus and they were through: the cluster had broken apart and now Accendare was shielded from them only by a Petit Chevalier, slightly larger than Temeraire, and another of Accendare's decoys.

They slowed; Maximus was heaving for breath, fighting to keep elevation. Harcourt waved wildly at Laurence from Lily's back, shouting hoarsely through her speaking trumpet, 'Go after her,' even while the formal signal was going up on Lily's back. Laurence touched Temeraire's side and sent him forward; Lily sprayed another burst of acid, and the two defending dragons recoiled, enough for Temeraire to dodge past them and get through.

Granby's voice came from below, yelling: ''Ware boarders!' So some Frenchmen had made the leap to Temeraire's back. Laurence had no time to look: directly before his face Accendare was twisting around, scarcely ten yards distant. Her right eye was milky, the left wicked and glaring, a pale yellow pupil in black sclera; she had long thin horns curving down from her forehead and to the very edge of her jaws, her opening jaws: a heat-shimmer distorted the air as flames came bursting out upon them. Very like looking into the mouth of Hell, he thought for that one narrow instant, staring into the red maw; then Temeraire snapped his wings shut and fell out of the way like a stone.

Laurence's stomach leaped; behind him he heard clatter and cries of surprise, the boarders and defenders alike losing their footing. It seemed only a moment before Temeraire opened his wings again and began to beat up hard, but they had plummeted some distance, and Accendare was flying rapidly away from them, back to the ships below.

The rearmost merchant ships of the French convoy had come within the accurate range of long guns of the British men-of-war: the steady roar of cannon-fire rose, mingled with sulphur and smoke. The quickest frigates had already moved on ahead, passing by the merchantmen under fire and continuing for the richer prizes at the front. In doing so, however, they had left the shelter of Excidium's formation, and Accendare now stooped towards them, her crew throwing the fist-sized iron incendiaries over her sides, which she bathed with flame as they fell towards the vulnerable British ships.

More than half the shells fell into the sea, much more; mindful of Temeraire's pursuit, Accendare had not gone very low, and aim could not be accurate from so high up. But Laurence could see a handful blooming into flame below: the thin metal shells broke as they struck the decks of the ships, and the naphtha within ignited against the hot metal, spreading a pool of fire across the deck.

Temeraire gave a low growl of anger as he saw fire catch the sails of one of the frigates, instantly putting on another burst of speed to go after Accendare; he had been hatched on deck, spent the first three weeks of his life at sea: the affection remained. Laurence urged him on with word and touch, full of the same anger. Intent on the pursuit and watching for other dragons who might be close enough to offer her support, Laurence was startled out of his single-minded focus unpleasantly: Croyn, one of the topmen, fell onto him before rolling away and off Temeraire's back, mouth round and open, hands reaching; his carabiner straps had been severed.

He missed the harness, his hands slipping over Temeraire's smooth hide; Laurence snatched at him, uselessly: the boy was falling, arms flailing at the empty air, down a quarter of a mile and gone into the water: only a small splash; he did not resurface. Another man went down just after him, one of the boarders, but already dead even as he tumbled slack-limbed through the air. Laurence loosened his own straps and stood, turning around as he drew his pistols. Seven boarders were still aboard, fighting very hard. One with lieutenant's bars on his shoulders was only a few paces away, engaged closely with Quarle, the second of the midwingmen who had been set to guard Laurence.

Even as Laurence got to his feet, the lieutenant knocked

44

aside Quarle's arm with his sword and drove a vicious-looking long knife into his side left-handed. Quarle dropped his own sword and put his hands around the hilt, sinking, coughing blood. Laurence had a wide-open shot, but just behind the lieutenant, one of the boarders had driven Martin to his knees: the midwingman's neck was bare to the man's cutlass.

Laurence levelled his pistol and fired: the boarder fell backwards with a hole in his chest spurting, and Martin heaved himself back to his feet. Before Laurence could take fresh aim and set off the other, the lieutenant took the risk of slashing his own straps and leaped over Quarle's body, catching Laurence's arm both for support and to push the pistol aside. It was an extraordinary manoeuvre, whether for bravery or recklessness; 'Bravo,' Laurence said, involuntarily. The Frenchman looked at him startled and then smiled, incongruously boyish in his blood-streaked face, before he brought his sword up.

Laurence had an unfair advantage, of course; he was useless dead, for a dragon whose captain had been killed would turn with utmost savagery on the enemy: uncontrolled but very dangerous nonetheless. The Frenchman needed him prisoner, not killed, and that made him overly cautious, while Laurence could freely aim for a killing blow and strike as best as ever he could.

But that was not very well, currently. It was an odd battle; they were upon the narrow base of Temeraire's neck, so closely engaged that Laurence was not at a disadvantage from the tall lieutenant's greater reach, but that same condition let the Frenchman keep his grip on Laurence, without which he would certainly have slipped off. They were more pushing at one another than truly sword-fighting; their blades hardly ever parted more than an inch or two before coming together again, and Laurence began to think the contest would only be ended if one or the other of them fell.

Laurence risked a step; it let him turn them both slightly,

so he could see the rest of the struggle over the lieutenant's shoulder. Martin and Ferris were both still standing, and several of the riflemen, but they were outnumbered, and if even a couple more of the boarders managed to get past, it would be very awkward for Laurence indeed. Several of the bellmen were trying to come up from below, but the boarders had detached a couple of men to fend them off: as Laurence watched, Johnson was stabbed through and fell.

'Vive l'Empereur,' the lieutenant shouted to his men encouragingly, looking also; he took heart from the favourable position and struck again, aiming for Laurence's leg. Laurence deflected the blow: his sword rang oddly with the impact, though, and he realized with an unpleasant shock that he was fighting with his dress sword, worn to the Admiralty the day before: he had never had a chance to exchange it.

He began to fight more narrowly, trying not to meet the Frenchman's sword anywhere below the midpoint of his sword: he did not want to lose his entire blade if it were going to snap. Another sharp blow, at his right arm: he blocked it as well, but this time five inches of steel did indeed snap off, scoring a thin line across his jaw before it tumbled away, red-gold in the reflected firelight.

The Frenchman had seen the weakness of the blade now, and was trying to batter it into pieces. Another crack and more of the blade went: Laurence was fighting with only six inches of steel now, with the paste brilliants on the silver-plated hilt sparkling at him mockingly, ridiculous. He clenched his jaw; he was not going to surrender and see Temeraire ordered to France: he would be damned first. If he jumped over the side, calling, there was some hope Temeraire might catch him; if not, then at least he would not be responsible for delivering Temeraire into Napoleon's hands after all.

Then a shout: Granby came swarming up the rear tail strap without benefit of carabiners, locked himself back on and lunged for the man guarding the left side of the belly strap.

The man fell dead, and six bellmen almost at once burst into the tops: the remaining boarders drew into a tight knot, but in a moment they would have to surrender or be killed. Martin had turned and was already clambering over Quarle's body, freed by the relief from below, and his sword was ready.

'Ah, voici un joli gâchis,' the lieutenant said in tones of despair, looking also, and he made a last gallant attempt, binding Laurence's hilt with his own blade, and using the length as a lever: he managed to pry it out of Laurence's hand with a great heave, but just as he did he staggered, surprised, and blood came out of his nose. He fell forward into Laurence's arms, senseless: young Digby was standing rather wobblingly behind him, holding the round-shot on the measuring cord; he had crept along from his lookout's post on Temeraire's shoulder, and struck the Frenchman on the head.

'Well done,' Laurence said, after he had worked out what had happened; the boy flushed up proudly. 'Mr. Martin, heave this fellow below to the infirmary, will you?' Laurence handed the Frenchman's limp form over. 'He fought quite like a lion.'

'Very good, sir.' Martin's mouth kept moving, he was saying something more, but a roar from above was drowning out his voice: it was the last thing Laurence heard.

The low and dangerous rumble of Temeraire's growl, just above him, penetrated the smothering unconsciousness. Laurence tried to move, to look around him, but the light stabbed painfully at his eyes, and his leg did not want to answer at all; groping blindly down along his thigh, he found it entangled with the leather straps of his harness, and felt a wet trickle of blood where one of the buckles had torn through his breeches and into his skin.

He thought for a moment perhaps they had been captured; but the voices he heard were English, and then he recognized Barham, shouting, and Granby saying fiercely, 'No, sir, no farther, not one damned step. Temeraire, if those men make ready, you may knock them down.'

Laurence struggled to sit up, and then suddenly there were anxious hands supporting him. 'Steady, sir, are you all right?' It was young Digby, pressing a dripping waterbag into his hands. Laurence wetted his lips, but he did not dare to swallow; his stomach was roiling. 'Help me stand,' he said, hoarsely, trying to squint his eyes open a little.

'No, sir, you mustn't,' Digby whispered urgently. 'You have had a nasty knock on the head, and those fellows, they have come to arrest you. Granby said we had to keep you out of sight and wait for the admiral.'

He was lying behind the protective curl of Temeraire's foreleg, with the hard-packed dirt of the clearing underneath him; Digby and Allen, the forward lookouts, were crouched down on either side of him. Small rivulets of dark blood were running down Temeraire's leg to stain the ground black, not far away. 'He is wounded,' Laurence said sharply, trying to get up again.

'Mr. Keynes is gone for bandages, sir; a Pêcheur hit us across the shoulders, but it is only a few scratches,' Digby said, holding him back; which attempt was successful, because Laurence could not make his wrenched leg even bend, much less carry any weight. 'You are not to get up, sir, Baylesworth is getting a stretcher.'

'Enough of this, help me rise,' Laurence said, sharply; Lenton could not possibly come quickly, so soon after a battle, and he did not mean to lie about letting matters get worse. He made Digby and Allen help him rise and limp out from the concealment, the two ensigns struggling under his weight.

Barham was there with a dozen Marines, these not the inexperienced boys of his escort in London but hard-bitten soldiers, older men, and they had brought with them a pepper gun: only a small, short-barrelled one, but at this range they hardly needed better. Barham was almost purple in the face, quarrelling with Granby at the side of the clearing; when he caught sight of Laurence his eyes went narrow. 'There you are; did you think you could hide here, like a coward? Stand down that animal, at once; Sergeant, go there and take him.'

'You are not to come anywhere near Laurence, at all,' Temeraire snarled at the soldiers, before Laurence could make any reply, and raised one deadly clawed foreleg, ready to strike. The blood streaking his shoulders and neck made him look truly savage, and his great ruff was standing up stiffly around his head.

The men flinched a little, but the sergeant said, stolidly, 'Run out that gun, Corporal,' and gestured to the rest of them to raise up their muskets.

In alarm, Laurence called out to him hoarsely, 'Temeraire, stop; for God's sake settle,' but it was useless; Temeraire was in a red-eyed rage, and did not take any notice. Even if the musketry did not cause him serious injury, the pepper gun would surely blind and madden him even further, and he could easily be driven into a truly uncontrolled frenzy, terrible both to himself and to others.

The trees to the west of them shook suddenly, and abruptly Maximus's enormous head and shoulders came rising up out of the growth; he flung his head back yawning tremendously, exposing rows of serrated teeth, and shook himself all over. 'Is the battle not over? What is all the noise?'

'You there!' Barham shouted at the big Regal Copper, pointing at Temeraire. 'Hold down that dragon!'

Like all Regal Coppers, Maximus was badly farsighted; to see into the clearing, he was forced to rear up onto his haunches to gain enough distance. He was twice Temeraire's size by weight and twenty feet more in length now; his wings, half-outspread for balance, threw a long shadow ahead of him, and with the sun behind him they glowed redly, veins standing out in the translucent skin.

Looming over them all, he drew his head back on his neck

49

and peered into the clearing. 'Why do you need to be held down?' he asked Temeraire, interestedly.

'I do not need to be held down!' Temeraire said, almost spitting in his anger, ruff quivering; the blood was running more freely down his shoulders. 'Those men want to take Laurence from me, and put him in prison, and execute him, and I will not let them, ever, and I do not *care* if Laurence tells me not to squash you,' he added, fiercely, to Lord Barham.

'Good God,' Laurence said, low and appalled; it had not occurred to him the real nature of Temeraire's fear. But the only time Temeraire had ever seen an arrest, the man taken had been a traitor, executed shortly thereafter before the eyes of the man's own dragon. The experience had left Temeraire and all the young dragons of the covert crushed with sympathetic misery for days; it was no wonder if he was panicked now.

Granby took advantage of the unwitting distraction Maximus had provided, and made a quick, impulsive gesture to the other officers of Temeraire's crew: Ferris and Evans jumped to follow him, Riggs and his riflemen scrambling after, and in a moment they were all ranged defensively in front of Temeraire, raising pistols and rifles. It was all bravado, their guns spent from the battle, but that did not in any way reduce the significance. Laurence shut his eyes in dismay. Granby and all his men had just flung themselves into the stew-pot with him, by such direct disobedience; indeed there was increasingly every justification to call this a mutiny.

The muskets facing them did not waver, though; the Marines were still hurrying to finish loading the gun, tamping down one of the big round pepper-balls with a small wad. 'Make ready!' the corporal said. Laurence could not think what to do; if he ordered Temeraire to knock down the gun, they would be attacking fellow soldiers, men only doing their duty: unforgivable, even to his own mind, and only a little less unthinkable than standing by while they injured Temeraire, or his own men.

'What the devil do you all mean here?' Keynes, the dragon-surgeon assigned to Temeraire's care, had just come back into the clearing, two staggering assistants behind him laden down with fresh white bandages and thin silk thread for stitching. He shoved his way through the startled Marines, his well-salted hair and blood-spattered coat giving him a badge of authority they did not choose to defy, and snatched the slow-match out of the hands of the man standing by the pepper gun.

He flung it to the ground and stamped it out, and glared all around, sparing neither Barham and the Marines nor Granby and his men, impartially furious. 'He is fresh from the field; have you all taken leave of your senses? You cannot be stirring up dragons like this after a battle; in half a minute we will have the rest of the covert looking in, and not just that great busybody there,' he added, pointing at Maximus.

Indeed more dragons had already lifted their heads up above the tree cover, trying to crane their heads over to see what was going on, making a great noise of cracking branches; the ground even trembled underfoot when the abashed Maximus dropped lower, back down to his haunches, in an attempt to make his curiosity less obvious. Barham uneasily looked around at the many inquisitive spectators: dragons ordinarily ate directly after a battle, and many of them had gore dripping from their jaws, bones cracking audibly as they chewed.

Keynes did not give him time to recover. 'Out, out at once, the lot of you; I cannot be operating in the middle of this circus, and as for you,' he snapped at Laurence, 'lie down again at once; I gave orders you were to be taken straight to the surgeons. Christ only knows what you are doing to that leg, hopping about on it. Where is Baylesworth with that stretcher?'

Barham, wavering, was caught by this. 'Laurence is damned well under arrest, and I have a mind to clap the rest of you

51

mutinous dogs into irons also,' he began, only to have Keynes wheel on him in turn.

'You can arrest him in the morning, after that leg has been seen to, and his dragon. Of all the blackguardly, unchristian notions; storming in on wounded men and beasts—' Keynes was literally shaking his fist in Barham's face; an alarming prospect, thanks to the wickedly-hooked ten-inch tenaculum clenched in his fingers, and the moral force of his argument was very great: Barham stepped back, involuntarily. The Marines gratefully took it as a signal, beginning to drag the gun back out of the clearing with them, and Barham, baffled and deserted, was forced to give way.

The delay thus won lasted only a short while. The surgeons scratched their heads over Laurence's leg; the bone was not broken, despite the breathtaking pain when they roughly palpated the limb, and there was no visible wound, save the great mottled bruises covering nearly every scrap of skin. His head ached fiercely also, but there was little they could do but offer him laudanum for the pain, which he refused, and order him to keep his weight off the leg: advice as practical as it was unnecessary, since he could not stand for any length of time without suffering a collapse.

Meanwhile, Temeraire's own wounds, thankfully minor, were sewed up, and with much coaxing Laurence persuaded him to eat a little, despite his agitation. By morning, it was plain Temeraire was healing well, with no sign of wound-fever, and there was no excuse for further delay; a formal summons had come from Admiral Lenton, ordering Laurence to report to the covert headquarters. He had to be carried in an elbow chair, leaving behind him an uneasy and restive Temeraire. 'If you do not come back by tomorrow morning, I will come and find you,' he vowed, and would not be dissuaded.

Laurence could do little in honesty to reassure him: there

was every likelihood he was to be arrested, if Lenton had not managed some miracle of persuasion, and after these multiple offences a court-martial might very well impose a death sentence. Ordinarily an aviator would not be hanged for anything less than outright treason. But Barham would surely have him up before a board of Navy officers, who would be far more severe, and consideration for preserving the dragon's service would not enter into their deliberations: Temeraire was already lost to England, as a fighting-dragon, by the demands of the Chinese.

It was by no means an easy or a comfortable situation, and still worse was the knowledge that he had imperilled his men; Granby would have to answer for his defiance, and the other lieutenants also, Evans and Ferris and Riggs; any or all of them might be dismissed the service: a terrible fate for an aviator, raised in the ranks from early childhood. Even those midwingmen who never passed for lieutenant were not usually sent away; some work would be found for them, in the breeding grounds or in the coverts, that they might remain in the society of their fellows.

Though his leg had improved some little way overnight, Laurence was still pale and sweating even from the short walk he risked taking up the front stairs of the building. The pain was increasing sharply, dizzying, and he was forced to stop and catch his breath before he went into the small office.

'Good Heavens; I thought you had been let go by the surgeons. Sit down, Laurence, before you fall down; take this,' Lenton said, ignoring Barham's scowl of impatience, and put a glass of brandy into Laurence's hand.

'Thank you, sir; you are not mistaken, I have been released,' Laurence said, and only sipped once for politeness's sake; his head was already clouded badly enough.

'That is enough; he is not here to be coddled,' Barham said. 'Never in my life have I seen such outrageous behaviour, and from an officer— By God, Laurence, I have never taken pleasure in a hanging, but on this occasion, I would call it good riddance. But Lenton swears to me your beast will become unmanageable; though how we should tell the difference I can hardly say.'

Lenton's lips tightened at this disdainful tone; Laurence could only imagine the humiliating lengths to which he had been forced in order to impress this understanding on Barham. Though Lenton was an admiral, and fresh from another great victory, even that meant very little in any larger sphere; Barham could offend him with impunity, where any admiral in the Navy would have had political influence and friends enough to require more respectful handling.

'You are to be dismissed the service, that is beyond question,' Barham continued. 'But the animal must be gotten off to China, and for that, I am sorry to say, we require your cooperation. Find some way to persuade him, and we will leave the matter there; any more of this recalcitrance, and I am damned if I will *not* hang you after all; yes, and have the animal shot, and be damned to those Chinamen also.'

This last very nearly brought Laurence out of his chair, despite his injury; only Lenton's hand on his shoulder, pressing down firmly, held him in place. 'Sir, you go too far,' Lenton said. 'We have never shot dragons in England for anything less than man-eating, and we are not going to start now; I would have a real mutiny on my hands.'

Barham scowled, and muttered something not quite intelligible under his breath about lack of discipline; which was a fine thing coming from a man who Laurence well knew had served during the great naval mutinies of '97, when half the fleet had risen up. 'Well, let us hope it does not come to any such thing. There is a transport in ordinary in harbour at Spithead, the *Allegiance*; she can be made ready for sea in a week. How then is the animal to be gotten aboard, since he is choosing to be balky?'

Laurence could not bring himself to answer; a week was a horribly short time, and for a moment he even wildly allowed himself to consider the prospect of flight. Temeraire could easily reach the Continent from Dover, and there were places in the forests of the German states where even now feral dragons lived; though only small breeds.

'It will require some consideration,' Lenton said. 'I will not scruple to say, sir, that the whole affair has been mismanaged from the beginning. The dragon has been badly stirred-up, now, and it is no joke to coax a dragon to do something he does not like to begin with.'

'Enough excuses, Lenton; quite enough,' Barham began, and then a tapping came on the door; they all looked in surprise as a rather pale-looking midwingman opened the door and said, 'Sir, sir—' only to hastily clear out of the way: the Chinese soldiers looked as though they would have trampled straight over him, clearing a path for Prince Yongxing into the room.

They were all of them so startled they forgot at first to rise, and Laurence was still struggling to get up to his feet when Yongxing had already come into the room. The attendants hurried to pull a chair – Lord Barham's chair – over for the prince; but Yongxing waved it aside, forcing the rest of them to keep on their feet. Lenton unobtrusively put a hand under Laurence's arm, giving him a little support, but the room still tilted and spun around him, the blaze of Yongxing's bright-coloured robes stabbing at his eyes.

'I see this is the way in which you show your respect for the Son of Heaven,' Yongxing said, addressing Barham. 'Once again you have thrown Lung Tien Xiang into battle; now you hold secret councils, and plot how you may yet keep the fruits of your thievery.'

Though Barham had been damning the Chinese five minutes before, now he went pale and stammered, 'Sir, Your Highness, not in the least—' but Yongxing was not slowed even a little.

'I have gone through this *covert*, as you call these animal pens,' he said. 'It is not surprising, when one considers your

55

barbaric methods, that Lung Tien Xiang should have formed this misguided attachment. Naturally he does not wish to be separated from the companion who is responsible for what little comfort he has been given.' He turned to Laurence, and looked him up and down disdainfully. 'You have taken advantage of his youth and inexperience; but this will not be tolerated. We will hear no further excuses for these delays. Once he has been restored to his home and his proper place, he will soon learn better than to value company so far beneath him.'

'Your Highness, you are mistaken; we have every intention to cooperate with you,' Lenton said bluntly, while Barham was still struggling for more polished phrases. 'But Temeraire will not leave Laurence, and I am sure you know well that a dragon cannot be sent, but only led.'

Yongxing said icily, 'Then plainly Captain Laurence must come also; or will you now attempt to convince us that *he* cannot be sent?'

They all stared, in blank confusion; Laurence hardly dared believe he understood properly, and then Barham blurted, 'Good God, if you want Laurence, you may damn well have him, and welcome.'

The rest of the meeting passed in a haze for Laurence, the tangle of confusion and immense relief leaving him badly distracted. His head still spun, and he answered to remarks somewhat randomly until Lenton finally intervened once more, sending him up to bed. He kept himself awake only long enough to send a quick note to Temeraire by way of the maid, and fell straightaway into a thick, unrefreshing sleep.

He clawed his way out of it the next morning, having slept fourteen hours. Captain Roland was drowsing by his bedside, head tipped against the chair back, mouth open; as he stirred, she woke and rubbed her face, yawning. 'Well, Laurence, are you awake? You have been giving us all a fright and no

mistake. Emily came to me because poor Temeraire was fretting himself to pieces: whyever did you send him such a
note?'

Laurence tried desperately to remember what he had written:
impossible; it was wholly gone, and he could remember very
little of the previous day at all, though the central, the essential point was quite fixed in his mind. 'Roland, I have not the
faintest idea what I said. Does Temeraire know that I am
going with him?'

'Well, now he does, since Lenton told me after I came
looking for you, but he certainly did not find it in here,' she
said, and gave him a piece of paper.

It was in his own hand, and with his signature, but wholly
unfamiliar, and nonsensical:

Temeraire—
Never fear; I am going; the Son of Heaven will not tolerate
delays, and Barham gives me leave. Allegiance will carry
us! Pray eat something.
—L.

Laurence stared at it in some distress, wondering how he
had come to write so. 'I do not remember a word of it; but
wait, no; *Allegiance* is the name of the transport, and Prince
Yongxing referred to the Emperor as the Son of Heaven,
though why I should have repeated such a blasphemous
thing I have no idea.' He handed her the note. 'My wits
must have been wandering. Pray throw it in the fire; and
go tell Temeraire that I am quite well now, and will be with
him again soon. Can you ring for someone to valet me? I
need to dress.'

'You look as though you ought to stay just where you are,'
Roland said. 'No: lie quiet a while. There is no great hurry at
present, as far as I understand, and I know this fellow Barham
wants to speak with you; also Lenton. I will go tell Temeraire

you have not died or grown a second head, and have Emily jog back and forth between you if you have messages.'

Laurence yielded to her persuasions; indeed he did not truly feel up to rising, and if Barham wanted to speak with him again, he thought he would need to conserve what strength he had. However, in the event, he was spared: Lenton came alone instead.

'Well, Laurence, you are in for a hellishly long trip, I am afraid, and I hope you do not have a bad time of it,' he said, drawing up a chair. 'My transport ran into a three-day gale going to India, back in the nineties; rain freezing as it fell, so the dragons could not fly above it for some relief. Poor Obversaria was ill the entire time. Nothing less pleasant than a sea-sick dragon, for them or you.'

Laurence had never commanded a dragon transport, but the image was a vivid one. 'I am glad to say, sir, that Temeraire has never had the slightest difficulty, and indeed he enjoys sea-travel greatly.'

'We will see how he likes it if you meet a hurricane,' Lenton said, shaking his head. 'Not that I expect either of you have any objections, under the circumstances.'

'No, not in the least,' Laurence said, heartfelt. He supposed it was merely a jump from frying-pan to fire, but he was grateful enough even for the slower roasting: the journey would last for many months, and there was room for hope: any number of things might happen before they reached China.

Lenton nodded. 'Well, you are looking moderately ghastly, so let me be brief. I have managed to persuade Barham that the best thing to do is pack you off bag and baggage, in this case your crew; some of your officers would be in for a good bit of unpleasantness, otherwise, and we had best get you on your way before he thinks better of it.'

Yet another relief, scarcely looked-for. 'Sir,' Laurence said, 'I must tell you how deeply indebted I am—'

'No, nonsense; do not thank me.' Lenton brushed his sparse

grey hair back from his forehead, and abruptly said, 'I am damned sorry about all this, Laurence. I would have run mad a good deal sooner, in your place; brutally done, all of it.'

Laurence hardly knew what to say; he had not expected anything like sympathy, and he did not feel he deserved it. After a moment, Lenton went on, more briskly. 'I am sorry not to give you a longer time to recover, but then you will not have much to do aboard ship but rest. Barham has promised them the *Allegiance* will sail in a week's time; though from what I gather, he will be hard put to find a captain for her by then.'

'I thought Cartwright was to have her?' Laurence asked, some vague memory stirring; he still read the *Naval Chronicle*, and followed the assignments of ships; Cartwright's name stuck in his head: they had served together in *Goliath*, many years before.

'Yes, when *Allegiance* was meant to go to Halifax; there is apparently some other ship being built for him there. But they cannot wait for him to finish a two years' journey to China and back,' Lenton said. 'Be that as it may, someone will be found; you must be ready.'

'You may be sure of it, sir,' Laurence said. 'I will be quite well again by then.'

His optimism was perhaps ill-founded; after Lenton had gone, Laurence tried to write a letter and found he could not quite manage it, his head ached too wretchedly. Fortunately, Granby came by an hour later to see him, full of excitement at the prospect of the journey, and contemptuous of the risks he had taken with his own career.

'As though I could give a cracked egg for such a thing, when that scoundrel was trying to have you hauled away, and pointing guns at Temeraire,' he said. 'Pray don't think of it, and tell me what you would like me to write.'

Laurence gave up trying to counsel him to caution; Granby's loyalty was as obstinate as his initial dislike had been, if more gratifying. 'Only a few lines, if you please – to Captain

Thomas Riley; tell him we are bound for China in a week's time, and if he does not mind a transport, he can likely get *Allegiance*, if only he goes straightaway to the Admiralty: Barham has no one for the ship; but be sure and tell him not to mention my name.'

'Very good,' Granby said, scratching away; he did not write a very elegant hand, the letters sprawling wastefully, but it was serviceable enough to read. 'Do you know him well? We will have to put up with whoever they give us for a long while.'

'Yes, very well indeed,' Laurence said. 'He was my third lieutenant in *Belize*, and my second in *Reliant*; he was at Temeraire's hatching: a fine officer and seaman. We could not hope for better.'

'I will run it down to the courier myself, and tell him to be sure it arrives,' Granby promised. 'What a relief it would be, not to have one of these wretched stiff-necked fellows—' and there he stopped, embarrassed; it was not so very long ago he had counted Laurence himself a 'stiff-necked fellow', after all.

'Thank you, John,' Laurence said hastily, sparing him. 'Although we ought not get our hopes up yet; the Ministry may prefer a more senior man in the role,' he added, though privately he thought the chances were excellent. Barham would not have an easy time of it, finding someone willing to accept the post.

Impressive though they might be, to the landsman's eye, a dragon transport was an awkward sort of vessel to command: often enough they sat in port endlessly, awaiting dragon passengers, while the crew dissipated itself in drinking and whoring. Or they might spend months in the middle of the ocean, trying to maintain a single position to serve as a resting point for dragons crossing long distances; like blockade-duty, only worse for lack of society. Little chance of battle or glory, less of prize-money; they were not desirable to any man who could do better.

But the *Reliant*, so badly dished in the gale after Trafalgar, would be in dry-dock for a long while. Riley, left on shore with no influence to help him to a new ship, virtually no seniority, would be as glad of the opportunity as Laurence would be to have him, and there was every chance Barham would seize on the first fellow who offered.

Laurence spent the next day labouring, with slightly more success, over other necessary letters. His affairs were not prepared for a long journey, much of it far past the limits of the courier circuit. Then too, over the last dreadful weeks he had entirely neglected his personal correspondence, and by now he owed several replies, particularly to his family. After the battle of Dover, his father had grown more tolerant of his new profession; although they still did not write one another directly, at least Laurence was no longer obliged to conceal his correspondence with his mother, and he had for some time now addressed his letters to her openly. His father might very well choose to suspend that privilege again, after this affair, but Laurence hoped he might not hear the particulars of it: fortunately, Barham had nothing to gain from embarrassing Lord Allendale; particularly not now when Wilberforce, their mutual political ally, meant to make another push for abolition in the next session of Parliament.

Laurence dashed off another dozen hasty notes, in a hand not very much like his usual, to other correspondents; most of them were naval men, who would well understand the exigencies of a hasty departure. Despite much abbreviation, the effort took its toll, and by the time Jane Roland came to see him once again, he had nearly prostrated himself once more, and was lying back against the pillows with eyes shut.

'Yes, I will post them for you, but you are behaving absurdly, Laurence,' she said, collecting up the letters. 'A knock on the head can be very nasty, even if you have not cracked your skull. When I had the yellow fever I did not prance about claiming I was well; I lay in bed and took my gruel and possets, and I was back on my feet quicker than any of the other fellows in the West Indies who took it.'

'Thank you, Jane,' he said, and did not argue with her; indeed he felt very ill, and he was grateful when she drew the curtains and cast the room into a comfortable dimness.

He briefly came out of sleep some hours later, hearing some commotion outside the door of his room: Roland saying, 'You are damned well going to leave now, or I will kick you down the hall. What do you mean, sneaking in here to pester him the instant I have gone out?'

'But I must speak with Captain Laurence; the situation is of the most urgent—' the protesting voice was unfamiliar, and rather bewildered. 'I have ridden straight from London—'

'If it is so urgent, you may go speak to Admiral Lenton,' Roland said. 'No; I do not care if you are from the Ministry; you look young enough to be one of my mids, and I do not for an instant believe you have anything to say that cannot wait until morning.'

With this she pulled the door shut behind her, and the rest of the argument was muffled; Laurence drifted again away. But the next morning there was no one to defend him, and scarcely had the maid brought in his breakfast – the threatened gruel and hot-milk posset, and quite unappetizing – than a fresh attempt at invasion was made, this time with more success.

'I beg your pardon, sir, for forcing myself upon you in this irregular fashion,' the stranger said, talking rapidly while he dragged up a chair to Laurence's bedside, uninvited. 'Pray allow me to explain; I realize the appearance is quite extraordinary—' He set down the heavy chair and sat down, or rather perched, at the very edge of the seat. 'My name is Hammond, Arthur Hammond; I have been deputized by the Ministry to accompany you to the court of China.'

Hammond was a surprisingly young man, perhaps twenty years of age, with untidy dark hair and a great intensity of expression that lent his thin, sallow face an illuminated quality. He spoke at first in half-sentences, torn between the forms of apology and his plain eagerness to come to his subject. 'The absence of an introduction, I beg you will forgive, we have been taken completely, completely by surprise, and Lord Barham has already committed us to the twenty-third as a sailing date. If you would prefer, we may of course press him for some extension—'

This of all things Laurence was eager to avoid, though he was indeed a little astonished by Hammond's forwardness; hastily he said, 'No, sir, I am entirely at your service; we cannot delay sailing to exchange formalities, particularly when Prince Yongxing has already been promised that date.'

'Ah! I am of a similar mind,' Hammond said, with a great deal of relief; Laurence suspected, looking at his face and measuring his years, that he had only received the appointment due to the lack of time. But Hammond quickly refuted the notion that a willingness to go to China on a moment's notice was his only qualification. Having settled himself, he drew out a thick sheaf of papers, which had been distending the front of his coat, and began to discourse in great detail and speed upon the prospects of their mission.

Laurence was almost from the first unable to follow him. Hammond unconsciously slipped into stretches of the Chinese language from time to time, when looking down at those of his papers written in that script, and while speaking in English dwelt largely on the subject of the Macartney embassy to China, which had taken place fourteen years prior. Laurence, who had been newly made lieutenant at the time and wholly occupied with naval matters and his own career, had hardly remembered the existence of the mission at all, much less any details.

He did not immediately stop Hammond, however: there was no convenient pause in the flow of his conversation, for one, and for another there was a reassuring quality to the monologue. Hammond spoke with authority beyond his years, an obvious command of his subject, and, still more importantly, without the least hint of the incivility which Laurence had come to expect from Barham and the Ministry. Laurence was grateful enough for any prospect of an ally to willingly listen, even if all he knew of the expedition himself was that Macartney's ship, the *Lion*, had been the first Western vessel to chart the Bay of Zhitao.

'Oh,' Hammond said, rather disappointed, when at last he realized how thoroughly he had mistaken his audience. 'Well, I suppose it does not much signify; to put it plainly, the embassy was a dismal failure. Lord Macartney refused to perform their ritual of obeisance before the Emperor, the kowtow, and they took offence. They would not even consider granting us a permanent mission, and he ended by being escorted out of the China Sea by a dozen dragons.'

'That I do remember,' Laurence said; indeed he had a vague recollection of discussing the matter among his friends in the gunroom, with some heat at the insult to Britain's envoy. 'But surely the kowtow was quite offensive; did they not wish him to grovel on the floor?'

'We cannot be turning up our noses at foreign customs when we are coming to their country, hat in hand,' Hammond said, earnestly, leaning forward. 'You can see yourself, sir, the evil consequences: I am sure that the bad blood from this incident continues to poison our present relationship.'

Laurence frowned; this argument was indeed persuasive, and made some better explanation why Yongxing had come to England so very ready to be offended. 'Do you think this same quarrel their reason for having offered Bonaparte a Celestial? After so long a time?'

'I will be quite honest with you, Captain, we have not the least idea,' Hammond said. 'Our only comfort, these last fourteen years – a very cornerstone of foreign policy – has been our certainty, our complete certainty, that the Chinese were no more interested in the affairs of Europe than we are in the affairs of the penguins. Now all our foundations have been shaken.'

Chapter Three

The *Allegiance* was a wallowing behemoth of a ship: just over four hundred feet in length and oddly narrow in proportion, except for the outsize dragondeck that flared out at the front of the ship, stretching from the foremast forward to the bow. Seen from above, she looked very strange, almost fan-shaped. But below the wide lip of the dragondeck, her hull narrowed quickly; the keel was fashioned out of steel rather than elm, and thickly covered with white paint against rust: the long white stripe running down her middle gave her an almost rakish appearance.

To give her the stability which she required to meet storms, she had a draught of more than twenty feet and was too large to come into the harbour proper, but had to be moored to enormous pillars sunk far out in the deep water and her supplies ferried to and fro by smaller vessels: a great lady surrounded by scurrying attendants. This was not the first transport which Laurence and Temeraire had travelled on, but she would be the first true ocean-going one; a poky three-dragon ship running from Gibraltar to Plymouth with barely a few planks in increased width could offer no comparison.

'It is very nice; I am more comfortable even than in my clearing.' Temeraire approved: from his place of solitary glory,

65

he could see all the ship's activity without being in the way, and the ship's galley with its ovens was placed directly beneath the dragondeck, which kept the surface warm. 'You are not cold at all, Laurence?' he asked, for perhaps the third time, craning his head down to peer closely at him.

'No, not in the least,' Laurence said shortly; he was a little annoyed by the continuing oversolicitude. Though the dizziness and headache had subsided together with the lump upon his head, his bruised leg remained stubborn, prone to giving out at odd moments and throbbing with an almost constant ache. He had been hoisted aboard in a bo'sun's chair, very offensive to his sense of his own capabilities, then put directly into an elbow-chair and carried up to the dragondeck, swathed in blankets like an invalid, and now had Temeraire very carefully coiling himself about to serve as a windbreak.

There were two sets of stairs rising to the dragondeck, one on either side of the foremast, and the area of the forecastle stretching from the foot of these and halfway to the mainmast was by custom allocated to the aviators, while the foremast jacks ruled the remainder of the space up to the mainmast. Already Temeraire's crew had taken possession of their rightful domain, pointedly pushing several piles of coiled cables across the invisible dividing line; bundles of leather harness and baskets full of rings and buckles had been laid down in their place, all to put the Navy men on notice that the aviators were not to be taken advantage of. Those men not occupied in putting away their gear were ranged along the line in various attitudes of relaxation and affected labour; Roland and the other two cadet runners, Morgan and Dyer, had been set to playing there by the ensigns, who had conveyed their duty to defend the rights of the Corps. Being so small they could walk the ship's rail with ease and were dashing back and forth with a fine show of recklessness.

Laurence watched them, broodingly; he was still uneasy about bringing Roland. 'Why would you leave her? Has she been misbehaving?' was all Jane had asked, when he had consulted her on the matter; impossibly awkward to try and explain his concerns, facing her. And of course, there was some sense in taking the girl along, young as she was: she would have to face every demand made of a male officer, when she came to be Excidium's captain on her mother's retirement; it would be no kindness to leave her unprepared by being too soft on her now.

Even so, now that he was aboard he was sorry. This was not a covert, and he had already seen that as with any naval crew there were some ugly, some very ugly fellows among the lot: drunkards, brawlers, gaol-birds. He felt too heavily the responsibility of watching over a young girl among such men; not to mention that he would be best pleased if the secret that women served in the Corps did not come out here and make a noise.

He did not mean to instruct Roland to lie, by no means, and of course he could not give her different duties than otherwise; but he privately and intensely hoped the truth might remain concealed. Roland was only eleven, and no cursory glance would take her for a girl in her trousers and short jacket; he had once mistaken her for a boy himself. But he also desired to see the aviators and the sailors friendly, or at least not hostile, and a close acquaintance could hardly fail to notice Roland's real gender for long.

At present his hopes looked more likely to be answered in her case than the general. The foremast hands, engaged in the business of loading the ship, were talking none too quietly about fellows who had nothing better to do but sit about and be passengers; a couple of men made loud comments about how the shifted cables had been cast all ahoo, and set to recoiling them, unnecessarily. Laurence shook his head and kept his silence; his own men had been within their rights, and he could not reprove Riley's men, nor would it do any good.

However, Temeraire had noticed also; he snorted, his ruff coming up a little. 'That cable looks perfectly well to me,' he said. 'My crew were very careful moving it.'

'It is all right, my dear; can never hurt to recoil a cable,' Laurence said hurriedly. It was not very surprising that Temeraire had begun to extend his protective and possessive instincts over the crew as well; they had been with him now for several months. But the timing was wretchedly inconvenient: the sailors would likely be nervous to begin with at the presence of a dragon, and if Temeraire involved himself in any dispute, taking the part of his crew, that could only increase the tensions on board.

'Pray take no offence,' Laurence added, stroking Temeraire's flank to draw his attention. 'The beginning of a journey is so very important; we wish to be good shipmates, and not encourage any sort of rivalry among the men.'

'Hm, I suppose,' Temeraire said, subsiding. 'But we have done nothing wrong; it is disagreeable of them to complain so.'

'We will be underway soon,' Laurence said, by way of distraction. 'The tide has turned, and I think that is the last of the embassy's luggage coming aboard now.'

Allegiance could carry as many as ten mid-weight dragons, in a pinch; Temeraire alone scarcely weighed her down, and there was a truly astonishing amount of storage space aboard. Yet the sheer quantity of the baggage the embassy carried began to look as though it would strain even her great capacity: shocking to Laurence, used to travelling with little more than a single sea-chest, and seeming quite out of proportion to the size of the entourage, which was itself enormous.

There were some fifteen soldiers, and no less than three physicians: one for the prince himself, one for the other two envoys, and one for the remainder of the embassy, each with assistants. After these and the translator, there were besides a pair of cooks with assistants, perhaps a dozen body servants, and an equal number of other men who seemed to have no clear function at all, including one gentleman who had been introduced as a poet, although Laurence could not believe this had been an accurate translation: more likely the man was a clerk of some sort.

The prince's wardrobe alone required some twenty chests, each one elaborately carved and with golden locks and hinges: the bo'sun's whip flew loud and cracking more than once, as the more enterprising sailors tried to pry them off. The innumerable bags of food had also to be slung aboard, and having already come once from China, they were beginning to show wear. One enormous eighty-pound sack of rice split wide open as it was handed across the deck, to the universal joy and delectation of the hovering seagulls, and afterwards the sailors were forced to wave the frenzied clouds of birds away every few minutes as they tried to keep on with their work.

There had already been a great fuss about boarding, earlier. Yongxing's attendants had demanded, at first, a walkway leading *down* to the ship – wholly impossible, even if the *Allegiance* could have been brought close enough to the dock to make a walkway of any sort practical, because of the height of her decks. Poor Hammond had spent the better part of an hour trying to persuade them that there was no dishonour or danger either in being lifted up to the deck, and pointing at frustrated intervals at the ship herself, a mute argument.

Hammond had eventually said to him, quite desperately, 'Captain, is this a dangerously high sea?' An absurd question, with a swell less than five feet, though in the brisk wind the waiting barge had occasionally bucked against the ropes holding her to the dock, but even Laurence's surprised negative had not satisfied the attendants. It had seemed they might never get aboard, but at last Yongxing himself had grown tired of waiting and ended the argument by emerging from his heavily-draped sedan chair, and climbing down into the boat, ignoring both the flurry of his anxious attendants and the hastily offered hands of the barge's crew.

The Chinese passengers who had waited for the second barge were still coming aboard now, on the starboard side, to the stiff and polished welcome of a dozen Marines and the most respectable-looking of the sailors, interleaved in a row along the inner edge of the gangway, decorative in their bright red coats and the white trousers and short blue jackets of the sailors.

Sun Kai, the younger envoy, leapt easily down from the bo'sun's chair and stood a moment looking around the busy deck thoughtfully. Laurence wondered if perhaps he did not approve the clamour and disarray of the deck, but no, it seemed he was only trying to get his feet underneath him: he took a few tentative steps back and forth, then stretched his sea-legs a little further and walked the length of the gangway and back more surely, with his hands clasped behind his back, and gazed with frowning concentration up at the rigging, trying evidently to trace the maze of ropes from their source to their conclusion.

This was much to the satisfaction of the men on display, who could at last stare their own fill in return. Prince Yongxing had disappointed them all by vanishing almost at once to the private quarters which had been arranged for him at the stern; Sun Kai, tall and properly impassive with his long black queue and shaved forehead, in splendid blue robes picked out with red and orange embroidery, was very nearly as good, and he showed no inclination to seek out his own quarters.

A moment later they had a still better piece of entertainment; shouts and cries rose from below, and Sun Kai sprang to the side to look over. Laurence sat up, and saw Hammond running to the edge, pale with horror: there had been a noisy splashing. But a few moments later, the older envoy finally appeared over the side, dripping water from the sodden lower half of his robes. Despite his misadventure, the grey-bearded man climbed down with a roar of good-humoured laughter at his own expense, waving off what looked like Hammond's

70

urgent apologies; he slapped his ample belly with a rueful expression, and then went away in company with Sun Kai.

'He had a narrow escape,' Laurence observed, sinking back into his chair. 'Those robes would have dragged him down in a moment, if he had properly fallen in.'

'I am sorry they did not all fall in,' Temeraire muttered, quietly for a twenty-ton dragon; which was to say, not very. There were sniggers on the deck, and Hammond glanced over at them anxiously.

The rest of the retinue were gotten aboard without further incident, and stowed away almost as quickly as their baggage. Hammond looked much relieved when the operation was at last completed, blotting his sweating forehead on the back of his hand, though the wind was knife-cold and bitter, and sat down quite limply on a locker along the gangway, much to the annoyance of the crew. They could not get the barge back aboard with him in the way, and yet he was a passenger and an envoy himself, too important to be bluntly told to move.

Taking pity on them all, Laurence looked for his runners: Roland, Morgan, and Dyer had been told to stay quiet on the dragondeck and out of the way, and so were sitting in a row at the very edge, dangling their heels into space. 'Morgan,' Laurence said, and the dark-haired boy scrambled up and towards him, 'go and invite Mr. Hammond to come and sit with me, if he would like.'

Hammond brightened at the invitation and came up to the dragondeck at once; he did not even notice as behind him the men immediately began rigging the tackles to hoist aboard the barge. 'Thank you, sir, thank you, it is very good of you,' he said, taking a seat on a locker which Morgan and Roland together pushed over for him, and accepting with still more gratitude the offer of a glass of brandy. 'How I should have managed, if Liu Bao had drowned, I have not the least notion.'

'Is that the gentleman's name?' Laurence said; all he remembered of the older envoy from the Admiralty meeting was his rather whistling snore. 'It would have been an inauspicious start to the journey, but Yongxing could scarcely have blamed you for his taking a misstep.'

'No, there you are quite wrong,' Hammond said. 'He is a prince; he can blame anyone he likes.'

Laurence was disposed to take this as a joke, but Hammond seemed rather glumly serious about it; and after drinking the best part of his glass of brandy in what already seemed to Laurence, despite their brief acquaintance, an uncharacteristic silence, Hammond added abruptly, 'And pray forgive me – I must mention, how very prejudicial such remarks may be – the consequences of a moment's thoughtless offence—'

It took Laurence a moment to puzzle out that Hammond referred to Temeraire's earlier resentful mutterings; Temeraire was quicker and answered for himself. 'I do not care if they do not like me,' he said. 'Maybe then they will let me alone, and I will not have to stay in China.' This thought visibly struck him, and his head came up with sudden enthusiasm. 'If I were very offensive, do you suppose they would go away now?' he asked. 'Laurence, what would be particularly insulting?'

Hammond looked like Pandora, the box open and horrors loosed upon the world; Laurence was inclined to laugh, but he stifled it out of sympathy. Hammond was young for his work, and surely, however brilliant his talents, felt his own lack of experience; it could not help but make him over-cautious.

'No, my dear, it will not do,' Laurence said. 'Likely they would only blame us for teaching you ill-manners, and resolve all the more on keeping you.'

'Oh.' Temeraire disconsolately let his head sink back down onto his forelegs. 'Well, I suppose I do not mind so much going, except that everyone else will be fighting without me,' he said in resignation. 'But the journey will be very inter- esting, and I suppose I would like to see China; only they *will* try to take Laurence away from me again, I am sure of it, and I am not going to have any of it.'

Hammond prudently did not engage him on this subject, but hurried instead to say, 'How long this business of loading has all taken – surely it is not typical? I made sure we would be halfway down the Channel by noon; here we have not even yet made sail.'

'I think they are nearly done,' Laurence said; the last immense chest was being swung aboard into the hands of the waiting sailors with the help of a block and line. The men looked all tired and surly, as well they might, having spent time enough for loading ten dragons on loading instead one man and his accoutrements; and their dinner was a good half-hour overdue already.

As the chest vanished below, Captain Riley climbed the stairs from the quarterdeck to join them, taking his hat off long enough to wipe sweat away from his brow. 'I have no notion how they got themselves and the lot to England. I suppose they did not come by transport?'

'No, or else we would surely be returning by their ship,' Laurence said. He had not considered the question before and realized only now that he had no idea how the Chinese embassy had made their voyage. 'Perhaps they came overland.' Hammond was silent and frowning, evidently wondering himself.

'That must be a very interesting journey, with so many different places to visit,' Temeraire observed. 'Not that I am sorry to be going by sea: not at all,' he added, hastily, peering down anxiously at Riley to be sure he had not offended. 'Will it be much faster, going by sea?'

'No, not in the least,' Laurence said. 'I have heard of a courier going from London to Bombay in two months, and we will be lucky to reach Canton in seven. But there is no secure route by land: France is in the way, unfortunately, and there is a great deal of banditry, not to mention the mountains and the Taklamakan desert to cross.'

'I would not wager on less than eight months, myself,' Riley said. 'If we make six knots with the wind anywhere but dead astern, it will be more than I look for, judging by her log.' Below and above now there was a great scurry of activity, all hands preparing to unmoor and make sail; the ebbing tide was lapping softly against the windward side. 'Well, we must get about it. Laurence, tonight I must be on deck, I need to take the measure of her; but I hope you will dine with me tomorrow? And you also, of course, Mr. Hammond.'

'Captain,' Hammond said, 'I am not familiar with the ordinary course of a ship's life – I beg your indulgence. Would it be suitable to invite the members of the embassy?'

'Why—' Riley said, astonished, and Laurence could not blame him; it was a bit much to be inviting people to another man's table. But Riley caught himself, and then said, more politely, 'Surely, sir, it is for Prince Yongxing to issue such an invitation first.'

'We will be in Canton before that happens, in the present state of relations,' Hammond said. 'No; we must make shifts to engage them, somehow.'

Riley offered a little more resistance; but Hammond had taken the bit between his teeth and managed, by a skilful combination of coaxing and deafness to hints, to carry his point. Riley might have struggled longer, but the men were all waiting impatiently for the word to weigh anchor, the tide was going every minute, and at last Hammond ended by saying, 'Thank you, sir, for your indulgence; and now I will beg you gentlemen to excuse me. I am a fair enough hand at their script on land, but I imagine it will take me some more time to draft an acceptable invitation aboard ship.' With this, he rose and escaped before Riley could retract the surrender he had not quite made.

'Well,' Riley said, gloomily, 'before he manages it, I am going to go and get us as far out to sea as I can; if they are mad as fire at my cheek, at least with this wind I can say in

74

perfect honesty that I cannot get back into port for them to kick me ashore. By the time we reach Madeira they may get over it.'

He jumped down to the forecastle and gave the word; in a moment the men at the great quadruple-height capstans were straining, their grunting and bellowing carrying up from the lower decks as the cable came dragging over the iron catheads: the *Allegiance*'s smallest kedge anchor as large as the best bower of another ship, its flukes spread wider than the height of a man.

Much to the relief of the men, Riley did not order them to warp her out; a handful of men pushed off from the pilings with iron poles, and even that was scarcely necessary: the wind was from the northwest, full on her starboard beam, and that with the tide carried her now easily away from the harbour. She was only under topsails, but as soon as they had cleared moorings Riley called for topgallants and courses, and despite his pessimistic words they were soon going through the water at a respectable clip: she did not make much leeway, with that long deep keel, but went straight down the Channel in a stately manner.

Temeraire had turned his head forward to enjoy the wind of their progress: he looked rather like the figurehead of some old Viking ship. Laurence smiled at the notion. Temeraire saw his expression and nudged at him affectionately. 'Will you read to me?' he asked hopefully. 'We will have only another couple hours of light.'

'With pleasure,' said Laurence, and sat up to look for one of his runners. 'Morgan,' he called, 'will you be so good as to go below and fetch me the book in the top of my sea-chest, by Gibbon; we are in the second volume.'

The great admiral's cabin at the stern had been hastily converted into something of a state apartment for Prince Yongxing, and the captain's cabin beneath the poop deck divided for the other two senior envoys, the smaller quarters nearby given over to the crowd of guards and attendants, displacing not only Riley himself, but the ship's first lieutenant, Lord Purbeck, the surgeon, the master, and several other of his officers. Fortunately, the quarters at the fore of the ship, ordinarily reserved for the senior aviators aboard, were all but empty with Temeraire the only dragon aboard: even shared out among them all, there was no shortage of room; and for the occasion, the ship's carpenters had knocked down the bulkheads of their individual cabins and made a grand dining space.

Too grand, at first: Hammond had objected. 'We cannot seem to have more room than the prince,' he explained, and so had the bulkheads shifted a good six feet forward: the collected tables were suddenly cramped.

Riley had benefited from the enormous prize-money awarded for the capture of Temeraire's egg almost as much as Laurence himself had; fortunately he could afford to keep a good table and a large one. The occasion indeed called for every stick of furniture which could be found on board: the instant he had recovered from the appalling shock of having his invitation even partly accepted, Riley had invited all the senior members of the gunroom, Laurence's own lieutenants, and any other man who might reasonably be expected to make civilized conversation.

'But Prince Yongxing is not coming,' Hammond said, 'and the rest of them have less than a dozen words of English between them. Except for the translator, and he is only one man.'

'Then at least we can make enough noise amongst ourselves we will not all be sitting in grim silence,' Riley said.

But this hope was not answered: the moment the guests arrived, a paralysed silence descended, bidding fair to continue throughout the meal. Though the translator had accompanied them, none of the Chinese spoke at first. The older envoy Liu Bao had stayed away also, leaving Sun Kai as the senior representative; but even he made only a spare, formal greeting on their arrival, and afterwards maintained a calm and silent dignity, though he stared intently at the barrel-thick column of the foremast, painted in yellow stripes, which came down through the ceiling and passed directly through the middle of the table, and went so far as to look beneath the table-cloth, to see it continuing down through the deck below.

Riley had left the right side of the table entirely for the Chinese guests, and had them shown to places there, but they did not move to sit when he and the officers did, which left the British in confusion, some men already half-seated and trying to keep themselves suspended in mid-air. Bewildered, Riley pressed them to take their seats; but he had to urge them several times before at last they would sit. It was an inauspicious beginning, and did not encourage conversation.

The officers at first began by taking refuge in their dinners, but even that semblance of good manners did not last very long. The Chinese did not eat with knife and fork, but with lacquered sticks they had brought with them. These they somehow manoeuvred one-handed to bring food to their lips, and shortly the British half of the company were staring in helplessly rude fascination, every new dish presenting a fresh opportunity to observe the technique. The guests were briefly puzzled by the platter of roast mutton, large slices carved from the leg, but after a moment one of the younger atten-dants carefully proceeded to roll up a slice, still only using the sticks, and picked it up entire to eat in three bites, leading the way for the rest.

By now Tripp, Riley's youngest midshipman, a plump and unlovely twelve-year-old aboard by virtue of his family's three votes in Parliament, and invited for his own education rather than his company, was surreptitiously trying to imitate the style, using his fork and knife turned upside-down in place of the sticks, his efforts meeting without notable success, except in doing damage to his formerly-clean breeches. He was too far down the table to be quelled by hard looks, and the men around him were too busy gawking themselves to notice.

Sun Kai had the seat of honour nearest Riley, and desperate to keep his attention from the boy's antics, Riley tentatively raised a glass to him, watching Hammond out of the corner of his eye for direction, and said, 'To your health, sir.' Hammond murmured a hasty translation across the table, and Sun Kai nodded, raised his own glass, and sipped politely, though not very much: it was a heady Madeira well-fortified with brandy, chosen to survive rough seas. For a moment it seemed this might rescue the occasion: the rest of the officers were belatedly recalled to their duty as gentlemen, and began to salute the rest of the guests; the pantomime of raised glasses was perfectly comprehensible without any translation, and led naturally to a thawing of relations. Smiles and nods began to traverse the table, and Laurence heard Hammond, beside him, heave out an almost inaudible sigh through open lips, and finally take some little food.

Laurence knew he was not doing his own part; but his knee was lodged up against a trestle of the table, preventing him from stretching out his now-aching leg, and though he had drunk as sparingly as was polite, his head felt thick and clouded. By now he only hoped he might avoid embarrassment, and resigned himself to making apologies to Riley after the meal for his dullness.

Riley's third lieutenant, a fellow named Franks, had spent the first three toasts in rude silence, sitting woodenly and raising his glass only with a mute smile, but sufficient flow of wine loosened his tongue at last. He had served on an East Indiaman as a boy, during the peace, and evidently had acquired a few stumbling words of Chinese; now he tried the less-obscene of them on the gentleman sitting across from him: a young, clean-shaven man named Ye Bing, gangly beneath the camouflage of his fine robes, who brightened and proceeded to respond with his own handful of English.

78

'A very— A fine—' he said, and stuck, unable to find the rest of the compliment he wished to make, shaking his head as Franks offered, alternatively, the options which seemed to him most natural: *wind*, *night*, and *dinner*; at last Ye Bing beckoned over the translator, who said on his behalf, 'Many compliments to your ship: it is most cleverly devised.'

Such praise was an easy way to a sailor's heart; Riley, over-hearing, broke off from his disjointed bilingual conversation with Hammond and Sun Kai, on their likely southward course, and called down to the translator, 'Pray thank the gentleman for his kind words, sir; and tell him that I hope you will all find yourselves quite comfortable.'

Ye Bing bowed his head and said, through the translator, 'Thank you, sir, we are already much more so than on our journey here. Four ships were required to carry us here, and one proved unhappily slow.'

'Captain Riley, I understand you have gone round the Cape of Good Hope before?' Hammond interrupted: rudely, and Laurence glanced at him in surprise.

Riley also looked startled, but politely turned back to answer him, but Franks, who had spent nearly all of the last two days below in the stinking hold, directing the stowage of all the baggage, said in slightly drunken irreverence, 'Four ships only? I am surprised it did not take six; you must have been packed like sardines.'

Ye Bing nodded and said, 'The vessels were small for so long a journey, but in the service of the Emperor all discomfort is a joy, and in any case, they were the largest of your ships in Canton at the time.'

'Oh; so you hired East Indiamen for the passage?' Macready asked; he was the Marine lieutenant, a rail-thin, wiry stump of a man who wore spectacles incongruous on his much-scarred face. There was no malice but undeniably a slight edge of superiority in the question, and in the smiles exchanged by the naval men. That the French could build ships but not sail them, that the Dons were excitable and undisciplined, that the Chinese had no fleet at all to speak of, these were the oft-repeated bywords of the service, and to have them so confirmed was always pleasant, always heartening.

'Four ships in Canton harbour, and you filled their holds with baggage instead of silk and porcelain; they must have charged you the earth,' Franks added.

'How very strange that you should say so,' Ye Bing said. 'Although we were travelling under the Emperor's seal, it is true, one captain did try to demand payment, and then even tried to sail away without permission. Some evil spirit must have seized hold of him and made him act in such a crazy manner. But I believe your Company officials were able to find a doctor to treat him, and he was allowed to apologize.'

Franks stared, as well he might. 'But then why did they take you, if you did not pay them?'

Ye Bing stared back, equally surprised to have been asked. 'The ships were confiscated by Imperial edict. What else could they have done?' He shrugged his shoulders, as if to dismiss the subject, and turned his attention back to the dishes; he seemed to think the piece of intelligence less significant than the small jam tartlets Riley's cook had provided with the latest course.

Laurence abruptly put down knife and fork; his appetite had been weak to begin with, and now was wholly gone. That they could speak so casually of the seizure of British ships and property – the forced servitude of British seamen to a foreign throne— For a moment almost he convinced himself he had misunderstood: every newspaper in the country would have been shrieking of such an incident; the Government would surely have made a formal protest. Then he looked at Hammond: the diplomat's face was pale and alarmed, but unsurprised; and all remaining doubt vanished as Laurence recalled all of Barham's sorry behaviour, so nearly grovelling, and Hammond's attempts to change the course of the conversation.

Comprehension was only a little slower in coming to the rest of the British, running up and down the table on the backs of low whispers, as the officers murmured back and forth to one another. Riley's reply to Hammond, which had been going forward all this time, slowed and stopped: though Hammond prompted Riley again, urgently, asking, 'Did you have a rough crossing of it? I hope we do not need to fear bad weather along the way,' this came too late; a complete silence fell, except for young Tripp chewing noisily.

Garnett, the master, elbowed the boy sharply, and even this sound failed. Sun Kai put down his wine glass and looked frowning up and down along the table; he had noticed the change of atmosphere: the feel of a brewing storm. There had already been a great deal of hard drinking, though they were scarcely halfway through the meal, and many of the officers were young, and flushing now with mortification and anger. Many a Navy man, cast on shore during an intermittent peace or by a lack of influence, had served aboard the ships of the East India Company; the ties between Britain's Navy and her merchant marine were strong, and the insult all the more keenly felt.

The translator was standing back from the chairs with an anxious expression, but most of the other Chinese attendants had not yet perceived. One laughed aloud at some remark of his neighbour's: it made a queer solitary noise in the cabin.

'By God,' Franks said, suddenly, out loud, 'I have a mind to—'

His seat-mates caught him by the arms, hurriedly, and kept him in his chair, hushing him with many anxious looks up towards the senior officers, but other whispers grew louder. One man was saying, '—sitting at our table!' to snatches of violent agreement; an explosion might come at any moment, certainly disastrous. Hammond was trying to speak, but no one was attending to him.

'Captain Riley,' Laurence said, harshly and over-loud,

quelling the furious whispers, 'will you be so good as to lay out our course for the journey? I believe Mr. Granby was curious as to the route we would follow.'

Granby, sitting a few chairs down, his face pale under his sunburn, started; then after a moment he said, 'Yes, indeed; I would take it as a great favour, sir,' nodding to Riley.

'Of course,' Riley said, if a little woodenly; he leaned over to the locker behind him, where his maps lay: bringing one onto the table, he traced the course, speaking somewhat more loudly than normal. 'Once out of the Channel, we must swing a ways out to skirt France and Spain; then we will come in a little closer and keep to the coastline of Africa as best we can. We will put in at the Cape until the summer monsoon begins, perhaps a week or three depending on our speed, and then ride the wind all the way to the South China Sea.'

The worst of the grim silence was broken, and slowly a thin obligatory conversation began again. But no one now said a word to the Chinese guests, except occasionally Hammond speaking to Sun Kai, and under the weight of disapproving stares even he faltered and was silent. Riley resorted to calling for the pudding, and the dinner wandered to a disastrous close, far earlier than usual.

There were Marines and seamen standing behind every sea-officer's chair to act as servants, already muttering to each other; by the time Laurence regained the deck, pulling himself up the ladderway more by the strength of his arms than by properly climbing, they had gone out, and the news had gone from one end of the deck to another, the aviators even speaking across the line with the sailors.

Hammond came out onto the deck and stared at the taut, muttering groups of men, biting his lips to bloodlessness; the anxiety made his face look queerly old and drawn. Laurence felt no pity for him, only indignation: there was no question that Hammond had deliberately tried to conceal the shameful matter.

Riley was beside him, not drinking the cup of coffee in his hand: boiled if not burnt, by the smell of it. 'Mr. Hammond,' he said, very quiet but with authority, more authority than Laurence, who for most of their acquaintance had known him as a subordinate, had ever heard him use; an authority which quite cleared away all traces of his ordinary easy-going humour, 'pray convey to the Chinamen that it is essential they stay below; I do not give a damn what excuse you like to give them, but I would not wager tuppence for their lives if they came on this deck now. Captain,' he added, turning to Laurence, 'I beg you send your men to sleep at once; I don't like the mood.'

'Yes,' Laurence said, in full understanding: men so stirred could become violent, and from there it was a short step to mutiny; the original cause of their rage would not even necessarily matter by then. He beckoned Granby over. 'John, send the fellows below, and have a word with the officers to keep them quiet; we want no disturbance.'

Granby nodded. 'By God, though—' he said, hard-eyed with his own anger, but he stopped when Laurence shook his head, and went. The aviators broke up and went below quietly; the example might have been of some good, for the sailors did not grow quarrelsome when ordered to do the same. Then, also, they knew very well that their officers were in this case not their enemies: anger was a living thing in every breast, shared sentiment bound them all together, and little more than mutters followed when Lord Purbeck, the first lieutenant, walked out upon the deck among them and ordered them below in his drawling, affected accent. 'Go along now, Jenkins; go along, Harvey.'

Temeraire was waiting on the dragondeck with head raised high and eyes bright; he had overheard enough to be on fire with curiosity. Having had the rest of the story, he snorted and said, 'If their own ships could not have carried them, they had much better have stayed home.' This was less indignation at the offence than simple dislike, however, and he was not inclined to great resentment; like most dragons, he had a very casual view of property, saving, of course, jewels and gold belonging to himself: even as he spoke he was busy polishing the great sapphire pendant which Laurence had given him, and which he never removed save for that purpose.

'It is an insult to the Crown,' Laurence said, rubbing his hand over his leg with short, pummelling strokes, resentful of the injury; he wanted badly to pace. Hammond was standing at the quarterdeck rail smoking a cigar, the dim red light of the burning embers flaring with his inhalations, illuminating his pale and sweat-washed face. Laurence glared at him along the length of the near-empty deck, bitterly. 'I wonder at him; at him and at Barham, to have swallowed such an outrage, with so little noise: it is scarcely to be borne.'

Temeraire blinked at him. 'But I thought we must at all costs avoid war with China,' he said, very reasonably, as he had been lectured on the subject without end for weeks, and even by Laurence himself.

'I should rather settle with Bonaparte, if the lesser evil had to be chosen,' Laurence said, for the moment too angry to consider the question rationally. 'At least he had the decency to declare war before seizing our citizens, instead of this cavalier offhand flinging of insults in our face, as if we did not dare to answer them. Not that Government have given them any reason to think otherwise: like a pack of damned curs, rolling over to show their bellies. And to think,' he added, smouldering, 'that scoundrel was trying to persuade me to kowtow, knowing it should be coming after *this*—'

Temeraire gave a snort of surprise at his vehemence, and nudged him gently with his nose. 'Pray do not be so angry; it cannot be good for you.'

Laurence shook his head, not in disagreement, and fell silent, leaning against Temeraire. It could do no good to vent his fury so, where some of the men left on deck might yet overhear and take it as encouragement to some rash act, and he did not want to distress Temeraire. But much was suddenly made plain to him: after swallowing such an insult, of course the Government would hardly strain at handing over a single dragon; the entire Ministry would likely be glad to rid themselves of so unpleasant a reminder, and to see the whole business hushed up all the more thoroughly.

He stroked Temeraire's side for comfort. 'Will you stay above deck with me a while?' Temeraire asked him, coaxing. 'You had much better sit down and rest, and not fret yourself so.'

Indeed Laurence did not want to leave him; it was curious how he could feel his lost calm restore itself under the influence of that steady heartbeat beneath his fingers. The wind was not too high, at the moment, and not all of the night watch could be sent below; an extra officer on the deck would not be amiss. 'Yes, I will stay; in any case I do not like to leave Riley alone with such a mood over the ship,' he answered, and went limping for his wraps.

Chapter Four

The wind was freshening from the northeast, very cold; Laurence stirred out of his half-sleep and looked up at the stars: only a few hours had passed. He huddled deeper into his blankets by Temeraire's side and tried to ignore the steady ache in his leg. The deck was strangely quiet; under Riley's grim and watchful eye there was scarcely any conversation at all among the remaining crew, though occasionally Laurence could hear indistinct murmurs from the rigging above, men whispering to each other. There was no moon, only a handful of lanterns on deck.

'You are cold,' Temeraire said unexpectedly, and Laurence turned to see the great deep-blue eyes studying him. 'Go inside, Laurence; you must get well, and I will not let anyone hurt Riley. Or the Chinese, I suppose, if you would not like it,' he added, though without much enthusiasm.

Laurence nodded, tiredly, and heaved himself up again; the moment of danger was over, he thought, at least for the moment, and there was no real sense in his staying above. 'You are comfortable enough?'

'Yes, with the heat from below I am perfectly warm,' Temeraire said; indeed Laurence could feel the warmth of the dragondeck even through the soles of his boots.

It was a great deal more pleasant in out of the wind; his leg stabbed unpleasantly twice as he climbed down to the upper berth deck, but his arms were up to his weight and held him until the spasm passed; he managed to reach his cabin without falling.

Laurence had several pleasant small round windows, not draughty, and near the ship's galley as he was, the cabin was still warm despite the wind; one of the runners had lit the hanging lantern, and Gibbon's book was lying still open on the lockers. He slept almost at once, despite the pain; the easy sway of his hanging cot was more familiar than any bed, and the low susurration of the water along the sides of the ship a wordless and constant reassurance.

He came awake all at once, breath jolted out of his body before his eyes even quite opened: noise more felt than heard. The deck abruptly slanted, and he flung out a hand to keep from striking the ceiling; a rat went sliding across the floor and fetched up against the fore lockers before scuttling into the dark again, indignant.

The ship righted almost at once: there was no unusual wind, no heavy swell; at once he understood that Temeraire had taken flight. Laurence flung on his boat-cloak and rushed out in nightshirt and bare feet; the drummer was beating to quarters, the crisp flying staccato echoing off the wooden walls, and even as Laurence staggered out of his room the carpenter and his mates were rushing past him to clear away the bulkheads. Another crash came: bombs, he now recognized, and then Granby was suddenly at his side, a little less disordered since he had been sleeping in breeches. Laurence accepted his arm without hesitation and with his help managed to push through the crowd and get back up to the dragondeck through the confusion. Sailors were running with frantic haste to the pumps, flinging buckets out over the sides for water to slop onto the decks and wet down the sails. A bloom of orange-yellow was trying to grow on the edge of the furled

mizzen topsail; one of the midshipmen, a spotty boy of thirteen Laurence had seen skylarking that morning, flung himself
gallantly out onto the yard with his shirt in his hand, dripping, and smothered it out.

There was no other light, nothing to show what might be
going on aloft, and too much shouting and noise to hear
anything of the battle above at all: Temeraire might have been
roaring at full voice for all they would have known of it. 'We
must get a flare up, at once,' Laurence said, taking his boots
from Roland; she had come running with them, and Morgan
with his breeches.

'Calloway, go and fetch a box of flares, and the flash-
powder,' Granby called. 'It must be a Fleur-de-Nuit; no other
breed could see without at least moonlight. If only they would
stop that noise,' he added, squinting uselessly up.

The loud crack warned them; Laurence fell as Granby tried
to pull him down to safety, but only a handful of splinters
came flying; screams rose from below: the bomb had gone
through a weak place in the wood and down into the galley.
Hot steam came up through the vent, and the smell of salt
pork, steeping already for the next day's dinner: tomorrow
was Thursday, Laurence remembered, ship's routine so deeply
engrained that the one thought followed instantly on the other
in his mind.

'We must get you below,' Granby said, taking his arm
again, calling, 'Martin!'

Laurence gave him an astonished, appalled look; Granby
did not even notice, and Martin, taking his left arm, seemed
to think nothing more natural. 'I am not leaving the deck,'
Laurence said sharply.

The gunner Calloway came panting with the box; in a
moment, the whistle of the first rising flare cut through the
low voices, and the yellow-white flash lit the sky. A dragon
bellowed: not Temeraire's voice, too low, and in the too-short
moment while the light lingered, Laurence caught sight of

Temeraire hovering protectively over the ship. The Fleur-de-Nuit had evaded him in the dark and was a little way off, twisting its head away from the light.

Temeraire roared at once and darted for the French dragon, but the flare died out and fell, left all again black as pitch. 'Another, another; damn you,' Laurence shouted to Calloway, who was still staring aloft just as they all were. 'He must have light; keep them going aloft.'

More of the crewmen rushed to help him, too many: three more flares went up at once, and Granby sprang to keep them from any further waste. Shortly they had the time marked: one flare followed after another in steady progression, a fresh burst of light just as the previous one failed. Smoke curled around Temeraire, trailed from his wings in the thin yellow light as he closed with the Fleur-de-Nuit, roaring; the French dragon dived to avoid him, and bombs scattered into the water harmlessly, the sound of the splashes travelling over the water.

'How many flares have we left?' Laurence asked Granby, low.

'Four dozen or so, no more,' Granby said, grimly: they were going very fast. 'And that is already with what the *Allegiance* was carrying besides our own; their gunner brought us all they had.'

Calloway slowed the rate of firing to stretch the dwindling supply longer, so that the dark returned full-force between bursts of light. Their eyes were all stinging with smoke and the strain of trying to see in the thin, always-fading light of the flares; Laurence could only imagine how Temeraire was managing, alone, half-blind, against an opponent fully manned and prepared for battle.

'Sir, Captain,' Roland cried, waving at him from the starboard rail; Martin helped Laurence over, but before they had reached her, one of the last handful of flares went off, and for a moment the ocean behind the *Allegiance* was illuminated clearly: two French heavy frigates coming on behind them, with the wind in their favour, and a dozen boats in the water crammed with men sweeping towards their either side.

The lookout above had seen also; 'Sail ho; boarders,' he bellowed out, and all was suddenly confusion once more: sailors running across the deck to stretch the boarding-netting, and Riley at the great double wheel with his coxswain and two of the strongest seamen; they were putting the *Allegiance* about with desperate haste, trying to bring her broadside to bear. There was no sense in trying to outrun the French ships; in this wind the frigates could make a good ten knots at least, and the *Allegiance* would never escape them.

Ringing along the galley chimney, words and the pounding of many feet echoed up hollowly from the gundecks: Riley's midshipmen and lieutenants were already hurrying men into place at the guns, their voices high and anxious as they repeated instructions, over and over, trying to drum what ought to have occupied the practice of months into the heads of men half-asleep and confused.

'Calloway, save the flares,' Laurence said, hating to give the order: the darkness would leave Temeraire vulnerable to the Fleur-de-Nuit. But with so few left, they had to be conserved, until there was some better hope of being able to do real damage to the French dragon.

'Stand by to repel boarders,' the bo'sun bellowed; the *Allegiance* was finally coming up through the wind, and there was a moment of silence: out in the darkness, the oars kept splashing, a steady count in French drifting faintly towards them over the water, and then Riley called, 'Fire as she bears.'

The guns below roared, red fire and smoke spitting: impossible to tell what damage had been done, except by the mingled sounds of screaming and splintering wood to let them know at least some of the shot had gone home. On went the guns, a rolling broadside as the *Allegiance* made her ponderous turn; but after they had spoken once, the inexperience of the crew began to tell.

At last the first gun spoke again, four minutes at least between shots; the second gun did not fire at all, nor the third; the fourth and fifth went together, with some more audible damage, but the sixth ball could be heard splashing into clear water; also the seventh, and then Purbeck called, "Vast firing.' The *Allegiance* had carried too far; now she could not fire again until she made her turn once more; and all the while the boarding party would be approaching, the rowers only encouraged to greater speed.

The guns died away; the clouds of thick grey smoke drifted over the water. The ship was again in darkness, but for the small, swaying pools of light cast off by the lanterns on deck. 'We must get you aboard Temeraire,' Granby said. 'We are not too far from shore yet for him to make the flight, and in any case there may be ships closer by: the transport from Halifax may be in these waters by now.'

'I am not going to run away and hand a hundred-gun transport over to the French,' Laurence said, very savagely.

'I am sure we can hold out, and in any case there is every likelihood of recapturing her before they can bring her into port, if you can warn the fleet,' Granby argued; no Navy officer would have persisted so against his commander, but aviator discipline was far more loose, and he would not be denied; it was indeed his duty as first lieutenant to see to the captain's safety.

'They could easily take her to the West Indies or a port in Spain, far from the blockades, and man her from there; we cannot lose her,' Laurence said.

'It would still be best to have you aboard, where they cannot lay hands on you unless we are forced to surrender,' Granby said. 'We must find some way to get Temeraire clear.'

'Sir, begging your pardon,' Calloway said, looking up from the box of flares, 'if you was to get me one of those pepper guns, we might pack up a ball with flash-powder, and maybe give himself a bit of breathing room.' He jerked his chin up towards the sky.

'I'll speak to Macready,' Ferris said at once, and dashed away to find the ship's Marine lieutenant.

The pepper gun was brought from below, two of the Marines carrying the halves of the long rifled barrel up while Calloway cautiously pried open one of the pepper-balls. The gunner shook out perhaps half the pepper and opened the locked box of flash-powder, taking out a single paper twist and sealing the box again. He held the twist far out over the side, two of his mates holding his waist to keep him steady while he unwound the twist and carefully spilled the yellow powder into the case, watching with only one eye, the other squinted up and his face half-turned away; his cheek was spotted with black scars, reminders of previous work with the powder: it needed no fuse and would go off on any careless impact, burning far hotter than gunpowder, if spent more quickly.

He sealed up the ball and plunged the rest of the twist into a bucket of water. His mates threw it overboard while he smeared the seal of the ball with a little tar and covered it all over with grease before loading the gun; then the second half of the barrel was screwed on. 'There; I don't say it will go off, but I allow as it may,' Calloway said, wiping his hands clean with no little relief.

'Very good,' Laurence said. 'Stand ready and save the last three flares to give us light for the shot; Macready, have you a man for the gun? Your best, mind you; he must strike the head to do any good.'

'Harris, you take her,' Macready said, pointing one of his men to the gun, a gangly, rawboned fellow of perhaps eighteen, and added to Laurence, 'Young eyes for a long shot, sir; never fear she'll go astray.'

A low angry rumble of voices drew their attention below, to the quarterdeck: the envoy Sun Kai had come on deck with

93

two of the servants trailing behind, carrying one of the enormous trunks out of their luggage. The sailors and most of Temeraire's crew were clustered along the rails to fend off the boarders, cutlasses and pistols in every hand; but even with the French ships gaining, one fellow with a pike went so far as to take a step towards the envoy, before the bo'sun started him with the knotted end of his rope, bawling, 'Keep the line, lads; keep the line.'

Laurence had all but forgotten the disastrous dinner in the confusion: it seemed already weeks ago, but Sun Kai was still wearing the same embroidered gown, his hands folded calmly into the sleeves, and the angry, alarmed men were primed for just such a provocation. 'Oh, his soul to the devil. We must get him away. Below, sir; below at once,' he shouted, pointing at the gangway, but Sun Kai only beckoned his men on, and came climbing up to the dragondeck while they heaved the great trunk up more slowly behind him.

'Where is that damned translator?' Laurence said. 'Dyer, go see—' But by then the servants had gotten the trunk up; they unlocked it and flung back the lid, and there was no need for translation: the rockets that lay in the padding of straw were wildly elaborate, red and blue and green like something out of a child's nursery, painted with swirls of colour, gold and silver, and unmistakable.

Calloway snatched one at once, blue with white and yellow stripes, one of the servants anxiously miming for him how the match should be set to the fuse. 'Yes, yes,' he said, impatiently, bringing over the slow-match; the rocket caught at once and hissed upwards, vanishing from sight far above where the flares had gone.

The white flash came first, then a great thunderclap of sound, echoing back from the water, and a more faintly glimmering circle of yellow stars spread out and hung lingering in the air. The Fleur-de-Nuit squawked audibly, undignified, as the fireworks went off: it was revealed plainly, not a hundred yards above, and Temeraire immediately flung himself upwards, teeth bared, hissing furiously.

Startled, the Fleur-de-Nuit dived, slipping under Temeraire's outstretched claws but coming into their range. 'Harris, a shot, a shot!' Macready yelled, and the young Marine squinted through the sight. The pepper-ball flew straight and true, if a little high; but the Fleur-de-Nuit had narrow curving horns flaring out from its forehead, just above the eyes; the ball broke open against them and the flash-powder burst white-hot and flaring. The dragon squalled again, this time in real pain, and flew wildly and fast away from the ships, deep into the dark; it swept past the ship so low that the sails shuddered noisily in the wind of its wings.

Harris stood up from the gun and turned, grinning wide and gap-toothed, then fell with a look of surprise, his arm and shoulder gone. Macready was knocked down by his falling body; Laurence jerked a knife-long splinter out of his own arm and wiped spattered blood from his face. The pepper gun was a blasted wreck: the crew of the Fleur-de-Nuit had flung down another bomb even as their dragon fled, and hit the gun dead-on.

A couple of the sailors dragged Harris's body to the side and flung him overboard; no one else had been killed. The world was queerly muffled; Calloway had sent up another pair of fireworks, a great starburst of orange streaks spreading almost over half the sky, but Laurence could hear the explosion only in his left ear.

With the Fleur-de-Nuit thus distracted, Temeraire dropped back down onto the deck, rocking the ship only a little. 'Hurry, hurry,' he said, ducking his head down beneath the straps as the harness-men scrambled to get him rigged out. 'She is very quick, and I do not think the light hurts her as much as it did the other one, the one we fought last fall; there is something different about her eyes.' He was heaving for breath, and his wings trembled a little: he had been hovering a great deal, and it was not a manoeuvre he was accustomed to perform for any length of time.

Sun Kai, who had remained upon deck, observing, did not protest the harnessing; perhaps, Laurence thought bitterly, they did not mind it when it was their own necks at risk. Then he noticed that drops of deep, red-black blood were dripping onto the deck. 'Where are you hurt?'

'It is not bad; she only caught me twice,' Temeraire said, twisting his head around and licking at his right flank; there was a shallow cut there, and another gouged claw-mark further up on his back.

Twice was a good deal more than Laurence cared for; he snapped at Keynes, who had been sent along with them, as the man was boosted up and began to pack the wound with bandages. 'Ought you not sew them up?'

'Nonsense,' Keynes said. 'He'll do as he is; barely worth calling them flesh wounds. Stop fretting.' Macready had regained his feet, wiping his forehead with the back of his hand; he gave the surgeon a dubious look at this reply and glanced at Laurence sidelong; the more so as Keynes continued his work muttering audibly about overanxious captains and mother hens.

Laurence himself was too grateful to object, full of relief. 'Are you ready, gentlemen?' he asked, checking his pistols and his sword: this time it was his good heavy cutlass, proper Spanish steel and a plain hilt; he was glad to feel its solid weight under his hand.

'Ready for you, sir,' Fellowes said, pulling the final strap tight; Temeraire reached out and lifted Laurence up to his shoulder. 'Give her a pull up there; does she hold?' he called, once Laurence was settled and locked on again.

'Well enough,' Laurence called back down, having thrown his weight against the stripped-down harness. 'Thank you, Fellowes; well done. Granby, send the riflemen to the tops with the Marines, and the rest to repel boarders.'

'Very good; and Laurence—' Granby said, clearly meaning to once again encourage him to take Temeraire away from the battle. Laurence cut him short by the expedient of giving Temeraire a quick nudge with his knee. The *Allegiance* heaved again beneath the weight of his leap, and they were airborne together at last.

The air above the *Allegiance* was thick with the harsh, sulphurous smoke of the fireworks, like the smell of flint-locks, cloying on his tongue and skin despite the cold wind. 'There she is,' Temeraire said, beating back aloft; Laurence followed his gaze and saw the Fleur-de-Nuit approaching again from high above: she had indeed recovered very quickly from the blinding light, judging by his previous experience with the breed, and he wondered if perhaps she was some sort of new cross. 'Shall we go after her?'

Laurence hesitated; for the sake of keeping Temeraire out of their hands, disabling the Fleur-de-Nuit was of the most urgent necessity, for if the *Allegiance* were forced to surrender and Temeraire had to attempt a return to shore, she could harry them in the darkness all the way back home. And yet the French frigates could do far more damage to the ship: a raking fire would mean a very slaughter of the men. If the *Allegiance* were taken it would be a terrible blow to the Navy and the Corps both: they had no large transports to spare.

'No,' he said finally. 'Our first duty must be to preserve the *Allegiance* – we must do something about those frigates.' He spoke more to convince himself than Temeraire; he felt the decision was in the right, but a terrible doubt lingered; what was courage in an ordinary man might often be called recklessness in an aviator, with the responsibility for a rare and precious dragon in his hands. It was Granby's duty to be overcautious, but it did not follow that he was in the wrong. Laurence had not been raised in the Corps, and he knew his nature balked at many of the restraints placed upon a dragon captain; he could not help but wonder if he were consulting his own pride too far.

Temeraire was always enthusiastic for battle; he made no argument, but only looked down at the frigates. 'Those ships look much smaller than the *Allegiance*,' Temeraire said doubtfully. 'Is she truly in danger?'

'Very great danger; they mean to rake her.' Even as Laurence spoke, another of the fireworks went off. The explosion came startlingly near, now that he was aloft on Temeraire's back; he was forced to shield his dazzled eyes with a hand. When the spots at last faded from his eyes, he saw in alarm that the leeward frigate had suddenly club-hauled to come about: a risky manoeuvre and not one he would himself have undertaken simply for an advantage of position, though in justice he could not deny it had been brilliantly performed. Now the *Allegiance* had her vulnerable stern wholly exposed to the French ship's larboard guns. 'Good God; there!' he said urgently, pointing even though Temeraire could not see the gesture.

'I see her,' Temeraire said: already diving. His sides were swelling out with the gathering breath required for the divine wind, the gleaming black hide going drumhide-taut as his deep chest expanded. Laurence could feel a palpable low rumbling echo already building beneath Temeraire's skin, a herald of the destructive power to come.

The Fleur-de-Nuit had made out his intentions: she was coming on behind them. He could hear her wings beating, but Temeraire was the faster, his greater weight not hampering him in the dive. Gunpowder cracked noisily as her riflemen took shots, but their attempts were only guesswork in the dark; Laurence laid himself close to Temeraire's neck and silently willed him to greater speed.

Below them, the frigate's cannon erupted in a great cloud of smoke and fury; flames licked out from the ports and flung an appalling scarlet glow up against Temeraire's breast. A fresh cracking of rifle-fire came from the frigate's decks, and he jerked, sharply, as if struck: Laurence called out his name in anxiety, but Temeraire had not paused in his drive towards the ship: he levelled out to blast her, and the sound of Laurence's voice was lost in the terrible thundering noise of the divine wind.

Temeraire had never before used the divine wind to attack a ship; but in the battle of Dover Laurence had seen the deadly resonance work against Napoleon's troop-carriers, shattering their light wood. He had expected something similar here: the deck splintering, damage to the yards, perhaps even breaking the masts. But the French frigate was solidly built, with oak planking as much as two foot thick, and her masts and yards were well-secured for battle with iron chains to reinforce the rigging.

Instead the sails caught and held the force of Temeraire's roar: they shivered for a moment, then bulged out full and straining. A score of braces snapped like violin strings, the masts all leaning away; yet still they held, wood and sailcloth groaning, and for a moment Laurence's heart sank: no great damage, it seemed, would be done.

But if part would not yield, then all must perforce bend: even as Temeraire stopped his roaring and went flashing by, the whole ship turned away, driven broadside to the wind, and slowly toppled over onto her side. The tremendous force left her all but on her beam-ends, men hanging loose from the rigging and the rails, their feet kicking in mid-air, some falling into the ocean.

Laurence twisted about to look back towards her as they swept on, Temeraire skimming past, low to the water. *Valérie* was emblazoned in lovingly bright gold letters upon her stern, illuminated by lanterns hung in the cabin windows: now swinging crazily, half overturned. Her captain knew his work: Laurence could hear shouts carrying across the water, and already the men were crawling up onto the side with every sort of sea-anchor in their hands, hawsers run out, ready to try and right her.

But they had no time. In Temeraire's wake, churned up by the force of the divine wind upon the water, a tremendous wave was climbing out of the swell. Slow and high it mounted, as if with some deliberate intent. For a moment all hung still, the ship suspended in blackness, the great shining wall of water blotting out even the night; then, falling, the wave heeled her over like a child's toy, and the ocean quenched all the fire of her guns.

She did not come up again. A pale froth lingered, and a half-dozen smaller waves chased the great one and broke upon the curve of the hull, which remained above the surface. A moment only: then it slipped down beneath the waters, and a hail of golden fireworks lit the sky. The Fleur-de-Nuit circled low over the churning waters, belling out in its deep lonely voice, as though unable to understand the sudden absence of the ship.

There was no sound of cheering from the *Allegiance*, though they must have seen. Laurence himself was silent, dismayed: three hundred men, perhaps more, the ocean smooth and glassy, unbroken. A ship might founder in a gale, in high winds and forty-foot waves; a ship might occasionally be sunk in an action, burnt or exploded after a long battle, run aground on rocks. But she had been untouched, in open ocean with no more than a ten-foot swell and winds of fourteen knots; and now obliterated whole.

Temeraire coughed, wetly, and made a sound of pain; Laurence hoarsely called, 'Back to the ship, at once,' but already the Fleur-de-Nuit was beating furiously towards them: against the next brilliant flare he could see the silhouettes of the boarders waiting, ready to leap aboard, knives and swords and pistols glittering white along their edges. Temeraire was flying so very awkwardly, laboured; as the Fleur-de-Nuit came close, he put on a desperate effort and lunged away, but he was no longer quicker in the air, and he could not get around the other dragon to reach the safety of the *Allegiance*.

Laurence might almost have let them come aboard, to treat the wound; he could feel the quivering labour of Temeraire's wings, and his mind was full of that scarlet moment, the terrible muffled impact of the ball: every moment aloft now might worsen the injury. But he could hear the shouting voices of the French dragon's crew, full of a grief and horror that required no translation; and he did not think they would accept a surrender.

'I hear wings,' Temeraire gasped, voice gone high and thin with pain; meaning another dragon, and Laurence vainly searched the impenetrable night: British or French? The Fleur-de-Nuit abruptly darted at them again; Temeraire gathered himself for another convulsive burst of speed, and then, hissing and spitting, Nitidus was there, beating about the head of the French dragon in a flurry of silver-grey wings: Captain Warren on his back standing in harness and waving his hat wildly at Laurence, yelling, 'Go, go!'

Dulcia had come about them on the other side, nipping at the Fleur-de-Nuit's flanks, forcing it to double back and snap at her; the two light dragons were the quickest of their formation-mates, and though not up to the weight of the big French dragon, they might harry it a little while. Temeraire was already turning in a slow arc, his wings working in shuddering sweeps. As they closed with the ship, Laurence could see the crew scrambling to clear the dragondeck for him to land: it was littered with splinters and ends of rope, twisted metal; the *Allegiance* had suffered badly from the raking, and the second frigate was keeping up a steady fire on her lower decks.

Temeraire did not properly land, but half-fell clumsily onto the deck and set the whole ship to rocking; Laurence was casting off his straps before they were even properly down. He slid down behind the withers without a hand on the harness; his leg gave way beneath him as he came down heavily upon the deck, but he only dragged himself up again and staggered half-falling to Temeraire's head.

Keynes was already at work, elbow-deep in black blood; to better give him access, Temeraire was leaning slowly over onto his side under the guidance of many hands, the harness-men holding up the light for the surgeon. Laurence went to his knees by Temeraire's head and pressed his cheek to the soft muzzle; blood soaked warm through his trousers, and his eyes were stinging, blurred. He did not quite know what he was saying, nor whether it made any sense, but Temeraire blew out warm air against him in answer, though he did not speak.

'There, I have it; now the tongs. Allen, stop that foolishness or go put your head over the side,' Keynes said, somewhere behind his back. 'Good. Is the iron hot? Now, then; Laurence, he must keep steady.'

'Hold fast, dear heart,' Laurence said, stroking Temeraire's nose. 'Hold as still as ever you may; hold still.' Temeraire gave a hiss only, and his breath wheezed in loudly through his red, flaring nostrils; one heartbeat, two, then the breath burst out of him, and the spiked ball rang as Keynes dropped it into the waiting tray. Temeraire gave another small hissing cry as the hot iron was clapped to the wound; Laurence nearly heaved at the scorched, roasting smell of meat.

'There; it is over; a clean wound. The ball had fetched up against the breastbone,' Keynes said; the wind blew the smoke clear, and suddenly Laurence could hear the crash and echo of the long guns again, and all the noise of the ship; the world once again had meaning and shape.

Laurence dragged himself up to his feet, swaying. 'Roland,' he said, 'you and Morgan go run and see what odds and ends of sailcloth and wadding they may have to spare; we must try and put some padding around him.'

'Morgan is dead, sir,' Roland said, and in the lantern-light he saw abruptly that her face was tracked with tears, not sweat; pale streaks through grime. 'Dyer and I will go.'

The two of them did not wait for him to nod, but darted away at once, shockingly small in and among the burly forms of the sailors; he followed after them with his eyes for a moment, and turned back, his face hardening.

The quarterdeck was so thickly slimed with blood that portions shone glossy black as though freshly painted. By the slaughter and lack of destruction in the rigging, Laurence thought the French must have been using canister shot, and indeed he could see some parts of the broken casings lying about on the deck. The French had crammed every man who could be spared into the boats, and there were a great many of those: two hundred desperate men were struggling to come aboard, enraged with the loss of their ship. They were four and five deep along the grappling-lines in places, or clinging to the rails, and the British sailors trying to hold them back had all the broad and empty deck behind them. Pistol-shot rang clear, and the clash of swords; sailors with long pikes were jabbing into the mass of boarders as they heaved and pushed.

Laurence had never seen a boarding fight from such a strange, in-between distance, at once near and yet removed; he felt very queer and unsettled, and drew his pistols out for comfort. He could not see many of his crew: Granby missing, and Evans, his second lieutenant too; down on the forecastle below, Martin's yellow hair shone bright in the lanterns for a moment as he leaped to cut a man off; then he disappeared under a blow from a big French sailor carrying a club.

'Laurence.' He heard his name, or at least something like it, strangely drawn out into three syllables more like *Lao-ren-tse*, and turned to look; Sun Kai was pointing northwards, along the line of the wind, but the last burst of fireworks was already fading, and Laurence could not see what he meant to point out.

Above, the Fleur-de-Nuit suddenly gave a roar; she banked sharply away from Nitidus and Dulcia, who were still darting at her flanks, and set off due eastward, flying fast, vanishing very quickly into the darkness. Almost on her heels came the deep belly-roar of a Regal Copper, and the higher shrieks of Yellow Reapers: the wind of their passage set all the shrouds snapping back and forth as they swept overhead, firing flares off in every direction.

The remaining French frigate doused her lights all at once, hoping to escape into the night, but Lily led the formation past her, low enough to rattle her masts; two passes, and in a fading crimson starburst Laurence saw the French colours slowly come drooping down, while all across the deck the boarders flung down their weapons and sank to the deck in surrender.

Chapter Five

. . . and the Conduct of your son was in all ways both heroic and gentlemanly. His Loss must grieve all those who shared in the Privilege of his Acquaintance, and none more so than those honoured to serve alongside him, and to see in him already formed the noble Character of a wise and courageous Officer and a loyal Servant of his Country and King. I pray that you may find some Comfort in the sure Knowledge that he died as he would have lived, valiant, fearing nothing but Almighty God, and certain to find a Place of Honour among those who have sacrificed All for their Nation.

Yours, etc.,
William Laurence

He laid the pen down and folded over the letter; it was miserably awkward, inadequate, and yet he could do no better. He had lost friends near his own age enough as a mid and a young lieutenant, and one thirteen-year-old boy under his own first command; even so he had never before had to write a letter for a ten-year-old, who by rights ought still to have been in his schoolroom playing with tin soldiers.

It was the last of the obligatory letters, and the thinnest:

there had not been very much to say of earlier acts of valour. Laurence set it aside and wrote a few lines of a more personal nature, these to his mother: news of the engagement would certainly be published in the *Gazette*, and he knew she would be anxious. It was difficult to write easily, after the earlier task; he confined himself to assuring her of his health and Temeraire's, dismissing their collective injuries as inconsequential. He had written a long and grinding description of the battle in his report for the Admiralty; he did not have the heart to paint a lighter picture of it for her eyes.

Having done at last, he shut up his small writing-desk and collected the letters, each one sealed and wrapped in oilcloth against rain or sea-water. He did not get up right away, but sat looking out the windows at the empty ocean, in silence.

Making his way back up to the dragondeck was a slow affair of easy stages. Having gained the forecastle, he limped for a moment to the larboard rail to rest, pretending it was to look over at their prize, the *Chanteuse*. Her sails were all hung out loose and billowing; men were clambering over her masts, getting her rigging back into order, looking much like busy ants at this distance.

The scene upon the dragondeck was very different now, with nearly all the formation crammed aboard. Temeraire had been allotted the entire starboard section, the better to ease his wound, but the rest of the dragons lay in a complicated many-coloured heap of entangled limbs, stirring rarely. Maximus alone took up virtually all the space remaining, and lay on the bottom; even Lily, who ordinarily considered it beneath her dignity to curl up with other dragons, was forced to let her tail and wing drape over him, while Messoria and Immortalis, older dragons and smaller, made not even such pretensions, and simply sprawled upon his great back, a limb dangling loose here and there.

They were all drowsing and looked perfectly happy with their circumstances; Nitidus only was too fidgety to like lying still very long, and he was presently aloft, circling the frigate curiously: a little too low for the comfort of the sailors, judging by the nervous way heads on the *Chanteuse* often turned skyward. Dulcia was nowhere in sight, perhaps already gone to carry news of the engagement back to England.

Crossing the deck had become something of an adventure, particularly with his uncooperative and dragging leg; Laurence only narrowly managed to avoid falling over Messoria's hanging tail when she twitched in her sleep. Temeraire was soundly asleep as well; when Laurence came to look at him, one eye slid halfway open, gleamed at him deep blue, and slid at once closed again. Laurence did not try to rouse him, very glad to see him comfortable; Temeraire had eaten well that morning, two cows and a large tunny, and Keynes had pronounced himself satisfied with the present progress of the wound.

'A nasty sort of weapon,' he had said, taking a ghoulish pleasure in showing Laurence the extracted ball; staring unhappily at its many squat spikes, Laurence could only be grateful it had been cleaned before he had been obliged to look at it. 'I have not seen its like before, though I hear the Russians use something of the sort; I should not have enjoyed working it out if it had gone any deeper, I can tell you.'

But by good fortune, the ball had come up against the breastbone, and lodged scarcely half a foot beneath the skin; even so, the ball itself and the extraction had torn the muscles of the breast cruelly, and Keynes said Temeraire ought not fly at all for as long as two weeks, perhaps even a month. Laurence rested a hand upon the broad, warm shoulder; he was glad to have only so much of a price to pay.

The other captains were sitting at a small folding-table wedged up against the galley chimney, very nearly the only open space available on the deck, playing cards; Laurence joined them and gave Harcourt the bundle of letters. 'Thank you for taking them,' he said, sitting down heavily to catch his breath.

They all paused in the game to look at the large packet. 'I am so very sorry, Laurence.' Harcourt put the whole into her satchel. 'You have been wretchedly mauled about.'

'Damn cowardly business,' Berkley shook his head. 'More like spying than proper combat, this skulking about at night.'

Laurence was silent; he was grateful for their sympathy, but at present he was too much oppressed to manage conversation. The funerals had been ordeal enough, keeping his feet for an hour against his leg's complaints, while one after another the bodies were slipped over the side, sewn into their hammocks with round-shot at their feet for the sailors, iron shells for the aviators, as Riley read slowly through the service.

He had spent the remainder of the morning closeted with Lieutenant Ferris, now his acting second, telling over the butcher's bill; a sadly long list. Granby had taken a musket-ball in his chest; thankfully it had cracked against a rib and gone straight out again in back, but he had lost a great deal of blood, and was already feverish. Evans, his second lieutenant, had a badly broken leg and was to be sent back to England; Martin at least would recover, but his jaw was presently so swollen he could not speak except in mumbles, and he could not yet see out of his left eye.

Two more of the topmen wounded, less severely; one of the riflemen, Dunne, wounded, and another, Donnell, killed; Miggsy of the bellmen killed; and worst-hit, the harness-men: four of them had been killed by a single cannon-ball, which had caught them belowdecks while they had been carrying away the extra harness. Morgan had been with them, carrying the box of spare buckles: a wretched waste.

Perhaps seeing something of the tally in his face, Berkley said, 'At least I can leave you Portis and Macdonaugh,' referring to two of Laurence's topmen, who had been transferred to Maximus during the confusion after the envoys' arrival.

'Are you not short-handed yourself?' Laurence asked. 'I cannot rob Maximus; you will be on active duty.'

'The transport coming from Halifax, the *William of Orange*, has a dozen likely fellows for Maximus,' Berkley said. 'No reason you cannot have your own back again.'

'I ought not argue with you; Heaven knows I am desperately short,' Laurence said. 'But the transport may not arrive for a month, if her crossing has been slow.'

'Oh; you were below earlier, so you did not hear us tell Captain Riley,' Warren said. '*William* was sighted only a few days ago, not far from here. So we have sent Chenery and Dulcia off to fetch her, and she will take us and the wounded home. Also, I believe Riley was saying that this boat needs something; it could not have been stars, Berkley?'

'Spars,' Laurence said, looking up at the rigging; in the daylight he could see that the yards which supported the sails did indeed look very ugly, much splintered and pockmarked with bullets. 'It will certainly be a relief if she can spare us some supplies. But you must know, Warren, this is a ship, not a boat.'

'Is there a difference?' Warren was unconcerned, scandalizing Laurence. 'I thought they were simply two words for the same thing; or is it a matter of size? This is certainly a behemoth, although Maximus is like to fall off her deck at any moment.'

'I am not,' Maximus said, but he opened his eyes and peered over at his hindquarters, only settling back to sleep when he had satisfied himself that he was not in present danger of tipping into the water.

Laurence opened his mouth and closed it again without venturing on an explanation; he felt the battle was already lost. 'You will be with us for a few days, then?'

'Until tomorrow only,' Harcourt said. 'If it looks to be longer than that, I think we must take the flight; I do not like to strain the dragons without need, but I like leaving Lenton short at Dover still less, and he will be wondering where on earth we have got to: we were only meant to be doing night manoeuvres with the fleet off Brest, before we saw you all firing off like Guy Fawkes' day.'

Riley had asked them all to dinner, of course; and the captured French officers as well. Harcourt was obliged to plead seasickness as an excuse for avoiding the close quarters where her gender might too easily be revealed, and Berkley was a taciturn fellow, disinclined to speak in sentences of more than five words at a time. But Warren was both free and easy in his speech, the more so after a glass or two of strong wine, and Sutton had a fine store of anecdotes, having been in service nearly thirty years; together they carried the conversation along in an energetic if somewhat ramshackle way.

But the Frenchmen were silent and shocked, and the British sailors only a little less so; their oppression only grew more apparent over the course of the meal. Lord Purbeck was stiff and formal, Macready grim; even Riley was quiet, inclined to uncharacteristic and long periods of silence, and plainly uncomfortable.

On the dragondeck afterwards, over coffee, Warren said, 'Laurence, I do not mean to insult your old service or your shipmates, but Lord! They make it heavy going. Tonight I should have thought we had offended them mortally, not saved them a good long fight and whoever knows how many bucketsful of blood.'

'I expect they feel we came rather late to save them very much.' Sutton leaned against his dragon Messoria companionably and lit a cigar. 'So instead we have robbed them of the full glory, not to mention that we have a share in the prize, you know, having arrived before the French ship struck. Would you care for a draught, my dear?' he asked, holding the cigar where Messoria could breathe the smoke.

'No, you have mistaken them entirely, I assure you,' Laurence said. 'We should never have taken the frigate if you had not come; she was not so badly mauled she could not have shown us her heels whenever she chose; every man aboard was wholly glad to see you come.' He did not very much wish to explain, but he did not like to leave them with so ill an impression, so he added briefly, 'It is the other frigate, the *Valérie*, which we sank before you came; the loss of men was very great.'

They perceived his own disquiet and pressed him no further; when Warren made as if to ask, Sutton nudged him into silence and called his runner for a deck of cards. They settled to a casual game of speculation, Harcourt having joined them now that they had parted from the naval officers. Laurence finished his cup and slipped quietly away.

Temeraire was himself sitting and looking out across the empty sea; he had slept all the day, and roused just lately for another large meal. He shifted himself to make a place for Laurence upon his foreleg, and curled about him with a small sigh.

'Do not take it to heart.' Laurence was aware he was giving advice he could not himself follow; but he feared that Temeraire might brood on the sinking too long, and drive himself into a melancholy. 'With the second frigate on our larboard, we should likely have been brought by the lee, and had they doused all the lights and stopped our fireworks, Lily and the others could hardly have found us in the night. You saved many lives, and the *Allegiance* herself.'

'I do not feel guilty,' Temeraire said. 'I did not intend to sink her like that, but I am not sorry for that; they meant to kill a great many of my crew, and of course I would not let them. It is the sailors: they look at me so queerly now, and they do not like to come near at all.'

Laurence could neither deny the truth of this observation, nor offer any false comfort. Sailors preferred to see a dragon as a fighting machine, very much like a ship which happened to breathe and fly: a mere instrument of man's will. They could accept without great difficulty his strength and brute

111

force, natural as a reflection of his size; if they feared him for it, so might a large, dangerous man be feared. The divine wind however bore an unearthly tinge, and the wreck of the *Valérie* was too implacable to be human: it woke every wild old legend of fire and destruction from the sky.

Already the battle seemed very like a nightmare in his own memory: the endless gaudy stream of the fireworks and the red light of the cannons firing, the ash-white eyes of the Fleur-de-Nuit in the dark, bitter smoke on his tongue, and above all the slow descent of the wave, like a curtain lowering upon a play. He stroked Temeraire's arm in silence, and together they watched the wake of the ship slipping gently by.

The cry of 'Sail' came at the first dim light: the *William of Orange* clear on the horizon, two points off the starboard bow. Riley squinted through his glass. 'We will pipe the hands to breakfast early; she will be in hailing distance well before nine.'

The *Chanteuse* lay between the two larger ships and was already hailing the oncoming transport: she herself would be going back to England to be condemned as a prize, carrying the prisoners. The day was clear and very cold, the sky that peculiarly rich shade of blue reserved for winter, and the *Chanteuse* looked cheerful with her white topgallants and royals set. It being rare for a transport to take a prize, the mood ought to have been celebratory; a handsome forty-four-gun ship and a trim sailer, she would certainly be bought into the service, and there would be head-money for the prisoners besides. But the unsettled mood had not quite cleared overnight, and the men were mostly quiet as they worked. Laurence himself had not slept very well, and now he stood on the forecastle watching the *William of Orange* draw near, wistfully; soon they would once again be quite alone.

'Good morning, Captain,' Hammond said, joining him at the rail. The intrusion was unwelcome, and Laurence did not make much attempt to hide it, but this made no immediate impression: Hammond was too busy gazing upon the *Chanteuse*, an indecent satisfaction showing on his face. 'We could not have asked for a better start to the journey.'

Several of the crew were at work nearby repairing the shattered deck, the carpenter and his mates; one of them, a cheerful, slant-shouldered fellow named Leddowes, brought aboard at Spithead and already established as the ship's jester, sat up on his heels at this remark and stared at Hammond in open disapproval, until the carpenter Eklof, a big silent Swede, thumped him on the shoulder with his big fist, drawing him back down to the work.

'I am surprised you think so,' Laurence said. 'Would you not have preferred a first-rate?'

'No, no,' Hammond said, oblivious to sarcasm. 'It is just as one could wish; do you know one of the balls passed quite through the prince's cabin? One of his guards was killed, and another, badly wounded, passed away during the night; I understand he is in a towering rage. The French navy has done us more good in one night than months of diplomacy. Do you suppose the captain of the captured ship might be presented to him? Of course I have told them our attackers were French, but it would be as well to give them incontrovertible proof.'

'We are not going to march a defeated officer about like a prize in some Roman triumph,' Laurence said levelly; he had been made prisoner once himself, and though he had been scarcely a boy at the time, a young midshipman, he still remembered the perfect courtesy of the French captain, asking him quite seriously for his parole.

'Of course, I do see. It would not look very well, I suppose,' Hammond said, but only as a regretful concession, and he added, 'Although it would be a pity if—'

'Is that all?' Laurence interrupted him, unwilling to hear any more.

'Oh— I beg your pardon; forgive my having intruded,' Hammond said, uncertainly, finally looking at Laurence. 'I meant only to inform you: the prince has expressed a desire of seeing you.'

'Thank you, sir,' Laurence said, with finality. Hammond looked as though he would have liked to say something more, perhaps to urge Laurence to go at once, or give him some advice for the meeting; but in the end he did not dare, and with a short bow went abruptly away.

Laurence had no desire to speak with Yongxing, still less to be trifled with, and his mood was not much improved by the physical unpleasantness of making his halting way to the prince's quarters, all the way to the stern of the ship. When the attendants tried to make him wait in the antechamber, he said shortly, 'He may send word when he is ready,' and turned at once to go. There was a hasty and huddled conference, one man going so far as to stand in the doorway to bar the way out, and after a moment Laurence was ushered directly into the great cabin.

The two gaping holes in the walls, opposite one another, had been stuffed with wads of blue silk to keep out the wind; but still the long banners of inscribed parchment hanging upon the walls blew and rattled now and again in the draught. Yongxing sat straight-backed upon an armchair draped in red cloth, at a small writing-table of lacquered wood; despite the motion of the ship, his brush moved steadily from ink-pot to paper, never dripping, the shining-wet characters formed up in neat lines and rows.

'You wished to see me, sir,' Laurence said.

Yongxing completed a final line and set aside his brush without immediately answering; he took a stone seal, resting in a small pool of red ink, and pressed it at the bottom of the page; then folded up the page and laid it to one side, atop another similar sheet, and folded these both into a piece of waxed cloth. 'Feng Li,' he called.

114

Laurence started; he had not even noticed the attendant standing in the corner, nondescript in plain robes of dark blue cotton, who now came forward. Feng was a tall fellow but so permanently stooped that all Laurence could see of him was the perfect line running across his head, ahead of which his dark hair was shaven to the skin. He gave Laurence one quick darting glance, mutely curious, then lifted the whole table up and carried it away to the side of the room, not spilling a drop of the ink.

He hurried back quickly with a footrest for Yongxing, then drew back into the corner of the room: plainly Yongxing did not mean to send him away for the interview. The prince sat up erect with his arms resting upon the chair, and did not offer Laurence a seat, though two more chairs stood against the far wall. This set the tone straightaway; Laurence felt his shoulders stiffening even before Yongxing had begun.

'Though you have only been brought along for necessity's sake,' Yongxing said coldly, 'you imagine that you remain companion to Lung Tien Xiang and may continue to treat him as your property. And now the worst has been realized: through your vicious and reckless behaviour, he has come to grave injury.'

Laurence pressed his lips together; he did not trust himself to make anything resembling a civilized remark in response. He had questioned his own judgement, both before taking Temeraire into the battle and all through the long following night, remembering the sound of the dreadful impact, and Temeraire's laboured and painful breath; but to have Yongxing question it was another matter.

'Is that all?' he said.

Yongxing had perhaps expected him to grovel, or beg forgiveness; certainly this short answer made the prince more voluble with anger. 'Are you so lacking in all right principles?' he said. 'You have no remorse; you would have taken Lung Tien Xiang to his death as easily as ridden a horse to foundering. You are not to go aloft with him again, and you will keep these low servants of yours away. I will set my own guards around him—'

'Sir,' Laurence said, bluntly, 'you may go to the devil.' Yongxing broke off, looking more taken aback than offended at finding himself interrupted, and Laurence added, 'And as for your guards, if any one of them sets foot upon my dragondeck, I will have Temeraire pitch him overboard. Good day.'

He made a short bow and did not stay to hear a response, if Yongxing even made one, but turned and went directly from the room. The attendants stared as he went past them and did not this time attempt to block his way; he was forcing his leg to obey his wishes, moving swiftly. He paid for the bravado: by the time he reached his own cabin, at the very other end of the ship's interminable length, his leg had begun to twitch and shudder with every step as if palsied; he was glad to reach the safety of his chair, and to soothe his ruffled temper with a private glass of wine. Perhaps he had spoken intemperately, but he did not regret it in the least; Yongxing should at least know that not all British officers and gentlemen were prepared to bow and scrape to his every tyrannous whim.

As satisfying a resolution as this was, however, Laurence could not help but acknowledge to himself that his defiance was a good deal strengthened by the conviction that Yongxing would never willingly bend on the central, the essential point, of his separation from Temeraire. The Ministry, in Hammond's person, might have something to gain in exchange for all their crawling; for his own part Laurence had nothing of great importance left to lose. This was a lowering thought, and he put down his glass and sat in silent gloom a while instead, rubbing his aching leg, propped upon a locker. Six bells rang on deck, and faintly he heard the pipe shrilling away, the scrape and clatter of the hands going to their breakfast on the berth deck below, and the smell of strong tea came drifting over from the galley.

Having finished his glass and eased his leg a little, Laurence at last got himself back onto his feet, and he crossed to Riley's cabin and tapped on the door. He meant to ask Riley to station several of the Marines to keep the threatened guards off the deck, and he was startled and not at all pleased to find Hammond already there, sitting before Riley's writing-desk, with a shadow of conscious guilt and anxiety upon his face.

'Laurence,' Riley said, after offering him a chair, 'I have been speaking with Mr. Hammond, about the passengers,' and Laurence noticed that Riley himself was looking tired and anxious. 'He has brought to my attention that they have all been keeping belowdecks, since this news about the Indiamen came out. It cannot go on like this for seven months: we must let them come on deck and take the air somehow. I am sure you will not object. I think we must let them walk about the dragondeck, we do not dare put them near the hands.'

No suggestion could have possibly been more unwelcome, nor come at a worse moment; Laurence eyed Hammond in mingled irritation and something very near despair; the man already seemed to be possessed of an evil genius for disaster, at least from Laurence's view, and the prospect of a long journey spent suffering one after another of his diplomatic machinations was increasingly grim.

'I am sorry for the inconvenience,' Riley said, when Laurence did not immediately reply. 'Only I do not see what else is to be done. There surely is no shortage of room?'

This, too, was indisputable; with so few aviators aboard, and the ship's complement so nearly full, it was unfair to ask the sailors to give up any portion of their space, and could only aggravate the tensions, already high. As a practical matter, Riley was perfectly correct, and it was his right as the ship's captain to decide where the passengers might be at liberty; but Yongxing's threat had made the matter a question of principle. Laurence would have liked to unburden himself plainly to Riley, and if Hammond had not been there, he would have done so; as it was—

'Perhaps,' Hammond put in, hurriedly, 'Captain Laurence is concerned that they might irritate the dragon. May I suggest that we set aside one portion for them, and that plainly demarcated? A cord, perhaps, might be strung; or else paint would do.'

'That would do nicely, if you would be so kind as to explain the boundaries to them, Mr. Hammond,' Riley said.

Laurence could make no open protest without explanation, and he did not choose to be laying out his actions in front of Hammond, inviting him to comment upon them; not when there was likely nothing to gain. Riley would sympathize – or at least Laurence hoped he would, though abruptly he was less certain; but sympathy or no, the difficulty would remain, and Laurence did not know what else could be done.

He was not resigned; he was not resigned in the least, but he did not mean to complain and make Riley's situation more difficult. 'You will also make plain, Mr. Hammond,' Laurence said, 'that they are none of them to bring small-arms onto the deck, neither muskets nor swords, and in any action they are to go belowdecks at once: I will brook no interference with my crew, or with Temeraire.'

'But sir, there are soldiers among them,' Hammond protested. 'I am sure they would wish to drill, from time to time—'

'They may wait until they reach China,' Laurence said.

Hammond followed him out of the cabin and caught him at the door to his own quarters; inside, two ground crewmen had just brought in more chairs, and Roland and Dyer were busily laying plates out upon the cloth: the other dragons' captains were joining Laurence for breakfast before they took their leave. 'Sir,' Hammond said, 'pray allow me a moment. I must beg your pardon for having sent you to Prince Yongxing in such a way, knowing him to be in an intemperate mood, and I assure you I blame only myself for the consequences, and your quarrel; still, I must beg you to be forbearing—'

Laurence listened to this much, frowning, and now with mounting incredulity said, 'Are you saying that you were already aware—? That you made this proposal to Captain Riley, knowing I had forbidden them the deck?'

His voice was rising as he spoke, and Hammond darted his eyes desperately towards the open door of the cabin: Roland and Dyer were staring wide-eyed and interested at them both, not attending to the great silver platters they were holding. 'You must understand, we *cannot* put them in such a position. Prince Yongxing has issued a command; if we defy it openly, we humiliate him before his own—'

'Then he had best learn not to issue commands to me, sir,' Laurence said angrily, 'and you would do better to tell him so, instead of carrying them out for him, in this underhanded—'

'For Heaven's sake! Do you imagine I have any desire to see you barred from Temeraire? All we have to bargain with is the dragon's refusal to be separated from you,' Hammond said, growing heated himself. 'But that alone will not get us very far without goodwill, and if Prince Yongxing cannot enforce his commands so long as we are at sea, our positions will be wholly reversed in China. Would you have us sacrifice an alliance to your pride? To say nothing,' Hammond added, with a contemptible attempt at wheedling, 'of any hope of keeping Temeraire.'

'I am no diplomat,' Laurence said, 'but I will tell you, sir, if you imagine you are likely to get so much as a thimbleful of goodwill from this prince, no matter how you truckle to him, then you are a damned fool; and I will thank you not to imagine that I may be bought by castles in the air.'

Laurence had meant to send Harcourt and the others off in a creditable manner, but his table was left to bear the social

119

burden alone, without any assistance from his conversation. Thankfully he had laid in good stores, and there was some advantage in being so close to the galley: bacon, ham, eggs, and coffee came to the table steaming hot, even as they sat down, along with a portion of a great tunny, rolled in pounded ship's biscuit and fried, the rest of which had gone to Temeraire; also a large dish of cherry preserves, and an even larger of marmalade. He ate only a little, and seized gladly on the distraction when Warren asked him to sketch the course of the battle for them. He pushed aside his mostly untouched plate to demonstrate the manoeuvres of the ships and the Fleur-de-Nuit with bits of crumbled bread, the salt-cellar standing for the *Allegiance*.

The dragons were just completing their own somewhat less-civilized breakfast as Laurence and the other captains came back above to the dragondeck. Laurence was deeply gratified to find Temeraire wide awake and alert, looking much more easy with his bandages showing clean white, and engaged in persuading Maximus to try a piece of the tunny.

'It is a particularly nice one, and fresh-caught this very morning,' he said. Maximus eyed the fish with deep suspicion: Temeraire had already eaten perhaps half, but its head had not been removed, and it lay gap-mouthed and staring glassily on the deck. A good fifteen hundred pounds when first taken, Laurence guessed; even half was still impressive.

Less so, however, when Maximus finally bent his head down and took it: the whole bulk made a single bite for him, and it was amusing to see him chewing with a sceptical expression. Temeraire waited expectantly; Maximus swallowed and licked his chops, and said, 'It would not be so very bad, I suppose, if there were nothing else handy, but it is too slippery.'

Temeraire's ruff flattened with disappointment. 'Perhaps one must develop a taste for it. I dare say they can catch you another.'

Maximus snorted. 'No; I will leave the fish to you. Is there

120

any more mutton, at all?' he asked, peering over at the herds-master with interest.

'How many have you et up already?' Berkley demanded, heaving himself up the stairs towards him. 'Four? That is enough; if you grow any more, you will never get yourself off the ground.'

Maximus ignored this and cleaned the last haunch of sheep out of the slaughtering-tub; the others had finished also, and the herdsmaster's mates began pumping water over the drag-ondeck to sluice away the blood: shortly there was a veri-table frenzy of sharks in the waters before the ship.

The *William of Orange* was nearly abreast of them, and Riley had gone across to discuss the supplies with her captain; now he reappeared on her deck and was rowed back over, while her men began laying out fresh supplies of wooden spars and sail-cloth. 'Lord Purbeck,' Riley said, climbing back up the side, 'we will send the launch to fetch over the supplies, if you please.'

'Shall we bring them for you instead?' Harcourt asked, calling down from the dragondeck. 'We will have to clear Maximus and Lily off the deck in any case; we can just as easily ferry supplies as fly circles.'

'Thank you, sir; you would oblige me greatly,' Riley said, looking up and bowing, with no evident suspicion: Harcourt's hair was pulled back tightly, the long braid concealed beneath her flying-hood, while her dress coat hid her figure well enough.

Maximus and Lily went aloft, without their crews, clearing room on the deck for the others to make ready; the crews rolled out the harnesses and armour, and began rigging the smaller dragons out, while the two larger flew over to the *William of Orange* for the supplies. The moment of depar-ture was drawing close, and Laurence limped over to Temeraire's side; he was conscious suddenly of a sharp, unan-ticipated regret.

'I do not know that dragon,' Temeraire said to Laurence, looking across the water at the other transport; there was a large beast sprawled sullenly upon their dragondeck, a stripy brown-and-green, with red streaks on his wings and neck rather like paint: Laurence had never seen the breed before.

'He is an Indian breed, from one of those tribes in Canada,' Sutton said, when Laurence pointed out the strange dragon. 'I think Dakota, if I am pronouncing the name correctly; I understand he and his rider – they do not use crews over there, you know, only one man to a dragon, no matter the size – were captured raiding a settlement on the frontier. It is a great coup: a vastly different breed, and I understand they are very fierce fighters. They meant to use him at the breeding grounds in Halifax, but I believe it was agreed that once Praecursoris was sent to them, they should send that fellow here in exchange; and a proper bloody-minded creature he looks.'

'It seems hard to send him so very far from home, and to stay,' Temeraire said, rather low, looking at the other dragon. 'He does not look at all happy.'

'He would only be sitting in the breeding grounds at Halifax instead of here, and that does not make much difference,' Messoria said, stretching her wings out for the convenience of her harness-crewmen, who were climbing over her to get her rigged out. 'They are all much alike, and not very interesting, except for the breeding part,' she added, with somewhat alarming frankness; she was a much older dragon than Temeraire, being over thirty years of age.

'That does not sound very interesting, either,' Temeraire said, and glumly laid himself back down. 'Do you suppose they will put me in a breeding ground in China?'

'I am sure not,' Laurence said; privately, he was quite determined he would not leave Temeraire to any such fate, no matter what the Emperor of China or anyone else had to say about it. 'They would hardly be making such a fuss, if that were all they wanted.'

Messoria snorted indulgently. 'You may not think it so terrible, anyway, after you have tried it.'

'Stop corrupting the morals of the young.' Captain Sutton slapped her side good-humouredly, and gave the harness a final reassuring tug. 'There, I think we are ready. Goodbye a second time, Laurence,' he said, as they clasped hands. 'I expect you have had enough excitement to stand you for the whole voyage; may the rest be less eventful.'

The three smaller dragons leaped one after another off the deck, Nitidus scarcely even making the *Allegiance* dip in the water, and flew over to the *William of Orange*; then Maximus and Lily came back in turns to be rigged-out themselves, and for Berkley and Harcourt to make Laurence their farewells. At last the whole formation was transferred to the other transport, leaving Temeraire alone on the *Allegiance* once more.

Riley gave the order to make sail directly; the wind coming from east-southeast and not over-strong, even the studding-sails were set, a fine and blooming display of white. *William of Orange* fired a gun to leeward as they passed, answered in a moment by Riley's order, and a cheer came to them across the water as the two transports drew finally away from one another, slow and majestic.

Maximus and Lily had gone aloft for a frolic, with the energy of young dragons lately fed; they could be seen for a long while chasing one another through the clouds above the ship, and Temeraire kept his gaze on them until distance reduced them to the size of birds. He sighed a little then, and drew his head back down, curling in upon himself. 'It will be a long time before we see them again, I suppose,' he said.

Laurence put his hand on the sleek neck, silently. This parting felt somehow more final: no great bustle and noise, no sense of new adventure unfolding, only the crew going about their work still subdued, with nothing to be seen but the long blue miles of empty ocean, an uncertain road to a more uncertain destination. 'The time will pass more quickly than you expect,' he said. 'Come, let us have the book again.'

II

Chapter Six

The weather held clear for the first brief stage of their journey, with that peculiar winter cleanliness: the water very dark and the sky cloudless, and the air gradually warming as they continued the journey southward. A brisk, busy time, replacing the damaged yards and hanging the sails fresh, so that their pace daily increased as they restored the ship to her old self. They saw only a couple of small merchantmen in the distance, who gave them a wide berth, and once high overhead a courier-dragon going on its rounds with dispatches: certainly a Greyling, one of the long-distance fliers, but too far away for even Temeraire to recognize if it was anyone they knew.

The Chinese guards had appeared promptly at dawn, the first day after the arrangement, a broad stripe of paint having marked off a section of the larboard dragondeck; despite the absence of any visible weapons they did indeed stand watch, as formal as Marines on parade, in shifts of three. The crew were by now well aware of the quarrel, which had taken place near enough the stern windows to be overheard on deck, and were naturally inclined to be resentful of the guards' presence, and still more so of the senior members of the Chinese party, who were one and all eyed darkly, without distinction.

Laurence however was beginning to discern some individual

traces among them, at least those who chose to come on deck. A few of the younger men showed some real enthusiasm for the sea, standing near the larboard end of the deck to best enjoy the spray as the *Allegiance* ploughed onwards. One young fellow, Li Honglin, was particularly adventurous, going so far as to imitate the habits of some of the midshipmen and hang off the yards despite his unsuitable clothes: the skirts of his half-robe looked likely to entangle with the ropes, and his short black boots had soles too thick to have much purchase on the edge of the deck, unlike the bare feet or thin slippers of the sailors. His compatriots were much alarmed each time he tried it, and urged him back onto the deck loudly and with urgent gestures.

The rest took the air more sedately, and stayed well back from the edges; they often brought up low stools to sit upon, and spoke freely among themselves in the strange rise-and-fall of their language, which Laurence could not so much as break into sentences; it seemed wholly impenetrable to him. But despite the impossibility of direct conversation, he quickly came to feel that most of the attendants had no strong hostility of their own towards the British: uniformly civil, at least in expression and gesture, and usually making polite bows as they came and went.

They omitted such courtesies only on those occasions when they were in Yongxing's company: at such times, they followed his practice, and neither nodded nor made any gesture at all towards the British aviators, but came and went as if there were no other people at all aboard. But the prince came on deck infrequently; his cabin with its wide windows was spacious enough he did not need to do so for exercise. His main purpose seemed to be to frown and to look over Temeraire, who did not benefit from these inspections, as he was almost always asleep: still recovering from his wound, he was as yet napping nearly all the day, and lay oblivious, now and again sending a small rumble through the deck with a wide and drowsy yawn, while the life of the ship went on unheeded about him.

Liu Bao did not even make brief visits such as these, but remained closeted in his apartments: permanently, as far as any of them could tell; no one had seen so much of him as the tip of his nose since his first coming aboard, though he was quartered in the cabin under the poop deck, and had only to open his front door and step outside. He did not even leave to go down below to take meals or consult with Yongxing, and only a few servants trotted back and forth between his quarters and the galley, once or twice a day.

Sun Kai, by contrast, scarcely spent a moment of daylight indoors; he took the air after every meal and remained on deck for long stretches at a time. On those occasions when Yongxing came above, Sun Kai always bowed formally to the prince, and then kept himself quietly to one side, set apart from the retinue of servants, and the two of them did not much converse. Sun Kai's own interest was centred upon the life of the ship, and her construction; and he was particularly fascinated by the great-gun exercises.

These, Riley was forced to curtail more than he would have liked, Hammond having argued that they could not be disturbing the prince regularly; so on most days the men only ran out the guns in dumb-show, without firing, and only occasionally engaged in the thunder and crash of a live exercise. In either case, Sun Kai always appeared promptly the moment the drum began to beat, if he were not already on deck at the time, and watched the proceedings intently from start to finish, not flinching even at the enormous eruption and recoil. He was careful to place himself so that he was not in the way, even as the men came racing up to the dragondeck to man its handful of guns, and by the second or third occasion the gun crews ceased to pay him any notice.

When there was no exercise in train, he studied the nearby guns at close-range. Those upon the dragondeck were the short-barrelled carronades, great forty-two-pound smashers, less accurate than the long guns but with far less recoil, so they did not require much room; and Sun Kai was fascinated by the fixed mounting in particular, which allowed the heavy iron barrel to slide back and forth along its path of recoil. He did not seem to think it rude to stare, either, as the men went about their work, aviators and sailors alike, though he could not have understood a word of what they were saying; and he studied the *Allegiance* herself with as much interest: the arrangement of her masts and sails, and with particular attention to the design of her hull. Laurence saw him often peering down over the edge of the dragondeck at the white line of the keel, and making sketches upon the deck in an attempt to outline her construction.

Yet for all his evident curiosity, he had a quality of deep reserve which went beyond the exterior, the severity of his foreign looks; his study was somehow more intense than eager, less a scholar's passion than a matter of industry and diligence, and there was nothing inviting in his manner. Hammond, undaunted, had already made a few overtures, which were received with courtesy but no warmth, and to Laurence it seemed almost painfully obvious that Sun Kai was not welcoming: not the least change of emotion showed on his face at Hammond's approach or departure, no smiles, no frowns, only a controlled, polite attention.

Even if conversation had been possible, Laurence did not think he could bring himself to intrude, after Hammond's example; though Sun Kai's study of the ship would certainly have benefited from some guidance, and thus offered an ideal subject of conversation. But tact forbade it as much as the barrier of language, so for the moment, Laurence contented himself with observation.

At Madeira, they watered and repaired their supplies of livestock from the damage which the formation's visit had done

130

them, but did not linger in port. 'All this shifting of the sails has been to some purpose – I am beginning to have a better notion of what suits her,' Riley said to Laurence. 'Would you mind Christmas at sea? I would be just as happy to put her to the test, and see if I can bring her up as far as seven knots.'

They sailed out of Funchal roads majestically, with a broad spread of sail, and Riley's jubilant air announced his hopes for greater speed had been answered even before he said, 'Eight knots, or nearly; what do you say to that?'

'I congratulate you indeed,' Laurence said. 'I would not have thought it possible, myself; she is going beyond anything.' He felt a curious kind of regret at their speed, wholly unfamiliar. As a captain he had never much indulged in real cracking on, feeling it inappropriate to be reckless with the King's property, but like any seaman he liked his ship to go as well as she could. He would ordinarily have shared truly in Riley's pleasure, and never looked back at the smudge of the island receding behind them.

Riley had invited Laurence and several of the ship's officers to dine, in a celebratory mood over the ship's newfound speed. As if for punishment, a brief squall blew up from nowhere during the meal, while only the hapless young Lieutenant Beckett was standing watch: he could have sailed around the world six times without a pause if only ships were to be controlled directly by mathematical formulae, and yet invariably managed to give quite the wrong order in any real weather. There was a mad rush from the dinner table as soon as the *Allegiance* first pitched beneath them, putting her head down and protesting, and they heard Temeraire make a startled small roar; even so, the wind nearly carried away the mizzentopgallant sail before Riley and Purbeck could get back on deck and put things to rights.

The storm blew away as quickly as it had come, the hurrying dark clouds leaving the sky washed shell-pink and blue behind them; the swell died to a comfortable height, a few feet, which the *Allegiance* scarcely noticed; and while there was yet enough light to read by on the dragondeck, a party of the Chinese came up on deck: several servants first manoeuvring Liu Bao out through his door, trundling him across the quarterdeck and forecastle, and then at last up to the dragondeck. The older envoy was greatly altered from his last appearance, having shed perhaps a stone in weight and gone a distinctly greenish shade under his beard and pouched cheeks, so visibly uncomfortable that Laurence could not help but be sorry for him. The servants had brought a chair for him; he was eased into it and his face turned into the cool wet wind, but he did not look at all as though he were improving, and when another of the attendants tried to offer him a plate of food, he only waved it away.

'Do you suppose he is going to starve to death?' Temeraire inquired, more in a spirit of curiosity than concern, and Laurence answered absently, 'I hope not; though he is old to be taking to sea for the first time,' even as he sat up and beckoned. 'Dyer, go down to Mr. Pollitt and ask if he would be so good as to step up for a moment.'

Shortly Dyer came back with the ship's surgeon puffing along behind him in his awkward way; Pollitt had been Laurence's own surgeon in two commands, and did not stand on ceremony, but heaved himself into a chair and said, 'Well, now, sir; is it the leg?'

'No, thank you, Mr. Pollitt; I am improving nicely; but I am concerned for the Chinese gentleman's health.' Laurence pointed out Liu Bao, and Pollitt, shaking his head, opined that if he went on losing weight at such a pace, he should scarcely reach the equator. 'I do not suppose they know any remedies for sea-sickness of this virulent sort, not being accustomed to long voyages,' Laurence said. 'Would you not make up some physic for him?'

'Well, he is not my patient, and I would not like to be accused of interference; I do not suppose their medical men take any kinder view of it than do we,' Pollitt said apologetically. 'But in any case, I think I should rather prescribe a course of ship's biscuit. There is very little offence any stomach can take at biscuit, I find, and who knows what sort of foreign cookery he has been teasing himself with. A little biscuit and perhaps a light wine will set him up properly again, I am sure.'

Of course the foreign cookery was native to Liu Bao, but Laurence saw nothing to argue with in this course of action, and later that evening sent over a large packet of biscuit, picked-over by a reluctant Roland and Dyer to remove the weevils, and the real sacrifice, three bottles of a particular sprightly Riesling: very light, indeed almost airy, and purchased at a cost of 6s. 3d. apiece from a Portsmouth wine-merchant.

Laurence felt a little odd in making the gesture; he hoped he would have done as much in any case, but there was more calculation in it than he had ever been used to make, and there was just a shade of dishonesty, a shade of flattery to it, which he could not entirely like, or approve of in himself. And indeed he felt some general qualms about any overture at all, given the insult of the confiscation of the East India Company ships, which he had no more forgotten than any of the sailors who still watched the Chinese with sullen dislike.

But he excused himself to Temeraire privately that night, having seen his offering delivered into Liu Bao's cabin. 'After all, it is not their fault personally, any more than it would be mine if the King were to do the same to them. If Government makes not a sound over the matter, they can hardly be blamed for treating it so lightly: *they* at least have not made the slightest attempt at concealing the incident, nor been dishonest in the least.'

Even as he said it, he was still not quite satisfied. But there was no other choice; he did not mean to be sitting about doing nothing, nor could he rely upon Hammond: skill and wit the diplomat might possess, but Laurence was by now convinced that there was no intention, on his part, of expending much effort to keep Temeraire; to Hammond the dragon was only a bargaining-chip. There was certainly no hope of persuading Yongxing, but so far as the other members of the embassy might be won over, in good faith, he meant to try, and if the effort should tax him in his pride, that was small sacrifice.

It proved worthwhile: Liu Bao crept from his cabin again the next day, looking less wretched, and by the subsequent morning was well enough to send for the translator, and ask Laurence to come over to their side of the deck and join him: some colour back in his face, and much relief. He had also brought along one of the cooks: the biscuits, he reported, had worked wonders, taken on his physician's recommendation with a little fresh ginger, and he was urgent to know how they might be made.

'Well, they are mostly flour and a bit of water, but I cannot tell you anything more, I am afraid,' Laurence said. 'We do not bake them aboard, you see; but I assure you we have enough in the bread-room to last you twice around the world, sir.'

'Once has been more than enough for me,' Liu Bao said. 'An old man like me has no business going so far away from home and being tossed around on the waves. Since we came on this ship, I have not been able to eat anything, not even a few pancakes, until those biscuits! But this morning I was able to have some congee and fish, and I was not sick at all. I am very grateful to you.'

'I am happy to have been of service, sir; indeed you look much improved,' Laurence said.

'That is very polite, even if it is not very truthful,' Liu Bao said. He held out his arm ruefully and shook it, the robe hanging rather loose. 'I will take some fattening up to look like myself again.'

'If you feel equal to it, sir, may I invite you to join us for dinner tomorrow evening?' Laurence asked, thinking this overture, though barely, enough encouragement to justify the invitation. 'It is our holiday, and I am giving a dinner for my officers; you would be very welcome, and any of your compatriots who might wish to join you.'

This dinner proved far more successful than the last. Granby was still laid up in the sickberth, forbidden rich food, but Lieutenant Ferris was bent on making the most of his opportunity to impress and in any direction which offered. He was a young officer and energetic, very lately promoted to Temeraire's captain of topmen on account of a fine boarding engagement he had led at Trafalgar. In ordinary course it would have been at least another year and more likely two or three before he could hope to become a second lieutenant in his own right, but with poor Evans sent home, he had stepped into his place as acting-second, and plainly hoped to keep the position.

In the morning, Laurence with some amusement overheard him sternly lecturing the midwingmen on the need to behave in a civilized manner at the table, and not sit around like lumps. Laurence suspected that he even primed the junior officers with a handful of anecdotes, as occasionally during the meal he glared significantly at one or the other of the boys, and the target would hastily gulp his wine and start in on a story rather improbable for an officer of such tender years.

Sun Kai accompanied Liu Bao, but as before had the air of an observer rather than a guest. But Liu Bao displayed no similar restraint and had plainly come ready to be pleased, though indeed it would have been a hard man who could have resisted the suckling pig, spit-roasted since that morning and glowing under its glaze of butter and cream. They neither of them disdained a second helping and Liu Bao was also loud in his approval of the crackling-brown goose, a handsome specimen acquired specially for the occasion at Madeira and still smug and fat at the time of its demise, unlike the usual poultry to be had at sea.

The civil exertions of the officers had an effect also, as stumbling and awkward as some of the younger fellows were about it; Liu Bao had a generous laugh easily provoked, and he shared many amusing stories of his own, mostly about hunting misadventures. Only the poor translator was unhappy, as he had a great deal of work scurrying back and forth around the table, alternately putting English into Chinese and then the reverse; almost from the beginning, the atmosphere was wholly different, and wholly amiable.

Sun Kai remained quiet, listening more than speaking, and Laurence could not be sure he was enjoying himself; he ate still in an abstemious fashion and drank very little, though Liu Bao, himself not at all lacking in capacity, would good-naturedly scold him from time to time, and fill his glass again to the brim. But after the great Christmas pudding was ceremoniously borne out, flickering blue with brandied flames, to shared applause, to be dismantled, served, and enjoyed, Liu Bao turned and said to him, 'You are being very dull tonight. Here, sing "The Hard Road" for us, that is the proper poem for this journey!'

For all his reserve, Sun Kai seemed quite willing to oblige; he cleared his throat and recited:

'Pure wine costs, for the golden bowl, ten thousand
    coppers a flagon,
And a jade platter of dainty food calls for a million
    coins.
I fling aside my bowl and meat, I cannot eat or
    drink . . .
I raise my talons to the sky, I peer four ways in vain.
I would cross the Yellow River, but ice takes hold of
    my limbs;
I would fly above the Tai-hang Mountains, but the sky
    is blind with snow.

I would sit and watch the golden carp, lazy by a
      brook—
But I suddenly dream of crossing the waves, sailing for
      the sun . . .
Journeying is hard,
Journeying is hard.
There are many turnings—
Which am I to follow?
I will mount a long wind some day and break the
      heavy bank of clouds,
And set my wings straight to bridge the wide, wide
      sea.'

If there was any rhyme or metre to the piece, they vanished
in the translation, but the content the aviators uniformly
approved and applauded. 'Is it your own work, sir?' Laurence
asked with interest. 'I do not believe I have ever heard a poem
from the view of a dragon.'

'No, no,' Sun Kai said. 'It is one of the works of the
honoured Lung Li Po, of the Tang Dynasty. I am only a poor
scholar, and my verses are not worthy of being shared in
company.' He was perfectly happy, however, to give them
several other selections from classical poets, all recited from
memory, in what seemed to Laurence a prodigious feat of
recall.

All the guests rolled away at last on the most harmonious
of terms, having carefully avoided any discussion of British
and Chinese sovereignty regarding either ships or dragons. 'I
will be so bold as to say it was a success,' Laurence said afterwards, sipping coffee upon the dragondeck while Temeraire
ate his sheep. 'They are not so very stiff-necked in company,
after all, and I can call myself really satisfied with Liu Bao;
I have been in many a ship where I should have been grateful
to dine with as good company.'

'Well, I am glad you had a pleasant evening,' Temeraire

said, grinding thoughtfully upon the leg bones. 'Can you say that poem over again?'

Laurence had to canvass his officers to attempt to reconstruct the poem; they were still at it the next morning, when Yongxing came up to take the air, and listened to them mangling the translation; after they had made a few attempts, he frowned and then turned to Temeraire, and himself recited the poem.

Yongxing spoke in Chinese, without translation; but nevertheless, after a single hearing, Temeraire was able to repeat the verses back to him in the same language, with not the least evidence of difficulty. It was not the first time that Laurence had been surprised by Temeraire's skill with language: like all dragons, Temeraire had learned speech during the long maturity in the shell, but unlike most, he had been exposed to three different tongues, and evidently remembered even what must have been his earliest.

'Laurence,' Temeraire said, turning his head towards him with excitement, after exchanging a few more words in Chinese with Yongxing, 'he says that it was written by a dragon, not a man at all.'

Laurence, still taken aback to find that Temeraire could speak the language, blinked yet again at this intelligence. 'Poetry seems an odd sort of occupation for a dragon, but I suppose if other Chinese dragons like books as well as you do, it is not so surprising one of them should have tried his hand at verse.'

'I wonder how he wrote it,' Temeraire said thoughtfully. 'I might like to try, but I do not see how I would ever put it down; I do not think I could hold a pen.' He raised his own foreleg and examined the five-fingered claw dubiously.

'I would be happy to take your dictation,' Laurence said, amused by the notion. 'I expect that is how he managed.'

He thought nothing more of it until two days later, when he came back on deck grim and worried after sitting a long

138

while again in the sickberth: the stubborn fever had recurred, and Granby lay pale and half-present, his blue eyes wide and fixed sightlessly upon the distant recesses of the ceiling, his lips parted and cracked; he took only a little water, and when he spoke his words were confused and wandering. Pollitt would give no opinion, and only shook his head a little.

Ferris was standing anxiously at the bottom of the dragondeck stairs, waiting for him; and at his expression Laurence quickened his still-limping pace. 'Sir,' Ferris said, 'I did not know what to do; he has been talking to Temeraire all morning, and we cannot tell what he is saying.'

Laurence hastened up the steps and found Yongxing seated in an armchair on the deck and conversing with Temeraire in Chinese, the prince speaking rather slowly and loudly, enunciating his words, and correcting Temeraire's own speech in return; he had also brought up several sheets of paper, and had painted a handful of their odd-looking characters upon them in large size. Temeraire indeed looked fascinated; his attention was wholly engaged, and the tip of his tail was flicking back and forth in mid-air, as when he was particularly excited.

'Laurence, look, that is "dragon" in their writing,' Temeraire said, catching sight of him and calling him forward: Laurence obediently stared at the picture, rather blankly; to him it looked like nothing more than the patterns sometimes left marked on a sandy shore after a tide, even when Temeraire had pointed out the portion of the symbol which represented the dragon's wings, and then the body.

'Do they only have a single letter for the entire word?' Laurence said, dubiously. 'How is it pronounced?'

'It is said *lung*,' Temeraire said, 'like in my Chinese name, Lung Tien Xiang, and *tien* is for Celestials,' he added, proudly, pointing to another symbol.

Yongxing was watching them both, with no very marked outward expression, but Laurence thought perhaps a suggestion of triumph in his eyes. 'I am very glad you have been so pleasantly occupied,' Laurence said to Temeraire, and turning to Yongxing, made a deliberate bow, addressing him without invitation. 'You are very kind, sir, to take such pains.'

Yongxing answered him stiffly, 'I consider it a duty. The study of the classics is the path to understanding.'

His manner was hardly welcoming, but if he chose to ignore the boundary and speak with Temeraire, Laurence considered it the equivalent of a formal call, and himself justified in initiating conversation. Whether or not Yongxing privately agreed, Laurence's forwardness did not deter him from future visits: every morning now began to find him upon the deck, giving Temeraire daily lessons in the language and offering him further samples of Chinese literature to whet his appetite.

Laurence at first suffered only irritation at these transparent attempts at enticement; Temeraire looked much brighter than he had since parting from Maximus and Lily, and though he might dislike the source, Laurence could not begrudge Temeraire the opportunity for so much new mental occupation, when he was as yet confined to the deck by his wound. As for the notion that Temeraire's loyalty would be swayed by any number of Oriental blandishments, Yongxing might entertain such a belief if he liked; Laurence had no doubts.

But he could not help but feel a rather sinking sensation as the days went on and Temeraire did not tire of the subject; their own books were now often neglected in favour of recitation of one or another piece of Chinese literature, which Temeraire liked to get by rote, as he could not write them down or read them. Laurence was well aware he was nothing like a scholar; his own notion of pleasant occupation was to spend an afternoon in conversation, perhaps writing letters or reading a newspaper when one not excessively out of date could be gotten. Although under Temeraire's influence he had gradually come to enjoy books far more than he had ever imagined he could, it was a good deal harder to share

Temeraire's excitement over works in a language he could not make head or tail of himself.

He did not mean to give Yongxing the satisfaction of seeing him at all discomfited, but it did feel like a victory for the prince at his own expense, particularly on those occasions when Temeraire mastered a new piece and visibly glowed under Yongxing's rare and hard-won praise. Laurence worried, also, that Yongxing seemed almost surprised by Temeraire's progress, and often especially pleased; Laurence naturally thought Temeraire remarkable among dragons, but this was not an opinion he desired Yongxing to share: the prince scarcely needed any additional motive to try and take Temeraire away.

As some consolation, Temeraire was constantly shifting into English, that he might draw Laurence in; and Yongxing had perforce to make polite conversation with him, or risk losing what advantage he had gained. But while this might be satisfying in a petty sort of way, Laurence could not be said to *enjoy* these conversations much. Any natural kinship of spirit must have been inadequate in the face of so violent a practical opposition, and they would scarcely have been inclined towards one another in any case.

One morning Yongxing came on deck early, with Temeraire still sleeping; and while his attendants brought out his chair and draped it, and arranged for him the scrolls which he meant to read to Temeraire that day, the prince came to the edge of the deck to gaze out at the ocean. They were in the midst of a lovely stretch of blue-water sailing, no shore in sight and the wind coming fresh and cool off the sea, and Laurence was himself standing in the bows to enjoy the vista: dark water stretching endless to the horizon, occasional little waves overlapping one another in a white froth, and the ship all alone beneath the curving bowl of the sky.

'Only in the desert can one find so desolate and uninteresting a view,' Yongxing said abruptly; as Laurence had been on the point of offering a polite remark about the beauty of the scene, he was left dumb and baffled, and still more so when Yongxing added, 'You British are forever sailing off to some new place; are you so discontented with your own country?' He did not wait for an answer, but shook his head and turned away, leaving Laurence again confirmed in his belief that he could hardly have found a man less in sympathy with himself on any point.

Temeraire's shipboard diet would ordinarily have been mostly fish, caught by himself; Laurence and Granby had planned on it in their calculations of supply, cattle and sheep intended for variety's sake, and in case of bad weather which might keep Temeraire confined to the ship. But barred from flying because of his wound, Temeraire could not hunt, and so he was consuming their stores at a far more rapid pace than they had originally counted upon.

'We will have to keep close to the Saharan coastline in any case, or risk being blown straight across to Rio by the trade winds,' Riley said. 'We can certainly stop at Cape Coast to take on supplies.' This was meant to console him; Laurence only nodded and went away.

Riley's father had plantations in the West Indies, and several hundred slaves to work them, while Laurence's own father was a firm supporter of Wilberforce and Clarkson, and had made several very cutting speeches in the Lords against the trade, on one occasion even mentioning Riley's father by name in a list of slave-holding gentlemen who, as he had mildly put it, 'disgrace the name of Christian, and blight the character and reputation of their country.'

The incident had made a coolness between them at the time: Riley was deeply attached to his father, a man of far greater personal warmth than Lord Allendale, and naturally resented the public insult. Laurence, while lacking a particularly strong degree of affection for his own father and angry to be put in so unhappy a position, was yet not at all willing to offer any sort of apology. He had grown up with the pamphlets and books put out by Clarkson's committee all about the house, and at the age of nine had been taken on a tour of a former slave-ship, about to be broken up; the nightmares had lingered afterwards for several months, and made upon his young mind a profound impression. They had never made peace on the subject but only settled into a truce; they neither of them mentioned the subject again, and studiously avoided discussing either parent. Laurence could not now speak frankly to Riley about how very reluctant he was to put in at a slave port, though he was not at all easy in his mind at the prospect.

Instead he privately asked Keynes whether Temeraire was not healing well, and might be permitted short flights again, for hunting. 'Best not,' the surgeon said, reluctantly; Laurence looked at him sharply, and at last drew from Keynes the admission that he had some concern: the wound was not healing as he would like. 'The muscles are still warm to the touch, and I believe I feel some drawn flesh beneath the hide,' Keynes said. 'It is far too soon to have any real concern, however I do not intend to take any risks: no flying, for at least another two weeks.'

So by this conversation Laurence merely gained one additional source of private care. There were sufficient others already, besides the shortage of food and the now-unavoidable stop at Cape Coast. With Temeraire's injury as well as Yongxing's steadfast opposition precluding any work aloft, the aviators had been left almost entirely idle, while at the same time the sailors had been particularly busy with repairing the damage to the ship and making her stores, and a host of not unpredictable evils had followed.

Thinking to offer Roland and Dyer some distraction, Laurence had called the two of them up to the dragondeck shortly before the arrival in Madeira, to examine them in their schoolwork. They had stared at him with such guilty expressions that he was not surprised to find they had neglected their studies entirely since having become his runners: very little notion of arithmetic, none at all of the more advanced mathematics, no French whatsoever, and when he handed them Gibbon's book, which he had brought to the deck meaning to read to Temeraire later, Roland stuttered so over the words that Temeraire put back his ruff and began to correct her from memory. Dyer was a little better off: when quizzed, he at least had his multiplication tables mostly by heart, and some sense of grammar; Roland stumbled over anything higher than eight and professed herself surprised to learn that speech even had parts. Laurence no longer wondered how he would fill their time; he only reproached himself for having been so lax about their schooling, and set about his newly self-appointed task as their schoolmaster with a will.

The runners had always been rather pets of the entire crew; since Morgan's death, Roland and Dyer had been cosseted still more. Their daily struggles with participles and division were now looked on by the other aviators with great amusement, but only until the *Allegiance*'s midshipmen made some jeering noises. Then the ensigns took it on themselves to repay the insult, and a few scuffles ensued in dark corners of the ship.

At first, Laurence and Riley entertained themselves by a comparison of the wooden excuses which were offered them for the collection of black eyes and bleeding lips. But the petty squabbling began to take a more ominous shape when older men started to present similar excuses: a deeper resentment on the sailors' part, founded in no small part in the uneven balance of labour and their fear of Temeraire, was finding expression in the near-daily exchange of insults, no longer even touching upon Roland and Dyer's studies. In their turn, the aviators had taken a reciprocal offence at the complete lack of gratitude that seemed to them due to Temeraire's valour.

The first true explosion occurred just as they began to make the turn eastward, past Cape Palmas, and headed towards Cape Coast. Laurence was drowsing on the dragondeck, sheltered by the shadow of Temeraire's body from the direct force of the sun; he did not see himself what had happened, but he was roused by a heavy thump, sudden shouts and cries, and climbing hurriedly to his feet saw the men in a ring. Martin was gripping Blythe, the armourer's mate, by the arm; one of Riley's officers, an older midshipman, was stretched out on the deck, and Lord Purbeck was shouting from the poop deck, 'Set that man in irons, Cornell, straightaway.'

Temeraire's head came straight up, and he roared: not raising the divine wind, thankfully, but he made a great and thundering noise nonetheless, and the men all scattered back from it, many with pale faces. 'No one is putting any of my crew in prison,' Temeraire said angrily, his tail lashing the air; he raised himself and spread wide his wings, and the whole ship shivered: the wind was blowing out from the Saharan coast, abaft the beam, the sails close-hauled to keep them on their southeast course, and Temeraire's wings were acting as an independent and contrary sail.

'Temeraire! Stop that at once; at once, do you hear me?' Laurence said sharply; he had never spoken so, not since the first weeks of Temeraire's existence, and Temeraire dropped down in surprise, his wings furling in tight on instinct. 'Purbeck, you will leave my men to me, if you please; stand down, master-at-arms,' Laurence said, snapping orders quickly: he did not mean to allow the scene to progress further, nor turn into some open struggle between the aviators and seamen. 'Mr. Ferris,' he said, 'take Blythe below and confine him.'

'Yes, sir,' Ferris said, already shoving through the crowd, and pushing the aviators back around him, breaking up the knots of angry men even before he reached Blythe.

Watching the progress with hard eyes, Laurence added, loudly, 'Mr. Martin, to my cabin at once. Back to your work, all of you; Mr. Keynes, come here.'

145

He stayed another moment, but he was satisfied: the pressing danger had been averted. He turned from the rail, trusting to ordinary discipline to break up the rest of the crowd. But Temeraire was huddled down very nearly flat, looking at him with a startled, unhappy expression; Laurence reached out to him and flinched as Temeraire twitched away: not out of reach, but the impulse plainly visible.

'Forgive me,' Laurence said, dropping his hand, a tightness in his throat. 'Temeraire,' he said, and stopped; he did not know what to say, for Temeraire could not be allowed to act so: he might have caused real damage to the ship, and aside from that if he carried on in such a fashion the crew would shortly grow too terrified of him to do their work. 'You have not hurt yourself?' he asked, instead, as Keynes hurried over.

'No,' Temeraire said, very quietly. 'I am perfectly well.' He submitted to being examined, in silence, and Keynes pronounced him unharmed by the exertion.

'I must go speak with Martin,' Laurence said, still at a loss; Temeraire did not answer, but curled himself up and swept his wings forward, around his head, and after a long moment, Laurence left the deck and went below.

The cabin was close and hot, even with all the windows standing open, and not calculated to improve Laurence's temper. Martin was pacing the length of the cabin in agitation; he was untidy in a suit of warm-weather slops, his face two days unshaven and presently flushed, his hair too long and flopping over his eyes. He did not recognize the degree of Laurence's real anger, but burst out talking the moment Laurence came in.

'I am so very sorry; it was all my fault. I oughtn't have spoken at all,' he said, even while Laurence limped to his chair and sat down heavily. 'You cannot punish Blythe, Laurence.'

Laurence had grown used to the lack of formality among aviators, and ordinarily did not balk at this liberty in passing,

146

but for Martin to make use of it under the circumstances was so egregious that Laurence sat back and stared at him, outrage plainly written on his face. Martin went pale under his freckled skin, swallowed and hurriedly said, 'I mean, Captain, sir.'

'I will do whatever I must to keep order among this crew, Mr. Martin, which appears to be more than I thought necessary,' Laurence said, and moderated his volume only with a great effort; he felt truly savage. 'You will tell me at once what happened.'

'I didn't mean to,' Martin said, much subdued. 'That fellow Reynolds has been making remarks all week, and Ferris told us to pay him no mind, but I was walking by, and he said—'

'I am not interested in hearing you bear tales,' Laurence said. 'What did you do?'

'Oh—' Martin said, flushing. 'I only said— Well, I said something back, which I should rather not repeat; and then he—' Martin stopped, and looked somewhat confused as to how to finish the story without seeming to accuse Reynolds again, and finished lamely, 'At any rate, sir, he was on the point of offering me a challenge, and that was when Blythe knocked him down; he only did it because he knew I could not fight, and did not want to see me have to refuse in front of the sailors; truly, sir, it is my fault, and not his.'

'I cannot disagree with you in the least,' Laurence said, brutally, and was glad in his anger to see Martin's shoulders hunch forward, as if struck. 'And when I have to have Blythe flogged on Sunday for striking an officer, I hope you will keep in mind that he is paying for your lack of self-restraint. You are dismissed; you are to keep belowdecks and to your quarters for the week, save when defaulters are called.'

Martin's lips worked a moment; his 'Yes, sir,' emerged only faintly, and he was almost stumbling as he left the room. Laurence sat still breathing harshly, almost panting in the thick air; the anger slowly deserted him in spite of every effort, and gave way to a heavier, bitter oppression. Blythe had saved not only Martin's reputation but that of the aviators as a whole; if Martin had openly refused a challenge made in front of the entire crew, it would have blackened all their characters; no matter that it was forced on them by the regulations of the Corps, which forbade duelling.

And yet there was no room for leniency in the matter whatsoever. Blythe had openly struck an officer before witnesses, and Laurence would have to sentence him to sufficient punishment to give the sailors satisfaction, and all of the men pause against any future capers of the sort. And the punishment would be carried out by the bo'sun's mate: a sailor, like as not to relish the chance to be severe on an aviator, particularly for such an offence.

He would have to go speak with Blythe; but a tapping at the door broke in upon him before he could rise, and Riley came in: unsmiling, in his coat and with his hat under his arm, neckcloth freshly tied.

Chapter Seven

They drew near Cape Coast a week later with the atmosphere of ill-will a settled and living thing among them, as palpable as the heat. Blythe had taken ill from his brutal flogging; he still lay nearly senseless in the sickbay, the other ground crew hands taking it in turn to sit by him and fan the bloody weals, and to coax him to take some water. They had taken the measure of Laurence's temper, and so their bitterness against the sailors was not expressed in word or direct action, but in sullen, black looks and murmurs, and abrupt silences whenever a sailor came in earshot.

Laurence had not dined in the great cabin since the incident: Riley had been offended at having Purbeck corrected on the deck; Laurence had grown short in turn when Riley refused to unbend and made it plain he was not satisfied by the dozen lashes which were all Laurence would sentence. In the heat of discussion, Laurence had let slip some suggestion of his distaste for going to the slave port, Riley had resented the implication, and they had ended not in shouting but in cold formality.

But worse by far than this, Temeraire's spirits were very low. He had forgiven Laurence the moment of harshness, and been persuaded to understand that some punishment was necessary for the offence. But he had not been at all reconciled to the actual event, and during the flogging he had growled savagely when Blythe had screamed towards the end. Some good had come of that: the bo'sun's mate Hingley, who had been wielding the cat with more than usual energy, had been alarmed, and the last couple of strokes had been mild; but the damage had already been done.

Temeraire had since remained unhappy and quiet, answering only briefly, and he was not eating well. The sailors, for their part, were as dissatisfied with the light sentence; the aviators with the brutality; poor Martin, set to tanning hides with the harness-master for punishment, was more wretched with guilt than from his punishment, and spent every spare moment at Blythe's bedside; and the only person at all satisfied with the situation was Yongxing, who seized the opportunity to hold several more long conversations with Temeraire in Chinese: privately, as Temeraire made no effort to include Laurence.

Yongxing looked less pleased, however, at the conclusion of the last of these, when Temeraire hissed, put back his ruff, and then proceeded to all but knock Laurence off his feet in coiling possessively around him. 'What has he been saying to you?' Laurence demanded, trying futilely to peer above the great black sides rising around him; he had already reached a state of high irritation at Yongxing's continued interference, and was very nearly at the end of his patience.

'He has been telling me about China, and how things are managed there for dragons,' Temeraire said, evasively, by which Laurence suspected that Temeraire had liked these described arrangements. 'But then he told me I should have a more worthy companion there, and you would be sent away.'

By the time he could be persuaded to uncoil himself again, Yongxing had gone, 'looking mad as fire,' Ferris reported, with glee unbecoming a senior lieutenant.

This scarcely contented Laurence. 'I am not going to have

Temeraire distressed in this manner,' he said to Hammond angrily, trying without success to persuade the diplomat to carry a highly undiplomatic message to the prince.

'You are taking a very short-sighted view of the matter,' Hammond said, maddeningly. 'If Prince Yongxing can be convinced over the course of this journey that Temeraire will not agree to be parted from you, all the better for us: they will be far more ready to negotiate when finally we arrive in China.' He paused and asked, with still more infuriating anxiousness, 'You are quite certain, that he will not agree?'

Granby said that evening, 'I say we heave Hammond and Yongxing over the side together some dark night, and good riddance,' on hearing the account, expressing Laurence's private sentiments more frankly than Laurence himself felt he could. He was speaking, with no regard for manners, between bites of a light meal of soup, toasted cheese, potatoes fried in pork fat with onions, an entire roast chicken, and a mince pie: he had finally been released from his sickbed, pallid and much reduced in weight, and Laurence had invited him to supper. 'What else was that prince saying to him?'

'I have not the least idea; he has not said three words together in English the last week,' Laurence said. 'And I do not mean to press Temeraire to tell me; it would be the most officious, prying sort of behaviour.'

'That none of his friends should ever be flogged there, I expect,' Granby said, darkly. 'And that he should have a dozen books to read every day, and heaps of jewels. I have heard stories about this sort of thing, but if a fellow ever really tried it, they would drum him out of the Corps quick as lightning; if the dragon did not carve him into joints, first.'

Laurence was silent a moment, twisting his wineglass in his fingers. 'Temeraire is only listening to it at all because he is unhappy.'

'Oh Hell.' Granby sat back heavily. 'I am damned sorry I have been sick so long; Ferris is a right 'un, but he hasn't been on a transport before, he couldn't know how the sailors get, and how to properly teach the fellows to take no notice,' he said glumly. 'And I can't give you any advice for cheering him up; I served with Laetificat longest, and she is easy-going even for a Regal Copper: no temper to speak of, and no mood I ever saw could dampen her appetite. Maybe it is not being allowed to fly.'

They came into the harbour the next morning: a broad semi-circle with a golden beach, dotted with attractive palms under the squat white walls of the overlooking castle. A multitude of rough canoes, many with branches still attached to the trunks from which they had been hollowed, were plying the waters of the harbour, and besides these there could be seen an assortment of brigs and schooners, and at the western end a snow of middling size, with her boats swarming back and forth, crowded with blacks who were being herded along from a tunnel mouth that came out onto the beach itself.

The *Allegiance* was too large to come into the harbour proper, but she had anchored close enough; the day was calm, and the cracking of the whips perfectly audible over the water, mingled with cries and the steady sound of weeping. Laurence came frowning onto the deck and ordered Roland and Dyer away from their wide-eyed staring, sending them below to tidy his cabin. Temeraire could not be protected in the same manner, and was observing the proceedings with some confusion, the slitted pupils of his eyes widening and narrowing as he stared.

'Laurence, those men are all in chains; what can so many of them have done?' he demanded, roused from his apathy. 'They cannot all have committed crimes; look, that one over there is a small child, and there is another.'

'No,' Laurence said. 'That is a slaver; pray do not watch.' Fearing this moment, he had made a vague attempt at explaining the idea of slavery to Temeraire, with his lack of success due as much to his own distaste as to Temeraire's difficulty with the notion of property. Temeraire did not listen now, but kept watching, his tail switching rapidly in anxiety. The loading of the vessel continued throughout the morning, and the hot wind blowing from the shore carried the sour smell of unwashed bodies, sweating and ill with misery.

At length the boarding was finished, and the snow with her unhappy cargo came out of the harbour and spread her sails to the wind, throwing up a fine furrow as she went past them, already moving at a steady pace, sailors scrambling in the rigging; but full half her crew were only armed landsmen, sitting idly about on deck with their muskets and pistols and mugs of grog. They stared openly at Temeraire, curious, their faces unsmiling, sweating and grimy from the work; one of them even picked up his gun and sighted along it at Temeraire, as if for sport. 'Present arms!' Lieutenant Riggs snapped, before Laurence could even react, and the three riflemen on deck had their guns ready in an instant; across the water, the fellow lowered his musket and grinned, showing strong yellowed teeth, and turned back to his shipmates laughing.

Temeraire's ruff was flattened, not out of any fear, as a musket-ball fired at such a range would have done him less injury than a mosquito to a man, but with great distaste. He gave a low rumbling growl, and almost drew a deep preparatory breath; Laurence laid a hand on his side and quietly said, 'No; it can do no good,' and stayed with him until at last the snow shrank away over the horizon, and passed out of their sight.

Even after she had gone, Temeraire's tail continued to flick unhappily back and forth. 'No, I am not hungry,' he said, when Laurence suggested some food, and stayed very quiet again, occasionally scraping at the deck with his claws, unconsciously, making a dreadful grating noise.

Riley was at the far end of the ship, walking the poop deck, but there were many sailors in earshot, getting the launch and the officers' barge over the side, preparing to begin the process of supply, and Lord Purbeck was overseeing; in any case you could not say anything on deck in full voice and not expect it to have travelled to the other end and back in less time than it would take to walk the distance. Laurence was conscious of the plain rudeness of seeming to criticize Riley on the deck of his own ship, even without the quarrel already lingering between them, but at last he could not forbear.

'Pray do not be so distressed,' he said, trying to console Temeraire, without going so far as to speak too bluntly against the practice. 'There is reason to hope that the trade will soon be stopped; the question will come before Parliament again this very session.'

Temeraire brightened perceptibly at the news, but he was unsatisfied with so bare an explanation and proceeded to inquire with great energy into the prospects of abolition; Laurence perforce had to explain Parliament and the distinction between the Commons and the Lords and the various factions engaged in the debate, relying for his particulars on his father's activities, but aware all the while that he was overheard and trying as best he could to be politic.

Even Sun Kai, who had been on deck the whole morning, and seen the progress of the snow and its effects on Temeraire's mood, gazed upon him thoughtfully, evidently guessing at some of the conversation; he had come as near as he could without crossing the painted border, and during a break, he asked Temeraire to translate for him. Temeraire explained a little; Sun Kai nodded, and then inquired of Laurence, 'Your father is an official then, and feels this practice dishonourable?'

Such a question, put baldly, could not be evaded however much it might offend; silence would be very nearly dishonest. 'Yes, sir, he does,' Laurence said, and before Sun Kai could prolong the conversation with further inquiries, Keynes came up to the deck; Laurence hailed him to ask him for permission to take Temeraire on a short flight to shore, and so was able to cut short the discussion. Even so abbreviated, however, it did no good for relations aboard ship; the sailors, mostly without strong opinions on the subject, naturally took their own captain's part, and felt Riley ill-used by the open expression of such sentiments on his ship when his own family connections to the trade were known.

The post was rowed back shortly before the hands' dinnertime, and Lord Purbeck chose to send the young midshipman Reynolds, who had set off the recent quarrel, to bring over the letters for the aviators: nearly a piece of deliberate provocation. The boy himself, his eye still blacked from Blythe's powerful blow, smirked so insolently that Laurence instantly resolved on ending Martin's punishment duty, nearly a week before he had otherwise intended, and said quite deliberately, 'Temeraire, look; we have a letter from Captain Roland; it will have news of Dover, I am sure.' Temeraire obligingly put his head down to inspect the letter; the ominous shadow of the ruff and the serrated teeth gleaming so nearby made a profound impression on Reynolds: the smirk vanished, and almost as quickly so did he himself, hastily retreating from the dragondeck.

Laurence stayed on deck to read the letters with Temeraire. Jane Roland's letter, scarcely a page long, had been sent only a few days after their departure and had very little news, only a cheerful account of the life of the covert; heartening to read, even if it left Temeraire sighing a little for home, and Laurence with much the same sentiments. He was a little puzzled, however, at receiving no other letters from his colleagues; since a courier had come through, he had expected to have something from Harcourt, at least, whom he knew to be a good correspondent, and perhaps one of the other captains.

He did have one more letter, from his mother, which had been forwarded on from Dover. Aviators received their mail quicker than anyone else, post-dragons making their rounds from covert to covert, whence the mail went out by horse and rider, and she had evidently written and sent it before receiving Laurence's own letter informing her of their departure.

He opened it and read most of it aloud for Temeraire's entertainment: she wrote mainly of his oldest brother George, who had just added a daughter to his three sons, and his father's political work, as being one of the few subjects on which Laurence and Lord Allendale were in sympathy, and which now was of fresh interest to Temeraire as well. Midway, however, Laurence abruptly stopped, as he read to himself a few lines which she had made in passing, which explained the unexpected silence of his fellow officers:

Naturally we were all very much shocked by the dreadful news of the Disaster in Austria, and they say that Mr. Pitt has taken ill, which of course much grieves your Father, as the Prime Minister has always been a Friend to the Cause. I am afraid I hear much talk in town of how Providence is favouring Bonaparte. It does seem strange that one man should make so great a difference in the course of War, when on both sides numbers are equal. But it is shameful in the extreme, how quickly Lord Nelson's great victory at Trafalgar is Forgot, and your own noble defence of our shores, and men of less resolution begin to speak of peace with the Tyrant.

She had of course written expecting him to be still at Dover, where news from the Continent came first, and where he would have long since heard all there was to know; instead it came as a highly unpleasant shock, particularly as she gave no further particulars. He had heard reports in Madeira of several battles fought in Austria, but nothing so decisive. At once he begged Temeraire to forgive him and hastened below to Riley's cabin, hoping there might be more news, and indeed found Riley numbly reading an express dispatch which Hammond had just given him, received from the Ministry.

'He has smashed them all to pieces, outside Austerlitz,' Hammond said, and they searched out the place on Riley's maps: a small town deep in Austria, northeast of Vienna. 'I have not been told a great deal, the Government is reserving the particulars, but he has taken at least thirty thousand men dead, wounded, or prisoner; the Russians are fleeing, and the Austrians have signed an armistice already.'

These spare facts were grim enough without elaboration, and they all fell silent together, looking over the few lines of the message, which disobligingly refused to offer more information regardless of the number of times they were re-read. 'Well,' Hammond said finally, 'we will just have to starve him out. Thank God for Nelson and Trafalgar! And he cannot mean to invade by air again, not with three Longwings stationed in the Channel now.'

'Ought we not return?' Laurence ventured, awkwardly; it seemed so self-serving a proposal he felt guilty in making it, and yet he could not imagine they were not badly needed, back in Britain. Excidium, Mortiferus, and Lily with their formations were indeed a deadly force to be reckoned with, but three dragons could not be everywhere, and Napoleon had before this found means of drawing one or the other away.

'I have received no orders to turn back,' Riley said, 'though I will say it does feel damned peculiar to be sailing on to China devil-may-care after news like this, with a hundred-and-fifty-gun ship and a heavy-combat dragon.'

'Gentlemen, you are in error,' Hammond said sharply. 'This disaster only renders our mission all the more urgent. If Napoleon is to be beaten, if our nation is to preserve a place as anything more besides an inconsequential island off the coast of a French Europe, only trade will do it. The Austrians may have been beaten for the moment, and the Russians; but so long as we can supply our Continental allies with funds and with resources, you may be sure they will resist Bonaparte's tyranny. We *must* continue on; we must secure at least neutrality

157

from China, if not some advantage, and protect our Eastern trade; no military goal could be of greater significance.'

He spoke with great authority, and Riley nodded in quick agreement. Laurence was silent as they began to discuss how they might speed the journey, and shortly he excused himself to return to the dragondeck; he could not argue, he was not impartial by any means, and Hammond's arguments had a great deal of weight; but he was not satisfied, and he felt an uneasy distress at the lack of sympathy between their thinking and his own.

'I cannot understand how they let Napoleon beat them,' Temeraire said, ruff bristling, when Laurence had broken the unhappy news to him and his senior officers. 'He had more ships and dragons than we did, at Trafalgar and at Dover, and we still won; and this time the Austrians and the Russians outnumbered him.'

'Trafalgar was a sea-battle,' Laurence said. 'Bonaparte has never really understood the navy; he is an artilleryman himself by training. And the battle of Dover we won only thanks to you; otherwise I dare say Bonaparte would be having himself crowned in Westminster directly. Do not forget how he managed to trick us into sending the better part of the Channel forces south and concealed the movements of his own dragons, before the invasion; if he had not been taken by surprise by the divine wind, the outcome could have been quite different.'

'It still does not seem to me that the battle was cleverly managed,' Temeraire said, dissatisfied. 'I am sure if we had been there, with our friends, we should not have lost, and I do not see why we are going to China when other people are fighting.'

'I call that a damned good question,' Granby said. 'A great pack of nonsense to begin with, giving away one of our very best dragons in the middle of a war when we are so desperate hard-up to begin with; Laurence, oughtn't we go home?'

Laurence only shook his head; he was too much in agree-

158

ment, and too powerless to make any alteration. Temeraire and the divine wind *had* changed the course of the war, at Dover. As little as the Ministry might like to admit it, or give credit for a victory to so narrow a cause; Laurence too well remembered the hopeless uneven struggle of that day, before Temeraire had turned the tide. To be meekly surrendering Temeraire and his extraordinary abilities seemed to Laurence a wilful blindness, and he did not believe the Chinese would yield to any of Hammond's requests at all.

But 'We have our orders' was all he said; even if Riley and Hammond had been of like mind with him, Laurence knew very well this would scarcely be accepted by the Ministry as even a thin excuse for violating their standing orders. 'I am sorry,' he added, seeing that Temeraire was inclined to be unhappy, 'but come; here is Mr. Keynes, to see if you can be allowed to take some exercise on shore; let us clear away and let him make his examination.'

'Truly it does not pain me at all,' Temeraire said anxiously, peering down at himself as Keynes at last stepped back from his chest. 'I am sure I am ready to fly again, and I will only go a short way.'

Keynes shook his head. 'Another week perhaps. No; do not set up a howl at me,' he said sternly, as Temeraire sat up to protest. 'It is not a question of the length of the flight; launching is the difficulty,' he added, to Laurence, by way of grudging explanation. 'The strain of getting aloft will be the most dangerous moment, and I am not confident the muscles are yet prepared to bear it.'

'But I am so very tired of only lying on deck,' Temeraire said disconsolately, almost a wail. 'I cannot even turn around properly.'

'It will only be another week, and perhaps less,' Laurence said, trying to comfort him; he was already regretting that he had ever made the proposal, and raised Temeraire's hopes only to be dashed. 'I am very sorry; but Mr. Keynes's opinion is worth more than either of ours on the subject, and we had better listen to him.'

Temeraire was not so easily appeased. 'I do not see why his opinion should be worth more than mine. It is my muscle, after all.'

Keynes folded his arms and said coolly, 'I am not going to argue with a patient. If you want to do yourself an injury and spend another two months lying about instead, by all means go jumping about as much as you like.'

Temeraire snorted back at this reply, and Laurence, annoyed, hurried to dismiss Keynes before the surgeon could be any more provoking: he had every confidence in the man's skill, but his tact could have stood much improvement, and though Temeraire was by no means contrary by nature, this was a hard disappointment to bear.

'I have a little better news, at least,' he told Temeraire, trying to rally his spirits. 'Mr. Pollitt was kind enough to bring me several new books from his visit ashore; shall I not fetch one now?'

Temeraire made only a grumble for answer, head unhappily drooping over the edge of the ship and gazing towards the denied shore. Laurence went down for the book, hoping that the interest of the material would rouse him, but while he was still in his cabin, the ship abruptly rocked, and an enormous splash outside sent water flying in through the opened round windows and onto the floor; Laurence ran to look through the nearest porthole, hastily rescuing his dampened letters, and saw Temeraire, with an expression at once guilty and self-satisfied, bobbing up and down in the water.

He dashed back up to the deck; Granby and Ferris were peering over the side in alarm, and the small boats that had been crowding around the sides of the ship, full of whores and enterprising fishermen, were already making frantic haste away and back to the security of the harbour, with much shrieking and splashing of oars. Temeraire rather abashed looked after them in dismay. 'I did not mean to frighten them,' he said. 'There is no need to run away,' he called, but the boats did not pause for an instant. The sailors, deprived of their entertainments, glared disapprovingly; Laurence was more concerned for Temeraire's health.

'Well, I have never seen anything so ridiculous in my life, but it is not likely to hurt him. The air-sacs will keep him afloat, and salt water never hurt a wound,' Keynes said, having been summoned back to the deck. 'But how we will ever get him back aboard, I have not the least idea.'

Temeraire plunged for a moment under the surface and came almost shooting up again, propelled by his buoyancy. 'It is very pleasant,' he called out. 'The water is not cold at all, Laurence; will you not come in?'

Laurence was by no means a strong swimmer, and uneasy at the notion of leaping into the open ocean: they were a good mile out from the shore. But he took one of the ship's small boats and rowed himself out, to keep Temeraire company and to be sure the dragon did not over-tire himself after so much enforced idleness on deck. The skiff was tossed about a little by the waves resulting from Temeraire's frolics, and occasionally swamped, but Laurence had prudently worn only an old pair of breeches and his most threadbare shirt.

His own spirits were very low; the defeat at Austerlitz was not merely a single battle lost, but the overthrow of Prime Minister Pitt's whole careful design, and the destruction of the coalition assembled to stop Napoleon: Britain alone could not field an army half so large as Napoleon's Grande Armée, nor easily land it on the Continent, and with the Austrians and Russians now driven from the field, their situation was plainly grim. But even with such cares, he could not help but smile to see Temeraire so full of energy and uncomplicated joy, and after a little while he even yielded to Temeraire's coaxing and let himself over the side. Laurence did not swim very long but soon climbed up onto Temeraire's back, while Temeraire paddled himself about enthusiastically, and nosed the skiff about as a sort of toy.

He might shut his eyes and imagine them back in Dover, or at Loch Laggan, with only the ordinary cares of war to burden them, and work to be done which he understood, with all the confidence of friendship and a nation united behind them; even the present disaster hardly insurmountable, in such a situation. The *Allegiance* only another ship in the harbour, their familiar clearing a short flight away, and no politicians and princes to trouble with. He lay back and spread his hands open against the warm side, the black scales warmed by the sun, and for a little while indulged the fancy enough to drowse.

'Do you suppose you will be able to climb back aboard the *Allegiance*?' Laurence said presently; he had been worrying the problem in his head.

Temeraire craned his head around to look at him. 'Could we not wait here on shore until I have gotten better, and rejoin the ship after?' he suggested. 'Or,' and his ruff quivered with sudden excitement, 'we might fly across the continent, and meet them on the opposite side: there are no people in the middle of Africa, I remember from your maps, so there cannot be any French to shoot us down.'

'No, but by report there are a great many feral dragons, not to mention any number of other dangerous creatures, and the perils of disease,' Laurence said. 'We cannot go flying over the uncharted interior, Temeraire; the risk cannot be justified, particularly not now.'

Temeraire sighed a little at giving up this ambitious project, but agreed to make the attempt to climb up onto the deck; after a little more play he swam back over to the ship, and rather bemused the waiting sailors by handing the skiff up to them, so they did not have to haul her back aboard. Laurence, having climbed up the side from Temeraire's shoulder, held a huddled conference with Riley. 'Perhaps if we let the starboard sheet anchor down as a counterweight?' he suggested. 'That with the best bower ought to keep her steady, and she is already loaded heavy towards the stern.'

'Laurence, what the Admiralty will say to me, if I get a transport sunk on a clear blue day in harbour, I should not like to think,' Riley said, unhappy at the notion. 'I dare say I should be hanged, and deserve it too.'

'If there is any danger of capsizing, he can always let go in an instant,' Laurence said. 'Otherwise we must sit in port a week at least, until Keynes is willing to grant him leave to fly again.'

'I am not going to sink the ship,' Temeraire said indignantly, poking his head up over the quarterdeck rail and entering into the conversation, much to Riley's startlement. 'I will be very careful.'

Though Riley was still dubious, he finally gave leave. Temeraire managed to rear up out of the water and get a grip with his foreclaws on the ship's side; the *Allegiance* listed towards him, but not too badly, held by the two anchors, and having gotten his wings out of the water, Temeraire beat them a couple of times, and half-leaped, half-scrambled up the side of the ship.

He fell heavily onto the deck without much grace, hind legs scrabbling for an undignified moment, but he indeed got aboard, and the *Allegiance* did not do more than bounce a little beneath him. He hastily settled his legs underneath him again and busied himself shaking water off his ruff and long tendrils, pretending he had not been clumsy. 'It was not very difficult to climb back on at all,' he said to Laurence, pleased. 'Now I can swim every day until I can fly again.'

Laurence wondered how Riley and the sailors would receive this news, but was unable to feel much dismay; he would have suffered far more than black looks to see Temeraire's spirits so restored; and when he presently suggested

163

something to eat, Temeraire gladly assented, and devoured two cows and a sheep down to the hooves.

When Yongxing once again ventured to the deck the following morning, he thus found Temeraire in good humour: fresh from another swim, well-fed, and highly pleased with himself. He had clambered aboard much more gracefully this second time, though Lord Purbeck at least found something to complain of, in the scratches to the ship's paint, and the sailors were still unhappy at having the bumboats frightened off. Yongxing himself benefited, as Temeraire was in a forgiving mood and disinclined to hold even what Laurence considered a well-deserved grudge, but the prince did not look at all satisfied; and spent the morning visit watching silently and brooding as Laurence read to Temeraire out of the new books procured by Mr. Pollitt on his visit ashore.

Yongxing soon left again; and shortly thereafter, his servant Feng Li came up to the deck to ask Laurence below, making clear his meaning through gestures and pantomime, Temeraire having settled down to nap through the heat of the day. Unwilling and wary, Laurence insisted on first going to his quarters to dress: he was again in shabby clothes, having accompanied Temeraire on his swim, and did not feel prepared to face Yongxing in his austere and elegant apartment without the armour of his dress coat and best trousers, and a fresh-pressed neckcloth.

There was no theatre about his arrival, this time; he was ushered in at once, and Yongxing sent even Feng Li away, that they might be private, but he did not speak at once and only stood in silence, hands clasped behind his back, gazing frowningly out the stern windows: then, as Laurence was on the point of speaking, abruptly turned and said, 'You have sincere affection for Lung Tien Xiang, and he for you; this I have come to see. Yet in your country, he is treated like an animal, exposed to all the dangers of war. Can you desire this fate for him?'

Laurence was much astonished at meeting so direct an appeal, and supposed Hammond proven right: there could be no explanation for this change but a growing conviction in Yongxing's mind of the futility of luring Temeraire away. But as pleased as he would otherwise have been to see Yongxing give up his attempts to divide them from one another, Laurence grew only more uneasy: there was plainly no common ground to be had between them, and he did not feel he understood Yongxing's motives for seeking to find any.

'Sir,' he said, after a moment, 'your accusations of ill-treatment I must dispute; and the dangers of war are the common hazard of those who take service for their country. Your Highness can scarcely expect me to find such a choice, willingly made, objectionable; I myself have so chosen, and such risks I hold it an honour to endure.'

'Yet you are a man of ordinary birth, and a soldier of no great rank; there may be ten thousand men such as you in England,' Yongxing said. 'You cannot compare yourself to a Celestial. Consider his happiness, and listen to my request. Help us restore him to his rightful place, and then part from him cheerfully: let him think you are not sorry to go, that he may forget you more easily, and find happiness with a companion appropriate to his station. Surely it is your duty not to hold him down to your own level, but to see him brought up to all the advantages which are his right.'

Yongxing made these remarks not in an insulting tone, but as stating plain fact, almost earnestly. 'I do not believe in that species of kindness, sir, which consists in lying to a loved one, and deceiving them for their own good,' Laurence said, as yet unsure whether he ought to be offended, or to view this as some attempt to appeal to his better nature.

But his confusion was sharply dispelled in another moment, as Yongxing persisted: 'I know that what I ask is a great sacrifice. Perhaps the hopes of your family will be disappointed; and you were given a great reward for bringing him to your

165

country, which may now be confiscated. We do not expect you to face ruin: do as I ask, and you will receive ten thousand taels of silver, and the gratitude of the Emperor.'

Laurence stared first, then flushed to an ugly shade of mortification, and said, when he had mastered himself well enough to speak, with bitter resentment, 'A noble sum indeed; but there is not silver enough in China, sir, to buy me.'

He would have turned to go at once; but Yongxing said in real exasperation, this refusal at last driving him past the careful façade of patience which he had so far maintained throughout the interview, 'You are foolish; you *cannot* be permitted to remain companion to Lung Tien Xiang, and in the end you will be sent home. Why not accept my offer?'

'That you may separate us by force, in your own country, I have no doubt,' Laurence said. 'But that will be *your* doing, and none of mine; and he shall know me faithful as he is himself, to the last.' He meant to leave; he could not challenge Yongxing, nor strike him, and only such a gesture could have begun to satisfy his deep and violent sense of injury; but so excellent an invitation to quarrel at least gave his anger some vent, and he added with all the scorn which he could give the words, 'Save yourself the trouble of any further cajolery; all your bribes and machinations you may be sure will meet with equal failure, and I have too much faith in Temeraire to imagine that he will ever be persuaded to prefer a nation where discourse such as this is the *civilized* mode.'

'You speak in ignorant disdain of the foremost nation of the world,' Yongxing said, growing himself angry, 'like all your countrymen, who show no respect for that which is superior, and insult our customs.'

'For which I might consider myself as owing you some apology, sir, if you yourself had not so often insulted myself and my own country, or shown respect for any customs other than your own,' Laurence said.

'We do not desire anything that is yours, or to come and

force our ways upon you,' Yongxing said. 'From your small island you come to our country, and out of kindness you are allowed to buy our tea and silk and porcelain, which you so passionately desire. But still you are not content; you forever demand more and more, while your missionaries try to spread your foreign religion and your merchants smuggle opium in defiance of the law. We do not need your trinkets, your clockworks and lamps and guns; our land is sufficient unto itself. In so unequal a position, you should show threefold gratitude and submission to the Emperor, and instead you offer one insult heaped on another. Too long already has this disrespect been tolerated.'

These arrayed grievances, so far beyond the matter at hand, were spoken passionately and with great energy; more sincere than anything Laurence had formerly heard from the prince and more unguarded, and the surprise he could not help but display evidently recalled Yongxing to his circumstances, and checked his flow of speech. For a moment they stood in silence, Laurence still resentful, and as unable to form a reply as if Yongxing had spoken in his native tongue, baffled entirely by a description of the relations between their countries which should lump Christian missionaries together with smugglers and so absurdly refuse to acknowledge the benefits of free and open trade to both parties.

'I am no politician, sir, to dispute with you upon matters of foreign policy,' Laurence said at last, 'but the honour and dignities of my nation and my countrymen I will defend to my last breath; and you will not move me with any argument to act dishonourably, least of all to Temeraire.'

Yongxing had recovered his composure, yet looked still intensely dissatisfied; now he shook his head, frowning. 'If you will not be persuaded by consideration for Lung Tien Xiang or for yourself, will you at least serve your country's interests?' With deep and evident reluctance he added, 'That we should open ports to you, besides Canton, cannot be considered; but we will permit your ambassador to remain in Peking, as you so greatly desire, and we will agree not to go to war against you or your allies, so long as you maintain a respectful obedience to the Emperor: this much can be allowed, if you will ease Lung Tien Xiang's return.'

He ended expectantly; Laurence stood motionless, breath-taken, white; and then he said, 'No,' almost inaudibly, and without staying to hear another word turned and left the room, thrusting the drapery from his way.

He went blindly to the deck and found Temeraire sleeping, peaceful, tail curled around himself; Laurence did not touch him but sat down on one of the lockers by the edge of the deck and bowed his head down, that he should not meet anyone's eyes; his hands clasped, that they should not be seen to shake.

'You refused, I hope?' Hammond said, wholly unexpectedly; Laurence, who had steeled himself to face a furious reproach, was left staring. 'Thank Heaven; it had not occurred to me that he might attempt a direct approach, and so soon. I must beg you, Captain, to be sure and not commit us to any proposal whatsoever, without private consultation with me, no matter how appealing it may seem. Either here or after we have reached China,' he added, as an afterthought. 'Now pray tell me again; he offered a promise of neutrality, and a perma-nent envoy in Peking, outright?'

There was a quick predatory gleam in his expression, and Laurence was put to dredging the details of the conversation from his memory in answer to his many questions. 'But I am sure that I do not misremember; he was quite firm that no other ports should ever be opened,' Laurence protested, when Hammond had begun dragging over his maps of China and speculating aloud which might be the most advantageous, inquiring of Laurence which harbours he thought best for shipping.

'Yes, yes,' Hammond said, waving this aside. 'But if *he* may be brought so far as to admit the possibility of a permanent envoy, how much more progress may we not hope to make? You must be aware that his own opinions are fixed quite immovably against all intercourse with the West.'

'I am,' Laurence said; he was more surprised to find Hammond so aware, given the diplomat's continuing efforts to establish good relations.

'Our chances of winning Prince Yongxing himself over are small, though I hope we shall make some progress,' Hammond said, 'but I find it most encouraging indeed that he should be so anxious to obtain your cooperation at such a stage. Plainly he wishes to arrive in China *fait accompli*, which should only be the case if he imagines the Emperor may be persuaded to grant us terms less pleasing to himself.

'He is not the heir to the throne, you know,' Hammond added, seeing Laurence look doubtful. 'The Emperor has three sons, and the eldest, Prince Mianning, is grown already and the presumptive crown prince. Not that Prince Yongxing lacks in influence, certainly, or he would never have been given so much autonomy as to be sent to England, but this very attempt on his part gives me hope there may yet be more opportunity than we heretofore have realized. If only—'

Here he grew abruptly dismal, and sat down again with the charts neglected. 'If only the French have not already established themselves with the more liberal minds of the court,' he finished, low. 'But that would explain a great deal, I am afraid, and in particular why they were ever given the egg. I could tear my hair over it; here they have managed to thoroughly insinuate themselves, I suppose, while we have been sitting about congratulating ourselves on our precious dignity ever since Lord Macartney was sent packing, and making no real attempt to restore relations.'

Laurence left feeling very little less guilt and unhappiness than before; his refusal, he was well aware, had not been motivated by any such rational and admirable arguments, but a wholly reflexive denial. He would certainly never agree to lie to Temeraire, as Yongxing had proposed, nor abandon him to any unpleasant or barbaric situation, but Hammond might make other demands, less easy to refuse. If they were ordered to separate to ensure a truly advantageous treaty, it would be his own duty not only to go, but to convince Temeraire to obey, however unwillingly. Before now, he had consoled himself in the belief that the Chinese would offer no satisfactory terms; this illusory comfort was now stripped away, and all the misery of separation loomed closer with every sea-mile.

Two days later saw them leaving Cape Coast, gladly for Laurence's part. The morning of their departure, a party of slaves had been brought in overland, and were being driven into the waiting dungeons within sight of the ship. An even more dreadful scene ensued, for the slaves had not yet been worn down by long confinement nor become resigned to their fate, and as the cellar doors were opened to receive them, which must have looked very much like the mouth of a waiting grave, several of the younger men staged a revolt.

They had evidently found some means of getting loose along their journey. Two of the guards went down at once, bludgeoned with the very chains that had bound the slaves, and the others began to stumble back and away, firing indiscriminately in their panic. A troop of guards came running down from their posts, adding to the general melee.

It was a hopeless attempt, if gallant, and most of the loosed men saw the inevitable and dashed for their personal freedom; some scrambled down the beach, others fled into the city. The guards managed to cow the remaining bound slaves again, and started shooting at the escaping ones. Most were killed before they were out of sight, and search parties organized immediately to find the remainder, marked as they were by their nakedness and the galls from their former chains. The dirt road leading to the dungeons was muddy with blood, the small and huddled corpses lying terribly still among the living; many women and children had been killed in the action. The slavers were already forcing the remaining men and women down into the cellar, and setting some of the others to drag the bodies away. Not fifteen minutes had gone by.

There was no singing or shouting as the anchor was hauled up, and the operation went more slowly than usual; but even so the bo'sun, ordinarily vigorous at any sign of malingering, did not start anyone with his cane. The day was again stickily humid, and so hot that the tar grew liquid and fell in great black splotches from the rigging, some even landing upon Temeraire's hide, much to his disgust. Laurence set the runners and the ensigns on watch with buckets and rags, to clean him off as the drops fell, and by the end of the day they were all drooping and filthy themselves.

The next day only more of the same, and the three after that; the shore tangled and impenetrable to larboard, broken only by cliffs and jumbled rock falls, and a constant attention necessary to keep the ship at a safe distance in deep water, with the winds freakish and variable so close to land. The men went about their work silent and unsmiling in the heat of the day; the evil news of Austerlitz had spread among them.

Chapter Eight

Blythe at last emerged from the sickberth, much reduced, mostly to sit and doze in a chair on the deck: Martin was especially solicitous for his comfort, and apt to speak sharply to anyone who so much as jostled the makeshift awning they had rigged over him. Blythe could not so much as cough but a glass of grog was put in his hand; he could not speak slightingly of the weather but he would be offered, as appropriate, a rug, an oilskin, a cool cloth.

'I'm sorry he's taken it so to heart, sir,' Blythe told Laurence helplessly. 'I don't suppose any high-spirited fellow could have stood it kindly, the way them tars were going on, and no fault of his, I'm sure. I wish he wouldn't take on so.'

The sailors were not pleased to see the offender so cosseted, and by way of answer made much of their fellow Reynolds, already inclined to put on a martyr's airs. In ordinary course he was only an indifferent seaman, and the new degree of respect he was receiving from his company went to his head. He strutted about the deck like cock-robin, giving unnecessary orders for the pleasure of seeing them followed with such excess of bows, and nods, and forelock-pulling; even Purbeck and Riley did not much check him.

Laurence had hoped that at least the shared disaster of

Austerlitz might mute the hostility between the sailors and the aviators; but this display kept tempers on both sides at an elevated pitch. The *Allegiance* was now drawing close to the equatorial line, and Laurence thought it necessary to make special arrangements for managing the usual crossing ceremony. Less than half of the aviators had ever crossed the line before, and if the sailors were given licence to dunk and shave the lot of them under the present mood, Laurence did not think order could possibly be maintained. He consulted with Riley, and the agreement was reached that he would offer a general tithe on behalf of his men, namely three casks of rum which he had taken the precaution of acquiring in Cape Coast; the aviators would therefore be universally excused.

All the sailors were disgruntled by the alteration in their tradition, several going so far as to speak of bad luck to the ship as a consequence; undoubtedly many of them had privately been looking forward to the opportunity to humiliate their shipboard rivals. As a result, when at last they crossed the equator and the usual pageant came aboard, it was rather quiet and unenthusiastic. Temeraire at least was entertained, though Laurence had to shush him hastily when he said, very audibly, 'But Laurence, that is not Neptune at all; that is Griggs, and Amphitrite is Boyne,' recognizing the seamen through their shabby costumes, which they had not taken much trouble to make effective.

This produced a good deal of imperfectly-suppressed hilarity among the crew, and Badger-Bag – the carpenter's mate Leddowes, less recognizable under a scruffy mop-head for a judicial wig – had a fit of inspiration and declared that this time, all those who allowed laughter to escape should be Neptune's victims. Laurence gave Riley a quick nod, and Leddowes was given a free hand among both sailors and aviators. Fair numbers of each were seized, all the rest applauding, and to cap the occasion Riley sang out, 'An extra ration of grog for all, thanks to the toll paid by Captain Laurence's crew,' producing an enthusiastic cheer.

Some of the hands got up a set of music, and another of dancing; the rum worked its effect and soon even the aviators were clapping along, and humming the music to the shanties, though they did not know the words. It was perhaps not as wholeheartedly cheerful as some crossings, but much better than Laurence had feared.

The Chinese had come on deck for the event, though naturally not subjected to the ritual, and watched with much discussion amongst themselves. It was of course a rather vulgar kind of entertainment, and Laurence felt some embarrassment at having Yongxing witness it, but Liu Bao thumped his thigh in applause along with the entire crew, and let out a tremendous, booming laugh for each of Badger-Bag's victims. He at length turned to Temeraire, across the boundary, and asked him a question: 'Laurence, he would like to know what the purpose of the ceremony is, and which spirits are being honoured,' Temeraire said. 'But I do not know myself; what are we celebrating, and why?'

'Oh,' Laurence said, wondering how to explain the rather ridiculous ceremony. 'We have just crossed the equator, and it is an old tradition that those who have never crossed the line before must pay respects to Neptune – that is the Roman god of the sea; though of course he is not actually worshipped anymore.'

'Aah!' Liu Bao said, approvingly, when this had been translated for him. 'I like that. It is good to show respect to old gods, even if they are not yours. It must be very good luck for the ship. And it is only nineteen days until the New Year: we will have to have a feast on board, and that will be good luck too. The spirits of our ancestors will guide the ship back to China.'

Laurence was dubious, but the sailors listening in to the translation with much interest found much to approve in this speech: both the feast, and the promised good luck, which appealed to their superstitious habit of thought. Although the mention of spirits was cause for a great deal of serious belowdecks debate, being a little too close to ghosts for comfort, in the end it was generally agreed that as ancestor spirits, these would have to be benevolently inclined towards the descendants being carried by the ship, and therefore not to be feared.

'They have asked me for a cow and four sheep, and all eight of the remaining chickens, also; we will have to put in at St. Helena after all. We will make the turn westward tomorrow; at least it will be easier sailing than all this beating into the trades we have been doing,' Riley said, watching dubiously a few days later: several of the Chinese servants were busy fishing for sharks. 'I only hope the liquor is not too strong. I must give it to the hands in addition to their grog ration, not in its place, or it would be no celebration at all.'

'I am sorry to give you any cause for alarm, but Liu Bao alone can drink two of me under the table; I have seen him put away three bottles of wine in a sitting,' Laurence said ruefully, speaking from much painful experience: the envoy had dined with him convivially several more times since Christmas, and if he were suffering any lingering ill-effects whatsoever from the sea-sickness, it could not be told from his appetite. 'For that matter, though Sun Kai does not drink a great deal, brandy and wine are all the same to him, as far as I can tell.'

'Oh, to the devil with them,' Riley said, sighing. 'Well, perhaps a few dozen able seamen will get themselves into enough trouble that I can take away their grog for the night. What do you suppose they are going to do with those sharks? They have thrown back two porpoises already, and those are much better eating.'

Laurence was ill-prepared to venture upon a guess, but he

did not have to: at that moment the lookout called, 'Wing three points off the larboard bow,' and they hurried at once to the side, to pull out their telescopes and peer into the sky, while sailors stampeded to their posts in case it should be an attack.

Temeraire had lifted his head from his nap at the noise. 'Laurence, it is Volly,' he called down from the dragondeck. 'He has seen us, he is coming this way.' Following this announcement, he roared out a greeting that made nearly every man jump and rattled the masts; several of the sailors looked darkly towards him, though none ventured a complaint.

Temeraire shifted himself about to make room, and some fifteen minutes later the little Greyling courier dropped down onto the deck, furling his broad grey-and-white-streaked wings. 'Temrer!' he said, and butted Temeraire happily with his head. 'Cow?'

'No, Volly, but we can fetch you a sheep,' Temeraire said indulgently. 'Has he been hurt?' he asked James; the little dragon sounded queerly nasal.

Volly's captain, Langford James, slid down. 'Hello, Laurence, there you are. We have been looking for you up and down the coast,' he said, reaching out to take Laurence's hand. 'No need to fret, Temeraire; he has only caught this blasted cold going about Dover. Half the dragons moaning and sniffling about: they are the greatest children imaginable. But he will be right as rain in a week or two.'

More rather than less alarmed by these reassurances, Temeraire edged a little distance away from Volly; he did not look particularly eager to experience his first illness. Laurence nodded; the letter he had had from Jane Roland had mentioned the sickness in passing. 'I hope you have not strained him on our account, coming so far. Shall I send for my surgeon?' he offered.

'No, thank you; he has been doctored enough. It'll be another week before he forgets the medicine he swallowed and forgives me for slipping it into his dinner,' James said, waving away the request. 'Any road, we have not come so very far; we have been down here flying the southern route the last two weeks, and it is a damn sight warmer here than in jolly old England, you know. Volly's hardly shy about letting me know if he don't care to fly, either, so as long as he doesn't speak up, I'll keep him in the air.' He petted the little dragon, who bumped his nose against James's hand, and then lowered his head directly to sleep.

'What news is there?' Laurence asked, shuffling through the post that James had handed over: his responsibility rather than Riley's, as it had been brought by dragon courier. 'Has there been any change on the Continent? We heard news of Austerlitz at Cape Coast. Are we recalled? Ferris, see these to Lord Purbeck, and the rest among our crew,' he added, handing the other letters off: for himself he had a dispatch, and a couple of letters, though he politely tucked them into his jacket rather than looking at them at once.

'No to both, more's the pity, but at least we can make the trip a little easier for you; we have taken the Dutch colony at Capetown,' James said. 'Seized it last month, so you can break your journey there.'

The news leaped from one end of the deck to the other with speed fuelled by the enthusiasm of men who had been long brooding over the grim news of Napoleon's latest success, and the *Allegiance* was instantly afire with patriotic cheers; no further conversation was possible until some measure of calm had been restored. The post did some work to this effect, Purbeck and Ferris handing it out among the respective crews, and gradually the noise collected into smaller pockets, many of the other men deep into their letters.

Laurence sent for a table and chairs to be brought up to the dragondeck, inviting Riley and Hammond to join them and hear the news. James was happy to give them a more detailed account of the capture than was contained in the

brief dispatch: he had been a courier from the age of fourteen, and had a turn for the dramatic; though in this case he
had little material to work from. 'I'm sorry it doesn't make
a better story; it was not really a fight, you know,' he said
apologetically. 'We had the Highlanders there, and the Dutch
only some mercenaries; they ran away before we even reached
the town. The governor had to surrender; the people are still
a little uneasy, but General Baird is leaving local affairs to
them, and they have not kicked up much of a fuss.'

'Well, it will certainly make resupply easier,' Riley said. 'We
need not stop in St. Helena, either; and that will be a savings
of as much as two weeks. It is very welcome news indeed.'

'Will you stay for dinner?' Laurence asked James. 'Or must
you be going straightaway?'

Volly abruptly sneezed behind him, a loud and startling
noise. 'Ick,' the little dragon said, waking himself up out of
his sleep, and rubbed his nose against his foreleg in distaste,
trying to scrape the mucus from his snout.

'Oh, stop that, filthy wretch,' James said, getting up; he
took a large white linen square from his harness bags and
wiped Volly clean with the weary air of long practice. 'I suppose
we will stay the night,' he said, after contemplating Volly. 'No
need to press him, now that I have found you in time, and
you can write any letters you like me to take on: we are home-
ward bound after we leave you.'

. . . so my poor Lily, like Excidium and Mortiferus, has
been banished from her comfortable clearing to the Sand
Pits, for when she sneezes, she cannot help but spit some
of the acid, the muscles involved in this reflex (so the
surgeons tell me) being the very same. They all three are
very disgusted with their situation, as the sand cannot
be got rid of from day to day, and they scratch themselves like Dogs trying to cast off fleas no matter how
they bathe.

179

Maximus is in deep disgrace, for he began sneezing first, and all the other dragons like to have someone to blame for their Misery; however he bears it well, or as Berkley tells me to write, 'Does not give a Tinker's Dam for the lot of them and whines all the day, except when busy stuffing his gullet; has not hurt his appetite in the least.'

We all do very well otherwise, and all send their love; the dragons also, and bid you convey their greetings and affection to Temeraire. They indeed miss him badly, though I am sorry to have to tell you that we have lately discovered one ignoble cause for their pining, which is plain Greed. Evidently he had taught them how to pry open the Feeding Pen, and close it again after, so they were able to help themselves whenever they liked without anyone the wiser – their Guilty Secret discovered only after note was taken that the Herds were oddly diminished, and the dragons of our formation overfed, whereupon being questioned they confessed the Whole.

I must stop, for we have Patrol, and Volatilus goes south in the morning. All our prayers for your safe Journey and quick return.

Etc.,
Catherine Harcourt

'What is this I hear from Harcourt of your teaching the dragons to steal from the pen?' Laurence demanded, looking up from his letter; he was taking the hour before dinner to read his mail, and compose replies.

Temeraire started up with so very revealing an expression that his guilt could be in no doubt. 'That is not true, I did not teach anyone to steal,' he said. 'The herdsmen at Dover are very lazy, and do not always come in the morning, so we have to wait and wait at the pen, and the herds are meant for us, anyway; it cannot be called stealing.'

'I suppose I ought to have suspected something when you stopped complaining of them being always late,' Laurence said. 'But how on earth did you manage it?'

'The gate is perfectly simple,' Temeraire said. 'There is only a bar across the fence, which one can lift very easily, and then it swings open; Nitidus could do it best, for his forehands are the smallest. Though it is difficult to keep the animals inside the pen, and the first time I learned how to open it, they all ran away,' he added. 'Maximus and I had to chase after them for hours and hours, it was not funny, *at all*,' he said, ruffled, sitting back on his haunches and contemplating Laurence with great indignation.

'I beg your pardon,' Laurence said, after he had regained his breath. 'I truly beg your pardon, it was only the notion of you, and Maximus, and the sheep— Oh dear,' Laurence said, and dissolved again, try as he might to contain himself: astonished stares from his crew, and Temeraire haughtily offended.

'Is there any other news in the letter?' Temeraire asked, coolly, when Laurence had finally done.

'Not news, but all the dragons have sent you greetings and their love,' Laurence said, now conciliatory. 'You may console yourself that they are all sick, and if you were there you certainly would be also,' he added, seeing Temeraire inclined to droop when reminded of his friends.

'I would not care if I were sick, if I were home. Anyway, I am sure to catch it from Volly,' Temeraire said gloomily, glancing over: the little Greyling was snuffling thickly in his sleep, bubbles of mucus swelling and shrinking over his nostrils as he breathed, and a small puddle of saliva had collected beneath his half-open mouth.

Laurence could not in honesty hold out much hope to the contrary, so he shifted the subject. 'Have you any messages? I will go below now and write my replies, so James can carry them back: the last chance of sending a word by courier we

181

will have for a long time, I am afraid, for ours do not go to the Far East except for some truly urgent matter.'

'Only to send my love,' Temeraire said, 'and to tell Captain Harcourt and also Admiral Lenton it was not stealing in the least. Oh, and also, tell Maximus and Lily about the poem written by the dragon, for that was very interesting, and perhaps they will like to hear of it. And also about my learning to climb aboard the ship, and that we have crossed the equator, and about Neptune and Badger-Bag.'

'Enough, enough; you will have me writing a novel,' Laurence said, rising easily: thankfully his leg had at last put itself right, and he was no longer forced to limp about the deck like an old man. He stroked Temeraire's side. 'Shall we come and sit with you while we have our port?'

Temeraire snorted and nudged him affectionately with his nose. 'Thank you, Laurence; that would be pleasant, and I would like to hear any news James has of the others, besides what is in your letters.'

The replies finished at the stroke of three, Laurence and his guests dined in unusual comfort: ordinarily, Laurence kept to his habit of formal decorum, and Granby and his own officers followed his lead, while Riley and his subordinates did so of their own accord and naval custom; they one and all sweltered through every meal under thick broadcloth and their snugly-tied neckcloths. But James had a born aviator's disregard for propriety coupled with the assurance of a man who had been a captain, even if only of a single-man courier, since the age of fourteen. With hardly a pause, he discarded his outer garments on coming below, saying, 'Good God, it is close in here; you must stifle, Laurence.'

Laurence was not sorry to follow his example, which he would have done regardless out of a desire not to make him feel out of place. Granby immediately followed suit, and after a brief surprise, Riley and Hammond matched them, though Lord Purbeck kept his coat and his expression fixed, clearly disapproving. The dinner went cheerfully enough, though at Laurence's request, James reserved his own news until they were comfortably ensconced on the dragondeck with their cigars and port, where Temeraire could hear, and with his body provide a bulwark against the rest of the crew's eaves-dropping. Laurence dismissed the aviators down to the fore-castle, this leaving only Sun Kai, as usual taking the air in the reserved corner of the dragondeck, close enough to over-hear what should be quite meaningless to him.

James had much to tell them of formation movements: nearly all the dragons of the Mediterranean division had been reassigned to the Channel, Laetificat and Excursius and their respective formations, to provide a thoroughly-impenetrable opposition should Bonaparte once again attempt invasion through the air, emboldened by his success on the Continent.

'Not much left to stop them from trying for Gibraltar, though, with all this shifting about,' Riley said. 'And we must keep watch over Toulon: we may have taken twenty prizes at Trafalgar, but now Bonaparte has every forest in Europe at his disposal, he can build more ships. I hope the Ministry have a care for it.'

'Oh, hell,' James said, sitting up with a thump; his chair had been tilted rather precariously backwards as he reclined with his feet on the rail. 'I am being a dunce; I suppose you haven't heard about Mr. Pitt.'

'He is not still ill?' Hammond said anxiously.

'Not ill in the least,' James said. 'Dead, this last fortnight and more. The news killed him, they say; he took his bed after we heard of the armistice, and never got out of it again.'

'God rest his soul,' Riley said.

'Amen,' Laurence said, deeply shocked. Pitt had not been an old man; younger than his father, certainly.

'Who is Mr. Pitt?' Temeraire inquired, and Laurence paused to explain to him the post of Prime Minister.

'James, have you any word on who will form the new

government?' he asked, already wondering what this might mean for himself and Temeraire, if the new Minister felt China ought to be dealt with differently, either in more conciliatory or more belligerent manner.

'No, I was off before more than the bare word had reached us,' James said. 'I promise if anything has changed when I get back, I will do my best and bring you the news at Capetown. But,' he added, 'they send us down here less than once in a sixmonth, ordinarily, so I shouldn't hope for it. The landing sites are too uncertain, and we have lost couriers without a trace down here before, trying to go overland or even just spend a night on shore.'

James set off again the next morning, waving at them from Volly's back until the little grey-white dragon disappeared entirely into the thready, low-hanging clouds. Laurence had managed to pen a brief reply to Harcourt as well as appending to his already-begun letters for his mother and Jane, and the courier had carried them all away: the last word they would receive from him for months, almost certainly.

There was little time for melancholy: he was at once called below, to consult with Liu Bao on the appropriate substitute for some sort of monkey organ which was ordinarily used in a dish. Having suggested lamb kidneys, Laurence was instantly solicited for assistance with another task, and the rest of the week passed in increasingly frantic preparations, the galley going day and night at full steam, until the dragondeck grew so warm that even Temeraire began to feel it a little excessive. The Chinese servants also set to clearing the ship of vermin; a hopeless task, but one in which they persevered. They came up to the deck sometimes five or six times in a day to fling the bodies of rats overboard into the sea, while the midshipmen looked on in outrage, these ordinarily serving, late in a voyage, as part of their own meals.

Laurence had not the least idea what to expect from the

occasion, but was careful to dress with especial formality, borrowing Riley's steward Jethson to valet him: his best shirt, starched and ironed; silk stockings and knee-breeches instead of trousers with his polished Hessian boots; his dress coat, bottle-green, with gold bars on the shoulders, and his decorations: the gold medal of the Nile, where he had been a naval lieutenant, on its broad blue ribbon, and the silver pin voted recently to the captains of the Dover battle.

He was very glad to have taken so many pains when he entered the Chinese quarters: passing through the door, he had to duck beneath a sweep of heavy red cloth and found the room so richly draped with hangings it might have been taken for a grand pavilion on land, except for the steady motion of the ship beneath their feet. The table was laid with delicate porcelain, each piece of different colour, many edged with gold and silver; and the lacquered eating sticks which Laurence had been dreading all week were at every place.

Yongxing was already seated at the head of the table, in imposing state and wearing his most formal robes, in the deep golden silk embroidered with dragons in blue and black thread. Laurence was seated close enough to see that there were small chips of gemstones for the dragons' eyes and talons, and in the very centre of the front, covering the chest, was a single dragon-figure larger than the rest, embroidered in pure white silk, with chips of rubies for its eyes and five outstretched talons on each foot.

Somehow they were all gotten in, down to little Roland and Dyer, the younger officers fairly squashed together at their separate table and their faces already shining and pink in the heat. The servants began pouring the wine directly everyone was seated, others coming in from the galley to lay down great platters along the length of the tables: cold sliced meats, interspersed with an assortment of dark yellow nuts, preserved cherries, and prawns with their heads and dangling forelegs intact.

185

Yongxing took up his cup for the first toast and all hurried to drink with him; the rice wine was served warm, and went down with dangerous ease. This was evidently the signal for a general beginning; the Chinese started in on the platters, and the younger men at least had little hesitation in following suit. Laurence was embarrassed to see, when he glanced over, that Roland and Dyer were having not the least difficulty with their chopsticks and were already round-cheeked from stuffing food into their mouths.

He himself had only just managed to get a piece of the beef to his mouth by dint of puncturing it with one of his sticks; the meat had a smoky, not unpleasant quality. No sooner had he swallowed than Yongxing raised the cup for another toast, and he had to drink again; this succession repeated itself several times more, until he was uncomfortably warm, his head nearly swimming.

Growing slowly braver with the sticks, he risked a prawn, though the other officers about him were avoiding them; the sauce made them slippery and awkward to manage. It wobbled precariously, the beady black eyes bobbing at him; he followed the Chinese example and bit it off just behind the attached head. At once he groped for the cup again, breathing deeply through his nose: the sauce was shockingly hot, and broke a fresh sweat out upon his forehead, the drops trickling down the side of his jaw into his collar. Liu Bao laughed uproariously at his expression and poured him more wine, leaning across the table and thumping him approvingly on the shoulder.

The platters were shortly taken off the tables and replaced with an array of wooden dishes, full of dumplings, some with thin crepe-paper skins and others of thick, yeasty white dough. These were at least easier to get hold of with the sticks, and could be chewed and swallowed whole. The cooks had evidently exercised some ingenuity, lacking essential ingredients; Laurence found a piece of seaweed in one, and the lamb kidneys made their appearance also. Three further courses of small dishes ensued, then a strange dish of uncooked fish, pale pink and fleshy, with cold noodles and pickled greens gone dull brown with long storage. A strange crunchy substance in the mixture was identified after inquiry by Hammond as dried jellyfish, which intelligence caused several men to surreptitiously pick the bits out and drop them onto the floor.

Liu Bao with motions and his own example encouraged Laurence to literally fling the ingredients into the air to mix them together, and Hammond informed them by translation that this was intended to ensure good luck: the higher the better. The British were not unwilling to make the attempt; their coordination was less equal to the task, however, and shortly both uniforms and the table were graced by bits of fish and pickled greens. Dignity was thus dealt a fatal blow: after nearly a jug of rice wine to every man, even Yongxing's presence was not enough to dampen the hilarity ensuing from watching their fellow officers fling bits of fish all over themselves.

'It is a dashed sight better than we had in the *Normandy*'s cutter,' Riley said to Laurence, over-loud, meaning the raw fish; to the more general audience, interest having been expressed by Hammond and Liu Bao both, he expanded on the story: 'We were wrecked in the *Normandy* when Captain Yarrow ran her onto a reef, all of us thrown on a desert island seven hundred miles from Rio. We were sent off in the cutter for rescue, though Laurence was only second lieutenant at the time, the captain and premier knew less about the sea than trained apes, which is how they came to run us aground. They wouldn't go themselves for love or money, or give us much in the way of supply, either,' he added, still smarting at the memory.

'Twelve men with nothing but hard tack and a bag of cocoanuts; we were glad enough for fish to eat it raw, with our fingers, the moment we caught it,' Laurence said. 'But I

187

cannot complain; I am tolerably sure Foley tapped me for his first lieutenant in *Goliath* because of it, and I would have eaten a good deal more raw fish for the chance. But this is much nicer, by far,' he added, hastily, thinking this conversation implied that raw fish was fit only for consumption in desperate circumstances, which opinion he privately held true, but not to be shared at present.

This story launched several more anecdotes from various of the naval officers, tongues loosened and backs unstiffened by so much gluttony. The translator was kept busy rendering these for the benefit of the highly interested Chinese audience; even Yongxing followed the stories; he had still not deigned to break his silence, save for the formal toasts, but there was something of a mellowing about his eyes.

Liu Bao was less circumspect about his curiosity. 'You have been to a great many places, I see, and had unusual adventures,' he observed to Laurence. 'Admiral Zheng He sailed all the way to Africa, but he died on his seventh voyage, and his tomb is empty. You have gone around the world more than once. Have you never been worried that you would die at sea, and no one would perform the rites at your grave?'

'I have never thought very much about it,' Laurence said, with a little dishonesty: in truth he had never given the matter any consideration whatsoever. 'But after all, Drake and Cook, and so many other great men, have been buried at sea; I really could not complain about sharing their tomb, sir, and with your own navigator as well.'

'Well, I hope you have many sons at home,' Liu Bao said, shaking his head.

The casual air with which he made so personal a remark took Laurence quite aback. 'No, sir; none,' he said, too startled to think of anything to do but answer. 'I have never married,' he added, seeing Liu Bao about to assume an expression of great sympathy, which on this answer being translated became a look of open astonishment; Yongxing and even Sun

Kai turned their heads to stare. Beleaguered, Laurence tried to explain. 'There is no urgency; I am a third son, and my eldest brother has three boys already himself.'

'Pardon me, Captain, if I may,' Hammond broke in, rescuing him, and said to them, 'Gentlemen, among us, the eldest son alone inherits the family estates, and the younger are expected to make their own way; I know it is not the same with you.'

'I suppose your father is a soldier, like you?' Yongxing said abruptly. 'Does he have a very small estate, that he cannot provide for all his sons?'

'No, sir; my father is Lord Allendale,' Laurence said, rather nettled by the suggestion. 'Our family seat is in Nottinghamshire; I do not think anyone would call it small.'

Yongxing looked startled and somewhat displeased by this answer, but perhaps he was only frowning at the soup which was at that moment being laid out before them: a very clear broth, pale gold and queer to the taste, smoky and thin, with pitchers of bright red vinegar as accompaniment and to add sharp flavour, and masses of short dried noodles in each bowl, strangely crunchy.

All the while the servants were bringing it in, the translator had been murmuring quietly in answer to some question from Sun Kai, and now on his behalf leaned across the table and asked, 'Captain, is your father a relation of the King?'

Though surprised by the question, Laurence was grateful enough for any excuse to put down his spoon; he would have found the soup difficult eating even had he not already gone through six courses. 'No, sir; I would hardly be so bold as to call His Majesty a relation. My father's family are of Plantagenet descent; we are only very distantly connected to the present house.'

Sun Kai listened to this translated, then persisted a little further. 'But are you more closely related to the King than the Lord Macartney?'

As the translator pronounced the name a little awkwardly, Laurence had some difficulty in recognizing the name as that of the earlier ambassador, until Hammond, whispering hastily in his ear, made it clear to whom Sun Kai was referring. 'Oh, certainly,' Laurence said. 'He was raised to the peerage for service to the Crown, himself; not that that is held any less honourable with us, I assure you, but my father is eleventh Earl of Allendale, and his creation dates from 1529.'

Even as he spoke, he was amused at finding himself so absurdly jealous of his ancestry, halfway around the world, in the company of men to whom it could be of no consequence whatsoever, when he had never trumpeted it among his acquaintance at home. Indeed, he had often rebelled against his father's lectures upon the subject, of which there had been many, particularly after his first abortive attempt to run away to sea. But four weeks of being daily called into his father's office to endure another repetition had evidently had some effect he had not previously suspected, if he could be provoked to so stuffy a response by being compared to a great diplomat of very respectable lineage.

But quite contrary to his expectations, Sun Kai and his countrymen showed a deep fascination with this intelligence, betraying an enthusiasm for genealogy Laurence had heretofore only encountered in a few of his more stiff-necked relations, and he shortly found himself pressed for details of the family history which he could only vaguely dredge out of his memory. 'I beg your pardon,' he said at last, growing rather desperate. 'I cannot keep it straight in my head without writing it down; you must forgive me.'

It was an unfortunate choice of gambit: Liu Bao, who had also been listening with interest, promptly said, 'Oh, that is easy enough,' and called for brush and ink; the servants were clearing away the soup, and there was room on the table for the moment. At once all those nearby leaned forward to look on, the Chinese in curiosity, the British in self-defence: there

190

was another course waiting in the wings, and no one was in a hurry for it to arrive but the cooks.

Feeling that he was being excessively punished for his moment of vanity, Laurence was forced to write out a chart on a long roll of rice paper under all their eyes. The difficulty of forming the Latin alphabet with a paintbrush was added to that of trying to remember the various begats; he had to leave several given names blank, marking them with interrogatives, before finally reaching Edward III after several contortions and one leap through the Salic line. The result said nothing complimentary about his penmanship, but the Chinese passed it around more than once, discussing it amongst themselves with energy, though the writing could hardly have made any more sense to them than theirs to him. Yongxing himself stared at it a long time, though his face remained devoid of emotion, and Sun Kai, receiving it last, rolled it away with an expression of intense satisfaction, apparently for safe-keeping.

Thankfully, that was an end to it; but now there was no more delaying the next dish, and the sacrificed poultry was brought out, all eight at once, on great platters and steaming with a pungent, liquored sauce. They were laid on the table and hacked expertly into small pieces by the servants using a broad-bladed cleaver, and again Laurence rather despairingly allowed his plate to be filled. The meat was delicious, tender and rich with juices, but almost a punishment to eat; nor was this the conclusion: when the chicken was taken away, nowhere close to finished, whole fish were brought out, fried in the rich slush from the hands' salt pork. No one could do more than pick at this dish, or the course of sweets that followed: seedcake, and sticky-sweet dumplings in syrup, filled with a thick red paste. The servants were especially anxious to press them onto the youngest officers, and poor Roland could be heard saying plaintively, 'Can I not eat it tomorrow?'

When finally they were allowed to escape, almost a dozen

191

men had to be bodily lifted up by their seat-mates and helped from the cabin. Those who could still walk unaided escaped to the deck, there to lean on the rail in various attitudes of pretended fascination, which were mostly a cover for waiting their turn in the seats of ease below. Laurence unashamedly took advantage of his private facility, and then heaved himself back up to sit with Temeraire, his head protesting almost as much as his belly.

Laurence was taken aback to find Temeraire himself being feasted in turn by a delegation of the Chinese servants, who had prepared for him delicacies favoured by dragons in their own land: the entrails of the cow, stuffed with its own liver and lungs chopped fine and mixed with spices, looking very much like large sausages; also a haunch, very lightly seared and touched with what looked very like the same fiery sauce which had been served to the human guests. The deep maroon flesh of an enormous tunny, sliced into thick steaks and layered with whole delicate sheets of yellow noodles, was his fish course, and after this, with great ceremony, the servants brought out an entire sheep, its meat cooked rather like mince and dressed back up in its skin, which had been dyed a deep crimson, with pieces of driftwood for legs.

Temeraire tasted this dish and said, in surprise, 'Why, it is sweet,' and asked the servants something in their native Chinese; they bowed many times, replying, and Temeraire nodded; then he daintily ate the contents, leaving the skin and wooden legs aside. 'They are only for decoration,' he told Laurence, settling down with a sigh of deep contentment; the only guest so comfortable. From the quarterdeck below, the faint sound of retching could be heard, as one of the older midshipmen suffered the consequences of overindulgence. 'They tell me that in China, dragons do not eat the skins, any more than people do.'

'Well, I only hope you will not find it indigestible, from so much spice,' Laurence said, and was sorry at once, recognizing in himself a species of jealousy that did not like to see Temeraire enjoying any Chinese customs. He was unhappily conscious that it had never occurred to him to offer Temeraire prepared dishes, or any greater variety than the difference between fish and mutton, even for a special occasion.

But Temeraire only said, 'No, I like it very well,' unconcerned and yawning; he stretched himself very long and flexed his claws. 'Do let us go for a long flight tomorrow?' he said, curling up again more compactly. 'I have not been tired at all, this whole last week, coming back; I am sure I can manage a longer journey.'

'By all means,' Laurence said, glad to hear that he was feeling stronger. Keynes had at last put a period to Temeraire's convalescence, shortly after their departure from Cape Coast. Yongxing's original prohibition against Laurence's taking Temeraire aloft again had never been withdrawn, but Laurence had no intention of abiding by this restriction, or begging him to lift it; but Hammond with some ingenuity and quiet discussion arranged matters diplomatically: Yongxing came on deck after Keynes's final pronouncement, and granted the permission audibly, 'for the sake of ensuring Lung Tien Xiang's welfare through healthy exercise,' as he put it. So they were free to take to the air again without any threat of quarrelling, but Temeraire had been complaining of soreness, and growing weary with unusual speed.

The feast had lasted so long that Temeraire had begun eating only at twilight; now full darkness spread, and Laurence lay back against Temeraire's side and looked over the less-familiar stars of the southern hemisphere; it was a perfectly clear night, and the master ought to be able to fix a good longitude, he hoped, through the constellations. The hands had been turned up for the evening to celebrate, and the rice wine had flowed freely at their mess tables also; they were singing a boisterous and highly explicit song, and Laurence made sure with a look that Roland and Dyer were not on deck to be interested in it: no sign of either, so they had probably sought their beds after dinner.

One by one the men slowly began to drift away from the festivities and seek their hammocks. Riley came climbing up from the quarterdeck, taking the steps one at a time with both feet, very weary and scarlet in the face; Laurence invited him to sit, and out of consideration did not offer a glass of wine. 'You cannot call it anything but a rousing success; any political hostess would consider it a triumph to put on such a dinner,' Laurence said. 'But I confess I would have been happier with half so many dishes, and the servants might have been much less solicitous without leaving me hungry.'

'Oh yes, indeed,' Riley said; distracted, and now that Laurence looked at him more closely, plainly unhappy, discomfited.

'What has occurred? Is something amiss?' Laurence looked at once at the rigging, the masts; but all looked well, and in any case every sense and intuition together told him that the ship was running well: or as well as she ever did, being in the end a great lumbering hulk.

'Laurence, I very much dislike being a tale-bearer, but I cannot conceal this,' Riley said. 'That ensign, or I suppose cadet, of yours; Roland. He— That is, Roland was asleep in the Chinese cabin, and as I was leaving, the servants asked me, with their translator, where he slept, so they might carry him there.' Laurence was already dreading the conclusion, and not very surprised when Riley added, 'But the fellow said "she" instead; I was on the point of correcting him when I looked— Well, not to drag it out; Roland is a girl. I have not the least notion how she has concealed it so long.'

'Oh bloody hell,' Laurence said, too tired and irritable from the excess of food and drink to mind his language. 'You have not said anything about this, have you, Tom? To anyone else?' Riley nodded, warily, and Laurence said, 'I must beg you to keep it quiet; the plain fact of the matter is, Longwings will

194

not go into harness under a male captain. And some other breeds also, but those are of less material significance; Longwings are the kind we cannot do without, and so some girls must be trained up for them.'

Riley said, uncertainly, half-smiling, 'Are you—? But this is absurd; was not the leader of your formation here on this very ship, with his Longwing?' he protested, seeing that Laurence was not speaking in jest.

'Do you mean Lily?' Temeraire asked, cocking his head. 'Her captain is Catherine Harcourt; she is not a man.'

'It is quite true; I assure you,' Laurence said, while Riley stared at him and Temeraire in turn.

'But Laurence, the very notion,' Riley said; grown now appalled as he began to believe them. 'Every feeling must cry out against such an abuse. Why, if we are to send women to war, should we not take them to sea, also? We could double our numbers, and what matter if the deck of every ship become a brothel, and children left motherless and crying on shore?'

'Come, the one does not follow on the other in the slightest,' Laurence said, impatient with this exaggeration; he did not like the necessity himself, but he was not at all willing to be given such romantic arguments against it. 'I do not at all say it could or ought to answer in the general case; but where the willing sacrifice of a few may mean the safety and happiness of the rest, I cannot think it so bad. Those women officers whom I have met are not impressed into service, nor forced to the work even by the ordinary necessities that require men to seek employment, and I assure you no one in the service would dream of offering any insult.'

This explanation did not reconcile Riley at all, but he abandoned his general protest for the specific. 'And so you truly mean to keep this girl in service?' he said, in tones increasingly plaintive rather than shocked. 'And have her going about in male dress in this fashion; can it be allowed?'

'There is formal dispensation from the sumptuary laws for female officers of the Corps while engaged upon their duties, authorized by the Crown,' Laurence said. 'I am sorry that you should be put to any distress over the matter, Tom; I had hoped to avoid the issue entirely, but I suppose it was too much to ask for, seven months aboard ship. I promise you,' he added, 'I was as shocked as you might wish when I first learned of the practice; but since I have served with several, and they are indeed not at all like ordinary females. They are raised to the life, you know, and under such circumstances habit may trump even birth.'

For his part, Temeraire had been following this exchange with cocked head and increasing confusion; now he said, 'I do not understand in the least, why ought it make any difference at all? Lily is female, and she can fight just as well as I can, or almost,' he amended, with a touch of superiority.

Riley, still dissatisfied even after Laurence's reassurance, looked after this remark very much as though he had been asked to justify the tide, or the phase of the moon; Laurence was by long experience better prepared for Temeraire's radical notions, and said, 'Women are generally smaller and weaker than men, Temeraire, less able to endure the privations of service.'

'I have never noticed that Captain Harcourt is much smaller than any of the rest of you,' Temeraire said; well he might not, speaking from a height of some thirty feet and a weight topping eighteen tons. 'Besides, I am smaller than Maximus, and Messoria is smaller than me; but that does not mean we cannot still fight.'

'It is different for dragons than for people,' Laurence said. 'Among other things, women must bear children, and care for them through childhood, where your kind lay eggs and hatch ready to look to your own needs.'

Temeraire blinked at this intelligence. 'You do not hatch out of eggs?' he asked, in deep fascination. 'How then—'

'I beg your pardon, I think I see Purbeck looking for me,' Riley said, very hastily, and escaped at a speed remarkable, Laurence thought somewhat resentfully, in a man who had lately consumed nearly a quarter of his own weight again in food.

'I cannot really undertake to explain the process to you; I have no children of my own,' Laurence said. 'In any case, it is late; and if you wish to make a long flight tomorrow, you had better rest well tonight.'

'That is true, and I am sleepy,' Temeraire said, yawning and letting his long forked tongue unroll, tasting the air. 'I think it will keep clear; we will have good weather for the flight.' He settled himself. 'Good night, Laurence; you will come early?'

'Directly after breakfast, I am entirely at your disposal.' Laurence promised. He stayed stroking Temeraire gently until the dragon drifted into sleep; his hide was still very warm to the touch, likely from the last lingering heat of the galley, its ovens finally given some rest after the long preparations. At last, Temeraire's eyes closing to the thinnest of slits, Laurence got himself back onto his feet and climbed down to the quarterdeck.

The men had mostly cleared away or were napping on deck, save those surly few set as lookouts and muttering of their unhappy lot in the rigging, and the night air was pleasantly cool. Laurence walked a ways aft to stretch his legs before going below; the midshipman standing watch, young Tripp, was yawning almost as wide as Temeraire; he closed his mouth with a snap and jerked to embarrassed attention when Laurence passed.

'A pleasant evening, Mr. Tripp,' Laurence said, concealing his amusement; the boy was coming along well, from what Riley had said, and bore little resemblance anymore to the idle, spoiled creature who had been foisted upon them by his family. His wrists showed bare for several inches past the ends of his sleeves, and the back of his coat had split so many times that in the end it had been necessary to expand it by the insertion of a panel of blue-dyed sailcloth, not quite the same shade as the rest, so he had an odd stripe running down the middle. Also his hair had grown curly, and bleached to almost yellow by the sun; his own mother would likely not recognize him.

'Oh yes, sir,' Tripp said, enthusiastically. 'Such wonderful food, and they gave me a whole dozen of those sweet dumplings at the end, too. It is a pity we cannot always be eating so.'

Laurence sighed over this example of youthful resilience; his own stomach was not at all comfortable yet. 'Mind you do not fall asleep on watch,' he said; after such a dinner it would be astonishing if the boy was not sorely tempted, and Laurence had no desire to see him suffer the ignominious punishment.

'Never, sir,' Tripp said, swallowing a fresh yawn and finishing the sentence out in a squeak. 'Sir,' he asked, nervously, in a low voice, when Laurence would have gone, 'may I ask you— You do not suppose that Chinese spirits would show themselves to a fellow who was not a member of their family, do you?'

'I am tolerably certain you will not see any spirits on watch, Mr. Tripp, unless you have concealed some in your coat pocket,' Laurence said, dryly. This took a moment to puzzle out, then Tripp laughed, but still nervously, and Laurence frowned. 'Has someone been telling you stories?' he asked, well aware of what such rumours could do to the state of a ship's crew.

'No, it is only that— Well, I thought I saw someone, forward, when I went to turn the glass. But I spoke, and he quite vanished away; I am sure he was a Chinaman, and oh, his face was so white!'

'That is quite plain; you saw one of the servants who cannot speak our tongue, coming from the head, and startled him into ducking away from what he thought would be a scolding of some sort. I hope you are not inclined to superstition, Mr. Tripp; it is something which must be tolerated in the men, but a sad flaw in an officer.' He spoke sternly, hoping by firmness to keep the boy from spreading the tale, at least; and if the fear kept him wakeful for the rest of the night, it would be so much the better.

'Yes, sir,' Tripp said, rather dismally. 'Good night, sir.'

Laurence continued his circuit of the deck, at a leisurely pace that was all he could muster. The exercise was settling his stomach; he was almost inclined to take another turn, but the glass was running low, and he did not wish to disappoint Temeraire by rising late. But as he made to step down into the fore hatch, a sudden heavy blow landed on his back and he lurched, tripped, and pitched headfirst down the ladderway.

His hand grasped automatically for the guideline, and after a jangling twist he found the steps with his feet, catching himself against the ladder with a thump. Angry, he looked up and nearly fell again, recoiling from the pallid white face, incomprehensibly deformed, that was peering closely into his own out of the dark.

'Good God in Heaven,' he said, with great sincerity; then he recognized Feng Li, Yongxing's servant, and breathed again: the man only looked so strange because he was dangling upside down through the hatch, barely inches from falling himself. 'What the devil do you mean, lunging about deck like this?' he demanded, catching the man's flailing hand and setting it onto the guideline, so he could right himself. 'You ought to have better sea-legs by now.'

Feng Li only stared in mute incomprehension, then hauled himself back onto his feet and scrambled down the ladder past Laurence pell-mell, disappearing belowdecks to where the Chinese servants were quartered with speed enough to call it vanishing. With his dark blue clothing and black hair, as soon as his face was out of sight he was almost invisible in the dark. 'I cannot blame Tripp in the least,' Laurence said aloud, now more generously inclined towards the boy's silliness; his heart was still pounding disgracefully as he continued on to his quarters.

Laurence roused the next morning to yells of dismay and feet running overhead; he dashed at once for the deck to find the foremainsail yard tumbled to the deck in two pieces, the enormous sail draped half over the forecastle, and Temeraire looking at once miserable and embarrassed. 'I did not mean to,' he said, sounding gravelly and quite unlike himself, and sneezed again, this time managing to turn his head away from the ship: the force of the eruption cast up a few waves that slopped against the larboard side.

Keynes was already climbing up to the deck with his bag, and laid his ear against Temeraire's chest. 'Hm.' He said nothing more, listening in many places, until Laurence grew impatient and prompted him.

'Oh, it is certainly a cold; there is nothing to be done but wait it out, and dose him for coughing when that should begin. I am only seeing if I might hear the fluid moving in the channels which relate to the divine wind,' Keynes said absently. 'We have no notion of the anatomy of the particular trait; a pity we have never had a specimen to dissect.'

Temeraire drew back at this, putting his ruff down, and snorted; or rather tried to: instead he blew mucus out all over Keynes's head. Laurence himself sprang back only just in time, and could not feel particularly sorry for the surgeon: the remark had been thoroughly tactless.

Temeraire croaked out, 'I am quite well, we can still go flying,' and looked at Laurence in appeal.

'Perhaps a shorter flight now, and then again in the afternoon, if you are still not tired,' Laurence offered, looking at

Keynes, who was ineffectually trying to get the slime from his face.

'No, in warm weather like this he can fly just as usual if he likes to; no need to baby him,' Keynes said, rather shortly, managing to clear his eyes at least. 'So long as you are sure to be strapped on tight, or he will sneeze you clean off. Will you excuse me?'

So in the end Temeraire had his long flight after all: the *Allegiance* left dwindling behind in the blue-water depths, and the ocean shading to jewelled glass as they drew nearer the coast: old cliffs, softened by the years and sloping gently to the water under a cloak of unbroken green, with a fringe of jagged grey boulders at their base to break the water. There were a few small stretches of pale sand, none large enough for Temeraire to land even if they had not grown wary; but otherwise the trees were impenetrable, even after they had flown straight inland for nearly an hour.

It was lonely, and as monotonous as flying over empty ocean; the wind among the leaves instead of the lapping of the waves, only a different variety of silence. Temeraire looked eagerly at every occasional animal cry that broke the stillness, but saw nothing past the ground cover, so thickly overgrown were the trees. 'Does no one live here?' he asked, eventually.

He might have been keeping his voice low because of the cold, but Laurence felt the same inclination to preserve the quiet, and answered softly, 'No; we have flown too deep. Even the most powerful tribes live only along the coasts, and never venture so far inland; there are too many feral dragons and other beasts, too savage to confront.'

They continued on without speaking for some time; the sun was very strong, and Laurence drifted neither awake nor asleep, his head nodding against his chest. Unchecked, Temeraire kept on his course, the slow pace no challenge to his endurance; when at last Laurence roused, on Temeraire's

201

sneezing again, the sun was past its zenith: they would miss dinner.

Temeraire did not express a wish to stay longer when Laurence said they ought to turn around; and if anything he quickened his pace. They had gone so far that the coastline was out of sight, and they flew back only by Laurence's compass, with no landmarks to guide them through the unchanging jungle. The smooth curve of the ocean was very welcome, and Temeraire's spirits rose as they struck out again over the waves. 'At least I am not tiring anymore, even if I am sick,' he said, and then sneezed himself thirty feet directly upwards, with a sound not unlike cannon-fire.

They did not reach the *Allegiance* again until nearly dark, and Laurence discovered he had missed more than his dinner-hour. Another sailor besides Tripp had also spied Feng Li on deck the night before, with similar results, and during Laurence's absence the story of the ghost had already gone round the ship, magnified a dozen times over, and gotten thoroughly entrenched. All his attempted explanations were useless, the ship's company wholly convinced: three men now swore they had seen the ghost dancing a jig upon the foresail yard the night before, foretelling its doom; others from the middle watch claimed the ghost had been wafting about the rigging all night long.

Liu Bao himself flung fuel onto the fire; having inquired and heard the tale during his visit to the deck the next day, he shook his head and opined that the ghost was a sign that someone aboard had acted immorally with a woman. This qualified nearly every man aboard; they muttered a great deal about foreign ghosts with unreasonably prudish sensibilities, and discussed the subject anxiously at meals, each one trying to persuade himself and his messmates that *he* could not possibly be the guilty culprit; *his* infraction had been small and innocent, and in any case he had always meant to marry her, the instant he returned.

As yet general suspicion had not fallen onto a single individual, but it was only a matter of time; and then the wretch's life would hardly be worth living. In the meantime, the men went about their duties at night only reluctantly, going so far as to refuse orders which would have required them to be alone on any part of the deck. Riley attempted to set an example to the men by walking out of sight during his watches, but this had less effect than might have been desired by his having to visibly steel himself first. Laurence roundly scolded Allen, the first of his own crew to mention the ghost in his hearing, so no more was said in front of him; but the aviators showed themselves inclined to stay close to Temeraire on duty, and to come to and from their quarters in groups.

Temeraire was himself too uncomfortable to pay a great deal of attention. He found the degree of fear baffling, and expressed some disappointment at never seeing the spectre when so many others had evidently had a glimpse; but for the most part he was occupied in sleeping, and directing his frequent sneezes away from the ship. He tried to conceal his coughing at first when it developed, reluctant to be dosed: Keynes had been brewing the medicine in a great pot in the galley since the first evidence of Temeraire's illness, and the foul stench rose through the boards ominously. But late on the third day he was seized with a fit he could not suppress, and Keynes and his assistants trundled the pot of medicine up onto the dragondeck: a thick, almost gelatinous brownish mixture, swimming in a glaze of liquid orange fat.

Temeraire stared down into the pot unhappily. 'Must I?' he asked.

'It will do its best work drunk hot,' Keynes said, implacable, and Temeraire squeezed his eyes shut and bent his head to gulp.

'Oh; oh, *no*,' he said, after the first swallow; he seized the barrel of water which had been prepared for him and upended it into his mouth, spilling much over his chops and neck and onto the deck as he guzzled. 'I cannot possibly drink any more of it,' he said, putting the barrel down. But with much coaxing and exhortation, he at length got down the whole, miserable and retching all the while.

Laurence stood by, stroking him anxiously; he did not dare speak again, Keynes had been so very cutting at his first suggestion of a brief respite. Temeraire at last finished and slumped to the deck, saying passionately, 'I will *never* be ill again, *ever*,' but despite his unhappiness, his coughing was indeed silenced, and that night he slept more easily, breathing a good deal less laboured.

Laurence stayed on deck by his side as he had every night of the illness; with Temeraire sleeping quiet he had ample opportunity to witness the absurd lengths the men practised to avoid the ghost; going two at a time to the head, and huddling around the two lanterns left on deck instead of sleeping. Even the officer of the watch stayed uneasily close, and looked pale every time he took the walk along the deck to turn the glass and strike the bell.

Nothing would cure it but distraction, and of that there was little prospect: the weather was holding fair, and there was little chance of meeting any enemy who would offer battle; any ship which did not wish to fight could easily outrun them. Laurence could not really wish for either, in any case; the situation could only be tolerated until they reached port, where the break in the journey would hopefully dispel the myth.

Temeraire snuffled in his sleep and half-woke, coughing wetly, and sighed in misery. Laurence laid a hand on him and opened the book on his lap again; the lantern swaying beside him gave a light, if an unreliable one, and he read slowly aloud until Temeraire's eyelids sank heavily down again.

Chapter Nine

'I do not mean to tell you your business,' General Baird said, showing very little reluctance to do so. 'But the winds to India are damn unpredictable this time of year, with the winter monsoon barely over. You are as likely to find yourselves blown straight back here. You had much better wait for Lord Caledon to arrive, especially after this news about Pitt.'

He was a younger man, but long-faced and serious, with a very decided mouth; the high upstanding collar of his uniform pushed up his chin and gave his neck a stiff, elongated look. The new British governor not yet arrived, he was temporarily in command of the Capetown settlement, and ensconced in the great fortified castle in the midst of the town at the foot of the great flat-topped Table Mount. The courtyard was brilliant with sun, hazy glints cast off the bayonets of the troops drilling smartly on the grounds, and the encircling walls blocked the best part of the breeze which had cooled them on the walk up from the beach.

'We cannot be sitting in port until June,' Hammond said. 'It would be much better if we were to sail and be delayed at sea, with an obvious attempt to make haste, than to be idle in front of Prince Yongxing. He has already been asking me how much longer we expect the journey to take, and where else we may be stopping.'

'I am perfectly happy to get underway as soon as we are resupplied, for my part,' Riley said, putting down his empty teacup and nodding to the servant to fill it again. 'She is not a fast ship by any means, but I would lay a thousand pounds on her against any weather we might meet.'

'Not, of course,' he said to Laurence later, somewhat anxiously, as they walked back to the *Allegiance*, 'that I would really like to try her against a typhoon. I never meant anything of the sort; I was thinking only of ordinary bad weather, perhaps a little rain.'

Their preparations for the long remaining stretch of ocean went ahead: not merely buying livestock, but also packing and preserving more salt meat, as there were no official naval supplies yet to be had from the port. Fortunately there was no shortage of supply; the settlers did not greatly resent the mild occupation, and they were happy enough to sell from their herds. Laurence was more occupied with the question of demand, for Temeraire's appetite was greatly diminished since he had been afflicted by the cold, and he had begun to pick querulously at his food, complaining of a lack of flavour.

There was no proper covert, but alerted by Volly, Baird had anticipated their arrival and arranged the clearing of a large green space near the landing ground so Temeraire could rest comfortably. Temeraire having flown to this stable location, Keynes could perform a proper inspection: Temeraire was directed to lay his head flat and open his jaws wide, and the surgeon climbed inside with a lantern, picking his way carefully among the hand-sized teeth to peer down into Temeraire's throat.

Watching anxiously from outside with Granby, Laurence could see that Temeraire's narrow forked tongue, ordinarily pale pink, was presently coated thickly with white, mottled with virulent red spots.

206

'I expect that is why he cannot taste anything; there is nothing out of the ordinary in the condition of his passages,' Keynes said, shrugging as he climbed out of Temeraire's jaws, to applause: a crowd of children, both settlers and natives, had gathered around the clearing's fence to watch, fascinated as if at a circus. 'And they use their tongues for scent also, which must be contributing to the difficulties.'

'Surely this is not a usual symptom?' Laurence asked.

'I don't recall ever seeing a dragon lose his appetite over a cold,' Granby put in, worriedly. 'In the ordinary line of things, they get hungrier.'

'He is only pickier than most about his food,' Keynes said. 'You will just have to force yourself to eat until the illness has run its course,' he added, to Temeraire, sternly. 'Come, here is some fresh beef; let us see you finish the whole.'

'I will try,' Temeraire said, heaving a sigh that came rather like a whine through his stuffed nose. 'But it is very tiresome chewing on and on when it does not taste like anything.' He obediently but unenthusiastically downed several large hunks, but only mauled a few more pieces about without swallowing much of them, and then went back to blowing his nose into the small pit which had been dug for this purpose, wiping it against a heap of broad palm leaves.

Laurence watched silently, then took the narrow pathway winding from the landing grounds back to the castle: he found Yongxing resting in the formal guest quarters with Sun Kai and Liu Bao. Thin curtains had been pinned up to dim the sunlight instead of the heavy velvet drapes, and two servants were making a breeze by standing at the full-open windows and waving great fans of folded paper; another stood by unobtrusively, refilling the envoys' cups with tea. Laurence felt untidy and hot in contrast, his collar wet and limp against his neck after the day's exertions, and dust thick on his boots, spattered also with blood from Temeraire's unfinished dinner.

After the translator was summoned and some pleasantries

207

exchanged, he explained the situation and said, as gracefully as he could manage, 'I would be grateful if you would lend me your cooks to make some dish for Temeraire, in your style, which might have some stronger flavour than fresh meat alone.'

He had scarcely finished asking before Yongxing was giving orders in their language; the cooks were dispatched to the kitchens at once. 'Sit and wait with us,' Yongxing said, unexpectedly, and had a chair brought for him, draped over with a long narrow silk cloth.

'No, thank you, sir; I am all over dirt,' Laurence said, eyeing the beautiful drapery, pale orange and patterned with flowers. 'I do very well.'

But Yongxing only repeated the invitation; yielding, Laurence gingerly sat down upon the very edge of the chair, and accepted the cup of tea which he was offered. Sun Kai nodded at him, in an odd approving fashion. 'Have you heard anything from your family, Captain?' he inquired through the translator. 'I hope all is well with them.'

'I have had no fresh news, sir, though I thank you for the concern,' Laurence said, and passed another quarter of an hour in further small talk of the weather and the prospects for their departure, wondering a little at this sudden change in his reception.

Shortly a couple of lamb carcasses, on a bed of pastry and dressed with a gelatinous, red-orange sauce, emerged from the kitchens and were trundled along the path to the clearing on great wooden trays. Temeraire brightened at once, the intensity of the spice penetrating even his dulled senses, and made a proper meal. 'I was hungry after all,' he said, licking sauce from his chops and putting his head down to be cleaned off more thoroughly. Laurence hoped he was not doing Temeraire some harm by the measure: some traces of the sauce got upon on his hand as he wiped Temeraire clean, and it literally burned upon the skin, leaving marks. But Temeraire

208

seemed comfortable enough, not even asking more water than usual, and Keynes opined that keeping him eating was of the greater importance.

Laurence scarcely needed to ask for the extended loan of the cooks; Yongxing not only agreed but made it a point to supervise and press them to do more elaborate work, and his own physician was called for and recommended the introduction of various herbs into the dishes. The poor servants were sent out into the markets to collect whatever ingredients they could find with silver as the only language they shared with the local merchants, the more exotic and expensive the better.

Keynes was sceptical but unworried, and Laurence, being more conscious of owing gratitude than truly grateful, and guilty over his lack of sincerity, did not try to interfere with the menus, even as the servants daily trooped back from the markets with a succession of increasingly bizarre ingredients: penguins, served stuffed with grain and berries and their own eggs; smoked elephant meat brought in by hunters willing to risk the dangerous journey inland; shaggy, fat-tailed sheep with hair instead of wool; and the still-stranger spices and vegetables. The Chinese insisted on these last, swearing they were healthy for dragons, though the English custom had always been to feed them a steady diet of meat alone. Temeraire, for his part, ate the complicated dishes one after another with no ill-effects other than a tendency to belch foully afterwards.

The local children had become regular visitors, emboldened by seeing Dyer and Roland so frequently climbing on and about Temeraire; they began to view the search for ingredients as a game, cheering every new dish, or occasionally hissing those they felt insufficiently imaginative. The native children were members of the various tribes which lived about the region. Most lived by herding, but others by foraging in the mountains and the forests beyond, and these in particular joined in the fun, daily bringing items which their older relations had found too bizarre for their own consumption.

The crowning triumph was a misshapen and overgrown fungus brought back to the clearing by a group of five children with an air of triumph, its roots still covered with wet black dirt: mushroom-like, but with three brown-spotted caps instead of one, arranged one atop the other along the stem, the largest nearly two feet across, and so fetid they carried it with faces averted, passing it among one other with much shrieking laughter.

The Chinese servants took it back to the castle kitchens with great enthusiasm, paying the children with handfuls of coloured ribbons and shells. Only shortly thereafter, General Baird appeared in the clearing, to complain: Laurence followed him back to the castle and understood the objections before he had fairly entered the complex. There was no visible smoke, but the air was suffused with the cooking smell, something like a mixture of stewed cabbage and the wet green mould which grew on the deck beams in humid weather; sour, cloying, and lingering upon the tongue. The street on the other side of the wall from the kitchens, ordinarily thronged with local merchants, was deserted; and the halls of the castle were nearly uninhabitable from the miasma. The envoys were quartered in a different building, well away from the kitchens, and so had not been personally affected, but the soldiers were quartered directly by and could not possibly be asked to eat in the repulsive atmosphere.

The labouring cooks, whose sense of smell, Laurence could only think, had been dulled by the week of producing successively more pungent dishes, protested through the interpreter that the sauce was not done, and all the persuasion Laurence and Baird together could muster was required to make them surrender the great stew-pot. Baird shamelessly ordered a couple of unlucky privates to carry it over to the clearing, the pot suspended between them on a broad tree branch. Laurence followed after them, trying to breathe shallowly.

However, Temeraire received it with enthusiasm, far more pleased that he could actually perceive the smell than put off by its quality. 'It seems perfectly nice to me,' he said, and nodded impatiently for it to be poured over his meat. He devoured an entire one of the local humpbacked oxen slathered in the stuff, and licked the insides of the pot clean, while Laurence watched dubiously from as far a distance as was polite.

Temeraire sprawled into a blissful somnolence after his meal, murmuring approval and hiccoughing a little between words, almost drunkenly. Laurence came closer, a little alarmed to see him so quickly asleep, but Temeraire roused at the prodding, beaming and enthusiastic, and insisted on nuzzling at Laurence closely. His breath had grown as unbearable as the original stench; Laurence averted his face and tried not to retch, very glad to escape when Temeraire fell asleep again and he could climb out of the affectionate embrace of the dragon's forelegs.

Laurence had to wash and shift his clothes before he could consider himself presentable. Even afterwards, he could still catch the lingering odour in his hair; too much to bear, he thought, and felt himself justified in carrying the protest back to the Chinese. It gave no offence, but it was not received with quite the gravity he had hoped for: indeed Liu Bao laughed uproariously when Laurence had described the effects of the mushroom; and when Laurence suggested that perhaps they might organize a more regular and limited set of dishes, Yongxing dismissed the notion, saying, 'We cannot insult a Tien-Lung by offering him the same day in and day out; the cooks will just have to be more careful.'

Laurence left without managing to carry his point, and with the suspicion that his control over Temeraire's diet had been usurped. His fears were soon confirmed. Temeraire woke the next day after an unusually long sleep, much improved and no longer so congested. The cold vanished entirely after few days more, but though Laurence hinted repeatedly that there was no further need for assistance, the prepared dishes continued to come. Temeraire certainly made no objections, even as his sense of smell began to be restored. 'I think I am beginning to be able to tell the spices from one another,' he said, licking his claws daintily clean: he had taken to picking up the food in his forelegs to eat, rather than simply feeding from the tubs. 'Those red things are called hua jiao, I like them very much.'

'So long as you are enjoying your meals,' Laurence said. 'I can hardly say anything more without being churlish,' he confided to Granby later that evening, over their own supper in his cabin. 'If nothing else at least their efforts made him more comfortable, and kept him eating healthily; I cannot now say thank you, no, especially when he likes it.'

'If you ask me, it is still nothing less than interference,' Granby said, rather disgruntled on his behalf. 'And however are we to keep him fed in this style, when we have gotten him back home?'

Laurence shook his head, both at the question and at the use of *when*; he would gladly have accepted uncertainty on the former point, if he might have had any assurance of the latter.

The *Allegiance* left Africa behind sailing almost due east with the current, which Riley thought better than trying to beat up along the coast into the capricious winds that still blew more south than north for the moment, and not liking to strike out across the main body of the Indian Ocean. Laurence watched the narrow hook of the land darken and fade into the ocean behind them; four months into the journey, and they were now more than halfway to China.

A similarly disconsolate mood prevailed among the rest of

the ship's company as they left behind the comfortable port and all its attractions. There had been no letters waiting in Capetown, as Volly had brought their mail with him, and little prospect of receiving any word from home ahead, unless some faster-sailing frigate or merchantman passed them by; but few of those would be sailing to China so early in the season. They thus had nothing to anticipate with pleasure, and the ghost still loomed ominously in all their hearts.

Preoccupied by their superstitious fears, the sailors were not as attentive as they ought to have been. Three days out of port, Laurence woke before dawn out of an uneasy sleep to the sound, penetrating easily through the bulkhead that separated his quarters from the next cabin, of Riley savaging poor Lieutenant Beckett, who had been on the middle watch. The wind had shifted and risen during the night, and in confusion Beckett had put them on the wrong heading and neglected to reef the main and mizzen: ordinarily his mistakes were corrected by the more experienced sailors, who would cough meaningfully until he hit upon the right order to give, but more anxious to avoid the ghost and stay out of the rigging, no one had on this occasion given him warning, and now the *Allegiance* had been blown far north out of her course.

The swell was rising some fifteen feet in height under a lightening sky, the waves pale, green-tinted and translucent as glass under their soapy white lather, leaping up into sharp peaks and spilling down again over themselves in great clouds of spray. Climbing to the dragondeck, Laurence pulled the hood of his sou'wester further forward, lips already dry and stiff with salt. Temeraire was curled tightly in upon himself, as far from the edge of the deck as he could manage, his hide wet and glossy in the lantern light.

'I do not suppose they could build up the fires a little in the galley?' Temeraire asked, a little plaintively, poking his head out from under his wing, eyes squinted down to slits to

213

avoid the spray; he coughed a little for emphasis. This was quite possibly a piece of dramatics, for Temeraire had otherwise gotten well over his cold before their leaving port, but Laurence had no desire to risk its recurrence. Though the water was bathwater-warm, the wind still gusting erratically from the south had a chill. He marshalled the crew to collect oilskins to cover Temeraire in, and had the harness-men stitch them together so they would stay.

Temeraire looked very odd under the makeshift quilt, only his nose visible, and shuffling awkwardly like an animated heap of laundry whenever he wished to change position. Laurence was perfectly content so long as he was warm and dry, and ignored the muffled sniggering from the forecastle; also Keynes, who made noises about coddling patients and encouraging malingering. The weather precluded reading on deck, so he climbed a little ways under the covers himself to sit with Temeraire and keep him company. The insulation kept in not only the heat from the galley below but the steady warmth of Temeraire's own body; Laurence soon needed to shed his coat, and grew drowsy against Temeraire's side, responding only vaguely and without much attention to the conversation.

'Are you asleep, Laurence?' Temeraire asked; Laurence roused with the question, and wondered if he had indeed been asleep a long time, or whether perhaps a fold of the oilskin quilt had fallen down to obscure the opening: it was grown very dark.

He pushed his way out from under the heavy oilskins; the ocean had smoothed out almost to a polished surface, and directly ahead a solid bank of purple-black clouds stretched across the whole expanse of the eastern horizon, its puffy, windswept fringe lit from behind by the sunrise into thick red colour; and deeper in the interior, flashes of sudden lightning briefly limning the edges of towering cloud masses. Far to the north, a ragged line of clouds was marching to join the greater multitude ahead of them, curving across the sky to a point just past the ship. The sky directly above was still clear.

'Pray have the storm-chains fetched, Mr. Fellowes,' Laurence said, putting down his glass. The rigging was already full of activity.

'Perhaps you should ride the storm out aloft,' Granby suggested, coming to join him at the rail. It was a natural suggestion to make: though Granby had been on transports before, he had served at Gibraltar and the Channel almost exclusively and did not have much experience of the open sea. Most dragons could stay aloft a full day, if only coasting on the wind, and well-fed and watered beforehand. It was a common way to keep them out of the way when a transport came into a thunderstorm or a squall: this was neither.

In answer, Laurence only shook his head briefly. 'It is just as well we have put together the oilskins; he will be much easier with them beneath the chains,' he said, and saw Granby take his meaning.

The storm-chains were brought up piecemeal from below, each iron link as thick around as a boy's wrist, and lain over Temeraire's back in crosswise bands. Heavy cables, wormed and parcelled to strengthen them, were laced through all the chain links and secured to the four double-post bitts in the corners of the dragondeck. Laurence inspected all the knots anxiously, and had several redone before he pronounced himself satisfied.

'Do the bonds catch you anywhere?' he asked Temeraire. 'They are not too tight?'

'I cannot move with all of these chains upon me,' Temeraire said, trying the narrow limits of his movement, the end of his tail twitching back and forth uneasily as he pushed against the restraints. 'It is not at all like the harness; what are these for? Why must I wear them?'

'Pray do not strain the ropes,' Laurence said, worried, and went to look: fortunately none had frayed. 'I am sorry for the need,' he added, returning, 'but if the seas grow heavy, you must be fast to the deck: else you could slide into the ocean, or by your movement throw the ship off her course. Are you very uncomfortable?'

'No, not very,' Temeraire said, but unhappily. 'Will it be for long?'

'While the storm lasts,' Laurence said, and looked out past the bow: the cloudbank was fading into the dim and leaden mass of the sky; the newly-risen sun swallowed up already. 'I must go look at the glass.'

The mercury was very low in Riley's cabin: empty, and no smell of breakfast beyond the brewing coffee. Laurence took a cup from the steward and drank it standing, hot, and went back on deck; in his brief absence the sea had risen perhaps another ten feet, and now the *Allegiance* was showing her true mettle, her iron-bound prow slicing the waves cleanly, and her enormous weight pressing them away to either side.

Storm covers were being laid down over the hatches; Laurence made a final inspection of Temeraire's restraints, then said to Granby, 'Send the men below; I will take the first watch.' He ducked under the oilskins by Temeraire's head again and stood by him, stroking the soft muzzle. 'We are in for a long blow, I am afraid,' he said. 'Could you eat something more?'

'I ate yesterday late, I am not hungry,' Temeraire said; in the dark recesses of the hood his pupils had widened, liquid and black, with only the thinnest crescent rims of blue. The iron chains moaned softly as he shifted his weight again, a higher note against the steady deep creaking of the timber, the ship's beams working. 'We have been in a storm before, on the *Reliant*,' he said. 'I did not have to wear such chains then.'

'You were much smaller, and so was the storm,' Laurence said, and Temeraire subsided, but not without a wordless grumbling murmur of discontent; he did not pursue conversation, but lay silently, occasionally scraping his talons against the edges of the chains. He was lying with his head pointed away from the bow, to avoid the spray; Laurence could look out past his muzzle and watch the sailors, busy getting on the storm lashings and taking in the topsails, all noise muffled by the thick layer of fabric but the low metallic grating.

By two bells in the forenoon watch, the ocean was coming over the bulwarks in thick overlapping sheets, an almost constant waterfall pouring over the edge of the dragondeck onto the forecastle. The galleys had gone cold; there would be no fires aboard until the storm had blown over. Temeraire huddled low to the deck and complained no more but drew the oilskin more closely around them, his muscles twitching beneath the hide to shake off the rivulets that burrowed deep between the layers. 'All hands, all hands,' Riley was saying, distantly, through the wind; the bo'sun took up the call with his bellowing voice cupped in his hand, and the men came scrambling up onto the deck, thump-thump of many hurrying feet through the planking, to begin the work of shortening sail and getting her before the wind.

The bell was rung without fail at every turn of the half-hourglass, their only measure of time; the light had failed early on, and sunset was only an incremental increase of darkness. A cold blue phosphorescence washed the deck, carried on the surface of the water, and illuminated the cables and edges of the planks; by its weak glimmering the crests of the waves could be seen, growing steadily higher.

Even the *Allegiance* could not break the present waves, but must go climbing slowly up their faces, rising so steeply that Laurence could look straight down along the deck and see the bottom of the wave trenches below. Then at last her bow would get over the crest: almost with a leap she would tilt over onto the far side of the collapsing wave, gather herself, and plunge deep and with shattering force into the surging froth at the bottom of the trench. The broad fan of the dragondeck then rose streaming, scooping a hollow out of the next wave's face; and she began the slow climb again from the beginning, only the drifting sand in the glass to mark the difference between one wave and the next.

Morning: the wind as savage, but the swell a little lighter, and Laurence woke from a restless, broken sleep. Temeraire refused food. 'I cannot eat anything, even if they could bring it me,' he said, when Laurence asked, and closed his eyes again: exhausted more than sleeping, and his nostrils caked white with salt.

Granby had relieved him on watch; he and a couple of the crew were on deck, huddled against Temeraire's other side. Laurence called Martin over and sent him to fetch some rags. The present rain was too mixed with spray to be fresh, but fortunately they were not short of water, and the fore scuttlebutt had been full before the storm. Clinging with both hands to the lifelines stretched fore and aft the length of the deck, Martin crept slowly along to the barrel, and brought the rags dripping back. Temeraire barely stirred as Laurence gently wiped the salt rims away from his nose.

A strange, dingy uniformity above with neither clouds nor sun visible; the rain came only in short drenching bursts flung at them by the wind, and at the summit of the waves the whole curving horizon was full of the heaving, billowing sea. Laurence sent Granby below when Ferris came up, and took some biscuit and hard cheese himself; he did not care to leave the deck. The rain increased as the day wore on, colder now than before; a heavy cross-sea pounded the *Allegiance* from either side, and one towering monster broke its crest nearly at the height of the foremast, the mass of water coming down like a blow upon Temeraire's body and jarring him from his fitful sleep with a start.

The flood knocked the handful of aviators off their feet, sent them swinging wildly from whatever hold they could get upon the ship. Laurence caught Portis before the midwingman could be washed off the edge of the dragondeck and tumbled down the stairs; but then he had to hold on until Portis could grip the lifeline and steady himself. Temeraire was jerking against the chains, only half awake and panicked, calling for Laurence; the deck around the base of the bitts was beginning to warp under his strength.

Scrambling over the wet deck to lay hands back on Temeraire's side, Laurence called reassurance. 'It was only a wave; I am here,' he said urgently. Temeraire stopped fighting the bonds and lowered himself panting to the deck: but the ropes had been stretched. The chains were looser now just when they were needed most, and the sea was too violent for landsmen, even aviators, to be trying to resecure the knots.

The *Allegiance* took another wave on her quarter and leaned alarmingly; Temeraire's full weight slid against the chains, further straining them, and instinctively he dug his claws into the deck to try and hold on; the oak planking splintered where he grasped at it. 'Ferris, here; stay with him,' Laurence bellowed, and himself struck out across the deck. Waves flooding the deck in succession now; he moved from one line to the next blindly, his hands finding purchase for him without conscious direction.

The knots were soaked through and stubborn, drawn tight by Temeraire's pulling against them. Laurence could only work upon them when the ropes came slack, in the narrow spaces between waves; every inch gained by hard labour. Temeraire was lying as flat as he could manage, the only help he could provide; all his other attention was given to keeping his place.

Laurence could see no one else across the deck, obscured by flying spray, nothing solid but the ropes burning his hands and the squat iron posts, and Temeraire's body a slightly darker region of the air. Two bells in the first dog watch: somewhere behind the clouds, the sun was setting. Out of the corner of his eye he saw a couple of shadows moving nearby; in a moment Leddowes was kneeling beside him, helping with the ropes. Leddowes hauled while Laurence tightened the knots, both of them clinging to each other and the iron bitts as the waves came; until at last the metal of the chains was beneath their hands: they had taken up the slack.

Nearly impossible to speak over the howl; Laurence simply pointed at the second larboard bitt, Leddowes nodded, and they set off. Laurence led, staying by the rail; easier to climb over the great guns than keep their footing out in the middle of the deck. A wave passed by and gave them a moment of calm; he was just letting go the rail to clamber over the first carronade when Leddowes shouted.

Turning, Laurence saw a dark shape coming at his head and flung up a protective hand only from instinct: a terrific blow like being struck with a poker landed on his arm. He managed to get a hand on the breeching of the carronade as he fell; he had only a confused impression of another shadow moving above him, and Leddowes, terrified and staring, was scrambling back away with both hands raised. A wave crashed over the side and Leddowes was abruptly gone.

Laurence clung to the gun and choked on salt water, kicking for some purchase: his boots were full of water and heavy as stone. His hair had come loose; he threw his head back to get it out of his eyes, and managed to catch the descending pry-bar with his free hand. Behind it he saw with a shock of recognition Feng Li's face looming white, terrified and desperate. Feng Li tried to pull the bar away for another attempt, and they wrestled it back and forth, Laurence half-sprawling on the deck with his bootheels skidding over the wet planks.

The wind was a third party to the battle, trying to drive them apart, and ultimately victorious: the bar slipped from Laurence's rope-numb fingers. Feng Li, still standing, went staggering back with arms flung wide as if to embrace the blast of the wind: full willing, it carried him backwards over the railing and into the churning water; he vanished without trace.

Laurence clawed back to his feet and looked over the rail: no sign of Feng Li or Leddowes either; he could not even see the surface of the water for the great clouds of mist and fog rising from the waves. No one else had even seen the brief struggle. Behind him, the bell was clanging again for the turn of the glass.

Too confused with fatigue to make any sense of the murderous attack, Laurence said nothing, other than to briefly tell Riley the men had been lost overboard; he could not think what else to do, and the storm occupied all the attention he could muster. The wind began to fall the next morning; by the start of the afternoon watch, Riley was confident enough to send the men to dinner, though by shifts. The heavy mass of cloud cover broke into patches by six bells, the sunlight streaming down in broad, dramatic swaths from behind the still-dark clouds; and all the hands privately and deeply satisfied despite their fatigue.

They were sorry over Leddowes, who had been well-liked and a favourite with all, but as for a long-expected loss rather than a dreadful accident: he was now proven to have been the prey of the ghost all along, and his mess-mates had already begun magnifying his erotic misdeeds in hushed voices to the rest of the crew. Feng Li's loss passed without much comment, nothing more than coincidence to their minds: if a foreigner with no sea-legs liked to go frolicking about on deck in a typhoon, there was nothing more to be expected, and they had not known him well.

The aftersea was still very choppy, but Temeraire was too unhappy to keep bound; Laurence gave the word to set him loose as soon as the crew had returned from their own dinner. The knots had swelled in the warm air, and the ropes had to be hacked through with axes. Set free, Temeraire shrugged the chains to the deck with a heavy thump, turned his head around and dragged the oilskin blanket off with his teeth; then he shook himself all over, water running down in streams off his hide, and announced militantly, 'I am going flying.'

He leapt aloft without harness or companion, leaving them all behind and gaping. Laurence made an involuntary startled gesture after him, useless and absurd, and then dropped his arm, sorry to have so betrayed himself. Temeraire was only stretching his wings after the long confinement, nothing more; or so he told himself. He was deeply shocked, alarmed; but he could only feel the sensation dully, the exhaustion like a smothering weight lying over all his emotions.

'You have been on deck for three days,' Granby said, and led him down below carefully. Laurence's fingers felt thick and clumsy, and did not quite want to grip the ladder rails. Granby gripped his arm once, when he nearly slipped, and Laurence could not quite stifle an exclamation of pain: there was a tender, throbbing line where the first blow from the pry-bar had struck across his upper arm.

Granby would have taken him to the surgeon at once, but Laurence refused. 'It is only a bruise, John; and I had rather not make any noise about it yet.' But then he had perforce to explain why: disjointedly, but the story came out as Granby pressed him.

'Laurence, this is outrageous. The fellow tried to murder you; we must do something,' Granby said.

'Yes,' Laurence answered, meaninglessly, climbing into his cot; his eyes were already closing. He had the dim awareness of a blanket being laid over him, and the light dimming; nothing more.

He woke clearer in his head, if not much less sore in body; and hurried from his bed at once: the *Allegiance* was low enough in the water he could at least tell that Temeraire had returned, but with the blanketing fatigue gone, Laurence had full consciousness to devote to worry. Coming out of his cabin thus preoccupied, he nearly fell over Willoughby, one of the harness-men, who was sleeping stretched across the doorway. 'What are you doing?' Laurence demanded.

'Mr. Granby set us on watches, sir,' the young man said, yawning and rubbing his face. 'Will you be going up on deck then now?'

Laurence protested in vain; Willoughby trailed after him like an overzealous sheepdog all the way up to the drag-ondeck. Temeraire sat up alertly as soon as he caught sight of them, and nudged Laurence along into the shelter of his body, while the rest of the aviators drew closed their ranks behind him: plainly Granby had not kept the secret.

'How badly are you hurt?' Temeraire nosed him all over, tongue flickering out for reassurance.

'I am perfectly well, I assure you, nothing more than a bump on the arm,' Laurence said, trying to fend him off; though he could not help being privately glad to see that Temeraire's fit of temper had at least for the moment subsided.

Granby ducked into the curve of Temeraire's body, and unrepentantly ignored Laurence's cold looks. 'There; we have worked out watches between us all. Laurence, you do not suppose it was some sort of accident, or that he mistook you for someone else, do you?'

'No.' Laurence hesitated, then reluctantly admitted, 'This was not the first attempt. I did not think anything of it at the time, but now I am almost certain he tried to knock me down the fore hatch, after the New Year's dinner.'

Temeraire growled deeply, and only with difficulty restrained himself from clawing at the deck, which already bore deep grooves from his thrashing about during the storm. 'I am glad he fell overboard,' he said venomously. 'I hope he was eaten by sharks.'

'Well, I am not,' Granby said. 'It will make it a sight more difficult to prove whyever he was at it.'

'It cannot have been anything of a personal nature,' Laurence said. 'I had not spoken ten words to him, and he would not have understood them if I had. I suppose he could have run mad,' he said, but with no real conviction.

'Twice, and once in the middle of a typhoon,' Granby said, contemptuously, dismissing the suggestion. 'No; I am not going to stretch that far: for my part, he must have done it under orders, and that means their prince is most likely behind it all, or I suppose one of those other Chinamen; we had better find out double-quick who, before they try it again.'

This notion Temeraire seconded with great energy, and Laurence blew out a heavy sigh. 'We had better call Hammond to my cabin in private and tell him about it,' he said. 'He may have some idea what their motives might be, and we will need his help to question the lot of them, anyway.'

Summoned below, Hammond listened to the news with visible and increasing alarm, but his ideas were of quite another sort. 'You seriously propose we should interrogate the Emperor's brother and his retinue like a gang of common criminals; accuse them of conspiracy to murder; demand alibis and evidence. You may as well put a torch to the magazine and scuttle the ship; our mission will have as much chance of success that way as the other. Or, no: more chance, because at least if we are all dead and at the bottom of the ocean there can be no cause for quarrel.'

'Well what do you propose, then, that we ought to just sit and smile at them until they do manage to kill Laurence?' Granby demanded, growing angry in his turn. 'I suppose that would suit you just as well; one less person to object to your handing Temeraire over to them, and the Corps can go hang for all you care.'

Hammond wheeled round on him. 'My first care is for our country, and not for any one man or dragon, as yours ought to be if you had any proper sense of duty—'

'That is quite enough, gentlemen,' Laurence cut in. 'Our first duty is to establish a secure peace with China, and our first hope must be to achieve it without the loss of Temeraire's strength; on either score there can be no dispute.'

'Then neither duty nor hope will be advanced by this course of action,' Hammond snapped. 'If you did manage to find any evidence, what do you imagine could be done? Do you think we are going to put Prince Yongxing in chains?'

He stopped and collected himself for a moment. 'I see no reason, no evidence whatsoever, to suggest Feng Li was not acting alone. You say the first attack came after the New Year; you might well have offended him at the feast unknowingly. He might have been a fanatic angered by your possession of Temeraire, or simply mad; or you might be mistaken entirely. Indeed, that seems to me the most likely – both incidents in such dim, confused conditions; the first under the influence of strong drink, the second in the midst of the storm—'

'For the love of Christ,' Granby said rudely, making Hammond stare. 'And Feng Li was shoving Laurence down hatchways and trying to knock his head in for some perfectly good reason, of course.'

Laurence himself had been momentarily bereft of speech at this offensive suggestion. 'If, sir, any of your suppositions are true, then any investigation would certainly reveal as much. Feng Li could not have concealed lunacy or such zealotry from all his countrymen, as he could from us; if I had offended him surely he would have spoken of it.'

'And in ascertaining as much, this investigation would only require offering a profound insult to the Emperor's brother, who may determine our success or failure in Peking,' Hammond said. 'Not only will I not abet it, sir, I absolutely forbid it; and if you make any such ill-advised, reckless attempt, I will do my very best to convince the captain of the ship that it is his duty to the King to confine you.'

This naturally ended the discussion, so far as Hammond was concerned in it; but Granby came back after closing the door behind him, with more force than strictly necessary. 'I don't know that I have ever been more tempted to push a fellow's nose in for him. Laurence, Temeraire could translate for us, surely, if we brought the fellows up to him.'

Laurence shook his head and went for the decanter; he was roused and knew it, and he did not immediately rely upon his own judgement. He gave Granby a glass, took his own to the stern lockers, and sat there drinking and looking out at the ocean: a steady dark swell of five feet, no more, rolling against her larboard quarter.

He set the glass aside at last. 'No: I am afraid we must think better of it, John. Little as I like Hammond's mode of address, I cannot say that he is wrong. Only think, if we did offend him and the Emperor with such an investigation, and yet found no evidence, or worse yet some rational explanation—'

'—we could say hail and farewell to any chance of keeping Temeraire,' Granby finished for him, with resignation. 'Well, I suppose you are right and we will have to lump it for now; but I am damned if I like it.'

Temeraire took a still dimmer view of this resolution. 'I do not care if we do not have any proof,' he said angrily. 'I am not going to sit and wait for him to kill you. The next time he comes out on deck I will kill *him*, instead, and that will put an end to it.'

'No, Temeraire, you cannot!' Laurence said, appalled.

'I am perfectly sure I can,' Temeraire disagreed. 'I suppose he might not come out on deck again,' he added, thoughtfully, 'but then I could always knock a hole through the stern windows and come at him that way. Or perhaps we could throw in a bomb after him.'

'You *must* not,' Laurence amended hastily. 'Even had we proof, we could hardly move against him; it would be grounds for an immediate declaration of war.'

'If it would be so terrible to kill him, why is it not so

terrible for him to kill *you*?' Temeraire demanded. 'Why is he not afraid of our declaring war on him?'

'Without proper evidence, I am sure the Government would hardly take such a measure,' Laurence said; he was fairly certain the Government would not declare war *with* evidence, but that, he felt, was not the best argument for the moment.

'But we are not allowed to *get* evidence,' Temeraire said. 'And also I am not allowed to kill him, and we are supposed to be polite to him, and all of it for the sake of the Government. I am very tired of this Government, which I have never seen, and which is always insisting that I must do disagreeable things, and does no good to anybody.'

'All politics aside, we cannot be sure Prince Yongxing had anything to do with the matter,' Laurence said. 'There are a thousand unanswered questions: why he should even wish me dead, and why he would set a manservant on to do it, rather than one of his guards; and after all, Feng Li could have had some reason of his own of which we know nothing. We cannot be killing people only on suspicion, without evidence; that would be to commit murder ourselves. You could not be comfortable afterwards, I assure you.'

'But I could, too,' Temeraire muttered, and subsided into glowering.

To Laurence's great relief, Yongxing did not come back up on deck for several days after the incident, which served to let the first heat of Temeraire's temper cool, and when at last he did make another appearance, it was with no alteration of manner at all: he greeted Laurence with the same cool and distant civility, and proceeded to give Temeraire another recitation of poetry, which after a little while caught Temeraire's interest, despite himself, and made him forget to keep glaring: he did not have a resentful nature. If Yongxing were conscious of any guilt whatsoever, it did not show in the slightest, and Laurence began to question his own judgement.

'I could easily have been mistaken,' he said unhappily, to

Granby and Temeraire, after Yongxing had quitted the deck again. 'I cannot find I remember the details anymore; and after all I was half-stunned with fatigue. Maybe the poor fellow only came up to try and help, and I am inventing things out of whole cloth; it seems more fantastic to me with every moment, that the Emperor of China's brother should be trying to have me assassinated, as though I were any threat to him, is absurd. I will end by agreeing with Hammond, and calling myself a drunkard and a fool.'

'Well, I'll call you neither,' Granby said. 'I can't make any sense of it myself, but the notion Feng Li just took a fancy to knock you on the head is all stuff. But we will just have to keep a guard on you, and hope this prince doesn't prove Hammond wrong.'

Chapter Ten

It was nearly three weeks more, passing wholly without incident, before they sighted the island of New Amsterdam: Temeraire delighted by the glistening heaps of seals, most sunbathing lazily upon the beaches and the more energetic coming to the ship to frolic in her wake. They were not shy of the sailors, nor even of the Marines who were inclined to use them for target practice, but when Temeraire descended into the water, they vanished away at once, and even those on the beach humped themselves sluggishly further away from the waterline.

Deserted, Temeraire swam about the ship in a disgruntled circle, then climbed back aboard: he had grown more adept at this manoeuvre with practice, and now barely set the *Allegiance* to bobbing. The seals gradually returned, and did not seem to object to him peering down at them more closely, though they dived deep again if he put his head too far into the water.

They had been carried southward by the storm nearly into the forties and had lost almost all their easting as well; a cost of more than a week's sailing. 'The one benefit is that I think the monsoon has set in, finally,' Riley said, consulting Laurence over his charts. 'From here, we can strike out for the Dutch East Indies directly; it will be a good month and a half without landfall, but I have sent the boats to the island, and with a

229

few days of sealing to add to what we already have, we should do nicely.'

The barrels of seal meat, salted down, stank profoundly; and two dozen more fresh carcasses were hung in meat-lockers from the catheads to keep them cool. The next day, out at sea again, the Chinese cooks butchered almost half of these on deck, throwing the heads, tails, and entrails overboard with shocking waste, and served Temeraire a heap of steaks, lightly seared. 'It is not bad, with a great deal of pepper, and perhaps more of those roasted onions,' he said after tasting, now grown particular.

Still as anxious to please as ever, they at once altered the dish to his liking. He then devoured the whole with pleasure and laid himself down for a long nap; wholly oblivious to the great disapproval of the ship's cook and quartermasters, and the crew in general. The cooks had not cleaned after themselves, and the upper deck was left nearly awash in blood; this having taken place in the afternoon, Riley did not see how he could ask the men to wash the decks a second time for the day. The smell was overpowering as Laurence sat down to dinner with him and the other senior officers, especially as the small windows were obliged to be kept shut to avoid the still more pungent smell of the remaining carcasses hanging outside.

Unhappily, Riley's cook had thought along the same lines as the Chinese cooks: the main dish upon the table was a beautifully golden pie, a week's worth of butter gone into the pastry along with the last of the fresh peas from Capetown, accompanied by a bowl of bubbling-hot gravy; but when cut into, the smell of the seal meat was too distinctly recognizable, and the entire table picked at their plates.

'It is no use,' Riley said, with a sigh, and scraped his serving back into the platter. 'Take it down to the midshipmen's mess, Jethson, and let them have it; it would be a pity to waste.' They all followed suit and made do with the remaining dishes, but it created a sad vacancy on the table, and as the steward carried away the platter, he could be heard through the door, talking loudly of 'foreigners what don't know how to behave civilized, and spoil people's appetite'.

They were passing around the bottle for consolation when the ship gave a queer jerk, a small hop in the water unlike anything Laurence had ever felt. Riley was already going to the door when Purbeck said suddenly, 'Look there,' and pointed out the window: the chain of the meat-locker was dangling loose, and the cage was gone.

They all stared; then a confusion of yells and screams erupted on deck, and the ship yawed abruptly to starboard, with the gunshot sound of cracking wood. Riley rushed out, the rest of them hard on his heels. As Laurence went up the ladder-way another crash shook her; he slipped down four rungs, and nearly knocked Granby off the ladder.

They popped out onto the deck jack-in-the-box fashion, all of them together; a bloody leg with buckled shoe and silk stocking was lying across the larboard gangway, all that was left of Reynolds, who had been the midshipman on duty, and two more bodies had fetched up against a splintered half-moon gap in the railing, apparently bludgeoned to death. On the dragondeck, Temeraire was sitting up on his haunches, looking around wildly; the other men on deck were leaping up into the rigging or scrambling for the forward ladder-way, struggling against the midshipmen who were trying to come up.

'Run up the colours,' Riley said, shouting over the noise, even as he leaped to try and grapple with the double-wheel, calling several other sailors to come and help him; Basson, the coxswain, was nowhere to be seen, and the ship was still drifting off her course. She was moving steadily, so they had not grounded on a reef, and there was no sign of any other ship, the horizon clear all around. 'Beat to quarters.'

The drumroll started and drowned out any hope of learning what was going on, but it was the best means of getting the panicking men back into order, the most urgent matter of business. 'Mr. Garnett, get the boats over the side, if you please,' Purbeck called loudly, striding out to the middle of the rail, fixing on his hat; he had as usual worn his best coat to dinner, and made a tall, official figure. 'Griggs, Masterson, what do you mean by this?' he said, addressing a couple of the hands peering down fearfully from the tops. 'Your grog is stopped for a week; get down and go along to your guns.'

Laurence pushed forward along the gangway, forcing a lane against the men now running to their proper places: one of the Marines hopping past, trying to pull on a freshly-blacked boot, his hands greasy and slipping on the leather; the gun crews for the aft carronades scrambling over one another. 'Laurence, Laurence, what is it?' Temeraire called, seeing him. 'I was asleep; what has happened?'

The *Allegiance* rocked abruptly over to one side, and Laurence was thrown against the railing; on the far side of the ship, a great jet of water fountained up and came splashing down upon the deck, and a monstrous draconic head lifted up above the railing: enormous, luridly orange eyes set behind a rounded snout, with ridges of webbing tangled with long trailers of black seaweed. An arm was still dangling from the creature's mouth, limply; it opened its maw and threw its head back with a jerk, swallowing the rest: its teeth were washed bright red with blood.

Riley called for the starboard broadside, and on deck Purbeck was drawing three of the gun crews together around one of the carronades: he meant them to point it at the creature directly. They were casting loose its tackles, the strongest men blocking the wheels; all sweating and utterly silent but for low grunting, working as fast as they could, greenish-pale; the forty-two-pounder could not be easily handled.

'Fire, fire, you fucking yellow-arsed millers!' Macready yelling hoarsely in the tops, already reloading his own gun. The other Marines belatedly set off a ragged volley, but the bullets did not penetrate; the serpentine neck was clad in thickly overlapping scales, blue and silver-gilt. The sea-serpent made a low croaking noise and lunged at the deck, striking two men flat and seizing another in its mouth; Doyle's shrieks could be heard even from within, his legs kicking frantically.

'No!' Temeraire said. 'Stop; arrêtez!' and followed this with a string of words in Chinese also; the serpent looked at him incuriously, with no sign of understanding, and bit down: Doyle's legs fell abruptly back to the deck, severed, blood spurting briefly in mid-air before they struck.

Temeraire held quite motionless with staring horror, his eyes fixed on the serpent's crunching jaws and his ruff completely flattened against his neck; Laurence shouted his name, and he came alive again. The fore- and mainmasts lay between him and the sea-serpent; he could not come at the creature directly, so he leaped off the bow and winged around the ship in a tight circle to come up behind it.

The sea-serpent's head turned to follow his movement, rising higher out of the water; it lay spindly forelegs on the *Allegiance*'s railing as it lifted itself out, webbing stretched between unnaturally long taloned fingers. Its body was much narrower than Temeraire's, thickening only slightly along its length, but in size its head was larger, with eyes larger than dinner platters, terrible in their unblinking, dull savagery.

Temeraire dived; his talons skidded along the silver hide, but he managed to find purchase by putting his forearms nearly around the body: despite the serpent's length, it was narrow enough for him to grasp. The serpent croaked again, gurgling deep in its throat, and clung to the *Allegiance*, the sagging jowly folds of flesh along its throat working with its cries. Temeraire set himself and hauled back, wings beating the air furiously: the ship leaned dangerously under their combined force, and yells could be heard from the hatchways, where water was coming in through the lowest gunports.

'Temeraire, cut loose,' Laurence shouted. 'She will overset.'

Temeraire was forced to let go; the serpent seemed to only

have a mind to get away from him now: it crawled forward onto the ship, knocking askew the mainsail yards and tearing the rigging as it came, head weaving from side to side. Laurence saw his own reflection, weirdly elongated, in the black pupil; then the serpent blinked sideways, a thick translucent sheath of skin sliding over the orb, and moved on past; Granby was pulling him back towards the ladder-way.

The creature's body was immensely long; its head and forelegs vanished beneath the waves on the other side of the ship, and its hindquarters had not yet emerged, the scales shading to deeper blue and purple iridescence as the length of it kept coming, undulating onwards. Laurence had never seen one even a tenth the size; the Atlantic serpents reached no more than twelve feet even in the warm waters off the coast of Brazil, and those in the Pacific dived when ships drew near, rarely seen as anything more than fins breaking the water.

The master's mate Sackler was coming up the ladder-way, panting, with a big sliver spade, seven inches wide, hastily tied onto a spar: he had been first mate on a South Seas whaler before being pressed. 'Sir, sir; tell them to 'ware; oh Christ, it'll loop us,' he yelled up, seeing Laurence through the opening, even as he threw the spade onto the deck and hauled himself out after.

With the reminder, Laurence remembered on occasion seeing a swordfish or tunny hauled up with a sea-serpent wrapped about it, strangling: it was their favourite means of seizing prey. Riley had heard the warning also; he was calling for axes, swords. Laurence seized one from the first basket handed up the ladder-way, and began chopping next to a dozen other men. But the body moved on without stopping; they made some cuts into pale, grey-white blubber, but did not even reach flesh, nowhere near cutting through.

'The head, watch for the head,' Sackler said, standing at the rail with the cutting-spade ready, hands clenched and shifting anxiously around the pole; Laurence handed off his axe and went to try and give Temeraire some direction: he was still hovering above in frustration, unable to grapple with the sea-serpent while it was so entangled with the ship's masts and rigging.

The sea-serpent's head broke the water again, on the same side, just as Sackler had warned, and the coils of the body began to draw tight; the *Allegiance* groaned, and the railing cracked and began to give way under the pressure.

Purbeck had the gun positioned and ready. 'Steady, men; wait for the downroll.'

'Wait, wait!' Temeraire called: Laurence could not see why.

Purbeck ignored him and called out, 'Fire!' The carronade roared, and the shot went flying across the water, struck the sea-serpent on the neck, and flew onward before sinking. The creature's head was knocked sideways by the impact, and a burning smell of cooked meat rose; but the blow was not mortal: it only gargled in pain and began to tighten still further.

Purbeck never flinched, steady though the serpent's body was scarcely half a foot away from him now. 'Spunge your gun,' he said as soon as the smoke had died away, setting the men on another round. But it would be another three minutes at least before they could fire again, hampered by the awkward position of the gun and the confusion of three gun crews flung together.

Abruptly a section of the starboard railing just by the gun burst under the pressure into great jagged splinters, as deadly as those scattered by cannon-fire. One stabbed Purbeck deep in the flesh of the arm, purple staining his coat sleeve instantly. Chervins threw up his arms, gargling around the shard in his throat, and slumped over the gun; Dyfydd hauled his body off onto the floor, never flagging despite the splinter stuck right through his jaw, the other end poking out the underside of his chin and dripping blood.

Temeraire was still hovering back and forth near the serpent's head, growling at it. He had not roared, perhaps afraid of doing so close to the *Allegiance*: a wave like that which had destroyed the *Valérie* would sink them just as easily as the serpent itself. Laurence was on the verge of ordering him to take the risk regardless: the men were hacking frantically, but the tough hide was resisting them, and in any moment the *Allegiance* might be broken beyond repair: if her futtocks cracked, or worse the keel bent, they might never be able to bring her into port again.

But before he could call, Temeraire suddenly gave a low frustrated cry, beat up into the air, and folded his wings shut: he fell like a stone, claws outstretched, and struck the sea-serpent's head directly, driving it below the water's surface. His momentum drove him beneath the waves also, and a deep purpling cloud of blood filled the water. 'Temeraire!' Laurence cried, scrambling heedless over the shuddering, jerking body of the serpent, half-crawling and half-running along the length of the blood-slippery deck; he climbed out over the rail and onto the mainmast chains, while Granby grabbed at him and missed.

He kicked his boots off into the water, no very coherent plan in mind; he could swim only a little, and he had no knife or gun. Granby was trying to climb out to join him, but could not keep his feet with the ship sawing to and fro like a nursery rocking-horse. Abruptly a great shiver travelled in reverse along the silver-grey length of the serpent's body that was all which was visible; its hindquarters and tail surfaced in a convulsive leap, then fell back into the water with a tremendous splash; and it lay still at last.

Temeraire popped back out through the surface like a cork, bouncing partway out of the water and splashing down again: he coughed and spluttered, and spat: there was blood all over his jaws. 'I think she is dead,' he said, between his wheezing gasps for air, and slowly paddled himself to the ship's side: he did not climb aboard, but leaned against the *Allegiance*, breathing deeply and relying on his native buoyancy to keep him afloat. Laurence clambered over to him on the fretwork like a boy, and perched there stroking him, as much for his own comfort as Temeraire's.

Temeraire being too weary to climb back aboard at once, Laurence took one of the small boats and pulled Keynes around to inspect him for any signs of injury. There were some scratches, in one wound an ugly, saw-edged tooth lodged, but none severe; Keynes however listened to Temeraire's chest again and looked grave, and opined that some water had entered the lungs.

With much encouragement from Laurence, Temeraire pulled himself back aboard; the *Allegiance* sagged more than usual, both from his fatigue and her own state of disarray, but he eventually managed to climb back aboard, though causing some fresh damage to the railing. Not even Lord Purbeck, devoted as he was to the ship's appearance, begrudged Temeraire the cracked banisters; indeed a tired but wholehearted cheer went up as he thumped down at last.

'Put your head down over the side,' Keynes said, once Temeraire was fairly established on the deck; he groaned a little, wanting only to sleep, but obeyed. After leaning precariously far, and complaining in a stifled voice that he was growing dizzy, he did manage to cough up some quantity of salt water. Having satisfied Keynes, he shuffled himself slowly backwards until his position on the deck was more secure, and curled into a heap.

'Will you have something to eat?' Laurence said. 'Something fresh; a sheep? I will have them prepare it for you however you like.'

'No, Laurence, I cannot eat anything, not at all,' Temeraire said, muffled, his head hidden under his wing and a shudder visible between his shoulderblades. 'Pray let them take her away.'

The body of the sea-serpent still lay sprawled across the *Allegiance*: the head had bobbed to the surface on the larboard side, and now the whole impressive extent of it could be seen.

Riley sent men in boats to measure it from nose to tail: more than 250 feet, at least twice the length of the largest Regal Copper Laurence had ever heard of, which had rendered it thus capable of encircling the whole vessel, though its body was less than twenty feet in diameter.

'Kiao, a sea-dragon,' Sun Kai called it, having come up on deck to see what had happened; he informed them that there were similar creatures in the China Sea, though ordinarily smaller.

No one suggested eating it. After the measurements had been done, and the Chinese poet, also something of an artist, permitted to render an illustration, the axes were applied to once more. Sackler led the effort with practised strokes of the cutting-spade, and Pratt severed the thick armoured column of the spine with three heavy blows. After this its own weight and the slow forward motion of the *Allegiance* did the rest of the work almost at once: the remaining flesh and hide parted with a sound like tearing fabric, and its separate halves slid away off the opposite sides.

There was already a great deal of activity in the waters around the body: sharks tearing at the head, and other fishes also; now an increasingly furious struggle arose around the hacked and bloody ends of the two halves. 'Let us get underway as best we can,' Riley said to Purbeck; though the main and mizzen sails and rigging had been badly mauled, the foremast and its rigging were untouched but for a few tangled ropes, and they managed to get a small spread of sail before the wind.

They left the corpse drifting on the surface behind them and got underway; in an hour or so it was little more than a silvery line on the water. Already the deck had been washed down, freshly scrubbed and sanded with holystone, and sluiced clean again, water pumped up with great enthusiasm, and the carpenter and his mates were engaged in cutting a couple of spars to replace the mainsail and mizzen topsail yards.

The sails had suffered greatly: spare sailcloth had to be brought up from stores, and this was found to have been rat-chewed, to Riley's fury. Some hurried patchwork was done, but the sun was setting, and the fresh cordage could not be rigged until morning. The men were let go by watches to supper, and then to sleep without the usual inspection.

Still barefoot, Laurence took some coffee and ship's biscuit when Roland brought it him, but stayed by Temeraire, who remained subdued and without appetite. Laurence tried to coax him out of the low spirits, worried that perhaps he had taken some deeper injury, not immediately apparent, but Temeraire said dully, 'No, I am not hurt at all, nor sick; I am perfectly well.'

'Then what has distressed you so?' Laurence at length asked, tentatively. 'You did so very well today, and saved the ship.'

'All I did was kill her; I do not see it is anything to be so proud of,' Temeraire said. 'She was not an enemy, fighting us for some cause; I think she only came because she was hungry, and then I suppose we frightened her, with the shooting, and that is why she attacked us; I wish I could have made her understand and leave.'

Laurence stared: it had not occurred to him that Temeraire might not have viewed the sea-serpent as the monstrous creature it seemed to him. 'Temeraire, you cannot think that beast anything like a dragon,' he said. 'It had no speech, nor intelligence; I dare say you are right that it came looking for food, but any animal can hunt.'

'Why should you say such things?' Temeraire said. 'You mean that she did not speak English, or French, or Chinese, but she was an ocean creature; how ought she have learned any human languages, if she was not tended by people in the shell? I would not understand them myself otherwise, but that would not mean I did not have intelligence.'

'But surely you must have seen she was quite without reason,' Laurence said. 'She ate four of the crew, and killed six others: men, not seals, and plainly not dumb beasts; if she

239

were intelligent, it would have been inhuman, uncivilized,' he amended, stumbling over his choice of words. 'No one has ever been able to tame a sea-serpent; even the Chinese do not say differently.'

'You may as well say, that if a creature will not serve people, and learn their habits, it is not intelligent, and had just as well be killed,' Temeraire said, his ruff quivering; he had lifted his head, stirred-up.

'Not at all,' Laurence said, trying to think of how he could give comfort; to him the lack of sentience in the creature's eyes had been wholly obvious. 'I am saying only that if they were intelligent, they would be able to be learn to communicate, and we would have heard of it. After all, many dragons do not choose to take on a handler, and refuse to speak with men at all; it does not happen so very often, but it does, and no one thinks dragons unintelligent for it,' he added, thinking he had chanced on a happy example.

'But what happens to them, if they do?' Temeraire said. 'What should happen to me, if I were to refuse to obey? I do not mean a single order; what if I did not wish to fight in the Corps at all.'

So far this had all been general; the suddenly narrower question startled Laurence, giving the conversation a more ominous cast. Fortunately, there was little work to be done with so light a spread of sail: the sailors were gathered on the forecastle, gambling with their grog rations and intent on their game of dice; the handful of aviators remaining on duty were talking together softly at the rail. There was no one likely to overhear, for which Laurence was grateful: others might misunderstand, and think Temeraire unwilling, even disloyal in some way. For his own part he could not believe there was any real risk of Temeraire's choosing to leave the Corps and all his friends; he tried to answer calmly. 'Feral dragons are housed in the breeding grounds, very comfortably. If you chose, you might live there also; there is a large

one in the north of Wales, on Cardigan Bay, which I understand is very beautiful.'

'And if I did not care to live there, but wished to go somewhere else?'

'But how would you eat?' Laurence said. 'Herds which could
feed a dragon would be raised by men, and their property.'

'If men have penned up all the animals and left none wild,
I cannot think it reasonable of them to complain if I take one
now and again,' Temeraire said. 'But even making such
allowance, I could hunt for fish. What if I chose to live near
Dover, and fly as I liked, and eat fish, and did not bother
anyone's herds; should I be allowed?'

Too late Laurence saw he had gotten himself onto dangerous
ground, and bitterly regretted having led the conversation in
this direction. He knew perfectly well Temeraire would be
allowed nothing of the sort. People would be terrified at the
notion of a dragon living loose among them, no matter how
peaceable the dragon might be. The objections to such a scheme
would be many and reasonable, and yet of course from
Temeraire's perspective the denial would of course represent
an unjust curtailment of his liberties. Laurence could not think
how to reply without aggravating his sense of injury.

Temeraire took his silence for the answer it was, and nodded.
'If I would not go, I should be put in chains again, and
dragged off,' he said. 'I would be forced to go to the breeding
grounds, and if I tried to leave, I would not be allowed; and
the same for any other dragon. So it seems to me,' he added,
grimly, a suggestion of a low growling anger beneath his voice,
'that we are just like slaves; only there are fewer of us, and
we are much bigger and dangerous, so we are treated generously where they are treated cruelly; but we are still not free.'

'Good God, that is not so,' Laurence said, standing up:
appalled, dismayed, at his own blindness as much as the
remark. Small wonder if Temeraire had flinched from the
storm-chains, if such a train of thought had been working

through his imagination before now, and Laurence did not believe that it could be the result solely of the recent battle.

'No, it is not so; wholly unreasonable,' Laurence repeated; he knew himself inadequate to debate with Temeraire on most philosophical grounds, but the notion was inherently absurd, and he felt he must be able to convince Temeraire of the fact, if only he could find the words. 'It is as much to say that I am a slave, because I am expected to obey the orders of the Admiralty: if I refused, I would be dismissed the service and very likely hanged; that does not mean I am a slave.'

'But you have chosen to be in the Navy and the Corps,' Temeraire said. 'You might resign, if you wished, and go elsewhere.'

'Yes, but then I should have to find some other profession to support myself, if I did not have enough capital to live off the interest. And indeed, if you did not wish to be in the Corps, I have enough to purchase an estate, somewhere in the north, or perhaps Ireland, and stock the grounds. You might live there exactly as you liked, and no one could object.' Laurence breathed again as Temeraire mulled this over; the militant light had faded a little from his eyes, and gradually his tail ceased its restless mid-air twitching and coiled again into a neatly spiralled heap upon the deck, the curving horns of his ruff laying more easily against his neck.

Eight bells rang softly, and the sailors left their dice game, the new watch coming on deck to put out the last handful of lights. Ferris came up the dragondeck stairs, yawning, with a handful of fresh crewmen still rubbing the sleep from their eyes; Baylesworth led the earlier watch below, the men saying, 'Good night, sir; good night, Temeraire,' as they went by, many of them patting Temeraire's flank.

'Good night, gentlemen,' Laurence answered, and Temeraire gave a low warm rumble.

'The men may sleep on deck if they like, Mr. Tripp,' Purbeck was saying, his voice carrying along from the stern. The ship's night settled upon her, the men gladly dropping along the forecastle, heads pillowed on coiled hawsers and rolled-up shirts; all darkness but for the solitary stern lantern, winking far at the other end of the ship, and the starlight; there was no moon, but the Magellanic Clouds were particularly bright, and the long cloudy mass of the Milky Way. Presently silence fell; the aviators also had disposed themselves along the larboard railing, and they were again as nearly alone as they might be on board. Laurence had sat down once more, leaning against Temeraire's side; there was a waiting quality to Temeraire's silence.

And at length Temeraire said, 'But if you did,' as if there had been no break in the conversation; although not with the same heat of anger as before. 'If you purchased an estate for me, that would still be your doing, and not mine. You love me, and would do anything you could to ensure my happiness; but what of a dragon like poor Levitas, with a captain of Rankin's sort, who did not care for his comfort? I do not understand what precisely capital is, but I am sure I have none of my own, nor any way of getting it.'

He was at least not so violently distressed as before, but rather now sounded weary, and a little sad. Laurence said, 'You do have your jewels, you know; the pendant alone is worth some ten thousand pounds, and it was a clear gift; no one could dispute that it is your own property in law.'

Temeraire bent his head to inspect the piece of jewellery, the breastplate which Laurence had purchased for him with much of the prize-money for the *Amitie*, the frigate which had carried his egg. The platinum had suffered some small dents and scratches in the course of the journey, which remained because Temeraire would not suffer to be parted from it long enough for them to be sanded out, but the pearl and sapphires were as brilliant as ever. 'So is that what capital is, then? Jewels? No wonder it is so nice. But Laurence, that makes no difference; it was still your present, after all, not something which I won myself.'

'I suppose no one has ever thought of offering dragons a salary, or prize-money. It is no lack of respect, I promise you; only that money does not seem to be of much use to dragons.'

'It is of no use, because we are not permitted to go anywhere, or do as we like, and so have nothing to spend it upon,' Temeraire said. 'If I had money, I am sure I still could not go to a shop and buy more jewels, or books; we are even chided for taking our food out of the pen when it suits us.'

'But it is not because you are a slave that you cannot go where you like, but because people would naturally be disturbed by it, and the public good must be consulted,' Laurence said. 'It would do you no good to go into town and to a shop if the keeper had fled before you came.'

'It is not fair that we should be thus restricted by others' fears, when we have not done anything wrong; you must see it is so, Laurence.'

'No, it is not just,' Laurence said, reluctantly. 'But people will be afraid of dragons no matter how they are told it is safe; it is plain human nature, foolish as it may be, and there is no managing around it. I am very sorry, my dear.' He laid his hand on Temeraire's side. 'I wish I had better answers for your objections; I can only add to these, that whatever inconveniences society may impose upon you, I would no more consider you a slave than myself, and I will always be glad to serve you in overcoming these as I may.'

Temeraire huffed out a low sigh, but nudged Laurence affectionately and drew a wing down more closely about him; he said no more on the subject, but instead asked for the latest book, a French translation of the *Arabian Nights*, which they had found in Capetown. Laurence was glad enough to be allowed to thus escape, but uneasy: he did not think he had been very successful in the task of reconciling Temeraire to a situation with which Laurence had always thought him well-satisfied.

III

Chapter Eleven

Allegiance, Macao

Jane, I must ask you to forgive the long gap in this Letter, and the few hasty Words that are all by which I can amend the same now. I have not had Leisure to take up my pen these three weeks – since we passed out of Banka Strait we have been much afflicted by malarial Fevers. I have escaped sickness myself, and most of my men, for which Keynes opines we must be grateful to Temeraire, believing that the heat of his body in some wise dispels the Miasmas which cause the ague, and our close association thus affords some protection.

But we have been spared only to increase of Labour: Captain Riley has been confined to his bed since almost the very first, and Lord Purbeck falling ill, I have stood watch in turn with the ship's third and fourth lieutenants, Franks and Beckett. Both are willing young men, and Franks does his best, but is by no means yet prepared for the Duty of overseeing so vast a Ship as the *Allegiance*, nor to maintain discipline among her Crew – stammers, I am sorry to say, which explains his seeming Rudeness at table, which I had earlier remarked upon.

This being summer, and Canton proper barred to

Westerners, we will put in at Macao tomorrow morning, where the ship's surgeon hopes to find Jesuit's bark to replenish our supply, and I some British merchantman, here out of season, to bear this home to you and to England. This will be my last Opportunity, as by special dispensation from Prince Yongxing we have Permission to continue on northwards to the Gulf of Zhi-Li, so we may reach Peking through Tien-sing. The savings of time will be enormous, but as no Western ships are permitted north of Canton ordinarily, we cannot hope to find any British vessels once we have left port.

We have passed three French merchantmen already in our Approach, more than I had been used to see in this part of the World, though it has been some seven years since the occasion of my last visit to Canton, and foreign Vessels of all kinds are more numerous than formerly. At the present hour, a sometimes obscuring Fog lies over the harbour, and impedes the view of my glass, so I cannot be certain, but I fear there may also be a Man-of-War, though perhaps Dutch rather than French; certainly it is not one of our own. The *Allegiance* is of course in no direct danger, being on a wholly different Scale and under the Protection of the Imperial Crown, which the French cannot dare to slight in these Waters, but we fear that the French may have some Embassy of their own in train, which must naturally have or shortly form the Design of disrupting our own Mission.

On the subject of my earlier Suspicions, I can say nothing more. No further Attempts have been made, at least, though our sadly reduced Numbers would have made easier any such stroke, and I begin to hope that Feng Li acted from some inscrutable motive of his own, and not at the Behest of another.

The Bell has rung – I must go on Deck. Allow me to

send with this all my Affection and Respect, and believe
me always,
    Yr. obdt. srvt,
    Wm. Laurence
    June 16, 1806

The fog persisted through the night, lingering as the *Allegiance*
made her final approach to Macao harbour. The long curving
stretch of sand, circled by tidy, square buildings in the
Portuguese style and a neatly planted row of saplings, had all
the comfort of familiarity, and most of the junks having their
sails still furled might almost have been small dinghies at
anchor in Funchal or Portsmouth roads. Even the softly eroded,
green-clad mountains revealed as the grey fog trailed away
would not have been out of place in any Mediterranean port.

Temeraire had been perched up on his hindquarters with
eager anticipation; now he gave up looking and lowered
himself to the deck in dissatisfaction. 'Why, it does not look
at all different,' he said, cast down. 'I do not see any other
dragons, either.'

The *Allegiance* herself, coming in off the ocean, was under
heavier cover, and her shape was not initially clear to those on
shore, revealed only as the sluggishly creeping sun burned off
the mists and she came further into the harbour, a breath of
wind pushing the fog off her bows. Then a nearly violent notice
was taken: Laurence had put in at the colony before, and
expected some bustle, perhaps exaggerated by the immense size
of the ship, quite unknown in these waters, but was taken aback
by the noise which arose almost explosively from the shore.

'Tien-lung, tien-lung!' The cry carried across the water, and
many of the smaller junks, more nimble, came bounding
across the water to meet them, crowding each other so closely
they often bumped each other's hulls and the *Allegiance* herself,
with all the hooting and shouting the crew could do to try
and fend them off.

More boats were being launched from the shore even as they let go the anchor, with much caution necessitated by their unwelcome close company. Laurence was startled to see Chinese women coming down to the shore in their queer, mincing gait, some in elaborate and elegant dress, with small children and even infants in tow; and cramming themselves aboard any junk that had room to spare with no care for their garments. Fortunately the wind was not strong and the current gentle, or the wallowing, overloaded vessels would certainly have been overset with a terrible loss of life. As it were they somehow made their way near the *Allegiance*, and as they drew near, the women seized their children and held them up over their heads, almost waving them in their direction.

'What on earth do they mean by it?' Laurence had never seen such an exhibition: by all his prior experience the Chinese women were exceedingly careful to seclude themselves from Western gaze, and he had not even known so many lived in Macao at all. Their antics were drawing the curious attention of the Westerners of the port also now, both along the shore and upon the decks of the other ships with which they shared the harbour. Laurence saw with sinking feelings that his previous night's assessment had not been incorrect: indeed rather short of the mark, for there were two French warships in the harbour, both handsome and trim, one a two-decker of some sixty-four guns and the smaller a heavy frigate of forty-eight.

Temeraire had been observing with a great deal of interest, snorting in amusement at some of the infants, who looked very ridiculous in their heavily-embroidered gowns, like sausages in silk and gold thread, and mostly wailing unhappily at being dangled in mid-air. 'I will ask them,' he said, and bent over the railing to address one of the more energetic women, who had actually knocked over a rival to secure a place at the boat's edge for herself and her offspring, a fat boy of maybe two who somehow managed to bear a resigned, phlegmatic expression on his round-cheeked face despite being thrust nearly into Temeraire's teeth.

He blinked at her reply, and settled back on his haunches. 'I am not certain, because she does not sound quite the same,' he said, 'but I think she says they are here to see me.' Affecting unconcern, he turned his head and with what he evidently thought were covert motions rubbed at his hide with his nose, polishing away imaginary stains, and further indulged his vanity by arranging himself to best advantage, his head poised high and his wings shaken out and folded more loosely against his body. His ruff was standing broadly out in excitement.

'It is good luck to see a Celestial.' Yongxing seemed to think this perfectly obvious, when applied to for some additional explanation. 'They would never have a chance to see one otherwise; they are only merchants.'

He turned from the spectacle dismissively. 'We with Liu Bao and Sun Kai will be going on to Guangzhou to speak with the superintendant and the viceroy, and to send word of our arrival to the Emperor,' he said, using the Chinese name for Canton, and waited expectantly; so that Laurence had perforce to offer him the use of the ship's barge for the purpose.

'I beg you will allow me to remind you, your Highness, we may confidently expect to reach Tien-sing in three weeks' time, so you may consider whether to hold any communications for the capital.' Laurence meant only to save him some effort; the distance was certainly better than a thousand miles.

But Yongxing very energetically made clear that he viewed this suggestion as nearly scandalous in its neglect of due respect to the throne, and Laurence was forced to apologize for having made it, excusing himself by a lack of knowledge of local custom. Yongxing was not mollified; in the end Laurence was glad to pack him and the other two envoys off at the cost of the services of the barge, though it left him and Hammond only the jollyboat to convey them to their own

251

rendezvous ashore: the ship's launch was already engaged in ferrying over fresh supplies of water and livestock.

'Is there anything I can bring you for your relief, Tom?' Laurence asked, putting his head into Riley's cabin.

Riley lifted his head from the pillows where he lay before the windows and waved a weak, yellow-tinged hand. 'I am a good deal better. But I would not say no to a good port, if you can find a decent bottle in the place; I think my mouth has been turned down forever from the godawful quinine.'

Reassured, Laurence went to take his leave of Temeraire, who had managed to coax the ensigns and runners into scrubbing him down, quite unnecessarily. The Chinese visitors were grown more ambitious, and had begun to throw gifts of flowers aboard, and other things also, less innocuous. Running up to Laurence very pale, Lieutenant Franks forgot to stutter in his alarm. 'Sir, they are throwing burning incense onto the ship, pray, pray make them stop.'

Laurence climbed up to the dragondeck. 'Temeraire, will you please tell them nothing lit can be thrown at the ship. Roland, Dyer, mind what they throw, and if you see anything else that may carry a risk of fire, throw it back over at once. I hope they have better sense than to try setting off crackers,' he added, without much confidence.

'I will stop them if they do,' Temeraire promised. 'You will see if there is someplace I can come ashore?'

'I will, but I cannot hold out much hope; the entire territory is scarcely four miles square, and thoroughly built-up,' Laurence said. 'But at least we can fly over it, and perhaps even over Canton, if the mandarins do not object.'

The English Factory was built facing directly onto the main beach, so there was no difficulty in finding it; indeed, their attention drawn by the gathered crowd, the Company commissioners had sent a small welcoming party to await them on shore, led by a tall young man in the uniform of the East India Company's private service, with aggressive sideburns and a prominent aquiline nose, giving him a predatory look rather increased than diminished by the alert light in his eyes. 'Major Heretford, at your service,' he said, bowing. 'And may I say, sir, we are damned glad to see you,' he added, with a soldier's frankness, once they were indoors. 'Sixteen months; we had begun to think no notice would be taken of it at all.'

With an unpleasant shock Laurence was recalled to the memory of the seizure of the East India merchant ships by the Chinese, all the long months ago: preoccupied by his own concerns over Temeraire's status and distracted by the voyage, he had nearly forgotten the incident entirely; but of course it could hardly have been concealed from the men stationed here. They would have spent the intervening months on fire to answer the profound insult.

'No action has been taken, surely?' Hammond asked, with an anxiety that gave Laurence a fresh distaste for him; there was a quality of fear to it. 'It would of all things be most prejudicial.'

Heretford eyed him sidelong. 'No, the commissioners thought best under the circumstances to conciliate the Chinese, and await some more official word,' in a tone that left very little doubt of where his own inclinations would have led him.

Laurence could not but find him sympathetic, though in the ordinary course he did not think very highly of the Company's private forces. But Heretford looked intelligent and competent, and the handful of men under his command showed signs of good discipline: their weapons well-kept, and their uniforms crisp despite the nearly sopping heat.

The boardroom was shuttered against the heat of the climbing sun, with fans laid ready at their places to stir the moist, stifling air. Glasses of claret punch, cooled with ice from the cellars, were brought once the introductions had been completed. The commissioners were happy enough to take the post which Laurence had brought, and promised to see it conveyed back to England; this concluding the exchange of pleasantries, they launched a delicate but pointed inquiry after the aims of the mission.

'Naturally we are pleased to hear that Government has compensated Captains Mestis and Holt and Greggson, and the Company, but I cannot possibly overstate the damage which the incident has done to our entire operations.' Sir George Staunton spoke quietly, but forcefully for all that; he was the chief of the commissioners despite his relative youth by virtue of his long experience of the nation. As a boy of twelve, he had accompanied the Macartney embassy itself in his father's train, and was one of the few British men perfectly fluent in the language.

Staunton described for them several more instances of bad treatment, and went on to say, 'These are entirely characteristic, I am sorry to say. The insolence and rapacity of the administration has markedly increased, and towards us only; the Dutch and the French meet with no such treatment. Our complaints, which previously they treated with some degree of respect, are now summarily dismissed, and in fact only draw worse down upon us.'

'We have been almost daily fearing to be ordered out entirely,' Mr. Grothing-Pyle added to this; he was a portly man, his white hair somewhat disordered by the vigorous action of his fan. 'With no insult to Major Heretford or his men,' he nodded to the officer, 'we would be hard-pressed to withstand such a demand, and you can be sure the French would be happy to help the Chinese enforce it.'

'And to take our establishments for their own once we were expelled,' Staunton added, to a circle of nodding heads. 'The arrival of the *Allegiance* certainly puts us in a different position, vis-à-vis the possibility of resistance—'

Here Hammond stopped him. 'Sir, I must beg leave to interrupt you. There is no contemplation of taking the *Allegiance* into action against the Chinese Empire: none; you must put such a thought out of your minds entirely.' He spoke very decidedly, though he was certainly the youngest man at the table, except for Heretford; a palpable coolness resulted. Hammond paid no attention. 'Our first and foremost goal is to restore our nation to enough favour with the court to keep the Chinese from entering into an alliance with France. All other designs are insignificant by comparison.'

'Mr. Hammond,' Staunton said, 'I cannot believe there is any possibility of such an alliance; nor that it can be so great a threat as you seem to imagine. The Chinese Empire is no Western military power, impressive as their size and their ranks of dragons may be to the inexperienced eye,' Hammond flushed at this small jab, perhaps not unintentional, 'and they are militantly uninterested in European affairs. It is a matter of policy with them to affect even if not feel a lack of concern with what passes beyond their borders, engrained over centuries.'

'Their having gone to the lengths of dispatching Prince Yongxing to Britain must surely weigh with you, sir, as showing that a change in policy may be achieved, if the impetus be sufficient,' Hammond said coolly.

They argued the point and many others with increasing politeness, over the course of several hours. Laurence had a struggle to keep his attention on the conversation, liberally laced as it was with references to names and incidents and concerns of which he knew nothing: some local unrest among the peasants and the state of affairs in Thibet, where apparently some sort of outright rebellion was in progress; the trade deficit and the necessity of opening more Chinese markets; difficulties with the Inca over the South American route.

But little though Laurence felt able to form his own conclusions, the conversation served another purpose for him. He grew convinced that while Hammond was thoroughly informed, his view of the situation was in direct contradiction on virtually all points with the established opinions of the commissioners. In one instance, the question of the kowtow

255

ceremony was raised and treated by Hammond as inconsequential: naturally they would perform the full ritual of genuflection, and by so doing hopefully amend the insult given by Lord Macartney's refusal to do so in the previous embassy.

Staunton objected forcefully. 'Yielding on this point with no concessions in return can only further degrade our standing in their eyes. The refusal was not made without reason. The ceremony is meant for envoys of tributary states, vassals of the Chinese throne, and having objected to it on these grounds before, we cannot now perform it without appearing to give way to the outrageous treatment they have meted out to us. It would of all things be most prejudicial to our cause, as giving them encouragement to continue.'

'I can scarcely admit that anything could be more prejudicial to our cause, than to wilfully resist the customs of a powerful and ancient nation in their own territory, because they do not meet our own notions of etiquette,' Hammond said. 'Victory on such a point can only be won by the loss of every other, as proved by the complete failure of Lord Macartney's embassy.'

'I find I must remind you that the Portuguese prostrated themselves not only to the Emperor but to his portrait and letters, at every demand the mandarins made, and their embassy failed quite as thoroughly,' Staunton said.

Laurence did not like the notion of grovelling before any man, Emperor of China or no; but he thought it was not merely his own preferences which inclined him to Staunton's opinion on the matter. Abasement of such a degree could not help but provoke disgust even in a recipient who demanded the gesture, it seemed to him, and only lead to even more contemptuous treatment. He was seated on Staunton's left for dinner, and through their more casual conversation grew increasingly convinced of the man's good judgement; and all the more doubtful of Hammond's.

At length they took their leave and returned to the beach

to await the boat. 'This news about the French envoy worries me more than all the rest together,' Hammond said, more to himself than to Laurence. 'De Guignes is dangerous; how I wish Bonaparte had sent anyone else!'

Laurence made no response; he was unhappily conscious that his own sentiments were much the same towards Hammond himself, and he would gladly have exchanged the man if he could.

Prince Yongxing and his companions returned from their errand late the following day, but when applied to for permission to continue the journey, or even to withdraw from the harbour, he refused point-blank; insisting that the *Allegiance* should have to wait for further instructions. Whence these were to come, and when, he did not say; and in the meantime the local ships continued their pilgrimages even into the night, carrying great hanging paper lanterns in the bows to light their way.

Laurence struggled out of sleep very early the next morning to the sound of an altercation outside his door: Roland, sounding very fierce despite her clear, high treble, saying something in a mixture of English and Chinese, which she had begun to acquire from Temeraire. 'What is that damned noise there?' he called strongly.

She peered in through the door, which she held only a little ajar, wide enough for her eye and mouth; over her shoulder he could see one of the Chinese servants making impatient gestures, and trying to get at the doorknob. 'It is Huang, sir, he is making a fuss and says the prince wants you to come up to the deck at once, though I told him you had only gone to sleep after the middle watch.'

He sighed and rubbed his face. 'Very good, Roland; tell him I will come.' He was in no humour to be up; late in his evening's watch, another visiting boat piloted by a young man more entrepreneurial than skilled had been caught broadside by a wave. Her anchor, improperly set, had come flying up and struck the *Allegiance* from beneath, jabbing a substantial hole in her hold and soaking much of the newly-purchased grain. At the same time the little boat had overturned herself, and though the harbour was not distant, the passengers in their heavy silk garments could not make their own way to safety, but had to be fished out by lantern light. It had been a long and tiresome night, and he had been up watch and watch dealing with the mess before finally gaining his bed only in the small hours of the morning. He splashed his face with the tepid water in the basin and put on his coat with reluctance before going up to the deck.

Temeraire was talking with someone; Laurence had to look twice before he even realized that the other was in fact a dragon, like none he had ever seen before. 'Laurence, this is Lung Yu Ping,' Temeraire said, when Laurence had climbed up to the dragondeck. 'She has brought us the post.'

Facing her, Laurence found their heads were nearly on a level: she was smaller even than a horse, with a broad curving forehead and a long arrow-shaped muzzle, and an enormously deep chest rather along greyhound proportions. She could not have carried anyone on her back except a child, and wore no harness but a delicate collar of yellow silk and gold, from which hung a fine mesh like thin chainmail which covered her chest snugly, fixed to her forearms and talons by golden rings.

The mesh was washed with gold, striking against her pale green hide; her wings were a darker shade of green, and striped with narrow bands of gold. They were also unusual in appearance: narrow and tapered, and longer than she was; even folded upon her back, their long tips dragged along the ground behind her like a train.

When Temeraire had repeated the introductions in Chinese, the little dragon sat up on her haunches and bowed. Laurence bowed in return, amused to greet a dragon thus on an equal plane. The forms satisfied, she poked her head forward to inspect him more closely, leaning over to look him up and down on both sides with great interest; her eyes were very large and liquid, amber in colour, and thickly lidded.

Hammond was standing and talking with Sun Kai and Liu Bao, who were inspecting a curious letter, thick and with many seals, the black ink liberally interspersed with vermilion markings. Yongxing stood a little way apart, reading a second missive written in oddly large characters upon a long rolled sheet of paper; he did not share this letter, but rolled it shut again and put it away privately, and rejoined the other three.

Hammond bowed to them and came to translate the news for Laurence. 'We are directed to let the ship continue on to Tien-sing, while we come on ahead by air,' he said, 'and they insist we must leave at once.'

'Directed?' Laurence asked, in confusion. 'But I do not understand; where have these orders come from? We cannot have had word from Peking already; Prince Yongxing sent word only three days ago.'

Temeraire addressed a question to Ping, who tilted her head and replied in deep, unfeminine tones which came echoing from her barrel chest. 'She says she brought it from a relay station at Heyuan, which is 400 of something called *li* from here, and the flight is a little more than two hours,' he said. 'But I do not know what that means in terms of distance.'

'One mile is three li,' Hammond said, frowning as he tried to work it out; Laurence, quicker at figuring in his head, stared at her: if there was no exaggeration, that meant Yu Ping had covered better than 120 miles in her flight. At such a rate, with couriers flying in relays, the message could indeed have come from Peking, nearly two thousand miles distant; the idea was incredible.

Yongxing, overhearing, said impatiently, 'Our message is of highest priority, and travelled by Jade Dragons the entire route; of course we have received word back. We cannot delay

259

in this fashion when the Emperor has spoken. How quickly can you be ready to leave?'

Still staggered, Laurence collected himself and protested that he could not leave the *Allegiance* at present, but would have to wait until Riley was well enough to rise from his bed. In vain: Yongxing did not even have a chance to protest before Hammond was vociferously arguing his point. 'We cannot possibly begin by offending the Emperor,' he said. 'The *Allegiance* can certainly remain here in port until Captain Riley is recovered.'

'For God's sake, that will only worsen the situation,' Laurence said impatiently. 'Half the crew is already gone to fever; she cannot lose the other half to desertion.' But the argument was a compelling one, particularly once it had been seconded by Staunton, who had come across to the ship by prior arrangement to take breakfast with Laurence and Hammond.

'Whatever assistance Major Hereford and his men can give Captain Riley, I am happy to promise,' Staunton said. 'But I do agree; they stand very much on ceremony here, and neglect of the outward forms is as good as a deliberate insult: I beg you not to delay.'

With this encouragement, and after some consultation with Franks and Beckett, who with more courage than truth pronounced themselves prepared to handle the duty alone, and a visit to Riley belowdecks, Laurence at last yielded. 'After all, we are not at the docks anyway because of her draught, and we have enough fresh supplies by now that Franks can haul in the boats and keep all the men aboard,' Riley pointed out. 'We will be sadly held up behind you no matter what, but I am much better, and Purbeck also; we will press on as soon as we can, and rendezvous with you at Peking.'

But this only set off a fresh series of problems: the packing was already underway when Hammond's cautious inquiries determined that the Chinese invitation was by no means a general one. Laurence himself was from necessity accepted as an adjunct to Temeraire, Hammond as the King's representative only grudgingly permitted to come along, but the suggestion that Temeraire's crew should come along, riding in harness, was rejected with horror.

'I am not going anywhere without the crew along to guard Laurence,' Temeraire put in, hearing of the difficulty, and conveyed this to Yongxing directly in suspicious tones; for emphasis he settled himself on the deck with finality, his tail drawn about him, looking quite immovable. A compromise was shortly offered that Laurence should choose ten of his crew, to be conveyed by some other Chinese dragons whose dignity would be less outraged by performing the service.

'What use ten men will be in the middle of Peking, I should like to know,' Granby observed tartly, when Hammond brought this offer back to the cabin; he had not forgiven the diplomat for his refusal to investigate the attempt on Laurence's life.

'What use you imagine a hundred men would be, in the case of any real threat from the Imperial armies, I should like to know,' Hammond answered with equal sharpness. 'In any case, it is the best we can do; I had a great deal of work to gain their permission for so many.'

'Then we will have to manage.' Laurence scarcely even looked up; he was at the same time sorting through his clothing, and discarding those garments which had been too badly worn by the journey to be respectable. 'The more important point, so far as safety is concerned, is to make certain the *Allegiance* is brought to anchor within a distance which Temeraire can reach in a single flight, without difficulty. Sir,' he said, turning to Staunton, who had come down to sit with them, at Laurence's invitation, 'may I prevail upon you to accompany Captain Riley, if your duties will allow it? Our departure will at one stroke rob him of all interpreters, and the authority of the envoys; I am concerned for any difficulties which he may encounter on the journey north.'

'I am entirely at his service and yours,' Staunton said, inclining his head; Hammond did not look entirely satisfied, but he could not object under the circumstances, and Laurence was privately glad to have found this politic way of having Staunton's advice on hand, even if his arrival would be delayed.

Granby would naturally accompany him, and so Ferris had to remain to oversee those men of the crew who could not come; the rest of the selection was a more painful one. Laurence did not like to seem to be showing any kind of favouritism, and indeed he did not want to leave Ferris without all of the best men. He settled finally for Keynes and Willoughby, of the ground crew: he had come to rely on the surgeon's opinion, and despite having to leave the harness behind, he felt it necessary to have at least one of the harness-men along, to direct the others in getting Temeraire rigged-out in some makeshift way if some emergency required.

Lieutenant Riggs interrupted his and Granby's deliberations with a passionate claim to come along, and bring his four best shots also. 'They don't need us here; they have the Marines aboard, and if anything should go wrong the rifles will do you best, you must see,' he said. As a point of tactics this was quite true; but equally true, the riflemen were the rowdiest of his young officers as a group, and Laurence was dubious about taking so many of them to court after they had been nearly seven months at sea. Any insult to a Chinese lady would certainly be resented harshly, and his own attention would be too distracted to keep close watch over them.

'Let us have Mr. Dunne and Mr. Hackley,' Laurence said finally. 'No; I understand your arguments, Mr. Riggs, but I want steady men for this work, men who will not go astray; I gather you take my meaning. Very good. John, we will have Blythe along also, and Martin from the topmen.'

'That leaves two,' Granby said, adding the names to the tally.

'I cannot take Baylesworth also; Ferris will need a reliable second,' Laurence said, after briefly considering the last of his lieutenants. 'Let us have Therrows from the bellmen instead. And Digby for the last: he is a trifle young, but he has handled himself well, and the experience will do him good.'

'I will have them on deck in fifteen minutes, sir,' Granby said, rising.

'Yes; and send Ferris down,' Laurence said, already writing his orders. 'Mr. Ferris, I rely on your good judgement,' he said, when the acting second lieutenant had come. 'There is no way to guess one tenth part of what may arise under the circumstances. I have written you a formal set of orders, in case Mr. Granby and myself should be lost. If that be the case your first concern must be Temeraire's safety, and following that the crew's, and their safe return to England.'

'Yes, sir,' Ferris said, downcast, and accepted the sealed packet; he did not try to argue for his inclusion, but left the cabin with unhappily bowed shoulders.

Laurence finished repacking his sea-chest: thankfully he had at the beginning of the voyage set aside his very best coat and hat, wrapped in paper and oilskin at the bottom of his chest, with a view towards preserving them for the embassy. He shifted now into the leather coat and trousers of heavy broadcloth which he wore for flying; these had not been too badly worn, being both more resilient and less called-on during the course of the journey. Only two of his shirts were worth including, and a handful of neckcloths; the rest he laid aside in a small bundle, and left in the cabin locker.

'Boyne,' he called, putting his head out the door and spying a seaman idly splicing some rope. 'Light this along to the deck, will you?' The sea-chest dispatched, he penned a few words to his mother and to Jane and took them to Riley, the small ritual only heightening the sensation which had crept upon him, as of being on the eve of battle.

The men were assembled on deck when he came up, their

various chests and bags being loaded upon the launch. The envoys' baggage would mostly be remaining aboard, after Laurence had pointed out nearly a day would be required to unload it; even so, their bare necessities outweighed all the baggage of the crewmen. Yongxing was on the dragondeck handing over a sealed letter to Lung Yu Ping; he seemed to find nothing at all unusual in entrusting it directly to the dragon, riderless as she was, and she herself took it with practised skill, holding it so delicately between her long taloned claws she might almost have been gripping it. She tucked it carefully into the gold mesh she wore, to rest against her belly.

After this, she bowed to him and then to Temeraire and waddled forward, her wings ungainly for walking. But at the edge of the deck, she snapped them out wide, fluttered them a little, then sprang with a tremendous leap nearly her full length into the air, already beating furiously, and in an instant had diminished into a tiny speck above.

'Oh,' Temeraire said, impressed, watching her go. 'She flies very high; I have never gone so far aloft.'

Laurence was not unimpressed either, and stood watching through his glass for a few minutes more himself; by then she was wholly out of sight, though the day was clear.

Staunton drew Laurence aside. 'May I make a suggestion? Take the children along. If I may speak from my own experience as a boy, they may well be useful. There is nothing like having children present to convey peaceful intentions, and the Chinese have an especial respect for filial relations, both by adoption as well as by blood. You can quite naturally be said to be their guardian, and I am certain I can persuade the Chinese they ought not be counted against your tally.'

Roland overheard: instantly she and Dyer stood shining-eyed and hopeful before Laurence, full of silent pleading, and with some hesitation he said, 'Well, if the Chinese have no objection to their addition to the party—' This was enough encouragement; they vanished belowdecks for their own bags, and came scrambling back up even before Staunton had finished negotiating for their inclusion.

'It still seems very silly to me,' Temeraire said, in what was meant to be an undertone. 'I could easily carry all of you, and everything in that boat besides. If I must fly alongside, it will surely take much longer.'

'I do not disagree with you, but let us not reopen the discussion,' Laurence said tiredly, leaning against Temeraire and stroking his nose. '*That* will take more time than could possibly be saved by any other means of transport.'

Temeraire nudged him comfortingly, and Laurence closed his eyes a moment; the moment of quiet after the three hours of frantic hurry brought all his fatigue from the missed night of sleep surging back to the fore. 'Yes, I am ready,' he said, straightening up; Granby was there. Laurence settled his hat upon his head and nodded to the crew as he went by, the men touching their foreheads; a few even murmured, 'Good luck, sir,' and 'Godspeed, sir.'

He shook Franks's hand, and stepped over the side to the yowling accompaniment of pipes and drums, the rest of the crew already aboard the launch. Yongxing and the other envoys had already been lowered down by means of the bo'sun's chair, and were ensconced in the stern under a canopy for shelter from the sun. 'Very well, Mr. Tripp; let us get underway,' Laurence said to the midshipman, and they were off, the high sloping sides of the *Allegiance* receding as they raised the gaff mainsail and took the southerly wind past Macao and into the great sprawling delta of the Pearl River.

Chapter Twelve

They did not follow the usual curve of the river to Whampoa and Canton, but instead took an earlier eastern branch towards the city of Dongguan: now drifting with the wind, now rowing against the slow current, past the broad square-bordered rice fields on either side of the river, verdant green with the tops of the shoots beginning to protrude beyond the water's surface. The stench of manure hung over the river like a cloud.

Laurence drowsed nearly the entire journey, only vaguely conscious of the futile attempts made by the crew to be quiet, their hissing whispers causing instructions to be repeated three times, gradually increasing to the usual volume. Any occasional slip, such as dropping a coil of rope too heavily, or stumbling over one of the thwarts, brought forth a stream of invective and injunctions to be quiet that were considerably louder than the ordinary noise would have been. Nevertheless he slept, or something close to it; every so often he would open his eyes and look up, to be sure of Temeraire's form still pacing them overhead.

He woke from a deeper sleep only after dark: the sail was being furled, and a few moments later the launch bumped gently against a dock, followed by the quiet ordinary cursing of the sailors tying-up. There was very little light immediately at hand but the boat's lanterns, only enough to show a broad stairway leading down into the water, the lowest steps disappearing beneath the river's surface; to either side of these only the dim shadows of native junks drawn up onto the beach.

A parade of lanterns came towards them from further in on the shore, the locals evidently warned to expect their arrival: great glowing spheres of deep orange-red silk, stretched taut over thin bamboo frames, reflecting like flames in the water. The lamp-bearers spread out along the edges of the walls in careful procession, and suddenly a great many Chinese were climbing aboard the ship, seizing on the various parts of the baggage, and transferring these off without so much as a request for permission, calling out to one another cheerfully as they worked.

Laurence was at first disposed to complain, but there was no cause: the entire operation was being carried out with admirable efficiency. A clerk had seated himself at the base of the steps with something like a drawing-table upon his lap, making a tally of the different parcels on a paper scroll as they passed by him, and at the same time marking each one plainly. Instead Laurence stood up and tried to unstiffen his neck surreptitiously by small movements to either side, without any undignified stretching. Yongxing had already gotten off the boat and gone into the small pavilion on the shore; from inside, Liu Bao's booming voice could be heard calling for what even Laurence had come to recognize as the word for wine, and Sun Kai was on the bank speaking with the local mandarin.

'Sir,' Laurence said to Hammond. 'Will you be so good as to ask the local officials where Temeraire has come to ground?'

Hammond made some inquiries of the men on the bank, frowned, and said to Laurence in an undertone, 'They say he has been taken to the Pavilion of Quiet Waters, and that we are to go elsewhere for the night; pray make some objection at once, loudly, so I may have an excuse to argue with them;

we ought not set a precedent of allowing ourselves to be separated from him.'

Laurence, who if not prompted would have at once made a great noise, found himself cast into confusion by the request to playact; he stammered a little, and said in a raised but awkwardly tentative voice, 'I must see Temeraire at once, and be sure he is well.'

Hammond turned back at once to the attendants, spreading his hands in apology, and spoke urgently; under their scowls, Laurence did his best to look stern and unyielding, feeling thoroughly ridiculous and angry all at once, and eventually Hammond turned back with satisfaction and said, 'Excellent; they have agreed to take us to him.'

Relieved, Laurence nodded and turned back to the ship's crew. 'Mr. Tripp, let these gentlemen show you and the men where to sleep; I will speak with you in the morning before you return to the *Allegiance*,' he told the midshipman, who touched his hat, and then he climbed up onto the stairs.

Without discussion, Granby arranged the men in a loose formation around him as they walked along the broad, paved roads, following the guide's bobbing lantern; Laurence had the impression of many small houses on either side, and deep wheel-ruts were cut into the paving-stones, all sharp edges worn soft and curving with the impression of long years. He felt wide-awake after the long day drowsing, and yet there was something curiously dreamlike about walking through the foreign dark, the soft black boots of the guide making hushing noises over the stones, the smoke of cooking fires drifting from the nearby houses, muted light filtering from behind screens and out of windows, and once a snatch of unfamiliar song in a woman's voice.

They came at last to the end of the wide straight road, and the guide led them up the broad stairway of a pavilion and between massive round columns of painted wood, the roof so far overhead that its shape was lost in the darkness. The low rumbled breathing of dragons echoed loudly in the half-enclosed space, close all around them, and the tawny lantern light gleamed on scales in every direction, like heaped mounds of treasure around the narrow aisle through the centre. Hammond drew unconsciously closer to the centre of their party, and caught his breath once, as the lantern reflected from a dragon's half-open eye, and turned it into a disk of flat, shining gold.

They passed through another set of columns and into an open garden, with water trickling somewhere in the darkness, and the whisper of broad leaves rubbing against one another overhead. A few more dragons lay sleeping here, one sprawled across the path; the guide poked him with the stick of the lantern until he grudgingly moved away, never even opening his eyes. They climbed more stairs up to another pavilion, smaller than the first, and here at last found Temeraire, curled up alone in the echoing vastness.

'Laurence?' Temeraire said, lifting his head as they came in, and nuzzled at him gladly. 'Will you stay? It is very strange to be sleeping on land again. I almost feel as though the ground is moving.'

'Of course,' Laurence said, and the crew laid themselves down without complaint: the night was pleasantly warm, and the floor made of inlaid squares of wood, smoothed down by years, and not uncomfortably hard. Laurence took his usual place upon Temeraire's forearm; after sleeping through the journey, he was wakeful, and told Granby he would take the first watch. 'Have you been given something to eat?' he asked Temeraire, once they were settled.

'Oh yes,' Temeraire said drowsily. 'A roasted pig, very large, and some stewed mushrooms. I am not at all hungry. It was not a very difficult flight, after all, and nothing very interesting either to see before the sun went down; except those fields were strange, that we came past, full of water.'

'The rice fields,' Laurence said, but Temeraire was already

asleep, and shortly began to snore: the noise was decidedly louder in the confines of the pavilion even though it had no walls. The night was very quiet, and the mosquitoes were not too much of a torment, thankfully; they evidently did not care for the dry heat given off by a dragon's body. There was very little to mark the time, with the sky concealed by the roof, and Laurence lost track of the hours. No interruption in the stillness of the night, except that once a noise in the courtyard drew his attention: a dragon landing, turning a milky pearlescent gaze towards them, reflecting the moonlight very much like a cat's eyes; but it did not come near the pavilion, and only padded away deeper into the darkness.

Granby woke for his turn at watch; Laurence composed himself to sleep: he too felt the old familiar illusion of the earth shifting, his body remembering the movement of the ocean even now that they had left it behind.

He woke startled: the riot of colour overhead was strange until he understood he was looking at the decoration upon the ceiling, every scrap of wood painted and enamelled in brilliant peacocky colours and shining gilt. He sat up and looked about himself with fresh interest: the round columns were painted a solid red, set upon square bases of white marble, and the roof was at least thirty feet overhead: Temeraire would have had no difficulty coming in underneath it.

The front of the pavilion opened onto a prospect of the courtyard which he found interesting rather than beautiful: paved with grey stones around a winding path of reddish ones, full of queerly shaped rocks and trees, and of course dragons: there were five sprawled over the grounds in various attitudes of repose, except for one already awake and grooming itself fastidiously by the enormous pool which covered the northeast corner of the grounds. The dragon was a shade of greyish blue not very different from the present colour of the sky, and curiously the tips of its four claws were painted a bright red; as Laurence watched it finished its morning ablutions, and took to the air.

Most of the dragons in the yard seemed of a similar breed, though there was a great deal of variety among them in size, in the precise shade of their colour, and in the number and placement of their horns; some were smooth-backed and others had spiked ridges. Shortly a very different kind of dragon came out of the large pavilion to the south: larger and crimson-red, with gold-tinted talons and a bright yellow crest running from its many-horned head and along its spine. It drank from the pool and yawned enormously, displaying a double row of small but wicked teeth, and a set of four larger curving fangs among them. Narrower halls, with walls interspersed with small archways, ran to east and west of the courtyard, joining the two pavilions; the red dragon went over to one of the archways now and yelled something inside.

A few moments later a woman came stumbling out through the archway, rubbing her face and making wordless groaning noises. Laurence stared, then embarrassed looked away; she was naked to the waist. The dragon nudged her hard and knocked her back entirely into the pond. It certainly had a reviving effect: she rose up spluttering and wide-eyed, and then yammered back at the grinning dragon in a passion before going back inside the hall. She came out again a few minutes later, now fully dressed in what seemed to be a sort of padded jerkin, dark blue cotton edged with broad bands of red, with wide sleeves, and carrying a rig made also of fabric: silk, Laurence thought. This she threw upon the dragon all by herself, still talking loudly and obviously disgruntled all the while; Laurence was irresistibly reminded of Berkley and Maximus, even though Berkley had never spoken so many words together in his life: something in the irreverent quality of their relations.

The rig secured, the Chinese aviator scrambled aboard and the two went aloft with no further ceremony, disappearing from the pavilion to whatever their day's duties might be. All the dragons were now beginning to stir, another three of the big scarlet ones coming out of the pavilion, and more people to come from the halls: men from the east, and a few more women from the west.

Temeraire himself twitched under Laurence, and then opened his eyes. 'Good morning,' he said, yawning, then, 'Oh!' his eyes wide as he looked around, taking in the opulent decoration and the bustle going on in the courtyard. 'I did not realize there were so many other dragons here, or that it was so grand,' he said, a little nervously. 'I hope they are friendly.'

'I am sure they cannot but be gracious, when they realize you have come from so far,' Laurence said, climbing down so Temeraire could stand. The air was close and heavy with moisture, the sky remaining uncertain and grey; it would be hot again, he thought. 'You ought to drink as much as you can,' he said. 'I have no notion how often they will want to stop and rest along the way today.'

'I suppose,' Temeraire said, reluctantly, and stepped out of the pavilion and into the court. The increasing hubbub came to an abrupt and complete halt; the dragons and their companions alike staring openly, and then there was a general movement back and away from him. Laurence was for a moment shocked and offended; then he saw that they were all, men and dragons, bowing themselves very low to the ground. They had only been opening a clear path to the pond.

There was perfect silence. Temeraire uncertainly walked through the parted ranks of the other dragons to the pond, rather hastily drank his fill, and retreated back to the raised pavilion; only when he had gone again did the general activity resume, with much less noise than earlier, and a good deal of peering into the pavilion, while pretending to do nothing of the sort. 'They were very nice to let me drink,' Temeraire said, almost whispering, 'but I wish they would not stare so.'

The dragons seemed disposed to linger, but one after another they all set off, except for a few plainly older ones, their scales faded at the edges, who returned to basking upon the courtyard stones. Granby and the rest of the crew had woken over the intervening time, sitting up to watch the spectacle with as much interest as the other dragons had taken in Temeraire; now they roused fully, and began to straighten their clothing. 'I suppose they will send someone for us,' Hammond was saying, brushing futilely at his wrinkled breeches; he had been dressed formally, rather than in the riding gear which all the aviators had put on. At that very moment, Ye Bing, one of the young Chinese attendants from the ship, came through the courtyard, waving to draw their attention.

Breakfast was not what Laurence was used to, being a sort of thin rice porridge mixed with dried fish and slices of horrifically discoloured eggs, served with greasy sticks of crisp, very light bread. The eggs he pushed to the side, and forced himself to eat the rest, on the same advice which he had given to Temeraire; but he would have given a great deal for some properly-cooked eggs and bacon. Liu Bao poked Laurence in the arm with his chopsticks and pointed at the eggs with some remark: he was eating his own with very evident relish.

'What do you suppose is the matter with them?' Granby asked in an undertone, prodding his own eggs doubtfully.

Hammond, inquiring of Liu Bao, said just as doubtfully, 'He says they are thousand-year eggs.' Braver than the rest of them, he picked one of the slices up and ate it; chewed, swallowed, and looked thoughtful while they waited his verdict. 'It tastes almost pickled,' he said. 'Not rotten, at any rate.' He tried another piece, and ended by eating the whole serving; for his own part, Laurence left the lurid yellow and green things alone.

They had been brought to a sort of guest hall not far from the dragon pavilion for the meal; the sailors were there waiting and joined them for the breakfast, grinning rather maliciously.

They were no more pleased at being left out of the adventure than the rest of the aviators had been, and not above making remarks about the quality of food which the party could expect for the rest of their journey. Afterwards, Laurence took his final parting from Tripp. 'And be sure you tell Captain Riley that all is ship-shape, in those exact words,' he said; it had been arranged between them that any other message, regardless how reassuring, would mean something had gone badly wrong.

A couple of mule-led carts were waiting for them outside, rather rough-hewn and clearly without springs; their baggage had gone on ahead. Laurence climbed in and held on grimly to the side as they rattled along down the road. The streets at least were not more impressive by daylight: very broad, but paved with old rounded cobblestones, whose mortar had largely worn away. The wheels of the cart ran along in deep sloping ruts between stones, bumping and leaping over the uneven surface.

There was a great bustle of people all around, who stared with great curiosity at them, often putting down their work to follow after them for some short distance. 'And this is not even a city?' Granby looked around with interest, making some attempt to tally the numbers. 'There seem to be a great many people, for only a town.'

'There are some two hundred millions of people in the country, by our latest intelligence,' Hammond said absently, himself busy taking down notes in a journal; Laurence shook his head at the appalling number, more than ten times the size of England's population.

Laurence was more startled for his part to see a dragon come walking down the road in the opposite direction. Another of the blue-grey ones; it was wearing a queer sort of silk harness with a prominent breast pad, and when they had passed it by, he saw that three little dragonets, two of the same variety and one of the red colour, were tramping along behind, each attached to the harness also as if on leading-strings.

Nor was this dragon the only one in the streets: they shortly passed by a military station, with a small troop of blue-clad infantrymen drilling in its courtyard, and a couple of the big red dragons were sitting outside the gate talking and exclaiming over a dice game which their captains were playing. No one seemed to take any particular notice of them; the hurrying peasants carrying their loads went by without a second glance, occasionally climbing over one of the splayed-out limbs when other routes were blocked.

Temeraire was waiting for them in an open field, with two of the blue-grey dragons also on hand, wearing mesh harnesses that were being loaded up with baggage by attendants. The other dragons were whispering amongst themselves and eyeing Temeraire sidelong. He looked uncomfortable, and greatly relieved to see Laurence.

Having been loaded, the dragons now crouched down onto all fours so the attendants could climb aloft and raise small pavilions on their backs: very much like the tents which were used for long flights among British aviators. One of the attendants spoke to Hammond, and gestured to one of the blue dragons. 'We are to ride on that one,' Hammond said to Laurence aside, then asked something else of the attendant, who shook his head, and answered forcefully, pointing again to the second dragon.

Before the reply could even be translated, Temeraire sat up indignantly. 'Laurence is not riding any other dragon,' he said, putting out a possessive claw and nearly knocking Laurence off his feet, herding him closer; Hammond scarcely had to repeat the sentiments in Chinese.

Laurence had not quite realized the Chinese did not mean for even him to ride with Temeraire. He did not like the idea of Temeraire having to fly with no company on the long trip, and yet he could not help but think the point a small one; they would be flying in company, in sight of one another, and Temeraire could be in no real danger. 'It is only for the one journey,' he said to Temeraire, and was surprised to find himself overruled at once not by Temeraire, but by Hammond.

'No; the suggestion is unacceptable, cannot be entertained,' Hammond said.

'Not at all,' Temeraire said, in perfect agreement, and actually growled when the attendant tried to continue the argument.

'Mr. Hammond,' Laurence said, with happy inspiration, 'pray tell them, if it is the notion of harness which is at issue, I can just as easily lock onto the chain of Temeraire's pendant; as long as I do not need to go climbing about it will be secure enough.'

'They cannot possibly argue with that,' Temeraire said, pleased, and interrupted the argument immediately to make the suggestion, which was grudgingly accepted.

'Captain, may I have a word?' Hammond drew him aside. 'This attempt is of a piece with last night's arrangements. I must urge you, sir, by no means agree to continue on should we somehow come to be parted; and be on your guard if they should make further attempts to separate you from Temeraire.'

'I take your point, sir; and thank you for the advice,' Laurence said, grimly, and looked narrowly at Yongxing. Though the prince had never stooped to involve himself directly in any of the discussions, Laurence suspected his hand behind them, and he had hoped that the failure of the shipboard attempts to part them would at least have precluded these efforts.

After these tensions at the journey's outset, the long day's flight itself was uneventful, except for the occasional leap in Laurence's stomach when Temeraire would swoop down for a closer look at the ground: the breastplate did not keep entirely still throughout the flight, and shifted far more than harness. Temeraire was considerably quicker than the other two dragons, with more endurance, and could easily catch them up even if he lingered half an hour in sight-seeing at a time. The most striking feature, to Laurence, was the exuberance of the population: they scarcely passed any long stretch of land that was not under cultivation of some form, and every substantial body of water was crammed full of boats going either direction. And of course the real immensity of the country: they travelled from morning to night, with only an hour's pause for dinner each day at noon, and the days were long.

An almost endless expanse of broad, flat plains, checkered with rice fields and interspersed with many streams, yielded after some two days' travel to hills, and then to the slow puckering rise of mountains. Towns and villages of varying size punctuated the countryside below, and occasionally people working in the fields would stop and watch them flying overhead, if Temeraire came low enough to be recognized as a Celestial. Laurence at first thought the Yangtze another lake; one of respectable size but not extraordinary, being something less than a mile wide, with its east and west banks shrouded in a fine, grey drizzle; only when they had come properly overhead could he see the mighty river sprawling endlessly away, and the slow procession of junks appearing and vanishing through the mists.

After having passed two nights in smaller towns, Laurence had begun to think their first establishment an unusual case, but their residence that night in the city of Wuchang dwarfed it into insignificance: eight great pavilions arranged in a symmetric octagonal shape, joined by narrower enclosed halls, around a space deserving to be called a park more than a garden. Roland and Dyer made at first a game of trying to count the dragons inhabiting it, but gave up the attempt somewhere after thirty; they lost track of their tally when a group of small purple dragons landed and darted in a flurry of wings and limbs across the pavilion, too many and too quick to count.

Temeraire drowsed; Laurence put aside his bowl: another plain dinner of rice and vegetables. Most of the men were already asleep, huddled in their cloaks, the rest silent; rain still coming down in a steady, steaming curtain beyond the walls of the pavilion, the overrun clattering off the upturned corners of the tiled roof. Along the slopes of the river valley, faintly visible, small yellow beacons burned beneath open-walled huts to mark the way for dragons flying through the night. Soft grumbling breath echoing from the neighbouring pavilions, and far away a more piercing cry, ringing clear despite the muffling weight of the rain.

Yongxing had been spending his nights apart from the rest of the company, in more private quarters, but now he came out of seclusion and stood at the edge of the pavilion looking out into the valley: in another moment the call came again, nearer. Temeraire lifted up his head to listen, the ruff around his neck rising up alertly; then Laurence heard the familiar leathery snapping of wings, mist and steam rolling away from the stones for the descending dragon, a white ghostly shadow coalescing from the silver rain. She folded great white wings and came pacing towards them, her talons clicking on the stones; the attendants going between pavilions shrank away from her, averting their faces, hurrying by, but Yongxing walked down the steps into the rain, and she lowered her great, wide-ruffed head towards him, calling his name in a clear, sweet voice.

'Is that another Celestial?' Temeraire asked him, hushed and uncertain; Laurence only shook his head and could not answer: she was a shockingly pure white, a colour he had never before seen in a dragon even in spots or streaks. Her scales had the translucent gleam of fine, much-scraped vellum, perfectly colourless, and the rims of her eyes were a glassy pink mazed with blood vessels so engorged as to be visible even at a distance. Yet she had the same great ruff, and the long narrow tendrils fringing her jaws, just as Temeraire did: the colour alone was unnatural. She wore a heavy golden torque set with rubies around the base of her neck, and gold talon-sheaths tipped with rubies upon all of her foreleg claws, the deep colour echoing the hue of her eyes.

She nudged Yongxing caressingly back into the shelter of the temple and came in after him, first shivering her wings quickly to let cascades of rain roll away in streams; she allotted them barely a glance, her eyes flickering rapidly over them and away, before she jealously coiled herself around Yongxing, to murmur quietly with him in the far corner of the pavilion. Servants came bringing her some dinner, but dragging their heels, uneasily, though they had shown no such similar reluctance around any of the other dragons, and indeed visible satisfaction in Temeraire's presence. She did not seem to merit their fear; she ate quickly and daintily, not letting so much as a drop spill out of the dish, and otherwise paid them no mind.

The next morning Yongxing briefly presented her to them as Lung Tien Lien, and then led her away to breakfast in private; Hammond had made quiet inquiries enough to tell them a little more over their own meal: 'She is certainly a Celestial,' he said. 'I suppose it is a kind of albinism; I have no idea why it should make them all so uneasy.'

'She was born in mourning colours, of course she is unlucky,' Liu Bao said, when he was cautiously applied to for information, as if this were self-evident, and he added, 'The Qianlong Emperor was going to give her to a prince out in Mongolia, so her bad luck wouldn't hurt any of his sons, but Yongxing insisted on having her himself instead of letting a Celestial go outside the Imperial family. He could have been Emperor himself, but of course you couldn't have an Emperor with a cursed dragon, it would be a disaster for the state. So now his brother is the Jiaqing Emperor. Such is the will of Heaven!' With this philosophical remark, he shrugged and ate another piece of fried bread. Hammond took this news bleakly, and Laurence shared his dismay: pride was one thing; principle implacable enough to sacrifice a throne for, something else entirely.

The two bearer dragons accompanying them had been changed for another one of the blue-grey breed and one of a slightly larger kind, deep green with blue streaks and a sleek hornless head; they still regarded Temeraire with the same staring awe, however, and Lien with nervous respect, and kept well to themselves. Temeraire had by now reconciled himself to the state of majestic solitude, however; and in any case he was thoroughly occupied in glancing sidelong at Lien with fascinated curiosity, until she turned to stare pointedly at him in return and he ducked his head, abashed.

She wore this morning an odd sort of headdress, made of thin silk draped between gold bars, which stood out over her eyes rather like a canopy and shaded them; Laurence wondered that she should find it necessary, with the sky still unrelieved and grey. But the hot, sullen weather broke almost abruptly during their first few hours of flight, through gorges winding among old mountains: their sloping southern faces lush and green, and the northern almost barren. A cool wind met their faces as they came out into the foothills, and the sun breaking from the clouds was almost painfully bright. The rice fields did not reappear, but long expanses of ripening wheat took their place, and once they saw a great herd of brown oxen creeping slowly across a grassy plain, heads to the ground as they munched away.

A little shed was planted on a hill, overlooking the herd, and beside it several massive spits turned, entire cows roasting upon them, a fragrant smoky smell rising upwards. 'Those look tasty,' Temeraire observed, a little wistfully. He was not alone in the sentiment: as they approached, one of their companion dragons put on a sudden burst of speed and swooped down. A man came out of the shed and held a discussion with the dragon, then went inside again; he came out carrying a large plank of wood and laid it down before the dragon, which carved a few Chinese symbols into the plank with its talon.

The man took away the plank, and the dragon took away a cow: plainly it had been making a purchase. It lifted back up into the air at once to rejoin them, crunching its cow happily as it flew: it evidently did not think it necessary to let its passengers off for any of the proceedings. Laurence thought he could see poor Hammond looking faintly green as it slurped the intestines up with obvious pleasure.

'We could try to purchase one, if they will take guineas,' Laurence offered to Temeraire, a little dubiously; he had brought gold rather than paper money with him, but had no idea if the herdsman would accept it.

'Oh, I am not really hungry,' Temeraire said, preoccupied by a wholly different thought. 'Laurence, that was writing, was it not? What he did on the plank?'

'I believe so, though I do not set myself up as an expert on Chinese writing,' Laurence said. 'You are more likely to recognize it than I.'

'I wonder if all Chinese dragons know how to write,' Temeraire said, dismal at the notion. 'They will think me very stupid if I am the only one who cannot. I must learn somehow; I always thought letters had to be made with a pen, but I am sure I could do that sort of carving.'

Perhaps in courtesy to Lien, who seemed to dislike bright sunlight, they now paused during the heat of the day at another wayside pavilion for some dinner and for the dragons to rest, and flew on into the evening instead; beacons upon the ground lighted their way at irregular intervals, and in any case Laurence could chart their course by the stars: turning now more sharply to the northeast, with the miles slipping quickly past. The days continued hot, but no longer so extraordinarily humid, and the nights were wonderfully cool and pleasant; signs of the force of the northern winters were apparent, however: the pavilions were walled on three sides, and set up from the ground on stone platforms which held stoves so the floors could be heated.

Peking sprawled out a great distance from beyond the city walls, which were numerous and grand, with many square towers and battlements not unlike the style of European castles. Broad streets of grey stone ran in straight lines to the gates and within, so full of people, of horses, of carts, all of them moving, that from above they seemed like rivers. They saw many dragons also, both on the streets and in the sky, leaping into the air for short flights from one quarter of the city to another, sometimes with a crowd of people hanging off them and evidently travelling in this manner. The city was divided with extraordinary regularity into square sections, except for the curving sprawl of four small lakes actually within the walls. To the east of these lay the great Imperial palace itself, not a single building but formed of many smaller pavilions, walled in and surrounded by a moat of murky water: in the setting sun, all the roofs within the complex shone as if gilded, nestled among trees with their spring growth still fresh and yellow-green, throwing long shadows into the plazas of grey stone.

A smaller dragon met them in mid-air as they drew near: black with canary-yellow stripes and wearing a collar of dark green silk, he had a rider upon his back, but spoke to the other dragons directly. Temeraire followed the other dragons down, to a small round island in the southernmost lake, less than half a mile from the palace walls. They landed upon a broad pier of white marble which jutted out into the lake, for the convenience of dragons only, as there were no boats in evidence.

This pier ended in an enormous gateway: a red structure more than a wall and yet too narrow to be considered a building, with three square archways as openings, the two smallest many times higher than Temeraire's head and wide enough for four of him to walk abreast; the central was even larger. A pair of enormous Imperial dragons stood at attention on either side, very like Temeraire in conformity but without his distinctive ruff, one black and the other a deep blue, and beside them a long file of soldiers: infantrymen in shining steel caps and blue robes, with long spears.

The two companion dragons walked directly through the smaller archways, and Lien paced straightaway through the middle, but the yellow-striped dragon barred Temeraire from following, bowed low, and said something in apologetic tones while gesturing to the centre archway. Temeraire answered back shortly, and sat down on his haunches with an air of finality, his ruff stiff and laid back against his neck in obvious displeasure. 'Is something wrong?' Laurence asked quietly; through the archway he could see a great many people and dragons assembled in the courtyard beyond, and obviously some ceremony was intended.

'They want you to climb down, and go through one of the small archways, and for me to go through the large one,' Temeraire said. 'But I am not putting you down alone. It sounds very silly to me, anyway, to have three doors all going to the same place.'

Laurence wished rather desperately for Hammond's advice, or anyone's for that matter; the striped dragon and his rider were equally nonplussed at Temeraire's recalcitrance, and Laurence found himself looking at the other man and meeting with an almost identical expression of confusion. The dragons and soldiers in the archway remained as motionless and precise as statues, but as the minutes passed those assembled on the other side must have come to realize something was wrong. A man in richly embroidered blue robes came hurrying through the side corridor, and spoke to the striped dragon and his rider; then looked askance at Laurence and Temeraire and hurried back to the other side.

A low murmur of conversation began, echoing down the archway, and then abruptly cut off; the people on the far side parted, and a dragon came through the archway towards them, a deep glossy black very much like Temeraire's own colouring, with the same deep blue eyes and wing-markings, and a great standing ruff of translucent black stretched among ribbed horns of vermilion, another Celestial. She stopped before them and spoke in deep resonant tones; Laurence felt Temeraire first stiffen and then tremble, his own ruff rising slowly up, and Temeraire said, low and uncertainly, 'Laurence, this is my mother.'

Chapter Thirteen

Laurence later learned from Hammond that passage through the central gate was reserved for the use of the Imperial family, and dragons of that breed and the Celestials only, hence their refusal to let Laurence himself pass through. At the moment, however, Qian simply led Temeraire in a short flight over the gateway and into the central courtyard beyond, thus neatly severing the Gordian knot.

The problem of etiquette resolved, they were all ushered into an enormous banquet, held within the largest of the dragon pavilions, with two tables waiting. Qian was herself seated at the head of the first table, with Temeraire upon her left and Yongxing and Lien upon her right. Laurence was directed to sit some distance down the table, with Hammond across and several more seats down; the rest of the British party was placed at the second table. Laurence did not think it politic to object: the separation was not even the length of the room, and in any case Temeraire's attention was entirely engaged at present. He was speaking to his mother with an almost timid air, very unlike himself and clearly overawed: she was larger than he, and the faint translucence of her scales indicated a great age, as well as her very grand manners. She wore no harness, but her ruff was adorned with enormous yellow topazes affixed to the spines, and a deceptively fragile neckpiece of filigree gold, studded with more topazes and great pearls.

Truly gigantic platters of brass were set before the dragons, each bearing an entire roasted deer, antlers intact: oranges stuck with cloves were impaled upon them, creating a fragrance not at all unpleasant to human senses, and their bellies were stuffed with a mixture of nuts and very bright red berries. The humans were served with a sequence of eight dishes, smaller though equally elaborate. After the dismal food along the course of the journey, even the highly exotic repast was very welcome, however.

Laurence had assumed there should be no one for him to talk to, as he sat down, unless he tried to shout across to Hammond, there being no translator present so far as he could tell. On his left side sat a very old mandarin, wearing a hat with a pearlescent white jewel perched on top and a peacock feather dangling down from the back over a truly impressive queue, still mostly black despite the profusion of wrinkles engraved upon his face. He ate and drank with single-minded intensity, never even trying to address Laurence at all: when the neighbour on his other side leaned over and shouted in the man's ear, Laurence realized that he was very deaf, as well as being unable to speak English.

But shortly after he had seated himself, he was taken aback to be addressed from his other side in English, heavy with French accents: 'I hope you have had a comfortable journey,' said the smiling, cheerful voice. It was the French ambassador, dressed in long robes in the Chinese style rather than in European dress; that and his dark hair accounted for Laurence not having distinguished him at once from the rest of the company.

'You will permit that I make myself known to you, I hope, despite the unhappy state of affairs between our countries,' De Guignes continued. 'I can claim an informal acquaintance,

286

you see; my nephew tells me he owes his life to your magnanimity.'

'I beg your pardon, sir, I have not the least notion to what you refer,' Laurence said, puzzled by this address. 'Your nephew?'

'Jean-Claude De Guignes; he is a lieutenant in our Armée de l'Air,' the ambassador said, bowing, still smiling. 'You encountered him this last November over your Channel, when he made an attempt to board you.'

'Good God,' Laurence said, exclaiming, distantly recalling the young lieutenant who had fought so vigorously in the convoy action, and he willingly shook De Guignes's hand. 'I remember; most extraordinary courage. I am so very happy to hear that he has quite recovered, I hope?'

'Oh yes, in his letter he expected to rise from his hospital any day; to go to prison of course, but that is better than going to a grave,' De Guignes said, with a prosaic shrug. 'He wrote me of your interesting journey, knowing I had been dispatched here to your destination; I have been with great pleasure expecting you this last month since his letter arrived, with hopes of expressing my admiration for your generosity.'

From this happy beginning, they exchanged some more conversation on neutral topics: the Chinese climate, the food, and the startling number of dragons. Laurence could not help but feel a certain kinship with him, as a fellow Westerner in the depths of the Oriental enclave, and though De Guignes was himself not a military man, his familiarity with the French aerial corps made him sympathetic company. They walked out together at the close of the meal, following the other guests into the courtyard, where most of these were being carried away by dragon in the same manner they had seen earlier in the city.

'It is a clever mode of transport, is it not?' De Guignes said, and Laurence, watching with interest, agreed wholeheartedly: the dragons, mostly of what he now considered the common blue variety, wore light harnesses of many silk straps draped over their backs, to which were hung numerous loops of broad silk ribbons. The passengers climbed up the loops to the topmost empty one, which they slid down over their arms and underneath the buttocks: they could then sit in comparative stability, clinging to the main strap, so long as the dragon flew level.

Hammond emerged from the pavilion and caught sight of them, eyes widening, and hastened to join them; he and De Guignes smiled and spoke with great friendliness, and as soon as the Frenchman had excused himself and departed in company with a pair of Chinese mandarins, Hammond instantly turned to Laurence and demanded to have the whole of their conversation recounted, in a perfectly shameless manner.

'Expecting us for a month!' Hammond was appalled by the intelligence, and managed to imply without actually saying anything openly offensive that he thought Laurence had been a simpleton to take De Guignes at face value. 'God only knows what mischief he may have worked against us in that time; pray have no more private conversation with him.'

Laurence did not respond to these remarks as he rather wanted to, and instead went away to Temeraire's side. Qian had been the last to depart, taking a caressing leave of Temeraire, nudging him with her nose before leaping aloft; her sleek black form disappeared into the night quickly, and Temeraire stood watching after her very wistfully.

The island had been prepared for their residence as a compromise measure; the property of the Emperor, it possessed several large and elegant dragon pavilions, with establishments intended for human use conjoined to these. Laurence and his party were allowed to establish themselves in a residence attached to the largest of the pavilions, facing across a broad courtyard. The building was a handsome one, and large, but the upper floor was wholly taken up by a host of servants greatly exceeding their needs; although seeing how these ranged themselves almost underfoot throughout the house, Laurence began to suspect them intended equally as spies and guards.

His sleep was heavy, but broken before dawn by servants poking their heads in to see if he were awake; after the fourth such attempt in ten minutes, Laurence yielded with no good grace and rose with a head still aching from the previous day's free flow of wine. He had little success in conveying his desire for a washbasin, and at length resorted to stepping outside into the courtyard to wash in the pond there. This posed no difficulty, as there was an enormous circular window little less than his height set in the wall, the lower sill barely off the ground.

Temeraire was sprawled luxuriously across the far end, lying flattened upon his belly with even his tail stretched out to its full extent, still fast asleep and making occasional small pleased grunts as he dreamed. A system of bamboo pipes emerged from beneath the pavement, evidently used to heat the stones, and these spilled a cloud of hot water into the pond, so Laurence could make more comfortable ablutions than he had expected. The servants hovered in visible impatience all the time, and looked rather scandalized at his stripping to the waist to wash. When at last he came back in, they pressed Chinese dress upon him: soft trousers and the stiff-collared gown which seemed nearly universal among them. He resisted a moment, but a glance over at his own clothes showed them sadly wrinkled from the travel; the native dress was at least neat, if not what he was used to, and not physically uncomfortable, though he felt very nearly indecent without a proper coat or neckcloth.

A functionary of some sort had come to breakfast with them and was already waiting at the table, which was evidently the source of the servants' urgency. Laurence bowed rather shortly to the stranger, named Zhao Wei, and let Hammond

289

carry the conversation while he drank a great deal of the tea: fragrant and strong, but not a dish of milk to be seen, and the servants only looked blank when the request was translated for them.

'His Imperial Majesty has in his benevolence decreed you are to reside here for the length of your visit,' Zhao Wei was saying; his English was by no means polished, but understandable; he had a rather prim and censorious look, and eyed Laurence's still unskilled use of the chopsticks with an expression of disdain hovering about his mouth. 'You may walk in the courtyard as you desire, but you are not to leave the residence without making a formal request and receiving permission.'

'Sir, we are most grateful, but you must be aware that if we are not to be allowed free movement during the day, the size of this house is by no means adequate to our needs,' Hammond said. 'Why, only Captain Laurence and myself had private rooms last night, and those small and ill-befitting our standing, while the rest of our compatriots were housed in shared quarters and very cramped.'

Laurence had noticed no such inadequacy, and found both the attempted restrictions on their movement and Hammond's negotiations for more space mildly absurd, the more so as it transpired, from their conversation, that the whole of the island had been vacated in deference to Temeraire. The complex could have accommodated a dozen dragons in extreme comfort, and there were sufficient human residences that every man of Laurence's crew might have had a building to himself. Still, their residence was in perfectly good repair, comfortable, and far more spacious than their shipboard quarters for the last seven months; he could not see the least reason for desiring additional space any more than for denying them the liberty of the island. But Hammond and Zhao Wei continued to negotiate the matter with a measured gravity and politeness.

Zhao Wei at length consented to their being allowed to take walks around the island in the company of the servants, 'so long as you do not go to the shores or the docks, and do not interfere in the patrols of the guardsmen.' With this Hammond pronounced himself satisfied. Zhao Wei sipped at his tea, and then added, 'Of course, His Majesty wishes Lung Tien Xiang to see something of the city. I will conduct him upon a tour after he has eaten.'

'I am certain Temeraire and Captain Laurence will find it most edifying,' Hammond said immediately, before Laurence could even draw breath. 'Indeed, sir, it was very kind of you to arrange for native clothing for Captain Laurence, so he will not suffer from excessive curiosity.'

Zhao Wei only now took notice of Laurence's clothing, with an expression that made it perfectly plain he was nothing whatsoever involved; but he bore his defeat in reasonably good part. He said only, 'I hope you will be ready to leave shortly, Captain,' with a small inclination of the head.

'And we may walk through the city itself?' Temeraire asked, with much excitement, as he was scrubbed and sluiced clean after his breakfast, holding out his forehands one at a time with the talons outspread to be brushed vigorously with soapy water. His teeth even received the same treatment, a young serving-maid ducking inside his mouth to scrub the back ones.

'Of course?' Zhao Wei said, showing some sincere puzzlement at the question.

'Perhaps you may see something of the training grounds of the dragons here, if there are any within the city bounds,' Hammond suggested: he had accompanied them outside. 'I am sure you would find it of interest, Temeraire.'

'Oh yes,' Temeraire said; his ruff was already up and half-quivering.

Hammond gave Laurence a significant glance, but Laurence chose to ignore it entirely: he had little desire to play the spy, or to prolong the tour, however interesting the sights might be. 'Are you quite ready, Temeraire?' he asked instead.

They were transported to the shore by an elaborate but awkward barge, which wallowed uncertainly under Temeraire's weight even in the placidity of the tiny lake; Laurence kept close to the tiller and watched the lubberly pilot with a grim and censorious eye: he would dearly have loved to take her away from the fellow. The scant distance to shore took twice as long to cover as it ought to have. A substantial escort of armed guards had been detached from their patrols on the island to accompany them on the tour. Most of these fanned out ahead to force a clear path through the streets, but some ten kept close on Laurence's heels, jostling one another out of any kind of formation in what seemed to be an attempt to keep him blocked almost by a human wall from wandering away.

Zhao Wei took them through another of the elaborate red-and-gold gateways, this one set in a fortified wall and yielding onto a very broad avenue. It was manned by several guards in the Imperial livery, as well as by two dragons also under gear: one of the by-now-familiar red ones, and the other a brilliant green with red markings. Their captains were sitting together sipping tea under an awning, their padded jerkins removed against the day's heat, and both were women.

'I see you have women captains also,' Laurence said to Zhao Wei. 'Do they serve with particular breeds, then?'

'Women are companions to those dragons that go into the army,' Zhao Wei said. 'Naturally only the lower breeds would choose to do that sort of work. Over there, that green one is one of the Emerald Glass. They are too lazy and slow to do well on the examinations, and the Scarlet Flower breed all like fighting too much, so they are not good for anything else.'

'Do you mean to say that only women serve in your aerial corps?' Laurence asked, sure he had misunderstood; but Zhao Wei only nodded a confirmation. 'But what reason can there be for such a policy; surely you do not ask women to serve in your infantry, or navy?' Laurence protested.

His dismay was evident, and Zhao Wei, perhaps feeling a need to defend his nation's unusual practice, proceeded to narrate the legend which was its foundation. The details were of course romanticized: a girl had supposedly disguised herself as a man to fight in her father's stead, had become companion to a military dragon and saved the empire by winning a great battle; as a consequence, the Emperor of the time had pronounced girls acceptable for service with dragons.

But these colourful exaggerations aside, it seemed that the nation's policy itself was accurately described: in times of conscription, the head of each family had at one time been required to serve or send a child in his stead. Girls being considerably less valued than boys, they had become the preferred choice to fill out the quota when possible. As they could only serve in the aerial corps, they had come to dominate this branch of the service until eventually the force became exclusive.

The telling of the legend, complete with recitation of its traditional poetic version, which Laurence suspected lost a great deal of colour in the translation, carried them past the gate and some distance along the avenue towards a broad grey-flagged plaza set back from the road itself, and full of children and hatchlings. The boys sat cross-legged on the floor in front, the hatchlings coiled up neatly behind, and all together in a queer mixture of childish voices and the more resonant draconic tones were parroting a human teacher who stood on a podium in front, reading loudly from a great book and beckoning the students to repeat after every line.

Zhao Wei waved his hand towards them. 'You wanted to see our schools. This is a new class, of course; they are only just beginning to study the Analects.'

Laurence was privately baffled at the notion of subjecting dragons to study and written examinations. 'They do not seem paired off,' he said, studying the group.

Zhao Wei looked blankly at him, and Laurence clarified, 'I mean, the boys are not sitting with their own hatchlings, and the children seem rather young for them, indeed.'

'Oh, those dragonets are much too young to have chosen any companions yet,' Zhao Wei said. 'They are only a few weeks old. When they have lived fifteen months, then they will be ready to choose, and the boys will be older.'

Laurence halted in surprise, and turned to stare at the little hatchlings again; he had always heard that dragons had to be tamed directly at hatching, to keep them from becoming feral and escaping into the wild, but this seemed plainly contradicted by the Chinese example. Temeraire said, 'It must be very lonely. I would not have liked to be without Laurence when I hatched, at all.' He lowered his head and nudged Laurence with his nose. 'And it would also be very tiresome to have to hunt all the time for yourself when you are first hatched; I was always hungry,' he added, more prosaically.

'Of course the hatchlings do not have to hunt for themselves,' Zhao Wei said. 'They must study. There are dragons who tend the eggs and feed the young. That is much better than having a person do it. Otherwise a dragonet could not help but become attached, before he was wise enough to properly judge the character and virtues of his proposed companion.'

This was a pointed remark indeed, and Laurence answered it coolly, 'I suppose that may be a concern, if you have less regulation of how men are to be chosen for such an opportunity. Among us, of course, a man must ordinarily serve for many years in the Corps before he can be considered worthy even to be presented to a hatchling. In such circumstances, it seems to me that an early attachment such as you decry may be instead the foundation of a lasting deeper affection, more rewarding to both parties.'

They continued on into the city proper, and now with a view of his surroundings from a more ordinary perspective than from the air, Laurence was struck afresh by the great breadth of the streets, which seemed to almost have been designed with dragons in mind. They gave the city a feeling of spaciousness altogether different from London; though the absolute number of people was, he guessed, nearly equal. Temeraire was here more staring than stared-at; the populace of the capital were evidently used to the presence of the more exalted breeds, while he had never been out into a city before, and his head craned nearly in a loop around his own neck as he tried to look in three directions at once.

Guards roughly pushed ordinary travellers out of the way of green sedan chairs, carrying mandarins on official duties. Along one broad way a wedding procession brilliant with scarlet and gold were winding their shouting, clapping way through the streets, with musicians and spitting fireworks in their train and the bride well-concealed in a draped chair: a wealthy match to judge by the elaborate proceedings. Occasional mules plodded along under cartloads, inured to the presence of the dragons, their hooves clopping along the stones; but Laurence did not see any horses on the main avenues, nor carriages: likely they could not be tamed to bear the presence of so many dragons. The air smelled quite differently: none of the sour grassy stench of manure and horse piss inescapable in London, but instead the faintly sulphurous smell of dragon waste, more pronounced when the wind blew from the northeast; Laurence suspected some larger cesspools lay in that quarter of the city.

And everywhere, everywhere dragons: the blue ones, most common, were engaged in the widest variety of tasks. In addition to those Laurence saw ferrying people about with their carrying harnesses, others bore loads of freight; but a sizeable number also seemed to be travelling alone on more important business, wearing collars of varying colours, very like the different colours of the mandarins' jewels. Zhao Wei confirmed these were signifiers of rank, and the dragons so adorned members of the civil service. 'The Lung Shen are like people, some are clever and some are lazy,' he said, and added, to Laurence's great interest, 'Many superior breeds have risen from the best of them, and the wisest may even be honoured with an Imperial mating.' Dozens of other breeds also were to be seen, some with and others without human companions, engaged on many errands. Temeraire drew some attention, but not nearly so much as in the south, the populace here evidently being used to the presence of the more exalted breeds: at one point two Imperial dragons came by going in the opposite direction, and inclined their heads to Temeraire politely as they passed.

They came shortly into a market district, the stores lavishly decorated with carving and gilt, and full of goods. Silks of glorious colour and texture, some of much finer quality than anything Laurence had ever seen in London; great skeins and wrapped yards of the plain blue cotton as yarn and cloth, in different grades of quality both by thickness and the intensity of the dye. And porcelain, which in particular caught Laurence's attention; unlike his father, he was no connoisseur of the art, but the precision in the blue-and-white designs seemed also superior to those dishes which he had seen imported, and the coloured dishes particularly lovely.

'Temeraire, will you ask if he would take gold?' he asked; Temeraire was peering into the shop with much interest, while the merchant eyed his looming head in the doorway anxiously; this at least seemed one place even in China where dragons were not quite welcome. The merchant looked doubtful, and addressed some questions to Zhao Wei; after this, he consented at least to take a half-guinea and inspect it. He rapped it on the side of the table and then called in his son from a back room: having few teeth left himself, he gave it to the younger man to bite upon. A woman seated in the back peeped around the corner, interested by the noise, and was admonished loudly and without effect until she stared her fill at Laurence and withdrew again; but her voice came from the back room stridently, so she seemed also to be participating in the debate.

At last the merchant seemed satisfied, but when Laurence picked up the vase which he had been examining, he immediately jumped forward and took it away, with a torrent of words; motioning Laurence to stay, he went into the back room. 'He says that is not worth so much,' Temeraire explained.

'But I have only given him half a pound,' Laurence protested; the man came back carrying a much larger vase, in a deep, nearly glowing red, shading delicately to a pure white at the top, and with an almost mirrored gloss. He put it down on the table and they all looked at it with admiration; even Zhao Wei did not withhold a murmur of approval, and Temeraire said, 'Oh, that is very pretty.'

Laurence pressed another few guineas on the shopkeeper with some difficulty, and still felt guilty at carrying it away, swathed in many protective layers of cotton rags; he had never seen a piece so lovely before, and he was already anxious for its survival through the long journey. Emboldened by this first success, he embarked on other purchases, of silk and other porcelain, and after that a small pendant of jade, which Zhao Wei, his façade of disdain gradually yielding to enthusiasm for the shopping expedition, pointed out to him, explaining that the symbols upon it were the start of the poem about the legendary woman dragon-soldier. It was apparently a good-luck symbol often bought for a girl about to embark upon such a career. Laurence rather thought Jane Roland would like it, and added it to the growing pile; very soon Zhao Wei had to detail several of his soldiers to carry the various packages: they no longer seemed so concerned about Laurence's potential escape as about his loading them down like carthorses.

Prices for many of the goods seemed considerably lower than Laurence was used to, in general; more than could be accounted for by the cost of freight. This alone was not a surprise, after hearing the Company commissioners in Macao talk about the rapacity of the local mandarins and the bribes they demanded, on top of the state duties. But the difference was so high that Laurence had to revise significantly upwards his guesses of the degree of extortion. 'It is a great pity,' Laurence said to Temeraire, as they came to the end of the avenue. 'If only the trade were allowed to proceed openly, I suppose these merchants could make a much better living, and the craftsmen too; having to send all their wares through Canton is what allows the mandarins there to be so unreasonable. Probably they do not even want to bother, if they can sell the goods here, so we receive only the dregs of their market.'

'Perhaps they do not want to sell the nicest pieces so far away. That is a very pleasant smell,' Temeraire said, approvingly, as they crossed a small bridge into another district, surrounded by a narrow moat of water and a low stone wall. Open shallow trenches full of smouldering coals lined the street to either side, with animals cooking over them, spitted on metal spears and being basted with great swabs by sweating, half-naked men: oxen, pigs, sheep, deer, horses, and smaller, less-identifiable creatures; Laurence did not look very closely. The sauces dripped and scorched upon the stones, raising thick wafting clouds of aromatic smoke. Only a handful of people were buying here, nimbly dodging among the dragons who made up the better part of the clientele.

Temeraire had eaten heartily that morning: a couple of young venison, with some stuffed ducks as a relish; he did not ask to eat, but looked a little wistfully at a smaller purple dragon eating roast suckling pigs off a skewer. But down a smaller alley Laurence also saw a tired-looking blue dragon, his hide marked with old sores from the silk carrying-harness he wore, turning sadly away from a beautifully roasted cow and pointing instead at a small, rather burnt sheep left off to the side: he took it away to a corner and began eating it very slowly, stretching it out, and he did not disdain the offal or the bones.

It was natural that if dragons were expected to earn their bread, there should be some less fortunate than others; but Laurence felt it somehow criminal to see one going hungry, particularly when there was so much extravagant waste at their residence and elsewhere. Temeraire did not notice, his gaze fixed on the displays. They came out of the district over another small bridge which led them back onto the broad avenue where they had begun. Temeraire sighed deeply with pleasure, releasing the aroma only slowly from his nostrils.

Laurence, for his part, was fallen quiet; the sight had dispelled his natural fascination with all the novelty of their surroundings and the natural interest inherent in a foreign capital of such extents, and without such distraction he was inescapably forced to recognize the stark contrast in the treatment of dragons. The city streets were not wider than in London by some odd coincidence, or a question of taste, or even for the greater grandeur which they offered; but plainly designed that dragons might live in full harmony with men, and that this design was accomplished, to the benefit of all parties, he could not dispute: the case of misery which he had seen served rather to illustrate the general good.

The dinner hour was hard upon them, and Zhao Wei turned their route back towards the island; Temeraire also grown quieter as they left the market precincts behind, and they walked along in silence until they reached the gateway; there pausing he looked back over his shoulder at the city, its activity undiminished. Zhao Wei caught the look and said something to him in Chinese. 'It is very nice,' Temeraire answered him, and added, 'but I cannot compare it: I have never walked in London, or even in Dover.'

They took their leave from Zhao Wei briefly, outside the pavilion, and went in again together. Laurence sat heavily down upon a wooden bench, while Temeraire began to pace restlessly back and forth, his tail-tip switching back and forth with agitation. 'It is not true, at all,' he burst out at last. 'Laurence, we have gone everywhere we liked; I have been in the streets and to shops, and no one has run away or been frightened: not in the south and not here. People are not afraid of dragons, not in the least.'

'I must beg your pardon,' Laurence said quietly. 'I confess I was mistaken: plainly men can be accustomed. I expect with so many dragons about, all men here are raised with close experience of them, and lose their fear. But I assure you I have not lied to you deliberately; the same is not true in Britain. It must be a question of use.'

'If use can make men stop being afraid, I do not see why we should be kept penned up so they may continue to be frightened,' Temeraire said.

To this Laurence could make no answer, and did not try; instead he retreated to his own room to take a little dinner; Temeraire lay down for his customary afternoon nap in a brooding, restless coil, while Laurence sat alone, picking unenthusiastically over his plate. Hammond came to inquire after what they had seen; Laurence answered him as briefly as he could, his irritation of spirit ill-concealed, and in short order Hammond went away rather flushed and thin-lipped.

'Has that fellow been pestering you?' Granby said, looking in.

'No,' Laurence said tiredly, getting up to rinse his hands in the basin he had filled from the pond. 'Indeed, I am afraid I was plainly rude to him just now, and he did not deserve it in the least: he was only curious how they raise the dragons here, so he could argue with them that Temeraire's treatment in England has not been so ill.'

'Well, as far as I am concerned he deserved a trimming,' Granby said. 'I could have pulled out my hair when I woke up and he told me smug as a deacon that he had packed you off alone with some Chinaman; not that Temeraire would let any harm come to you, but anything could happen in a crowd, after all.'

'No, nothing of the kind was attempted at all; our guide was a little rude to begin, but perfectly civil by the end.' Laurence glanced over at the bundles stacked in the corner, where Zhao Wei's men had left them. 'I begin to think Hammond was right, John; and it was all old-maid flutters and imagination,' he said, unhappily; it seemed to him, after the long day's tour, that the prince hardly needed to stoop to murder, with the many advantages of his country to serve as gentler and no less persuasive arguments.

'More likely Yongxing gave up trying aboard ship, and has just been waiting to get you settled in under his eyes,' Granby said pessimistically. 'This is a nice enough cottage, I suppose, but there are a damned lot of guards skulking about.'

'All the more reason not to fear,' Laurence said. 'If they meant to kill me, they could have done so by now, a dozen times over.'

'Temeraire would hardly stay here if the Emperor's own guards killed you, and him already suspicious,' Granby said. 'Most like he would do his best to kill the lot of them, and then I hope go find the ship again and go back home; though it takes them very hard, losing a captain, and he might just as easily go and run into the wild.'

'We can argue ourselves in circles this way forever.' Laurence lifted his hands impatiently and let them drop again. 'At least today, the only wish which I saw put in action was to make a desirable impression upon Temeraire.' He did not say that this goal had been thoroughly accomplished and with little effort; he did not know how to draw a contrast against the treatment of dragons in the West without sounding at best a complainer and at worst nearly disloyal: he was conscious afresh that he had not been raised an aviator, and he was unwilling to say anything that might wound Granby's feelings.

'You are a damned sight too quiet,' Granby said, unexpectedly, and Laurence gave a guilty start: he had been sitting and brooding in silence. 'I am not surprised he took a liking to the city, he is always on fire for anything new; but is it that bad?'

'It is not only the city,' Laurence said finally. 'It is the respect which is given to dragons; and not only to himself: they all of them have a great deal of liberty, as a matter of course. I think I saw a hundred dragons at least today, wandering through the streets, and no one took any notice of them.'

'And God forbid we should take a flight over Regent's Park but we have shrieks of murder and fire and flood all at once, and ten memoranda sent us from the Admiralty,' Granby agreed, with a quick flash of resentment. 'Not that we *could* set down in London if we wanted to: the streets are too narrow for anything bigger than a Winchester. From what we have seen even just from the air, this place is laid out with a good deal more sense. It is no wonder they have ten beasts to our one, if not more.'

Laurence was deeply relieved to find Granby taking no offence against him, and so willing to discuss the subject. 'John, do you know, here they do not assign handlers until the dragon is fifteen months of age; until then they are raised by other dragons.'

'Well, that seems a rotten waste to me, letting dragons sit around nursemaiding,' Granby said. 'But I suppose they can afford it. Laurence, when I think what we could do with a round dozen of those big scarlet fellows, that they have sitting around getting fat everywhere; it makes you weep.'

'Yes; but what I meant to say was, they seem not to have any ferals at all,' Laurence said. 'Is it not one in ten that we lose?'

'Oh, not nearly so many, not in modern times,' Granby said. 'We used to lose Longwings by the dozen, until Queen Elizabeth had the bright idea of setting her serving-maid to one and we found they would take to girls like lambs, and then it turned out the Xenicas would too. And Winchesters often used to nip off like lightning before you could get a stitch of harness on them, but nowadays we hatch them inside and let them flap about for a bit before bringing out the food. Not more than one in thirty, at the most, if you do not count the eggs we lose in the breeding grounds: the ferals already there hide them from us sometimes.'

Their conversation was interrupted by a servant; Laurence tried to wave the man away, but with apologetic bows and a tug on Laurence's sleeve, he made clear he wished to lead them out to the main dining chamber: Sun Kai, unexpectedly, had come to take tea with them.

Laurence was in no mood for company, and Hammond, who joined them to serve as translator, as yet remained stiff and unfriendly; they made an awkward and mostly-silent company. Sun Kai inquired politely about their accommodations, and then about their enjoyment of the country, which Laurence answered very shortly; he could not help some suspicion that this might be some attempt at probing Temeraire's state of mind, and still more so when Sun Kai at last came however to the purpose for his visit.

'Lung Tien Qian sends you an invitation,' Sun Kai said. 'She hopes you and Temeraire will take tea with her tomorrow in the Ten Thousand Lotus palace, in the morning before the flowers open.'

'Thank you, sir, for bearing the message,' Laurence said, polite but flat. 'Temeraire is anxious to know her better.' The invitation could hardly be refused, though he was by no means happy to see further lures thrown out to Temeraire.

Sun Kai nodded equably. 'She too is anxious to know more of her offspring's condition. Her judgement carries much weight with the Son of Heaven.' He sipped his tea and added, 'Perhaps you will wish to tell her of your nation, and the respect which Lung Tien Xiang has won there.'

Hammond translated this, and then added, quickly enough that Sun Kai might think it part of the translation of his own words, 'Sir, I trust you see this is a tolerably clear hint. You must make every effort to win her favour.'

'I cannot see why Sun Kai would give me any advice at all in the first place,' Laurence said, after the envoy had left them again. 'He has always been polite enough, but not what anyone would call friendly.'

'Well, it's not much advice, is it?' Granby said. 'He only said to tell her that Temeraire is happy: that's hardly something you couldn't have thought of alone, and it makes a polite noise.'

'Yes; but we would not have known to value her good opinion quite so highly, or think this meeting of any particular importance,' Hammond said. 'No; for a diplomat, he has said a great deal indeed, as much as he could, I imagine, without committing himself quite openly to us. This is most heartening,' he added, with what Laurence felt was excessive optimism, likely born of frustration: Hammond had so far written five times to the Emperor's ministers, to ask for a meeting where he might present his credentials: every note been returned unopened, and a flat refusal had met his request to go out from the island to meet the handful of other Westerners in the town.

'She cannot be so very maternal, if she agreed to send him so far away in the first place,' Laurence said to Granby, shortly after dawn the next morning; he was inspecting his best coat and trousers, which he had set out to air overnight, in the early light: his cravat needed pressing, and he thought he had noticed some frayed threads on his best shirt.

'They usually aren't, you know,' Granby said. 'Or at least, not after the hatching, though they get broody over the eggs when they are first laid. Not that they don't care at all, but after all, a dragonet can take the head off a goat five minutes after it breaks the shell; they don't need mothering. Here, let me have that; I can't press without scorching, but I can do up a seam.' He took the shirt and needle from Laurence and set to repairing the tear in the cuff.

'Still, she would not care to see him neglected, I am sure,' Laurence said. 'Though I wonder that she is so deeply in the Emperor's counsel; I would have imagined that if they sent any Celestial egg away, it would only have been of a lesser line. Thank you, Dyer; set it there,' he said, as the young runner came in bearing the hot iron from the stove.

His appearance polished so far as he could manage, Laurence joined Temeraire in the courtyard; the striped dragon had returned to escort them. The flight was only a short one, but curious: they flew so low they could see small clumps of ivy and rootlings that had managed to establish themselves upon the yellow-tiled roofs of the palace buildings, and see the colours of the jewels upon the mandarins' hats as the ministers went hurrying through the enormous courtyards and walkways below, despite the early hour of the morning.

The particular palace lay within the walls of the immense Forbidden City, easily identifiable from aloft: two immense dragon pavilions on either side of a long pond almost choked with water-lilies, the flowers still closed within their buds. Wide sturdy bridges spanned the pond, arched high for decoration, and a courtyard flagged with black marble lay to the south, just now being touched with first light.

The yellow-striped dragon landed here and bowed them along; as Temeraire padded by, Laurence could see other dragons stirring in the early light under the eaves of the great pavilions. An ancient Celestial was creeping stiffly out from the bay furthest to the southeast, the tendrils about his jaw long and drooping as moustaches. His enormous ruff was leached of colour, and his hide gone so translucent the black was now redly tinted with the colour of the flesh and blood beneath. Another of the yellow-striped dragons paced him carefully, nudging him occasionally with his nose towards the sun-drenched courtyard; the Celestial's eyes were a milky blue, the pupils barely visible beneath the cataracts.

A few other dragons emerged also: Imperials rather than Celestials, lacking the ruff and tendrils, and with more variety in their hue: some were as black as Temeraire, but others a deep indigo-washed blue; all very dark, however, except for Lien, who emerged at the same time out of a separate and private pavilion, set back and alone among the trees, and came to the pond to drink. With her white hide, she looked almost unearthly among the rest; Laurence felt it would be difficult to fault anyone for indulging in superstition towards her, and indeed the other dragons consciously gave her a wide berth. She ignored them entirely in return and yawned wide and red, shaking her head vigorously to scatter away the clinging drops of water, and then paced away into the gardens in solitary dignity.

Qian herself was waiting for them at one of the central pavilions, flanked by two Imperial dragons of particularly graceful appearance, all of them adorned with elaborate jewels. She inclined her head courteously and flicked a talon against a standing bell nearby to summon servants; the attending dragons shifted their places to make room for Laurence and Temeraire on her right, and the human servants brought Laurence a comfortable chair. Qian made no immediate conversation, but gestured towards the lake; the line of the morning sun was now travelling swiftly northwards over the water as the sun crept higher, and the lotus buds were unfolding in almost balletic progression; they numbered literally in the thousands, and made a spectacle of glowing pink colour against the deep green of their leaves.

As the last unfurled flowers came to rest, the dragons all tapped their claws against the flagstones in a clicking noise, a kind of applause. Now a small table was brought for

Laurence and great porcelain bowls painted in blue and white for the dragons, and a black, pungent tea poured for them all. To Laurence's surprise the dragons drank with enjoyment, even going so far as to lick up the leaves in the bottom of their cups. He himself found the tea curious and over-strong in flavour: almost the aroma of smoked meat, though he drained his cup politely as well. Temeraire drank his own enthusiastically and very fast, and then sat back with a peculiar uncertain expression, as though trying to decide whether he had liked it or not.

'You have come a very long way,' Qian said, addressing Laurence; an unobtrusive servant had stepped forward to her side to translate. 'I hope you are enjoying your visit with us, but surely you must miss your home?'

'An officer in the King's service must be used to go where he is required, madam,' Laurence said, wondering if this was meant as a suggestion. 'I have not spent more than a sixmonth at my own family's home since I took ship the first time, and that was as a boy of twelve.'

'That is very young, to go so far away,' Qian said. 'Your mother must have had great anxiety for you.'

'She had the acquaintance of Captain Mountjoy, with whom I served, and we knew his family well,' Laurence said, and seized the opening to add, 'You yourself had no such advantage, I regret, on being parted from Temeraire; I would be glad to satisfy you on whatever points I might, if only in retrospect.'

She turned her head to the attending dragons. 'Perhaps Mei and Shu will take Xiang to see the flowers more closely,' she said, using Temeraire's Chinese name. The two Imperials inclined their heads and stood up expectantly waiting for Temeraire.

Temeraire looked a little worriedly at Laurence, and said, 'They are very nice from here?'

Laurence felt rather anxious himself at the prospect of a

solitary interview, with so little sense of what might please Qian, but he mustered a smile for Temeraire and said, 'I will wait here with your mother; I am sure you will enjoy them.'

'Be sure not to bother Grandfather or Lien,' Qian added to the Imperial dragons, who nodded as they led Temeraire away.

The servants refilled his cup and Qian's bowl from a fresh kettle, and she lapped at it in a more leisurely way. Presently she said, 'I understand Temeraire has been serving in your army.'

There was unmistakably a note of censure in her voice, which did not need translation. 'Among us, all those dragons who can, serve in defence of their home: that is no dishonour, but the fulfilment of our duty,' Laurence said. 'I assure you we could not value him more highly. There are very few dragons among us: even the least are greatly prized, and Temeraire is of the highest order.'

She rumbled low and thoughtfully. 'Why are there so few dragons, that you must ask your most valued to fight?'

'We are a small nation, nothing like your own,' Laurence said. 'Only a handful of smaller wild breeds were native to the British Isles, when the Romans came and began to tame them. Since then, by crossbreeding our lines have multiplied, and thanks to careful tending of our cattle herds, we have been able to increase our numbers, but still we cannot support nearly so many as you here possess.'

She lowered her head and regarded him keenly. 'And among the French, how are dragons treated?'

Instinctively Laurence was certain British treatment of dragons was superior and more generous than that of any other Western nation; but he was unhappily aware he would have considered it also superior to China's, if he had not come and already seen plainly otherwise. A month before, he could easily have spoken with pride of how British dragons were cared for. Like all of them, Temeraire had been fed and housed on raw meat and in bare clearings, with constant training and little entertainment. Laurence thought he might as well brag of raising children in a pigsty to the Queen, as speak of such conditions to this elegant dragon in her flower-decked palace. If the French were no better, they were hardly worse; and he would have thought very little of anyone who covered the faults in his own service by blackening another's.

'In ordinary course, the practices in France are much the same as ours, I believe,' he said at last. 'I do not know what promises were made you, in Temeraire's particular case, but I can tell you that Emperor Napoleon himself is a military man: even as we left England he was in the field, and any dragon who was his companion would hardly remain behind while he went to war.'

'You are yourself descended from kings, I understand,' Qian said unexpectedly, and turning her head spoke to one of the servants, who hurried forward with a long rice-paper scroll and unrolled it upon the table: with amazement, Laurence saw it was a copy, in a much finer hand and larger, of the familial chart which he had drawn so long ago at the New Year banquet. 'This is correct?' she inquired, seeing him so startled.

It had never occurred to him that the information would come to her ears, nor that she would find it of interest. But he at once swallowed any reluctance: he would puff off his consequence to her day and night if it would win her approval. 'My family is indeed an old one, and proud; you see I myself have gone into service in the Corps, and count it an honour,' he said, though guilt pricked at him; certainly no one in the circles of his birth would have called it as much.

Qian nodded, apparently satisfied, and sipped again at her tea while the servant carried the chart away again. Laurence cast about for something else to say. 'If I may be so bold, I think I may with confidence say on behalf of my Government that we would gladly agree to whatever conditions the French accepted, on your first sending Temeraire's egg to them.'

'Many considerations beside remain,' was all she said in response to this overture, however.

Temeraire and the two Imperials were already coming back from their walk, Temeraire having evidently set a rather hurried pace; at the same time, the white dragon came walking past as she returned to her own quarters with Yongxing now by her side, speaking with her in low voices, one hand affectionately resting upon her side. She walked slowly, so he could keep pace, and also the several attendants trailing reluctantly after burdened with large scrolls and several books: still the Imperials held well back and waited to let them pass before coming back into the pavilion.

'Qian, why is she that colour?' Temeraire asked, peeking back out at Lien after she had gone by. 'She looks so very strange.'

'Who can understand the workings of Heaven?' Qian said repressively. 'Do not be disrespectful. Lien is a great scholar; she was *chuang-yuan*, many years ago, though she did not need to submit to the examinations at all, being a Celestial, and also she is your elder cousin. She was sired by Chu, who was hatched of Xian, as was I.'

'Oh,' Temeraire said, abashed. More timidly he asked, 'Who was my sire?'

'Lung Qin Gao,' Qian said, and twitched her tail; she looked rather pleased by the recollection. 'He is an Imperial dragon, and is at present in the south in Hangzhou: his companion is a prince of the third rank, and they are visiting the West Lake.'

Laurence was startled to learn Celestials could so breed true with Imperials: but on his tentative inquiry Qian confirmed as much. 'That is how our line continues. We cannot breed among ourselves,' she said, and added, quite unconscious of how she was staggering him, 'There are only myself

310

and Lien now, who are female, and besides Grandfather and Chu, there are only Chuan and Ming and Zhi, and we are all cousins at most.'

'Only eight of them, altogether?' Hammond stared and sat down blankly: as well he might.

'I don't see how they can possibly continue on like that forever,' Granby said. 'Are they so mad to keep them only for the emperors, that they'll risk losing the whole line?'

'Evidently from time to time a pair of Imperials will give birth to a Celestial,' Laurence said, between bites; he was sitting down at last to his painfully late dinner, in his bedroom: seven o'clock and full darkness outside, and he had swelled himself near to bursting with tea in an effort to stave off hunger over the visit which had stretched to many hours. 'That is how the oldest fellow there now was born; and he is sire to the lot of them, going back four or five generations.'

'I cannot make it out in the least,' Hammond said, paying no attention to the rest of the conversation. 'Eight Celestials; why on earth would they ever have given him away? Surely, at least for breeding— I cannot, I *cannot* credit it; Bonaparte cannot have impressed them so, not secondhand and from a continent away. There must be something else, something which I have not grasped. Gentlemen, you will excuse me,' he added, distractedly, and rose and left them alone. Laurence finished his meal without much appetite and set down his chopsticks.

'She did not say no to our keeping him, at any rate,' Granby said into the silence, but dismally.

Laurence said, after a moment, more to quell his own inner voices, 'I could not be so selfish to even try and deny him the pleasure of making the better acquaintance of his own kindred, or learning about his native land.'

'It is all stuff and nonsense in the end, Laurence,' Granby said, trying to comfort him. 'A dragon won't be parted from

311

his captain for all the gems in Araby, and all the calves in Christendom too, for that matter.'

Laurence rose and went to the window. Temeraire had curled up for the night upon the heated courtyard stones once again. The moon had risen, and he was very beautiful to look at in the silver light, with the blossom-heavy trees on either side hanging low above him and a dappled reflection in the pond, all his scales gleaming.

'That is true; a dragon will endure a great deal sooner than be parted from his captain. It does not follow that a decent man would ask it of him,' Laurence said, very low, and let the curtain fall.

Chapter Fourteen

Temeraire himself was quiet the day after their visit. Laurence went out to sit with him, and gazed at him with anxiety; but he did not know how to broach the subject of what distressed him, nor what to say. If Temeraire was grown discontented with his lot in England, and wished to stay, there was nothing to be done. Hammond would hardly argue, so long as he were able to complete his negotiations; he cared a good deal more for establishing a permanent embassy and winning some sort of treaty than for getting Temeraire home. Laurence was by no means inclined to force the issue early.

Qian had told Temeraire, on their departure, to make himself free of the palace, but the same invitation had not been extended to Laurence. Temeraire did not ask permission to go, but he looked wistfully into the distance, and paced the courtyard in circles, and refused Laurence's offer to read together. At last growing sick of himself, Laurence said, 'Would you wish to go see Qian again? I am sure she would welcome your visit.'

'She did not ask you,' Temeraire said, but his wings fanned halfway out, irresolute.

'There can be no offence intended in a mother liking to see her offspring privately,' Laurence said, and this excuse was sufficient; Temeraire very nearly glowed with pleasure and set off at once. He returned only late that evening, jubilant and full of plans to return.

'They have started teaching me to write,' he said. 'I have already learned twenty-five characters today; shall I show you?'

'By all means,' Laurence answered, and not only to humour him; grimly he set himself to studying the symbols Temeraire laid down, and copying them down as best he could with a quill instead of a brush while Temeraire pronounced them for his benefit, though he looked rather doubtful at Laurence's attempts to reproduce the sounds. He did not make much progress, but the effort alone made Temeraire so very happy that he could not begrudge it, and concealed the intense strain which he had suffered under the entire seeming endless day.

Infuriatingly, however, Laurence had to contend not only with his own feelings, but with Hammond on the subject. '*One* visit, in your company, could serve as reassurance and give her the opportunity of making your acquaintance,' the diplomat said. 'But this continued solitary visiting cannot be allowed. If he comes to prefer China and agrees of his own volition to stay, we will lose any hope of success: they will pack us off at once.'

'That is enough, sir,' Laurence said angrily. 'I have no intention of insulting Temeraire by suggesting that his natural wish to become acquainted with his kind in any way represents a lack of fidelity.'

Hammond pressed the point, and the conversation grew heated; at last Laurence concluded by saying, 'If I must make this plain, so be it: I do not consider myself as under your command. I have been given no instructions to that effect, and your attempt to assert an authority without official foundation is entirely improper.'

Their relations had already been tolerably cool; now they became frigid, and Hammond did not come to have dinner with Laurence and his officers that night. The next day, however, he came early into the pavilion, before Temeraire had left on his visit, accompanied by Prince Yongxing. 'His Highness has been kind enough to come and see how we do; I am sure you will join me in welcoming him,' he said, with rather hard emphasis on the last words, and Laurence rather reluctantly rose to make his most formal leg.

'You are very kind, sir; as you see you find us very comfortable,' he said, with stiff politeness, and wary; he still did not trust Yongxing's intentions in the least.

Yongxing inclined his head a very little, equally stiff and unsmiling, and then turned and beckoned to a young boy following him: no more than thirteen years of age, wearing wholly nondescript garments of the usual indigo-dyed cotton. Glancing up at him, the boy nodded and walked past Laurence, directly up to Temeraire, and made a formal greeting: he raised his hands up in front of himself, fingers wrapped over one another, and inclined his head, saying something in Chinese at the same time. Temeraire looked a little puzzled, and Hammond interjected hastily, 'Tell him yes, for Heaven's sake.'

'Oh,' said Temeraire, uncertainly, but said something to the boy, evidently affirmative. Laurence was startled to see the boy climb up onto Temeraire's foreleg, and arrange himself there. Yongxing's face was as always difficult to read, but there was a suggestion of satisfaction to his mouth; then he said, 'We will go inside and take tea,' and turned away.

'Be sure not to let him fall,' Hammond added hastily to Temeraire, with an anxious look at the boy, who was sitting crosslegged, with great poise, and seemed as likely to fall off as a Buddha statue to climb off its pediment.

'Roland,' Laurence called; she and Dyer had been working their trigonometry in the back corner. 'Pray see if he would like some refreshment.'

She nodded and went to talk to the boy in her broken

Chinese while Laurence followed the other men across the courtyard and into the residence. Already the servants had hastily rearranged the furniture: a single draped chair for Yongxing, with a footstool, and armless chairs placed at right angles to it for Laurence and Hammond. They brought the tea with great ceremony and attention, and throughout the process Yongxing remained perfectly silent. Nor did he speak once the servants had at last withdrawn, but sipped at his tea, very slowly.

Hammond at length broke the silence with polite thanks for the comfort of their residence, and the attentions which they had received. 'The tour of the city, in particular, was a great kindness; may I ask, sir, if it was your doing?'

Yongxing said, 'It was the Emperor's wish. Perhaps, Captain,' he added, 'you were favourably impressed?'

It was very little a question, and Laurence said, shortly, 'I was, sir; your city is remarkable.' Yongxing smiled, a small dry twist of the lips, and did not say anything more, but then he scarcely needed to; Laurence looked away, all the memory of the coverts in England and the bitter contrast fresh in his mind.

They sat in dumb-show a while longer; Hammond ventured again, 'May I inquire as to the Emperor's health? We are most eager, sir, as you can imagine, to pay the King's respects to His Imperial Majesty, and to convey the letters which I bear.'

'The Emperor is in Chengde,' Yongxing said dismissively. 'He will not return to Peking soon; you will have to be patient.'

Laurence was increasingly angry. Yongxing's attempt to insinuate the boy into Temeraire's company was as blatant as any of the previous attempts to separate the two of them, and yet now Hammond was making not the least objection, and still trying to make polite conversation in the face of insulting rudeness. Pointedly, Laurence said, 'Your Highness's companion seems a very likely young man; may I inquire if he is your son?'

Yongxing frowned at the question and said only, 'No,' coldly.

Hammond, sensing Laurence's impatience, hastily intervened before Laurence could say anything more. 'We are of course only too happy to attend the Emperor's convenience; but I hope we may be granted some additional liberty, if the wait is likely to be long; at least as much as has been given the French ambassador. I am sure, sir, you have not forgotten their murderous attack upon us, at the outset of our journey, and I hope you will allow me to say, once again, that the interests of our nations march far more closely together than yours with theirs.'

Unchecked by any reply, Hammond went on; he spoke passionately and at length about the dangers of Napoleon's domination of Europe, the stifling of the trade which should otherwise bring great wealth to China; and the threat of an insatiable conqueror spreading his empire ever wider, perhaps, he added, ending on their very doorstop, 'For Napoleon has already made one attempt, sir, to come at us in India, and he makes no secret that his ambition is to exceed Alexander. If he should ever be successful, you must realize his rapacity will not be satisfied there.'

The idea that Napoleon should subdue Europe, conquer the Russian and the Ottoman Empires both, cross the Himalayas, establish himself in India, and still have energy left to wage war on China, was to Laurence a piece of exaggeration that would hardly convince anyone; and as for trade, he knew that argument carried no weight at all with Yongxing, who had so fervently spoken of China's self-sufficiency. Nevertheless the prince did not interrupt Hammond at all from beginning to end, listened to the entire long speech frowning, and then at the end of it, when Hammond concluded with a renewed plea to be granted the same freedoms as De Guignes, Yongxing received it in silence, sat a long time, and then said only, 'You have as much liberty as he does; anything more would be unsuitable.'

'Sir,' Hammond said, 'perhaps you are unaware that we have not been permitted to leave the island, nor to communicate with any official even by letter.'

'Neither is he permitted,' Yongxing said. 'It is not proper for foreigners to wander through Peking, disrupting the affairs of the magistrates and the ministers: they have much to occupy them.'

Hammond was left baffled by this reply, confusion writ plain on his face, and Laurence, for his part, had sat through enough; plainly Yongxing meant nothing but to waste their time, while the boy flattered and fawned over Temeraire. As the child was not his own son, Yongxing had surely chosen him from his relations especially for great charm of personality and instructed him to be as insinuating as ever he might. Laurence did not truly fear that Temeraire would take a preference to the boy, but he had no intention of sitting here playing the fool for the benefit of Yongxing's scheming.

'We cannot be leaving the children unattended this way,' he said abruptly. 'You will excuse me, sir,' and rose from the table already bowing.

As Laurence had suspected, Yongxing had no desire to sit and make conversation with Hammond except to provide the boy an open field, and he rose also to take his leave of them. They returned all together to the courtyard, where Laurence found, to his private satisfaction, that the boy had climbed down from Temeraire's arm and was engaged in a game of jacks with Roland and Dyer, all of them munching on ship's biscuit, and Temeraire had wandered out to the pier, to enjoy the breeze coming off the lake.

Yongxing spoke sharply, and the boy sprang up with a guilty expression; Roland and Dyer looked equally abashed, with glances towards their abandoned books. 'We thought it was only polite to be hospitable,' Roland said hurriedly, looking to see how Laurence would take this.

'I hope he has enjoyed the visit,' Laurence said, mildly, to their relief. 'Back to your work, now.' They hurried back to their books, and, the boy called to heel, Yongxing swept away with a dissatisfied mien, exchanging a few words with Hammond in Chinese; Laurence gladly watched him go.

'At least we may be grateful that De Guignes is as restricted in his movements as we are,' Hammond said after a moment. 'I cannot think Yongxing would bother to lie on the subject, though I cannot understand how—' he stopped in puzzlement and shook his head. 'Well, perhaps I may learn a little more tomorrow.'

'I beg your pardon?' Laurence said, and Hammond absently said, 'He said he would come again, at the same time; he means to make a regular visit of it.'

'He may mean whatever he likes,' Laurence said, angrily, at finding Hammond had thus meekly accepted further intrusions on his behalf, 'but *I* will not be playing attendance on him; and why you should choose to waste your time cultivating a man you know very well has not the least sympathy for us is beyond me.'

Hammond answered with some heat, 'Of course Yongxing has no natural sympathy for us; why should he or any other man here? Our work is to win them over, and if he is willing to give us the chance to persuade him, it is our duty to try, sir; I am surprised that the effort of remaining civil and drinking a little tea should so try your patience.'

Laurence snapped, 'And I am surprised to find you so unconcerned over this attempt at supplanting me, after all your earlier protests.'

'What, with a twelve-year-old boy?' Hammond said, so very incredulous it was nearly offensive. 'I, sir, in my turn, am astonished at your taking alarm *now*; and perhaps if you had not been so quick to dismiss my advice before, you should not have so much need to fear.'

'I do not fear in the least,' Laurence said, 'but neither am I disposed to tolerate so blatant an attempt, or to have us

319

submit tamely to a daily invasion whose only purpose is to give offence.'

'I will remind you, Captain, as you did me not so very long ago, that just as you are not under my authority, *I* am not under *yours*,' Hammond said. 'The conduct of our diplomacy has very clearly been placed in my hands, and thank Heaven: if we were relying upon you, by now I dare say you would be blithely flying back to England, with half our trade in the Pacific sinking to the bottom of the ocean behind you.'

'Very well; you may do as you like, sir,' Laurence said, 'but you had best make plain to him that I do not mean to leave this protégé of his alone with Temeraire anymore, and I think you will find him less eager to be *persuaded* afterwards; and do not imagine,' he added, 'that I will tolerate having the boy let in when my back is turned, either.'

'As you are disposed to think me a liar and an unscrupulous schemer, I see very little purpose in denying I should do any such thing,' Hammond said angrily, colouring up.

He departed instantly, leaving Laurence still angry but ashamed and conscious of having been unfair; he would himself have called it grounds for a challenge. By the next morning, when from the pavilion he saw Yongxing going away with the boy, having evidently cut short the visit on being denied access to Temeraire, his guilt was sharp enough that he made some attempt to apologize, with little success: Hammond would have none of it.

'Whether he took offence at your refusing to join us, or whether you were correct about his aims, can make no difference now,' he said, very coldly. 'If you will excuse me, I have letters to write,' and so quitted the room.

Laurence gave it up and instead went to say farewell to Temeraire, only to have his guilt and unhappiness both renewed at seeing in Temeraire's manner an almost furtive excitement, a very great eagerness to be gone. Hammond was hardly wrong: the idle flattery of a child was nothing to the danger of the company of Qian and the Imperial dragons, no matter how devious Yongxing's motives or how sincere Qian's; there was only less honest excuse for complaining of her.

Temeraire would be gone for hours, but the house being small and the chambers separated mainly by screens of rice paper, Hammond's angry presence was nearly palpable inside, so Laurence stayed in the pavilion after he had gone, attending to his correspondence: unnecessarily, as it was now five months since he had received any letters, and little of any interest had occurred since the welcoming dinner party, now two weeks old; he was not disposed to write of the quarrel with Hammond.

He dozed off over the writing, and woke rather abruptly, nearly knocking heads with Sun Kai, who was bending over him and shaking him. 'Captain Laurence, you must wake up,' Sun Kai was saying.

Laurence said automatically, 'I beg your pardon; what is the matter?' and then stared: Sun Kai had spoken in quite excellent English, with an accent more reminiscent of Italian than Chinese. 'Good Lord, have you been able to speak English all this time?' he demanded, his mind leaping to every occasion on which Sun Kai had stood on the dragondeck, privy to all their conversations, and now revealed as having understood every word.

'There is no time at present for explanations,' Sun Kai said. 'You must come with me at once: men are coming here to kill you, and all your companions also.'

It was near on five o'clock in the afternoon, and the lake and trees, framed in the pavilion doors, were golden in the setting light; birds were speaking occasionally from up in the rafters where they nested. The remark, delivered in perfectly calm tones, was so ludicrous Laurence did not at first understand it, and then stood up in outrage. 'I am not going anywhere in response to such a threat, with so little explanation,' he said, and raised his voice. 'Granby!'

321

'Everything all right, sir?' Blythe had been occupying himself in the neighbouring courtyard on some busy-work, and now poked his head in, even as Granby came running.

'Mr. Granby, we are evidently to expect an attack,' Laurence said. 'As this house does not admit of much security, we will take the small pavilion to the south, with the interior pond. Establish a lookout, and let us have fresh locks in all the pistols.'

'Very good,' Granby said, and dashed away again; Blythe, in his customary silence, picked up the cutlasses he had been sharpening and offered Laurence one before wrapping up the others and carrying them with his whetstone to the pavilion.

Sun Kai shook his head. 'This is great foolishness,' he said, following after Laurence. 'The very largest gang of hunhun are coming from the city. I have a boat waiting just here, and there is time yet for you and all your men to get your things and come away.'

Laurence inspected the pavilion entryway; as he had remembered, the pillars were made of stone rather than wood, and nearly two feet in diameter, very sturdy, and the walls of a smooth grey brick under their layer of red paint. The roof was of wood, which was a pity, but he thought the glazed tile would not catch fire easily. 'Blythe, will you see if you can arrange some elevation for Lieutenant Riggs and his riflemen out of those stones in the garden? Pray assist him, Willoughby; thank you.'

Turning around, he said to Sun Kai, 'Sir, you have not said where you would take me, nor who these assassins are, nor whence they have been sent; still less have you given us any reason to trust you. You have certainly deceived us so far as your knowledge of our language. Why you should so abruptly reverse yourself, I have no idea, and after the treatment which we have received, I am in no humour to put myself into your hands.'

Hammond came with the other men, looking confused, and

came to join Laurence, greeting Sun Kai in Chinese. 'May I inquire what is happening?' he asked stiffly.

'Sun Kai has told me to expect another attempt at assassination,' Laurence said. 'See if you can get anything more clear from him; in the meantime, I must assume we are shortly to come under attack, and make arrangements. He can speak perfect English,' he added. 'You need not resort to Chinese.' He left Sun Kai with a visibly startled Hammond, and joined Riggs and Granby at the entryway.

'If we could knock a couple of holes in this front wall, we could shoot down at any of them coming,' Riggs said, tapping the brick. 'Otherwise, sir, we're best off laying down a barricade mid-room, and shooting as they come in; but then we can't have fellows with swords at the entryway.'

'Lay and man the barricade,' Laurence said. 'Mr. Granby, block as much of this entryway as you can, so they cannot come in more than three or four abreast if you can manage it. We will form up the rest of the men to either side of the opening, well clear of the field of fire, and hold the door with pistols and cutlasses between volleys while Mr. Riggs and his fellows reload.'

Granby and Riggs both nodded. 'Right you are,' Riggs said. 'We have a couple of spare rifles along, sir; we could use you at the barricade.'

This was rather transparent, and Laurence treated it with the contempt which it deserved. 'Use them for second shots as you can; we cannot waste the guns in the hands of any man who is not a trained rifleman.'

Keynes came in almost staggering under a basket of sheets, with three of the elaborate porcelain vases from their residence laid on top. 'You are not my usual kind of patients,' he said, 'but I can bandage and splint you, at any rate. I will be in the back by the pond. And I have brought these to carry water in,' he added, sardonic, jerking his chin at the vases. 'I suppose they would bring fifty pounds each in auction, so let that be an encouragement not to drop them.'

'Roland, Dyer; which of you is the better hand at reloading?' Laurence asked. 'Very well; you will both help Mr. Riggs for the first three volleys, then Dyer, you are to go help Mr. Keynes, and run back and forth with the water jugs as that duty permits.'

'Laurence,' Granby said in an undertone, when the others had gone, 'I don't see any sign of all those guards anywhere, and they have always been used to patrol at this hour; they must have been called away by someone.'

Laurence nodded silently and waved him back to work. 'Mr. Hammond, you will pray go behind the barricade,' he said, as the diplomat came to his side, Sun Kai with him.

'Captain Laurence, I beg you to listen to me,' Hammond said urgently. 'We had much better go with Sun Kai at once. These attackers he expects are young bannermen, members of the Tartar tribes, who from poverty and lack of occupation have gone into a sort of local brigandage, and there may be a great many of them.'

'Will they have any artillery?' Laurence asked, paying no attention to the attempt at persuasion.

'Cannon? No, of course not; they do not even have muskets,' Sun Kai said, 'but what does that matter? There may be one hundred of them or more, and I have heard rumours that some among them have even studied Shaolin Quan, in secret, though it is against the law.'

'And some of them may be, however distantly, kin to the Emperor,' Hammond added. 'If we were to kill one, it could easily be used as a pretext for taking offence, and casting us out of the country; you must see we ought to leave at once.'

'Sir, you will give us some privacy,' Laurence said to Sun Kai, flatly, and the envoy did not argue, but silently bowed his head and moved some distance away.

'Mr. Hammond,' Laurence said, turning to him, 'you yourself warned me to beware of attempts to separate me from Temeraire, now only consider: if he should return here, to

324

find us gone, with no explanation and all our baggage gone also, how should he ever find us again? Perhaps he might even be convinced that we had been given a treaty and left him deliberately behind, as Yongxing once desired me to do.'

'And how will the case be improved if he returns and finds you dead, and all of us with you?' Hammond said impatiently. 'Sun Kai has before now given us cause to trust him.'

'I give less weight to a small piece of inconsequential advice than you do, sir, and more to a long and deliberate lie of omission; he has unquestionably spied on us from the very beginning of our acquaintance,' Laurence said. 'No; we are not going with him. It will not be more than a few hours before Temeraire returns, and I am confident in our holding out that long.'

'Unless they have found some means of distracting him, and keeping him longer at his visit,' Hammond said. 'If the Chinese government meant to separate us from him, they could have done so by force at any time during his absence. I am sure Sun Kai can arrange to have a message sent to him at his mother's residence once we have gone to safety.'

'Then let him go and send the message now, if he likes,' Laurence said. 'You are welcome to go with him.'

'No, sir,' Hammond said, flushing, and turned on his heel to speak with Sun Kai. The former envoy shook his head and left, and Hammond went to take a cutlass from the ready heap.

They worked for another quarter of an hour, hauling in three of the queer-shaped boulders from outside to make the barricade for the riflemen, and dragging over the enormous dragon-couch to block off most of the entryway. The sun had gone by now, but the usual lanterns did not make their appearance around the island, nor any signs of human life at all.

'Sir!' Digby hissed suddenly, pointing out into the grounds. 'Two points to starboard, outside the doors of the house.'

'Away from the entry,' Laurence said; he could not see

anything in the twilight, but Digby's young eyes were better than his. 'Willoughby, douse that light.'

The soft click-click of the guns being cocked, the echo of his own breath in his ears, the constant untroubled hum of the flies and mosquitoes outside; these were at first the only noise, until use filtered them out and he could hear the light running footsteps outside: a great many men, he thought. Abruptly there was a crash of wood, several yells. 'They've broken into the house, sir,' Hackley whispered hoarsely from the barricades.

'Quiet, there,' Laurence said, and they kept a silent vigil while the sound of breaking furniture and shattering glass came from the house. The flare of torches outside cast shadows into the pavilion, weaving and leaping in strange angles as a search commenced. Laurence heard men calling to each other outside, the sound coming down from the eaves of the roof. He glanced back; Riggs nodded, and the three riflemen raised their guns.

The first man appeared in the entrance and saw the wooden slab of the dragon-couch blocking it. 'My shot,' Riggs said clearly, and fired: the Chinaman fell dead with his mouth open to shout.

But the report of the gun brought more cries from outside, and men came bursting in with swords and torches in their hands; a full volley fired off, killing another three, then one more shot from the last rifle, and Riggs called, 'Prime and reload!'

The quick slaughter of their fellows had checked the advance of the larger body of men, and clustered them in the opening left in the doorway. Yelling 'Temeraire!' and 'England!' the aviators launched themselves from the shadows, and engaged the attackers close at hand.

The torchlight was painful to Laurence's eyes after the long wait in the dark, and the smoke of the burning wood mingled with that from the musketry. There was no room for any real swordplay; they were engaged hilt-to-hilt, except when one of the Chinese swords broke – they smelled of rust – and a few men fell over. Otherwise they were all simply heaving back against the pressure of dozens of bodies, trying to come through the narrow opening.

Digby, being too slim to be of much use in the human wall, was stabbing at the attackers between their legs, their arms, through any space left open. 'My pistols,' Laurence shouted at him; no chance to pull them free himself: he was holding his cutlass with two hands, one upon the hilt and another laid upon the flat of the blade, keeping off three men. They were packed so close together they could not move either way to strike at him, but could only raise and lower their swords in a straight line, trying to break his blade through sheer weight.

Digby pulled one of the pistols out of its holster, and fired, taking the man directly before Laurence between the eyes. The other two involuntarily pulled back, and Laurence managed to stab one in the belly, then seized the other by the sword-arm and threw him to the ground; Digby put a sword into his back, and he lay still.

'Present arms!' Riggs yelled, from behind, and Laurence bellowed, 'Clear the door! Back aways!' He swung a cut at the head of the man engaged with Granby, making him flinch back, and they scrambled back together, the polished stone floor already slick under their boot-heels. Someone pushed the dripping jug into his hand; he swallowed a couple of times and passed it on, wiping his mouth and his forehead against his sleeve. The rifles all fired at once, and another couple of shots after; then they were back into the fray.

The attackers had already learned to fear the rifles, and they had left a little clear space before the door, many milling about a few paces off under the torches; they nearly filled the courtyard before the pavilion: Sun Kai's estimate had not been exaggerated. Laurence shot a man six paces away, then flipped the pistol in his hand; as they came rushing back on, he clubbed another in the side of the head, and then he was again pushing back against the weight of the swords, until Riggs shouted again.

'Well done, gentlemen,' Laurence said, breathing deeply. The Chinese had retreated at the shout and were not immediately at the door; Riggs had experience enough to hold the volley until they advanced again. 'For the moment, the advantage is ours. Mr. Granby, we will divide into two parties. Stay back this next wave, and we shall alternate. Therrows, Willoughby, Digby, with me; Martin, Blythe, and Hammond, with Granby.'

'I can go with both, sir,' Digby said. 'I'm not tired at all, truly; it's less work for me, since I can't help to hold them.'

'Very well, but be sure to take water between, and stay back on occasion,' Laurence said. 'There are a damned lot of them, as I dare say you have all seen,' he said candidly. 'But our position is a good one, and I have no doubt we can hold them as long as ever need be, so long as we pace ourselves properly.'

'And go see Keynes at once to be tied up if you take a cut or a blow – we cannot afford to lose anyone to slow bleeding,' Granby added to this, while Laurence nodded. 'Only sing out, and someone will come to take your place in line.'

A sudden feverish many-voiced yell rose from outside, the men working themselves up to facing the volley, then a pounding of running feet, and Riggs shouted, 'Fire!' as the attackers stormed the entryway again.

The fighting at the door was a greater strain now with fewer of them to hand, but the opening was sufficiently narrow that they could hold it even so. The bodies of the dead were forming a grisly addition to their barrier, piled now two and even three deep, and some of the attackers were forced to stretch over them to fight. The reloading time seemed queerly long, an illusion; Laurence was very glad of the rest when at last the next volley was ready. He leaned against the wall, drinking again from the vase; his arms and shoulders were aching from the constant pressure, and his knees.

'Is it empty, sir?' Dyer was there, anxious, and Laurence handed him the vase: he trotted away back towards the pond, through the haze of smoke shrouding the middle of the room; it was drifting slowly upwards, into the cavernous emptiness above.

Again the Chinese did not immediately storm the door, with the volley waiting. Laurence stepped a little way back into the pavilion and tried to look out, to see if he could make anything out beyond the front line of the struggle. But the torches dazzled his eyes too much: nothing but an impenetrable darkness beyond the first row of shining faces staring intently towards the entryway, feverish with the strain of battle. The time seemed long; he missed the ship's glass, and the steady telling of the bell. Surely it had been an hour or two, by now; Temeraire would come soon.

A sudden clamour from outside, and a new rhythm of clapping hands. His hand went without thought to the cutlass hilt; the volley went off with a roar. 'For England and the King!' Granby shouted, and led his group into the fray.

But the men at the entry were drawing back to either side, Granby and his fellows were left standing uneasily in the opening. Laurence wondered if maybe they had some artillery after all. But instead abruptly a man came running at them down the open aisle, alone, as if intent on throwing himself onto their swords: they stood set, waiting. Not three paces distant he leaped into the air, landed somehow sideways against the column, and sprang off it literally over their heads, diving, and tucked himself neatly into a rolling somersault along the stone floor.

The manoeuvre defied gravity more thoroughly than any skylarking Laurence had ever seen done; ten feet into the air and down again with no propulsion but his own legs. The

329

man leaped up at once, unbruised, now at Granby's back with the main wave of attackers charging the entryway again. 'Therrows, Willoughby,' Laurence bellowed to the men in his group, unnecessarily: they were already running to hold him back.

The man had no weapon, but his agility was beyond anything; he jumped away from their swinging swords in a manner that made them seem accomplices in a stage play rather than in deadly earnest, trying to kill him; and from his greater distance, Laurence could see he was drawing them steadily back, towards Granby and the others, where their swords could only become dangers to their comrades.

Laurence clapped on to his pistol and drew it out, his hands following the practised sequence despite the dark and the furore; in his head he listened to the chant of the great guns exercise, so nearly parallel. Ramrod down the muzzle with a rag, twice, and then he pulled back the hammer to half-cocked; groping after the paper cartridge in his hip pouch.

Therrows suddenly screamed and fell, clutching his knee. Willoughby's head turned to look; his sword was held defensively, at the level of his chest, but in that one moment of incaution the Chinese man leaped again impossibly high and struck him full on the jaw with both feet. The sound of his neck snapping was grisly; he was lifted an inch straight up off the ground, arms splaying out wide, and then collapsed into a heap, his head lolling side to side upon the ground. The Chinese man tumbled to the ground from his leap, landed on his shoulder, rolling lightly back up, and turned to look at Laurence.

Riggs was yelling from behind him, 'Make ready! Faster, damn you, make ready!'

Laurence's hands were still working. Tearing open the cartridge of black powder with his teeth, a few grains like sand bitter on his tongue. Powder straight down the muzzle, then the round lead ball after, the paper in for wadding, rammed down hard; no time to check the primer, and he raised the gun and blew out the man's brains, barely more than arm's reach away.

Laurence and Granby dragged Therrows back over to Keynes while the Chinese backed away from the waiting volley. He was sobbing quietly, his leg dangling useless; 'I'm sorry, sir,' he kept saying, choked.

'For Heaven's sake, enough moan,' Keynes said sharply, when they put him down, and slapped Therrows across the face with a distinct lack of sympathy. The young man gulped, but stopped, and hastily scrubbed an arm across his face. 'The kneecap is broken,' Keynes said, after a moment. 'A clean enough break, but he won't be standing again for a month.'

'Get over to Riggs when you have been splinted, and reload for them,' Laurence told Therrows, then he and Granby dashed back to the entryway.

'We'll take rest by turns,' Laurence said, kneeling down by the others. 'Hammond, you first; go and tell Riggs to keep one rifle back, loaded, at all times, if they should try and send another fellow over that way.'

Hammond was visibly heaving for breath, his cheeks marked with spots of bright red; he nodded and said hoarsely, 'Leave your pistols, I will reload.'

Blythe, gulping water from the vase, abruptly choked, spat out a fountain and yelled, 'Sweet Christ in Heaven!' and made them all jump. Laurence looked around wildly: a bright orange goldfish two fingers long was wriggling on the stones in the puddled water. 'Sorry,' Blythe said, panting. 'I felt the bugger squirming in my mouth.'

Laurence stared, then Martin started laughing, and for a moment they were all grinning at one another; then the rifles cracked off, and they were back to the door.

The attackers made no attempt at setting the pavilion on fire, which surprised Laurence; they had torches enough, and wood

331

was plentiful around the island. They did try smoke, building small bonfires to either side of the building under the eaves, but either through some trick of the pavilion's design, or simply the prevailing wind, a drifting air current carried the smoke up and out through the yellow tile roof. It was unpleasant enough, but not deadly, and near the pond the air was fresh. Each round the one man resting would go back there, to drink and clear his lungs, and have the handful of scratches they had all by now accumulated smeared with salve and bound up if still bleeding.

The gang tried a battering ram, a fresh-cut tree with the branches and leaves still attached, but Laurence called, 'Stand aside as they come, and cut at their legs.' The bearers ran themselves directly onto the blades with great courage, trying to break through, but even the three steps that led up to the pavilion door were enough to break their momentum. Several at the head fell with gashes showing bone, to be clubbed to death with pistol-butts, and then the tree itself toppled forward and halted their progress. The British had a few frantic minutes of hacking off the branches, to clear the view for the riflemen; by then the next volley was more than ready, and the attackers gave up the attempt.

After this the battle settled into a sort of grisly rhythm; each round of fire won them even more time to rest now, the Chinese evidently disheartened by their failure to break in through the small British line, and by the very great slaughter. Every bullet found its mark; Riggs and his men had been trained to make shots from the back of a dragon, flying sometimes at thirty knots in the heat of battle, and with less than thirty yards to the entryway, they could scarcely miss. It was a slow, grinding way to fight, every minute seeming to consume five times its proper length; Laurence began to count the time by volleys.

'We had better go to three shots only a volley, sir,' Riggs said, coughing, when Laurence knelt to speak with him, his next rest spell. 'It'll hold them all the same, now they've had a taste, and though I brought all the cartridges we had, we're not bloody infantry. I have Therrows making us more, but we have enough powder for another thirty rounds at most, I think.'

'That will have to do,' Laurence said. 'We will try and hold them longer between volleys. Start resting one man every other round, also.' He emptied his own cartridge box and Granby's into the general pile: only another seven, but that meant two rounds more at least, and the rifles were of more value than the pistols.

He splashed his face with water at the pond, smiling a little at the darting fish which he could see more clearly now, his eyes perhaps adjusting to the dark. His neckcloth was soaked quite through with sweat; he took it off and wrung it out over the stones, then could not bring himself to put it back on once he had exposed his grateful skin to the air. He rinsed it clean and left it spread out to dry, then hurried back.

Another measureless stretch of time, the faces of the attackers growing blurry and dim in the doorway. Laurence was struggling to hold off a couple of men, shoulder to shoulder with Granby, when he heard Dyer's high treble cry out, 'Captain! Captain!' from behind. He could not turn and look; there was no opportunity for pause.

'I have them,' Granby panted, and kicked the man in front in the balls with his heavy Hessian boot; he engaged the other hilt to hilt, and Laurence pulled away and turned hurriedly around.

A couple of men were standing dripping on the edge of the pond, and another pulling himself out: they had somehow found whatever reservoir fed the pond, and swum through it underneath the wall. Keynes was sprawled unmoving on the floor, and Riggs and the other riflemen were running over, still reloading frantically as they went. Hammond had been resting: he was swinging furiously at the two other men, pushing them back towards the water, but he did not have much science: they had short knives, and would get under his guard in a moment.

Little Dyer seized one of the great vases and flung it, still full of water, into the man bending over Keynes's body with his knife; it shattered against his head and knocked him down to the floor, dazed and slipping in the water. Roland, running over, snatched up Keynes's tenaculum, and dragged the sharp hooked end across the man's throat before he could arise, blood spurting in a furious jet from the severed vein, through his grasping fingers.

More men were coming out of the pond. 'Fire at will,' Riggs shouted, and three went down, one of them shot with only his head protruding from the water, sinking back down below the surface in a spreading cloud of blood. Laurence was up beside Hammond, and together they forced the two he was struggling against back into the water: while Hammond kept swinging, Laurence stabbed one with the point of his cutlass, and clubbed the other with the hilt; he fell unconscious into the water, open-mouthed, and bubbles rose in a profusion from his lips.

'Push them all into the water,' Laurence said. 'We must block up the passage.' He climbed into the pond, pushing the bodies against the current; he could feel a greater pressure coming from the other side, more men trying to come through. 'Riggs, get your men back to the front and relieve Granby,' he said, 'Hammond and I can hold them here.'

'I can help also,' Therrows said, limping over: he was a tall fellow, and could sit down on the edge of the pond and put his good leg against the mass of bodies.

'Roland, Dyer, see if there is anything to be done for Keynes,' Laurence said over his shoulder, and then looked when he did not hear a response immediately: they were both being sick in the corner, quietly.

Roland wiped her mouth and got up, looking rather like

an unsteady-legged foal. 'Yes, sir,' she said, and she and Dyer tottered over to Keynes. He groaned as they turned him over: there was a great clot of blood on his head, above the eyebrow, but he opened his eyes dazedly as they bound it up.

The pressure on the other side of the mass of bodies weakened, and slowly ceased; behind them the guns spoke again and again with suddenly quickened pace, Riggs and his men firing almost at the rate of redcoats. Laurence, trying to look over his shoulder, could not see anything through the haze of smoke.

'Therrows and I can manage, go!' Hammond gasped out. Laurence nodded and slogged out of the water, his full boots dragging like stones; he had to stop and pour them out before he could run to the front.

Even as he came, the shooting stopped: the smoke so thick and queerly bright they could not see anyone through it, only the broken heap of bodies around the floor at their feet. They stood waiting, Riggs and his men reloading more slowly, their fingers shaking. Then Laurence stepped forward, using a hand on the column for balance: there was nowhere to stand but on the corpses.

They came out blinking through the haze, into the early morning sunlight, startling up a flock of crows that lifted from the bodies in the courtyard and fled shrieking hoarsely over the water of the lake. There was no one left moving in sight: the rest of the attackers had fled. Martin abruptly fell over onto his knees, his cutlass clanging unmusically on the stones; Granby went to help him up and ended by falling down also. Laurence groped to a small wooden bench before his own legs gave out; not caring very much that he was sharing it with one of the dead, a smooth-faced young man with a trail of red blood drying on his lips and a purpled stain around the ragged bullet wound in his chest.

There was no sign of Temeraire. He had not come.

Chapter Fifteen

Sun Kai found them scarcely more than dead themselves, an hour later; he had come warily into the courtyard from the pier with a small group of armed men: perhaps ten or so and formally dressed in guard uniforms, unlike the scruffy and unkempt members of the gang. The smouldering bonfires had gone out of their own accord, for lack of fuel; the British were dragging the corpses into the deepest shade, so they would putrefy less horribly.

They were all of them half-blind and numb with exhaustion, and could offer no resistance; helpless to account for Temeraire's absence and with no other idea of what to do, Laurence submitted to being led to the boat, and thence to a stuffy, enclosed palanquin, whose curtains were drawn tight around him. He slept instantly upon the embroidered pillows, despite the jostling and shouts of their progress, and knew nothing more until at last the palanquin was set down, and he was shaken back to wakefulness.

'Come inside,' Sun Kai said, and pulled on him until he rose; Hammond and Granby and the other crewmen were emerging in similarly dazed and battered condition from other sedan chairs behind him. Laurence followed unthinking up the stairs into the blessedly cool interior of a house, fragrant with traces of incense; along a narrow hallway and to a room which faced onto the garden courtyard. There he at once surged forward and leaped over the low balcony railing: Temeraire was lying curled asleep upon the stones.

'Temeraire,' Laurence called, and went towards him; Sun Kai exclaimed in Chinese and ran after him, catching his arm before he could touch Temeraire's side; then the dragon raised up his head and looked at them, curiously, and Laurence stared: it was not Temeraire at all.

Sun Kai tried to drag Laurence down to the ground, kneeling down himself; Laurence shook him off, managing with difficulty to keep his balance. He noticed only then a young man of perhaps twenty, dressed in elegant silk robes of dark yellow embroidered with dragons, sitting on a bench.

Hammond had followed Laurence and now caught at his sleeve. 'For God's sake, kneel,' he whispered. 'This must be Prince Mianning, the crown prince.' He himself went down to both knees, and pressed his forehead to the ground just as Sun Kai was doing.

Laurence stared a little stupidly down at them both, looked at the young man, and hesitated; then he bowed deeply instead, from the waist: he was mortally certain he could not bend a single knee without falling down to both, or more ignominiously upon his face, and he was not yet willing to perform the kowtow to the Emperor, much less the prince.

The prince did not seem offended, but spoke in Chinese to Sun Kai; he rose, and Hammond also, very slowly. 'He says we can rest here safely,' Hammond said to Laurence. 'I beg you to believe him, sir; he can have no need to deceive us.'

Laurence said, 'Will you ask him about Temeraire?' Hammond looked at the other dragon blankly. 'That is not him,' Laurence added. 'It is some other Celestial, it is not Temeraire.'

Sun Kai said, 'Lung Tien Xiang is in seclusion in the Pavilion of Endless Spring. A messenger is waiting to bring him word, as soon as he emerges.'

338

'He is well?' Laurence asked, not bothering to try and make sense of this; the most urgent concern was to understand what might have kept Temeraire away.

'There is no reason to think otherwise,' Sun Kai said, which seemed evasive. Laurence did not know how to press him further; he was too thick with fatigue. But Sun Kai took pity on his confusion and added more gently, 'He is well. We cannot interrupt his seclusion, but he will come out sometime today, and we will bring him to you then.'

Laurence still did not understand, but he could not think of anything else to do at the moment. 'Thank you,' he managed. 'Pray thank his Highness for his hospitality, for us; pray convey our very deep thanks. I beg he will excuse any inadequacy in our address.'

The prince nodded and dismissed them with a wave. Sun Kai herded them back over the balcony into their rooms, and stood watching over them until they had collapsed upon the hard wooden bed platforms; perhaps he did not trust them not to leap up and go wandering again. Laurence almost laughed at the improbability of it, and fell asleep mid-thought.

'Laurence, Laurence,' Temeraire said, very anxiously; Laurence opened his eyes and found Temeraire's head poked in through the balcony doors, and a darkening sky beyond. 'Laurence, you are not hurt?'

'Oh!' Hammond had woken, and fallen off his bed in startlement at finding himself cheek to jowl with Temeraire's muzzle. 'Good God,' he said, painfully climbing to his feet and sitting back down upon the bed. 'I feel like a man of eighty with gout in both legs.'

Laurence sat up with only a little less effort; every muscle had stiffened up during his rest. 'No, I am quite well,' he said, reaching out gratefully to put a hand on Temeraire's muzzle and feel the reassurance of his solid presence. 'You have not been ill?'

He did not mean it to sound accusing, but he could hardly imagine any other excuse for Temeraire's apparent desertion, and perhaps some of his feeling was clear in his tone. Temeraire's ruff drooped. 'No,' he said, miserably. 'No, I am not sick at all.'

He volunteered nothing more, and Laurence did not press him, conscious of Hammond's presence: Temeraire's shy behaviour did not bode a very good explanation for his absence, and as little as Laurence might relish the prospect of confronting him, he liked the notion of doing so in front of Hammond even less. Temeraire withdrew his head to let them come out into the garden. No acrobatic leaping this time: Laurence levered himself out of bed and stepped slowly and carefully over the balcony rail. Hammond, following, was almost unable to lift his foot high enough to clear the rail, though it was scarcely two feet off the ground.

The prince had left, but the dragon, whom Temeraire introduced to them as Lung Tien Chuan, was still there. He nodded to them politely, without much interest, then went straight back to working upon a large tray of wet sand in which he was scratching symbols with a talon: writing poetry, Temeraire explained.

Having made his bow to Chuan, Hammond groaned again as he lowered himself onto a stool, muttering under his breath with a degree of profanity more appropriate to the seamen from whom he had likely first heard the oaths. It was not a very graceful performance, but Laurence was perfectly willing to forgive him that and more after the previous day's work. He had never expected Hammond to do as much, untrained, untried, and in disagreement with the whole enterprise.

'If I may be so bold, sir, allow me to recommend you take a turn around the garden instead of sitting,' Laurence said. 'I have often found it answer well.'

'I suppose I had better,' Hammond said, and after a few deep breaths heaved himself back up to his feet, not disdaining the offer of Laurence's hand, and walking very slowly at first. But Hammond was a young man: he was already walking more easily after they had gone halfway round. With the worst of his pain relieved, Hammond's curiosity revived: as they continued walking around the garden he studied the two dragons closely, his steps slowing as he turned first from one to the other and back. The courtyard was longer than it was wide. Stands of tall bamboo and a few smaller pine trees clustered at the ends, leaving the middle mostly open, so the two dragons lay opposite each other, head to head, making the comparison easier.

They were indeed as like as mirror images, except for the difference in their jewels: Chuan wore a net of gold draped from his ruff down the length of his neck, studded with pearls: very splendid, but it looked likely to be inconvenient in any sort of violent activity. Temeraire had also battle-scars, of which Chuan had none: the round knot of scales on his breast from the spiked ball, now several months old, and the smaller scratches from other battles. But these were difficult to see, and aside from these the only difference was a certain undefinable quality in their posture and expression, which Laurence could not have adequately described for another's interpretation.

'Can it be chance?' Hammond said. 'All Celestials may be related, but such a degree of similarity? I cannot tell them apart.'

'We are hatched from twin eggs,' Temeraire said, lifting up his head as he overheard this. 'Chuan's egg was first, and then mine.'

'Oh, I have been unutterably slow,' Hammond said, and sat down limply on the bench. 'Laurence— Laurence—' His face was almost shining from within, and he reached out groping towards Laurence, and seized his hand and shook it. 'Of course, of *course*: they did not want to set up another prince as a rival for the throne, that is why they sent away the egg. My God, how relieved I am!'

341

'Sir, I hardly dispute your conclusions, but I cannot see what difference it makes to our present situation,' Laurence said, rather taken aback by this enthusiasm.

'Do you not see?' Hammond said. 'Napoleon was only an excuse, because he is an emperor on the other side of the world, as far away as they could manage from their own court. And all this time I have been wondering how the devil De Guignes ever managed to approach them, when they would scarcely let me put my nose out of doors. Ha! The French have no alliance, no real understanding with them at all.'

'That is certainly cause for relief,' Laurence said. 'But their lack of success does not seem to me to directly improve our position; plainly the Chinese have now changed their minds, and desire Temeraire's return.'

'No, do you not see? Prince Mianning still has every reason to want Temeraire gone, if he could render another claimant eligible for the throne,' Hammond said. 'Oh, this makes all the difference in the world. I have been groping in the dark; now I have some sense of their motives, a great deal more comes clear. How much longer will it be until the *Allegiance* arrives?' he asked suddenly, looking up at Laurence.

'I know too little about the likely currents and the prevailing winds in the Bay of Zhitao to make any accurate estimate,' Laurence said, taken aback. 'A week at least, I should think.'

'I wish to God Staunton were here already. I have a thousand questions and not enough answers,' Hammond said. 'But I can at least try and coax a little more information from Sun Kai: I hope he will be a little more forthright now. I will go seek him; I beg your pardon.'

At this, he turned and ducked back into the house. Laurence called after him belatedly, 'Hammond, your clothes—!' for his breeches were unbuckled at the knee, they and his shirt hideously bloodstained besides, and his stockings thoroughly laddered: he looked a proper spectacle. But it was too late: he had gone.

Laurence supposed no one could blame them for their appearance, as they had been brought over without baggage. 'Well, at least he is gone to some purpose; and we cannot but be relieved by this news that there is no alliance with France,' he said to Temeraire.

'Yes,' Temeraire said, but unenthusiastically. He had been quite silent all this time, brooding and coiled about the garden. The tip of his tail continued flicking back and forth restlessly at the edge of the nearer pond and spattering thick black spots onto the sun-heated flagstones, which dried almost as quickly as they appeared.

Laurence did not immediately press him for explanation, even now Hammond had gone, but came and sat by his head. He hoped deeply that Temeraire would speak of his own volition, and not require questioning.

'Are all the rest of my crew all right also?' Temeraire asked after a moment.

Laurence said, 'Willoughby has been killed, I am very sorry to tell you. A few injuries besides, but nothing else mortal, thankfully.'

Temeraire trembled and made a low keening sound deep in his throat. 'I ought to have come. If I had been there, they could never have done it.'

Laurence was silent, thinking of poor Willoughby: a damned ugly waste. 'You did very wrong not to send word,' he said finally. 'I cannot hold you culpable in Willoughby's death. He was killed early, before you would ordinarily have come back, and I do not think I would have done anything differently, had I known you were not returning. But certainly you have violated your leave.'

Temeraire made another small unhappy noise and said, low, 'I have failed in my duty; have I not? So it was my fault, then, and there is nothing else to be said about it.'

Laurence said, 'No, if you had sent word, I would have thought nothing of agreeing to your extended absence: we had every reason to think our position perfectly secure. And in all justice, you have never been formally instructed in the rules of leave in the Corps, as they have never been necessary for a dragon, and it was my responsibility to be sure you understood.

'I am not trying to comfort you,' he added, seeing that Temeraire shook his head. 'But I wish you to feel what you have in fact done wrong, and not to distract yourself improperly with false guilt over what you could not have controlled.'

'Laurence, you do not understand,' Temeraire said. 'I have always understood the rules quite well; that is not why I did not send word. I did not mean to stay so long, only I did not notice the time passing.'

Laurence did not know what to say. The idea that Temeraire had not noticed the passage of a full night and day, when he had always been used to come back before dark, was difficult to swallow, if not impossible. If such an excuse had been given him by one of his men, Laurence would have outright called it a lie; as it was, his silence betrayed what he thought of it.

Temeraire hunched his shoulders and scratched a little at the ground, his claws scraping the stones with a noise that made Chuan look up and put his ruff back, with a quick rumble of complaint. Temeraire stopped; then all at once he said abruptly, 'I was with Mei.'

'With who?' Laurence said, blankly.

'Lung Qin Mei,' Temeraire said, '—she is an Imperial.'

The shock of understanding was near a physical blow. There was a mixture of embarrassment, guilt, and confused pride in Temeraire's confession which made everything plain.

'I see,' Laurence said with an effort, as controlled as ever he had been in his life. 'Well—' He stopped, and mastered himself. 'You are young, and— And have never courted before; you cannot have known how it would take you,' he said. 'I am glad to know the reason; that is some excuse.' He tried to believe his own words; he did believe them; only he did not particularly want to forgive Temeraire's absence on such grounds. Despite his quarrel with Hammond over Yongxing's attempts to supplant him with the boy, Laurence had never really feared losing Temeraire's affections; it was bitter, indeed, to find himself so unexpectedly with real cause for jealousy after all.

They buried Willoughby in the grey hours of the morning, in a vast cemetery outside the city walls, to which Sun Kai brought them. It was crowded for a burial place, even considering the extent, with many small groups of people paying respects at the tombs. These visitors' interest was caught by both Temeraire's presence and the Western party, and shortly something of a procession had formed behind them, despite the guards who pushed off any too-curious onlookers.

But though the crowd shortly numbered several hundreds of people, they maintained an attitude of respect, and fell to perfect silence while Laurence sombrely spoke a few words for the dead and led his men in the Lord's Prayer. The tomb was above-ground, and built of white stone, with an upturned roof very like the local houses; it looked elaborate even in comparison to the neighbouring mausoleums. 'Laurence, if it wouldn't be disrespectful, I think his mother would be glad of a sketch,' Granby said quietly.

'Yes, I ought to have thought of it myself,' Laurence said. 'Digby, do you think you could knock something together?'

'Please allow me to have an artist prepare one,' Sun Kai interjected. 'I am ashamed not to have offered before. And assure his mother that all the proper sacrifices will be made; a young man of good family has already been selected by Prince Mianning to carry out all the rites.' Laurence assented to these arrangements without investigating further; Mrs. Willoughby was, as he recalled, a rather strict Methodist, and he was sure would be happier not to know more than that her son's tomb was so elegant and would be well maintained.

Afterwards Laurence returned to the island with Temeraire and a few of the men to collect their possessions, which had been left behind in the hurry and confusion. All the bodies had been cleared away already, but the smoke-blackened patches remained upon the outer walls of the pavilion where they had sheltered, and dried bloodstains upon the stones; Temeraire looked at them a long time, silently, and then turned his head away. Inside the residence, furniture had been wildly overturned, the rice-paper screens torn through, and most of their chests smashed open, clothing flung onto the floor and trampled upon.

Laurence walked through the rooms as Blythe and Martin began collecting whatever they could find in good enough condition to bother with. His own chamber had been thoroughly pillaged, the bed itself flung up on its side against the wall, as if they had thought him maybe cowering underneath, and his many bundles from the shopping expedition thrown rudely about the room. Powder and bits of shattered porcelain trickled out across the floor behind some of them like a trail, strips of torn and frayed silk hanging almost decoratively about the room. Laurence bent down and lifted up the large shapeless package of the red vase, fallen over in a corner of the room, and slowly took off the wrappings; and then he found himself looking upon it through an unaccountable blurring of his vision: the shining surface wholly undamaged, not even chipped, and in the afternoon sun it poured out over his hands a living richness of deep and scarlet light.

The true heart of the summer had struck the city now: the stones grew hot as worked anvils during the day, and the wind blew an endless stream of fine yellow dust from the enormous deserts of the Gobi to the west. Hammond was engaged in a slow elaborate dance of negotiations, which so far as Laurence could see proceeded only in circles: a sequence

346

of wax-sealed letters coming back and forth from the house, some small trinkety gifts received and sent in return, vague promises and less action. In the meantime, they were all growing short-tempered and impatient, except for Temeraire, who was occupied still with his education and his courting. Mei now came to the residence to teach him daily, elegant in an elaborate collar of silver and pearls; her hide was a deep shade of blue, with dapplings of violet and yellow upon her wings, and she wore many golden rings upon her talons.

'Mei is a very charming dragon,' Laurence said to Temeraire after her first visit, feeling he might as well be properly martyred; it had not escaped his attention that Mei was very lovely, at least as far as he was a judge of draconic beauty.

'I am glad you think so also,' Temeraire said, brightening; the points of his ruff raised and quivered. 'She was hatched only three years ago, and has just passed the first examinations with honour. She has been teaching me how to read and write, and has been very kind; she has not at all made fun of me, for not knowing.'

She could not have complained of her pupil's progress, Laurence was sure. Already Temeraire had mastered the technique of writing in the sand tray-tables with his talons, and Mei praised his calligraphy done in clay; soon she promised to begin teaching him the more rigid strokes used for carving in soft wood. Laurence watched him scribbling industriously late into the afternoon, while the light lasted, and often played audience for him in Mei's absence: the rich sonorous tones of Temeraire's voice pleasant though the words of the Chinese poetry were meaningless, except when he stopped in a particularly nice passage to translate.

The rest of them had little to occupy their time: Mianning occasionally gave them a dinner, and once an entertainment consisting of a highly unmusical concert and the tumbling of some remarkable acrobats, nearly all young children and limber as mountain goats. Occasionally they drilled with their small-arms in the courtyard behind the residence, but it was not very pleasant in the heat, and they were glad to return to the cool walks and gardens of the palace after.

Some two weeks following their remove to the palace, Laurence sat reading in the balcony overlooking the courtyard, where Temeraire slept, while Hammond worked on papers at the writing-desk within the room. A servant came bearing them a letter: Hammond broke the seal and scanned the lines, telling Laurence, 'It is from Liu Bao, he has invited us to dine at his home.'

'Hammond, do you suppose there is any chance he might be involved?' Laurence asked reluctantly, after a moment. 'I do not like to suggest such a thing, but after all, we know he is not in Mianning's service, like Sun Kai is; could he be in league with Yongxing?'

'It is true we cannot rule out his possible involvement,' Hammond said. 'As a Tartar himself, Liu Bao would likely have been able to organize the attack upon us. Still, I have learned he is a relation of the Emperor's mother, and an official in the Manchu White Banner; his support would be invaluable, and I find it hard to believe he would openly invite us if he meant anything underhanded.'

They went warily, but their plans for caution were thoroughly undermined as they arrived, met unexpectedly at the gates by the rich savoury smell of roasted beef. Liu Bao had ordered his now well-travelled cooks to prepare a traditional British dinner for them, and if there was rather more curry than one would expect in the fried potatoes, and the currant-studded pudding inclined to be somewhat liquid, none of them found anything to complain of in the enormous crown roast, the upstanding ribs jewelled with whole onions, and the Yorkshire pudding was improbably successful.

Despite their very best efforts, the last plates were again carried away almost full, and there was some doubt whether

348

a number of the guests would not have to be carted off in the same manner, including Temeraire. He had been served with plain, freshly butchered prey, in the British manner, but the cooks could not restrain themselves entirely and had served him not merely a cow or sheep, but two of each, as well as a pig, a goat, a chicken, and a lobster. Having done his duty by each course, he now crawled out into the garden uninvited with a little moan and collapsed into a stupor.

'That is all right, let him sleep!' Liu Bao said, waving away Laurence's apology. 'We can sit in the moon-viewing terrace and drink wine.'

Laurence girded himself, but for once Liu Bao did not press the wine on them too enthusiastically. It was quite pleasant to sit, suffused with the steady genial warmth of inebriation, the sun going down behind the smoke-blue mountains and Temeraire drowsing in an aureate glow before them. Laurence had entirely if irrationally given up the idea of Liu Bao's involvement: it was impossible to be suspicious of a man while sitting in his garden, full of his generous dinner; and even Hammond was half-unwillingly at his ease, blinking with the effort of keeping awake.

Liu Bao expressed some curiosity as to how they had come to take up residence with Prince Mianning. For further proofs of his innocence, he received the news of the gang attack with real surprise, and shook his head sympathetically. 'Something has to be done about these hunhun, they are really getting out of hand. One of my nephews got involved with them a few years ago, and his poor mother worried herself almost to death. But then she made a big sacrifice to Guanyin and built her a special altar in the nicest place in their south garden, and now he has gotten married and taken up studying.' He poked Laurence in the side. 'You ought to try studying yourself! It will be embarrassing for you if your dragon passes the examinations and you don't.'

'Good God, could that possibly make a difference in their

minds, Hammond?' Laurence asked, sitting up appalled. For all his efforts, Chinese remained to him as impenetrable as if it were enciphered ten times over, and as for sitting examinations next to men who had been studying for them since the age of seven—

But, 'I am only teasing you,' Liu Bao said good-humouredly, much to Laurence's relief. 'Don't be afraid. I suppose if Lung Tien Xiang really wants to stay companion to an unlettered barbarian, no one can argue with him.'

'He is joking about calling you that, of course,' Hammond added to the translation, but a little doubtfully.

'I *am* an unlettered barbarian, by their standards of learning, and not stupid enough to make pretensions to be anything else,' Laurence said. 'I only wish that the negotiators took your view of it, sir,' he added to Liu Bao. 'But they are quite fixed that a Celestial may only be companion to the Emperor and his kin.'

'Well, if the dragon will not have anyone else, they will have to live with it,' Liu Bao said, unconcerned. 'Why doesn't the Emperor adopt you? That would save face for everyone.'

Laurence was disposed to think this a joke, but Hammond stared at Liu Bao with quite a different expression. 'Sir, would such a suggestion be seriously entertained?'

Liu Bao shrugged and filled their cups again with wine. 'Why not? The Emperor has three sons to perform the rites for him, he doesn't need to adopt anyone; but another doesn't hurt.'

'Do you mean to pursue the notion?' Laurence asked Hammond, rather incredulous, as they made their staggering way out to the sedan chairs waiting to bear them back to the palace.

'With your permission, certainly,' Hammond said. 'It is an extraordinary idea to be sure, but after all it would be understood on all sides as only a formality. Indeed,' he continued, growing more enthusiastic, 'I think it would answer in every possible respect. Surely they would not lightly declare war upon a nation related by such intimate ties, and only consider the advantages to our trade of such a connection.'

Laurence could more easily consider his father's likely reaction. 'If you think it a worthwhile course to pursue, I will not forestall you,' he said reluctantly, but he did not think the red vase, which he had been hoping to use as something of a peace-offering, would be in any way adequate to mend matters if Lord Allendale should learn that Laurence had given himself up for adoption like a foundling, even to the Emperor of China.

Chapter Sixteen

'It was a close-run affair before we arrived, that much I can tell you,' Riley said, accepting a cup of tea across the breakfast table with more eagerness than he had taken the bowl of rice porridge. 'I have never seen the like: a fleet of twenty ships, with two dragons for support. Of course they were only junks, and not half the size of a frigate, but the Chinese Navy ships were hardly any bigger. I cannot imagine what they were about, to let a lot of pirates get so out of hand.'

'I was impressed by their admiral, however; he seemed a rational sort of man,' Staunton put in. 'A lesser man would not have liked being rescued.'

'He would have been a great gaby to prefer being sunk,' Riley said, less generous.

The two of them had arrived only that morning, with a small party from the *Allegiance*; having been shocked by the story of the murderous gang attack, they were now describing the adventure of their own passage through the China Sea. A week out of Macao, they had encountered a Chinese fleet attempting to subdue an enormous band of pirates, who had established themselves in the Zhoushan Islands to prey upon both domestic shipping and the smaller ships of the Western trade.

'There was not much trouble once we were there, of course,' Riley went on. 'The pirate dragons had no armaments – the crews tried to fire arrows at us, if you can credit it – and no sense of range at all; dived so low we could hardly miss them at musket-shot, much less with the pepper guns. They sheered off pretty quick after a taste of that, and we sank three of the pirates with a single broadside.'

'Did the admiral say anything about how he would report the incident?' Hammond asked Staunton.

'I can only tell you that he was punctilious in expressing his gratitude. He came aboard our ship, which was I believe a concession on his part.'

'And let him have a good look at our guns,' Riley said. 'I fancy he was more interested in those than in being polite. But at any rate, we saw him to port, and then came on; she's anchored in Tien-sing harbour now. No chance of our leaving soon?'

'I do not like to tempt fate, but I hardly think so,' Hammond said. 'The Emperor is still away on his summer hunting trip up to the north, and he will not return to the Summer Palace for several weeks more. At that time I expect we will be given a formal audience.

'I have been putting forward this notion of adoption, which I described to you, sir,' he added to Staunton. 'We have already received some small amount of support, not only from Prince Mianning, and I have high hopes that the service which you have just performed for them will sway opinion decisively in our favour.'

'Is there any difficulty in the ship's remaining where she is?' Laurence asked with concern.

'For the moment, no, but I must say, supplies are dearer than I had looked for,' Riley said. 'They have nothing like salt meat for sale, and the prices they ask for cattle are outrageous; we have been feeding the men on fish and chickens.'

'Have we outrun our funds?' Laurence too late began to

354

regret his purchases. 'I have been a little extravagant, but I do have some gold left, and they make no bones about taking it once they see it is real.'

'Thank you, Laurence, but I don't need to rob you; we are not in dun territory yet,' Riley said. 'I am mostly thinking about the journey home – with a dragon to feed, I hope?'

Laurence did not know how to answer the question; he made some evasion, and fell silent to let Hammond carry on the conversation.

After their breakfast, Sun Kai came by to inform them that a feast and an entertainment would be held that evening, to welcome the new arrivals: a great theatrical performance. 'Laurence, I am going to go see Qian,' Temeraire said, poking his head into the room while Laurence contemplated his clothing. 'You will not go out, will you?'

He had grown singularly more protective since the assault, refusing to leave Laurence unattended; the servants had all suffered his narrow and suspicious inspection for weeks, and he had put forward several thoughtful suggestions for Laurence's protection, such as devising a schedule which should arrange for Laurence's being kept under a five-man guard at all hours, or drawing in his sand-table a proposed suit of armour which would not have been unsuited to the battle-fields of the Crusades.

'No, you may rest easy; I am afraid I will have enough to do to make myself presentable,' Laurence said. 'Pray give her my regards; will you be there long? We cannot be late tonight, this engagement is in our honour.'

'No, I will come back very soon,' Temeraire said, and true to his word returned less than an hour later, ruff quivering with suppressed excitement and clutching a long narrow bundle carefully in his forehand.

Laurence came out into the courtyard at his request, and Temeraire nudged the package over to him rather abashedly. Laurence was so taken aback he only stared at first, then he slowly removed the silk wrappings and opened the lacquered box: an elaborate smooth-hilted sabre lay next to its scabbard on a yellow silk cushion. He lifted it from its bed: well-balanced, broad at the base, with the curved tip sharpened along both edges; the surface watered like good Damascus steel, with two blood grooves cut along the back edge to lighten the blade.

The hilt was wrapped in black ray-skin, the fittings of gilded iron adorned with gold beads and small pearls, and a gold dragon-head collar at the base of the blade with two small sapphires for eyes. The scabbard itself of black lacquered wood was also decorated with broad gold bands of gilded iron, and strung with strong silk cords: Laurence took his rather shabby if serviceable cutlass off his belt and buckled the new one on.

'Does it suit you?' Temeraire asked anxiously.

'Very well indeed,' Laurence said, drawing out the blade for practice: the length admirably fitted to his height. 'My dear, this is beyond anything; however did you get it?'

'Well, it is not all my doing,' Temeraire said. 'Last week, Qian admired my breastplate, and I told her you had given it to me; then I thought I would like to give you a present also. She said it was usual for the sire and dame to give a gift when a dragon takes a companion, so I might choose one for you from her things, and I thought this was the nicest.' He turned his head to one side and another, inspecting Laurence with deep satisfaction.

'You must be quite right; I could not imagine a better,' Laurence said, attempting to master himself; he felt quite absurdly happy and absurdly reassured, and on going back inside to complete his dress could not help but stand and admire the sword in the mirror.

Hammond and Staunton had both adopted the Chinese scholar-robes; the rest of his officers wore their bottle-green coats, trousers, and Hessians polished to a gleam; neckcloths had been washed and pressed, and even Roland and Dyer were perfectly smart, having been set on chairs and admonished not to move the moment they were bathed and dressed. Riley was similarly elegant in Navy blue, knee-breeches and slippers, and the four Marines that he had brought from the ship in their lobster-red coats brought up the end of their company in style as they left the residence.

A curious stage had been erected in the middle of the plaza where the performance was to be held: small, but marvellously painted and gilded, with three different levels. Qian presided at the centre of the northern end of the court, Prince Mianning and Chuan on her left, and a place for Temeraire and the British party reserved upon her right. Besides the Celestials, there were also several Imperials present, including Mei, seated further down the side and looking very graceful in a rig of gold set with polished jade: she nodded to Laurence and Temeraire from her place as they took their seats. The white dragon Lien was there also, seated with Yongxing to one side, a little apart from the rest of the guests; her albino coloration again startling by contrast with the dark-hued Imperials and Celestials on every side, and her proudly raised ruff today adorned with a netting of fine gold mesh, with a great pendant ruby lying upon her forehead.

'Oh, there is Miankai,' Roland said in undertones to Dyer, and waved quickly across the square to a boy sitting by Mianning's side. The boy wore robes similar to the crown prince's, of the same dark shade of yellow, and an elaborate hat; he sat very stiff and proper. Seeing Roland's wave, he lifted his hand partway to respond, then dropped it again hastily, glanced down the table towards Yongxing, as if to see if he had been noticed in the gesture, and sat back relieved when he realized he had not drawn the older man's attention.

'How on earth do you know Prince Miankai? Has he ever come by the crown prince's residence?' Hammond asked. Laurence also would have liked to know, as on his orders the

357

runners had not been allowed out of their quarters alone at all, and ought not have had any opportunity of getting to know anyone else, even another child.

Roland looking up at him said surprised, 'Why, you presented him to us, on the island,' and Laurence looked hard again. It might have been the boy that had visited them before, in Yongxing's company, but it was almost impossible to tell; swathed in the formal clothing, the boy looked entirely different.

'Prince Miankai?' Hammond said. 'The boy Yongxing brought was Prince Miankai?' He might have said something more; certainly his lips moved. But nothing at all could be heard over the sudden roll of drums: the instruments evidently hidden somewhere within the stage, but the sound quite unmuffled and about the volume of a moderate broadside, perhaps twenty-four guns, at close range.

The performance was baffling, of course, being entirely transacted in Chinese, but the movement of the scenery and the participants was clever: figures rose and dropped between the three different levels, flowers bloomed, clouds floated by, the sun and moon rose and set; all amid elaborate dances and mock swordplay. Laurence was fascinated by the spectacle, though the noise was scarcely to be imagined, and after some time his head began to ache sadly. He wondered if even the Chinese could understand the words being spoken, what with the din of drums and jangling instruments and the occasional explosion of firecrackers.

He could not apply to Hammond or Staunton for explanation: through the entire proceeding the two of them were attempting to carry on a conversation in pantomime, and paying no attention whatsoever to the stage. Hammond had brought an opera glass, which they used only to peer across the courtyard at Yongxing, and the gouts of smoke and flame which formed part of the first act's extraordinary finale only drew their exclamations of annoyance at disrupting the view.

358

There was a brief gap in the proceedings while the stage was reset for the second act, and the two of them seized the few moments to converse. 'Laurence,' Hammond said, 'I must beg your pardon; you were perfectly right. Plainly Yongxing did mean to make the boy Temeraire's companion in your place, and now at last I understand *why*: he must mean to put the boy on the throne, somehow, and establish himself as regent.'

'Is the Emperor ill, or an old man?' Laurence said, puzzled.

'No,' Staunton said meaningfully. 'Not in the least.'

Laurence stared. 'Gentlemen, you sound as though you are accusing him of regicide and fratricide both; you cannot be serious.'

'I only wish I were not,' Staunton said. 'If he does make such an attempt, we might end in the middle of a civil war, with nothing more likely for us than disaster regardless of the outcome.'

'It will not come to that now,' Hammond said, confidently. 'Prince Mianning is no fool, and I expect the Emperor is not either. Yongxing brought the boy to us incognito for no good reason, and they will not fail to see that, nor that it is of a piece with the rest of his actions, once I lay them all before Prince Mianning. First his attempts to bribe you, with terms that I now wonder if he had the authority to offer, and then his servant attacking you on board the ship; and recall, the hunhun gang came at us directly after you refused to allow him to throw Temeraire and the boy into each other's company; all of it forms a very neat and damning picture.'

He spoke almost exultantly, not very cautious, and started when Temeraire, who had overheard all, said with dawning anger, 'Are you saying that we have evidence, now, then? That Yongxing has been behind all of this— That he is the one who tried to hurt Laurence, and had Willoughby killed?' His great head rose and swivelled at once towards Yongxing, his slit pupils narrowing to thin black lines.

'Not here, Temeraire,' Laurence said hurriedly, laying a hand on his side. 'Pray do nothing for the moment.'

'No, no,' Hammond said also, alarmed. 'I am not yet certain, of course; it is only hypothetical, and we cannot take any action against him ourselves. We must leave it in their hands—'

The actors moved to take their places upon the stage, putting an end to the immediate conversation; yet beneath his hand Laurence could feel the angry resonance deep within Temeraire's breast, a slow rolling growl that found no voice but lingered just short of sound. His talons gripped at the edges of the flagstones, his spiked ruff at half-mast and his nostrils red and flaring; he paid no more mind to the spectacle, all his attention given over to watching Yongxing.

Laurence stroked his side again, trying to distract him: the square was crowded full of guests and scenery, and he did not like to imagine the results if Temeraire were to leap to some sort of action, for all he would gladly have liked to indulge his own anger and indignation towards the man. Worse, Laurence could not think how Yongxing was to be dealt with. The man was still the Emperor's brother, and to him the plot which Hammond and Staunton imagined too outrageous to be easily believed.

A crash of cymbals and deep-voiced bells came from behind the stage, and two elaborate rice-paper dragons descended, crackling sparks flying from their nostrils; beneath them nearly the entire company of actors came running out around the base of the stage, swords and paste-jewelled knives waving, to enact a great battle. The drums again rolled out their thunder, the noise so vast it was almost like the shock of a blow, driving air out of his lungs. Laurence gasped for breath, then slowly put a groping hand up to his shoulder and found a short dagger's hilt jutting from below his collarbone.

'Laurence!' Hammond said, reaching for him, and Granby was shouting at the men and thrusting aside the chairs: he and Blythe put themselves in front of Laurence. Temeraire was turning his head to look down at him.

'I am not hurt,' Laurence said, confusedly: there was queerly no pain at first, and he tried to stand up, to lift his arm, and then felt the wound; blood was spreading in a warm stain around the base of the knife.

Temeraire gave a shrill, terrible cry, cutting through all the noise and music; every dragon reared back on its hindquarters to stare, and the drums stopped abruptly: in the sudden silence Roland was crying out, 'He threw it, over there, I saw him!' and pointing at one of the actors.

The man was empty-handed, in the midst of all the others still carrying their counterfeit weapons, and dressed in plainer clothing. He saw that his attempt to hide among them had failed and turned to flee too late; the troupe ran screaming in all directions as Temeraire flung himself almost clumsily into the square.

The man shrieked, once, as Temeraire's claws caught and dragged mortally deep furrows through his body. Temeraire threw the bloody corpse savaged and broken to the ground; for a moment he hung over it low and brooding, to be sure the man was dead, and then raised his head and turned on Yongxing; he bared his teeth and hissed, a murderous sound, and stalked towards him. At once Lien sprang forward, placing herself protectively in front of Yongxing; she struck down Temeraire's reaching talons with a swipe of her own foreleg and growled.

In answer, Temeraire's chest swelled out, and his ruff, queerly, stretched: something Laurence had never seen before, the narrow horns which made it up expanding outwards, the webbing drawn along with it. Lien did not flinch at all, but snarled almost contemptuously at him, her own parchment-pale ruff unfolding wide; the blood vessels in her eyes swelled horribly, and she stepped farther into the square to face him.

At once there was a general hasty movement to flee the

courtyard. Drums and bells and twanging strings made a terrific noise as the rest of the actors decamped from the stage, dragging their instruments and costumes with them; the audience members picked up the skirts of their robes and hurried away with a little more dignity but no less speed.

'Temeraire, no!' Laurence called, understanding too late. Every legend of dragons duelling in the wild invariably ended in the destruction of one or both: and the white dragon was clearly the elder and larger. 'John, get this damned thing out,' he said to Granby, struggling to unwind his neckcloth with his good hand.

'Blythe, Martin, hold his shoulders,' Granby directed them, laid hold of the knife and pulled it loose, grating against bone; the blood spurted for a single dizzy moment, and then they clapped a pad made of their neckcloths over the wound, and tied it firmly down.

Temeraire and Lien were still facing each other, feinting back and forth in small movements, barely more than a twitch of the head in either direction. They did not have much room to manoeuvre, the stage occupying so much of the courtyard, and the rows of empty seats still lining the edges. Their eyes never left each other.

'There's no use,' Granby said quietly, gripping Laurence by the arm, helping him to his feet. 'Once they've set themselves on to duel like that, you can only get killed, trying to get between them, or distract him from the battle.'

'Yes, very well,' Laurence said harshly, putting off their hands. His legs had steadied, though his stomach was knotted and uncertain; the pain was not worse than he could manage. 'Get well clear,' he ordered, turning around to the crew. 'Granby, take a party back to the residence and bring back our arms, in case that fellow should try to set any of the guards on him.'

Granby dashed away with Martin and Riggs, while the other men climbed hastily over the seats and got back from the fighting. The square was now nearly deserted, except for a few curiosity-seekers with more bravery than sense, and those most intimately concerned: Qian observing with a look at once anxious and disapproving, and Mei some distance behind her, having retreated in the general rush and then crept partway back.

Prince Mianning also remained, though withdrawn a prudent distance: even so, Chuan was fidgeting and plainly concerned. Mianning laid a quieting hand on Chuan's side and spoke to his guards: they snatched up the young prince Miankai and carried him off to safety, in spite of his loud protests. Yongxing watched the boy taken away and nodded to Mianning coolly in approval, himself disdaining to move from his place.

The white dragon abruptly hissed and struck out: Laurence flinched, but Temeraire had reared back in the bare nick of time, the red-tipped talons passing scant inches from his throat. Now up on his powerful back legs, he crouched and sprang, claws outstretched, and Lien was forced to retreat, hopping back awkwardly and off-balance. She spread her wings partway to catch her footing, and sprang aloft when Temeraire pressed her again; he followed her up at once.

Laurence snatched Hammond's opera glass away unceremoniously and tried to follow their path. The white dragon was the larger, and her wingspan greater; she quickly outstripped Temeraire and looped about gracefully, her deadly intentions plain: she meant to plummet down on him from above. But the first flush of battle-fury past, Temeraire had recognized her advantage, and put his experience to use; instead of pursuing her, he angled away and flew out of the radiance of the lanterns, melting into the darkness.

'Oh, well done,' Laurence said. Lien was hovering uncertainly mid-air, head darting this way and that, peering into the night with her queer red eyes; abruptly Temeraire came flashing straight down towards her, roaring. But she flung herself aside with unbelievable quickness: unlike most dragons, the attack from above did not cause her more than a moment's hesitation, and as she rolled away she managed to score Temeraire flying past: three bloody gashes opened red against his black hide. Drops of thick blood splashed onto the court-yard, shining black in the lantern light. Mei crept closer with a small whimpering cry; Qian turned on her, hissing, but Mei only ducked down submissively and offered no target, coiling anxiously against a stand of trees to watch more closely.

Lien was making good use of her greater speed, darting back and away from Temeraire, encouraging him to spend his strength in useless attempts to hit her; but Temeraire grew wily: the speed of his slashes was just a little less than he could manage, a fraction slow. At least so Laurence hoped; rather than the wound giving him so much pain. Lien was successfully tempted closer: Temeraire suddenly flashed out with both foreclaws at once, and caught her in belly and breast; she shrieked out in pain and beat away frantically.

Yongxing's chair fell over clattering as the prince surged to his feet, all pretence of calm gone; now he stood watching with fists clenched by his sides. The wounds did not look very deep, but the white dragon seemed quite stunned by them, keening in pain and hovering to lick the gashes. Certainly none of the palace dragons had any scars; it occurred to Laurence that very likely they had never been in real battle.

Temeraire hung in the air a moment, talons flexing, but when she did not turn back to close with him again, he seized the opening and dived straight down towards Yongxing, his real target. Lien's head snapped up; she shrieked again and threw herself after him, beating with all her might, injury forgotten. She caught even with him just shy of the ground and flung herself upon him, wings and bodies tangling, and wrenched him aside from his course.

They struck the ground rolling together, a single hissing, savage, many-limbed beast clawing at itself, neither dragon paying any attention now to scratches or gouges, neither able to draw in the deep breaths that could let them use the divine wind against one another. Their thrashing tails struck everywhere, knocking over potted trees and scalping a mature stand of bamboo with a single stroke; Laurence seized Hammond's arm and dragged him ahead of the crashing hollow trunks as they collapsed down upon the chairs with an echoing drumlike clatter.

Shaking leaves from his hair and the collar of his coat, Laurence awkwardly raised himself on his one good arm from beneath the branches. In their frenzy, Temeraire and Lien had just knocked askew a column of the stage. The entire grandiose structure began to lean over, sliding by degrees towards the ground, almost stately. Its progress towards destruction was quite plain to see, but Mianning did not take shelter: the prince had stepped over to offer Laurence a hand to rise, and perhaps had not understood his very real danger; his dragon Chuan, too, was distracted, trying to keep himself between Mianning and the duel.

Thrusting himself up with an effort from the ground, Laurence managed to knock Mianning down even as the whole gilt-and-painted structure smashed into the courtyard stones, bursting into foot-long shards of wood. He bent low over the prince to shield them both, covering the back of his neck with his good arm. Splinters jabbed him painfully even through the padded broadcloth of his heavy coat, one sticking him badly in the thigh where he had only his trousers, and another, razor-sharp, sliced his scalp above the temple as it flew.

Then the deadly hail was past, and Laurence straightened wiping blood from the side of his face to see Yongxing, with a deeply astonished expression, fall over: a great jagged splinter protruding from his eye.

Temeraire and Lien managed to disentangle themselves and sprang apart into facing crouches, still growling, their tails waving angrily. Temeraire glanced back over his shoulder towards Yongxing first, meaning to make another try, and halted in surprise: one foreleg poised in the air. Lien snarled and leaped at him, but he dodged instead of meeting her attack, and then she saw.

For a moment she was perfectly still, only the tendrils of her ruff lifting a little in the breeze, and the thin runnels of red-black blood trickling down her legs. She walked very slowly over to Yongxing's body and bent her head low, nudging him just a little, as if to confirm for herself what she must already have known.

There was no movement, not even a last nerveless twitching of the body, as Laurence had sometimes seen in the suddenly killed. Yongxing lay stretched out his full height; the surprise had faded with the final slackening of the muscles, and his face was now composed and unsmiling, his hands lying one outflung and slightly open, the other fallen across his breast, and his jewelled robes still glittering in the sputtering torch-light. No one else came near; the handful of servants and guards who had not abandoned the clearing huddled back at the edges, staring, and the other dragons all kept silent.

Lien did not scream out, as Laurence had dreaded, or even make any sound at all; she did not turn again on Temeraire, either, but very carefully with her talons brushed away the smaller splinters that had fallen onto Yongxing's robes, the broken pieces of wood, a few shredded leaves of bamboo; then she gathered the body up in both her foreclaws, and carrying it flew silently away into the dark.

Chapter Seventeen

Laurence twitched away from the restless, pinching hands, first in one direction then the other: but there was no escape, either from them or from the dragging weight of the yellow robes, stiff with gold and green thread, and pulled down by the gemstone eyes of the dragons embroidered all over them. His shoulder ached abominably under the burden, even a week after the injury, and they would keep trying to move his arm to adjust the sleeves.

'Are you not ready yet?' Hammond said anxiously, putting his head into the room. He admonished the tailors in rapid-fire Chinese; and Laurence closed his mouth on an exclamation as one managed to poke him with a too-hasty needle.

'Surely we are not late; are we not expected at two o'clock?' Laurence asked, making the mistake of turning around to see a clock, and being shouted at from three directions for his pains.

'One is expected to be many hours early for any meeting with the Emperor, and in this case we must be more punctilious than less,' Hammond said, sweeping his own blue robes out of the way as he pulled over a stool. 'You are quite sure you remember the phrases, and their order?'

Laurence submitted to being drilled once more; it was at

least good for distraction from his uncomfortable position. At last he was let go, one of the tailors following them halfway down the hall, making a last adjustment to the shoulders while Hammond tried to hurry him.

The young Prince Miankai's innocent testimony had quite damned Yongxing: the boy had been promised his own Celestial, and had been asked how he would like to be Emperor himself, though with no great details on how this was to be accomplished. Yongxing's whole party of supporters, men who like him believed all contact with the West ought to be severed, had been cast quite into disgrace, leaving Prince Mianning once more ascendant in the court: and as a result, further opposition to Hammond's proposal of adoption had collapsed. The Emperor had sent his edict approving the arrangements, and as this was to the Chinese the equivalent of commanding them done instantly, their progress now became as rapid as it had been creeping heretofore. Scarcely had the terms been settled than servants were swarming through their quarters in Mianning's palace, sweeping away all their possessions into boxes and bundles.

The Emperor had taken up residence now at his summer palace in the Yuanmingyuan Garden: a half-day's journey from Peking by dragon, and thence they had been conveyed almost pell-mell. The vast granite courtyards of the Forbidden City had turned anvils under the punishing summer sun, which was muted in the Yuanmingyuan by the lush greenery and the expanses of carefully tended lakes; Laurence had found it little wonder the Emperor preferred this more comfortable estate.

Only Staunton had been granted permission to accompany Laurence and Hammond into the actual ceremony of adoption, but Riley and Granby led the other men as an escort: their numbers fleshed out substantially by guards and mandarins loaned by Prince Mianning to give Laurence what they considered a respectable number. As a party they left the elaborate complex where they had been housed, and began the journey to the audience hall where the Emperor would meet them. After an hour's walk, crossing some six streams and ponds, their guides pausing at regular intervals to point out to them particularly elegant features of the landscaped grounds, Laurence began to fear they had indeed not left in good time: but at last they came to the hall, and were led to the walled court to await the Emperor's pleasure.

The wait itself was interminable: slowly soaking the robes through with sweat as they sat in the hot, breathless court-yard. Cups of ices were brought to them, also many dishes of hot food, which Laurence had to force himself to sample; bowls of milk and tea, and presents: a large pearl on a golden chain, quite perfect, and some scrolls of Chinese literature, and for Temeraire a set of gold-and-silver talon sheaths, such as his mother occasionally wore. Temeraire was alone among them unfazed by the heat; delighted, he put the talon sheaths on at once and entertained himself by flashing them in the sunlight, while the rest of the party lay in an increasing stupor.

At last the mandarins came out again and with deep bows led Laurence within, followed by Hammond and Staunton, and Temeraire behind them. The audience chamber itself was open to the air, hung with graceful light draperies, the fragrance of peaches rising from a heaped bowl of golden fruit. There were no chairs but the dragon couch at the back of the room, where a great male Celestial presently sprawled, and the simple but beautifully polished rosewood chair which held the Emperor.

He was a stocky, broad-jawed man, unlike the thin-faced and rather sallow Mianning, and with a small moustache squared off at the corners of his mouth, not yet touched with grey though he was nearing fifty. His clothes were very magnif-icent, in the brilliant yellow hue which they had seen nowhere else but on the private guard outside the palace, and he wore them entirely unconsciously; Laurence thought not even the

King had looked so casually in state robes, on those few occasions when he had attended at court.

The Emperor was frowning, but thoughtful rather than displeased, and nodded expectantly as they came in; Mianning stood among many other dignitaries to either side of the throne, and inclined his head very slightly. Laurence took a deep breath and lowered himself carefully to both knees, listening to the mandarin hissing off the count to time each full genuflection. The floor was of polished wood covered with gorgeously woven rugs, and the act itself was not uncomfortable; he could just glimpse Hammond and Staunton following along behind him as he bowed each time to the floor.

Still it went against the grain, and Laurence was glad to rise at last with the formality met; thankfully the Emperor made no unwelcome gesture of condescension, but only ceased to frown: there was a general air of release from tension in the room. The Emperor now rose from his chair and led Laurence to the small altar on the eastern side of the hall. Laurence lit the stands of incense upon the altar and parroted the phrases which Hammond had so laboriously taught him, relieved to see Hammond's small nod: he had made no mistakes, then, or at least none unforgivable.

He had to genuflect once more, but this time before the altar, which Laurence was ashamed to acknowledge even to himself was easier by far to bear, though closer to real blasphemy; hurriedly, under his breath, he said a Lord's Prayer, and hoped that should make quite clear that he did not really mean to be breaking the commandment. Then the worst of the business was over: now Temeraire was called forward for the ceremony which would formally bind them as companions, and Laurence could make the required oaths with a light heart.

The Emperor had seated himself again to oversee the proceedings; now he nodded approvingly, and made a brief gesture to one of his attendants. At once a table was brought into the room, though without any chairs, and more of the cool ices served while the Emperor made inquiries of Laurence about his family, through Hammond's mediation. The Emperor was taken aback to learn that Laurence was himself unmarried and without children, and Laurence was forced to submit to being lectured on the subject at great length, quite seriously, and to agree that he had been neglecting his family duties. He did not mind very much: he was too happy not to have misspoken, and for the ordeal to be so nearly over.

Hammond himself was pale with relief as they left, and had actually to stop and sit down upon a bench on their way to their quarters. A couple of servants brought him some water and fanned him until the colour came back into his face and he could stagger on. 'I congratulate you, sir,' Staunton said, shaking Hammond's hand as they at last left him to lie down in his chamber. 'I am not ashamed to say I would not have believed it possible.'

'Thank you; thank you,' Hammond could only repeat, deeply affected; he was nearly toppling over.

Hammond had won for them not only Laurence's formal entrée into the Imperial family, but the grant of an estate in the Tartar city itself. It was not quite an official embassy, but as a practical matter it was much the same, as Hammond could now reside there indefinitely at Laurence's invitation. Even the kowtow had been dealt with to everyone's satisfaction: from the British point of view, Laurence had made the gesture not as a representative of the Crown, but as an adopted son, while the Chinese were content to have their proper forms met.

'We have already had several very friendly messages from the mandarins at Canton through the Imperial post, did Hammond tell you?' Staunton said to Laurence, as they stood together outside their own rooms. 'The Emperor's gesture to remit all duties on British ships for the year will of course be a tremendous benefit to the Company, but in the long run this new mind-set among them will by far prove the more valuable. I suppose—' Staunton hesitated; his hand was already on the screen-frame, ready to go inside. 'I suppose you could not find it consistent with your duty to stay? I need scarcely say that it would be of tremendous value to have you here, though of course I know how great our need for dragons is, back home.'

Retiring at last, Laurence gladly exchanged his clothes for plain cotton robes, and went outside to join Temeraire in the fragrant shade of a bank of orange trees. Temeraire had a scroll laid out in his frame, but was gazing out across the nearby pond rather than reading. In view, a graceful nine-arched bridge crossed the pond, mirrored in black shadows against the water now dyed yellow-orange with the reflections of the late sunlight, the lotus flowers closing up for the night.

He turned his head and nudged Laurence in greeting. 'I have been watching: there is Lien,' he said, pointing with his nose across the water. The white dragon was crossing over the bridge, all alone except for a tall, dark-haired man in blue scholar-robes walking by her side, who looked somehow unusual; after a moment squinting, Laurence realized the man did not have a shaved forehead nor a queue. Midway Lien paused and turned to look at them: Laurence put a hand on Temeraire's neck, instinctively, in the face of that unblinking red gaze.

Temeraire snorted, and his ruff came up a little way, but she did not stay: her neck proudly straight and haughty, she turned away again and continued past, vanishing shortly among the trees. 'I wonder what she will do now,' Temeraire said.

Laurence wondered also; certainly she would not find another willing companion, when she had been held unlucky even before her late misfortunes. He had even heard several courtiers make remarks to the effect that she was responsible for Yongxing's fate; deeply cruel, if she had heard them, and still less forgiving opinion held that she ought to be banished entirely. 'Perhaps she will go into some secluded breeding grounds.'

'I do not think they have particular grounds set aside for breeding here,' Temeraire said. 'Mei and I did not have to—' Here he stopped, and if it were possible for a dragon to blush, he certainly would have undertaken it. 'But perhaps I am wrong,' he said hastily.

Laurence swallowed. 'You have a great deal of affection for Mei.'

'Oh yes,' Temeraire said, wistfully.

Laurence was silent; he picked up one of the hard little yellow fruits that had fallen unripe, and rolled it in his hands. 'The *Allegiance* will sail with the next favourable tide, if the wind permits,' he said finally, very low. 'Would you prefer us to stay?' Seeing that he had surprised Temeraire, he added, 'Hammond and Staunton tell me we could do a great deal of good for Britain's interests here. If you wish to remain, I will write to Lenton, and let him know we had better be stationed here.'

'Oh,' Temeraire said, and bent his head over the reading frame: he was not paying attention to the scroll, but only thinking. 'You would rather go home, though, would you not?'

'I would be lying if I said otherwise,' Laurence said heavily. 'But I would rather see you happy; and I cannot think how I could make you so in England, now you have seen how dragons are treated here.' The disloyalty nearly choked him; he could go no further.

'The dragons here are not all smarter than British dragons,' Temeraire said. 'There is no reason Maximus or Lily could not learn to read and write, or carry on some other kind of profession. It is not right that we are kept penned up like animals, and never taught anything but how to fight.'

'No,' Laurence said. 'No, it is not.' There was no possible answer to make, all his defence of British custom undone by the examples which he had seen before him in every corner of China. If some dragons went hungry, that was hardly a counter. He himself would gladly have starved sooner than give up his own liberty, and he would not insult Temeraire by mentioning it even as a sop.

They were silent together for a long space of time, while the servants came around to light the lamps; the quarter-moon rising hung mirrored in the pond, luminous silver, and Laurence idly threw pebbles into the water to break the reflection into gilt ripples. It was hard to imagine what he would do in China, himself, other than serve as a figurehead. He would have to learn the language somehow after all, at least spoken if not the script.

'No, Laurence, it will not do. I cannot stay here and enjoy myself, while back home they are still at war, and need me,' Temeraire said finally. 'And more than that, the dragons in England do not even know that there is any other way of doing things. I will miss Mei and Qian, but I could not be happy while I knew Maximus and Lily were still being treated so badly. It seems to me my duty to go back and arrange things better there.'

Laurence did not know what to say. He had often chided Temeraire for revolutionary thoughts, a tendency to sedition, but only jokingly; it had never occurred to him Temeraire would ever make any such attempt deliberately, outright. Laurence had no idea what the official reaction would be, but he was certain it would not be taken calmly. 'Temeraire, you cannot possibly—' he said, and stopped, the great blue eyes expectantly upon him.

'My dear,' he said quietly, after a moment, 'you put me to shame. Certainly we ought not be content to leave things as they are, now we know there is a better way.'

374

'I thought you would agree,' Temeraire said, in satisfaction. 'Besides,' he added, more prosaically, 'my mother tells me that Celestials are not supposed to fight, at all, and only studying all the time does not sound very exciting. We had much better go home.' He nodded, and looked back at his poetry. 'Laurence,' he said, 'the ship's carpenter could make some more of these reading frames, could he not?'

'My dear, if it will make you happy he shall make you a dozen,' Laurence said, and leaned against him, full of gratitude despite his concerns, to calculate by the moon when the tide should turn again for England and for home.

Acknowledgments

A second novel poses a fresh set of challenges and alarms, and I am especially grateful to my editors, Betsy Mitchell of Del Rey, and Jane Johnson and Emma Coode of HarperCollins UK, for their insights and excellent advice on this one. I also owe many thanks to my team of beta readers for all their help and encouragement: Holly Benton, Francesca Coppa, Dana Dupont, Doris Egan, Diana Fox, Vanessa Len, Shelley Mitchell, Georgina Paterson, Sara Rosenbaum, L. Salom, Micole Sudberg, Kaa Takenaka, Rebecca Tushnet, and Cho We Zen.

Many thanks to my sterling agent, Cynthia Manson, for all her help and guidance, and to my family for all their continuing advice and support and enthusiasm. I'm lucky beyond measure in my very best and in-house reader, my husband Charles.

And I want to say a special thanks to Dominic Harman, who has been doing one brilliant cover after another for both the American and British editions; it's a thrill beyond measure to see my dragons given life in his art.

Kate Greenaway.

8/6

THE PERENNIAL PHILOSOPHY

By Aldous Huxley

*

Novels

TIME MUST HAVE A STOP
AFTER MANY A SUMMER
EYELESS IN GAZA
BRAVE NEW WORLD
POINT COUNTER POINT
THOSE BARREN LEAVES
ANTIC HAY
CROME YELLOW

Biography

GREY EMINENCE

Short Stories

BRIEF CANDLES
TWO OR THREE GRACES
LITTLE MEXICAN
MORTAL COILS
LIMBO

Essays and Belles Lettres

SCIENCE, LIBERTY AND PEACE
THE ART OF SEEING
ENDS AND MEANS
MUSIC AT NIGHT
VULGARITY IN LITERATURE
DO WHAT YOU WILL
PROPER STUDIES
JESTING PILATE
ALONG THE ROAD
ON THE MARGIN
TEXTS AND PRETEXTS
BEYOND THE MEXIQUE BAY
THE OLIVE TREE

Poetry

THE CICADAS
LEDA

Drama

THE WORLD OF LIGHT

*

Chatto & Windus

ALDOUS HUXLEY

The Perennial Philosophy

1947

Chatto & Windus

LONDON

PUBLISHED BY
Chatto & Windus
LONDON

*

Oxford University Press
TORONTO

Applications regarding translation rights in any
work by Aldous Huxley should be addressed
to Chatto & Windus, 40 William IV Street,
London, W.C. 2

FIRST PUBLISHED 1946
SECOND IMPRESSION 1947
PRINTED IN GREAT BRITAIN
IN COMPLETE CONFORMITY WITH
THE AUTHORIZED ECONOMY STANDARDS

Contents

v

Acknowledgments

For permission to use the following selections, grateful acknowledgment and thanks are extended to the following authors and publishers:

George Allen & Unwin Ltd.: MONKEY and THE WAY AND ITS POWER, translated by Arthur Waley; LETTERS, by Spinoza.

Burns, Oates & Washbourne Ltd.: THE CLOUD OF UNKNOWING, edited by McCann; THE WORKS OF ST. JOHN OF THE CROSS, translated by Allison Piers.

Cambridge University Press: STUDIES IN ISLAMIC MYSTICISM, by R. A. Nicholson.

J. M. Dent & Sons Ltd.: ADORNMENT OF THE SPIRITUAL MARRIAGE, by Ruysbroeck, translated by Winschenk Dom.

P. J. and A. E. Dobell: CENTURIES OF MEDITATION, by Thomas Traherne.

Dwight Goddard Estate: A BUDDHIST BIBLE, by Dwight Goddard.

Kegan Paul, Trench, Trubner & Co. Ltd.: MASNAVI, by Jalaluddin Rumi, translated by Whinfield.

Longmans, Green & Co. Ltd.: THE SPIRIT OF ST. FRANCIS DE SALES, by Jean Pierre Camus, translated by Lear; CATHERINE OF SIENA, by Johannes Jorgensen.

Macmillan & Co. Ltd.: THEOLOGIA GERMANICA, translated by Winkworth; THE SPIRITUAL REFORMERS, by Rufus Jones; MYSTICISM EAST AND WEST, by Rudolph Otto; ONE HUNDRED POEMS OF KABIR, by Rabindranath Tagore.

John Murray and *Mr. Lionel Giles:* MUSINGS OF A CHINESE MYSTIC, from THE WISDOM OF THE EAST series, translated by Herbert Giles.

Oxford University Press and *Harvard University Press:* THE TRANSFORMATION OF NATURE IN ART, by Amanda K. Coomaraswamy.

Oxford University Press and *The Pali Text Society:* THE PATH OF PURITY, by Buddhaghosha.

Oxford University Press: THE TIBETAN BOOK OF THE DEAD, translated by Dr. Evans-Wentz.

Paramananda and the publishers of BHAGAVAD-GITA.

George Routledge & Sons Ltd.: STUDIES IN THE LANKAVATARA SUTRA, by Suzuki.

Sheed & Ward Ltd.: THE MYSTICAL THEOLOGY OF ST. BERNARD, by Étienne Gilson.

The Society for Promoting Christian Knowledge: DIONYSIUS THE AREOPAGITE, translated by C. E. Rolt.

John M. Watkins: WORKS OF MEISTER ECKHART, translated by Evans; THE CREST-JEWEL OF WISDOM, by Shankara, translated by Charles Johnston.

INTRODUCTION

PHILOSOPHIA PERENNIS—the phrase was coined by Leibniz; but the thing—the metaphysic that recognizes a divine Reality substantial to the world of things and lives and minds; the psychology that finds in the soul something similar to, or even identical with, divine Reality; the ethic that places man's final end in the knowledge of the immanent and transcendent Ground of all being—the thing is immemorial and universal. Rudiments of the Perennial Philosophy may be found among the traditionary lore of primitive peoples in every region of the world, and in its fully developed forms it has a place in every one of the higher religions. A version of this Highest Common Factor in all preceding and subsequent theologies was first committed to writing more than twenty-five centuries ago, and since that time the inexhaustible theme has been treated again and again, from the standpoint of every religious tradition and in all the principal languages of Asia and Europe. In the pages that follow I have brought together a number of selections from these writings, chosen mainly for their significance—because they effectively illustrated some particular point in the general system of the Perennial Philosophy—but also for their intrinsic beauty and memorableness. These selections are arranged under various heads and embedded, so to speak, in a commentary of my own, designed to illustrate and connect, to develop and, where necessary, to elucidate.

Knowledge is a function of being. When there is a change in the being of the knower, there is a corresponding change in the nature and amount of knowing. For example, the being of a child is transformed by growth and education into that of a man; among the results of this transformation is a revolutionary change in the way of knowing and the amount and character of the things known. As the individual grows up, his knowledge becomes more conceptual and systematic in form, and its

A

factual, utilitarian content is enormously increased. But these gains are offset by a certain deterioration in the quality of immediate apprehension, a blunting and a loss of intuitive power. Or consider the change in his being which the scientist is able to induce mechanically by means of his instruments. Equipped with a spectroscope and a sixty-inch reflector an astronomer becomes, so far as eyesight is concerned, a superhuman creature; and, as we should naturally expect, the knowledge possessed by this superhuman creature is very different, both in quantity and quality, from that which can be acquired by a stargazer with unmodified, merely human eyes.

Nor are changes in the knower's physiological or intellectual being the only ones to affect his knowledge. What we know depends also on what, as moral beings, we choose to make ourselves. 'Practice,' in the words of William James, 'may change our theoretical horizon, and this in a twofold way: it may lead into new worlds and secure new powers. Knowledge we could never attain, remaining what we are, may be attainable in consequence of higher powers and a higher life, which we may morally achieve.' To put the matter more succinctly, 'Blessed are the pure in heart, for they shall see God.' And the same idea has been expressed by the Sufi poet, Jalal-uddin Rumi, in terms of a scientific metaphor: 'The astrolabe of the mysteries of God is love.'

This book, I repeat, is an anthology of the Perennial Philosophy; but, though an anthology, it contains but few extracts from the writings of professional men of letters and, though illustrating a philosophy, hardly anything from the professional philosophers. The reason for this is very simple. The Perennial Philosophy is primarily concerned with the one, divine Reality substantial to the manifold world of things and lives and minds. But the nature of this one Reality is such that it cannot be directly and immediately apprehended except by those who have chosen to fulfil certain conditions, making themselves loving, pure in heart, and poor in spirit. Why should this be so? We do not know. It is just one of those facts which we have to accept, whether we like them or not and however implausible and unlikely they may seem. Nothing in our everyday experience gives us any reason for supposing that water is made up of hydrogen and oxygen; and yet when we subject water to certain rather drastic treatments, the nature of its constituent elements becomes manifest. Similarly, nothing in our everyday experience gives us much reason for supposing that the mind of the average sensual man has, as one of its constituents, something resembling, or identical with, the Reality substantial to the manifold world; and yet, when that mind is subjected to certain rather drastic treatments, the divine element, of which it is in part at least composed, becomes manifest, not only to the mind itself, but also, by its reflection in external behaviour, to other minds. It is only by making physical experiments that we can discover the intimate nature of matter and its potentialities. And it is only by making psychological and moral experiments that we can discover the intimate nature of mind and its potentialities. In the ordinary circumstances of average sensual life these potentialities of the mind remain latent and unmanifested. If we would realize them, we must fulfil certain conditions and obey certain rules, which experience has shown empirically to be valid.

In regard to few professional philosophers and men of letters is there any evidence that they did very much in the way of fulfilling the necessary conditions of direct spiritual knowledge. When poets or metaphysicians talk about the subject matter of the Perennial Philosophy, it is generally at second hand. But in every age there have been some men and women who chose to fulfil the conditions upon which alone, as a matter of brute empirical fact, such immediate knowledge can be had; and of these a few have left accounts of the Reality they were thus enabled to apprehend and have tried to relate, in one comprehensive system of thought, the given facts of this experience with the given facts of their other experiences. To such first-hand exponents of the Perennial Philosophy those who knew them have generally given the name of 'saint' or 'prophet,' 'sage' or 'enlightened one.' And it is mainly to these, because there is good reason for supposing that they knew what they were talking about, and not to the professional philosophers or men of letters, that I have gone for my selections.

In India two classes of scripture are recognized: the Shruti, or inspired writings which are their own authority, since they are the product of immediate insight into ultimate Reality; and the Smriti, which are based upon the Shruti and from them derive such authority as they have. 'The Shruti,' in Shankara's words, 'depends upon direct perception. The Smriti plays a part analogous to induction, since, like induction, it derives its authority from an authority other than itself.' This book, then, is an anthology, with explanatory comments, of passages drawn from the Shruti and Smriti of many times and places. Unfortunately, familiarity with traditionally hallowed writings tends to breed, not indeed contempt, but something which, for practical purposes, is almost as bad—namely a kind of reverential insensibility, a stupor of the spirit, an inward deafness to the meaning of the sacred words. For this reason, when selecting material to illustrate the doctrines of the Perennial Philosophy, as they were formulated in the West, I have gone almost always to sources other than the Bible. This Christian Smriti, from which I have drawn, is based upon the Shruti of the canonical books, but has the great advantage of being less well known and therefore more vivid and, so to say, more audible than they are. Moreover, much of this Smriti is the work of genuinely saintly men and women, who have qualified themselves to know at first hand what they are talking about. Consequently it may be regarded as being itself a form of inspired and self-validating Shruti—and this in a much higher degree than many of the writings now included in the Biblical canon.

In recent years a number of attempts have been made to work out a system of empirical theology. But in spite of the subtlety and intellectual power of such writers as Sorley, Oman and Tennant, the effort has met with only a partial success. Even in the hands of its ablest exponents empirical theology is not particularly convincing. The reason, it seems to me, must be sought in the fact that the empirical theologians have confined their attention more or less exclusively to the

experience of those whom the theologians of an older school
called 'the unregenerate'—that is to say, the experience of
people who have not gone very far in fulfilling the necessary
conditions of spiritual knowledge. But it is a fact, confirmed
and re-confirmed during two or three thousand years of religious history, that the ultimate Reality is not clearly and
immediately apprehended, except by those who have made
themselves loving, pure in heart and poor in spirit. This being
so, it is hardly surprising that a theology based upon the experience of nice, ordinary, unregenerate people should carry so
little conviction. This kind of empirical theology is on precisely the same footing as an empirical astronomy, based upon
the experience of naked-eye observers. With the unaided eye
a small, faint smudge can be detected in the constellation of
Orion, and doubtless an imposing cosmological theory could
be based upon the observation of this smudge. But no amount
of such theorizing, however ingenious, could ever tell us as
much about the galactic and extra-galactic nebulae as can direct
acquaintance by means of a good telescope, camera and spectroscope. Analogously, no amount of theorizing about such hints
as may be darkly glimpsed within the ordinary, unregenerate
experience of the manifold world can tell us as much about
divine Reality as can be directly apprehended by a mind in a
state of detachment, charity and humility. Natural science is
empirical; but it does not confine itself to the experience of
human beings in their merely human and unmodified condition. Why empirical theologians should feel themselves
obliged to submit to this handicap, goodness only knows.
And of course, so long as they confine empirical experience
within these all too human limits, they are doomed to the perpetual stultification of their best efforts. From the material
they have chosen to consider, no mind, however brilliantly
gifted, can infer more than a set of possibilities or, at the very
best, specious probabilities. The self-validating certainty of
direct awareness cannot in the very nature of things be
achieved except by those equipped with the moral 'astrolabe
of God's mysteries.' If one is not oneself a sage or saint, the

best thing one can do, in the field of metaphysics, is to study the works of those who were, and who, because they had modified their merely human mode of being, were capable of a more than merely human kind and amount of knowledge.

Chapter 1

THAT ART THOU

IN studying the Perennial Philosophy we can begin either at the bottom, with practice and morality; or at the top, with a consideration of metaphysical truths; or, finally, in the middle, at the focal point where mind and matter, action and thought have their meeting place in human psychology.

The lower gate is that preferred by strictly practical teachers —men who, like Gautama Buddha, have no use for speculation and whose primary concern is to put out in men's hearts the hideous fires of greed, resentment and infatuation. Through the upper gate go those whose vocation it is to think and speculate—the born philosophers and theologians. The middle gate gives entrance to the exponents of what has been called 'spiritual religion'—the devout contemplatives of India, the Sufis of Islam, the Catholic mystics of the later Middle Ages, and, in the Protestant tradition, such men as Denk and Franck and Castellio, as Everard and John Smith and the first Quakers and William Law.

It is through this central door, and just because it is central, that we shall make our entry into the subject matter of this book. The psychology of the Perennial Philosophy has its source in metaphysics and issues logically in a characteristic way of life and system of ethics. Starting from this mid-point of doctrine, it is easy for the mind to move in either direction.

In the present section we shall confine our attention to but a single feature of this traditional psychology—the most important, the most emphatically insisted upon by all exponents of the Perennial Philosophy and, we may add, the least psychological. For the doctrine that is to be illustrated in this section belongs to autology rather than psychology—to the science, not of the personal ego, but of that eternal Self in the depth of particular, individualized selves, and identical with, or at least akin to, the divine Ground. Based upon the direct experience of those who have fulfilled the necessary conditions of such knowledge, this teaching is expressed most succinctly in the Sanskrit formula, *tat tvam asi* ('That art thou'); the Atman, or immanent eternal Self, is one with Brahman, the Absolute Principle of all existence; and the last end of every human being is to discover the fact for himself, to find out Who he really is.

> The more God is in all things, the more He is outside them. The more He is within, the more without.
>
> *Eckhart*

Only the transcendent, the completely other, can be immanent without being modified by the becoming of that in which it dwells. The Perennial Philosophy teaches that it is desirable and indeed necessary to know the spiritual Ground of things, not only within the soul, but also outside in the world and, beyond world and soul, in its transcendent otherness—'in heaven.'

> Though GOD is everywhere present, yet He is only present to thee in the deepest and most central part of thy soul. The natural senses cannot possess God or unite thee to Him; nay, thy inward faculties of understanding, will and memory can only reach after God, but cannot be the place of His habitation in thee. But there is a root or depth of thee from whence all these faculties come forth, as lines from a centre, or as branches from the body of the tree. This depth is called the centre, the fund or bottom of the soul. This depth is the unity, the eternity—I had almost said the infinity—of thy soul; for it is so infinite that nothing can satisfy it or give it rest but the infinity of God.
>
> *William Law*

This extract seems to contradict what was said above; but the contradiction is not a real one. God within and God without —these are two abstract notions, which can be entertained by the understanding and expressed in words. But the facts to which these notions refer cannot be realized and experienced except in 'the deepest and most central part of the soul.' And this is true no less of God without than of God within. But though the two abstract notions have to be realized (to use a spatial metaphor) in the same place, the intrinsic nature of the realization of God within is qualitatively different from that of the realization of God without, and each in turn is different from that of the realization of the Ground as simultaneously within and without—as the Self of the perceiver and at the same time (in the words of the Bhagavad-Gita) as 'That by which all this world is pervaded.'

When Svetaketu was twelve years old he was sent to a teacher, with whom he studied until he was twenty-four. After learning all the Vedas, he returned home full of conceit in the belief that he was consummately well educated, and very censorious.

His father said to him, 'Svetaketu, my child, you who are so full of your learning and so censorious, have you asked for that knowledge by which we hear the unhearable, by which we perceive what cannot be perceived and know what cannot be known?'

'What is that knowledge, sir?' asked Svetaketu.

His father replied, 'As by knowing one lump of clay all that is made of clay is known, the difference being only in name, but the truth being that all is clay—so, my child, is that knowledge, knowing which we know all.'

'But surely these venerable teachers of mine are ignorant of this knowledge; for if they possessed it they would have imparted it to me. Do you, sir, therefore give me that knowledge.'

'So be it,' said the father. . . . And he said, 'Bring me a fruit of the nyagrodha tree.'

'Here is one, sir.'

'Break it.'

'It is broken, sir.'

'What do you see there?'

'Some seeds, sir, exceedingly small.'

'Break one of these.'

'It is broken, sir.'

'What do you see there?'

'Nothing at all.'

The father said, 'My son, that subtle essence which you do not perceive there—in that very essence stands the being of the huge nyagrodha tree. In that which is the subtle essence all that exists has its self. That is the True, that is the Self, and thou, Svetaketu, art That.'

'Pray, sir,' said the son, 'tell me more.'

'Be it so, my child,' the father replied; and he said, 'Place this salt in water, and come to me tomorrow morning.'

The son did as he was told.

Next morning the father said, 'Bring me the salt which you put in the water.'

The son looked for it, but could not find it; for the salt, of course, had dissolved.

The father said, 'Taste some of the water from the surface of the vessel. How is it?'

'Salty.'

'Taste some from the middle. How is it?'

'Salty.'

'Taste some from the bottom. How is it?'

'Salty.'

The father said, 'Throw the water away and then come back to me again.'

The son did so; but the salt was not lost, for salt exists for ever.

Then the father said, 'Here likewise in this body of yours, my son, you do not perceive the True; but there in fact it is. In that which is the subtle essence, all that exists has its self. That is the True, that is the Self, and thou, Svetaketu, art That.'

From the Chandogya Upanishad

The man who wishes to know the 'That' which is 'thou' may set to work in any one of three ways. He may begin by looking inwards into his own particular *thou* and, by a process of 'dying to self'—self in reasoning, self in willing, self in feeling—come at last to a knowledge of the Self, the Kingdom of God that is within. Or else he may begin with the *thous* existing outside himself, and may try to realize their essential unity with God and, through God, with one another and with his own being. Or, finally (and this is doubtless the best way), he may seek to approach the ultimate That both from within and from without, so that he comes to realize God experimentally as at once the principle of his own *thou* and of all other *thous*, animate and inanimate. The completely illuminated human being knows, with Law, that God 'is present in the deepest and most central part of his own soul'; but he is also and at the same time one of those who, in the words of Plotinus,

> see all things, not in process of becoming, but in Being, and see themselves in the other. Each being contains in itself the whole intelligible world. Therefore All is everywhere. Each is there All, and All is each. Man as he now is has ceased to be the All. But when he ceases to be an individual, he raises himself again and penetrates the whole world.

It is from the more or less obscure intuition of the oneness that is the ground and principle of all multiplicity that philosophy takes its source. And not alone philosophy, but natural science as well. All science, in Meyerson's phrase, is the reduction of multiplicities to identities. Divining the One within and beyond the many, we find an intrinsic plausibility in any explanation of the diverse in terms of a single principle.

The philosophy of the Upanishads reappears, developed and enriched, in the Bhagavad-Gita and was finally systematized, in the ninth century of our era, by Shankara. Shankara's teaching (simultaneously theoretical and practical, as is that of all true exponents of the Perennial Philosophy) is summarized in his versified treatise, *Viveka-Chudamani* ('The Crest-Jewel of Wisdom'). All the following passages are taken from this conveniently brief and untechnical work.

> The Atman is that by which the universe is pervaded, but which nothing pervades; which causes all things to shine, but which all things cannot make to shine. . . .

The nature of the one Reality must be known by one's own clear spiritual perception; it cannot be known through a pandit (learned man). Similarly the form of the moon can only be known through one's own eyes. How can it be known through others?

Who but the Atman is capable of removing the bonds of ignorance, passion and self-interested action? . . .

Liberation cannot be achieved except by the perception of the identity of the individual spirit with the universal Spirit. It can be achieved neither by Yoga (physical training), nor by Sankhya (speculative philosophy), nor by the practice of religious ceremonies, nor by mere learning. . . .

Disease is not cured by pronouncing the name of medicine, but by taking medicine. Deliverance is not achieved by repeating the word 'Brahman,' but by directly experiencing Brahman. . . .

The Atman is the Witness of the individual mind and its operations. It is absolute knowledge. . . .

The wise man is one who understands that the essence of Brahman and of Atman is Pure Consciousness, and who realizes their absolute identity. The identity of Brahman and Atman is affirmed in hundreds of sacred texts. . . .

Caste, creed, family and lineage do not exist in Brahman. Brahman has neither name nor form, transcends merit and demerit, is beyond time, space and the objects of sense-experience. Such is Brahman, and 'thou art That.' Meditate upon this truth within your consciousness.

Supreme, beyond the power of speech to express, Brahman may yet be apprehended by the eye of pure illumination. Pure, absolute and eternal Reality—such is Brahman, and 'thou art That.' Meditate upon this truth within your consciousness. . . .

Though One, Brahman is the cause of the many. There is no other cause. And yet Brahman is independent of the law of causation. Such is Brahman, and 'thou art That.' Meditate upon this truth within your consciousness. . . .

The truth of Brahman may be understood intellectually. But (even in those who so understand) the desire for personal separateness is deep-rooted and powerful, for it exists from beginningless time. It creates the notion, 'I am the actor, I am he who experiences.' This notion is the cause of bondage to conditional existence, birth and death. It can be removed only by the earnest effort to live constantly in union with Brahman. By the sages, the eradication of this notion and the craving for personal separateness is called Liberation.

It is ignorance that causes us to identify ourselves with the body, the ego, the senses, or anything that is not the Atman. He is a wise man who overcomes this ignorance by devotion to the Atman. . . .

When a man follows the way of the world, or the way of the flesh, or the way of tradition (i.e. when he believes in religious rites and the letter of the scriptures, as though they were intrinsically sacred), knowledge of Reality cannot arise in him.

The wise say that this threefold way is like an iron chain, binding the feet of him who aspires to escape from the prison-house of this world. He who frees himself from the chain achieves Deliverance.

Shankara

In the Taoist formulations of the Perennial Philosophy there is an insistence, no less forcible than in the Upanishads, the Gita and the writings of Shankara, upon the universal immanence of the transcendent spiritual Ground of all existence. What follows is an extract from one of the great classics of Taoist literature, the Book of Chuang Tzu, most of which seems to have been written around the turn of the fourth and third centuries B.C.

> Do not ask whether the Principle is in this or in that; it is in all beings. It is on this account that we apply to it the epithets of supreme, universal, total. . . . It has ordained that all things should be limited, but is Itself unlimited, infinite. As to what pertains to manifestation, the Principle causes the succession of its phases, but is not this succession. It is the author of causes and effects, but is not the causes and effects. It is the author of condensations and dissipations (birth and death, changes of state), but is not itself condensations and dissipations. All proceeds from It and is under its influence. It is in all things, but is not identical with beings, for it is neither differentiated nor limited.
>
> *Chuang Tzu*

From Taoism we pass to that Mahayana Buddhism which, in the Far East, came to be so closely associated with Taoism, borrowing and bestowing until the two came at last to be fused in what is known as Zen. The Lankavatara Sutra, from which the following extract is taken, was the scripture which the founder of Zen Buddhism expressly recommended to his first disciples.

> Those who vainly reason without understanding the truth are lost in the jungle of the Vijnanas (the various forms of relative knowledge), running about here and there and trying to justify their view of ego-substance.
>
> The self realized in your inmost consciousness appears in its purity; this is the Tathagata-garbha (literally, Buddha-womb), which is not the realm of those given over to mere reasoning. . . .
>
> Pure in its own nature and free from the category of finite and infinite, Universal Mind is the undefiled Buddha-womb, which is wrongly apprehended by sentient beings.
>
> *Lankavatara Sutra*

One Nature, perfect and pervading, circulates in all natures,
One Reality, all-comprehensive, contains within itself all realities.
The one Moon reflects itself wherever there is a sheet of water,

And all the moons in the waters are embraced within the one
    Moon.
The Dharma-body (the Absolute) of all the Buddhas enters into
    my own being.
And my own being is found in union with theirs. . . .
The Inner Light is beyond praise and blame;
Like space it knows no boundaries,
Yet it is even here, within us, ever retaining its serenity and
    fullness.
It is only when you hunt for it that you lose it;
You cannot take hold of it, but equally you cannot get rid of it,
And while you can do neither, it goes on its own way.
You remain silent and it speaks; you speak, and it is dumb;
The great gate of charity is wide open, with no obstacles before it.

Yung-chia Ta-shih

I am not competent, nor is this the place to discuss the doctrinal differences between Buddhism and Hinduism. Let it
suffice to point out that, when he insisted that human beings
are by nature 'non-Atman,' the Buddha was evidently speaking about the personal self and not the universal Self. The
Brahman controversialists, who appear in certain of the Pali
scriptures, never so much as mention the Vedanta doctrine of
the identity of Atman and Godhead and the non-identity of
ego and Atman. What they maintain and Gautama denies is
the substantial nature and eternal persistence of the individual
psyche. 'As an unintelligent man seeks for the abode of music
in the body of the lute, so does he look for a soul within the
skandhas (the material and psychic aggregates, of which the
individual mind-body is composed).' About the existence of
the Atman that is Brahman, as about most other metaphysical
matters, the Buddha declines to speak, on the ground that such
discussions do not tend to edification or spiritual progress
among the members of a monastic order, such as he had
founded. But though it has its dangers, though it may become
the most absorbing, because the most serious and noblest, of
distractions, metaphysical thinking is unavoidable and finally

necessary. Even the Hinayanists found this, and the later
Mahayanists were to develop, in connection with the practice
of their religion, a splendid and imposing system of cosmological, ethical and psychological thought. This system was
based upon the postulates of a strict idealism and professed to
dispense with the idea of God. But moral and spiritual experience was too strong for philosophical theory, and under the
inspiration of direct experience, the writers of the Mahayana
sutras found themselves using all their ingenuity to explain why
the Tathagata and the Bodhisattvas display an infinite charity
towards beings that do not really exist. At the same time they
stretched the framework of subjective idealism so as to make
room for Universal Mind; qualified the idea of soullessness
with the doctrine that, if purified, the individual mind can
identify itself with the Universal Mind or Buddha-womb; and,
while maintaining godlessness, asserted that this realizable Universal Mind is the inner consciousness of the eternal Buddha
and that the Buddha-mind is associated with 'a great compassionate heart' which desires the liberation of every sentient
being and bestows divine grace on all who make a serious effort
to achieve man's final end. In a word, despite their inauspicious vocabulary, the best of the Mahayana sutras contain an
authentic formulation of the Perennial Philosophy—a formulation which in some respects (as we shall see when we come to
the section, 'God in the World') is more complete than any
other.

In India, as in Persia, Mohammedan thought came to be
enriched by the doctrine that God is immanent as well as
transcendent, while to Mohammedan practice were added the
moral disciplines and 'spiritual exercises,' by means of which
the soul is prepared for contemplation or the unitive knowledge of the Godhead. It is a significant historical fact that the
poet-saint Kabir is claimed as a co-religionist both by Moslems
and Hindus. The politics of those whose goal is beyond time
are always pacific; it is the idolaters of past and future, of
reactionary memory and Utopian dream, who do the persecuting and make the wars.

Behold but One in all things; it is the second that leads you astray.

Kabir

That this insight into the nature of things and the origin of good and evil is not confined exclusively to the saint, but is recognized obscurely by every human being, is proved by the very structure of our language. For language, as Richard Trench pointed out long ago, is often 'wiser, not merely than the vulgar, but even than the wisest of those who speak it. Sometimes it locks up truths which were once well known, but have been forgotten. In other cases it holds the germs of truths which, though they were never plainly discerned, the genius of its framers caught a glimpse of in a happy moment of divination.' For example, how significant it is that in the Indo-European languages, as Darmsteter has pointed out, the root meaning 'two' should connote badness. The Greek prefix dys- (as in dyspepsia) and the Latin dis- (as in dishonourable) are both derived from 'duo.' The cognate bis- gives a pejorative sense to such modern French words as *bévue* ('blunder,' literally 'two-sight'). Traces of that 'second which leads you astray' can be found in 'dubious,' 'doubt' and *Zweifel*—for to doubt is to be double-minded. Bunyan has his Mr. Facing-both-ways, and modern American slang its 'two-timers.' Obscurely and unconsciously wise, our language confirms the findings of the mystics and proclaims the essential badness of division—a word, incidentally, in which our old enemy 'two' makes another decisive appearance.

Here it may be remarked that the cult of unity on the political level is only an idolatrous *ersatz* for the genuine religion of unity on the personal and spiritual levels. Totalitarian regimes justify their existence by means of a philosophy of political monism, according to which the state is God on earth, unification under the heel of the divine state is salvation, and all means to such unification, however intrinsically wicked, are right and may be used without scruple. This political monism leads in practice to excessive privilege and power for the few

B

and oppression for the many, to discontent at home and war abroad. But excessive privilege and power are standing temptations to pride, greed, vanity and cruelty; oppression results in fear and envy; war breeds hatred, misery and despair. All such negative emotions are fatal to the spiritual life. Only the pure in heart and poor in spirit can come to the unitive knowledge of God. Hence, the attempt to impose more unity upon societies than their individual members are ready for makes it psychologically almost impossible for those individuals to realize their unity with the divine Ground and with one another.

Among the Christians and the Sufis, to whose writings we now return, the concern is primarily with the human mind and its divine essence.

> My Me is God, nor do I recognize any other Me except my God Himself.
>
> *St. Catherine of Genoa*

> In those respects in which the soul is unlike God, it is also unlike itself.
>
> *St. Bernard*

> I went from God to God, until they cried from me in me, 'O thou I!'
>
> *Bayazid of Bistun*

Two of the recorded anecdotes about this Sufi saint deserve to be quoted here. 'When Bayazid was asked how old he was, he replied, "Four years." They said, "How can that be?" He answered, "I have been veiled from God by the world for seventy years, but I have seen Him during the last four years. The period during which one is veiled does not belong to one's life."' On another occasion someone knocked at the saint's door and cried, 'Is Bayazid here?' Bayazid answered, 'Is anybody here except God?'

To gauge the soul we must gauge it with God, for the Ground of God and the Ground of the Soul are one and the same.

Eckhart

The spirit possesses God essentially in naked nature, and God the spirit.

Ruysbroeck

For though she sink all sinking in the oneness of divinity, she never touches bottom. For it is of the very essence of the soul that she is powerless to plumb the depths of her creator. And here one cannot speak of the soul any more, for she has lost her nature yonder in the oneness of divine essence. There she is no more called soul, but is called immeasurable being.

Eckhart

The knower and the known are one. Simple people imagine that they should see God, as if He stood there and they here. This is not so. God and I, we are one in knowledge.

Eckhart

'I live, yet not I, but Christ in me.' Or perhaps it might be more accurate to use the verb transitively and say, 'I live, yet not I; for it is the Logos who *lives me*'—lives me as an actor lives his part. In such a case, of course, the actor is always infinitely superior to the rôle. Where real life is concerned, there are no Shakespearean characters, there are only Addisonian Catos or, more often, grotesque Monsieur Perrichons and Charley's Aunts mistaking themselves for Julius Caesar or the Prince of Denmark. But by a merciful dispensation it is always in the power of every *dramatis persona* to get his low, stupid lines pronounced and supernaturally transfigured by the divine equivalent of a Garrick.

O my God, how does it happen in this poor old world that Thou art so great and yet nobody finds Thee, that Thou callest so loudly and nobody hears Thee, that Thou art so near and nobody feels Thee, that Thou givest Thyself to everybody and nobody knows Thy name? Men flee from Thee and say they cannot find Thee; they turn their backs and say they cannot see Thee; they stop their ears and say they cannot hear Thee.

Hans Denk

Between the Catholic mystics of the fourteenth and fifteenth centuries and the Quakers of the seventeenth there yawns a wide gap of time made hideous, so far as religion is concerned, with interdenominational wars and persecutions. But the gulf was bridged by a succession of men, whom Rufus Jones, in the only accessible English work devoted to their lives and teachings, has called the 'Spiritual Reformers.' Denk, Franck, Castellio, Weigel, Everard, the Cambridge Platonists—in spite of the murdering and the madness, the apostolic succession remains unbroken. The truths that had been spoken in the *Theologia Germanica*—that book which Luther professed to love so much and from which, if we may judge from his career, he learned so singularly little—were being uttered once again by Englishmen during the Civil War and under the Cromwellian dictatorship. The mystical tradition, perpetuated by the Protestant Spiritual Reformers, had become diffused, as it were, in the religious atmosphere of the time when George Fox had his first great 'opening' and knew by direct experience:

that Every Man was enlightened by the Divine Light of Christ, and I saw it shine through all; And that they that believed in it came out of Condemnation and came to the Light of Life, and became the Children of it; And that they that hated it and did not believe in it, were condemned by it, though they made a profession of Christ. This I saw in the pure Openings of Light, without the help of any Man, neither did I then know where to find it in the Scriptures, though afterwards, searching the Scriptures, I found it.

From Fox's Journal

The doctrine of the Inner Light achieved a clearer formulation in the writings of the second generation of Quakers.
'There is,' wrote William Penn, 'something nearer to us than
Scriptures, to wit, the Word in the heart from which all Scriptures come.' And a little later Robert Barclay sought to explain the direct experience of *tat tvam asi* in terms of an
Augustinian theology that had, of course, to be considerably
stretched and trimmed before it could fit the facts. Man, he
declared in his famous theses, is a fallen being, incapable of
good, unless united to the Divine Light. This Divine Light is
Christ within the human soul, and is as universal as the seed
of sin. All men, heathen as well as Christian, are endowed
with the Inward Light, even though they may know nothing
of the outward history of Christ's life. Justification is for those
who do not resist the Inner Light and so permit of a new
birth of holiness within them.

> Goodness needeth not to enter into the soul, for it is there
> already, only it is unperceived.
>
> *Theologia Germanica*

> When the Ten Thousand things are viewed in their oneness, we
> return to the Origin and remain where we have always been.
>
> *Sen T'sen*

It is because we don't know Who we are, because we are
unaware that the Kingdom of Heaven is within us, that we
behave in the generally silly, the often insane, the sometimes
criminal ways that are so characteristically human. We are
saved, we are liberated and enlightened, by perceiving the
hitherto unperceived good that is already within us, by returning to our eternal Ground and remaining where, without
knowing it, we have always been. Plato speaks in the same
sense when he says, in the *Republic*, that 'the virtue of wisdom more than anything else contains a divine element which
always remains.' And in the *Theaetetus* he makes the point,
so frequently insisted upon by those who have practised spirit-

ual religion, that it is only by becoming Godlike that we can know God—and to become Godlike is to identify ourselves with the divine element which in fact constitutes our essential nature, but of which, in our mainly voluntary ignorance, we choose to remain unaware.

They are on the way to truth who apprehend God by means of the divine, Light by the light.

Philo

Philo was the exponent of the Hellenistic Mystery Religion which grew up, as Professor Goodenough has shown, among the Jews of the Dispersion, between about 200 B.C. and 100 A.D. Reinterpreting the Pentateuch in terms of a metaphysical system derived from Platonism, Neo-Pythagoreanism and Stoicism, Philo transformed the wholly transcendental and almost anthropomorphically personal God of the Old Testament into the immanent-transcendent Absolute Mind of the Perennial Philosophy. But even from the orthodox scribes and Pharisees of that momentous century which witnessed, along with the dissemination of Philo's doctrines, the first beginnings of Christianity and the destruction of the Temple at Jerusalem, even from the guardians of the Law we hear significantly mystical utterances. Hillel, the great rabbi whose teachings on humility and the love of God and man read like an earlier, cruder version of some of the Gospel sermons, is reported to have spoken these words to an assemblage in the courts of the Temple. 'If I am here' (it is Jehovah who is speaking through the mouth of his prophet), 'everyone is here. If I am not here, no one is here.'

The Beloved is all in all; the lover merely veils Him;
The Beloved is all that lives, the lover a dead thing.

Jalal-uddin Rumi

There is a spirit in the soul, untouched by time and flesh, flowing from the Spirit, remaining in the Spirit, itself wholly spiritual. In this principle is God, ever verdant, ever flowering in all the joy and glory of His actual Self. Sometimes I have called this principle the Tabernacle of the soul, sometimes a spiritual Light, anon I say it is a Spark. But now I say that it is more exalted over this and that than the heavens are exalted above the earth. So now I name it in a nobler fashion. . . . It is free of all names and void of all forms. It is one and simple, as God is one and simple, and no man can in any wise behold it.

Eckhart

Crude formulations of some of the doctrines of the Perennial Philosophy are to be found in the thought-systems of the uncivilized and so-called primitive peoples of the world. Among the Maoris, for example, every human being is regarded as a compound of four elements—a divine eternal principle, known as the *toiora*; an ego, which disappears at death; a ghost-shadow, or psyche, which survives death; and finally a body. Among the Oglala Indians the divine element is called the *sican*, and this is regarded as identical with the *ton*, or divine essence of the world. Other elements of the self are the *nagi*, or personality, and *niya*, or vital soul. After death the *sican* is reunited with the divine Ground of all things, the *nagi* survives in the ghost world of psychic phenomena and the *niya* disappears into the material universe.

In regard to no twentieth-century 'primitive' society can we rule out the possibility of influence by, or borrowing from, some higher culture. Consequently, we have no right to argue from the present to the past. Because many contemporary savages have an esoteric philosophy that is monotheistic with a monotheism that is sometimes of the 'That art thou' variety, we are not entitled to infer offhand that neolithic or palaeolithic men held similar views.

More legitimate and more intrinsically plausible are the inferences that may be drawn from what we know about our own physiology and psychology. We know that human minds have proved themselves capable of everything from imbecility to Quantum Theory, from *Mein Kampf* and sadism to the sanctity of Philip Neri, from metaphysics to crossword puzzles, power politics and the *Missa Solemnis*. We also know that human minds are in some way associated with human brains, and we have fairly good reasons for supposing that there have been no considerable changes in the size and conformation of human brains for a good many thousands of years. Consequently it seems justifiable to infer that human minds in the remote past were capable of as many and as various kinds and degrees of activity as are minds at the present time.

It is, however, certain that many activities undertaken by some minds at the present time were not, in the remote past, undertaken by any minds at all. For this there are several obvious reasons. Certain thoughts are practically unthinkable except in terms of an appropriate language and within the framework of an appropriate system of classification. Where these necessary instruments do not exist, the thoughts in question are not expressed and not even conceived. Nor is this all: the incentive to develop the instruments of certain kinds of thinking is not always present. For long periods of history and prehistory it would seem that men and women, though perfectly capable of doing so, did not wish to pay attention to problems which their descendants found absorbingly interesting. For example, there is no reason to suppose that, between the thirteenth century and the twentieth, the human mind underwent any kind of evolutionary change, comparable to the change, let us say, in the physical structure of the horse's foot during an incomparably longer span of geological time. What happened was that men turned their attention from certain aspects of reality to certain other aspects. The result, among other things, was the development of the natural sciences. Our perceptions and our understanding are directed, in large measure, by our will. We are aware of, and we think about, the things which, for one reason or another, we want to see and understand. Where there's a will there is always an intellectual way. The capacities of the human mind are almost indefinitely great. Whatever we will to do, whether it be to come to the unitive knowledge of the Godhead, or to manufacture self-propelled flame-throwers—that we are able to do, provided always that the willing be sufficiently intense and sustained. It is clear that many of the things to which modern men have chosen to pay attention were ignored by their predecessors. Consequently the very means for thinking clearly and fruitfully about those things remained uninvented, not merely during prehistoric times, but even to the opening of the modern era.

The lack of a suitable vocabulary and an adequate frame of reference, and the absence of any strong and sustained desire to invent these necessary instruments of thought—here are two sufficient reasons why so many of the almost endless potentialities of the human mind remained for so long unactualized. Another and, on its own level, equally cogent reason is this: much of the world's most original and fruitful thinking is done by people of poor physique and of a thoroughly unpractical turn of mind. Because this is so, and because the value of pure thought, whether analytical or integral, has everywhere been more or less clearly recognized, provision was and still is made by every civilized society for giving thinkers a measure of protection from the ordinary strains and stresses of social life. The hermitage, the monastery, the college, the academy and the research laboratory; the begging bowl, the endowment, patronage and the grant of taxpayers' money—such are the principal devices that have been used by actives to conserve that rare bird, the religious, philosophical, artistic or scientific contemplative. In many primitive societies conditions are hard and there is no surplus wealth. The born contemplative has to face the struggle for existence and social predominance without protection. The result, in most cases, is that he either dies young or is too desperately busy merely keeping alive to be able to devote his attention to anything else. When this happens the prevailing philosophy will be that of the hardy, extraverted man of action.

All this sheds some light—dim, it is true, and merely inferential—on the problem of the perennialness of the Perennial Philosophy. In India the scriptures were regarded, not as revelations made at some given moment of history, but as eternal gospels, existent from everlasting to everlasting, inasmuch as coeval with man, or for that matter with any other kind of corporeal or incorporeal being possessed of reason. A similar point of view is expressed by Aristotle, who regards the fundamental truths of religion as everlasting and indestructible. There have been ascents and falls, periods (literally 'roads around' or cycles) of progress and regress; but the great fact of God as the First Mover of a universe which partakes of his divinity has always been recognized. In the light of what we know about prehistoric man (and what we know amounts to nothing more than a few chipped stones, some paintings, drawings and sculptures) and of what we may legitimately infer from other, better documented fields of knowledge, what are we to think of these traditional doctrines? My own view is that they may be true. We know that born contemplatives in the realm both of analytic and of integral thought have turned up in fair numbers and at frequent intervals during recorded history. There is therefore every reason to suppose that they turned up before history was recorded. That many of these people died young or were unable to exercise their talents is certain. But a few of them must have survived. In this context it is highly significant that, among many contemporary primitives, two thought-patterns are found— an exoteric pattern for the unphilosophic many and an esoteric pattern (often monotheistic, with a belief in a God not merely of power, but of goodness and wisdom) for the initiated few. There is no reason to suppose that circumstances were any harder for prehistoric men than they are for many contemporary savages. But if an esoteric monotheism of the kind that seems to come natural to the born thinker is possible in modern savage societies, the majority of whose members accept the sort of polytheistic philosophy that seems to come natural to men of action, a similar esoteric doctrine might have been current in prehistoric societies. True, the modern esoteric doctrines may have been derived from higher cultures. But the significant fact remains that, if so derived, they yet had a meaning for certain members of the primitive society and were considered valuable enough to be carefully preserved. We have seen that many thoughts are unthinkable apart from an appropriate vocabulary and frame of reference. But the fundamental ideas of the Perennial Philosophy can be formulated in a very simple vocabulary, and the experiences to which the ideas refer can and indeed must be had immediately and apart from any vocabulary whatsoever. Strange openings and theophanies are granted to quite small children, who are often profoundly and permanently affected by these experiences. We have no reason to suppose that what happens now to persons with small vocabularies did not happen in remote antiquity. In the modern world (as Vaughan and Traherne and Wordsworth, among others, have told us) the child tends to grow out of his direct awareness of the one Ground of things; for the habit of analytical thought is fatal to the intuitions of integral thinking, whether on the 'psychic' or the spiritual level. Psychic preoccupations may be and often are a major obstacle in the way of genuine spirituality. In primitive societies now (and, presumably, in the remote past) there is much preoccupation with, and a widespread talent for, psychic thinking. But a few people may have worked their way through psychic into genuinely spiritual experience—just as, even in modern industrialized societies, a few people work their way out of the prevailing preoccupation with matter and through the prevailing habits of analytical thought into the direct experience of the spiritual Ground of things.

Such, then, very briefly are the reasons for supposing that the historical traditions of oriental and our own classical antiquity may be true. It is interesting to find that at least one distinguished contemporary ethnologist is in agreement with Aristotle and the Vedantists. 'Orthodox ethnology,' writes Dr. Paul Radin in his *Primitive Man as Philosopher*, 'has been nothing but an enthusiastic and quite uncritical attempt to apply the Darwinian theory of evolution to the facts of social experience.' And he adds that 'no progress in ethnology will be achieved until scholars rid themselves once and for all of the curious notion that everything possesses a history; until they realize that certain ideas and certain concepts are as ultimate for man, as a social being, as specific physiological reactions are ultimate for him, as a biological being.' Among these ultimate concepts, in Dr. Radin's view, is that of monotheism. Such monotheism is often no more than the recognition of a single dark and numinous Power ruling the world. But it may sometimes be genuinely ethical and spiritual.

The nineteenth century's mania for history and prophetic Utopianism tended to blind the eyes of even its acutest thinkers to the timeless facts of eternity. Thus we find T. H. Green writing of mystical union as though it were an evolutionary process and not, as all the evidence seems to show, a state which man, as man, has always had it in his power to realize. 'An animal organism, which has its history in time, gradually becomes the vehicle of an eternally complete consciousness, which in itself can have no history, but a history of the process by which the animal organism becomes its vehicle.' But in actual fact it is only in regard to peripheral knowledge that there has been a genuine historical development. Without much lapse of time and much accumulation of skills and information, there can be but an imperfect knowledge of the material world. But direct awareness of the 'eternally complete consciousness,' which is the ground of the material world, is a possibility occasionally actualized by some human beings at almost any stage of their own personal development, from childhood to old age, and at any period of the race's history.

Chapter 2

THE NATURE OF THE GROUND

OUR starting point has been the psychological doctrine, 'That art thou.' The question that now quite naturally presents itself is a metaphysical one: What is the That to which the thou can discover itself to be akin?

To this the fully developed Perennial Philosophy has at all times and in all places given fundamentally the same answer. The divine Ground of all existence is a spiritual Absolute, ineffable in terms of discursive thought, but (in certain circumstances) susceptible of being directly experienced and realized by the human being. This Absolute is the God-without-form of Hindu and Christian mystical phraseology. The last end of man, the ultimate reason for human existence, is unitive knowledge of the divine Ground—the knowledge that can come only to those who are prepared to 'die to self' and so make room, as it were, for God. Out of any given generation of men and women very few will achieve the final end of human existence; but the opportunity for coming to unitive knowledge will, in one way or another, continually be offered until all sentient beings realize Who in fact they are.

The Absolute Ground of all existence has a personal aspect. The activity of Brahman is Isvara, and Isvara is further manifested in the Hindu Trinity and, at a more distant remove, in the other deities or angels of the Indian pantheon. Analogously, for Christian mystics, the ineffable, attributeless Godhead is manifested in a Trinity of Persons, of whom it is possible to predicate such human attributes as goodness, wisdom, mercy and love, but in a supereminent degree.

Finally there is an incarnation of God in a human being, who possesses the same qualities of character as the personal God, but who exhibits them under the limitations necessarily imposed by confinement within a material body born into the world at a given moment of time. For Christians there has been and, *ex hypothesi*, can be but one such divine incarnation; for Indians there can be and have been many. In Christendom as well as in the East, contemplatives who follow the path of devotion conceive of, and indeed directly perceive, the incarnation as a constantly renewed fact of experience. Christ is for ever being begotten within the soul by the Father, and the play of Krishna is the pseudo-historical symbol of an everlasting truth of psychology and metaphysics — the fact that, in relation to God, the personal soul is always feminine and passive.

Mahayana Buddhism teaches these same metaphysical doctrines in terms of the 'Three Bodies' of Buddha—the absolute Dharmakaya, known also as the Primordial Buddha, or Mind, or the Clear Light of the Void; the Sambhogakaya, corresponding to Isvara or the personal God of Judaism, Christianity and Islam; and finally the Nirmanakaya, the material body, in which the Logos is incarnated upon earth as a living, historical Buddha.

Among the Sufis, Al Haqq, the Real, seems to be thought of as the abyss of Godhead underlying the personal Allah, while the Prophet is taken out of history and regarded as the incarnation of the Logos.

Some idea of the inexhaustible richness of the divine nature can be obtained by analysing, word by word, the invocation with which the Lord's Prayer begins—'Our Father who art in heaven.' God is ours—ours in the same intimate sense that our consciousness and life are ours. But as well as immanently ours, God is also transcendently the personal Father, who loves his creatures and to whom love and allegiance are owed by them in return. 'Our Father who *art*': when we come to consider the verb in isolation, we perceive that the immanent-transcendent personal God is also the immanent-transcendent One, the essence and principle of all existence. And finally God's being is 'in heaven'; the divine nature is other than, and incommensurable with, the nature of the creatures in whom God is immanent. That is why we can attain to the unitive

knowledge of God only when we become in some measure
Godlike, only when we permit God's kingdom to come by
making our own creaturely kingdom go.

God may be worshipped and contemplated in any of his
aspects. But to persist in worshipping only one aspect to the
exclusion of all the rest is to run into grave spiritual peril.
Thus, if we approach God with the preconceived idea that He
is exclusively the personal, transcendental, all-powerful ruler of
the world, we run the risk of becoming entangled in a religion
of rites, propitiatory sacrifices (sometimes of the most horrible
nature) and legalistic observances. Inevitably so; for if God
is an unapproachable potentate out there, giving mysterious
orders, this kind of religion is entirely appropriate to the cosmic
situation. The best that can be said for ritualistic legalism is that
it improves conduct. It does little, however, to alter character
and nothing of itself to modify consciousness.

Things are a great deal better when the transcendent, omnipotent personal God is regarded as also a loving Father. The
sincere worship of such a God changes character as well as
conduct, and does something to modify consciousness. But
the complete transformation of consciousness, which is 'enlightenment,' 'deliverance,' 'salvation,' comes only when God
is thought of as the Perennial Philosophy affirms Him to be—
immanent as well as transcendent, supra-personal as well as
personal—and when religious practices are adapted to this
conception.

When God is regarded as exclusively immanent, legalism
and external practices are abandoned and there is a concentration on the Inner Light. The dangers now are quietism and
antinomianism, a partial modification of consciousness that is
useless or even harmful, because it is not accompanied by the
transformation of character which is the necessary prerequisite of a total, complete and spiritually fruitful transformation
of consciousness.

Finally it is possible to think of God as an exclusively supra-
personal being. For many persons this conception is too
'philosophical' to provide an adequate motive for doing any-

thing practical about their beliefs. Hence, for them, it is of no value.

It would be a mistake, of course, to suppose that people who worship one aspect of God to the exclusion of all the rest must inevitably run into the different kinds of trouble described above. If they are not too stubborn in their ready-made beliefs, if they submit with docility to what happens to them in the process of worshipping, the God who is both immanent and transcendent, personal and more than personal, may reveal Himself to them in his fullness. Nevertheless, the fact remains that it is easier for us to reach our goal if we are not handicapped by a set of erroneous or inadequate beliefs about the right way to get there and the nature of what we are looking for.

Who is God? I can think of no better answer than, He who is. Nothing is more appropriate to the eternity which God is. If you call God good, or great, or blessed, or wise, or anything else of this sort, it is included in these words, namely, He is.

St. Bernard

The purpose of all words is to illustrate the meaning of an object. When they are heard, they should enable the hearer to understand this meaning, and this according to the four categories of substance, of activity, of quality and of relationship. For example, *cow* and *horse* belong to the category of substance. *He cooks* or *he prays* belongs to the category of activity. *White* and *black* belong to the category of quality. *Having money* or *possessing cows* belongs to the category of relationship. Now there is no class of substance to which the Brahman belongs, no common genus. It cannot therefore be denoted by words which, like 'being' in the ordinary sense, signify a category of things. Nor can it be denoted by quality, for it is without qualities; nor yet by activity, because it is without activity—'at rest, without parts or activity,' according to the Scriptures. Neither can it be denoted by relationship, for it is 'without a second' and is not the object of anything but its own self. Therefore it cannot be defined by word or idea; as the Scripture says, it is the One 'before whom words recoil.'

Shankara

It was from the Nameless that Heaven and Earth sprang;
The named is but the mother that rears the ten thousand creatures,
      each after its kind.
Truly, 'Only he that rids himself forever of desire can see the
      Secret Essences.'
He that has never rid himself of desire can see only the Outcomes.

Lao Tẓu

One of the greatest favours bestowed on the soul transiently in
this life is to enable it to see so distinctly and to feel so profoundly
that it cannot comprehend God at all. These souls are herein
somewhat like the saints in heaven, where they who know Him
most perfectly perceive most clearly that He is infinitely incomprehensible; for those who have the less clear vision do not
perceive so clearly as do these others how greatly He transcends
their vision.

St. John of the Cross

When I came out of the Godhead into multiplicity, then all things
proclaimed, 'There is a God' (the personal Creator). Now this
cannot make me blessed, for hereby I realize myself as creature.
But in the breaking through I am more than all creatures; I am
neither God nor creature; I am that which I was and shall remain, now and for ever more. There I receive a thrust which
carries me above all angels. By this thrust I become so rich that
God is not sufficient for me, in so far as He is only God in his
divine works. For in thus breaking through, I perceive what God
and I are in common. There I am what I was. There I neither
increase nor decrease. For there I am the immovable which moves
all things. Here man has won again what he is eternally and ever
shall be. Here God is received into the soul.

Eckhart

The Godhead gave all things up to God. The Godhead is poor,
naked and empty as though it were not; it has not, wills not,
wants not, works not, gets not. It is God who has the treasure
and the bride in him, the Godhead is as void as though it were not.

Eckhart

c

We can understand something of what lies beyond our experience by considering analogous cases lying within our experience. Thus, the relations subsisting between the world and God and between God and the Godhead seem to be analogous, in some measure at least, to those that hold between the body (with its environment) and the psyche, and between the psyche and the spirit. In the light of what we know about the second—and what we know is not, unfortunately, very much—we may be able to form some not too hopelessly inadequate notions about the first.

Mind affects its body in four ways—subconsciously, through that unbelievably subtle physiological intelligence, which Driesch hypostatized under the name of the entelechy; consciously, by deliberate acts of will; subconsciously again, by the reaction upon the physical organism of emotional states having nothing to do with the organs or processes reacted upon; and, either consciously or subconsciously, in certain 'supernormal' manifestations. Outside the body matter can be influenced by the mind in two ways—first, by means of the body, and second, by a 'supernormal' process, recently studied under laboratory conditions and described as 'the PK effect.' Similarly, the mind can establish relations with other minds either indirectly, by willing its body to undertake symbolic activities, such as speech or writing; or 'supernormally,' by the direct approach of mind-reading, telepathy, extra-sensory perception.

Let us now consider these relationships a little more closely. In some fields the physiological intelligence works on its own initiative, as when it directs the never-ceasing processes of breathing, say, or assimilation. In others it acts at the behest of the conscious mind, as when we will to accomplish some action, but do not and cannot will the muscular, glandular, nervous and vascular means to the desired end. The apparently simple act of mimicry well illustrates the extraordinary nature of the feats performed by the physiological intelligence. When a parrot (making use, let us remember, of the beak, tongue and throat of a bird) imitates the sounds produced by the lips, teeth, palate and vocal cords of a man articulating words, what precisely happens? Responding in some as yet entirely uncomprehended way to the conscious mind's desire to imitate some remembered or immediately perceived event, the physiological intelligence sets in motion large numbers of muscles, co-ordinating their efforts with such exquisite skill that the result is a more or less perfect copy of the original. Working on its own level, the conscious mind not merely of a parrot, but of the most highly gifted of human beings, would find itself completely baffled by a problem of comparable complexity.

As an example of the third way in which our minds affect matter, we may cite the all-too-familiar phenomenon of 'nervous indigestion.' In certain persons symptoms of dyspepsia make their appearance when the conscious mind is troubled by such negative emotions as fear, envy, anger or hatred. These emotions are directed towards events or persons in the outer environment; but in some way or other they adversely affect the physiological intelligence and this derangement results, among other things, in 'nervous indigestion.' From tuberculosis and gastric ulcer to heart disease and even dental caries, numerous physical ailments have been found to be closely correlated with certain undesirable states of the conscious mind. Conversely every physician knows that a calm and cheerful patient is much more likely to recover than one who is agitated and depressed.

Finally we come to such occurrences as faith healing and levitation—occurrences 'supernormally' strange, but nevertheless attested by masses of evidence which it is hard to discount completely. Precisely how faith cures diseases (whether at Lourdes or in the hypnotist's consulting room), or how St. Joseph of Cupertino was able to ignore the laws of gravitation, we do not know. (But let us remember that we are no less ignorant of the way in which minds and bodies are related in the most ordinary of everyday activities.) In the same way we are unable to form any idea of the *modus operandi* of what Professor Rhine has called the PK effect. Nevertheless the fact that the fall of dice can be influenced by the mental states of certain individuals seems now to have been established beyond the possibility of doubt. And if the PK effect can be demonstrated in the laboratory and measured by statistical methods, then, obviously, the intrinsic credibility of the scattered anecdotal evidence for the direct influence of mind upon matter, not merely within the body, but outside in the external world, is thereby notably increased. The same is true of extra-sensory perception. Apparent examples of it are constantly turning up in ordinary life. But science is almost impotent to cope with the particular case, the isolated instance. Promoting their methodological ineptitude to the rank of a criterion of truth, dogmatic scientists have often branded everything beyond the pale of their limited competence as unreal and even impossible. But when tests for ESP can be repeated under standardized conditions, the subject comes under the jurisdiction of the law of probabilities and achieves (in the teeth of what passionate opposition!) a measure of scientific respectability.

Such, very baldly and briefly, are the most important things we know about mind in regard to its capacity to influence matter. From this modest knowledge about ourselves, what are we entitled to conclude in regard to the divine object of our nearly total ignorance?

First, as to creation: if a human mind can directly influence matter not merely within, but even outside its body, then a divine mind, immanent in the universe or transcendent to it, may be presumed to be capable of imposing forms upon a pre-existing chaos of formless matter, or even, perhaps, of thinking substance as well as forms into existence.

Once created or divinely informed, the universe has to be sustained. The necessity for a continuous re-creation of the world becomes manifest, according to Descartes, 'when we consider the nature of time, or the duration of things; for this is of such a kind that its parts are not mutually dependent and never co-existent; and, accordingly, from the fact that we are now it does not necessarily follow that we shall be a moment afterwards, unless some cause, viz. that which first produced us, shall, as it were, continually reproduce us, that is, conserve us.' Here we seem to have something analogous, on the cosmic level, to that physiological intelligence which, in men and the lower animals, unsleepingly performs the task of seeing that bodies behave as they should. Indeed, the physiological intelligence may plausibly be regarded as a special aspect of the general re-creating Logos. In Chinese phraseology it is the Tao as it manifests itself on the level of living bodies.

The bodies of human beings are affected by the good or bad states of their minds. Analogously, the existence at the heart of things of a divine serenity and goodwill may be regarded as one of the reasons why the world's sickness, though chronic, has not proved fatal. And if, in the psychic universe, there should be other and more than human consciousnesses obsessed by thoughts of evil and egotism and rebellion, this would account, perhaps, for some of the quite extravagant and improbable wickedness of human behaviour.

The acts willed by our minds are accomplished either through the instrumentality of the physiological intelligence and the body, or, very exceptionally, and to a limited extent, by direct supernormal means of the PK variety. Analogously the physical situations willed by a divine Providence may be arranged by the perpetually creating Mind that sustains the universe—in which case Providence will appear to do its work by wholly natural means; or else, very exceptionally, the divine Mind may act directly on the universe from the outside, as it were—in which case the workings of Providence and the gifts of grace will appear to be miraculous. Similarly, the divine Mind may choose to communicate with finite minds either by manipulating the world of men and things in ways which the particular mind to be reached at that moment will find meaningful; or else there may be direct communication by something resembling thought transference.

In Eckhart's phrase, God, the creator and perpetual re-creator of the world, 'becomes and disbecomes.' In other words He is, to some extent at least, in time. A temporal God might have the nature of the traditional Hebrew God of the Old Testament; or He might be a limited deity of the kind described by certain philosophical theologians of the present century; or alternatively He might be an emergent God, starting unspiritually at Alpha and becoming gradually more divine as the aeons rolled on towards some hypothetical Omega. (Why the movement should be towards more and better rather than less and worse, upwards rather than downwards or in undulations, onwards rather than round and round, one really doesn't know. There seems to be no reason why a God who is exclusively temporal—a God who merely becomes and is ungrounded in eternity—should not be as completely at the mercy of time as is the individual mind apart from the spirit. A God who becomes is a God who also disbecomes, and it is the disbecoming which may ultimately prevail, so that the last state of emergent deity may be worse than the first.)

The ground in which the multifarious and time-bound psyche is rooted is a simple, timeless awareness. By making ourselves pure in heart and poor in spirit we can discover and be identified with this awareness. In the spirit we not only have, but are, the unitive knowledge of the divine Ground.

Analogously, God in time is grounded in the eternal now of the modeless Godhead. It is in the Godhead that things, lives and minds have their being; it is through God that they have their becoming—a becoming whose goal and purpose is to return to the eternity of the Ground.

Meanwhile, I beseech you by the eternal and imperishable truth, and by my soul, consider; grasp the unheard-of. God and Godhead are as distinct as heaven and earth. Heaven stands a thousand miles above the earth, and even so the Godhead is above God. God becomes and disbecomes. Whoever understands this preaching, I wish him well. But even if nobody had been here, I must still have preached this to the poor-box.

Eckhart

Like St. Augustine, Eckhart was to some extent the victim of his own literary talents. *Le style c'est l'homme.* No doubt. But the converse is also partly true. *L'homme c'est le style.* Because we have a gift for writing in a certain way, we find ourselves, in some sort, becoming our way of writing. We mould ourselves in the likeness of our particular brand of eloquence. Eckhart was one of the inventors of German prose, and he was tempted by his new-found mastery of forceful expression to commit himself to extreme positions—to be doctrinally the image of his powerful and over-emphatic sentences. A statement like the foregoing would lead one to believe that he despised what the Vedantists call the 'lower knowledge' of Brahman, not as the Absolute Ground of all things, but as the personal God. In reality he, like the Vedantists, accepts the lower knowledge as genuine knowledge and regards devotion to the personal God as the best preparation for the unitive knowledge of the Godhead. Another point to remember is that the attributeless Godhead of Vedanta, of Mahayana Buddhism, of Christian and Sufi mysticism is the Ground of all the qualities possessed by the personal God and the Incarnation. 'God is not good, I am good,' says Eckhart in his violent and excessive way. What he really meant was, 'I am just humanly good; God is supereminently good; the Godhead *is,* and his "isness" (*istigkeit,* in Eckhart's German) contains goodness, love, wisdom and all the rest in their essence and principle.' In consequence, the Godhead is never, for the exponent of the Perennial Philosophy, the mere Absolute of academic metaphysics, but something more purely perfect, more reverently to be adored than even the personal God or his human incarnation—a Being towards whom it is possible to feel the most intense devotion and in relation to whom it is necessary (if one is to come to that unitive knowledge which is man's final end) to practise a discipline more arduous and unremitting than any imposed by ecclesiastical authority.

There is a distinction and differentiation, according to our reason, between God and the Godhead, between action and rest. The

fruitful nature of the Persons ever worketh in a living differentiation. But the simple Being of God, according to the nature
thereof, is an eternal Rest of God and of all created things.

Ruysbroeck

(In the Reality unitively known by the mystic), we can speak no
more of Father, Son and Holy Spirit, nor of any creature, but
only one Being, which is the very substance of the Divine Persons. There were we all one before our creation, for this is our
super-essence. There the Godhead is in simple essence without
activity.

Ruysbroeck

The holy light of faith is so pure that, compared with it, particular lights are but impurities; and even ideas of the saints, of
the Blessed Virgin, and the sight of Jesus Christ in his humanity
are impediments in the way of the sight of God in His purity.

J. J. Olier

Coming as it does from a devout Catholic of the Counter-
Reformation, this statement may seem somewhat startling.
But we must remember that Olier (who was a man of saintly
life and one of the most influential religious teachers of the
seventeenth century) is speaking here about a state of consciousness, to which few people ever come. To those on the
ordinary levels of being he recommends other modes of knowledge. One of his penitents, for example, was advised to read,
as a corrective to St. John of the Cross and other exponents
of pure mystical theology, St. Gertrude's revelations of the
incarnate and even physiological aspects of the deity. In
Olier's opinion, as in that of most directors of souls, whether
Catholic or Indian, it was mere folly to recommend the worship of God-without-form to persons who are in a condition to
understand only the personal and the incarnate aspects of the
divine Ground. This is a perfectly sensible attitude, and we
are justified in adopting a policy in accordance with it—provided always that we clearly remember that its adoption may

be attended by certain spiritual dangers and disadvantages. The nature of these dangers and disadvantages will be illustrated and discussed in another section. For the present it will suffice to quote the warning words of Philo: 'He who thinks that God has any quality and is not the One, injures not God, but himself.'

Thou must love God as not-God, not-Spirit, not-person, not-image, but as He is, a sheer, pure absolute One, sundered from all two-ness, and in whom we must eternally sink from nothingness to nothingness.

Eckhart

What Eckhart describes as the pure One, the absolute not-God in whom we must sink from nothingness to nothingness is called in Mahayana Buddhism the Clear Light of the Void. What follows is part of a formula addressed by the Tibetan priest to a person in the act of death.

O nobly born, the time has now come for thee to seek the Path. Thy breathing is about to cease. In the past thy teacher hath set thee face to face with the Clear Light; and now thou art about to experience it in its Reality in the *Bardo* state (the 'intermediate state' immediately following death, in which the soul is judged—or rather judges itself by choosing, in accord with the character formed during its life on earth, what sort of an after-life it shall have). In this *Bardo* state all things are like the cloudless sky, and the naked, immaculate Intellect is like unto a translucent void without circumference or centre. At this moment know thou thyself and abide in that state. I, too, at this time, am setting thee face to face.

The Tibetan Book of the Dead

Going back further into the past, we find in one of the earliest Upanishads the classical description of the Absolute One as a Super-Essential No-Thing.

The significance of Brahman is expressed by *neti neti* (not so, not so); for beyond this, that you say it is not so, there is nothing further. Its name, however, is 'the Reality of reality.' That is to say, the senses are real, and the Brahman is their Reality.

Brihad Aranyaka Upanishad

In other words, there is a hierarchy of the real. The manifold world of our everyday experience is real with a relative reality that is, on its own level, unquestionable; but this relative reality has its being within and because of the absolute Reality, which, on account of the incommensurable otherness of its eternal nature, we can never hope to describe, even though it is possible for us directly to apprehend it.

The extract which follows next is of great historical significance, since it was mainly through the 'Mystical Theology' and the 'Divine Names' of the fifth-century author who wrote under the name of Dionysius the Areopagite that mediaeval Christendom established contact with Neoplatonism and thus, at several removes, with the metaphysical thought and discipline of India. In the ninth century Scotus Erigena translated the two books into Latin, and from that time forth their influence upon the philosophical speculations and the religious life of the West was wide, deep and beneficent. It was to the authority of the Areopagite that the Christian exponents of the Perennial Philosophy appealed, whenever they were menaced (and they were always being menaced) by those whose primary interest was in ritual, legalism and ecclesiastical organization. And because Dionysius was mistakenly identified with St. Paul's first Athenian convert, his authority was regarded as all but apostolic; therefore, according to the rules of the Catholic game, the appeal to it could not lightly be dismissed, even by those to whom the books meant less than nothing. In spite of their maddening eccentricity, the men and women who followed the Dionysian path had to be tolerated. And once left free to produce the fruits of the spirit, a number of them arrived at such a conspicuous degree of sanctity that it became impossible even for the heads of the Spanish

Inquisition to condemn the tree from which such fruits had sprung.

The simple, absolute and immutable mysteries of divine Truth are hidden in the super-luminous darkness of that silence which revealeth in secret. For this darkness, though of deepest obscurity, is yet radiantly clear; and, though beyond touch and sight, it more than fills our unseeing minds with splendours of transcendent beauty. . . . We long exceedingly to dwell in this translucent darkness and, through not seeing and not knowing, to see Him who is beyond both vision and knowledge—by the very fact of neither seeing Him nor knowing Him. For this is truly to see and to know and, through the abandonment of all things, to praise Him who is beyond and above all things. For this is not unlike the art of those who carve a life-like image from stone: removing from around it all that impedes clear vision of the latent form, revealing its hidden beauty solely by taking away. For it is, as I believe, more fitting to praise Him by taking away than by ascription; for we ascribe attributes to Him, when we start from universals and come down through the intermediate to the particulars. But here we take away all things from Him going up from particulars to universals, that we may know openly the unknowable, which is hidden in and under all things that may be known. And we behold that darkness beyond being, concealed under all natural light.

Dionysius the Areopagite

The world as it appears to common sense consists of an indefinite number of successive and presumably causally connected events, involving an indefinite number of separate, individual things, lives and thoughts, the whole constituting a presumably orderly cosmos. It is in order to describe, discuss and manage this common-sense universe that human languages have been developed.

Whenever, for any reason, we wish to think of the world, not as it appears to common sense, but as a continuum, we find that our traditional syntax and vocabulary are quite inadequate. Mathematicians have therefore been compelled to invent radically new symbol-systems for this express purpose. But the divine Ground of all existence is not merely a continuum, it is also out of time, and different, not merely in degree, but in kind from the worlds to which traditional language and the languages of mathematics are adequate. Hence, in all expositions of the Perennial Philosophy, the frequency of paradox, of verbal extravagance, sometimes even of seeming blasphemy. Nobody has yet invented a Spiritual Calculus, in terms of which we may talk coherently about the divine Ground and of the world conceived as its manifestation. For the present, therefore, we must be patient with the linguistic eccentricities of those who are compelled to describe one order of experience in terms of a symbol-system, whose relevance is to the facts of another and quite different order.

So far, then, as a fully adequate expression of the Perennial Philosophy is concerned, there exists a problem in semantics that is finally insoluble. The fact is one which must be steadily borne in mind by all who read its formulations. Only in this way shall we be able to understand even remotely what is being talked about. Consider, for example, those negative definitions of the transcendent and immanent Ground of being. In statements such as Eckhart's, God is equated with nothing. And in a certain sense the equation is exact; for God is certainly no thing. In the phrase used by Scotus Erigena God is not a what; He is a That. In other words, the Ground can be denoted as being *there*, but not defined as having qualities. This means that discursive knowledge *about* the Ground is not merely, like all inferential knowledge, a thing at one remove, or even at several removes, from the reality of immediate acquaintance; it is and, because of the very nature of our language and our standard patterns of thought, it must be, paradoxical knowledge. Direct knowledge *of* the Ground cannot be had except by union, and union can be achieved only by the annihilation of the self-regarding ego, which is the barrier separating the 'thou' from the 'That.'

Chapter 3

PERSONALITY, SANCTITY, DIVINE INCARNATION

IN English, words of Latin origin tend to carry overtones of intellectual, moral and aesthetic 'classiness'—overtones which are not carried, as a rule, by their Anglo-Saxon equivalents. 'Maternal,' for instance, means the same as 'motherly,' 'intoxicated' as 'drunk'—but with what subtly important shades of difference! And when Shakespeare needed a name for a comic character, it was Sir Toby Belch that he chose, not Cavalier Tobias Eructation.

The word 'personality' is derived from the Latin, and its upper partials are in the highest degree respectable. For some odd philological reason, the Saxon equivalent of 'personality' is hardly ever used. Which is a pity. For if it were used— used as currently as 'belch' is used for 'eructation'—would people make such a reverential fuss about the thing connoted as certain English-speaking philosophers, moralists and theologians have recently done? 'Personality,' we are constantly being assured, is the highest form of reality with which we are acquainted. But surely people would think twice about making or accepting this affirmation if, instead of 'personality,' the word employed had been its Teutonic synonym, 'selfness.' For 'selfness,' though it means precisely the same, carries none of the high-class overtones that go with 'personality.' On the contrary, its primary meaning comes to us embedded, as it were, in discords, like the note of a cracked bell. For, as all exponents of the Perennial Philosophy have constantly insisted, man's obsessive consciousness of, and insistence on being, a separate self is the final and most formidable obstacle to the unitive knowledge of God. To be a self is, for them, the original sin, and to die to self, in feeling, will and intellect, is the final and all-inclusive virtue. It is the memory of these utterances that calls up the unfavourable overtones with which the word 'selfness' is associated. The all too favourable overtones of 'personality' are evoked in part by its intrinsically solemn Latinity, but also by reminiscences of what has been said about the 'persons' of the Trinity. But the persons of the Trinity have nothing in common with the flesh-and-blood persons of our everyday acquaintance—nothing, that is to say, except that indwelling Spirit, with which we ought and are intended to identify ourselves, but which most of us prefer to ignore in favour of our separate selfness. That this God-eclipsing and anti-spiritual selfness should have been given the same name as is applied to the God who is a Spirit, is, to say the least of it, unfortunate. Like all such mistakes it is probably, in some obscure and subconscious way, voluntary and purposeful. We love our selfness; we want to be justified in our love; therefore we christen it with the same name as is applied by theologians to Father, Son and Holy Spirit.

But now thou askest me how thou mayest destroy this naked knowing and feeling of thine own being. For peradventure thou thinkest that if it were destroyed, all other hindrances were destroyed; and if thou thinkest thus, thou thinkest right truly. But to this I answer thee and I say, that without a full special grace full freely given by God, and also a full according ableness on thy part to receive this grace, this naked knowing and feeling of thy being may in nowise be destroyed. And this ableness is nought else but a strong and a deep ghostly sorrow. . . . All men have matter of sorrow; but most specially he feeleth matter of sorrow that knoweth and feeleth that he *is*. All other sorrows in comparison to this be but as it were game to earnest. For he may make sorrow earnestly that knoweth and feeleth not only what he is, but that he is. And whoso felt never this sorrow, let him make sorrow; for he hath never yet felt perfect sorrow. This sorrow, when it is had, cleanseth the soul, not only of sin, but also of pain that it hath deserved for sin; and also it maketh a soul able to receive that joy, the which reaveth from a man all knowing and feeling of his being.

This sorrow, if it be truly conceived, is full of holy desire; and else a man might never in this life abide it or bear it. For were it not that a soul were somewhat fed with a manner of comfort by his right working, he should not be able to bear that pain that he hath by the knowing and feeling of his being. For as oft as he would have a true knowing and a feeling of his God in purity of spirit (as it may be here), and then feeleth that he may not—for he findeth evermore his knowing and his feeling as it were occupied and filled with a foul stinking lump of himself, the which must always be hated and despised and forsaken, if he shall be God's perfect disciple, taught by Himself in the mount of perfection— so oft he goeth nigh mad for sorrow. . . .

This sorrow and this desire must every soul have and feel in itself (either in this manner or in another), as God vouchsafeth to teach his ghostly disciples according to his good will and their according ableness in body and in soul, in degree and disposition, ere the time be that they may perfectly be oned unto God in perfect charity—such as may be had here, if God vouchsafeth.

The Cloud of Unknowing

What is the nature of this 'stinking lump' of selfness or personality, which has to be so passionately repented of and so completely died to, before there can be any 'true knowing of God in purity of spirit'? The most meagre and non-committal hypothesis is that of Hume. 'Mankind,' he says, 'are nothing but a bundle or collection of different perceptions, which succeed each other with an inconceivable rapidity and are in a perpetual flux and movement.' An almost identical answer is given by the Buddhists, whose doctrine of *anatta* is the denial of any permanent soul, existing behind the flux of experience and the various psycho-physical *skandhas* (closely corresponding to Hume's 'bundles'), which constitute the more enduring elements of personality. Hume and the Buddhists give a sufficiently realistic description of selfness in action; but they fail to explain how or why the bundles ever became bundles. Did their constituent atoms of experience come together of their own accord? And, if so, why, or by what means, and within what kind of a non-spatial universe? To give a plausible answer to these questions in terms of *anatta* is so difficult that we are forced to abandon the doctrine in favour of the notion that, behind the flux and within the bundles, there exists some kind of permanent soul, by which experience is organized and which in turn makes use of that organized experience to become a particular and unique personality. This is the view of the orthodox Hinduism, from which Buddhist thought parted company, and of almost all European thought from before the time of Aristotle to the present day. But whereas most contemporary thinkers make an attempt to describe human nature in terms of a dichotomy of interacting psyche and physique, or an inseparable wholeness of these two elements within particular embodied selves, all the exponents of the Perennial Philosophy make, in one form or another, the affirmation that man is a kind of trinity composed of body, psyche and spirit. Selfness or personality is a product of the first two elements. The third element (that *quidquid increatum et increabile*, as Eckhart called it) is akin to, or even identical with, the divine Spirit that is the Ground of all being. Man's final end, the purpose of his existence, is to love, know and be united with the immanent and transcendent Godhead. And this identification of self with spiritual not-self can be achieved only by 'dying to' selfness and living to spirit.

What could begin to deny self, if there were not something in man different from self?

William Law

What is man? An angel, an animal, a void, a world, a nothing surrounded by God, indigent of God, capable of God, filled with God, if it so desires.

Bérulle

The separate creaturely life, as opposed to life in union with God, is only a life of various appetites, hungers and wants, and cannot possibly be anything else. God Himself cannot make a creature to be in itself, or in its own nature, anything else but a state of emptiness. The highest life that is natural and creaturely can go no higher than this; it can only be a bare capacity for goodness and cannot possibly be a good and happy life but by the life of God dwelling in and in union with it. And this is the twofold life that, of all necessity, must be united in every good and perfect and happy creature.

William Law

The Scriptures say of human beings that there is an outward man and along with him an inner man.

To the outward man belong those things that depend on the soul, but are connected with the flesh and are blended with it, and the co-operative functions of the several members, such as the eye, the ear, the tongue, the hand and so on.

The Scripture speaks of all this as the old man, the earthy man, the outward person, the enemy, the servant.

Within us all is the other person, the inner man, whom the Scripture calls the new man, the heavenly man, the young person, the friend, the aristocrat.

Eckhart

The seed of God is in us. Given an intelligent and hard-working farmer, it will thrive and grow up to God, whose seed it is; and accordingly its fruits will be God-nature. Pear seeds grow into pear trees, nut seeds into nut trees, and God seed into God.

Eckhart

The will is free and we are at liberty to identify our being either exclusively with our selfness and its interests, regarded as independent of indwelling Spirit and transcendent Godhead (in which case we shall be passively damned or actively fiend-ish), or exclusively with the divine within us and without (in which case we shall be saints), or finally with self at one moment or in one context and with spiritual not-self at other moments and in other contexts (in which case we shall be average citizens, too theocentric to be wholly lost, and too

D

egocentric to achieve enlightenment and a total deliverance).
Since human craving can never be satisfied except by the unitive
knowledge of God and since the mind-body is capable of an
enormous variety of experiences, we are free to identify ourselves with an almost infinite number of possible objects—with
the pleasures of gluttony, for example, or intemperance, or
sensuality; with money, power or fame; with our family,
regarded as a possession or actually an extension and projection of our own selfness; with our goods and chattels, our
hobbies, our collections; with our artistic or scientific talents;
with some favourite branch of knowledge, some fascinating
'special subject'; with our professions, our political parties,
our churches; with our pains and illnesses; with our memories
of success or misfortune, our hopes, fears and schemes for the
future; and finally with the eternal Reality within which and
by which all the rest has its being. And we are free, of course,
to identify ourselves with more than one of these things simultaneously or in succession. Hence the quite astonishingly improbable combination of traits making up a complex personality. Thus a man can be at once the craftiest of politicians and
the dupe of his own verbiage, can have a passion for brandy
and money, and an equal passion for the poetry of George
Meredith and under-age girls and his mother, for horse-racing
and detective stories and the good of his country—the whole
accompanied by a sneaking fear of hell-fire, a hatred of Spinoza
and an unblemished record for Sunday church-going. A person born with one kind of psycho-physical constitution will be
tempted to identify himself with one set of interests and
passions, while a person with another kind of temperament will
be tempted to make very different identifications. But these
temptations (though extremely powerful, if the constitutional
bias is strongly marked) do not have to be succumbed to;
people can and do resist them, can and do refuse to identify
themselves with what it would be all too easy and natural for
them to be; can and do become better and quite other than
their own selves. In this context the following brief article on
'How Men Behave in Crisis' (published in a recent issue of

Harper's Magazine) is highly significant. 'A young psychiatrist, who went as a medical observer on five combat missions of the Eighth Air Force in England, says that in times of great stress and danger men are likely to react quite uniformly, even though under normal circumstances they differ widely in personality. He went on one mission, during which the B-17 plane and crew were so severely damaged that survival seemed impossible. He had already studied the "on the ground" personalities of the crew and had found that they represented a great diversity of human types. Of their behaviour in crisis he reported:

'"Their reactions were remarkably alike. During the violent combat and in the acute emergencies that arose during it, they were all quietly precise on the interphone and decisive in action. The tail gunner, right waist gunner and navigator were severely wounded early in the fight, but all three kept at their duties efficiently and without cessation. The burden of emergency work fell on the pilot, engineer and ball turret gunner, and all functioned with rapidity, skilful effectiveness and no lost motion. The burden of the decisions, during, but particularly after the combat, rested essentially on the pilot and, in secondary details, on the co-pilot and bombardier. The decisions, arrived at with care and speed, were unquestioned once they were made, and proved excellent. In the period when disaster was momentarily expected, the alternative plans of action were made clearly and with no thought other than the safety of the entire crew. All at this point were quiet, unobtrusively cheerful and ready for anything. There was at no time paralysis, panic, unclear thinking, faulty or confused judgment, or self-seeking in any one of them.

'" One could not possibly have inferred from their behaviour that this one was a man of unstable moods and that that one was a shy, quiet, introspective man. They all became outwardly calm, precise in thought and rapid in action.

'" Such action is typical of a crew who know intimately what fear is, so that they can use, without being distracted by, its physiological concomitants; who are well trained, so that they can direct their action with clarity; and who have all the more than personal trust inherent in a unified team.'''

We see then that, when the crisis came, each of these young men forgot the particular personality which he had built up out of the elements provided by his heredity and the environment in which he had grown up; that one resisted the normally irresistible temptation to identify himself with his mood of the moment, another the temptation to identify himself with his private day-dreams, and so on with the rest; and that all of them behaved in the same strikingly similar and wholly admirable way. It was as though the crisis and the preliminary training for crisis had lifted them out of their divergent personalities and raised them to the same higher level.

Sometimes crisis alone, without any preparatory training, is sufficient to make a man forget to be his customary self and become, for the time being, something quite different. Thus the most unlikely people will, under the influence of disaster, temporarily turn into heroes, martyrs, selfless labourers for the good of their fellows. Very often, too, the proximity of death produces similar results. For example, Samuel Johnson behaved in one way during almost the whole of his life and in quite another way during his last illness. The fascinatingly complex personality, in which six generations of Boswellians have taken so much delight—the learned boor and glutton, the kind-hearted bully, the superstitious intellectual, the convinced Christian who was a fetishist, the courageous man who was terrified of death—became, while he was actually dying, simple, single, serene and God-centred.

Paradoxical as it may seem, it is, for very many persons, much easier to behave selflessly in time of crisis than it is when life is taking its normal course in undisturbed tranquillity. When the going is easy, there is nothing to make us forget our precious selfness, nothing (except our own will to mortification and the knowledge of God) to distract our minds from the distractions with which we have chosen to be identified; we are at perfect liberty to wallow in our personality to our heart's content. And how we wallow! It is for this reason that all the masters of the spiritual life insist so strongly upon the importance of little things.

God requires a faithful fulfilment of the merest trifle given us to do, rather than the most ardent aspiration to things to which we are not called.

St. François de Sales

There is no one in the world who cannot arrive without difficulty at the most eminent perfection by fulfilling with love obscure and common duties.

J. P. de Caussade

Some people measure the worth of good actions only by their natural qualities or their difficulty, giving the preference to what is conspicuous or brilliant. Such men forget that Christian virtues, which are God's inspirations, should be viewed from the side of grace, not that of nature. The dignity and difficulty of a good action certainly affects what is technically called its accidental worth, but all its essential worth comes from love alone.

Jean Pierre Camus
(quoting St. François de Sales)

The saint is one who knows that every moment of our human life is a moment of crisis; for at every moment we are called upon to make an all-important decision—to choose between the way that leads to death and spiritual darkness and the way that leads towards light and life; between interests exclusively temporal and the eternal order; between our personal will, or the will of some projection of our personality, and the will of God. In order to fit himself to deal with the emergencies of his way of life, the saint undertakes appropriate training of mind and body, just as the soldier does. But whereas the objectives of military training are limited and very simple, namely, to make men courageous, cool-headed and co-operatively efficient in the business of killing other men, with whom, personally, they have no quarrel, the objectives of spiritual training are much less narrowly specialized. Here the aim is primarily to bring human beings to a state in which, because there are no longer any God-eclipsing obstacles between themselves and Reality, they are able to be aware continuously of the divine Ground of their own and all other beings; secondarily, as a means to this end, to meet all, even the most trivial circumstances of daily living, without malice, greed, self-assertion or voluntary ignorance, but consistently with love and understanding. Because its objectives are not limited, because, for the lover of God, every moment is a moment of crisis, spiritual training is incomparably more difficult and searching than military training. There are many good soldiers, few saints.

We have seen that, in critical emergencies, soldiers specifically trained to cope with that kind of thing tend to forget the inborn and acquired idiosyncrasies with which they normally identify their being and, transcending selfness, to behave in the same, one-pointed, better-than-personal way. What is true of soldiers is also true of saints, but with this important difference —that the aim of spiritual training is to make people become selfless in *every* circumstance of life, while the aim of military training is to make them selfless only in certain very special circumstances and in relation to only certain classes of human beings. This could not be otherwise; for all that we are and will and do depends, in the last analysis, upon what we believe the Nature of Things to be. The philosophy that rationalizes power politics and justifies war and military training is always (whatever the official religion of the politicians and war makers) some wildly unrealistic doctrine of national, racial or ideological idolatry, having, as its inevitable corollaries, the notions of *Herrenvolk* and 'the lesser breeds without the Law.'

The biographies of the saints testify unequivocally to the fact that spiritual training leads to a transcendence of personality, not merely in the special circumstances of battle, but in all circumstances and in relation to all creatures, so that the saint 'loves his enemies' or, if he is a Buddhist, does not even recognize the existence of enemies, but treats all sentient beings, sub-human as well as human, with the same compassion and disinterested goodwill. Those who win through to the unitive knowledge of God set out upon their course from the most diverse starting points. One is a man, another a woman; one a born active, another a born contemplative. No two of them inherit the same temperament and physical constitution, and their lives are passed in material, moral and intellectual environments that are profoundly dissimilar. Nevertheless, in so far as they are saints, in so far as they possess the unitive knowledge that makes them 'perfect as their Father which is in heaven is perfect,' they are all astonishingly alike. Their actions are uniformly selfless and they are constantly recollected, so that at every moment they know who they are and what is their true relation to the universe and its spiritual Ground. Of even plain average people it may be said that their name is Legion— much more so of exceptionally complex personalities, who identify themselves with a wide diversity of moods, cravings and opinions. Saints, on the contrary, are neither double-minded nor half-hearted, but single and, however great their intellectual gifts, profoundly simple. The multiplicity of Legion has given place to one-pointedness—not to any of those evil one-pointednesses of ambition or covetousness, or lust for power and fame, not even to any of the nobler, but still all too human one-pointednesses of art, scholarship and science, regarded as ends in themselves, but to the supreme, more than human one-pointedness that is the very being of those souls who consciously and consistently pursue man's final end, the knowledge of eternal Reality. In one of the Pali scriptures there is a significant anecdote about the Brahman Drona who, 'seeing the Blessed One sitting at the foot of a tree, asked him, "Are you a *deva*?" And the Exalted One answered, "I am not." "Are you a *gandharva*?" "I am not." "Are you a *yaksha*?" "I am not." "Are you a man?" "I am not a man." On the Brahman asking what he might be, the Blessed One replied, "Those evil influences, those cravings, whose non-destruction would have individualized me as a *deva*, a *gandharva*, a *yaksha* (three types of supernatural being), or a man, I have completely annihilated. Know therefore that I am Buddha." '

Here we may remark in passing that it is only the one-pointed who are truly capable of worshipping one God. Monotheism as a theory can be entertained even by a person whose name is Legion. But when it comes to passing from theory to practice, from discursive knowledge about to immediate acquaintance with the one God, there cannot be monotheism except where there is singleness of heart. Knowledge is in the knower according to the mode of the knower. Where the knower is poly-psychic the universe he knows by immediate experience is polytheistic. The Buddha declined to make any statement in regard to the ultimate divine Reality. All he would talk about was *nirvana*, which is the name of the experience that comes to the totally selfless and one-pointed. To this same experience others have given the name of union with Brahman, with Al Haqq, with the immanent and transcendent Godhead. Maintaining, in this matter, the attitude of a strict operationalist, the Buddha would speak only of the spiritual experience, not of the metaphysical entity presumed by the theologians of other religions, as also of later Buddhism, to be the object and (since in contemplation the knower, the known and the knowledge are all one) at the same time the subject and substance of that experience.

When a man lacks discrimination, his will wanders in all directions, after innumerable aims. Those who lack discrimination may quote the letter of the scripture; but they are really denying its inner truth. They are full of worldly desires and hungry for the rewards of heaven. They use beautiful figures of speech; they teach elaborate rituals, which are supposed to obtain pleasure and power for those who practise them. But, actually, they understand nothing except the law of Karma that chains men to rebirth.

Those whose discrimination is stolen away by such talk grow deeply attached to pleasure and power. And so they are unable to develop that one-pointed concentration of the will, which leads a man to absorption in God.

Bhagavad-Gita

Among the cultivated and mentally active, hagiography is now a very unpopular form of literature. The fact is not at all surprising. The cultivated and the mentally active have an insatiable appetite for novelty, diversity and distraction. But the saints, however commanding their talents and whatever the nature of their professional activities, are all incessantly preoccupied with only one subject—spiritual Reality and the means by which they and their fellows can come to the unitive knowledge of that Reality. And as for their actions—these are as monotonously uniform as their thoughts; for in all circumstances they behave selflessly, patiently and with indefatigable charity. No wonder, then, if the biographies of such men and women remain unread. For one well-educated person who knows anything about William Law there are two or three hundred who have read Boswell's life of his younger contemporary. Why? Because, until he actually lay dying, Johnson indulged himself in the most fascinating of multiple personalities; whereas Law, for all the superiority of his talents, was almost absurdly simple and single-minded. Legion prefers to read about Legion. It is for this reason that, in the whole repertory of epic, drama and the novel, there are hardly any representations of true theocentric saints.

O Friend, hope for Him whilst you live, know whilst you live, understand whilst you live; for in life deliverance abides.
If your bonds be not broken whilst living, what hope of deliverance in death?
It is but an empty dream that the soul shall have union with Him because it has passed from the body;
If He is found now, He is found then;
If not, we do but go to dwell in the City of Death.

Kabir

This figure in the form of a sun (the description is of the engraved

frontispiece to the first edition of *The Rule of Perfection*) represents the will of God. The faces placed here in the sun represent
souls living in the divine will. These faces are arranged in three
concentric circles, showing the three degrees of this divine will.
The first or outermost degree signifies the souls of the active life;
the second, those of the life of contemplation; the third, those of
the life of supereminence. Outside the first circle are many tools,
such as pincers and hammers, denoting the active life. But round
the second circle we have placed nothing at all, in order to signify
that in this kind of contemplative life, without any other speculations or practices, one must follow the leading of the will of God.
The tools are on the ground and in shadow, inasmuch as outward
works are in themselves full of darkness. These tools, however,
are touched by a ray of the sun, to show that works may be
enlightened and illuminated by the will of God.

The light of the divine will shines but little on the faces of the
first circle; much more on those of the second; while those of
the third or innermost circle are resplendent. The features of the
first show up most clearly; the second, less; the third, hardly at
all. This signifies that the souls of the first degree are much in
themselves; those of the second degree are less in themselves and
more in God; those in the third degree are almost nothing in
themselves and all in God, absorbed in his essential will. All
these faces have their eyes fixed on the will of God.

Benet of Canfield

It is in virtue of his absorption in God and just because he has
not identified his being with the inborn and acquired elements
of his private personality, that the saint is able to exercise his
entirely non-coercive and therefore entirely beneficent influence on individuals and even on whole societies. Or, to be
more accurate, it is because he has purged himself of selfness
that divine Reality is able to use him as a channel of grace and
power. 'I live, yet not I, but Christ—the eternal Logos—
liveth in me.' True of the saint, this must *a fortiori* be true of
the Avatar, or incarnation of God. If, in so far as he was a
saint, St. Paul was 'not I,' then certainly Christ was 'not I';

and to talk, as so many liberal churchmen now do, of worshipping 'the personality of Jesus,' is an absurdity. For, obviously, had Jesus remained content merely to have a personality, like the rest of us, he would never have exercised the kind of influence which in fact he did exercise, and it would never have occurred to anyone to regard him as a divine incarnation and to identify him with the Logos. That he came to be thought of as the Christ was due to the fact that he had passed beyond selfness and had become the bodily and mental conduit through which a more than personal, supernatural life flowed down into the world.

Souls which have come to the unitive knowledge of God are, in Benet of Canfield's phrase, 'almost nothing in themselves and all in God.' This vanishing residue of selfness persists because, in some slight measure, they still identify their being with some innate psycho-physical idiosyncrasy, some acquired habit of thought or feeling, some convention or unanalysed prejudice current in the social environment. Jesus was almost wholly absorbed in the essential will of God; but in spite of this, he may have retained some elements of selfness. To what extent there was any 'I' associated with the more-than-personal, divine 'Not-I,' it is very difficult, on the basis of the existing evidence, to judge. For example, did Jesus interpret his experience of divine Reality and his own spontaneous inferences from that experience in terms of those fascinating apocalyptic notions current in contemporary Jewish circles? Some eminent scholars have argued that the doctrine of the world's imminent dissolution was the central core of his teaching. Others, equally learned, have held that it was attributed to him by the authors of the Synoptic Gospels, and that Jesus himself did not identify his experience and his theological thinking with locally popular opinions. Which party is right? Goodness knows. On this subject, as on so many others, the existing evidence does not permit of a certain and unambiguous answer.

The moral of all this is plain. The quantity and quality of the surviving biographical documents are such that we have no means of knowing what the residual personality of Jesus was really like. But if the Gospels tell us very little about the 'I' which was Jesus, they make up for this deficiency by telling us inferentially, in the parables and discourses, a good deal about the spiritual 'not-I,' whose manifest presence in the mortal man was the reason why his disciples called him the Christ and identified him with the eternal Logos.

The biography of a saint or avatar is valuable only in so far as it throws light upon the means by which, in the circumstances of a particular human life, the 'I' was purged away so as to make room for the divine 'not-I.' The authors of the Synoptic Gospels did not choose to write such a biography, and no amount of textual criticism or ingenious surmise can call it into existence. In the course of the last hundred years an enormous sum of energy has been expended on the attempt to make documents yield more evidence than in fact they contain. However regrettable may be the Synoptists' lack of interest in biography, and whatever objections may be raised against the theologies of Paul and John, there can still be no doubt that their instinct was essentially sound. Each in his own way wrote about the eternal 'not-I' of Christ rather than the historical 'I'; each in his own way stressed that element in the life of Jesus, in which, because it is more-than-personal, all persons can participate. (The nature of selfness is such that one person cannot be a part of another person. A self can contain or be contained by something that is either less or more than a self, it can never contain or be contained by a self.)

The doctrine that God can be incarnated in human form is found in most of the principal historic expositions of the Perennial Philosophy—in Hinduism, in Mahayana Buddhism, in Christianity and in the Mohammedanism of the Sufis, by whom the Prophet was equated with the eternal Logos.

> When goodness grows weak,
> When evil increases,
> I make myself a body.

In every age I come back
To deliver the holy,
To destroy the sin of the sinner,
To establish righteousness.

He who knows the nature
Of my task and my holy birth
Is not reborn
When he leaves this body;
He comes to Me.

Flying from fear,
From lust and anger,
He hides in Me,
His refuge and safety.
Burnt clean in the blaze of my being,
In Me many find home.

Bhagavad-Gita

Then the Blessed One spoke and said: 'Know, Vasetha, that from time to time a Tathagata is born into the world, a fully Enlightened One, blessed and worthy, abounding in wisdom and goodness, happy with knowledge of the worlds, unsurpassed as a guide to erring mortals, a teacher of gods and men, a Blessed Buddha. He thoroughly understands this universe, as though he saw it face to face. . . . The Truth does he proclaim both in its letter and in its spirit, lovely in its origin, lovely in its progress, lovely in its consummation. A higher life doth he make known in all its purity and in all its perfectness.

Tevigga Sutta

Krishna is an incarnation of Brahman, Gautama Buddha of what the Mahayanists called the Dharmakaya, Suchness, Mind, the spiritual Ground of all being. The Christian doctrine of the incarnation of the Godhead in human form differs from that of India and the Far East inasmuch as it affirms that there has been and can be only one Avatar.

What we do depends in large measure upon what we think, and if what we do is evil, there is good empirical reason for supposing that our thought-patterns are inadequate to material, mental or spiritual reality. Because Christians believed that there had been only one Avatar, Christian history has been disgraced by more and bloodier crusades, interdenominational wars, persecutions and proselytizing imperialism than has the history of Hinduism and Buddhism. Absurd and idolatrous doctrines, affirming the quasi-divine nature of sovereign states and their rulers, have led oriental, no less than Western, peoples into innumerable political wars; but because they have not believed in an exclusive revelation at one sole instant of time, or in the quasi-divinity of an ecclesiastical organization, oriental peoples have kept remarkably clear of the mass murder for religion's sake, which has been so dreadfully frequent in Christendom. And while, in this important respect, the level of public morality has been lower in the West than in the East, the levels of exceptional sanctity and of ordinary individual morality have not, so far as one can judge from the available evidence, been any higher. If the tree is indeed known by its fruits, Christianity's departure from the norm of the Perennial Philosophy would seem to be philosophically unjustifiable.

The Logos passes out of eternity into time for no other purpose than to assist the beings, whose bodily form he takes, to pass out of time into eternity. If the Avatar's appearance upon the stage of history is enormously important, this is due to the fact that by his teaching he points out, and by his being a channel of grace and divine power he actually is, the means by which human beings may transcend the limitations of history. The author of the Fourth Gospel affirms that the Word became flesh; but in another passage he adds that the flesh profiteth nothing—nothing, that is to say, in itself, but a great deal, of course, as a means to the union with immanent and transcendent Spirit. In this context it is very interesting to consider the development of Buddhism. 'Under the forms of religious or mystical imagery,' writes R. E. Johnston in his *Buddhist China*, 'the Mahayana expresses the universal, whereas

Hinayana cannot set itself free from the domination of historical fact.' In the words of an eminent orientalist, Ananda K. Coomaraswamy, 'The Mahayanist believer is warned—precisely as the worshipper of Krishna is warned in the Vaishnavite scriptures that the Krishna Lila is not a history, but a process for ever unfolded in the heart of man—that matters of historical fact are without religious significance' (except, we should add, in so far as they point to or themselves constitute the means—whether remote or proximate, whether political, ethical or spiritual—by which men may come to deliverance from selfness and the temporal order.)

In the West, the mystics went some way towards liberating Christianity from its unfortunate servitude to historic fact (or, to be more accurate, to those various mixtures of contemporary record with subsequent inference and phantasy, which have, at different epochs, been accepted as historic fact). From the writings of Eckhart, Tauler and Ruysbroeck, of Boehme, William Law and the Quakers, it would be possible to extract a spiritualized and universalized Christianity, whose narratives should refer, not to history as it was, or as someone afterwards thought it ought to be, but to 'processes forever unfolded in the heart of man.' But unfortunately the influence of the mystics was never powerful enough to bring about a radical Mahayanist revolution in the West. In spite of them, Christianity has remained a religion in which the pure Perennial Philosophy has been overlaid, now more, now less, by an idolatrous preoccupation with events and things in time—events and things regarded not merely as useful means, but as ends, intrinsically sacred and indeed divine. Moreover, such improvements on history as were made in the course of centuries were, most imprudently, treated as though they themselves were a part of history—a procedure which put a powerful weapon into the hands of Protestant and, later, of Rationalist controversialists. How much wiser it would have been to admit the perfectly avowable fact that, when the sternness of Christ the Judge had been unduly emphasized, men and women felt the need of personifying the divine compassion in a new form, with the result that the figure of the Virgin, mediatrix to the mediator, came into increased prominence. And when, in course of time, the Queen of Heaven was felt to be too awe-inspiring, compassion was re-personified in the homely figure of St. Joseph, who thus became mediator to the mediatrix to the mediator. In exactly the same way Buddhist worshippers felt that the historic Sakyamuni, with his insistence on recollectedness, discrimination and a total dying to self as the principal means of liberation, was too stern and too intellectual. The result was that the love and compassion which Sakyamuni had also inculcated came to be personified in Buddhas such as Amida and Maitreya—divine characters completely removed from history, inasmuch as their temporal career was situated somewhere in the distant past or distant future. Here it may be remarked that the vast numbers of Buddhas and Bodhisattvas, of whom the Mahayanist theologians speak, are commensurate with the vastness of their cosmology. Time, for them, is beginningless, and the innumerable universes, every one of them supporting sentient beings of every possible variety, are born, evolve, decay and die, only to repeat the same cycle—again and again, until the final inconceivably remote consummation, when every sentient being in all the worlds shall have won to deliverance out of time into eternal Suchness or Buddhahood. This cosmological background to Buddhism has affinities with the world picture of modern astronomy—especially with that version of it offered in the recently published theory of Dr. Weiszäcker regarding the formation of planets. If the Weiszäcker hypothesis is correct, the production of a planetary system would be a normal episode in the life of every star. There are forty thousand million stars in our own galactic system alone, and beyond our galaxy other galaxies, indefinitely. If, as we have no choice but to believe, spiritual laws governing consciousness are uniform throughout the whole planet-bearing and presumably life-supporting universe, then certainly there is plenty of room, and at the same time, no doubt, the most agonizing and desperate need, for those innumerable redemptive incarnations of Suchness, upon whose shining multitudes the Mahayanists love to dwell.

For my part, I think the chief reason which prompted the invisible God to become visible in the flesh and to hold converse with men was to lead carnal men, who are only able to love carnally, to the healthful love of his flesh, and afterwards, little by little, to spiritual love.

St. Bernard

St. Bernard's doctrine of 'the carnal love of Christ' has been admirably summed up by Professor Étienne Gilson in his book, *The Mystical Theology of St. Bernard*. 'Knowledge of self already expanded into *social* carnal love of the neighbour, so like oneself in misery, is now a second time expanded into a carnal love of Christ, the model of compassion, since for our salvation He has become the Man of Sorrows. Here then is the place occupied in Cistercian mysticism by the meditation on the visible Humanity of Christ. It is but a beginning, but an absolutely necessary beginning.... Charity, of course, is essentially spiritual, and a love of this kind can be no more than its first moment. It is too much bound up with the senses, unless we know how to make use of it with prudence, and to lean on it only as something to be surpassed. In expressing himself thus, Bernard merely codified the teachings of his own experience; for we have it from him that he was much given to the practice of this sensitive love at the outset of his "conversion"; later on he was to consider it an advance to have passed beyond it; not, that is to say, to have forgotten it, but to have added another, which outweighs it as the rational and spiritual outweigh the carnal. Nevertheless, this beginning is already a summit.

'This sensitive affection for Christ was always presented by St. Bernard as love of a relatively inferior order. It is so precisely on account of its sensitive character, for charity is of a purely spiritual essence. In right the soul should be able to enter directly into union, in virtue of its spiritual powers, with

E

a God Who is pure spirit. The Incarnation, moreover, should be regarded as one of the consequences of man's transgression, so that love for the Person of Christ is, as a matter of fact, bound up with the history of a fall which need not, and should not, have happened. St. Bernard furthermore, and in several places, notes that this affection cannot stand safely alone, but needs to be supported by what he calls "science." He had examples before him of the deviations into which even the most ardent devotion can fall, when it is not allied with, and ruled by, a sane theology.'

Can the many fantastic and mutually incompatible theories of expiation and atonement, which have been grafted on to the Christian doctrine of divine incarnation, be regarded as indispensable elements in a 'sane theology'? I find it difficult to imagine how anyone who has looked into a history of these notions, as expounded, for example, by the author of the Epistle to the Hebrews, by Athanasius and Augustine, by Anselm and Luther, by Calvin and Grotius, can plausibly answer this question in the affirmative. In the present context, it will be enough to call attention to one of the bitterest of all the bitter ironies of history. For the Christ of the Gospels, lawyers seemed further from the Kingdom of Heaven, more hopelessly impervious to Reality, than almost any other class of human beings except the rich. But Christian theology, especially that of the Western churches, was the product of minds imbued with Jewish and Roman legalism. In all too many instances the immediate insights of the Avatar and the theocentric saint were rationalized into a system, not by philosophers, but by speculative barristers and metaphysical jurists. Why should what Abbot John Chapman calls 'the problem of *reconciling* (not merely uniting) Mysticism and Christianity' be so extremely difficult? Simply because so much Roman and Protestant thinking was done by those very lawyers whom Christ regarded as being peculiarly incapable of understanding the true Nature of Things. 'The Abbot (Chapman is apparently referring to Abbot Marmion) says St. John of the Cross is like a sponge full of Christianity. You can squeeze it all out, and the full mystical theory (in other words, the pure Perennial Philosophy) remains. Consequently for fifteen years or so I hated St. John of the Cross and called him a Buddhist. I loved St. Teresa and read her over and over again. She is first a Christian, only secondarily a mystic. Then I found I had wasted fifteen years, so far as prayer was concerned.'

Now see the meaning of these two sayings of Christ's. The one, 'No man cometh unto the Father but by me,' that is through my life. The other saying, 'No man cometh unto me except the Father draw him'; that is, he does not take my life upon him and follow after me, except he is moved and drawn of my Father, that is, of the Simple and Perfect Good, of which St. Paul saith, 'When that which is perfect is come, that which is in part shall be done away.'

Theologia Germanica

In other words, there must be imitation of Christ before there can be identification with the Father; and there must be essential identity or likeness between the human spirit and the God who is Spirit in order that the idea of imitating the earthly behaviour of the incarnate Godhead should ever cross anybody's mind. Christian theologians speak of the possibility of 'deification,' but deny that there is identity of substance between spiritual Reality and the human spirit. In Vedanta and Mahayana Buddhism, as also among the Sufis, spirit and Spirit are held to be the same substance; Atman is Brahman; That art thou.

When not enlightened, Buddhas are no other than ordinary beings; when there is enlightenment, ordinary beings at once turn into Buddhas.

Hui Neng

Every human being can thus become an Avatar by adoption, but not by his unaided efforts. He must be shown the way, and he must be aided by divine grace. That men and women may be thus instructed and helped, the Godhead assumes the form of an ordinary human being, who has to earn deliverance and enlightenment in the way that is prescribed by the divine Nature of Things—namely, by charity, by a total dying to self and a total, one-pointed awareness. Thus enlightened, the Avatar can reveal the way of enlightenment to others and help them actually to become what they already potentially are. *Tel qu'en Lui-même enfin l'éternité le change.* And of course the eternity which transforms us into Ourselves is not the experience of mere persistence after bodily death. There will be no experience of timeless Reality then, unless there is the same or a similar knowledge within the world of time and matter. By precept and by example, the Avatar teaches that this transforming knowledge is possible, that all sentient beings are called to it and that, sooner or later, in one way or another, all must finally come to it.

Chapter 4

GOD IN THE WORLD

'THAT art thou': 'Behold but One in all things'—God within and God without. There is a way to Reality in and through the soul, and there is a way to Reality in and through the world. Whether the ultimate goal can be reached by following either of these ways to the exclusion of the other is to be doubted. The third, best and hardest way is that which leads to the divine Ground simultaneously in the perceiver and in that which is perceived.

> The Mind is no other than the Buddha, and Buddha is no other than sentient being. When Mind assumes the form of a sentient being, it has suffered no decrease; when it has become a Buddha, it has added nothing to itself.
>
> *Huang-Po*

> All creatures have existed eternally in the divine essence, as in their exemplar. So far as they conform to the divine idea, all beings were, before their creation, one thing with the essence of God. (God creates into time what was and is in eternity.) Eternally, all creatures are God in God. . . . So far as they are in God, they are the same life, the same essence, the same power, the same One, and nothing less.
>
> *Suso*

> The image of God is found essentially and personally in all mankind. Each possesses it whole, entire and undivided, and all together not more than one alone. In this way we are all one, intimately united in our eternal image, which is the image of God and the source in us of all our life. Our created essence and our life are attached to it without mediation as to their eternal cause.
>
> *Ruysbroeck*

God who, in his simple substance, is all everywhere equally, nevertheless, in efficacy, is in rational creatures in another way than in irrational, and in good rational creatures in another way than in the bad. He is in irrational creatures in such a way as not to be comprehended by them; by all rational ones, however, he can be comprehended through knowledge; but only by the good is he to be comprehended also through love.

St. Bernard

When is a man in mere understanding? I answer, 'When a man sees one thing separated from another.' And when is a man above mere understanding? That I can tell you: 'When a man sees All in all, then a man stands beyond mere understanding.'

Eckhart

There are four kinds of Dhyana (spiritual disciplines). What are these four? They are, first, the Dhyana practised by the ignorant; second, the Dhyana devoted to the examination of meaning; third, the Dhyana with Suchness for its object; fourth, the Dhyana of the Tathagatas (Buddhas).

What is meant by the Dhyana practised by the ignorant? It is the one resorted to by the Yogins who exercise themselves in the disciplines of Sravakas and Pratyekabuddhas (contemplatives and 'solitary Buddhas' of the Hinayana school), who perceiving that there is no ego substance, that the body is a shadow and a skeleton which is transient, impure and full of suffering, persistently cling to these notions, which are regarded as just so and not otherwise, and who, starting from them, advance by stages until they reach the cessation, where there are no thoughts. This is called the Dhyana practised by the ignorant.

What then is the Dhyana devoted to the examination of meaning? It is the one practised by those who, having gone beyond the egolessness of things, beyond individuality and generality, beyond the untenability of such ideas as 'self,' 'other' and 'both,' which are held by the philosophers, proceed to examine and follow up the meaning of the various aspects of Bodhisattvahood. This is the Dhyana devoted to the examination of meaning.

What is the Dhyana with Tathata (or Suchness) as its object?
When the Yogin recognizes that the discrimination of the two
forms of egolessness is mere imagination and that where he estab-
lishes himself in the reality of Suchness there is no rising of discrimination—this I call the Dhyana with Suchness for its object.

What is the Dhyana of the Tathagata? When the Yogin,
entering upon the stage of Tathagatahood and abiding in the
triple bliss characterizing self-realization attained by noble wisdom, devotes himself for the sake of all beings to the accomplishment of incomprehensible works—this I call the Dhyana of the
Tathagata.

Lankavatara Sutra

When followers of Zen fail to go beyond the world of their senses
and thoughts, all their doings and movements are of no significance. But when the senses and thoughts are annihilated, all the
passages to Universal Mind are blocked, and no entrance then
becomes possible. The original Mind is to be recognized along
with the working of the senses and thoughts—only it does not
belong to them, nor yet is it independent of them. Do not build
up your views upon your senses and thoughts, do not base your
understanding upon your senses and thoughts; but at the same
time do not seek the Mind away from your senses and thoughts,
do not try to grasp Reality by rejecting your senses and thoughts.
When you are neither attached to, nor detached from, them, then
you enjoy your perfect unobstructed freedom, then you have
your seat of enlightenment.

Huang-Po

Every individual being, from the atom up to the most highly
organized of living bodies and the most exalted of finite minds,
may be thought of, in René Guénon's phrase, as a point where
a ray of the primordial Godhead meets one of the differenti-
ated, creaturely emanations of that same Godhead's creative
energy. The creature, as creature, may be very far from God,
in the sense that it lacks the intelligence to discover the nature
of the divine Ground of its being. But the creature in its

eternal essence—as the meeting place of creatureliness and primordial Godhead—is one of the infinite number of points where divine Reality is wholly and eternally present. Because of this, rational beings can come to the unitive knowledge of the divine Ground, non-rational and inanimate beings may reveal to rational beings the fullness of God's presence within their material forms. The poet's or the painter's vision of the divine in nature, the worshipper's awareness of a holy presence in the sacrament, symbol or image—these are not entirely subjective. True, such perceptions cannot be had by all perceivers, for knowledge is a function of being; but the thing known is independent of the mode and nature of the knower. What the poet and painter see, and try to record for us, is actually there, waiting to be apprehended by anyone who has the right kind of faculties. Similarly, in the image or the sacramental object the divine Ground is wholly present. Faith and devotion prepare the worshipper's mind for perceiving the ray of Godhead at its point of intersection with the particular fragment of matter before him. Incidentally, by being worshipped, such symbols become the centres of a field of force. The longings, emotions and imaginations of those who kneel and, for generations, have knelt before the shrine create, as it were, an enduring vortex in the psychic medium, so that the image lives with a secondary, inferior divine life projected on to it by its worshippers, as well as with the primary divine life which, in common with all other animate and inanimate beings, it possesses in virtue of its relation to the divine Ground. The religious experience of sacramentalists and image worshippers may be perfectly genuine and objective; but it is not always or necessarily an experience of God or the Godhead. It may be, and perhaps in most cases it actually is, an experience of the field of force generated by the minds of past and present worshippers and projected on to the sacramental object where it sticks, so to speak, in a condition of what may be called second-hand objectivity, waiting to be perceived by minds suitably attuned to it. How desirable this kind of experience really is will have to be discussed in another section. All that need be said here is that the iconoclast's contempt for sacraments and symbols, as being nothing but mummery with stocks and stones, is quite unjustified.

> The workmen still in doubt what course to take,
> Whether I'd best a saint or hog-trough make,
> After debate resolved me for a saint;
> And so famed Loyola I represent.

The all too Protestant satirist forgot that God is in the hog-trough no less than in the conventionally sacred image. 'Lift the stone and you will find me,' affirms the best known of the Oxyrhinchus Logia of Jesus, 'cleave the wood, and I am there.' Those who have personally and immediately realized the truth of this saying and, along with it, the truth of Brahmanism's 'That art thou' are wholly delivered.

The Sravaka (literally 'hearer,' the name given by Mahayana Buddhists to contemplatives of the Hinayana school) fails to perceive that Mind, as it is in itself, has no stages, no causation. Disciplining himself in the cause, he has attained the result and abides in the samadhi (contemplation) of Emptiness for ever so many aeons. However enlightened in this way, the Sravaka is not at all on the right track. From the point of view of the Bodhisattva, this is like suffering the torture of hell. The Sravaka has buried himself in Emptiness and does not know how to get out of his quiet contemplation, for he has no insight into the Buddha-nature itself.

Mo Tsu

When Enlightenment is perfected, a Bodhisattva is free from the bondage of things, but does not seek to be delivered from things. Samsara (the world of becoming) is not hated by him, nor is Nirvana loved. When perfect Enlightenment shines, it is neither bondage nor deliverance.

Prunabuddha-sutra

The touch of Earth is always reinvigorating to the son of Earth, even when he seeks a supraphysical Knowledge. It may even be said that the supraphysical can only be really mastered in its full-ness—to its heights we can always reach—when we keep our feet firmly on the physical. 'Earth is His footing,' says the Upani-shad, whenever it images the Self that manifests in the universe.

Sri Aurobindo

'To its heights we can always come.' For those of us who are still splashing about in the lower ooze, the phrase has a rather ironical ring. Nevertheless, in the light of even the most distant acquaintance with the heights and the fullness, it is pos-sible to understand what its author means. To discover the Kingdom of God exclusively within oneself is easier than to discover it, not only there, but also in the outer world of minds and things and living creatures. It is easier because the heights within reveal themselves to those who are ready to exclude from their purview all that lies without. And though this exclusion may be a painful and mortificatory process, the fact remains that it is less arduous than the process of inclusion, by which we come to know the fullness as well as the heights of spiritual life. Where there is exclusive concentration on the heights within, temptations and distractions are avoided and there is a general denial and suppression. But when the hope is to know God inclusively—to realize the divine Ground in the world as well as in the soul, temptations and distractions must not be avoided, but submitted to and used as opportunities for advance; there must be no suppression of outward-turning activities, but a transformation of them so that they become sacramental. Mortification becomes more searching and more subtle; there is need of unsleeping awareness and, on the levels of thought, feeling and conduct, the constant exercise of something like an artist's tact and taste.

It is in the literature of Mahayana and especially of Zen Buddhism that we find the best account of the psychology of the man for whom *samsara* and *nirvana*, time and eternity, are one and the same. More systematically perhaps than any

other religion, the Buddhism of the Far East teaches the way
to spiritual Knowledge in its fullness as well as in its heights,
in and through the world as well as in and through the soul.
In this context we may point to a highly significant fact, which
is that the incomparable landscape painting of China and Japan
was essentially a religious art, inspired by Taoism and Zen
Buddhism; in Europe, on the contrary, landscape painting and
the poetry of 'nature worship' were secular arts which arose
when Christianity was in decline, and derived little or no
inspiration from Christian ideals.

'Blind, deaf, dumb!
Infinitely beyond the reach of imaginative contrivances!'
In these lines Seccho has swept everything away for you—what
you see together with what you do not see, what you hear together with what you do not hear, and what you talk about
together with what you cannot talk about. All these are completely brushed off, and you attain the life of the blind, deaf and
dumb. Here all your imaginations, contrivances and calculations
are once and for all put an end to; they are no more made use of.
This is where lies the highest point of Zen, this is where we have
true blindness, true deafness and true dumbness, each in its artless
and effectless aspect.

'Above the heavens and below the heavens!
How ludicrous, how disheartening!'
Here Seccho lifts up with one hand and with the other puts down.
Tell me what he finds to be ludicrous, what he finds to be disheartening. It is ludicrous that this dumb person is not dumb
after all, that this deaf person is not after all deaf; it is disheparten-
ing that the one who is not at all blind is blind for all that, and
that the one who is not at all deaf is deaf for all that.

'Li-lou does not know how to discriminate right colour.'
Li-lou lived in the reign of the Emperor Huang. He is said to
have been able to distinguish the point of a soft hair at a distance
of one hundred paces. His eyesight was extraordinary. When
the Emperor Huang took a pleasure cruise on the River Ch'ih, he
dropped his precious jewel in the water and made Li fetch it up.

But he failed. The Emperor made Ch'ih-kou search for it; but he also failed to find it. Later Hsiang-wang was ordered to get it, and he got it. Hence,

> 'When Hsiang-wang goes down, the precious gem shines
> most brilliantly;
> But where Li-lou walks about, the waves rise even to the
> sky.'

When we come to these higher spheres, even the eyes of Li-lou are incapable of discriminating the right colour.

'How can Shih-kuang recognize the mysterious tune?'
Shih-kuang was the son of Ching-kuang of Chin in the province of Chiang under the Chou dynasty. His other name was Tzu-yeh. He could thoroughly distinguish the five sounds and the six notes; he could even hear the ants fighting on the other side of a hill. When Chin and Ch'u were at war, Shih-kuang could tell, just by softly fingering the strings of his lute, that the engagement would surely be unfavourable for Ch'u. In spite of his extraordinary sensitiveness Seccho declares that he is unable to recognize the mysterious tune. After all, one who is not at all deaf is really deaf. The most exquisite note in the higher spheres is beyond the hearing of Shih-kuang. Says Seccho, I am not going to be a Li-lou, nor a Shih-kuang; for

> 'What life can compare with this? Sitting quietly by the
> window,
> I watch the leaves fall and the flowers bloom, as the seasons
> come and go.'

When one reaches this stage of realization, seeing is no-seeing, hearing is no-hearing, preaching is no-preaching. When hungry one eats, when tired one sleeps. Let the leaves fall, let the flowers bloom as they like. When the leaves fall, I know it is the autumn; when the flowers bloom, I know it is the spring.

Having swept everything clean before you, Seccho now opens a passage-way, saying:

> 'Do you understand, or not?
> An iron bar without a hole!'

He has done all he could for you; he is exhausted—only able to turn round and present you with this iron bar without a hole. It is a most significant expression. Look and see with your own eyes! If you hesitate, you miss the mark for ever.

Yengo (the author of this commentary) now raised his staff and said, 'Do you see?' He then struck his chair and said, 'Do you hear?' Coming down from the chair, he said, 'Was anything talked about?'

What precisely is the significance of that iron bar without a hole? I do not pretend to know. Zen has always specialized in nonsense as a means of stimulating the mind to go forward to that which is beyond sense; so perhaps the point of the bar resides precisely in its pointlessness and in our disturbed, bewildered reaction to that pointlessness.

In the root divine Wisdom is all-Brahman; in the stem she is all-Illusion; in the flower she is all-World; and in the fruit, all-Liberation.

Tantra Tattva

The Sravakas and the Pratyekabuddhas, when they reach the eighth stage of the Bodhisattva's discipline, become so intoxicated with the bliss of mental tranquillity that they fail to realize that the visible world is nothing but the Mind. They are still in the realm of individuation; their insight is not yet pure. The Bodhisattvas, on the other hand, are alive to their original vows, flowing out of the all-embracing love that is in their hearts. They do not enter into Nirvana (as a state separate from the world of becoming); they know that the visible world is nothing but a manifestation of Mind itself.

Condensed from the Lankavatara Sutra

A conscious being alone understands what is meant by moving;
To those not endowed with consciousness the moving is unintelligible.
If you exercise yourself in the practice of keeping your mind unmoved,
The immovable you gain is that of one who has no consciousness.

If you are desirous for the truly immovable,
The immovable is in the moving itself,
And this immovable is the truly immovable one.
There is no seed of Buddhahood where there is no consciousness.

Mark well how varied are the aspects of the immovable one,
And know that the first reality is immovable.
Only when this reality is attained
Is the true working of Suchness understood.

Hui Neng

These phrases about the unmoving first mover remind one of
Aristotle. But between Aristotle and the exponents of the
Perennial Philosophy within the great religious traditions there
is this vast difference: Aristotle is primarily concerned with
cosmology, the Perennial Philosophers are primarily concerned with liberation and enlightenment: Aristotle is content
to know about the unmoving mover, from the outside and
theoretically; the aim of the Perennial Philosophers is to
become directly aware of it, to know it unitively, so that they
and others may actually become the unmoving One. This
unitive knowledge can be knowledge in the heights, or knowledge in the fullness, or knowledge simultaneously in the
heights and the fullness. Spiritual knowledge exclusively in
the heights of the soul was rejected by Mahayana Buddhism as
inadequate. The similar rejection of quietism within the Christian tradition will be touched upon in the section, 'Contemplation and Action.' Meanwhile it is interesting to find that the
problem which aroused such acrimonious debate throughout
seventeenth-century Europe had arisen for the Buddhists at a
considerably earlier epoch. But whereas in Catholic Europe
the outcome of the battle over Molinos, Mme Guyon and
Fénelon was to all intents and purposes the extinction of
mysticism for the best part of two centuries, in Asia the two
parties were tolerant enough to agree to differ. Hinayana
spirituality continued to explore the heights within, while the
Mahayanist masters held up the ideal not of the Arhat, but of

the Bodhisattva, and pointed the way to spiritual knowledge in its fullness as well as in its heights. What follows is a poetical account, by a Zen saint of the eighteenth century, of the state of those who have realized the Zen ideal.

Abiding with the non-particular which is in particulars,
Going or returning, they remain for ever unmoved.
Taking hold of the not-thought which lies in thoughts,
In their every act they hear the voice of Truth.
How boundless the sky of contemplation!
How transparent the moonlight of the four-fold Wisdom!
As the Truth reveals itself in its eternal tranquillity,
This very earth is the Lotus-Land of Purity,
And this body is the body of the Buddha.

Hakuin

Nature's intent is neither food, nor drink, nor clothing, nor comfort, nor anything else from which God is left out. Whether you like it or not, whether you know it or not, secretly Nature seeks and hunts and tries to ferret out the track in which God may be found.

Eckhart

Any flea as it is in God is nobler than the highest of the angels in himself.

Eckhart

My inner man relishes things not as creatures but as the gift of God. But to my innermost man they savour not of God's gift, but of ever and aye.

Eckhart

Pigs eat acorns, but neither consider the sun that gave them life, nor the influence of the heavens by which they were nourished, nor the very root of the tree from whence they came.

Thomas Traherne

Your enjoyment of the world is never right till every morning you awake in Heaven; see yourself in your Father's palace; and look upon the skies, the earth and the air as celestial joys; having such a reverend esteem of all, as if you were among the Angels. The bride of a monarch, in her husband's chamber, hath no such causes of delight as you.

You never enjoy the world aright till the sea itself floweth in your veins, till you are clothed with the heavens and crowned with the stars; and perceive yourself to be the sole heir of the whole world, and more than so, because men are in it who are every one sole heirs as well as you. Till you can sing and rejoice and delight in God, as misers do in gold, and kings in sceptres, you can never enjoy the world.

Till your spirit filleth the whole world, and the stars are your jewels; till you are as familiar with the ways of God in all ages as with your walk and table; till you are intimately acquainted with that shady nothing out of which the world was made; till you love men so as to desire their happiness with a thirst equal to the zeal of your own; till you delight in God for being good to all; you never enjoy the world. Till you more feel it than your private estate, and are more present in the hemisphere, considering the glories and the beauties there, than in your own house; till you remember how lately you were made, and how wonderful it was when you came into it; and more rejoice in the palace of your glory than if it had been made today morning.

Yet further, you never enjoyed the world aright, till you so love the beauty of enjoying it, that you are covetous and earnest to persuade others to enjoy it. And so perfectly hate the abominable corruption of men in despising it that you had rather suffer the flames of hell than willingly be guilty of their error.

The world is a mirror of Infinite Beauty, yet no man sees it. It is a Temple of Majesty, yet no man regards it. It is a region of Light and Peace, did not men disquiet it. It is the Paradise of God. It is more to man since he is fallen than it was before. It is the place of Angels and the Gate of Heaven. When Jacob waked out of his dream, he said, God is here, and I wist it not.

How dreadful is this place! This is none other than the House of
God and the Gate of Heaven.

Thomas Traherne

Before going on to discuss the means whereby it is possible
to come to the fullness as well as the height of spiritual knowledge, let us briefly consider the experience of those who have
been privileged to 'behold the One in all things,' but have
made no efforts to perceive it within themselves. A great deal
of interesting material on this subject may be found in Buck's
Cosmic Consciousness. All that need be said here is that such
'cosmic consciousness' may come unsought and is in the
nature of what Catholic theologians call a 'gratuitous grace.'
One may have a gratuitous grace (the power of healing, for
example, or foreknowledge) while in a state of mortal sin, and
the gift is neither necessary to, nor sufficient for, salvation. At
the best such sudden accessions of 'cosmic consciousness' as
are described by Buck are merely unusual invitations to further
personal effort in the direction of the inner height as well as
the external fullness of knowledge. In a great many cases the
invitation is not accepted; the gift is prized for the ecstatic
pleasure it brings; its coming is remembered nostalgically
and, if the recipient happens to be a poet, written about with
eloquence—as Byron, for example, wrote in a splendid passage
of *Childe Harold*, as Wordsworth wrote in *Tintern Abbey* and
The Prelude. In these matters no human being may presume
to pass definitive judgment upon another human being; but it
is at least permissible to say that, on the basis of the biographical evidence, there is no reason to suppose that either Wordsworth or Byron ever seriously did anything about the theophanies they described; nor is there any evidence that these
theophanies were of themselves sufficient to transform their
characters. That enormous egotism, to which De Quincey
and Keats and Haydon bear witness, seems to have remained
with Wordsworth to the end. And Byron was as fascinatingly
and tragi-comically Byronic after he had beheld the One in
all things as he was before.

F

In this context it is interesting to compare Wordsworth with another great nature lover and man of letters, St. Bernard. 'Let Nature be your teacher,' says the first; and he goes on to affirm that

> One impulse from the vernal wood
> Will tell you more of man,
> Of moral evil and of good,
> Than all the sages can.

St. Bernard speaks in what seems a similar strain. 'What I know of the divine sciences and Holy Scripture, I learnt in woods and fields. I have had no other masters than the beeches and the oaks.' And in another of his letters he says: 'Listen to a man of experience: thou wilt learn more in the woods than in books. Trees and stones will teach thee more than thou canst acquire from the mouth of a magister.' The phrases are similar; but their inner significance is very different. In Augustine's language, God alone is to be enjoyed; creatures are not to be enjoyed but used—used with love and compassion and a wondering, detached appreciation, as means to the knowledge of that which may be enjoyed. Wordsworth, like almost all other literary Nature-worshippers, preaches the enjoyment of creatures rather than their use for the attainment of spiritual ends—a use which, as we shall see, entails much self-discipline for the user. For Bernard it goes without saying that his correspondents are actively practising this self-discipline and that Nature, though loved and heeded as a teacher, is only being used as a means to God, not enjoyed as though she were God. The beauty of flowers and landscape is not merely to be relished as one 'wanders lonely as a cloud' about the country-side, is not merely to be pleasurably remembered when one is lying 'in vacant or in pensive mood' on the sofa in the library, after tea. The reaction must be a little more strenuous and purposeful. 'Here, my brothers,' says an ancient Buddhist author, 'are the roots of trees, here are empty places; meditate.' The truth is, of course, that the world is only for those

who have deserved it; for, in Philo's words, 'even though a
man may be incapable of making himself worthy of the creator
of the cosmos, yet he ought to try to make himself worthy of
the cosmos. He ought to transform himself from being a man
into the nature of the cosmos and become, if one may say so,
a little cosmos.' For those who have not deserved the world,
either by making themselves worthy of its creator (that is to
say, by non-attachment and a total self-naughting), or, less
arduously, by making themselves worthy of the cosmos (by
bringing order and a measure of unity to the manifold confusion of undisciplined human personality), the world is,
spiritually speaking, a very dangerous place.

That *nirvana* and *samsara* are one is a fact about the nature
of the universe; but it is a fact which cannot be fully realized
or directly experienced, except by souls far advanced in spirituality. For ordinary, nice, unregenerate people to accept this
truth by hearsay, and to act upon it in practice, is merely to
court disaster. All the dismal story of antinomianism is there
to warn us of what happens when men and women make
practical applications of a merely intellectual and unrealized
theory that all is God and God is all. And hardly less depress-
ing than the spectacle of antinomianism is that of the earnestly
respectable 'well-rounded life' of good citizens who do their
best to live sacramentally, but don't in fact have any direct
acquaintance with that for which the sacramental activity
really stands. Dr. Oman, in his *The Natural and the Supernatural*, writes at length on the theme that 'reconciliation to
the evanescent is revelation of the eternal'; and in a recent
volume, *Science, Religion and the Future*, Canon Raven applauds
Dr. Oman for having stated the principles of a theology in
which there could be no ultimate antithesis between nature and
grace, science and religion, in which, indeed, the worlds of the
scientist and the theologian are seen to be one and the same.
All this is in full accord with Taoism and Zen Buddhism and
with such Christian teachings as St. Augustine's *Ama et fac
quod vis* and Father Lallemant's advice to theocentric contemplatives to go out and act in the world, since their actions

are the only ones capable of doing any real good to the world. But what neither Dr. Oman nor Canon Raven makes sufficiently clear is that nature and grace, *samsara* and *nirvana*, perpetual perishing and eternity, are really and experientially one only to persons who have fulfilled certain conditions. *Fac quod vis* in the temporal world—but only when you have learnt the infinitely difficult art of loving God with all your mind and heart and your neighbour as yourself. If you haven't learnt this lesson, you will either be an antinomian eccentric or criminal or else a respectable well-rounded-lifer, who has left himself no time to understand either nature or grace. The Gospels are perfectly clear about the process by which, and by which alone, a man may gain the right to live in the world as though he were at home in it: he must make a total denial of selfhood, submit to a complete and absolute mortification. At one period of his career, Jesus himself seems to have undertaken austerities, not merely of the mind, but of the body. There is the record of his forty days' fast and his statement, evidently drawn from personal experience, that some demons cannot be cast out except by those who have fasted much as well as prayed. (The Curé d'Ars, whose knowledge of miracles and corporal penance was based on personal experience, insists on the close correlation between severe bodily austerities and the power to get petitionary prayer answered in ways that are sometimes supernormal.) The Pharisees reproached Jesus because he 'came eating and drinking,' and associated with 'publicans and sinners'; they ignored, or were unaware of, the fact that this apparently worldly prophet had at one time rivalled the physical austerities of John the Baptist and was practising the spiritual mortifications which he consistently preached. The pattern of Jesus' life is essentially similar to that of the ideal sage, whose career is traced in the 'Oxherding Pictures,' so popular among Zen Buddhists. The wild ox, symbolizing the unregenerate self, is caught, made to change its direction, then tamed and gradually transformed from black to white. Regeneration goes so far that for a time the ox is completely lost, so that nothing remains to be pictured but the full-orbed moon, symbolizing Mind, Suchness, the Ground. But this is not the final stage. In the end, the herdsman comes back to the world of men, riding on the back of his ox. Because he now loves, loves to the extent of being identified with the divine object of his love, he can do what he likes; for what he likes is what the Nature of Things likes. He is found in company with wine-bibbers and butchers; he and they are all converted into Buddhas. For him, there is complete reconciliation to the evanescent and, through that reconciliation, revelation of the eternal. But for nice ordinary unregenerate people the only reconciliation to the evanescent is that of indulged passions, of distractions submitted to and enjoyed. To tell such persons that evanescence and eternity are the same, and not immediately to qualify the statement, is positively fatal—for, in practice, they are not the same except to the saint; and there is no record that anybody ever came to sanctity who did not, at the outset of his or her career, behave as if evanescence and eternity, nature and grace, were profoundly different and in many respects incompatible. As always, the path of spirituality is a knife-edge between abysses. On one side is the danger of mere rejection and escape, on the other the danger of mere acceptance and the enjoyment of things which should only be used as instruments or symbols. The versified caption which accompanies the last of the 'Ox-herding Pictures' runs as follows:

Even beyond the ultimate limits there extends a passage-way,
By which he comes back to the six realms of existence.
Every worldly affair is now a Buddhist work,
And wherever he goes he finds his home air.
Like a gem he stands out even in the mud,
Like pure gold he shines even in the furnace.
Along the endless road (of birth and death) he walks sufficient
    unto himself.
In all circumstances he moves tranquil and unattached.

The means whereby man's final end is to be attained will be

described and illustrated at length in the section on 'Mortification and Non-attachment.' This section, however, is mainly
concerned with the disciplining of the will. But the disciplining of the will must have as its accompaniment a no less
thorough disciplining of the consciousness. There has to be
a conversion, sudden or otherwise, not merely of the heart,
but also of the senses and of the perceiving mind. What follows is a brief account of this *metanoia*, as the Greeks called it,
this total and radical 'change of mind.'

It is in the Indian and Far Eastern formulations of the
Perennial Philosophy that this subject is most systematically
treated. What is prescribed is a process of conscious discrimination between the personal self and the Self that is identical
with Brahman, between the individual ego and the Buddha-
womb or Universal Mind. The result of this discrimination
is a more or less sudden and complete 'revulsion' of consciousness, and the realization of a state of 'no-mind,' which may be
described as the freedom from perceptual and intellectual
attachment to the ego-principle. This state of 'no-mind'
exists, as it were, on a knife-edge between the carelessness of
the average sensual man and the strained over-eagerness of the
zealot for salvation. To achieve it, one must walk delicately
and, to maintain it, must learn to combine the most intense
alertness with a tranquil and self-denying passivity, the most
indomitable determination with a perfect submission to the
leadings of the spirit. 'When no-mind is sought after by a
mind,' says Huang-Po, 'that is making it a particular object of
thought. There is only testimony of silence; it goes beyond
thinking.' In other words, we, as separate individuals, must
not try to think it, but rather permit ourselves to be thought
by it. Similarly, in the Diamond Sutra we read that if a
Bodhisattva, in his attempt to realize Suchness, 'retains the
thought of an ego, a person, a separate being, or a soul, he is
no longer a Bodhisattva.' Al-Ghazzali, the philosopher of
Sufism, also stresses the need for intellectual humbleness and
docility. 'If the thought that he is effaced from self occurs to
one who is in *fana* (a term roughly corresponding to Zen's

"no-mind," or *mushin*), that is a defect. The highest state is to
be effaced from effacement.' There is an ecstatic effacement-
from-effacement in the interior heights of the Atman-Brahman;
and there is another, more comprehensive effacement-from-
effacement, not only in the inner heights, but also in and
through the world, in the waking, everyday knowledge of God
in his fullness.

A man must become truly poor and as free from his own creaturely will as he was when he was born. And I tell you, by the
eternal truth, that so long as you *desire* to fulfil the will of God
and have any hankering after eternity and God, for just so long
you are not truly poor. He alone has true spiritual poverty who
wills nothing, knows nothing, desires nothing.

Eckhart

The Perfect Way knows no difficulties,
Except that it refuses to make preferences.
Only when freed from hate and love
Does it reveal itself fully and without disguise.

A tenth of an inch's difference,
And heaven and earth are set apart.
If you wish to see it before your own eyes,
Have no fixed thoughts either for or against it.

To set up what you like against what you dislike—
This is the disease of the mind.
When the deep meaning of the Way is not understood,
Peace of mind is disturbed to no purpose. . . .

Pursue not the outer entanglements,
Dwell not in the inner void;
Be serene in the oneness of things,
And dualism vanishes of itself.

When you strive to gain quiescence by stopping motion,
The quiescence so gained is ever in motion.
So long as you tarry in such dualism,
How can you realize oneness?

And when oneness is not thoroughly grasped,
Loss is sustained in two ways:
The denying of external reality is the assertion of it,
And the assertion of Emptiness (the Absolute) is the denying
    of it. . . .

Transformations going on in the empty world that confronts us
Appear to be real because of Ignorance.
Do not strive to seek after the True,
Only cease to cherish opinions.

The two exist because of the One;
But hold not even to this One.
When a mind is not disturbed,
The ten thousand things offer no offence. . . .

If an eye never falls asleep,
All dreams will cease of themselves;
If the Mind retains its absoluteness,
The ten thousand things are of one substance.

When the deep mystery of one Suchness is fathomed,
All of a sudden we forget the external entanglements;
When the ten thousand things are viewed in their oneness,
We return to the origin and remain where we have always
    been. . . .

One in all,
All in One—
If only this is realized,
No more worry about not being perfect!

When Mind and each believing mind are not divided,
And undivided are each believing mind and Mind,
This is where words fail,
For it is not of the past, present or future.

The Third Patriarch of Zen

Do what you are doing now, suffer what you are suffering now;
to do all this with holiness, nothing need be changed but your
hearts. Sanctity consists in *willing* what happens to us by God's
order.

de Caussade

The seventeenth-century Frenchman's vocabulary is very different from that of the seventh-century Chinaman's. But the
advice they give is fundamentally similar. Conformity to the
will of God, submission, docility to the leadings of the Holy
Ghost—in practice, if not verbally, these are the same as conformity to the Perfect Way, refusing to have preferences and
cherish opinions, keeping the eyes open so that dreams may
cease and Truth reveal itself.

The world inhabited by ordinary, nice, unregenerate people
is mainly dull (so dull that they have to distract their minds
from being aware of it by all sorts of artificial 'amusements'),
sometimes briefly and intensely pleasurable, occasionally or
quite often disagreeable and even agonizing. For those who
have deserved the world by making themselves fit to see God
within it as well as within their own souls, it wears a very
different aspect.

The corn was orient and immortal wheat, which never should be
reaped, nor was ever sown. I thought it had stood from everlasting to everlasting. The dust and stones of the street were as
precious as gold. The gates at first were the end of the world.
The green trees, when I saw them first through one of the gates,
transported and ravished me; their sweetness and unusual beauty
made my heart to leap, and almost mad with ecstasy, they were
such strange and wonderful things. The Men! O what vener-

able and reverend creatures did the aged seem! Immortal Cherubim! And young men glittering and sparkling angels, and maids strange seraphic pieces of life and beauty! Boys and girls tumbling in the street, and playing, were moving jewels. I knew not that they were born or should die. But all things abided eternally as they were in their proper places. Eternity was manifested in the light of the day, and something infinite behind everything appeared; which talked with my expectation and moved my desire. The city seemed to stand in Eden, or to be built in Heaven. The streets were mine, the temple was mine, the people were mine, their clothes and gold and silver were mine, as much as their sparkling eyes, fair skins and ruddy faces. The skies were mine, and so were the sun and moon and stars, and all the world was mine; and I the only spectator and enjoyer of it. . . . And so it was that with much ado I was corrupted and made to learn the dirty devices of the world. Which now I unlearn, and become as it were a little child again, that I may enter into the Kingdom of God.

Thomas Traherne

Therefore I give you still another thought, which is yet purer and more spiritual: In the Kingdom of Heaven all is in all, all is one, and all is ours.

Eckhart

The doctrine that God is in the world has an important practical corollary—the sacredness of Nature, and the sinfulness and folly of man's overweening efforts to be her master rather than her intelligently docile collaborator. Sub-human lives and even things are to be treated with respect and understanding, not brutally oppressed to serve our human ends.

The ruler of the Southern Ocean was Shu, the ruler of the Northern Ocean was Hu, and the ruler of the Centre was Chaos. Shu and Hu were continually meeting in the land of Chaos, who treated them very well. They consulted together how they might repay his kindness, and said: 'Men all have seven orifices for the purpose of seeing, hearing, eating and breathing, while this ruler alone has not a single one. Let us try to make them for him.' Accordingly they dug one orifice in him every day. At the end of seven days Chaos died.

Chuang Tzu

In this delicately comic parable Chaos is Nature in the state of *wu-wei*—non-assertion or equilibrium. Shu and Hu are the living images of those busy persons who thought they would improve on Nature by turning dry prairies into wheat fields, and produced deserts; who proudly proclaimed the Conquest of the Air, and then discovered that they had defeated civilization; who chopped down vast forests to provide the newsprint demanded by that universal literacy which was to make the world safe for intelligence and democracy, and got wholesale erosion, pulp magazines and the organs of Fascist, Communist, capitalist and nationalist propaganda. In brief, Shu and Hu are devotees of the apocalyptic religion of Inevitable Progress, and their creed is that the Kingdom of Heaven is outside you, and in the future. Chuang Tzu, on the other hand, like all good Taoists, has no desire to bully Nature into subserving ill-considered temporal ends, at variance with the final end of men as formulated in the Perennial Philosophy. His wish is to work with Nature, so as to produce material and social conditions in which individuals may realize Tao on every level from the physiological up to the spiritual.

Compared with that of the Taoists and Far Eastern Buddhists, the Christian attitude towards Nature has been curiously insensitive and often downright domineering and violent. Taking their cue from an unfortunate remark in Genesis, Catholic moralists have regarded animals as mere things which men do right to exploit for their own ends. Like landscape painting, the humanitarian movement in Europe was an almost completely secular affair. In the Far East both were essentially religious.

The Greeks believed that *hubris* was always followed by *nemesis*, that if you went too far you would get a knock on the head to remind you that the gods will not tolerate insolence on the part of mortal men. In the sphere of human relations, the modern mind understands the doctrine of *hubris* and regards it as mainly true. We wish pride to have a fall, and we see that very often it does fall.

To have too much power over one's fellows, to be too rich, too violent, too ambitious—all this invites punishment, and in the long run, we notice, punishment of one sort or another duly comes. But the Greeks did not stop there. Because they regarded Nature as in some way divine, they felt that it had to be respected and they were convinced that a hubristic lack of respect for Nature would be punished by avenging *nemesis*. In 'The Persians,' Aeschylus gives the reasons—the ultimate, metaphysical reasons—for the barbarians' defeat. Xerxes was punished for two offences—overweening imperialism directed against the Athenians, and overweening imperialism directed against Nature. He tried to enslave his fellow-men, and he tried to enslave the sea, by building a bridge across the Hellespont.

> *Atossa.*   From shore to shore he bridged the Hellespont.
> *Ghost of Darius.*   What, could he chain the mighty Bosphorus?
> *Atossa.*   Even so, some god assisting his design.
> *Ghost of Darius.*   Some god of power to cloud his better sense.

Today we recognize and condemn the first kind of imperialism; but most of us ignore the existence and even the very possibility of the second. And yet the author of *Erewhon* was certainly not a fool, and now that we are paying the appalling price for our much touted 'conquest of Nature' his book seems more than ever topical. And Butler was not the only nineteenth-century sceptic in regard to Inevitable Progress. A generation or more before him, Alfred de Vigny was writing about the new technological marvel of his days, the steam engine—writing in a tone very different from the enthusiastic roarings and trumpetings of his great contemporary, Victor Hugo.

Sur le taureau de fer, qui fume, souffle et beugle,
L'homme est monté trop tôt. Nul ne connaît encor
Quels orages en lui porte ce rude aveugle,
Et le gai voyageur lui livre son trésor.

And a little later in the same poem he adds:

Tous se sont dit : 'Allons,' mais aucun n'est le maître
D'un dragon mugissant qu'un savant a fait naître.
Nous nous sommes joués à plus fort que nous tous.

Looking backwards across the carnage and the devastation, we can see that Vigny was perfectly right. None of those gay travellers, of whom Victor Hugo was the most vociferously eloquent, had the faintest notion where that first, funny little Puffing Billy was taking them. Or rather they had a very clear notion, but it happened to be entirely false. For they were convinced that Puffing Billy was hauling them at full speed towards universal peace and the brotherhood of man; while the newspapers which they were so proud of being able to read, as the train rumbled along towards its Utopian destination not more than fifty years or so away, were the guarantee that liberty and reason would soon be everywhere triumphant. Puffing Billy has now turned into a four-motored bomber loaded with white phosphorus and high explosives, and the free press is everywhere the servant of its advertisers, of a pressure group, or of the government. And yet, for some inexplicable reason, the travellers (now far from gay) still hold fast to the religion of Inevitable Progress—which is, in the last analysis, the hope and faith (in the teeth of all human experience) that one can get something for nothing. How much saner and more realistic is the Greek view that every victory has to be paid for, and that, for some victories, the price exacted is so high that it outweighs any advantage that may be obtained! Modern man no longer regards Nature as being in any sense divine and feels perfectly free to behave towards her as an overweening conqueror and tyrant. The spoils of recent technological imperialism have been enormous; but meanwhile *nemesis* has seen to it that we get our kicks as well as halfpence. For example, has the ability to travel in twelve hours from New York to Los Angeles given more pleasure to the human race than the dropping of bombs and fire has given pain? There is no known method of computing the amount of felicity or goodness in the world at large. What is obvious, however, is that the advantages accruing from recent technological advances—or, in Greek phraseology, from recent acts of *hubris* directed against Nature—are generally accompanied by corresponding disadvantages, that gains in one direction entail losses in other directions, and that we never get something except for something. Whether the net result of these elaborate credit and debit operations is a genuine Progress in virtue, happiness, charity and intelligence is something we can never definitely determine. It is because the reality of Progress can never be determined that the nineteenth and twentieth centuries have had to treat it as an article of religious faith. To the exponents of the Perennial Philosophy, the question whether Progress is inevitable or even real is not a matter of primary importance. For them, the important thing is that individual men and women should come to the unitive knowledge of the divine Ground, and what interests them in regard to the social environment is not its progressiveness or non-progressiveness (whatever those terms may mean), but the degree to which it helps or hinders individuals in their advance towards man's final end.

Chapter 5

CHARITY

He that loveth not knoweth not God, for God is love.

1 John iv

By love may He be gotten and holden, but by thought never.

The Cloud of Unknowing

Whosoever studies to reach contemplation (i.e. unitive knowledge) should begin by searchingly enquiring of himself how
much he loves. For love is the motive power of the mind
(*machina mentis*), which draws it out of the world and raises it
on high.

St. Gregory the Great

The astrolabe of the mysteries of God is love.

Jalal-uddin Rumi

Heavens, deal so still!
Let the superfluous and lust-dieted man
That slaves your ordinance, that will not see
Because he doth not feel, feel your power quickly.

Shakespeare

Love is infallible; it has no errors, for all errors are the want of
love.

William Law

WE can only love what we know, and we can never know
completely what we do not love. Love is a mode of
knowledge, and when the love is sufficiently disinterested and
sufficiently intense, the knowledge becomes unitive knowledge
and so takes on the quality of infallibility. Where there is no
disinterested love (or, more briefly, no charity), there is only

95

biased self-love, and consequently only a partial and distorted knowledge both of the self and of the world of things, lives, minds and spirit outside the self. The lust-dieted man 'slaves the ordinances of Heaven'—that is to say, he subordinates the laws of Nature and the spirit to his own cravings. The result is that 'he does not feel' and therefore makes himself incapable of knowledge. His ignorance is ultimately voluntary; if he cannot see, it is because 'he will not see.' Such voluntary ignorance inevitably has its negative reward. *Nemesis* follows *hubris*—sometimes in a spectacular way, as when the self-blinded man (Macbeth, Othello, Lear) falls into the trap which his own ambition or possessiveness or petulant vanity has prepared for him; sometimes in a less obvious way, as in the cases where power, prosperity and reputation endure to the end but at the cost of an ever-increasing imperviousness to grace and enlightenment, an ever completer inability to escape, now or hereafter, from the stifling prison of selfness and separateness. How profound can be the spiritual ignorance by which such 'enslavers of Heaven's ordinances' are punished is indicated by the behaviour of Cardinal Richelieu on his death-bed. The priest who attended him urged the great man to prepare his soul for its coming ordeal by forgiving all his enemies. 'I have never had any enemies,' the Cardinal replied with the calm sincerity of an ignorance which long years of intrigue and avarice and ambition had rendered as absolute as had been his political power, 'save only those of the State.' Like Napoleon, but in a different way, he was 'feeling heaven's power,' because he had refused to feel charity and therefore refused to know the whole truth about his own soul or anything else.

Here on earth the love of God is better than the knowledge of God, while it is better to know inferior things than to love them. By knowing them we raise them, in a way, to our intelligence, whereas by loving them we stoop towards them and may become subservient to them, as the miser to his gold.

St. Thomas Aquinas (paraphrased)

This remark seems, at first sight, to be incompatible with what
precedes it.   But in reality St. Thomas is merely distinguishing
between the various forms of love and knowledge.   It is better
to love-know God than just to know about God, without love,
through the reading of a treatise on theology.   Gold, on the
other hand, should never be known with the miser's love, or
rather concupiscence, but either abstractly, as the scientific
investigator knows it, or else with the disinterested love-knowledge of the artist in metal, or of the spectator, who love-knows
the goldsmith's work, not for its cash value, not for the sake of
possessing it, but just because it is beautiful.   And the same
applies to all created things, lives and minds.   It is bad to love-
know them with self-centred attachment and cupidity; it is
somewhat better to know them with scientific dispassion; it is
best to supplement abstract knowledge-without-cupidity with
true disinterested love-knowledge, having the quality of aesthetic delight, or of charity, or of both combined.

> We make an idol of truth itself; for truth apart from charity is
> not God, but his image and idol, which we must neither love nor
> worship.
>
> *Pascal*

By a kind of philological accident (which is probably no accident at all, but one of the more subtle expressions of man's
deep-seated will to ignorance and spiritual darkness), the word
'charity' has come, in modern English, to be synonymous with
'almsgiving,' and is almost never used in its original sense, as
signifying the highest and most divine form of love.   Owing
to this impoverishment of our, at the best of times, very inadequate vocabulary of psychological and spiritual terms, the
word 'love' has had to assume an added burden.   'God is love,'
we repeat glibly, and that we must 'love our neighbours as ourselves'; but 'love,' unfortunately, stands for everything from
what happens when, on the screen, two close-ups rapturously
collide to what happens when a John Woolman or a Peter
Claver feels a concern about Negro slaves, because they are

G

temples of the Holy Spirit—from what happens when crowds shout and sing and wave flags in the *Sport-Palast* or the Red Square to what happens when a solitary contemplative becomes absorbed in the prayer of simple regard. Ambiguity in vocabulary leads to confusion of thought; and, in this matter of love, confusion of thought admirably serves the purpose of an unregenerate and divided human nature that is determined to make the best of both worlds—to say that it is serving God, while in fact it is serving Mammon, Mars or Priapus.

Systematically or in brief aphorism and parable, the masters of the spiritual life have described the nature of true charity and have distinguished it from the other, lower forms of love. Let us consider its principal characteristics in order. First, charity is disinterested, seeking no reward, nor allowing itself to be diminished by any return of evil for its good. God is to be loved for Himself, not for his gifts, and persons and things are to be loved for God's sake, because they are temples of the Holy Ghost. Moreover, since charity is disinterested, it must of necessity be universal.

Love seeks no cause beyond itself and no fruit; it is its own fruit, its own enjoyment. I love because I love; I love in order that I may love. . . . Of all the motions and affections of the soul, love is the only one by means of which the creature, though not on equal terms, is able to treat with the Creator and to give back something resembling what has been given to it. . . . When God loves, He only desires to be loved, knowing that love will render all those who love Him happy.

St. Bernard

For as love has no by-ends, wills nothing but its own increase, so everything is as oil to its flame; it must have that which it wills and cannot be disappointed, because everything (including unkindness on the part of those loved) naturally helps it to live in its own way and to bring forth its own work.

William Law

Those who speak ill of me are really my good friends.
When, being slandered, I cherish neither enmity nor preference,
There grows within me the power of love and humility, which is
     born of the Unborn.

Kung-chia Ta-shih

Some people want to see God with their eyes as they see a cow,
and to love Him as they love their cow—for the milk and cheese
and profit it brings them. This is how it is with people who love
God for the sake of outward wealth or inward comfort. They do
not rightly love God, when they love Him for their own advantage. Indeed, I tell you the truth, any object you have in your
mind, however good, will be a barrier between you and the
inmost Truth.

Eckhart

A beggar, Lord, I ask of Thee
More than a thousand kings could ask.
Each one wants something, which he asks of Thee.
I come to ask Thee to give me Thyself.

Ansari of Herat

I will have nothing to do with a love which would be for God or
in God. This is a love which pure love cannot abide; for pure
love is God Himself.

St. Catherine of Genoa

As a mother, even at the risk of her own life, protects her son, her
only son, so let there be good will without measure between all
beings. Let good will without measure prevail in the whole
world, above, below, around, unstinted, unmixed with any feeling of differing or opposing interests. If a man remain steadfastly
in this state of mind all the time he is awake, then is come to pass
the saying, 'Even in this world holiness has been found.'

Metta Sutta

Learn to look with an equal eye upon all beings, seeing the one
Self in all.

Srimad Bhagavatam

The second distinguishing mark of charity is that, unlike the lower forms of love, it is not an emotion. It begins as an act of the will and is consummated as a purely spiritual awareness, a unitive love-knowledge of the essence of its object.

Let everyone understand that real love of God does not consist in tear-shedding, nor in that sweetness and tenderness for which usually we long, just because they console us, but in serving God in justice, fortitude of soul and humility.

St. Teresa

The worth of love does not consist in high feelings, but in detachment, in patience under all trials for the sake of God whom we love.

St. John of the Cross

By love I do not mean any natural tenderness, which is more or less in people according to their constitution; but I mean a larger principle of the soul, founded in reason and piety, which makes us tender, kind and gentle to all our fellow creatures as creatures of God, and for his sake.

William Law

The nature of charity, or the love-knowledge of God, is defined by Shankara, the great Vedantist saint and philosopher of the ninth century, in the thirty-second couplet of his *Viveka-Chudamani.*

Among the instruments of emancipation the supreme is devotion. Contemplation of the true form of the real Self (the Atman which is identical with Brahman) is said to be devotion.

In other words, the highest form of the love of God is an immediate spiritual intuition, by which 'knower, known and knowledge are made one.' The means to, and earlier stages of, this supreme love-knowledge of Spirit by spirit are described by Shankara in the preceding verses of his philosophical poem, and consist in acts of a will directed towards the denial of self-ness in thought, feeling and action, towards desirelessness and non-attachment or (to use the corresponding Christian term) 'holy indifference,' towards a cheerful acceptance of affliction, without self-pity and without thought of returning evil for evil, and finally towards unsleeping and one-pointed mindfulness of the Godhead who is at once transcendent and, because transcendent, immanent in every soul.

It is plain that no distinct object whatever that pleases the will can be God; and, for that reason, if the will is to be united with Him, it must empty itself, cast away every disorderly affection of the desire, every satisfaction it may distinctly have, high and low, temporal and spiritual, so that, purified and cleansed from all unruly satisfactions, joys and desires, it may be wholly occupied, with all its affections, in loving God. For if the will can in any way comprehend God and be united with Him, it cannot be through any capacity of the desire, but only by love; and as all the delight, sweetness and joy, of which the will is sensible, is not love, it follows that none of these pleasing impressions can be the adequate means of uniting the will to God. These adequate means consist in an act of the will. And because an act of the will is quite distinct from feeling, it is by an act that the will is united with God and rests in Him; that act is love. This union is never wrought by feeling or exertion of the desire; for these remain in the soul as aims and ends. It is only as motives of love that feelings can be of service, if the will is bent on going onwards, and for nothing else. . . .

He, then, is very unwise who, when sweetness and spiritual delight fail him, thinks for that reason that God has abandoned him; and when he finds them again, rejoices and is glad, thinking that he has in that way come to possess God.

More unwise still is he who goes about seeking for sweetness in God, rejoices in it, and dwells upon it; for in so doing he is not seeking after God with the will grounded in the emptiness of faith and charity, but only in spiritual sweetness and delight, which is a created thing, following herein in his own will and fond pleasure. . . . It is impossible for the will to attain to the sweetness and bliss of the divine union otherwise than in detachment, in refusing to the desire every pleasure in the things of heaven and earth.

St. John of the Cross

Love (the sensible love of the emotions) does not unify. True, it unites in act; but it does not unite in essence.

Eckhart

The reason why sensible love even of the highest object cannot unite the soul to its divine Ground in spiritual essence is that, like all other emotions of the heart, sensible love intensifies that selfness, which is the final obstacle in the way of such union. 'The damned are in eternal movement without any mixture of rest; we mortals, who are yet in this pilgrimage, have now movement, now rest. . . . Only God has repose without movement.' Consequently it is only if we abide in the peace of God that passes all understanding that we can abide in the knowledge and love of God. And to the peace that passes understanding we have to go by way of the humble and very ordinary peace which can be understood by everybody—peace between nations and within them (for wars and violent revolutions have the effect of more or less totally eclipsing God for the majority of those involved in them); peace between individuals and within the individual soul (for personal quarrels and private fears, loves, hates, ambitions and distractions are, in their petty way, no less fatal to the development of the spiritual life than are the greater calamities). We have to will the peace that it is within our power to get for ourselves and others, in order that we may be fit to receive that other peace, which is a fruit of the Spirit and the condition, as St. Paul implied, of the unitive knowledge-love of God.

It is by means of tranquillity of mind that you are able to transmute this false mind of death and rebirth into the clear Intuitive

Mind and, by so doing, to realize the primal and enlightening Essence of Mind. You should make this your starting point for spiritual practices. Having harmonized your starting point with your goal, you will be able by right practice to attain your true end of perfect Enlightenment.

If you wish to tranquillize your mind and restore its original purity, you must proceed as you would do if you were purifying a jar of muddy water. You first let it stand, until the sediment settles at the bottom, when the water will become clear, which corresponds with the state of the mind before it was troubled by defiling passions. Then you carefully strain off the pure water. ... When the mind becomes tranquillized and concentrated into perfect unity, then all things will be seen, not in their separateness, but in their unity, wherein there is no place for the passions to enter, and which is in full conformity with the mysterious and indescribable purity of Nirvana.

Surangama Sutra

This identity out of the One into the One and with the One is the source and fountainhead and breaking forth of glowing Love.

Eckhart

Spiritual progress, as we have had occasion to discover in several other contexts, is always spiral and reciprocal. Peace from distractions and emotional agitations is the way to charity; and charity, or unitive love-knowledge, is the way to the higher peace of God. And the same is true of humility, which is the third characteristic mark of charity. Humility is a necessary condition of the highest form of love, and the highest form of love makes possible the consummation of humility in a total self-naughting.

Would you become a pilgrim on the road of Love?
The first condition is that you make yourself humble as dust and
    ashes.

Ansari of Herat

I have but one word to say to you concerning love for your neighbour, namely that nothing save humility can mould you to it; nothing but the consciousness of your own weakness can make you indulgent and pitiful to that of others. You will answer, I quite understand that humility should produce forbearance towards others, but how am I first to acquire humility? Two things combined will bring that about; you must never separate them. The first is contemplation of the deep gulf, whence God's all-powerful hand has drawn you out, and over which He ever holds you, so to say, suspended. The second is the presence of that all-penetrating God. It is only in beholding and loving God that we can learn forgetfulness of self, measure duly the nothingness which has dazzled us, and accustom ourselves thankfully to decrease beneath that great Majesty which absorbs all things. Love God and you will be humble; love God and you will throw off the love of self; love God and you will love all that He gives you to love for love of Him.

Fénelon

Feelings, as we have seen, may be of service as motives of charity; but charity as charity has its beginning in the will—will to peace and humility in oneself, will to patience and kindness towards one's fellow-creatures, will to that disinterested love of God which 'asks nothing and refuses nothing.' But the will can be strengthened by exercise and confirmed by perseverance. This is very clearly brought out in the following record—delightful for its Boswellian vividness—of a conversation between the young Bishop of Belley and his beloved friend and master, François de Sales.

I once asked the Bishop of Geneva what one must do to attain perfection. 'You must love God with all your heart,' he answered, 'and your neighbour as yourself.'

'I did not ask wherein perfection lies,' I rejoined, 'but how to attain it.' 'Charity,' he said again, 'that is both the means and the end, the only way by which we can reach that perfection

which is, after all, but Charity itself. . . . Just as the soul is the
life of the body, so charity is the life of the soul.'

'I know all that,' I said. 'But I want to know *how* one is to love
God with all one's heart and one's neighbour as oneself.'

But again he answered, 'We must love God with all our
hearts, and our neighbour as ourselves.'

'I am no further than I was,' I replied. 'Tell me how to
acquire such love.'

'The best way, the shortest and easiest way of loving God with
all one's heart is to love Him wholly and heartily!'

He would give no other answer. At last, however, the Bishop
said, 'There are many besides you who want me to tell them of
methods and systems and secret ways of becoming perfect, and I
can only tell them that the sole secret is a hearty love of God, and
the only way of attaining that love is by loving. You learn to
speak by speaking, to study by studying, to run by running, to
work by working; and just so you learn to love God and man by
loving. All those who think to learn in any other way deceive
themselves. If you want to love God, go on loving Him more
and more. Begin as a mere apprentice, and the very power of
love will lead you on to become a master in the art. Those who
have made most progress will continually press on, never believing themselves to have reached their end; for charity should go
on increasing until we draw our last breath.'

Jean Pierre Camus

The passage from what St. Bernard calls the 'carnal love' of
the sacred humanity to the spiritual love of the Godhead, from
the emotional love that can only unite lover and beloved in act
to the perfect charity which unifies them in spiritual substance,
is reflected in religious practice as the passage from meditation,
discursive and affective, to infused contemplation. All Christian writers insist that the spiritual love of the Godhead is
superior to the carnal love of the humanity, which serves as
introduction and means to man's final end in unitive love-
knowledge of the divine Ground; but all insist no less strongly
that carnal love is a necessary introduction and an indispensable

means. Oriental writers would agree that this is true for many persons, but not for all, since there are some born contemplatives who are able to 'harmonize their starting point with their goal' and to embark directly upon the Yoga of Knowledge. It is from the point of view of the born contemplative that the greatest of Taoist philosophers writes in the following passage.

> Those men who in a special way regard Heaven as Father and have, as it were, a personal love for it, how much more should they love what is above Heaven as Father! Other men in a special way regard their rulers as better than themselves and they, as it were, personally die for them. How much more should they die for what is truer than a ruler! When the springs dry up, the fish are all together on dry land. They then moisten each other with their dampness and keep each other wet with their slime. But this is not to be compared with forgetting each other in a river or lake.
>
> *Chuang Tzu*

The slime of personal and emotional love is remotely similar to the water of the Godhead's spiritual being, but of inferior quality and (precisely because the love is emotional and therefore personal) of insufficient quantity. Having, by their voluntary ignorance, wrong-doing and wrong being, caused the divine springs to dry up, human beings can do something to mitigate the horrors of their situation by 'keeping one another wet with their slime.' But there can be no happiness or safety in time and no deliverance into eternity, until they give up thinking that slime is enough and, by abandoning themselves to what is in fact their element, call back the eternal waters. To those who seek first the Kingdom of God, all the rest will be added. From those who, like the modern idolaters of progress, seek first all the rest in the expectation that (after the harnessing of atomic power and the next revolution but three) the Kingdom of God will be added, everything will be taken away. And yet we continue to trust in progress, to regard personal slime as the highest form of spiritual moisture and to prefer an agonizing and impossible existence on dry land to love, joy and peace in our native ocean.

The sect of lovers is distinct from all others;
Lovers have a religion and a faith all their own.

Jalal-uddin Rumi

The soul lives by that which it loves rather than in the body which it animates. For it has not its life in the body, but rather gives it to the body and lives in that which it loves.

St. John of the Cross

Temperance is love surrendering itself wholly to Him who is its object; courage is love bearing all things gladly for the sake of Him who is its object; justice is love serving only Him who is its object, and therefore rightly ruling; prudence is love making wise distinctions between what hinders and what helps itself.

St. Augustine

The distinguishing marks of charity are disinterestedness, tranquillity and humility. But where there is disinterestedness there is neither greed for personal advantage nor fear for personal loss or punishment; where there is tranquillity, there is neither craving nor aversion, but a steady will to conform to the divine Tao or Logos on every level of existence and a steady awareness of the divine Suchness and what should be one's own relations to it; and where there is humility there is no censoriousness and no glorification of the ego or any projected alter-ego at the expense of others, who are recognized as having the same weaknesses and faults, but also the same capacity for transcending them in the unitive knowledge of God, as one has oneself. From all this it follows that charity is the root and substance of morality, and that where there is little charity there will be much avoidable evil. All this has been summed up in Augustine's formula: 'Love, and do what you like.' Among the later elaborations of the Augustinian theme we may cite the following from the writings of John Everard, one of those spiritually minded seventeenth-century divines whose teachings fell on the deaf ears of warring factions and, when the revolution and the military dictatorship were at an end, on the even deafer ears of Restoration clergymen and their successors in the Augustan age. (Just how deaf those ears could be we may judge by what Swift wrote of his beloved and morally perfect Houyhnhnms. The subject matter of their conversations, as of their poetry, consisted of such things as 'friendship and benevolence, the visible operations of nature or ancient traditions; the bounds and limits of virtue, the unerring rules of reason.' Never once do the ideas of God, or charity, or deliverance engage their minds. Which shows sufficiently clearly what the Dean of St. Patrick's thought of the religion by which he made his money.)

> Turn the man loose who has found the living Guide within him, and then let him neglect the outward if he can! Just as you would say to a man who loves his wife with all tenderness, "You are at liberty to beat her, hurt her or kill her, if you want to.'
>
> *John Everard*

From this it follows that, where there is charity, there can be no coercion.

> God forces no one, for love cannot compel, and God's service, therefore, is a thing of perfect freedom.
>
> *Hans Denk*

But just because it cannot compel, charity has a kind of authority, a non-coercive power, by means of which it defends itself and gets its beneficent will done in the world—not always, of course, not inevitably or automatically (for individuals and, still more, organizations can be impenetrably armoured against divine influence), but in a surprisingly large number of cases.

Heaven arms with pity those whom it would not see destroyed.

Lao Tzu

'He abused me, he beat me, he defeated me, he robbed me'—in those who harbour such thoughts hatred will never cease.

'He abused me, he beat me, he defeated me, he robbed me'—in those who do not harbour such thoughts hatred will cease.

For hatred does not cease by hatred at any time—this is an old rule.

Dhammapada

Our present economic, social and international arrangements are based, in large measure, upon organized lovelessness. We begin by lacking charity towards Nature, so that instead of trying to co-operate with Tao or the Logos on the inanimate and sub-human levels, we try to dominate and exploit, we waste the earth's mineral resources, ruin its soil, ravage its forests, pour filth into its rivers and poisonous fumes into its air. From lovelessness in relation to Nature we advance to lovelessness in relation to art—a lovelessness so extreme that we have effectively killed all the fundamental or useful arts and set up various kinds of mass-production by machines in their place. And of course this lovelessness in regard to art is at the same time a lovelessness in regard to the human beings who have to perform the fool-proof and grace-proof tasks imposed by our mechanical art-surrogates and by the interminable paper work connected with mass-production and mass-distribution. With mass-production and mass-distribution go mass-financing, and the three have conspired to expropriate ever-increasing numbers of small owners of land and productive equipment, thus reducing the sum of freedom among the majority and increasing the power of a minority to exercise a coercive control over the lives of their fellows. This coercively controlling minority is composed of private capitalists or governmental bureaucrats or of both classes of bosses acting in collaboration—and, of course, the coercive and therefore essentially loveless nature of the control remains the same, whether the bosses call them-

selves 'company directors' or 'civil servants.' The only difference between these two kinds of oligarchical rulers is that the
first derive more of their power from wealth than from position within a conventionally respected hierarchy, while the
second derive more power from position than from wealth.
Upon this fairly uniform groundwork of loveless relationships
are imposed others, which vary widely from one society to
another, according to local conditions and local habits of
thought and feeling. Here are a few examples: contempt and
exploitation of coloured minorities living among white majorities, or of coloured majorities governed by minorities of white
imperialists; hatred of Jews, Catholics, Freemasons or of any
other minority whose language, habits, appearance or religion
happens to differ from those of the local majority. And the
crowning superstructure of uncharity is the organized lovelessness of the relations between state and sovereign state—a lovelessness that expresses itself in the axiomatic assumption that
it is right and natural for national organizations to behave like
thieves and murderers, armed to the teeth and ready, at the
first favourable opportunity, to steal and kill. (Just how
axiomatic is this assumption about the nature of nationhood
is shown by the history of Central America. So long as the
arbitrarily delimited territories of Central America were called
provinces of the Spanish colonial empire, there was peace
between their inhabitants. But early in the nineteenth century
the various administrative districts of the Spanish empire
broke from their allegiance to the 'mother country' and decided to become nations on the European model. Result:
they immediately went to war with one another. Why?
Because, by definition, a sovereign national state is an organization that has the right and duty to coerce its members to
steal and kill on the largest possible scale.)

'Lead us not into temptation' must be the guiding principle
of all social organization, and the temptations to be guarded
against and, so far as possible, eliminated by means of appropriate economic and political arrangements are temptations
against charity, that is to say, against the disinterested love of

God, Nature and man. First, the dissemination and general acceptance of any form of the Perennial Philosophy will do something to preserve men and women from the temptation to idolatrous worship of things in time—church-worship, state-worship, revolutionary future-worship, humanistic self-worship, all of them essentially and necessarily opposed to charity. Next come decentralization, widespread private ownership of land and the means of production on a small scale, discouragement of monopoly by state or corporation, division of economic and political power (the only guarantee, as Lord Acton was never tired of insisting, of civil liberty under law). These social rearrangements would do much to prevent ambitious individuals, organizations and governments from being led into the temptation of behaving tyrannously; while co-operatives, democratically controlled professional organizations and town meetings would deliver the masses of the people from the temptation of making their decentralized individualism too rugged. But of course none of these intrinsically desirable reforms can possibly be carried out, so long as it is thought right and natural that sovereign states should prepare to make war on one another. For modern war cannot be waged except by countries with an over-developed capital goods industry; countries in which economic power is wielded either by the state or by a few monopolistic corporations which it is easy to tax and, if necessary, temporarily to nationalize; countries where the labouring masses, being without property, are rootless, easily transferable from one place to another, highly regimented by factory discipline. Any decentralized society of free, uncoerced small owners, with a properly balanced economy must, in a war-making world such as ours, be at the mercy of one whose production is highly mechanized and centralized, whose people are without property and therefore easily coercible, and whose economy is lop-sided. This is why the one desire of industrially undeveloped countries like Mexico and China is to become like Germany, or England, or the United States. So long as the organized lovelessness of war and preparation for war remains, there can be no mitigation, on any large, nation-wide or world-wide scale, of the organized lovelessness of our economic and political relationships. War and preparation for war are standing temptations to make the present bad, God-eclipsing arrangements of society progressively worse as technology becomes progressively more efficient.

Chapter 6

MORTIFICATION, NON-ATTACHMENT, RIGHT LIVELIHOOD

This treasure of the Kingdom of God has been hidden by time and multiplicity and the soul's own works, or briefly by its creaturely nature. But in the measure that the soul can separate itself from this multiplicity, to that extent it reveals within itself the Kingdom of God. Here the soul and the Godhead are one.

Eckhart

'OUR kingdom go' is the necessary and unavoidable corollary of 'Thy kingdom come.' For the more there is of self, the less there is of God. The divine eternal fullness of life can be gained only by those who have deliberately lost the partial, separative life of craving and self-interest, of egocentric thinking, feeling, wishing and acting. Mortification or deliberate dying to self is inculcated with an uncompromising firmness in the canonical writings of Christianity, Hinduism, Buddhism and most of the other major and minor religions of the world, and by every theocentric saint and spiritual reformer who has ever lived out and expounded the principles of the Perennial Philosophy. But this 'self-naughting' is never (at least by anyone who knows what he is talking about) regarded as an end in itself. It possesses merely an instrumental value, as the indispensable means to something else. In the words of one whom we have often had occasion to cite in earlier sections, it is necessary for all of us to 'learn the true nature and worth of all self-denials and mortifications.'

As to their nature, considered in themselves, they have nothing of goodness or holiness, nor are any real part of our sanctification, they are not the true food or nourishment of the Divine Life in our souls, they have no quickening, sanctifying power in them;

H 113

their only worth consists in this, that they remove the impediments of holiness, break down that which stands between God
and us, and make way for the quickening, sanctifying spirit of
God to operate on our souls, which operation of God is the one
only thing that can raise the Divine Life in the soul, or help it to
the smallest degree of real holiness or spiritual life. . . . Hence we
may learn the reason why many people not only lose the benefit,
but are even the worse for all their mortifications. It is because
they mistake the whole nature and worth of them. They practise
them for their own sakes, as things good in themselves; they
think them to be real parts of holiness, and so rest in them and
look no further, but grow full of self-esteem and self-admiration
for their own progress in them. This makes them self-sufficient,
morose, severe judges of all those that fall short of their mortifications. And thus their self-denials do only that for them which
indulgences do for other people: they withstand and hinder the
operation of God upon their souls, and instead of being really
self-denials, they strengthen and keep up the kingdom of self.

William Law

The rout and destruction of the passions, while a good, is not the
ultimate good; the discovery of Wisdom is the surpassing good.
When this is found, all the people will sing.

Philo

Living in religion (as I can speak by experience) if one is not in a
right course of prayer and other exercises between God and our
soul, one's nature groweth much worse than ever it would have
been, if one had lived in the world. For pride and self-love,
which are rooted in the soul by sin, find means to strengthen
themselves exceedingly in religion, if the soul is not in a course
that may teach her and procure her true humility. For by the
corrections and contradictions of the will (which cannot be
avoided by any living in a religious community) I find my heart
grown, as I may say, as hard as a stone; and nothing would
have been able to soften it but by being put into a course of

prayer, by which the soul tendeth towards God and learneth of Him the lesson of truly humbling herself.

Dame Gertrude More

Once, when I was grumbling over being obliged to eat meat and do no penance, I heard it said that sometimes there was more of self-love than desire of penance in such sorrow.

St. Teresa

That the mortified are, in some respects, often much worse than the unmortified is a commonplace of history, fiction and descriptive psychology. Thus, the Puritan may practise all the cardinal virtues—prudence, fortitude, temperance and chastity —and yet remain a thoroughly bad man; for, in all too many cases, these virtues of his are accompanied by, and indeed causally connected with, the sins of pride, envy, chronic anger and an uncharitableness pushed sometimes to the level of active cruelty. Mistaking the means for the end, the Puritan has fancied himself holy because he is stoically austere. But stoical austerity is merely the exaltation of the more creditable side of the ego at the expense of the less creditable. Holiness, on the contrary, is the total denial of the separative self, in its creditable no less than its discreditable aspects, and the abandonment of the will to God. To the extent that there is attachment to 'I,' 'me,' 'mine,' there is no attachment to, and therefore no unitive knowledge of, the divine Ground. Mortification has to be carried to the pitch of non-attachment or (in the phrase of St. François de Sales) 'holy indifference'; otherwise it merely transfers self-will from one channel to another, not merely without decrease in the total volume of that self-will, but sometimes with an actual increase. As usual, the corruption of the best is the worst. The difference between the mortified but still proud and self-centred stoic and the unmortified hedonist consists in this: the latter, being flabby, shiftless and at heart rather ashamed of himself, lacks the energy and the motive to do much harm except to his own body, mind and spirit; the former, because he has all the secondary virtues and looks down on those who are not like himself, is morally equipped to wish and to be able to do harm on the very largest scale and with a perfectly untroubled conscience. These are obvious facts; and yet, in the current religious jargon of our day the word 'immoral' is reserved almost exclusively for the carnally self-indulgent. The covetous and the ambitious, the respectable toughs and those who cloak their lust for power and place under the right sort of idealistic cant, are not merely unblamed; they are even held up as models of virtue and godliness. The representatives of the organized churches begin by putting haloes on the heads of the people who do most to make wars and revolutions, then go on, rather plaintively, to wonder why the world should be in such a mess.

Mortification is not, as many people seem to imagine, a matter, primarily, of severe physical austerities. It is possible that, for certain persons in certain circumstances, the practice of severe physical austerities may prove helpful in advance towards man's final end. In most cases, however, it would seem that what is gained by such austerities is not liberation, but something quite different—the achievement of 'psychic' powers. The ability to get petitionary prayer answered, the power to heal and work other miracles, the knack of looking into the future or into other people's minds—these, it would seem, are often related in some kind of causal connection with fasting, watching and the self-infliction of pain. Most of the great theocentric saints and spiritual teachers have admitted the existence of supernormal powers, only, however, to deplore them. To think that such *Siddhis*, as the Indians call them, have anything to do with liberation is, they say, a dangerous illusion. These things are either irrelevant to the main issue of life, or, if too much prized and attended to, an obstacle in the way of spiritual advance. Nor are these the only objections to physical austerities. Carried to extremes, they may be dangerous to health—and without health the steady persistence of effort required by the spiritual life is very difficult of achievement. And being difficult, painful and generally conspicuous, physical austerities are a standing temptation to vanity and the competitive spirit of record breaking. 'When thou didst give thyself up to physical mortification, thou wast great, thou wast admired.' So writes Suso of his own experiences—experiences which led him, just as Gautama Buddha had been led many centuries before, to give up his course of bodily penance. And St. Teresa remarks how much easier it is to impose great penances upon oneself than to suffer in patience, charity and humbleness the ordinary everyday crosses of family life (which did not prevent her, incidentally, from practising, to the very day of her death, the most excruciating forms of self-torture. Whether these austerities really helped her to come to the unitive knowledge of God, or whether they were prized and persisted in because of the psychic powers they helped to develop, there is no means of determining.)

Our dear Saint (François de Sales) disapproved of immoderate fasting. He used to say that the spirit could not endure the body when overfed, but that, if underfed, the body could not endure the spirit.

Jean Pierre Camus

When the will, the moment it feels any joy in sensible things rises upwards in that joy to God, and when sensible things move it to pray, it should not neglect them, it should make use of them for so holy an exercise; because sensible things, in these conditions, subserve the end for which God created them, namely to be occasions for making Him better known and loved.

St. John of the Cross

He who is not conscious of liberty of spirit among the things of sense and sweetness—things which should serve as motives to prayer—and whose will rests and feeds upon them, ought to abstain from the use of them; for to him they are a hindrance on the road to God.

St. John of the Cross

One man may declare that he cannot fast; but can he declare
that he cannot love God? Another may affirm that he cannot
preserve virginity or sell all his goods in order to give the price
to the poor; but can he tell me that he cannot love his enemies?
All that is necessary is to look into one's own heart; for what
God asks of us is not found at a great distance.

St. Jerome

Anybody who wishes to do so can get all, and indeed more than
all, the mortification he wants out of the incidents of ordinary,
day-to-day living, without ever resorting to harsh bodily
penance. Here are the rules laid down by the author of *Holy
Wisdom* for Dame Gertrude More.

First, that she should do all that belonged to her to do by any
law, human or Divine. Secondly, that she was to refrain from
doing those things that were forbidden her by human or Divine
Law, or by Divine inspiration. Thirdly, that she should bear
with as much patience or resignation as possible all crosses and
contradictions to her natural will, which were inflicted by the hand
of God. Such, for instance, were aridities, temptations, afflictions or bodily pain, sickness and infirmity; or again, the loss
of friends or want of necessaries and comforts. All this was to be
endured patiently, whether the crosses came direct from God or
by means of His creatures. . . . These indeed were mortifications
enough for Dame Gertrude, or for any other soul, and there
was no need for anyone to advise or impose others.

Augustine Baker

To sum up, that mortification is the best which results in the
elimination of self-will, self-interest, self-centred thinking,
wishing and imagining. Extreme physical austerities are not
likely to achieve this kind of mortification. But the acceptance
of what happens to us (apart, of course, from our own sins) in
the course of daily living *is* likely to produce this result. If
specific exercises in self-denial are undertaken, they should

be inconspicuous, non-competitive and uninjurious to health. Thus, in the matter of diet, most people will find it sufficiently mortifying to refrain from eating all the things which the experts in nutrition condemn as unwholesome. And where social relations are concerned, self-denial should take the form, not of showy acts of would-be humility, but of control of the tongue and the moods—in refraining from saying anything uncharitable or merely frivolous (which means, in practice, refraining from about fifty per cent. of ordinary conversation), and in behaving calmly and with quiet cheerfulness when external circumstances or the state of our bodies predisposes us to anxiety, gloom or an excessive elation.

When a man practises charity in order to be reborn in heaven, or for fame, or reward, or from fear, such charity can obtain no pure effect.

Sutra on the Distinction and Protection of the Dharma

When Prince Wen Wang was on a tour of inspection in Tsang, he saw an old man fishing. But his fishing was not real fishing, for he did not fish in order to catch fish, but to amuse himself. So Wen Wang wished to employ him in the administration of government, but feared lest his own ministers, uncles and brothers might object. On the other hand, if he let the old man go, he could not bear to think of the people being deprived of such an influence.

Chuang Tzu

God, if I worship Thee in fear of hell, burn me in hell. And if I worship Thee in hope of Paradise, exclude me from Paradise; but if I worship Thee for Thine own sake, withhold not Thine everlasting Beauty.

Rabi'a

Rabi'a, the Sufi woman-saint, speaks, thinks and feels in terms of devotional theism; the Buddhist theologian, in terms o im-

personal moral Law; the Chinese philosopher, with characteristic humour, in terms of politics; but all three insist on the need
for non-attachment to self-interest—insist on it as strongly as
does Christ when he reproaches the Pharisees for their egocentric piety, as does the Krishna of the Bhagavad-Gita when
he tells Arjuna to do his divinely ordained duty without personal craving for, or fear of, the fruits of his actions.

St. Ignatius Loyola was once asked what his feelings would be if
the Pope were to suppress the Company of Jesus. 'A quarter of
an hour of prayer,' he answered, 'and I should think no more
about it.'

This is, perhaps, the most difficult of all mortifications—to
achieve a 'holy indifference' to the temporal success or failure
of the cause to which one has devoted one's best energies. If
it triumphs, well and good; and if it meets defeat, that also
is well and good, if only in ways that, to a limited and time-
bound mind, are here and now entirely incomprehensible.

By a man without passions I mean one who does not permit good
or evil to disturb his inward economy, but rather falls in with
what happens and does not add to the sum of his mortality.

Chuang Tzu

The fitting disposition for union with God is not that the soul
should understand, feel, taste or imagine anything on the subject
of the nature of God, or any other thing whatever, but should
remain in that pureness and love which is perfect resignation and
complete detachment from all things for God alone.

St. John of the Cross

Disquietude is always vanity, because it serves no good. Yes,
even if the whole world were thrown into confusion and all
things in it, disquietude on that account would be vanity.

St. John of the Cross

Sufficient not only unto the day, but also unto the place, is the evil thereof. Agitation over happenings which we are powerless to modify, either because they have not yet occurred, or else are occurring at an inaccessible distance from us, achieves nothing beyond the inoculation of here and now with the remote or anticipated evil that is the object of our distress. Listening four or five times a day to newscasters and commentators, reading the morning papers and all the weeklies and monthlies—nowadays, this is described as 'taking an intelligent interest in politics.' St. John of the Cross would have called it indulgence in idle curiosity and the cultivation of disquietude for disquietude's sake.

I want very little, and what I do want I have very little wish for. I have hardly any desires, but if I were to be born again, I should have none at all. We should ask nothing and refuse nothing, but leave ourselves in the arms of divine Providence without wasting time in any desire, except to will what God wills of us.

St. François de Sales

Push far enough towards the Void,
Hold fast enough to Quietness,
And of the ten thousand things none but can be worked on by you.
I have beheld them, whither they go back.
See, all things howsoever they flourish
Return to the root from which they grew.
This return to the Root is called Quietness;
Quietness is called submission to Fate;
What has submitted to Fate becomes part of the always-so;
To know the always-so is to be illumined;
Not to know it means to go blindly to disaster.

Lao Tzu

I wish I could join the 'Solitaries' (on Caldey Island), instead of being Superior and having to write books. But I don't wish to have what I wish, of course.

Abbot John Chapman

We must not wish anything other than what happens from moment to moment, all the while, however, exercising ourselves in goodness.

St. Catherine of Genoa

In the practice of mortification as in most other fields, advance is along a knife-edge. On one side lurks the Scylla of ego-centric austerity, on the other the Charybdis of an uncaring quietism. The holy indifference inculcated by the exponents of the Perennial Philosophy is neither stoicism nor mere passivity. It is rather an active resignation. Self-will is renounced, not that there may be a total holiday from willing, but that the divine will may use the mortified mind and body as its instrument for good. Or we may say, with Kabir, that 'the devout seeker is he who mingles in his heart the double currents of love and detachment, like the mingling of the streams of Ganges and Jumna.' Until we put an end to particular attachments, there can be no love of God with the whole heart, mind and strength and no universal charity towards all creatures for God's sake. Hence the hard sayings in the Gospels about the need to renounce exclusive family ties. And if the Son of Man has nowhere to lay his head, if the Tathagata and the Bodhisattvas 'have their thoughts awakened to the nature of Reality without abiding in anything whatever,' this is because a truly Godlike love which, like the sun, shines equally upon the just and the unjust, is impossible to a mind imprisoned in private preferences and aversions.

The soul that is attached to anything, however much good there may be in it, will not arrive at the liberty of divine union. For whether it be a strong wire rope or a slender and delicate thread that holds the bird, it matters not, if it really holds it fast; for, until the cord be broken, the bird cannot fly. So the soul, held by the bonds of human affections, however slight they may be, cannot, while they last, make its way to God.

St. John of the Cross

There are some who are newly delivered from their sins and so, though they are resolved to love God, they are still novices and apprentices, soft and weak. . . . They love a number of superfluous, vain and dangerous things at the same time as Our Lord. Though they love God above all things, they yet continue to take pleasure in many things which they do not love according to God, but besides Him—things such as slight inordinations in word, gesture, clothing, pastimes and frivolities.

St. François de Sales

There are souls who have made some progress in divine love, and have cut off all the love they had for dangerous things; yet they still have dangerous and superfluous loves, because they love what God wills them to love, but with excess and too tender and passionate a love. . . . The love of our relations, friends and benefactors is itself according to God, but we may love them excessively; as also our vocations, however spiritual they be; and our devotional exercises (which we should yet love very greatly) may be loved inordinately, when we set them above obedience and the more general good, or care for them as an end, when they are only means.

St. François de Sales

The goods of God, which are beyond all measure, can only be contained in an empty and solitary heart.

St. John of the Cross

Suppose a boat is crossing a river and another boat, an empty one, is about to collide with it. Even an irritable man would not lose his temper. But suppose there was someone in the second boat. Then the occupant of the first would shout to him to keep clear. And if he did not hear the first time, nor even when called to three times, bad language would inevitably follow. In the first case there was no anger, in the second there was—because in the first case the boat was empty, in the second it was occupied. And so it is with man. If he could only pass empty through life, who would be able to injure him?

Chuang Tzu

When the heart weeps for what it has lost, the spirit laughs for what it has found.

Anonymous Sufi Aphorism

It is by losing the egocentric life that we save the hitherto latent and undiscovered life which, in the spiritual part of our being, we share with the divine Ground. This new-found life is 'more abundant' than the other, and of a different and higher kind. Its possession is liberation into the eternal, and liberation is beatitude. Necessarily so; for the Brahman, who is one with the Atman, is not only Being and Knowledge, but also Bliss, and, after Love and Peace, the final fruit of the Spirit is Joy. Mortification is painful, but that pain is one of the pre-conditions of blessedness. This fact of spiritual experience is sometimes obscured by the language in which it is described. Thus, when Christ says that the Kingdom of Heaven cannot be entered except by those who are as little children, we are apt to forget (so touching are the images evoked by the simple phrase) that a man cannot become childlike unless he chooses to undertake the most strenuous and searching course of self-denial. In practice the command to become as little children is identical with the command to lose one's life. As Traherne makes clear in the beautiful passage quoted in the section on 'God in the World,' one cannot know created Nature in all its essentially sacred beauty, unless one first unlearns the dirty devices of adult humanity. Seen through the dung-coloured spectacles of self-interest, the universe looks singularly like a dung-heap; and as, through long wearing, the spectacles have grown on to the eyeballs, the process of 'cleansing the doors of perception' is often, at any rate in the earlier stages of the spiritual life, painfully like a surgical operation. Later on, it is true, even self-naughting may be suffused with the joy of the Spirit. On this point the following passage from the fourteenth-century *Scale of Perfection* is illuminating.

Many a man hath the virtues of humility, patience and charity towards his neighbours, only in the reason and will, and hath no

spiritual delight nor love in them; for ofttimes he feeleth grudging, heaviness and bitterness for to do them, but yet nevertheless
he doth them, but 'tis only by stirring of reason for dread of God.
This man hath these virtues in reason and will, but not the love
of them in affection. But when, by the grace of Jesus and by
ghostly and bodily exercise, reason is turned into light and will
into love, then hath he virtues in affection; for he hath so gnawn
on the bitter bark or shell of the nut that at length he hath broken
it and now feeds on the kernel; that is to say, the virtues which
were first heavy for to practise are now turned into a very delight
and savour.

Walter Hilton

As long as I am this or that, or have this or that, I am not all
things and I have not all things. Become pure till you neither
are nor have either this or that; then you are omnipresent and,
being neither this nor that, are all things.

Eckhart

The point so dramatically emphasized by Eckhart in these lines
is one that has often been made by the moralists and psychologists of the spiritual life. It is only when we have renounced
our preoccupation with 'I,' 'me,' 'mine' that we can truly
possess the world in which we live. Everything is ours, provided that we regard nothing as our property. And not only
is everything ours; it is also everybody else's.

> True love in this differs from dross and clay,
> That to divide is not to take away.

There can be no complete communism except in the goods of
the spirit and, to some extent also, of the mind, and only when
such goods are possessed by men and women in a state of non-
attachment and self-denial. Some degree of mortification, it
should be noted, is an indispensable prerequisite for the creation and enjoyment even of merely intellectual and aesthetic
goods. Those who choose the profession of artist, philosopher or man of science, choose, in many cases, a life of

poverty and unrewarded hard work. But these are by no means the only mortifications they have to undertake. When he looks at the world, the artist must deny his ordinary human tendency to think of things in utilitarian, self-regarding terms. Similarly, the critical philosopher must mortify his common sense, while the research worker must steadfastly resist the temptations to over-simplify and think conventionally, and must make himself docile to the leadings of mysterious Fact. And what is true of the creators of aesthetic and intellectual goods is also true of the enjoyers of such goods, when created. That these mortifications are by no means trifling has been shown again and again in the course of history. One thinks, for example, of the intellectually mortified Socrates and the hemlock with which his unmortified compatriots rewarded him. One thinks of the heroic efforts that had to be made by Galileo and his contemporaries to break with the Aristotelian convention of thought, and the no less heroic efforts that have to be made today by any scientist who believes that there is more in the universe than can be discovered by employing the time-hallowed recipes of Descartes. Such mortifications have their reward in a state of consciousness that corresponds, on a lower level, to spiritual beatitude. The artist—and the philosopher and the man of science are also artists—knows the bliss of aesthetic contemplation, discovery and non-attached possession.

The goods of the intellect, the emotions and the imagination are real goods; but they are not the final good, and when we treat them as ends in themselves, we fall into idolatry. Mortification of will, desire and action is not enough; there must also be mortification in the fields of knowing, thinking, feeling and fancying.

Man's intellectual faculties are by the Fall in a much worse state than his animal appetites and want a much greater self-denial. And when own will, own understanding and own imagination have their natural strength indulged and gratified, and are made seemingly rich and honourable with the treasures acquired from

a study of the *Belles Lettres*, they will just as much help poor
fallen man to be like-minded with Christ as the art of cookery,
well and duly studied, will help a professor of the Gospel to the
spirit and practice of Christian abstinence.

William Law

Because it was German and spelt with a *K*, *Kultur* was an
object, during the First World War, of derisive contempt. All
this has now been changed. In Russia, Literature, Art and
Science have become the three persons of a new humanistic
Trinity. Nor is the cult of Culture confined to the Soviet
Union. It is practised by a majority of intellectuals in the
capitalist democracies. Clever, hard-boiled journalists, who
write about everything else with the condescending cynicism
of people who know all about God, Man and the Universe,
and have seen through the whole absurd caboodle, fairly fall
over themselves when it comes to Culture. With an earnest-
ness and enthusiasm that are, in the circumstances, unutterably ludicrous, they invite us to share their positively religious
emotions in the face of High Art, as represented by the latest
murals or civic centres; they insist that so long as Mrs. X goes
on writing her inimitable novels and Mr. Y his more than
Coleridgean criticism, the world, in spite of all appearances to
the contrary, makes sense. The same over-valuation of Culture,
the same belief that Art and Literature are ends in themselves
and can flourish in isolation from a reasonable and realistic
philosophy of life, have even invaded the schools and colleges.
Among 'advanced' educationists there are many people who
seem to think that all will be well so long as adolescents are
permitted to 'express themselves,' and small children are encouraged to be 'creative' in the art class. But, alas, plasticine
and self-expression will not solve the problems of education.
Nor will technology and vocational guidance; nor the classics
and the Hundred Best Books. The following criticisms of
education were made more than two and a half centuries ago;
but they are as relevant today as they were in the seventeenth
century.

He knoweth nothing as he ought to know, who thinks he knoweth anything without seeing its place and the manner how it relateth to God, angels and men, and to all the creatures in earth, heaven and hell, time and eternity.

Thomas Traherne

Nevertheless some things were defective too (at Oxford under the Commonwealth). There was never a tutor that did professly teach Felicity, though that be the mistress of all the other sciences. Nor did any of us study these things but as *aliens*, which we ought to have studied as our own enjoyments. We studied to inform our knowledge, but knew not for what end we studied. And for lack of aiming at a certain end, we erred in the manner.

Thomas Traherne

In Traherne's vocabulary 'felicity' means 'beatitude,' which is identical in practice with liberation, which, in its turn, is the unitive knowledge of God in the heights within and in the fullness without as well as within.

What follows is an account of the intellectual mortifications which must be practised by those whose primary concern is with the knowledge of the Godhead in the interior heights of the soul.

Happy is the man who, by continually effacing all images and through introversion and the lifting up of his mind to God, at last forgets and leaves behind all such hindrances. For by such means only, he operates inwardly, with his naked, pure, simple intellect and affections, about the most pure and simple object, God. Therefore see that thy whole exercise about God within thee may depend wholly and only on that naked intellect, affection and will. For indeed, this exercise cannot be discharged by any bodily organ, or by the external senses, but only by that which constitutes the essence of man—understanding and love. If, therefore, thou desirest a safe stair and short path to arrive at the end of true bliss, then, with an intent mind, earnestly desire and aspire after continual cleanness of heart and purity of mind. Add to this a constant calm and tranquillity of the senses, and a recollecting of the affections of the heart, continually fixing them above. Work to simplify the heart, that being immovable and at peace from any invading vain phantasms, thou mayest always stand fast in the Lord within thee, to that degree as if thy soul had already entered the always present now of eternity—that is, the state of the deity. To mount to God is to enter into oneself. For he who so mounts and enters and goes above and beyond himself, he truly mounts up to God. The mind must then raise itself above itself and say, 'He who above all I need is above all I know.' And so carried into the darkness of the mind, gathering itself into that all-sufficient good, it learns to stay at home and with its whole affection it cleaves and becomes habitually fixed in the supreme good within. Thus continue, until thou becomest immutable and dost arrive at that true life which is God Himself, perpetually, without any vicissitude of space or time, reposing in that inward quiet and secret mansion of the deity.

Albertus Magnus (?)

Some men love knowledge and discernment as the best and most excellent of all things. Behold, then knowledge and discernment come to be loved more than that which is discerned; for the false natural light loveth its knowledge and powers, which are itself, more than what is known. And were it possible that this false natural light should understand the simple Truth, as it is in God and in truth, it still would not lose its own property, that is, it could not depart from itself and its own things.

Theologia Germanica

The relationship between moral action and spiritual knowledge is circular, as it were, and reciprocal. Selfless behaviour makes possible an accession of knowledge, and the accession of knowledge makes possible the performance of further and more genuinely selfless actions, which in their turn enhance the agent's capacity for knowing. And so on, if all goes well and there is perfect docility and obedience, indefinitely. The process is summed up in a few lines of the Maitrayana Upanishad.

I

A man undertakes right action (which includes, of course, right recollectedness and right meditation), and this enables him to catch a glimpse of the Self that underlies his separate individuality. 'Having seen his own self as the Self, he becomes selfless (and therefore acts selflessly) and in virtue of selflessness he is to be conceived as unconditioned. This is the highest mystery, betokening emancipation; through selflessness he has no part in pleasure or pain (in other words, he enters a state of non-attachment or holy indifference), but achieves absoluteness' (or as Albertus Magnus phrases it, 'becomes immutable and arrives at that true life which is God Himself').

When mortification is perfect, its most characteristic fruit is simplicity.

> A simple heart will love all that is most precious on earth, husband or wife, parent or child, brother or friend, without marring its singleness; external things will have no attraction save inasmuch as they lead souls to Him; all exaggeration or unreality, affectation and falsehood must pass away from such a one, as the dews dry up before the sunshine. The single motive is to please God, and hence arises total indifference as to what others say and think, so that words and actions are perfectly simple and natural, as in his sight only. Such Christian simplicity is the very perfection of interior life—God, his will and pleasure, its sole object.
>
> *N. Grou*

And here is a more extended account of the matter by one of the greatest masters of psychological analysis.

> In the world, when people call anyone simple, they generally mean a foolish, ignorant, credulous person. But real simplicity, so far from being foolish, is almost sublime. All good men like and admire it, are conscious of sinning against it, observe it in others and know what it involves; and yet they could not precisely define it. I should say that simplicity is an uprightness of soul which prevents self-consciousness. It is not the same as sincerity, which is a much humbler virtue. Many people are sin-

cere who are not simple. They say nothing but what they believe to be true, and do not aim at appearing anything but what they are. But they are for ever thinking about themselves, weighing their every word and thought, and dwelling upon themselves in apprehension of having done too much or too little. These people are sincere but they are not simple. They are not at their ease with others, nor others with them. There is nothing easy, frank, unrestrained or natural about them. One feels that one would like less admirable people better, who were not so stiff.

To be absorbed in the world around and never turn a thought within, as is the blind condition of some who are carried away by what is pleasant and tangible, is one extreme as opposed to simplicity. And to be self-absorbed in all matters, whether it be duty to God or man, is the other extreme, which makes a person wise in his own conceit—reserved, self-conscious, uneasy at the least thing which disturbs his inward self-complacency. Such false wisdom, in spite of its solemnity, is hardly less vain and foolish than the folly of those who plunge headlong into worldly pleasures. The one is intoxicated by his outward surroundings, the other by what he believes himself to be doing inwardly; but both are in a state of intoxication, and the last is a worse state than the first, because it seems to be wise, though it is not really, and so people do not try to be cured. Real simplicity lies in a *juste milieu* equally free from thoughtlessness and affectation, in which the soul is not overwhelmed by externals, so as to be unable to reflect, nor yet given up to the endless refinements, which self-consciousness induces. That soul which looks where it is going without losing time arguing over every step, or looking back perpetually, possesses true simplicity. Such simplicity is indeed a great treasure. How shall we attain to it? I would give all I possess for it; it is the costly pearl of Holy Scripture.

The first step, then, is for the soul to put away outward things and look within so as to know its own real interest; so far all is right and natural; thus much is only a wise self-love, which seeks to avoid the intoxication of the world.

In the next step the soul must add the contemplation of God, whom it fears, to that of self. This is a faint approach to the real wisdom, but the soul is still greatly self-absorbed: it is not satisfied with fearing God; it wants to be certain that it does fear Him and fears lest it fear Him not, going round in a perpetual circle of self-consciousness. All this restless dwelling on self is very far from the peace and freedom of real love; but that is yet in the distance; the soul must needs go through a season of trial, and were it suddenly plunged into a state of rest, it would not know how to use it.

The third step is that, ceasing from a restless self-contemplation, the soul begins to dwell upon God instead, and by degrees forgets itself in Him. It becomes full of Him and ceases to feed upon self. Such a soul is not blinded to its own faults or indifferent to its own errors; it is more conscious of them than ever, and increased light shows them in plainer form, but this self-knowledge comes from God, and therefore it is not restless or uneasy.

Fénelon

How admirably acute and subtle this is! One of the most extraordinary, because most gratuitous, pieces of twentieth-century vanity is the assumption that nobody knew anything about psychology before the days of Freud. But the real truth is that most modern psychologists understand human beings less well than did the ablest of their predecessors. Fénelon and La Rochefoucauld knew all about the surface rationalization of deep, discreditable motives in the subconscious, and were fully aware that sexuality and the will to power were, all too often, the effective forces at work under the polite mask of the *persona*. Machiavelli had drawn Pareto's distinction between 'residues' and 'derivations'—between the real, self-interested motives for political action and the fancy theories, principles and ideals in terms of which such action is explained and justified to the credulous public. Like Buddha's and St. Augustine's, Pascal's view of human virtue and rationality could not have been more realistically low. But all these men, even La Rochefoucauld, even Machiavelli, were aware of certain facts which twentieth-century psychologists have chosen to ignore—the fact that human nature is tripartite, consisting of a spirit as well as of a mind and body; the fact that we live on the border-line between two worlds, the temporal and the eternal, the physical-vital-human and the divine; the fact that, though nothing in himself, man is 'a nothing surrounded by God, indigent of God, capable of God and filled with God, if he so desires.'

The Christian simplicity, of which Grou and Fénelon write, is the same thing as the virtue so much admired by Lao Tzu and his successors. According to these Chinese sages, personal sins and social maladjustments are all due to the fact that men have separated themselves from their divine source and live according to their own will and notions, not according to Tao —which is the Great Way, the Logos, the Nature of Things, as it manifests itself on every plane from the physical, up through the animal and the mental, to the spiritual. Enlightenment comes when we give up self-will and make ourselves docile to the workings of Tao in the world around us and in our own bodies, minds and spirits. Sometimes the Taoist philosophers write as though they believed in Rousseau's Noble Savage, and (being Chinese and therefore much more concerned with the concrete and the practical than with the merely speculative) they are fond of prescribing methods by which rulers may reduce the complexity of civilization and so preserve their subjects from the corrupting influences of man-made and therefore Tao-eclipsing conventions of thought, feeling and action. But the rulers who are to perform this task for the masses must themselves be sages; and to become a sage, one must get rid of all the rigidities of unregenerate adulthood and become again as a little child. For only that which is soft and docile is truly alive; that which conquers and outlives everything is that which adapts itself to everything, that which always seeks the lowest place—not the hard rock, but the water that wears away the everlasting hills. The simplicity and spontaneity of the perfect sage are the fruits of mortification— mortification of the will and, by recollectedness and medita-

tion, of the mind.   Only the most highly disciplined artist can
recapture, on a higher level, the spontaneity of the child with
its first paint-box.   Nothing is more difficult than to be
simple.

'May I ask,' said Yen Hui, 'in what consists the fasting of the
heart?'
'Cultivate unity,' replied Confucius. 'You do your hearing,
not with your ears, but with your mind; not with your mind, but
with your very soul.   But let the hearing stop with the ears.
Let the working of the mind stop with itself.   Then the soul will
be a negative existence, passively responsive to externals.   In such
a negative existence, only Tao can abide.   And that negative
state is the fasting of the heart.'
'Then,' said Yen Hui, 'the reason I could not get the use of
this method is my own individuality.   If I could get the use of it,
my individuality would have gone.   Is this what you mean by
the negative state?'
'Exactly so,' replied the Master.   'Let me tell you.   If you can
enter the domain of this prince (a bad ruler whom Yen Hui was
ambitious to reform) without offending his *amour propre*, cheerful if he hears you, passive if he does not; without science, without drugs, simply living there in a state of complete indifference
—you will be near success. . . . Look at that window.   Through
it an empty room becomes bright with scenery; but the landscape stops outside.   In this sense you may use your ears and
eyes to communicate within, but shut out all wisdom (in the
sense of conventional, copybook maxims) from your mind.   This
is the method for regenerating all creation.'

Chuang Tzu

Mortification may be regarded, in this context, as the process of
study, by which we learn at last to have unstudied reactions to
events—reactions in harmony with Tao, Suchness, the Will of
God.   Those who have made themselves docile to the divine
Nature of Things, those who respond to circumstances, not
with craving and aversion, but with the love that permits them

to do spontaneously what they like; those who can truthfully say, Not I, but God in me—such men and women are compared by the exponents of the Perennial Philosophy to children, to fools and simpletons, even sometimes, as in the following passage, to drunkards.

A drunken man who falls out of a cart, though he may suffer, does not die. His bones are the same as other people's; but he meets his accident in a different way. His spirit is in a condition of security. He is not conscious of riding in the cart; neither is he conscious of falling out of it. Ideas of life, death, fear and the like cannot penetrate his breast; and so he does not suffer from contact with objective existence. If such security is to be got from wine, how much more is it to be got from God?

Chuang Tzu

It is by long obedience and hard work that the artist comes to unforced spontaneity and consummate mastery. Knowing that he can never create anything on his own account, out of the top layers, so to speak, of his personal consciousness, he submits obediently to the workings of 'inspiration'; and knowing that the medium in which he works has its own self-nature, which must not be ignored or violently overriden, he makes himself its patient servant and, in this way, achieves perfect freedom of expression. But life is also an art, and the man who would become a consummate artist in living must follow, on all the levels of his being, the same procedure as that by which the painter or the sculptor or any other craftsman comes to his own more limited perfection.

Prince Hui's cook was cutting up a bullock. Every blow of his knife, every heave of his shoulders, every tread of his foot, every *whshh* of rent flesh, every *chhk* of the chopper, was in perfect harmony—rhythmical like the Dance of the Mulberry Grove, simultaneous like the chords of the Ching Shou.

'Well done!' cried the Prince. ' Yours is skill indeed.'

'Sire,' replied the cook, 'I have always devoted myself to Tao. It is better than skill. When I first began to cut up bullocks, I saw before me simply whole bullocks. After three years' practice I saw no more whole animals. And now I work with my mind and not with my eye. When my senses bid me stop, but my mind urges me on, I fall back upon eternal principles. I follow such openings or cavities as there may be, according to the natural constitution of the animal. I do not attempt to cut through joints, still less through large bones.

'A good cook changes his chopper once a year—because he cuts. An ordinary cook, once a month—because he hacks. But I have had this chopper nineteen years, and though I have cut up many thousands of bullocks, its edge is as if fresh from the whetstone. For at the joints there are always interstices, and the edge of a chopper being without thickness, it remains only to insert that which is without thickness into such an interstice. By these means the interstice will be enlarged, and the blade will find plenty of room. It is thus that I have kept my chopper for nineteen years, as though fresh from the whetstone.

'Nevertheless, when I come upon a hard part, where the blade meets with a difficulty, I am all caution. I fix my eyes on it. I stay my hand, and gently apply the blade, until with a *hwah* the part yields like earth crumbling to the ground. Then I withdraw the blade and stand up and look around; and at last I wipe my chopper and put it carefully away.'

'Bravo!' cried the Prince. 'From the words of this cook I have learnt how to take care of my life.'

Chuang Tzu

In the first seven branches of his Eightfold Path the Buddha describes the conditions that must be fulfilled by anyone who desires to come to that right contemplation which is the eighth and final branch. The fulfilment of these conditions entails the undertaking of a course of the most searching and comprehensive mortification—mortification of intellect and will, craving and emotion, thought, speech, action and, finally, means of livelihood. Certain professions are more or less completely incompatible with the achievement of man's final end; and there are certain ways of making a living which do so much physical and, above all, so much moral, intellectual and spiritual harm that, even if they could be practised in a non-attached spirit (which is generally impossible), they would still have to be eschewed by anyone dedicated to the task of liberating, not only himself, but others. The exponents of the Perennial Philosophy are not content to avoid and forbid the practice of criminal professions, such as brothel-keeping, forgery, racketeering and the like; they also avoid themselves, and warn others against, a number of ways of livelihood commonly regarded as legitimate. Thus, in many Buddhist societies, the manufacture of arms, the concoction of intoxicating liquors and the wholesale purveying of butcher's meat were not, as in contemporary Christendom, rewarded by wealth, peerages and political influence; they were deplored as businesses which, it was thought, made it particularly difficult for their practitioners and for other members of the communities in which they were practised to achieve enlightenment and liberation. Similarly, in mediaeval Europe, Christians were forbidden to make a living by the taking of interest on money or by cornering the market. As Tawney and others have shown, it was only after the Reformation that coupon-clipping, usury and gambling in stocks and commodities became respectable and received ecclesiastical approval.

For the Quakers, soldiering was and is a form of wrong livelihood—war being, in their eyes, anti-Christian, not so much because it causes suffering as because it propagates hatred, puts a premium on fraud and cruelty, infects whole societies with anger, fear, pride and uncharitableness. Such passions eclipse the Inner Light, and therefore the wars by which they are aroused and intensified must be regarded, whatever their immediate political outcome, as crusades to make the world safe for spiritual darkness.

It has been found, as a matter of experience, that it is dangerous to lay down detailed and inflexible rules for right livelihood—dangerous, because most people see no reason for being righteous overmuch and consequently respond to the imposition of too rigid a code by hypocrisy or open rebellion. In the Christian tradition, for example, a distinction is made between the precepts, which are binding on all and sundry, and the counsels of perfection, binding only upon those who feel drawn towards a total renunciation of 'the world.' The precepts include the ordinary moral code and the commandment to love God with all one's heart, strength and mind, and one's neighbour as oneself. Some of those who make a serious effort to obey this last and greatest commandment find that they cannot do so whole-heartedly unless they follow the counsels and sever all connections with the world. Nevertheless it is possible for men and women to achieve that 'perfection,' which is deliverance into the unitive knowledge of God, without abandoning the married state and without selling all they have and giving the price to the poor. Effective poverty (possessing no money) is by no means always affective poverty (being indifferent to money). One man may be poor, but desperately concerned with what money can buy, full of cravings, envy and bitter self-pity. Another may have money, but no attachment to money or the things, powers and privileges that money can buy. 'Evangelical poverty' is a combination of effective with affective poverty; but a genuine poverty of spirit is possible even in those who are not effectively poor. It will be seen, then, that the problems of right livelihood, in so far as they lie outside the jurisdiction of the common moral code, are strictly personal. The way in which any individual problem presents itself and the nature of the appropriate solution depend upon the degree of knowledge, moral sensibility and spiritual insight achieved by the individual concerned. For this reason no universally applicable rules can be formulated except in the most general terms. 'Here are my three treasures,' says Lao Tzu. 'Guard and keep them! The first is pity, the second frugality, the third refusal to be foremost of all things under heaven.' And when Jesus is asked by a stranger to settle a dispute between himself and his brother over an inheritance, he refuses (since he does not know the circumstances) to be a judge in the case and merely utters a general warning against covetousness.

> Ga-San instructed his adherents one day: 'Those who speak against killing, and who desire to spare the lives of all conscious beings, are right. It is good to protect even animals and insects. But what about those persons who kill time, what about those who destroy wealth, and those who murder the economy of their society? We should not overlook them. Again, what of the one who preaches without enlightenment? He is killing Buddhism.'
>
> *From 'One Hundred and One Zen Stories'*

Once the noble Ibrahim, as he sat on his throne,
Heard a clamour and noise of cries on the roof,
Also heavy footsteps on the roof of his palace.
He said to himself, 'Whose heavy feet are these?'
He shouted from the window, 'Who goes there?'
The guards, filled with confusion, bowed their heads, saying,
'It is we, going the rounds in search.'
He said, 'What seek ye?' They said, 'Our camels.'
He said, 'Who ever searched for camels on a housetop?'
They said, 'We follow thy example,
Who seekest union with God, while sitting on a throne.'

Jalal-uddin Rumi

Of all social, moral and spiritual problems that of power is the most chronically urgent and the most difficult of solution. Craving for power is not a vice of the body, consequently knows none of the limitations imposed by a tired or satiated physiology upon gluttony, intemperance and lust. Growing with every successive satisfaction, the appetite for power can manifest itself indefinitely, without interruption by bodily fatigue or sickness. Moreover, the nature of society is such that the higher a man climbs in the political, economic or religious hierarchy, the greater are his opportunities and resources for exercising power. But climbing the hierarchical ladder is ordinarily a slow process, and the ambitious rarely reach the top till they are well advanced in life. The older he grows, the more chances does the power lover have for indulging his besetting sin, the more continuously is he subjected to temptations and the more glamorous do those temptations become. In this respect his situation is profoundly different from that of the debauchee. The latter may never voluntarily leave his vices, but at least, as he advances in years, he finds his vices leaving him; the former neither leaves his vices nor is left by them. Instead of bringing to the power lover a merciful respite from his addictions, old age is apt to intensify them by making it easier for him to satisfy his cravings on a larger scale and in a more spectacular way. That is why, in Acton's words, 'all great men are bad.' Can we therefore be surprised if political action, undertaken, in all too many cases, not for the public good, but solely or at least primarily to gratify the power lusts of bad men, should prove so often either self-stultifying or downright disastrous?

'*L'état c'est moi*,' says the tyrant; and this is true, of course, not only of the autocrat at the apex of the pyramid, but of all the members of the ruling minority through whom he governs and who are, in fact, the real rulers of the nation. Moreover, so long as the policy which gratifies the power lusts of the ruling class is successful, and so long as the price of success is not too high, even the masses of the ruled will feel that the state is themselves—a vast and splendid projection of the individual's intrinsically insignificant ego. The little man can satisfy his lust for power vicariously through the activities of the imperialistic state, just as the big man does; the difference between them is one of degree, not of kind.

No infallible method for controlling the political manifestations of the lust for power has ever been devised. Since power is of its very essence indefinitely expansive, it cannot be checked except by colliding with another power. Hence, any society that values liberty, in the sense of government by law rather than by class interest or personal decree, must see to it that the power of its rulers is divided. National unity means national servitude to a single man and his supporting oligarchy. Organized and balanced disunity is the necessary condition of liberty. His Majesty's Loyal Opposition is the loyalest, because the most genuinely useful section of any liberty-loving community. Furthermore, since the appetite for power is purely mental and therefore insatiable and impervious to disease or old age, no community that values liberty can afford to give its rulers long tenures of office. The Carthusian Order, which was 'never reformed because never deformed,' owed its long immunity from corruption to the fact that its abbots were elected for periods of only a single year. In ancient Rome the amount of liberty under law was in inverse ratio to the length of the magistrates' terms of office. These rules for controlling the lust for power are very easy to formulate, but very difficult, as history shows, to enforce in practice. They are particularly difficult to enforce at a period like the present, when time-hallowed political machinery is being rendered obsolete by rapid technological change and when the salutary principle of organized and balanced disunity requires to be embodied in new and more appropriate institutions.

Acton, the learned Catholic historian, was of opinion that all great men are bad; Rumi, the Persian poet and mystic, thought that to seek for union with God while occupying a throne was an undertaking hardly less senseless than looking for camels among the chimney-pots. A slightly more optimistic note is sounded by St. François de Sales, whose views on the matter were recorded by his Boswellizing disciple, the young Bishop of Belley.

'*Mon Père*,' I said one day, 'how is it possible for those who are themselves high in office to practise the virtue of obedience?'

François de Sales replied, 'They have greater and more excellent ways of doing so than their inferiors.'

As I did not understand this reply, he went on to say, 'Those who are bound by obedience are usually subject to one superior only. . . . But those who are themselves superiors have a wider field for obedience, even while they command; for if they bear in mind that it is God who has placed them over other men, and gives them the rule they have, they will exercise it out of obedience to God, and thus, even while commanding, they will obey. Moreover, there is no position so high but that it is subject to a spiritual superior in what concerns the conscience and the soul. But there is a yet higher point of obedience to which all superiors may aspire, even that to which St. Paul alludes, when he says, "Though I be free from all men, yet have I made myself servant unto all." It is by such universal obedience to everyone that we become "all things to all men"; and serving everyone for Our Lord's sake, we esteem all to be our superiors.'

In accordance with this rule, I have often observed how François de Sales treated everyone, even the most insignificant persons who approached him, as though he were the inferior, never repulsing anyone, never refusing to enter into conversation, to speak or to listen, never betraying the slightest sign of weariness, impatience and annoyance, however importunate or ill-timed the interruption. To those who asked him why he thus wasted his time his constant reply was, 'It is God's will; it is what He requires of me; what more need I ask? While I am doing this, I am not required to do anything else. God's Holy Will is the centre from which all we do must radiate; all else is mere weariness and excitement.'

Jean Pierre Camus

We see, then, that a 'great man' can be good—good enough even to aspire to unitive knowledge of the divine Ground— provided that, while exercising power, he fulfils two conditions. First, he must deny himself all the personal advantages of power and must practise the patience and recollectedness without which there cannot be love either of man or God. And, second, he must realize that the accident of possessing temporal power does not give him spiritual authority, which belongs only to those seers, living or dead, who have achieved a direct insight into the Nature of Things. A society, in which the boss is mad enough to believe himself a prophet, is a society doomed to destruction. A viable society is one in which those who have qualified themselves to see indicate the goals to be aimed at, while those whose business it is to rule respect the authority and listen to the advice of the seers. In theory, at least, all this was well understood in India and, until the Reformation, in Europe, where 'no position was so high but that it was subject to a spiritual superior in what concerned the conscience and the soul.' Unfortunately the churches tried to make the best of both worlds—to combine spiritual authority with temporal power, wielded either directly or at one remove, from behind the throne. But spiritual authority can be exercised only by those who are perfectly disinterested and whose motives are therefore above suspicion. An ecclesiastical organization may call itself the Mystical Body of Christ; but if its prelates are slave-holders and the rulers of states, as they were in the past, or if the corporation is a large-scale capitalist, as is the case today, no titles, however honorific, can conceal the fact that, when it passes judgment, it does so as an interested party with some political or economic axe to grind. True, in matters which do not directly concern the temporal powers of the corporation, individual churchmen can be, and have actually proved themselves, perfectly disinterested—consequently can possess, and have possessed, genuine spiritual authority. St. Philip Neri's is a case in point. Possessing absolutely no temporal power, he yet exercised a prodigious influence over sixteenth-century Europe. But for that influence, it may be doubted whether the efforts of the Council of Trent to reform the Roman church from within would have met with much success.

In actual practice how many great men have ever fulfilled, or are ever likely to fulfil, the conditions which alone render power innocuous to the ruler as well as to the ruled? Obviously, very few. Except by saints, the problem of power is finally insoluble. But since genuine self-government is possible only in very small groups, societies on a national or supernational scale will always be ruled by oligarchical minorities, whose members come to power because they have a lust for power. This means that the problem of power will always arise and, since it cannot be solved except by people like François de Sales, will always make trouble.   And this, in its turn, means that we cannot expect the large-scale societies of the future to be much better than were the societies of the past during the brief periods when they were at their best.

Chapter 7

TRUTH

Why dost thou prate of God? Whatever thou sayest of Him is untrue.

Eckhart

IN religious literature the word 'truth' is used indiscriminately in at least three distinct and very different senses. Thus, it is sometimes treated as a synonym for 'fact,' as when it is affirmed that God is Truth—meaning that He is the primordial Reality. But this is clearly not the meaning of the word in such a phrase as 'worshipping God in spirit and in truth.' Here, it is obvious, 'truth' signifies direct apprehension of spiritual Fact, as opposed to second-hand knowledge *about* Reality, formulated in sentences and accepted on authority or because an argument from previously granted postulates was logically convincing. And finally there is the more ordinary meaning of the word, as in such a sentence as, 'This statement is the truth,' where we mean to assert that the verbal symbols of which the statement is composed correspond to the facts to which it refers. When Eckhart writes that 'whatever thou sayest of God is untrue,' he is not affirming that all theological statements are false. In so far as there can be any correspondence between human symbols and divine Fact, some theological statements are as true as it is possible for us to make them. Himself a theologian, Eckhart would certainly have admitted this. But besides being a theologian, Eckhart was a mystic. And being a mystic, he understood very vividly what the modern semanticist is so busily (and, also, so unsuccessfully) trying to drum into contemporary minds—namely, that words are not the same as things and that a knowledge of words about facts is in no sense equivalent to a direct and immediate apprehension of the facts themselves. What Eck-

K   145

hart actually asserts is this: whatever one may say about God can never in any circumstances be the 'truth' in the first two meanings of that much abused and ambiguous word. By implication St. Thomas Aquinas was saying exactly the same thing when, after his experience of infused contemplation, he refused to go on with his theological work, declaring that everything he had written up to that time was as mere straw compared with the immediate knowledge, which had been vouchsafed to him. Two hundred years earlier, in Bagdad, the great Mohammedan theologian, Al-Ghazzali, had similarly turned from the consideration of truths about God to the contemplation and direct apprehension of Truth-the-Fact, from the purely intellectual discipline of the philosophers to the moral and spiritual discipline of the Sufis.

The moral of all this is obvious. Whenever we hear or read about 'truth,' we should always pause long enough to ask ourselves in which of the three senses listed above the word is, at the moment, being used. By taking this simple precaution (and to take it is a genuinely virtuous act of intellectual honesty) we shall save ourselves a great deal of disturbing and quite unnecessary mental confusion.

Wishing to entice the blind,
The Buddha playfully let words escape from his golden mouth;
Heaven and earth are filled, ever since, with entangling briars.

Dai-o Kokushi

There is nothing true anywhere,
The True is nowhere to be found.
If you say you see the True,
This seeing is not the true one.
When the True is left to itself,
There is nothing false in it, for it is Mind itself.
When Mind in itself is not liberated from the false,
There is nothing true; nowhere is the True to be found.

Hui Neng

The truth indeed has never been preached by the Buddha, seeing
that one has to realize it within oneself.

Sutralamkara

The further one travels, the less one knows.

Lao Tẓu

'Listen to this!' shouted Monkey. 'After all the trouble we had
getting here from China, and after you specially ordered that we
were to be given the scriptures, Ananda and Kasyapa made a
fraudulent delivery of goods. They gave us blank copies to take
away; I ask you, what is the good of that to us?'

'You needn't shout,' said the Buddha, smiling. '... As a matter
of fact, it is such blank scrolls as these that are the true scriptures.
But I quite see that the people of China are too foolish and ignorant to believe this, so there is nothing for it but to give them
copies with some writing on.'

Wu Ch'êng-ên

The philosophers indeed are clever enough, but wanting in
    wisdom;
As to the others, they are either ignorant or puerile!
They take an empty fist as containing something real and the
    pointing finger as the object pointed at.
Because the finger is adhered to as though it were the Moon, all
    their efforts are lost.

Yoka Daishi

What is known as the teaching of the Buddha is not the teaching
of the Buddha.

Diamond Sutra

'What is the ultimate teaching of Buddhism?'
'You won't understand it until you have it.'

Shih-t'ou

The subject matter of the Perennial Philosophy is the nature
of eternal, spiritual Reality; but the language in which it must
be formulated was developed for the purpose of dealing with

phenomena in time. That is why, in all these formulations, we find an element of paradox. The nature of Truth-the-Fact cannot be described by means of verbal symbols that do not adequately correspond to it. At best it can be hinted at in terms of *non sequiturs* and contradictions.

To these unavoidable paradoxes some spiritual writers have chosen to add deliberate and calculated enormities of language —hard sayings, exaggerations, ironic or humorous extravagances, designed to startle and shock the reader out of that self-satisfied complacency which is the original sin of the intellect. Of this second kind of paradox the masters of Taoism and Zen Buddhism were particularly fond. The latter, indeed, made use of paralogisms and even of nonsense as a device for 'taking the kingdom of heaven by violence.' Aspirants to the life of perfection were encouraged to practise discursive meditation on some completely non-logical formula. The result was a kind of *reductio ad absurdum* of the whole self-centred and world-centred discursive process, a sudden breaking through from 'reason' (in the language of scholastic philosophy) to intuitive 'intellect,' capable of a genuine insight into the divine Ground of all being. This method strikes us as odd and eccentric : but the fact remains that it worked to the extent of producing in many persons the final *metanoia*, or transformation of consciousness and character.

Zen's use of almost comic extravagance to emphasize the philosophic truths it regarded as most important is well illustrated in the first of the extracts cited above. We are not intended seriously to imagine that an Avatar preaches in order to play a practical joke on the human race. But meanwhile what the author has succeeded in doing is to startle us out of our habitual complacency about the home-made verbal universe in which we normally do most of our living. Words are not facts, and still less are they the primordial Fact. If we take them too seriously, we shall lose our way in a forest of entangling briars. But if, on the contrary, we don't take them seriously enough, we shall still remain unaware that there is a way to lose or a goal to be reached. If the Enlightened did not preach, there would be no deliverance for anyone. But because human minds and human languages are what they are, this necessary and indispensable preaching is beset with dangers. The history of all the religions is similar in one important respect; some of their adherents are enlightened and delivered, because they have chosen to react appropriately to the words which the founders have let fall; others achieve a partial salvation by reacting with partial appropriateness; yet others harm themselves and their fellows by reacting with a total inappropriateness—either ignoring the words altogether or, more often, taking them too seriously and treating them as though they were identical with the Fact to which they refer.

That words are at once indispensable and, in many cases, fatal has been recognized by all the exponents of the Perennial Philosophy. Thus, Jesus spoke of himself as bringing into the world something even worse than briars—a sword. St. Paul distinguished between the letter that kills and the spirit that gives life. And throughout the centuries that followed, the masters of Christian spirituality have found it necessary to harp again and again upon a theme which has never been outdated because *homo loquax*, the talking animal, is still as naïvely delighted by his chief accomplishment, still as helplessly the victim of his own words, as he was when the Tower of Babel was being built. Recent years have seen the publication of numerous works on semantics and of an ocean of nationalistic, racialistic and militaristic propaganda. Never have so many capable writers warned mankind against the dangers of wrong speech—and never have words been used more recklessly by politicians or taken more seriously by the public. The fact is surely proof enough that, under changing forms, the old problems remain what they always were—urgent, unsolved and, to all appearances, insoluble.

All that the imagination can imagine and the reason conceive and understand in this life is not, and cannot be, a proximate means of union with God.

St. John of the Cross

Jejune and barren speculations may unfold the plicatures of Truth's garment, but they cannot discover her lovely face.

John Smith, the Platonist

In all faces is shown the Face of faces, veiled and in a riddle. Howbeit, unveiled it is not seen, until, above all faces, a man enter into a certain secret and mystic silence, where there is no knowing or concept of a face. This mist, cloud, darkness or ignorance, into which he that seeketh thy Face entereth, when he goeth beyond all knowledge or concept, is the state below which thy Face cannot be found, except veiled; but that very darkness revealeth thy Face to be there beyond all veils. Hence I observe how needful it is for me to enter into the darkness and to admit the coincidence of opposites, beyond all the grasp of reason, and there to seek the Truth, where impossibility meeteth us.

Nicholas of Cusa

As the Godhead is nameless, and all naming is alien to Him, so also the soul is nameless; for it is here the same as God.

Eckhart

God being, as He is, inaccessible, do not rest in the consideration of objects perceptible to the senses and comprehended by the understanding. This is to be content with what is less than God; so doing, you will destroy the energy of the soul, which is necessary for walking with Him.

St. John of the Cross

To find or know God in reality by any outward proofs, or by anything but by God Himself made manifest and self-evident in you, will never be your case either here or hereafter. For neither God, nor heaven, nor hell, nor the devil, nor the flesh, can be any otherwise knowable in you or by you but by their own existence and manifestation in you. And all pretended knowledge of any of these things, beyond and without this self-evident sensibility of their birth within you, is only such knowledge of them as the blind man hath of the light that hath never entered into him.

William Law

What follows is a summary by an eminent scholar of the
Indian doctrines concerning *jnana*, the liberating knowledge of
Brahman or the divine Ground.

Jnana is eternal, is general, is necessary and is not a personal
knowledge of this man or that man. It is there, as knowledge
in the *Atman* itself, and lies there hidden under all *avidya* (ignorance)—irremovable, though it may be obscured, unprovable, because self-evident, needing no proof, because itself giving to all
proof the ground of possibility. These sentences come near to
Eckhart's 'knowledge' and to the teaching of Augustine on the
Eternal Truth in the soul which, itself immediately certain, is the
ground of all certainty and is a possession, not of A or B, but of
'the soul.'

Rudolf Otto

The science of aesthetics is not the same as, nor even a proximate means to, the practice and appreciation of the arts. How
can one learn to have an eye for pictures, or to become a good
painter? Certainly not by reading Benedetto Croce. One
learns to paint by painting, and one learns to appreciate pictures
by going to picture galleries and looking at them.

But this is not to say that Croce and his fellows have wasted
their time. We should be grateful to them for their labours in
building up a system of thought, by means of which the immediately apprehended significance and value of art can be assessed
in the light of general knowledge, related to other facts of
experience and, in this way and to this extent, 'explained.'

What is true of aesthetics is also true of theology. Theological speculation is valuable in so far as it enables those who
have had immediate experience of various aspects of God to
form intelligible ideas about the nature of the divine Ground,
and of their own experience of the Ground in relation to other
experiences. And when a coherent system of theology has
been worked out, it is useful in so far as it convinces those who
study it that there is nothing inherently self-contradictory about
the postulate of the divine Ground and that, for those who are

ready to fulfil certain conditions, the postulate may become a
realized Fact.   In no circumstances, however, can the study of
theology or the mind's assent to theological propositions take
the place of what Law calls 'the birth of God within.'   For
theory is not practice, and words are not the things for which
they stand.

> Theology as we know it has been formed by the great mystics,
> especially St. Augustine and St. Thomas.   Plenty of other great
> theologians—especially St. Gregory and St. Bernard, even down
> to Suarez—would not have had such insight without mystic
> super-knowledge.
>
> *Abbot John Chapman*

Against this we must set Dr. Tennant's view—namely, that
religious experience is something real and unique, but does not
add anything to the experiencer's knowledge of ultimate Reality and must always be interpreted in terms of an idea of God
derived from other sources.   A study of the facts would suggest
that both these opinions are to some degree correct.   The facts
of mystical insight (together with the facts of what is taken to
be historic revelation) are rationalized in terms of general
knowledge and become the basis of a theology.   And, reciprocally, an existing theology in terms of general knowledge exercises a profound influence upon those who have undertaken
the spiritual life, causing them, if it is low, to be content with a
low form of experience, if it is high, to reject as inadequate the
experience of any form of reality having characteristics incompatible with those of the God described in the books.   Thus
mystics make theology, and theology makes mystics.
    A person who gives assent to untrue dogma, or who pays all
his attention and allegiance to one true dogma in a comprehensive system, while neglecting the others (as many Christians concentrate exclusively on the humanity of the Second
Person of the Trinity and ignore the Father and the Holy
Ghost), runs the risk of limiting in advance his direct apprehension of Reality.   In religion as in natural science, experience

is determined only by experience. It is fatal to prejudge it, to compel it to fit the mould imposed by a theory which either does not correspond to the facts at all, or corresponds to only some of the facts. 'Do not strive to seek after the true,' writes a Zen master, 'only cease to cherish opinions.' There is only one way to cure the results of belief in a false or incomplete theology and it is the same as the only known way of passing from belief in even the truest theology to knowledge or primordial Fact—selflessness, docility, openness to the datum of Eternity. Opinions are things which we make and can therefore understand, formulate and argue about. But 'to rest in the consideration of objects perceptible to the sense or comprehended by the understanding is to be content,' in the words of St. John of the Cross, 'with what is less than God.' Unitive knowledge of God is possible only to those who 'have ceased to cherish opinions'—even opinions that are as true as it is possible for verbalized abstractions to be.

> Up then, noble soul! Put on thy jumping shoes which are intellect and love, and overleap the worship of thy mental powers, overleap thine understanding and spring into the heart of God, into his hiddenness where thou art hidden from all creatures.
>
> *Eckhart*

> With the lamp of word and discrimination one must go beyond word and discrimination and enter upon the path of realization.
>
> *Lankavatara Sutra*

The word 'intellect' is used by Eckhart in the scholastic sense of immediate intuition. 'Intellect and reason,' says Aquinas, 'are not two powers, but distinct as the perfect from the imperfect. . . . The intellect means, an intimate penetration of truth; the reason, enquiry and discourse.' It is by following, and then abandoning, the rational and emotional path of 'word and discrimination' that one is enabled to enter upon the

intellectual or intuitive 'path of realization.' And yet, in spite
of the warnings pronounced by those who, through selflessness, have passed from letter to spirit and from theory to
immediate knowledge, the organized Christian churches have
persisted in the fatal habit of mistaking means for ends. The
verbal statements of theology's more or less adequate ration-
alizations of experience have been taken too seriously and
treated with the reverence that is due only to the Fact they are
intended to describe. It has been fancied that souls are saved
if assent is given to what is locally regarded as the correct
formula, lost if it is withheld. The two words, *filioque*, may
not have been the sole cause of the schism between the Eastern
and Western churches; but they were unquestionably the pretext and *casus belli*.

The over-valuation of words and formulae may be regarded
as a special case of that over-valuation of the things of time,
which is so fatally characteristic of historic Christianity. To
know Truth-as-Fact and to know it unitively, 'in spirit and in
truth-as-immediate-apprehension'—this is deliverance, in this
'standeth our eternal life.' To be familiar with the verbalized
truths, which symbolically correspond to Truth-as-Fact in so
far as it can be known in, or inferred from, truth-as-immediate-
apprehension, or truth-as-historic-revelation—this is not salvation, but merely the study of a special branch of philosophy.
Even the most ordinary experience of a thing or event in time
can never be fully or adequately described in words. The
experience of seeing the sky or having neuralgia is incommunicable; the best we can do is to say 'blue' or 'pain,' in the
hope that those who hear us may have had experiences similar
to our own and so be able to supply their own version of the
meaning. God, however, is not a thing or event in time, and
the time-bound words which cannot do justice even to temporal matters are even more inadequate to the intrinsic nature
and our own unitive experience of that which belongs to an
incommensurably different order. To suppose that people can
be saved by studying and giving assent to formulae is like supposing that one can get to Timbuctoo by poring over a map

of Africa. Maps are symbols, and even the best of them are
inaccurate and imperfect symbols. But to anyone who really
wants to reach a given destination, a map is indispensably useful as indicating the direction in which the traveller should set
out and the roads which he must take.

In later Buddhist philosophy words are regarded as one of
the prime determining factors in the creative evolution of
human beings. In this philosophy five categories of being are
recognized—Name, Appearance, Discrimination, Right Knowledge, Suchness. The first three are related for evil, the last two
for good. Appearances are discriminated by the sense organs,
then reified by naming, so that words are taken for things and
symbols are used as the measure of reality. According to this
view, language is a main source of the sense of separateness and
the blasphemous idea of individual self-sufficiency, with their
inevitable corollaries of greed, envy, lust for power, anger and
cruelty. And from these evil passions there springs the necessity of an indefinitely protracted and repeated separate existence
under the same, self-perpetuated conditions of craving and infatuation. The only escape is through a creative act of the will,
assisted by Buddha-grace, leading through selflessness to Right
Knowledge, which consists, among other things, in a proper
appraisal of Names, Appearances and Discrimination. In and
through Right Knowledge, one emerges from the infatuating
delusion of 'I,' 'me,' 'mine,' and, resisting the temptation to
deny the world in a state of premature and one-sided ecstasy, or
to affirm it by living like the average sensual man, one comes at
last to the transfiguring awareness that *samsara* and *nirvana* are
one, to the unitive apprehension of pure Suchness—the ultimate Ground, which can only be indicated, never adequately
described in verbal symbols.

In connection with the Mahayanist view that words play an
important and even creative part in the evolution of unregenerate human nature, we may mention Hume's arguments against
the reality of causation. These arguments start from the postulate that all events are 'loose and separate' from one another
and proceed with faultless logic to a conclusion that makes com-

plete nonsense of all organized thought or purposive action. The fallacy, as Professor Stout has pointed out, lies in the preliminary postulate. And when we ask ourselves what it was that induced Hume to make this odd and quite unrealistic assumption that events are 'loose and separate,' we see that his only reason for flying in the face of immediate experience was the fact that things and happenings are symbolically represented in our thought by nouns, verbs and adjectives, and that these words are, in effect, 'loose and separate' from one another in a way which the events and things they stand for quite obviously are not. Taking words as the measure of things, instead of using things as the measure of words, Hume imposed the discrete and, so to say, *pointilliste* pattern of language upon the continuum of actual experience—with the impossibly paradoxical results with which we are all familiar. Most human beings are not philosophers and care not at all for consistency in thought or action. Thus, in some circumstances they take it for granted that events are not 'loose and separate,' but co-exist or follow one another within the organized and organizing field of a cosmic whole. But on other occasions, where the opposite view is more nearly in accord with their passions or interests, they adopt, all unconsciously, the Humian position and treat events as though they were as independent of one another and the rest of the world as the words by which they are symbolized. This is generally true of all occurrences involving 'I,' 'me,' 'mine.' Reifying the 'loose and separate' names, we regard the things as also loose and separate—not subject to law, not involved in the network of relationships, by which in fact they are so obviously bound up with their physical, social and spiritual environment. We regard as absurd the idea that there is no causal process in nature and no organic connection between events and things in the lives of other people; but at the same time we accept as axiomatic the notion that our own sacred ego is 'loose and separate' from the universe, a law unto itself above the moral *dharma* and even, in many respects, above the natural law of causality. Both in Buddhism and Catholicism, monks and nuns were encouraged to avoid the personal pronoun and to speak of themselves in terms of circumlocutions that clearly indicated their real relationship with the cosmic reality and their fellow-creatures. The precaution was a wise one. Our responses to familiar words are conditioned reflexes. By changing the stimulus, we can do something to change the response. No Pavlov bell, no salivation; no harping on words like 'me' and 'mine,' no purely automatic and unreflecting egotism. When a monk speaks of himself, not as 'I,' but as 'this sinner' or 'this unprofitable servant,' he tends to stop taking his 'loose and separate' selfhood for granted, and makes himself aware of his real, organic relationship with God and his neighbours.

In practice words are used for other purposes than for making statements about facts. Very often they are used rhetorically, in order to arouse the passions and direct the will towards some course of action regarded as desirable. And sometimes, too, they are used poetically—that is to say, they are used in such a way that, besides making a statement about real or imaginary things and events, and besides appealing rhetorically to the will and the passions, they cause the reader to be aware that they are beautiful. Beauty in art or nature is a matter of relationships between things not in themselves intrinsically beautiful. There is nothing beautiful, for example, about the vocables 'time,' or 'syllable.' But when they are used in such a phrase as 'to the last syllable of recorded time,' the relationship between the sound of the component words, between our ideas of the things for which they stand, and between the overtones of association with which each word and the phrase as a whole are charged, is apprehended, by a direct and immediate intuition, as being beautiful.

About the rhetorical use of words nothing much need be said. There is rhetoric for good causes and there is rhetoric for bad causes—rhetoric which is tolerably true to facts as well as emotionally moving, and rhetoric which is unconsciously or deliberately a lie. To learn to discriminate between the different kinds of rhetoric is an essential part of intellectual morality; and intellectual morality is as necessary a pre-condition of the spiritual life as is the control of the will and the guard of heart and tongue.

We have now to consider a more difficult problem. How should the poetical use of words be related to the life of the spirit? (And, of course, what applies to the poetical use of words applies equally to the pictorial use of pigments, the musical use of sounds, the sculptural use of clay or stone—in a word, to all the arts.)

'Beauty is truth, truth beauty.' But unfortunately Keats failed to specify in which of its principal meanings he was using the word 'truth.' Some critics have assumed that he was using it in the third of the senses listed at the opening of this section, and have therefore dismissed the aphorism as non-sensical. $Zn + H_2SO_4 = ZnSO_4 + H_2$. This is a truth in the third sense of the word—and, manifestly, this truth is not identical with beauty. But no less manifestly Keats was not talking about this kind of 'truth.' He was using the word primarily in its first sense, as a synonym for 'fact,' and secondarily with the significance attached to it in the Johannine phrase, 'to worship God in truth.' His sentence, therefore, carries two meanings. 'Beauty is the Primordial Fact, and the Primordial Fact is Beauty, the principle of all particular beauties'; and 'Beauty is an immediate experience, and this immediate experience is identical with Beauty-as-Principle, Beauty-as-Primordial-Fact.' The first of these statements is fully in accord with the doctrines of the Perennial Philosophy. Among the trinities in which the ineffable One makes itself manifest is the trinity of the Good, the True, and the Beautiful. We perceive beauty in the harmonious intervals between the parts of a whole. In this context the divine Ground might be paradoxically defined as Pure Interval, independent of what is separated and harmonized within the totality.

With Keats's statement in its secondary meaning the exponents of the Perennial Philosophy would certainly disagree. The experience of beauty in art or in nature may be qualitatively akin to the immediate, unitive experience of the divine Ground or Godhead; but it is not the same as that experience, and the particular beauty-fact experienced, though partaking in some sort of the divine nature, is at several removes from the Godhead. The poet, the nature lover, the aesthete are granted apprehensions of Reality analogous to those vouchsafed to the selfless contemplative; but because they have not troubled to make themselves perfectly selfless, they are incapable of knowing the divine Beauty in its fullness, as it is in itself. The poet is born with the capacity of arranging words in such a way that something of the quality of the graces and inspirations he has received can make itself felt to other human beings in the white spaces, so to speak, between the lines of his verse. This is a great and precious gift; but if the poet remains content with his gift, if he persists in worshipping the beauty in art and nature without going on to make himself capable, through selflessness, of apprehending Beauty as it is, in the divine Ground, then he is only an idolater. True, his idolatry is among the highest of which human beings are capable; but an idolatry, none the less, it remains.

The experience of beauty is pure, self-manifested, compounded equally of joy and consciousness, free from admixture of any other perception, the very twin brother of mystical experience, and the very life of it is supersensuous wonder. . . . It is enjoyed by those who are competent thereto, in identity, just as the form of God is itself the joy with which it is recognized.

Visvanatha

What follows is the last composition of a Zen nun, who had been in her youth a great beauty and an accomplished poetess.

Sixty-six times have these eyes beheld the changing scenes of Autumn.
I have said enough about moonlight,
Ask me no more.
Only listen to the voice of pines and cedars, when no wind stirs.

Ryo-Nen

The silence under windless trees is what Mallarmé would call a *creux néant musicien*. But whereas the music for which the poet listened was merely aesthetic and imaginative, it was to pure Suchness that the self-naughted contemplative was laying herself open. 'Be still and know that I am God.'

> This truth is to be lived, it is not to be merely pronounced with
>   the mouth. . . .
> There is really nothing to argue about in this teaching;
> Any arguing is sure to go against the intent of it.
> Doctrines given up to controversy and argumentation lead of
>   themselves to birth and death.
>
> *Hui Neng*

Away, then, with the fictions and workings of discursive reason, either for or against Christianity! They are only the wanton spirit of the mind, whilst ignorant of God and insensible of its own nature and condition. Death and life are the only things in question; life is God living and working in the soul; death is the soul living and working according to the sense and reason of bestial flesh and blood. Both this life and this death are of their own growth, growing from their own seed within us, not as busy reason talks and directs, but as the heart turns either to the one or to the other.

> *William Law*

Can I explain the Friend to one for whom He is no Friend?
> *Jalal-uddin Rumi*

When a mother cries to her sucking babe, 'Come, O son, I am
    thy mother!'
Does the child answer, 'O mother, show a proof
That I shall find comfort in taking thy milk'?
> *Jalal-uddin Rumi*

Great truths do not take hold of the hearts of the masses. And now, as all the world is in error, how shall I, though I know the true path, how shall I guide? If I know that I cannot succeed and yet try to force success, this would be but another source of error. Better then to desist and strive no more. But if I do not strive, who will?

Chuang Tʒu

Between the horns of Chuang Tzu's dilemma there is no way but that of love, peace and joy. Only those who manifest their possession, in however small a measure, of the fruits of the Spirit can persuade others that the life of the spirit is worth living. Argument and controversy are almost useless; in many cases, indeed, they are positively harmful. But this, of course, is a thing that clever men with a gift for syllogisms and sarcasm find it peculiarly hard to admit. Milton, no doubt, genuinely believed that he was working for truth, righteousness and the glory of God by exploding in torrents of learned scurrility against the enemies of his favourite dictator and his favourite brand of nonconformity. In actual fact, of course, he and the other controversialists of the sixteenth and seventeenth centuries did nothing but harm to the cause of true religion, for which, on one side or the other, they fought with an equal learning and ingenuity and with the same foulmouthed intemperance of language. The successive controversies went on, with occasional lucid intervals, for about two hundred years—Papists arguing with anti-Papists, Protestants with other Protestants, Jesuits with Quietists and Jansenists. When the noise finally died down, Christianity (which, like any other religion, can survive only if it manifests the fruits of the Spirit) was all but dead; the real religion of most educated Europeans was now nationalistic idolatry. During the eighteenth century this change to idolatry seemed (after the atrocities committed in the name of Christianity by Wallenstein and Tilly) to be a change for the better. This was because the ruling classes were determined that the horrors of the wars of religion should not be repeated and therefore deliberately tempered power politics with gentlemanliness. Symptoms of gentlemanliness can still be observed in the Napoleonic and

Crimean wars. But the national Molochs were steadily devouring the eighteenth-century ideal. During the First and Second World Wars we have witnessed the total elimination of the old checks and self-restraints. The consequences of political idolatry now display themselves without the smallest mitigation either of humanistic honour and etiquette or of transcendental religion. By its internecine quarrels over words, forms of organization, money and power, historic Christianity consummated the work of self-destruction, to which its excessive preoccupation with things in time had from the first so tragically committed it.

Sell your cleverness and buy bewilderment;
Cleverness is mere opinion, bewilderment is intuition.

Jalal-uddin Rumi

Reason is like an officer when the King appears;
The officer then loses his power and hides himself.
Reason is the shadow cast by God; God is the sun.

Jalal-uddin Rumi

Non-rational creatures do not look before or after, but live in the animal eternity of a perpetual present; instinct is their animal grace and constant inspiration; and they are never tempted to live otherwise than in accord with their own animal *dharma*, or immanent law. Thanks to his reasoning powers and to the instrument of reason, language, man (in his merely human condition) lives nostalgically, apprehensively and hopefully in the past and future as well as in the present; has no instincts to tell him what to do; must rely on personal cleverness, rather than on inspiration from the divine Nature of Things; finds himself in a condition of chronic civil war between passion and prudence and, on a higher level of awareness and ethical sensibility, between egotism and dawning spirituality. But this 'wearisome condition of humanity' is the indispensable prerequisite of enlightenment and deliverance. Man must live in time in order to be able to advance into eternity, no longer on the animal, but on the spiritual level; he must be conscious of himself as a separate ego in order to be able consciously to transcend separate selfhood; he must do battle with the lower self in order that he may become identified with that higher Self within him, which is akin to the divine Not-Self; and finally he must make use of his cleverness in order to pass beyond cleverness to the intellectual vision of Truth, the immediate, unitive knowledge of the divine Ground. Reason and its works 'are not and cannot be a proximate means of union with God.' The proximate means is 'intellect,' in the scholastic sense of the word, or spirit. In the last analysis the use and purpose of reason is to create the internal and external conditions favourable to its own transfiguration by and into spirit. It is the lamp by which it finds the way to go beyond itself. We see, then, that as a means to a proximate means to an End, discursive reasoning is of enormous value. But if, in our pride and madness, we treat it as a proximate means to the divine End (as so many religious people have done and still do), or if, denying the existence of an eternal End, we regard it as at once the means to Progress and its ever-receding goal in time, cleverness becomes the enemy, a source of spiritual blindness, moral evil and social disaster. At no period in history has cleverness been so highly valued or, in certain directions, so widely and efficiently trained as at the present time. And at no time have intellectual vision and spirituality been less esteemed, or the End to which they are proximate means less widely and less earnestly sought for. Because technology advances, we fancy that we are making corresponding progress all along the line; because we have considerable power over inanimate nature, we are convinced that we are the self-sufficient masters of our fate and captains of our souls; and because cleverness has given us technology and power, we believe, in spite of all the evidence to the contrary, that we have only to go on being yet cleverer in a yet more systematic way to achieve social order, international peace and personal happiness.

In Wu Ch'êng-ên's extraordinary masterpiece (so admirably translated by Mr. Arthur Waley) there is an episode, at once comical and profound, in which Monkey (who, in the allegory, is the incarnation of human cleverness) gets to heaven and there causes so much trouble that at last Buddha has to be called in to deal with him. It ends in the following passage:

'I'll have a wager with you,' said Buddha. 'If you are really so clever, jump off the palm of my right hand. If you succeed, I'll tell the Jade Emperor to come and live with me in the Western Paradise, and you shall have his throne without more ado. But if you fail, you shall go back to earth and do penance there for many a kalpa before you come back to me with your talk.'

'This Buddha,' Monkey thought to himself, 'is a perfect fool. I can jump a hundred and eight thousand leagues, while his palm cannot be as much as eight inches across. How could I fail to jump clear of it?'

'You're sure you're in a position to do this for me?' he asked.

'Of course I am,' said Buddha.

He stretched out his right hand, which looked about the size of a lotus leaf. Monkey put his cudgel behind his ear, and leapt with all his might. 'That's all right,' he said to himself. 'I'm right off it now.' He was whizzing so fast that he was almost invisible, and Buddha, watching him with the eye of wisdom, saw a mere whirligig shoot along.

Monkey came at last to five pink pillars, sticking up into the air. 'This is the end of the World,' said Monkey to himself. 'All I have got to do is to go back to Buddha and claim my forfeit. The Throne is mine.'

'Wait a minute,' he said presently, 'I'd better just leave a record of some kind, in case I have trouble with Buddha.' He plucked a hair and blew on it with magic breath, crying 'Change!' It changed at once into a writing brush charged with heavy ink, and at the base of the central pillar he wrote, 'The Great Sage Equal to Heaven reached this place.' Then, to mark his disrespect, he relieved nature at the bottom of the first pillar, and somersaulted back to where he had come from. Standing on Buddha's palm, he said, 'Well, I've gone and come back. You can go and tell the Jade Emperor to hand over the palaces of Heaven.'

'You stinking ape,' said Buddha, 'you've been on the palm of my hand all the time.'

'You're quite mistaken,' said Monkey. 'I got to the end of the World, where I saw five flesh-coloured pillars sticking up into the sky. I wrote something on one of them. I'll take you there and show you, if you like.'

'No need for that,' said Buddha. 'Just look down.'

Monkey peered down with his fiery, steely eyes, and there at the base of the middle finger of Buddha's hand he saw written the words, 'The Great Sage Equal to Heaven reached this place,' and from the fork between the thumb and first finger came a smell of monkey's urine.

From Monkey

And so, having triumphantly urinated on the proffered hand of Wisdom, the Monkey within us turns back and, full of a bumptious confidence in his own omnipotence, sets out to re-fashion the world of men and things into something nearer to his heart's desire. Sometimes his intentions are good, sometimes consciously bad. But, whatever the intentions may be, the results of action undertaken by even the most brilliant cleverness, when it is unenlightened by the divine Nature of Things, unsubordinated to the Spirit, are generally evil. That this has always been clearly understood by humanity at large is proved by the usages of language. 'Cunning' and 'canny' are equivalent to 'knowing,' and all three adjectives pass a more or less unfavourable moral judgment on those to whom they are applied. 'Conceit' is just 'concept'; but what a man's mind conceives most clearly is the supreme value of his own ego. 'Shrewd,' which is the participial form of 'shrew,' meaning malicious, and is connected with 'beshrew,' to curse, is now applied, by way of rather dubious compliment, to astute business men and attorneys. Wizards are so called because they are wise—wise, of course, in the sense that, in American slang, a 'wise guy' is wise. Conversely, an idiot was once popularly known as an innocent. 'This use of innocent,' says Richard Trench, 'assumes that to hurt and harm is the chief employment, towards which men turn their intellectual powers; that where they are wise, they are oftenest wise to do evil.' Meanwhile it goes without saying that cleverness and accumulated knowledge are indispensable, but always as means to proximate means, and never as proximate means or, what is even worse, as ends in themselves. *Quid faceret eruditio sine dilectione?* says St. Bernard. *Inflaret. Quid, absque eruditione dilectio? Erraret.* What would learning do without love? It would puff up. And love without learning? It would go astray.

Such as men themselves are, such will God Himself seem to them to be.

John Smith, the Platonist

Men's minds perceive second causes,
But only prophets perceive the action of the First Cause.

Jalal-uddin Rumi

The amount and kind of knowledge we acquire depends first upon the will and, second, upon our psycho-physical constitution and the modifications imposed upon it by environment and our own choice. Thus, Professor Burkitt has pointed out that, where technological discovery is concerned 'man's desire has been the important factor. Once something is definitely wanted, again and again it has been produced in an extremely short time. . . . Conversely, nothing will teach the Bushmen of South Africa to plant and herd. They have no desire to do so.' The same is true in regard to ethical and spiritual discoveries. 'You are as holy as you wish to be,' was the motto given by Ruysbroeck to the students who came to visit him. And he might have added, 'You can therefore know as much of Reality as you wish to know'—for knowledge is in the knower according to the mode of the knower, and the mode of the knower is, in certain all-important respects, within the knower's control.

Liberating knowledge of God comes to the pure in heart and poor in spirit; and though such purity and poverty are enormously difficult of achievement, they are nevertheless possible to all.

She said, moreover, that if one would attain to purity of mind it was necessary to abstain altogether from any judgment on one's neighbour and from all empty talk about his conduct. In creatures one should always seek only for the will of God. With great force she said: 'For no reason whatever should one judge the actions of creatures or their motives. Even when we see that it is an actual sin, we ought not to pass judgment on it, but have holy and sincere compassion and offer it up to God with humble and devout prayer.'

From the Testament of St. Catherine of Siena, written down by Tommaso di Petra

This total abstention from judgment upon one's fellows is only one of the conditions of inward purity. The others have already been described in the section on 'Mortification.'

Learning consists in adding to one's stock day by day. The practice of Tao consists in subtracting day by day: subtracting and yet again subtracting until one has reached inactivity.

Lao Tzu

It is the inactivity of self-will and ego-centred cleverness that makes possible the activity within the emptied and purified soul of the eternal Suchness. And when eternity is known in the heights within, it is also known in the fullness of experience, outside in the world.

Didst thou ever descry a glorious eternity in a winged moment of time? Didst thou ever see a bright infinite in the narrow point of an object? Then thou knowest what spirit means—the spire-top, whither all things ascend harmoniously, where they meet and sit contented in an unfathomed Depth of Life.

Peter Sterry

Chapter 8

RELIGION AND TEMPERAMENT

IT seems best at this point to turn back for a moment from
ethics to psychology, where a very important problem awaits
us—a problem to which the exponents of the Perennial Philosophy have given a great deal of attention. What precisely is
the relation between individual constitution and temperament
on the one hand and the kind and degree of spiritual knowledge
on the other? The materials for a comprehensively accurate
answer to this question are not available—except, perhaps, in
the form of that incommunicable science, based upon intuition
and long practice, that exists in the minds of experienced
'spiritual directors.' But the answer that *can* be given, though
incomplete, is highly significant.

All knowledge, as we have seen, is a function of being. Or,
to phrase the same idea in scholastic terms, the thing known
is in the knower according to the mode of the knower. In the
Introduction reference was made to the effect upon knowledge
of changes of being along what may be called its vertical axis,
in the direction of sanctity or its opposite. But there is also
variation in the horizontal plane. Congenitally by psycho-
physical constitution, each one of us is born into a certain
position on this horizontal plane. It is a vast territory, still
imperfectly explored, a continent stretching all the way from
imbecility to genius, from shrinking weakness to aggressive
strength, from cruelty to Pickwickian kindliness, from self-
revealing sociability to taciturn misanthropy and love of solitude, from an almost frantic lasciviousness to an almost un-
tempted continence. From any point on this huge expanse of
possible human nature an individual can move almost indefinitely up or down, towards union with the divine Ground of
his own and all other beings, or towards the last, the infernal
extremes of separateness and selfhood. But where horizontal
168

movement is concerned there is far less freedom. It is impossible for one kind of physical constitution to transform itself into another kind; and the particular temperament associated with a given physical constitution can be modified only within narrow limits. With the best will in the world and the best social environment, all that anyone can hope to do is to make the best of his congenital psycho-physical make-up; to change the fundamental patterns of constitution and temperament is beyond his power.

In the course of the last thirty centuries many attempts have been made to work out a classification system in terms of which human differences could be measured and described. For example, there is the ancient Hindu method of classifying people according to the psycho-physico-social categories of caste. There are the primarily medical classifications associated with the name of Hippocrates, classifications in terms of two main 'habits'—the phthisic and the apoplectic—or of the four humours (blood, phlegm, black bile and yellow bile) and the four qualities (hot, cold, moist and dry). More recently there have been the various physiognomic systems of the eighteenth and early nineteenth centuries; the crude and merely psychological dichotomy of introversion and extraversion; the more complete, but still inadequate, psychophysical classifications proposed by Kretschmer, Stockard, Viola and others; and finally the system, more comprehensive, more flexibly adequate to the complex facts than all those which preceded it, worked out by Dr. William Sheldon and his collaborators.

In the present section our concern is with classifications of human differences in relation to the problems of the spiritual life. Traditional systems will be described and illustrated, and the findings of the Perennial Philosophy will be compared with the conclusions reached by the most recent scientific research.

In the West, the traditional Catholic classification of human beings is based upon the Gospel anecdote of Martha and Mary. The way of Martha is the way of salvation through action, the way of Mary is the way through contemplation. Following

Aristotle, who in this as in many other matters was in accord with the Perennial Philosophy, Catholic thinkers have regarded contemplation (the highest term of which is the unitive knowledge of the Godhead) as man's final end, and therefore have always held that Mary's was indeed the better way.

Significantly enough, it is in essentially similar terms that Dr. Radin classifies and (by implication) evaluates primitive human beings in so far as they are philosophers and religious devotees. For him there is no doubt that the higher monotheistic forms of primitive religion are created (or should one rather say, with Plato, *discovered?*) by people belonging to the first of the two great psycho-physical classes of human beings —the men of thought. To those belonging to the other class, the men of action, is due the creation or discovery of the lower, unphilosophical, polytheistic kinds of religion.

This simple dichotomy is a classification of human differences that is valid so far as it goes. But like all such dichotomies, whether physical (like Hippocrates' division of humanity into those of phthisic and those of apoplectic habit) or psychological (like Jung's classification in terms of introvert and extravert), this grouping of the religious into those who think and those who act, those who follow the way of Martha and those who follow the way of Mary, is inadequate to the facts. And of course no director of souls, no head of a religious organization, is ever, in actual practice, content with this all too simple system. Underlying the best Catholic writing on prayer and the best Catholic practice in the matter of recognizing vocations and assigning duties, we sense the existence of an implicit and unformulated classification of human differences more complete and more realistic than the explicit dichotomy of action and contemplation.

In Hindu thought the outlines of this completer and more adequate classification are clearly indicated. The ways leading to the delivering union with God are not two, but three—the way of works, the way of knowledge and the way of devotion. In the Bhagavad-Gita Sri Krishna instructs Arjuna in all three paths—liberation through action without attachment; liberation through knowledge of the Self and the Absolute Ground of all being with which it is identical; and liberation through intense devotion to the personal God or the divine incarnation.

Do without attachment the work you have to do; for a man who does his work without attachment attains the Supreme Goal verily. By action alone men like Janaka attained perfection.

But there is also the way of Mary.

Freed from passion, fear and anger, absorbed in Me, taking refuge in Me, and purified by the fires of Knowledge, many have become one with my Being.

And again:

Those who have completely controlled their senses and are of even mind under all conditions and thus contemplate the Imperishable, the Ineffable, the Unmanifest, the Omnipresent, the Incomprehensible, the Eternal—they, devoted to the welfare of all beings, attain Me alone and none else.

But the path of contemplation is not easy.

The task of those whose minds are set on the Unmanifest is the more difficult; for, to those who are in the body, the realization of the Unmanifest is hard. But those who consecrate all their actions to Me (as the personal God, or as the divine Incarnation), who regard Me as the supreme Goal, who worship Me and meditate upon Me with single-minded concentration—for those whose minds are thus absorbed in Me, I become ere long the Saviour from the world's ocean of mortality.

These three ways of deliverance are precisely correlated with the three categories, in terms of which Sheldon has worked out what is, without question, the best and most adequate classification of human differences. Human beings, he has shown, vary continuously between the viable extremes of a tri-polar system; and physical and psychological measurements can be devised, whereby any given individual may be accurately located in relation to the three co-ordinates. Or we can put the matter differently and say that any given individual is a mixture, in varying proportions, of three physical and three closely related psychological components. The strength of each component can be measured according to empirically determined procedures. To the three physical components Sheldon gives the names of endomorphy, mesomorphy and ectomorphy. The individual with a high degree of endomorphy is predominantly soft and rounded and may easily become grossly fat. The high mesomorph is hard, big-boned and strong-muscled. The high ectomorph is slender and has small bones and stringy, weak, unemphatic muscles. The endomorph has a huge gut, a gut that may be more than twice as heavy and twice as long as that of the extreme ectomorph. In a real sense his or her body is built around the digestive tract. The centrally significant fact of mesomorphic physique, on the other hand, is the powerful musculature, while that of the ectomorph is the over-sensitive and (since the ratio of body surface to mass is higher in ectomorphs than in either of the other types) relatively unprotected nervous system.

With endomorphic constitution is closely correlated a temperamental pattern, which Sheldon calls viscerotonia. Significant among the viscerotonic traits are love of food and, characteristically, love of eating in common; love of comfort and luxury; love of ceremoniousness; indiscriminate amiability and love of people as such; fear of solitude and craving for company; uninhibited expression of emotion; love of childhood, in the form of nostalgia towards one's own past and in an intense enjoyment of family life; craving for affection and social support, and need of people when in trouble. The temperament that is related to mesomorphy is called somatotonia. In this the dominating traits are love of muscular activity, aggressiveness and lust for power; indifference to pain; callousness in regard to other people's feelings; a love of combat and competitiveness; a high degree of physical courage; a nostalgic feeling, not for childhood, but for youth, the period of maximum muscular power; a need for activity when in trouble.

From the foregoing descriptions it will be seen how inadequate is the Jungian conception of extraversion, as a simple antithesis to introversion. Extraversion is not simple; it is of two radically different kinds. There is the emotional, sociable extraversion of the viscerotonic endomorph—the person who is always seeking company and telling everybody just what he feels. And there is the extraversion of the big-muscled somatotonic—the person who looks outward on the world as a place where he can exercise power, where he can bend people to his will and shape things to his heart's desire. One is the genial extraversion of the salesman, the Rotarian good mixer, the liberal Protestant clergyman. The other is the extraversion of the engineer who works off his lust for power on things, of the sportsman and the professional blood-and-iron soldier, of the ambitious business executive and politician, of the dictator, whether in the home or at the head of a state.

With cerebrotonia, the temperament that is correlated with ectomorphic physique, we leave the genial world of Pickwick, the strenuously competitive world of Hotspur, and pass into an entirely different and somewhat disquieting kind of universe —that of Hamlet and Ivan Karamazov. The extreme cerebrotonic is the over-alert, over-sensitive introvert, who is more concerned with what goes on behind his eyes—with the constructions of thought and imagination, with the variations of feeling and consciousness—than with that external world, to which, in their different ways, the viscerotonic and the somatotonic pay their primary attention and allegiance. Cerebrotonics have little or no desire to dominate, nor do they feel the viscerotonic's indiscriminate liking for people as people; on the contrary they want to live and let live, and their passion for privacy is intense. Solitary confinement, the most terrible punishment that can be inflicted on the soft, round, genial person, is, for the cerebrotonic, no punishment at all. For him the ultimate horror is the boarding school and the barracks. In company cerebrotonics are nervous and shy, tensely inhibited and unpredictably moody. (It is a significant fact that no extreme cerebrotonic has ever been a good actor or actress.) Cerebrotonics hate to slam doors or raise their voices, and suffer acutely from the unrestrained bellowing and trampling of the somatotonic. Their manner is restrained, and when it comes to expressing their feelings they are extremely reserved. The emotional gush of the viscerotonic strikes them as offensively shallow and even insincere, nor have they any patience with viscerotonic ceremoniousness and love of luxury and magnificence. They do not easily form habits and find it hard to adapt their lives to the routines which come so naturally to somatotonics. Owing to their over-sensitiveness, cerebrotonics are often extremely, almost insanely sexual; but they are hardly ever tempted to take to drink—for alcohol, which heightens the natural aggressiveness of the somatotonic and increases the relaxed amiability of the viscerotonic, merely makes them feel ill and depressed. Each in his own way, the viscerotonic and the somatotonic are well adapted to the world they live in; but the introverted cerebrotonic is in some sort incommensurable with the things and people and institutions that surround him. Consequently a remarkably high proportion of extreme cerebrotonics fail to make good as normal citizens and average pillars of society. But if many fail, many also become abnormal on the higher side of the average. In universities, monasteries and research laboratories —wherever sheltered conditions are provided for those whose small guts and feeble muscles do not permit them to eat or fight their way through the ordinary rough and tumble—the percentage of outstandingly gifted and accomplished cerebrotonics will almost always be very high. Realizing the importance of this extreme, over-evolved and scarcely viable type of human being, all civilizations have provided in one way or another for its protection.

In the light of these descriptions we can understand more clearly the Bhagavad-Gita's classification of paths to salvation.

The path of devotion is the path naturally followed by the person in whom the viscerotonic component is high. His inborn tendency to externalize the emotions he spontaneously feels in regard to persons can be disciplined and canalized, so that a merely animal gregariousness and a merely human kindliness become transformed into charity—devotion to the personal God and universal goodwill and compassion towards all sentient beings.

The path of works is for those whose extraversion is of the somatotonic kind, those who in all circumstances feel the need to 'do something.' In the unregenerate somatotonic this craving for action is always associated with aggressiveness, self-assertion and the lust for power. For the born *Kshatriya*, or warrior-ruler, the task, as Krishna explains to Arjuna, is to get rid of those fatal accompaniments to the love of action and to work without regard to the fruits of work, in a state of complete non-attachment to self. Which is, of course, like everything else, a good deal easier said than done.

Finally, there is the way of knowledge, through the modification of consciousness, until it ceases to be ego-centred and becomes centred in and united with the divine Ground. This is the way to which the extreme cerebrotonic is naturally drawn. His special discipline consists in the mortification of his innate tendency towards introversion for its own sake, towards thought and imagination and self-analysis as ends in themselves rather than as means towards the ultimate transcendence of phantasy and discursive reasoning in the timeless act of pure intellectual intuition.

Within the general population, as we have seen, variation is continuous, and in most people the three components are fairly evenly mixed. Those exhibiting extreme predominance of any one component are relatively rare. And yet, in spite of their rarity, it is by the thought-patterns characteristic of these extreme individuals that theology and ethics, at any rate on the theoretical side, have been mainly dominated. The reason for this is simple. Any extreme position is more uncompromisingly clear and therefore more easily recognized and understood than the intermediate positions, which are the natural thought-pattern of the person in whom the constituent components of personality are evenly balanced. These intermediate positions, it should be noted, do not in any sense contain or reconcile the extreme positions; they are merely other thought-patterns added to the list of possible systems. The construction of an all-embracing system of metaphysics, ethics and psychology is a task that can never be accomplished by any single individual, for the sufficient reason that he *is* an individual with one particular kind of constitution and temperament and therefore capable of knowing only according to the mode of his own being. Hence the advantages inherent in what may be called the anthological approach to truth.

The Sanskrit *dharma*—one of the key words in Indian formulations of the Perennial Philosophy—has two principal meanings. The *dharma* of an individual is, first of all, his essential nature, the intrinsic law of his being and development. But *dharma* also signifies the law of righteousness and piety. The implications of this double meaning are clear: a man's duty, how he ought to live, what he ought to believe and what he ought to do about his beliefs—these things are conditioned by his essential nature, his constitution and temperament. Going a good deal further than do the Catholics, with their doctrine of vocations, the Indians admit the right of individuals with different *dharmas* to worship different aspects or conceptions of the divine. Hence the almost total absence, among Hindus and Buddhists, of bloody persecutions, religious wars and proselytizing imperialism.

It should, however, be remarked that, within its own ecclesiastical fold, Catholicism has been almost as tolerant as Hinduism and Mahayana Buddhism. Nominally one, each of these religions consists, in fact, of a number of very different religions, covering the whole gamut of thought and behaviour from fetishism, through polytheism, through legalistic monotheism, through devotion to the sacred humanity of the Avatar, to the profession of the Perennial Philosophy and the practice of a purely spiritual religion that seeks the unitive knowledge of the Absolute Godhead. These tolerated religions-within-a-religion are not, of course, regarded as equally valuable or equally true. To worship polytheistically may be one's *dharma*; nevertheless the fact remains that man's final end is the unitive knowledge of the Godhead, and all the historical formulations of the Perennial Philosophy are agreed that every human being ought, and perhaps in some way or other actually will, achieve that end. 'All souls,' writes Father Garrigou-Lagrange, 're-ceive a general remote call to the mystical life; and if all were faithful in avoiding, as they should, not merely mortal but venial sin, if they were, each according to his condition, docile to the Holy Ghost, and if they lived long enough, a day would come when they would receive the proximate and efficacious vocation to a high perfection and to the mystical life properly so called.' With this statement Hindu and Buddhist theo-logians would probably agree; but they would add that every soul will in fact eventually attain this 'high perfection.' All are called, but in any given generation few are chosen, because few choose themselves. But the series of conscious existences, corporeal or incorporeal, is indefinitely long; there is therefore time and opportunity for everyone to learn the necessary lessons. Moreover, there will always be helpers. For periodi-cally there are 'descents' of the Godhead into physical form; and at all times there are future Buddhas ready, on the threshold of reunion with the Intelligible Light, to renounce the bliss of immediate liberation in order to return as saviours and teachers again and again into the world of suffering and time and evil, until at last every sentient being shall have been delivered into eternity.

The practical consequences of this doctrine are clear enough. The lower forms of religion, whether emotional, active or intellectual, are never to be accepted as final. True, each of them comes naturally to persons of a certain kind of constitu-tion and temperament; but the *dharma* or duty of any given individual is not to remain complacently fixed in the imperfect religion that happens to suit him; it is rather to transcend it, not by impossibly denying the modes of thought, behaviour

M

and feeling that are natural to him, but by making use of them, so that by means of nature he may pass beyond nature. Thus the introvert uses 'discrimination' (in the Indian phrase), and so learns to distinguish the mental activities of the ego from the principial consciousness of the Self, which is akin to, or identical with, the divine Ground. The emotional extravert learns to 'hate his father and mother' (in other words, to give up his selfish attachment to the pleasures of indiscriminately loving and being loved), concentrates his devotion on the personal or incarnate aspect of God, and comes at last to love the Absolute Godhead by an act, no longer of feeling, but of will illuminated by knowledge. And finally there is that other kind of extravert, whose concern is not with the pleasures of giving or receiving affection, but with the satisfaction of his lust for power over things, events and persons. Using his own nature to transcend his own nature, he must follow the path laid down in the Bhagavad-Gita for the bewildered Arjuna—the path of work without attachment to the fruits of work, the path of what St. François de Sales calls 'holy indifference,' the path that leads through the forgetting of self to the discovery of the Self.

In the course of history it has often happened that one or other of the imperfect religions has been taken too seriously and regarded as good and true in itself, instead of as a means to the ultimate end of all religion. The effects of such mistakes are often disastrous. For example, many Protestant sects have insisted on the necessity, or at least the extreme desirability, of a violent conversion. But violent conversion, as Sheldon has pointed out, is a phenomenon confined almost exclusively to persons with a high degree of somatotonia. These persons are so intensely extraverted as to be quite unaware of what is happening in the lower levels of their minds. If for any reason their attention comes to be turned inwards, the resulting self-knowledge, because of its novelty and strangeness, presents itself with the force and quality of a revelation and their *metanoia*, or change of mind, is sudden and thrilling. This change may be to religion, or it may be to something else—

for example, to psycho-analysis. To insist upon the necessity of violent conversion as the only means to salvation is about as sensible as it would be to insist upon the necessity of having a large face, heavy bones and powerful muscles. To those naturally subject to this kind of emotional upheaval, the doctrine that makes salvation dependent on conversion gives a complacency that is quite fatal to spiritual growth, while those who are incapable of it are filled with a no less fatal despair. Other examples of inadequate theologies based upon psychological ignorance could easily be cited. One remembers, for instance, the sad case of Calvin, the cerebrotonic who took his own intellectual constructions so seriously that he lost all sense of reality, both human and spiritual. And then there is our liberal Protestantism, that predominantly viscerotonic heresy, which seems to have forgotten the very existence of the Father, Spirit and Logos and equates Christianity with an emotional attachment to Christ's humanity or (to use the currently popular phrase) 'the personality of Jesus,' worshipped idolatrously as though there were no other God. Even within all-comprehensive Catholicism we constantly hear complaints of the ignorant and self-centred directors, who impose upon the souls under their charge a religious *dharma* wholly unsuited to their nature—with results which writers such as St. John of the Cross describe as wholly pernicious. We see, then, that it is natural for us to think of God as possessed of the qualities which our temperament tends to make us perceive in Him; but unless nature finds a way of transcending itself by means of itself, we are lost. In the last analysis Philo is quite right in saying that those who do not conceive God purely and simply as the One injure, not God of course, but themselves and, along with themselves, their fellows.

The way of knowledge comes most naturally to persons whose temperament is predominantly cerebrotonic. By this I do not mean that the following of this way is easy for the cerebrotonic. His specially besetting sins are just as difficult to overcome as are the sins which beset the power-loving somatotonic and the extreme viscerotonic with his gluttony for food and comfort and social approval. Rather I mean that the idea that such a way exists and can be followed (either by discrimination, or through non-attached work and one-pointed devotion) is one which spontaneously occurs to the cerebrotonic. At all levels of culture he is the natural monotheist; and this natural monotheist, as Dr. Radin's examples of primitive theology clearly show, is often a monotheist of the *tat tvam asi*, inner-light school. Persons committed by their temperament to one or other of the two kinds of extraversion are natural polytheists. But natural polytheists can, without much difficulty, be convinced of the theoretical superiority of monotheism. The nature of human reason is such that there is an intrinsic plausibility about any hypothesis which seeks to explain the manifold in terms of unity, to reduce apparent multiplicity to essential identity. And from this theoretical monotheism the half-converted polytheist can, if he chooses, go on (through practices suitable to his own particular temperament) to the actual realization of the divine Ground of his own and all other beings. He *can*, I repeat, and sometimes he actually does. But very often he does not. There are many theoretical monotheists whose whole life and every action prove that in reality they are still what their temperament inclines them to be—polytheists, worshippers not of the one God they sometimes talk about, but of the many gods, nationalistic and technological, financial and familial, to whom in practice they pay all their allegiance.

In Christian art the Saviour has almost invariably been represented as slender, small-boned, unemphatically muscled. Large, powerful Christs are a rather shocking exception to a very ancient rule. Of Rubens' crucifixions William Blake contemptuously wrote:

> I understood Christ was a carpenter
> And not a brewer's servant, my good sir.

In a word, the traditional Jesus is thought of as a man of predominantly ectomorphic physique and therefore, by implication, of predominantly cerebrotonic temperament. The central core of primitive Christian doctrine confirms the essential correctness of the iconographic tradition. The religion of the Gospels is what we should expect from a cerebrotonic—not, of course, from any cerebrotonic, but from one who had used the psycho-physical peculiarities of his own nature to transcend nature, who had followed his particular *dharma* to its spiritual goal. The insistence that the Kingdom of Heaven is within; the ignoring of ritual; the slightly contemptuous attitude towards legalism, towards the ceremonial routines of organized religion, towards hallowed days and places; the general other-worldliness; the emphasis laid upon restraint, not merely of overt action, but even of desire and unexpressed intention; the indifference to the splendours of material civilization and the love of poverty as one of the greatest of goods; the doctrine that non-attachment must be carried even into the sphere of family relationships and that even devotion to the highest goals of merely human ideals, even the righteousness of the Scribes and Pharisees, may be idolatrous distractions from the love of God—all these are characteristically cerebrotonic ideas, such as would never have occurred spontaneously to the extraverted power lover or the equally extraverted viscerotonic.

Primitive Buddhism is no less predominantly cerebrotonic than primitive Christianity, and so is Vedanta, the metaphysical discipline which lies at the heart of Hinduism. Confucianism, on the contrary, is a mainly viscerotonic system—familial, ceremonious and thoroughly this-worldly. And in Mohammedanism we find a system which incorporates strongly somatotonic elements. Hence Islam's black record of holy wars and persecutions—a record comparable to that of later Christianity, after that religion had so far compromised with unregenerate somatotonia as to call its ecclesiastical organization 'the Church Militant.'

So far as the achievement of man's final end is concerned, it is as much of a handicap to be an extreme cerebrotonic or an extreme viscerotonic as it is to be an extreme somatotonic. But whereas the cerebrotonic and the viscerotonic cannot do much harm except to themselves and those in immediate con-

tact with them, the extreme somatotonic, with his native aggressiveness, plays havoc with whole societies. From one point of
view civilization may be defined as a complex of religious, legal
and educational devices for preventing extreme somatotonics
from doing too much mischief, and for directing their irre-
pressible energies into socially desirable channels. Confucianism and Chinese culture have sought to achieve this end by
inculcating filial piety, good manners and an amiably viscerotonic epicureanism—the whole reinforced somewhat incongruously by the cerebrotonic spirituality and restraints of
Buddhism and classical Taoism. In India the caste system
represents an attempt to subordinate military, political and
financial power to spiritual authority; and the education given
to all classes still insists so strongly upon the fact that man's
final end is unitive knowledge of God that even at the present
time, even after nearly two hundred years of gradually acceler-
ating Europeanization, successful somatotonics will, in middle
life, give up wealth, position and power to end their days as
humble seekers after enlightenment. In Catholic Europe, as in
India, there was an effort to subordinate temporal power to
spiritual authority; but since the Church itself exercised temporal power through the agency of political prelates and mitred
business men, the effort was never more than partially successful. After the Reformation even the pious wish to limit
temporal power by means of spiritual authority was completely abandoned. Henry VIII made himself, in Stubbs's
words, 'the Pope, the whole Pope, and something more than
the Pope,' and his example has been followed by most heads of
states ever since. Power has been limited only by other
powers, not by an appeal to first principles as interpreted by
those who are morally and spiritually qualified to know what
they are talking about. Meanwhile, the interest in religion has
everywhere declined and even among believing Christians the
Perennial Philosophy has been to a great extent replaced by a
metaphysic of inevitable progress and an evolving God, by a
passionate concern, not with eternity, but with future time.
And almost suddenly, within the last quarter of a century,

there has been consummated what Sheldon calls a 'somatotonic revolution,' directed against all that is characteristically cerebrotonic in the theory and practice of traditional Christian culture. Here are a few symptoms of this somatotonic revolution.

In traditional Christianity, as in all the great religious formulations of the Perennial Philosophy, it was axiomatic that contemplation is the end and purpose of action. Today the great majority even of professed Christians regard action (directed towards material and social progress) as the end, and analytic thought (there is no question any longer of integral thought, or contemplation) as the means to that end.

In traditional Christianity, as in the other formulations of the Perennial Philosophy, the secret of happiness and the way to salvation were to be sought, not in the external environment, but in the individual's state of mind with regard to the environment. Today the all-important thing is not the state of the mind, but the state of the environment. Happiness and moral progress depend, it is thought, on bigger and better gadgets and a higher standard of living.

In traditional Christian education the stress was all on restraint; with the recent rise of the 'progressive school' it is all on activity and 'self-expression.'

Traditionally Christian good manners outlawed all expressions of pleasure in the satisfaction of physical appetites. 'You may love a screeching owl, but you must not love a roasted fowl'—such was the rhyme on which children were brought up in the nurseries of only fifty years ago. Today the young unceasingly proclaim how much they 'love' and 'adore' different kinds of food and drink; adolescents and adults talk about the 'thrills' they derive from the stimulation of their sexuality. The popular philosophy of life has ceased to be based on the classics of devotion and the rules of aristocratic good breeding, and is now moulded by the writers of advertising copy, whose one idea is to persuade everybody to be as extraverted and uninhibitedly greedy as possible, since of course it is only the possessive, the restless, the distracted, who spend money on the things that advertisers want to sell. Technological progress is in part the product of the somatotonic revolution, in part the producer and sustainer of that revolution. The extraverted attention results in technological discoveries. (Significantly enough, a high degree of material civilization has always been associated with the large-scale and officially sanctioned practice of polytheism.) In their turn, technological discoveries have resulted in mass-production; and mass-production, it is obvious, cannot be kept going at full blast except by persuading the whole population to accept the somatotonic *Weltanschauung* and act accordingly.

Like technological progress, with which it is so closely associated in so many ways, modern war is at once a cause and a result of the somatotonic revolution. Nazi education, which was specifically education for war, had two principal aims: to encourage the manifestation of somatotonia in those most richly endowed with that component of personality, and to make the rest of the population feel ashamed of its relaxed amiability, or its inward-looking sensitiveness and tendency towards self-restraint and tender-mindedness. During the war the enemies of Nazism have been compelled, of course, to borrow from the Nazis' educational philosophy. All over the world millions of young men and even of young women are being systematically educated to be 'tough' and to value 'toughness' beyond every other moral quality. With this system of somatotonic ethics is associated the idolatrous and polytheistic theology of nationalism—a pseudo-religion far stronger at the present time for evil and division than is Christianity, or any other monotheistic religion, for unification and good. In the past most societies tried systematically to discourage somatotonia. This was a measure of self-defence; they did not want to be physically destroyed by the power-loving aggressiveness of their most active minority, and they did not want to be spiritually blinded by an excess of extraversion. During the last few years all this has been changed. What, we may apprehensively wonder, will be the result of the current world-wide reversal of an immemorial social policy? Time alone will show.

Chapter 9

SELF-KNOWLEDGE

In other living creatures ignorance of self is nature; in man it is vice.

Boethius

VICE may be defined as a course of behaviour consented to by the will and having results which are bad, primarily because they are God-eclipsing and, secondarily, because they are physically or psychologically harmful to the agent or his fellows. Ignorance of self is something that answers to this description. In its origins it is voluntary; for by introspection and by listening to other people's judgments of our character we can all, if we so desire, come to a very shrewd understanding of our flaws and weaknesses and the real, as opposed to the avowed and advertised, motives of our actions. If most of us remain ignorant of ourselves, it is because self-knowledge is painful and we prefer the pleasures of illusion. As for the consequences of such ignorance, these are bad by every criterion, from the utilitarian to the transcendental. Bad because self-ignorance leads to unrealistic behaviour and so causes every kind of trouble for everyone concerned; and bad because, without self-knowledge, there can be no true humility, therefore no effective self-naughting, therefore no unitive knowledge of the divine Ground underlying the self and ordinarily eclipsed by it.

The importance, the indispensable necessity, of self-knowledge has been stressed by the saints and doctors of every one of the great religious traditions. To us in the West, the most familiar voice is that of Socrates. More systematically than Socrates the Indian exponents of the Perennial Philosophy harped on the same theme. There is, for example, the Buddha, whose discourse on 'The Setting-Up of Mindfulness' expounds (with that positively inexorable exhaustiveness characteristic of the Pali scriptures) the whole art of self-knowledge in all its branches—knowledge of one's body, one's senses, one's feelings, one's thoughts. This art of self-knowledge is practised with two aims in view. The proximate aim is that 'a brother, as to the body, continues so to look upon the body, that he remains ardent, self-possessed and mindful, having overcome both the hankering and dejection common in the world. And in the same way as to feelings, thoughts and ideas, he so looks upon each that he remains ardent, self-possessed and mindful, without hankering or dejection.' Beyond and through this desirable psychological condition lies the final end of man, knowledge of that which underlies the individualized self. In their own vocabulary, Christian writers express the same ideas.

A man has many skins in himself, covering the depths of his heart. Man knows so many things; he does not know himself. Why, thirty or forty skins or hides, just like an ox's or a bear's, so thick and hard, cover the soul. Go into your own ground and learn to know yourself there.

Eckhart

Fools regard themselves as awake now—so personal is their knowledge. It may be as a prince or it may be as a herdsman, but so cock-sure of themselves!

Chuang Tzu

This metaphor of waking from dreams recurs again and again in the various expositions of the Perennial Philosophy. In this context liberation might be defined as the process of waking up out of the nonsense, nightmares and illusory pleasures of what is ordinarily called real life into the awareness of eternity. The 'sober certainty of waking bliss'—that wonderful phrase in which Milton described the experience of the noblest kind of music—comes, I suppose, about as near as words can get to enlightenment and deliverance.

Thou (the human being) art that which is not. I am that I am.
If thou perceivest this truth in thy soul, never shall the enemy
deceive thee; thou shalt escape all his snares.

St. Catherine of Siena

Knowledge of ourselves teaches us whence we come, where we
are and whither we are going. We come from God and we are
in exile; and it is because our potency of affection tends towards
God that we are aware of this state of exile.

Ruysbroeck

Spiritual progress is through the growing knowledge of the
self as nothing and of the Godhead as all-embracing Reality.
(Such knowledge, of course, is worthless if it is merely theoretical; to be effective, it must be realized as an immediate,
intuitive experience and appropriately acted upon.) Of one
great master of the spiritual life Professor Étienne Gilson
writes: 'The displacement of fear by Charity by way of the
practice of humility—in that consists the whole of St. Bernard's ascesis, its beginning, its development and its term.'
Fear, worry, anxiety—these form the central core of individualized selfhood. Fear cannot be got rid of by personal
effort, but only by the ego's absorption in a cause greater than
its own interests. Absorption in any cause will rid the mind of
some of its fears; but only absorption in the loving and knowing of the divine Ground can rid it of *all* fear. For when the
cause is less than the highest, the sense of fear and anxiety is
transferred from the self to the cause—as when heroic self-
sacrifice for a loved individual or institution is accompanied
by anxiety in regard to that for which the sacrifice is made.
Whereas if the sacrifice is made for God, and for others for
God's sake, there can be no fear or abiding anxiety, since
nothing can be a menace to the divine Ground and even failure and disaster are to be accepted as being in accord with
the divine will. In few men and women is the love of God
intense enough to cast out this projected fear and anxiety for

cherished persons and institutions. The reason is to be sought in the fact that few men and women are humble enough to be capable of loving as they should. And they lack the necessary humility because they are without the fully realized knowledge of their own personal nothingness.

Humility does not consist in hiding our talents and virtues, in thinking ourselves worse and more ordinary than we are, but in possessing a clear knowledge of all that is lacking in us and in not exalting ourselves for that which we have, seeing that God has freely given it us and that, with all His gifts, we are still of infinitely little importance.

Lacordaire

As the light grows, we see ourselves to be worse than we thought. We are amazed at our former blindness as we see issuing from our heart a whole swarm of shameful feelings, like filthy reptiles crawling from a hidden cave. But we must be neither amazed nor disturbed. We are not worse than we were; on the contrary, we are better. But while our faults diminish, the light we see them by waxes brighter, and we are filled with horror. So long as there is no sign of cure, we are unaware of the depth of our disease; we are in a state of blind presumption and hardness, the prey of self-delusion. While we go with the stream, we are unconscious of its rapid course; but when we begin to stem it ever so little, it makes itself felt.

Fénelon

My daughter, build yourself two cells. First a real cell, so that you do not run about much and talk, unless it is needful, or you can do it out of love for your neighbour. Next build yourself a spiritual cell, which you can always take with you, and that is the cell of true self-knowledge; you will find there the knowledge of God's goodness to you. Here there are really two cells in one, and if you live in one you must also live in the other; otherwise the soul will either despair or be presumptuous. If you dwelt in self-knowledge alone, you would despair; if you dwelt in the knowledge of God alone, you would be tempted to presumption. One must go with the other, and thus you will reach perfection.

St. Catherine of Siena

Chapter 10

GRACE AND FREE WILL

DELIVERANCE is out of time into eternity, and is achieved by obedience and docility to the eternal Nature of Things. We have been given free will, in order that we may will our self-will out of existence and so come to live continuously in a 'state of grace.' All our actions must be directed, in the last analysis, to making ourselves passive in relation to the activity and the being of divine Reality. We are, as it were, aeolian harps, endowed with the power either to expose themselves to the wind of the Spirit or to shut themselves away from it.

> The Valley Spirit never dies.
> It is called the Mysterious Female.
> And the doorway of the Mysterious Female
> Is the base from which Heaven and Earth spring.
> It is there within us all the time.
> Draw upon it as you will, it never runs dry.
>
> *Lao Tzu*

In every exposition of the Perennial Philosophy the human soul is regarded as feminine in relation to the Godhead, the personal God and even the Order of Nature. *Hubris*, which is the original sin, consists in regarding the personal ego as self-sufficiently masculine in relation to the Spirit within and to Nature without, and in behaving accordingly.

St. Paul drew a very useful and illuminating distinction between the *psyche* and the *pneuma*. But the latter word never achieved any degree of popularity, and the hopelessly ambiguous term, *psyche*, came to be used indifferently for either the personal consciousness or the spirit. And why, in the Western church, did devotional writers choose to speak of man's *anima* (which for the Romans signified the lower, animal soul) instead of using the word traditionally reserved for the rational soul, namely *animus*? The answer, I suspect, is that they were anxious to stress by every means in their power the essential femininity of the human spirit in its relations with God. *Pneuma*, being grammatically neuter, and *animus*, being masculine, were felt to be less suitable than *anima* and *psyche*. Consider this concrete example; given the structure of Greek and Latin, it would have been very difficult for the speakers of these languages to identify anything but a grammatically feminine soul with the heroine of the Song of Songs—an allegorical figure who, for long centuries, played the same part in Christian thought and sentiment as the Gopi Maidens played in the theology and devotion of the Hindus.

Take note of this fundamental truth. Everything that works in nature and creature, except sin, is the working of God in nature and creature. The creature has nothing else in its power but the free use of its will, and its free will hath no other power but that of concurring with, or resisting, the working of God in nature. The creature with its free will can bring nothing into being, nor make any alteration in the working of nature; it can only change its own state or place in the working of nature, and so feel or find something in its state that it did not feel or find before.

William Law

Defined in psychological terms, grace is something other than our self-conscious personal self, by which we are helped. We have experience of three kinds of such helps—animal grace, human grace and spiritual grace. Animal grace comes when we are living in full accord with our own nature on the biological level—not abusing our bodies by excess, not interfering with the workings of our indwelling animal intelligence by conscious cravings and aversions, but living wholesomely and laying ourselves open to the 'virtue of the sun and the spirit of the air.' The reward of being thus in harmony with Tao or the Logos in its physical and physiological aspects is a sense of well-being, an awareness of life as good, not for any reason, but just because it is life. There is no question, when we are in a condition of animal grace, of *propter vitam vivendi perdere causas*; for in this state there is no distinction between the reasons for living and life itself. Life, like virtue, is then its own reward. But, of course, the fullness of animal grace is reserved for animals. Man's nature is such that he must live a self-conscious life in time, not in a blissful sub-rational eternity on the hither side of good and evil. Consequently animal grace is something that he knows only spasmodically in an occasional holiday from self-consciousness, or as an accompaniment to other states, in which life is not its own reward but has to be lived for a reason outside itself.

Human grace comes to us either from persons, or from social groups, or from our own wishes, hopes and imaginings projected outside ourselves and persisting somehow in the psychic medium in a state of what may be called second-hand objectivity. We have all had experience of the different types of human grace. There is, for example, the grace which, during childhood, comes from mother, father, nurse or beloved teacher. At a later stage we experience the grace of friends; the grace of men and women morally better and wiser than ourselves; the grace of the *guru*, or spiritual director. Then there is the grace which comes to us because of our attachment to country, party, church or other social organization—a grace which has helped even the feeblest and most timid individuals to achieve what, without it, would have been the impossible. And finally there is the grace which we derive from our ideals, whether low or high, whether conceived of in abstract terms or bodied forth in imaginary personifications. To this last type, it would seem, belong many of the graces experienced by the pious adherents of the various religions. The help received by those who devotedly adore or pray to some personal saint, deity or Avatar is often, we may guess, not a genuinely spiritual grace, but a human grace, coming back to the worshipper from the vortex of psychic power set up by repeated acts (his own and other people's) of faith, yearning and imagination.

Spiritual grace cannot be received continuously or in its fullness, except by those who have willed away their self-will to the point of being able truthfully to say, 'Not I, but God in me.' There are, however, few people so irremediably self-condemned to imprisonment within their own personality as to be wholly incapable of receiving the graces which are from instant to instant being offered to every soul. By fits and starts most of us contrive to forget, if only partially, our pre-occupation with 'I,' 'me,' 'mine,' and so become capable of receiving, if only partially, the graces which, in that moment, are being offered us.

. Spiritual grace originates from the divine Ground of all being, and it is given for the purpose of helping man to achieve his final end, which is to return out of time and selfhood to that Ground. It resembles animal grace in being derived from a source wholly other than our self-conscious, human selves; indeed, it is the same thing as animal grace, but manifesting itself on a higher level of the ascending spiral that leads from matter to the Godhead. In any given instance, human grace may be wholly good, inasmuch as it helps the recipient in the task of achieving the unitive knowledge of God; but because of its source in the individualized self, it is always a little sus-pect and, in many cases, of course, the help it gives is help towards the achievement of ends very different from the true end of our existence.

All our goodness is a loan; God is the owner. God works and his work is God.

                                        St. John of the Cross

Perpetual inspiration is as necessary to the life of goodness, holi-ness and happiness as perpetual respiration is necessary to animal life.

                                        William Law

Conversely, of course, the life of goodness, holiness and beatitude is a necessary condition of perpetual inspiration. The relations between action and contemplation, ethics and

N

spirituality are circular and reciprocal. Each is at once cause and effect.

It was when the Great Way declined that human kindness and morality arose.

Lao Tẕu

Chinese verbs are tenseless. This statement as to a hypothetical event in history refers at the same time to the present and the future. It means simply this: that with the rise of self-consciousness, animal grace is no longer sufficient for the conduct of life, and must be supplemented by conscious and deliberate choices between right and wrong—choices which have to be made in the light of a clearly formulated ethical code. But, as the Taoist sages are never tired of repeating, codes of ethics and deliberate choices made by the surface will are only a second best. The individualized will and the superficial intelligence are to be used for the purpose of recapturing the old animal relation to Tao, but on a higher, spiritual level. The goal is perpetual inspiration from sources beyond the personal self; and the means are 'human kindness and morality,' leading to the charity, which is unitive knowledge of Tao, as at once the Ground and Logos.

Lord, Thou hast given me my being of such a nature that it can continually make itself more able to receive thy grace and goodness. And this power, which I have of Thee, wherein I have a living image of Thine almighty power, is free will. By this I can either enlarge or restrict my capacity for Thy grace.

Nicholas of Cusa

Shun asked Ch'eng, saying, 'Can one get Tao so as to have it for oneself?'

'Your very body,' replied Ch'eng, 'is not your own. How should Tao be?'

'If my body,' said Shun, 'is not my own, pray whose is it?'

'It is the delegated image of God,' replied Ch'eng. 'Your life

is not your own. It is the delegated harmony of God. Your
individuality is not your own. It is the delegated adaptability of
God. Your posterity is not your own. It is the delegated
exuviae of God. You move, but know not how. You are at
rest, but know not why. You taste, but know not the cause.
These are the operations of God's laws. 'How then should you
get Tao so as to have it for your own?'

Chuang Tzu

It is within my power either to serve God, or not to serve Him.
Serving Him I add to my own good and the good of the whole
world. Not serving Him, I forfeit my own good and deprive
the world of that good, which was in my power to create.

Leo Tolstoy

God did not deprive thee of the operation of his love, but thou
didst deprive Him of thy cooperation. God would never have
rejected thee, if thou hadst not rejected his love. O all-good
God, thou dost not forsake unless forsaken, thou never takest
away thy gifts until we take away our hearts.

St. François de Sales

Ch'ing, the chief carpenter, was carving wood into a stand for
musical instruments. When finished, the work appeared to those
who saw it as though of supernatural execution; and the Prince
of Lu asked him, saying, 'What mystery is there in your art?'
    'No mystery, Your Highness,' replied Ch'ing. 'And yet there
is something. When I am about to make such a stand, I guard
against any diminution of my vital power. I first reduce my mind
to absolute quiescence. Three days in this condition, and I
become oblivious of any reward to be gained. Five days, and
I become oblivious of any fame to be acquired. Seven days,
and I become unconscious of my four limbs and my physical
frame. Then, with no thought of the Court present in my mind,
my skill becomes concentrated, and all disturbing elements from
without are gone. I enter some mountain forest, I search for a
suitable tree. It contains the form required, which is afterwards

elaborated. I see the stand in my mind's eye, and then set to work. Beyond that there is nothing. I bring my own native capacity into relation with that of the wood. What was suspected to be of supernatural execution in my work was due solely to this.'

Chuang Tẓu

The artist's inspiration may be either a human or a spiritual grace, or a mixture of both. High artistic achievement is impossible without at least those forms of intellectual, emotional and physical mortification appropriate to the kind of art which is being practised. Over and above this course of what may be called professional mortification, some artists have practised the kind of self-naughting which is the indispensable pre-condition of the unitive knowledge of the divine Ground. Fra Angelico, for example, prepared himself for his work by means of prayer and meditation; and from the foregoing extract from Chuang Tzu we see how essentially religious (and not merely professional) was the Taoist craftsman's approach to his art.

Here we may remark in passing that mechanization is incompatible with inspiration. The artisan could do and often did do a thoroughly bad job. But if, like Ch'ing, the chief carpenter, he cared for his art and were ready to do what was necessary to make himself docile to inspiration, he could and sometimes did do a job so good that it seemed 'as though of supernatural execution.' Among the many and enormous advantages of efficient automatic machinery is this: it is completely foolproof. But every gain has to be paid for. The automatic machine is fool-proof; but just because it is fool-proof it is also grace-proof. The man who tends such a machine is impervious to every form of aesthetic inspiration, whether of human or of genuinely spiritual origin. 'Industry without art is brutality.' But actually Ruskin maligns the brutes. The industrious bird or insect is inspired, when it works, by the infallible animal grace of instinct—by Tao as it manifests itself on the level immediately above the physiological. The industrial worker at his fool-proof and grace-proof machine does his job in a man-made universe of punctual automata—a universe that lies entirely beyond the pale of Tao on any level, brutal, human or spiritual.

In this context we may mention those sudden theophanies which are sometimes vouchsafed to children and sometimes to adults, who may be poets or Philistines, learned or unsophisticated, but who have this in common, that they have done nothing at all to prepare for what has happened to them. These gratuitous graces, which have inspired much literary and pictorial art, some splendid and some (where inspiration was not seconded by native talent) pathetically inadequate, seem generally to belong to one or other of two main classes —sudden and profoundly impressive perception of ultimate Reality as Love, Light and Bliss, and a no less impressive perception of it as dark, awe-inspiring and inscrutable Power. In memorable forms, Wordsworth has recorded his own experience of both these aspects of the divine Ground.

> There was a time when meadow, grove and stream,
> The earth and every common sight,
>   To me did seem
>   Apparelled in celestial light.

And so on.   But that was not the only vision.

>   Lustily
> I dipped my oars into the silent lake,
> And, as I rose upon the stroke, my boat
> Went heaving through the water like a swan;
> When, from behind that craggy steep, till then
> The horizon's bound, a huge peak, black and huge,
> As if with voluntary power instinct,
> Upreared its head.   I struck and struck again,
> And growing still in stature, the grim shape
> Towered up between me and the stars. . . .
>   But after I had seen
> That spectacle, for many days my brain

Worked with a dim and undetermined sense
Of unknown modes of being; o'er my thoughts
There hung a darkness, call it solitude,
Or blank desertion.

Significantly enough, it is to this second aspect of Reality that
primitive minds seem to have been most receptive. The formidable God, to whom Job at last submits, is an 'unknown
mode of Being,' whose most characteristic creations are
Behemoth and Leviathan. He is the sort of God who calls,
in Kierkegaard's phrase, for 'teleological suspensions of morality,' chiefly in the form of blood sacrifices, even human sacrifices. The Hindu goddess, Kali, in her more frightful aspects,
is another manifestation of the same unknown mode of Being.
And by many contemporary savages the underlying Ground is
apprehended and theologically rationalized as sheer, unmitigated Power, which has to be propitiatively worshipped and,
if possible, turned to profitable use by means of a compulsive
magic.

To think of God as mere Power, and not also, at the same
time as Power, Love and Wisdom, comes quite naturally to
the ordinary, unregenerate human mind. Only the totally selfless are in a position to know experimentally that, in spite of
everything, 'all will be well' and, in some way, already *is* well.
'The philosopher who denies divine providence,' says Rumi,
'is a stranger to the perception of the saints.' Only those who
have the perception of the saints can know all the time and by
immediate experience that divine Reality manifests itself as a
Power that is loving, compassionate and wise. The rest of us
are not yet in a spiritual position to do more than accept their
findings on faith. If it were not for the records they have left
behind, we should be more inclined to agree with Job and the
primitives.

Inspirations prevent us, and even before they are thought of make
themselves felt; but after we have felt them it is ours either to
consent to them, so as to second and follow their attractions, or

else to dissent and repulse them. They make themselves felt
without us, but they do not make us consent without us.

St. François de Sales

Our free will can hinder the course of inspiration, and when the
favourable gale of God's grace swells the sails of our soul, it is in
our power to refuse consent and thereby hinder the effect of the
wind's favour; but when our spirit sails along and makes its
voyage prosperously, it is not we who make the gale of inspiration blow for us, nor we who make our sails swell with it, nor we
who give motion to the ship of our heart; but we simply receive
the gale, consent to its motion and let our ship sail under it, not
hindering it by our resistance.

St. François de Sales

Grace is necessary to salvation, free will equally so—but grace in
order to give salvation, free will in order to receive it. Therefore
we should not attribute part of the good work to grace and part to
free will; it is performed in its entirety by the common and
inseparable action of both; entirely by grace, entirely by free
will, but springing from the first in the second.

St. Bernard

St. Bernard distinguishes between *voluntas communis* and
voluntas propria. *Voluntas communis* is common in two senses;
it is the will to share, and it is the will common to man and
God. For practical purposes it is equivalent to charity. *Voluntas propria* is the will to get and hold for oneself, and is
the root of all sin. In its cognitive aspect, *voluntas propria* is
the same as *sensum proprium*, which is one's own opinion,
cherished because it is one's own and therefore always morally
wrong, even though it may be theoretically correct.

Two students from the University of Paris came to visit Ruysbroeck and asked him to furnish them with a short phrase or
motto, which might serve them as a rule of life.

Vos estis tam sancti sicut vultis, Ruysbroeck answered. 'You
are as holy as you will to be.'

God is bound to act, to pour Himself into thee as soon as He shall find thee ready.

Eckhart

The will is that which has all power; it makes heaven and it makes hell; for there is no hell but where the will of the creature is turned from God, nor any heaven but where the will of the creature worketh with God.

William Law

O man, consider thyself! Here thou standest in the earnest perpetual strife of good and evil; all nature is continually at work to bring forth the great redemption; the whole creation is travailing in pain and laborious working to be delivered from the vanity of time; and wilt thou be asleep? Everything thou hearest or seest says nothing, shows nothing to thee but what either eternal light or eternal darkness has brought forth; for as day and night divide the whole of our time, so heaven and hell divide all our thoughts, words and actions. Stir which way thou wilt, do or design what thou wilt, thou must be an agent with the one or the other. Thou canst not stand still, because thou livest in the perpetual workings of temporal and eternal nature; if thou workest not with the good, the evil that is in nature carries thee along with it. Thou hast the height and depth of eternity in thee and therefore, be doing what thou wilt, either in the closet, the field, the shop or the church, thou art sowing that which grows and must be reaped in eternity.

William Law

God expects but one thing of you, and that is that you should come out of yourself in so far as you are a created being and let God be God in you.

Eckhart

For those who take pleasure in theological speculations based upon scriptural texts and dogmatic postulates, there are the thousands of pages of Catholic and Protestant controversy upon grace, works, faith and justification. And for students of comparative religion there are scholarly commentaries on the Bhagavad-Gita, on the works of Ramanuja and those later Vaishnavites, whose doctrine of grace bears a striking resemblance to that of Luther; there are histories of Buddhism which duly trace the development of that religion from the Hinayanist doctrine that salvation is the fruit of strenuous self-help to the Mahayanist doctrine that it cannot be achieved without the grace of the Primordial Buddha, whose inner consciousness and 'great compassionate heart' constitute the eternal Suchness of things. For the rest of us, the foregoing quotations from writers within the Christian and early Taoist tradition provide, it seems to me, an adequate account of the observable facts of grace and inspiration and their relation to the observable facts of free will.

Chapter 11

GOOD AND EVIL

DESIRE is the first datum of our consciousness; we are born into sympathy and antipathy, wishing and willing. Unconsciously at first, then consciously, we evaluate: 'This is good, that is bad.' And a little later we discover obligation. 'This, being good, ought to be done; that, being bad, ought not to be done.'

All evaluations are not equally valid. We are called upon to pass judgment on what our desires and dislikes affirm to be good or bad. Very often we discover that the verdict of the higher court is at variance with the decision reached so quickly and light-heartedly in the court of first instance. In the light of what we know about ourselves, our fellow-beings and the world at large, we discover that what at first seemed good may, in the long run or in the larger context, be bad; and that what at first seemed bad may be a good which we feel ourselves under obligation to accomplish.

When we say that a man is possessed of penetrating moral insight we mean that his judgment of value-claims is sound; that he knows enough to be able to say what is good in the longest run and the largest context. When we say that a man has a strong moral character, we mean that he is ready to act upon the findings of his insight, even when these findings are unpleasantly or even excruciatingly at variance with his first, spontaneous valuations.

In actual practice moral insight is never a strictly personal matter. The judge administers a system of law and is guided by precedent. In other words, every individual is the member of a community, which has a moral code based upon past findings of what in fact is good in the longer run and the wider context. In most circumstances most of the members of any given society permit themselves to be guided by the generally accepted code of morals; a few reject the code, either in its entirety or in part; and a few choose to live by another, higher and more exacting code. In Christian phraseology, there are the few who stubbornly persist in living in a state of mortal sin and antisocial lawlessness; there are the many who obey the laws, make the Precepts of Morality their guide, repent of mortal sins when they commit them, but do not make much effort to avoid venial sins; and finally there are the few whose righteousness 'exceeds the righteousness of the scribes and Pharisees,' who are guided by the Counsels of Perfection and have the insight to perceive and the character to avoid venial sins and even imperfections.

Philosophers and theologians have sought to establish a theoretical basis for the existing moral codes, by whose aid individual men and women pass judgment on their spontaneous evaluations. From Moses to Bentham, from Epicurus to Calvin, from the Christian and Buddhist philosophies of universal love to the lunatic doctrines of nationalism and racial superiority—the list is long and the span of thought enormously wide. But fortunately there is no need for us to consider these various theories. Our concern is only with the Perennial Philosophy and with the system of ethical principles which those who believe in that philosophy have used, when passing judgment on their own and other people's evaluations. The questions that we have to ask in this section are simple enough, and simple too are the answers. As always, the difficulties begin only when we pass from theory to practice, from ethical principle to particular application.

Granted that the ground of the individual soul is akin to, or identical with, the divine Ground of all existence, and granted that this divine Ground is an ineffable Godhead that manifests itself as personal God or even as the incarnate Logos, what is the ultimate nature of good and evil, and what the true purpose and last end of human life?

The answers to these questions will be given to a great extent in the words of that most surprising product of the English eighteenth century, William Law. (How very odd

our educational system is! Students of English literature are
forced to read the graceful journalism of Steele and Addison,
are expected to know all about the minor novels of Defoe and
the tiny elegances of Matthew Prior. But they can pass all
their examinations *summa cum laude* without having so much
as looked into the writings of a man who was not only a master
of English prose, but also one of the most interesting thinkers
of his period and one of the most endearingly saintly figures in
the whole history of Anglicanism.) Our current neglect of
Law is yet another of the many indications that twentieth-
century educators have ceased to be concerned with questions
of ultimate truth or meaning and (apart from mere vocational
training) are interested solely in the dissemination of a rootless and irrelevant culture, and the fostering of the solemn
foolery of scholarship for scholarship's sake.

Nothing burns in hell but the self.

Theologia Germanica

The mind is on fire, thoughts are on fire. Mind-consciousness
and the impressions received by the mind, and the sensations that
arise from the impressions that the mind receives—these too are
on fire.

And with what are they on fire? With the fire of greed, with
the fire of resentment, with the fire of infatuation; with birth, old
age and death, with sorrow and lamentation, with misery and
grief and despair they are on fire.

From the Buddha's Fire Sermon

If thou hast not seen the devil, look at thine own self.

Jalal-uddin Rumi

Your own self is your own Cain that murders your own Abel.
For every action and motion of self has the spirit of Anti-Christ
and murders the divine life within you.

William Law

The city of God is made by the love of God pushed to the contempt of self; the earthly city, by the love of self pushed to the contempt of God.

St. Augustine

The difference between a good and a bad man does not lie in this, that the one wills that which is good and the other does not, but solely in this, that the one concurs with the living inspiring spirit of God within him, and the other resists it, and can be chargeable with evil only because he resists it.

William Law

People should think less about what they ought to do and more about what they ought to be. If only their being were good, their works would shine forth brightly. Do not imagine that you can ground your salvation upon actions; it must rest on what you *are*. The ground upon which good character rests is the very same ground from which man's work derives its value, namely a mind wholly turned to God. Verily, if you were so minded, you might tread on a stone and it would be a more pious work than if you, simply for your own profit, were to receive the Body of the Lord and were wanting in spiritual detachment.

Eckhart

Man is made by his belief. As he believes, so he is.

Bhagavad-Gita

It is mind which gives to things their quality, their foundation and their being. Whoever speaks or acts with impure mind, him sorrow follows, as the wheel follows the steps of the ox that draws the cart.

Dhammapada

The nature of a man's being determines the nature of his actions; and the nature of his being comes to manifestation first of all in the mind. What he craves and thinks, what he believes and feels—this is, so to speak, the Logos, by whose agency an individual's fundamental character performs its creative acts. These acts will be beautiful and morally good if the being is God-centred, bad and ugly if it is centred in the personal self. 'The stone,' says Eckhart, 'performs its work without ceasing, day and night.' For even when it is not actually falling the stone has weight. A man's being is his potential energy directed towards or away from God; and it is by this potential energy that he will be judged as good or evil—for it is possible, in the language of the Gospel, to commit adultery and murder in the heart, even while remaining blameless in action.

Covetousness, envy, pride and wrath are the four elements of self, or nature, or hell, all of them inseparable from it. And the reason why it must be thus, and cannot be otherwise, is because the natural life of the creature is brought forth for the participation of some high supernatural good in the Creator. But it could have no fitness, no possible capacity to receive such good, unless it was in itself both an extremity of want and an extremity of desire for some high good. When therefore this natural life is deprived of or fallen from God, it can be nothing else in itself but an extremity of want continually desiring, and an extremity of desire continually wanting. And because it is that, its whole life can be nothing else but a plague and torment of covetousness, envy, pride and wrath, all which is precisely nature, self, or hell. Now covetousness, pride and envy are not three different things, but only three different names for the restless workings of one and the same will or desire. Wrath, which is a fourth birth from these three, can have no existence till one or all of these three are contradicted, or have something done to them that is contrary to their will. These four properties generate their own torment. They have no outward cause, nor any inward power of altering themselves. And therefore all self or nature must be in this state until some supernatural good comes into it, or gets a birth in it. Whilst man indeed lives among the vanities of time, his covetousness, envy, pride and wrath may be in a tolerable state, may hold him to a mixture of peace and trouble; they may have at times their gratifications as well as their torments. But when death has

put an end to the vanity of all earthly cheats, the soul that is not
born again of the supernatural Word and Spirit of God, must find
itself unavoidably devoured or shut up in its own insatiable, un-
changeable, self-tormenting covetousness, envy, pride and wrath.

William Law

It is true that you cannot properly express the degree of your
sinfulness; but that is because it is impossible, in this life, to
represent sins in all their true ugliness; nor shall we ever know
them as they really are except in the light of God.   God gives to
some souls an impression of the enormity of sin, by which He
makes them feel that sin is incomparably greater than it seems.
Such souls must conceive their sins as faith represents them (that
is, as they are in themselves), but must be content to describe
them in such human words as their mouth is able to utter.

Charles de Condren

Lucifer, when he stood in his natural nobility, as God had created
him, was a pure noble creature.   But when he kept to self, when
he possessed himself and his natural nobility as a property, he fell
and became, instead of an angel, a devil.   So it is with man.   If
he remains in himself and possesses himself of his natural nobility
as a property, he falls and becomes, instead of a man, a devil.

The Following of Christ

If a delicious fragrant fruit had a power of separating itself from
the rich spirit, fine taste, smell and colour, which it receives from
the virtue of the air and the spirit of the sun, or if it could, in the
beginning of its growth, turn away from the sun and receive no
virtue from it, then it would stand in its own first birth of wrath,
sourness, bitterness, astringency, just as the devils do, who have
turned back into their own dark root and have rejected the Light
and Spirit of God.   So that the hellish nature of a devil is nothing
but its own first forms of life withdrawn or separated from the
heavenly Light and Love; just as the sourness, bitterness and
astringency of a fruit are nothing else but the first form of its vege-
table life, before it has reached the virtue of the sun and the spirit

of the air. And as a fruit, if it had a sensibility of itself, would be full of torment as soon as it was shut up in the first forms of its life, in its own astringency, sourness and stinging bitterness, so the angels, when they had turned back into these very same first forms of their own life, and broke off from the heavenly Light and Love of God, became their own hell. No hell was made for them, no new qualities came into them, no vengeance or pains from the Lord of Love fell on them; they only stood in that state of division and separation from the Son and Holy Spirit of God, which by their own motion they had made for themselves. They had nothing in them but what they had from God, the first forms of a heavenly life; but they had them in a state of self-torment, because they had separated them from birth of Love and Light.

William Law

In all the possibility of things there is and can be but one happiness and one misery. The one misery is nature and creature left to itself, the one happiness is the Life, the Light, the Spirit of God, manifested in nature and creature. This is the true meaning of the words of Our Lord: There is but one that is good, and that is God.

William Law

Men are not in hell because God is angry with them; they are in wrath and darkness because they have done to the light, which infinitely flows forth from God, as that man does to the light of the sun, who puts out his own eyes.

William Law

Though the light and comfort of the outward world keeps even the worst of men from any constant strong sensibility of that wrathful, fiery, dark and self-tormenting nature that is the very essence of every fallen unregenerate soul, yet every man in the world has more or less frequent and strong intimations given him that so it is with him in the inmost ground of his soul. How many inventions are some people forced to have recourse to in order to keep off a certain inward uneasiness, which they are afraid of and know not whence it comes? Alas, it is because there is a fallen spirit, a dark aching fire within them, which has never had its proper relief and is trying to discover itself and calling out for help at every cessation of worldly joy.

William Law

In the Hebrew-Christian tradition the Fall is subsequent to creation and is due exclusively to the egocentric use of a free will, which ought to have remained centred in the divine Ground and not in the separate selfhood. The myth of Genesis embodies a very important psychological truth, but falls short of being an entirely satisfactory symbol, because it fails to mention, much less to account for, the fact of evil and suffering in the non-human world. To be adequate to our experience the myth would have to be modified in two ways. In the first place, it would have to make clear that creation, the incomprehensible passage from the unmanifested One into the manifest multiplicity of nature, from eternity into time, is not merely the prelude and necessary condition of the Fall; to some extent it *is* the Fall. And in the second place, it would have to indicate that something analogous to free will may exist below the human level.

That the passage from the unity of spiritual to the manifoldness of temporal being is an essential part of the Fall is clearly stated in the Buddhist and Hindu renderings of the Perennial Philosophy. Pain and evil are inseparable from individual existence in a world of time; and, for human beings, there is an intensification of this inevitable pain and evil when the desire is turned towards the self and the many, rather than towards the divine Ground. To this we might speculatively add the opinion that perhaps even sub-human existences may be endowed (both individually and collectively, as kinds and species) with something resembling the power of choice. There is the extraordinary fact that 'man stands alone'—that, so far as we can judge, every other species is a species of living fossils, capable only of degeneration and extinction, not of further evolutionary advance. In the phraseology of Scholastic

Aristotelianism, matter possesses an appetite for form—not necessarily for the best form, but for form as such. Looking about us in the world of living things, we observe (with a delighted wonder, touched occasionally, it must be admitted, with a certain questioning dismay) the innumerable forms, always beautiful, often extravagantly odd and sometimes even sinister, in which the insatiable appetite of matter has found its satisfaction. Of all this living matter only that which is organized as human beings has succeeded in finding a form capable, at any rate on the mental side, of further development. All the rest is now locked up in forms that can only remain what they are or, if they change, only change for the worse. It looks as though, in the cosmic intelligence test, all living matter, except the human, had succumbed, at one time or another during its biological career, to the temptation of assuming, not the ultimately best, but the immediately most profitable form. By an act of something analogous to free will every species, except the human, has chosen the quick returns of specialization, the present rapture of being perfect, but perfect on a low level of being. The result is that they all stand at the end of evolutionary blind alleys. To the initial cosmic Fall of creation, of multitudinous manifestation in time, they have added the obscurely biological equivalent of man's voluntary Fall. As species, they have chosen the immediate satisfaction of the self rather than the capacity for reunion with the divine Ground. For this wrong choice, the non-human forms of life are punished negatively, by being debarred from realizing the supreme good, to which only the unspecialized and therefore freer, more highly conscious human form is capable. But it must be remembered, of course, that the capacity for supreme good is achieved only at the price of becoming also capable of extreme evil. Animals do not suffer in so many ways, nor, we may feel pretty certain, to the same extent as do men and women. Further, they are quite innocent of that literally diabolic wickedness which, together with sanctity, is one of the distinguishing marks of the human species.

We see then that, for the Perennial Philosophy, good is the

separate self's conformity to, and finally annihilation in, the divine Ground which gives it being; evil, the intensification of separateness, the refusal to know that the Ground exists. This doctrine is, of course, perfectly compatible with the formulation of ethical principles as a series of negative and positive divine commandments, or even in terms of social utility. The crimes which are everywhere forbidden proceed from states of mind which are everywhere condemned as wrong; and these wrong states of mind are, as a matter of empirical fact, absolutely incompatible with that unitive knowledge of the divine Ground, which, according to the Perennial Philosophy, is the supreme good.

Chapter 12

TIME AND ETERNITY

THE universe is an everlasting succession of events; but its ground, according to the Perennial Philosophy, is the timeless now of the divine Spirit. A classical statement of the relationship between time and eternity may be found in the later chapters of the *Consolations of Philosophy*, where Boethius summarizes the conceptions of his predecessors, notably of Plotinus.

It is one thing to be carried through an endless life, another thing to embrace the whole presence of an endless life together, which is manifestly proper to the divine Mind.

The temporal world seems to emulate in part that which it cannot fully obtain or express, tying itself to whatever presence there is in this exiguous and fleeting moment—a presence which, since it carries a certain image of that abiding Presence, gives to whatever may partake of it the quality of seeming to have being. But because it could not stay, it undertook an infinite journey of time; and so it came to pass that, by going, it continued that life, whose plenitude it could not comprehend by staying.

Boethius

Since God hath always an eternal and present state, His knowledge, surpassing time's notions, remaineth in the simplicity of His presence and, comprehending the infinite of what is past and to come, considereth all things as though they were in the act of being accomplished.

Boethius

Knowledge of what is happening now does not determine the event. What is ordinarily called God's foreknowledge is in reality a timeless now-knowledge, which is compatible with the freedom of the human creature's will in time.

212

The manifest world and whatever is moved in any sort take their
causes, order and forms from the stability of the divine Mind.
This hath determined manifold ways for doing things; which
ways being considered in the purity of God's understanding are
named Providence; but being referred to those things which He
moveth and disposeth are called Fate. . . . Providence is the very
divine Reason itself, which disposeth all things. But Fate is a
disposition inherent in changeable things, by which Providence
connecteth all things in their due order. For Providence equally
embraceth all things together, though diverse, though infinite;
but Fate puts into motion all things, distributed by places, forms
and times; so that the unfolding of the temporal order, being
united in the foresight of the divine Mind, is Providence, and the
same uniting, being digested and unfolded in time, is called Fate.
. . . As a workman conceiving the form of anything in his mind,
taketh his work in hand and executeth by order of time that which
he had simply and in a moment foreseen, so God by his Providence disposeth whatever is to be done with simplicity and stability, and by Fate effecteth by manifold ways and in the order of
time those very things which He disposeth. . . . All that is under
Fate is also subject to Providence. But some things which are
under Providence are above the course of Fate. For they are
those things which, being stably fixed in virtue of their nearness
to the first divinity, exceed the order of Fate's mobility.

Boethius

The concept of a clock enfolds all succession in time. In the concept the sixth hour is not earlier than the seventh or eighth,
although the clock never strikes the hour, save when the concept
biddeth.

Nicholas of Cusa

From Hobbes onwards, the enemies of the Perennial Philosophy have denied the existence of an eternal now. According
to these thinkers, time and change are fundamental; there is
no other reality. Moreover, future events are completely inde-
terminate, and even God can have no knowledge of them.

Consequently God cannot be described as Alpha and Omega—merely as Alpha and Lambda, or whatever other intermediate letter of the temporal alphabet is now in process of being spelled out. But the anecdotal evidence collected by the Society for Psychical Research and the statistical evidence accumulated during many thousands of laboratory tests for extra-sensory perception point inescapably to the conclusion that even human minds are capable of foreknowledge. And if a finite consciousness can know what card is going to be turned up three seconds from now, or what shipwreck is going to take place next week, then there is nothing impossible or even intrinsically improbable in the idea of an infinite consciousness that can know now events indefinitely remote in what, for us, is future time. The 'specious present' in which human beings live may be, and perhaps always is, something more than a brief section of transition from known past to unknown future, regarded, because of the vividness of memory, as the instant we call 'now'; it may and perhaps always does contain a portion of the immediate and even of the relatively distant future. For the Godhead, the specious present may be precisely that *interminabilis vitae tota simul et perpetua possessio*, of which Boethius speaks.

The existence of the eternal now is sometimes denied on the ground that a temporal order cannot co-exist with another order which is non-temporal; and that it is impossible for a changing substance to be united with a changeless substance. This objection, it is obvious, would be valid if the non-temporal order were of a mechanical nature, or if the changeless substance were possessed of spatial and material qualities. But according to the Perennial Philosophy, the eternal now is a consciousness; the divine Ground is spirit; the being of Brahman is *chit*, or knowledge. That a temporal world should be known and, in being known, sustained and perpetually created by an eternal consciousness is an idea which contains nothing self-contradictory.

Finally we come to the arguments directed against those who have asserted that the eternal Ground can be unitively known by human minds. This claim is regarded as absurd because it

involves the assertion, 'At one time I am eternal, at another time
I am in time.' But this statement is absurd only if man is a
being of a twofold nature, capable of living on only one level.
But if, as the exponents of the Perennial Philosophy have
always maintained, man is not only a body and a psyche, but
also a spirit, and if he can at will live either on the merely human
plane or else in harmony and even in union with the divine
Ground of his being, then the statement makes perfectly good
sense. The body is always in time, the spirit is always timeless
and the psyche is an amphibious creature compelled by the laws
of man's being to associate itself to some extent with its body,
but capable, if it so desires, of experiencing and being identified
with its spirit and, through its spirit, with the divine Ground.
The spirit remains always what it eternally is; but man is so
constituted that his psyche cannot always remain identified
with the spirit. In the statement, 'At one time I am eternal,
at another time I am in time,' the word 'I' stands for the
psyche, which passes from time to eternity when it is identified
with the spirit and passes again from eternity to time, either
voluntarily or by involuntary necessity, when it chooses or is
compelled to identify itself with the body.

'The Sufi,' says Jalal-uddin Rumi, 'is the son of time
present.' Spiritual progress is a spiral advance. We start as
infants in the animal eternity of life in the moment, without
anxiety for the future or regret for the past; we grow up into
the specifically human condition of those who look before and
after, who live to a great extent, not in the present but in
memory and anticipation, not spontaneously but by rule and
with prudence, in repentance and fear and hope; and we can
continue, if we so desire, up and on in a returning sweep
towards a point corresponding to our starting place in animal-
ity, but incommensurably above it. Once more life is lived
in the moment—the life now, not of a sub-human creature,
but of a being in whom charity has cast out fear, vision has
taken the place of hope, selflessness has put a stop to the positive egotism of complacent reminiscence and the negative
egotism of remorse. The present moment is the only aperture

through which the soul can pass out of time into eternity, through which grace can pass out of eternity into the soul, and through which charity can pass from one soul in time to another soul in time. That is why the Sufi and, along with him, every other practising exponent of the Perennial Philosophy is, or tries to be, a son of time present.

Past and future veil God from our sight;
Burn up both of them with fire. How long
Wilt thou be partitioned by these segments, like a reed?
So long as a reed is partitioned, it is not privy to secrets,
Nor is it vocal in response to lip and breathing.

Jalal-uddin Rumi

This emptying of the memory, though the advantages of it are not so great as those of the state of union, yet merely because it delivers souls from much sorrow, grief and sadness, besides imperfections and sins, is in reality a great good.

St. John of the Cross

In the idealistic cosmology of Mahayana Buddhism memory plays the part of a rather maleficent demiurge. 'When the triple world is surveyed by the Bodhisattva, he perceives that its existence is due to memory that has been accumulated since the beginningless past, but wrongly interpreted' (Lankavatara Sutra). The word here translated as 'memory' means literally 'perfuming.' The mind-body carries with it the ineradicable smell of all that has been thought and done, desired and felt, throughout its racial and personal past. The Chinese translate the Sanskrit term by two symbols, signifying 'habit-energy.' The world is what (in our eyes) it is, because of all the consciously or unconsciously and physiologically remembered habits formed by our ancestors or by ourselves, either in our present life or in previous existences. These remembered bad habits cause us to believe that multiplicity is the sole reality and that the idea of 'I,' 'me,' 'mine' represents the ultimate truth. *Nirvana* consists in 'seeing into the abode of reality as it is,' and not reality *quoad nos*, as it seems to us. Obviously, this cannot be achieved so long as there is an 'us,' to which reality can be relative. Hence the need, stressed by every exponent of the Perennial Philosophy, for mortification, for dying to self. And this must be a mortification not only of the appetites, the feelings and the will, but also of the reasoning powers, of consciousness itself and of that which makes our consciousness what it is—our personal memory and our inherited habit-energies. To achieve complete deliverance, conversion from sin is not enough; there must also be a conversion of the mind, a *paravritti*, as the Mahayanists call it, or revulsion in the very depths of consciousness. As the result of this revulsion, the habit-energies of accumulated memory are destroyed and, along with them, the sense of being a separate ego. Reality is no longer perceived *quoad nos* (for the good reason that there is no longer a *nos* to perceive it), but as it is in itself. In Blake's words, 'If the doors of perception were cleansed, everything would be seen as it is, infinite.' By those who are pure in heart and poor in spirit, *samsara* and *nirvana*, appearance and reality, time and eternity are experienced as one and the same.

Time is what keeps the light from reaching us. There is no greater obstacle to God than time. And not only time but temporalities, not only temporal things but temporal affections; not only temporal affections but the very taint and smell of time.

Eckhart

Rejoice in God all the time, says St. Paul. He rejoices all the time who rejoices above time and free from time. Three things prevent a man from knowing God. The first is time, the second is corporeality, the third is multiplicity. That God may come in, these things must go out—except thou have them in a higher, better way: multitude summed up to one in thee.

Eckhart

Whenever God is thought of as being wholly in time, there

is a tendency to regard Him as a 'numinous' rather than a moral being, a God of mere unmitigated Power rather than a God of Power, Wisdom and Love, an inscrutable and dangerous potentate to be propitiated by sacrifices, not a Spirit to be worshipped in spirit. All this is only natural; for time is a perpetual perishing and a God who is wholly in time is a God who destroys as fast as He creates. Nature is as incomprehensibly appalling as it is lovely and bountiful. If the Divine does not transcend the temporal order in which it is immanent, and if the human spirit does not transcend its time-bound soul, then there is no possibility of 'justifying the ways of God to man.' God as manifested in the universe is the irresistible Being who speaks to Job out of the whirlwind, and whose emblems are Behemoth and Leviathan, the war horse and the eagle. It is this same Being who is described in the apocalyptic eleventh chapter of the Bhagavad-Gita. 'O Supreme Spirit,' says Arjuna, addressing himself to the Krishna whom he now knows to be the incarnation of the Godhead, 'I long to see your Isvara-form'—that is to say, his form as God of the world, Nature, the temporal order. Krishna answers, 'You shall behold the whole universe, with all things animate and inanimate, within this body of mine.' Arjuna's reaction to the revelation is one of amazement and fear.

> Ah, my God, I see all gods within your body;
> Each in his degree, the multitude of creatures;
> See Lord Brahma seated upon his lotus,
> See all the sages and the holy serpents.

> Universal Form, I see you without limit,
> Infinite of eyes, arms, mouths and bellies—
> See, and find no end, midst or beginning.

There follows a long passage, enlarging on the omnipotence and all-comprehensiveness of God in his Isvara-form. Then the quality of the vision changes, and Arjuna realizes, with fear and trembling, that the God of the universe is a God of destruction as well as of creation.

> Now with frightful tusks your mouths are gnashing,
> Flaring like the fires of Doomsday morning—
> North, south, east and west seem all confounded—
> Lord of devas, world's abode, have mercy! . . .

> Swift as many rivers streaming to the ocean,
> Rush the heroes to your fiery gullets,
> Moth-like to meet the flame of their destruction.
> Headlong these plunge into you and perish. . . .

> Tell me who you are, and were from the beginning,
> You of aspect grim.   O God of gods, be gracious.
> Take my homage, Lord.   From me your ways are hidden.

'Tell me who you are.'   The answer is clear and unequivocal.

> I am come as Time, the waster of the peoples,
> Ready for the hour that ripens to their ruin.

But the God who comes so terribly as Time also exists timelessly as the Godhead, as Brahman, whose essence is *Sat, Chit, Ananda,* Being, Awareness, Bliss; and within and beyond man's time-tortured psyche is his spirit, 'uncreated and uncreatable,' as Eckhart says, the Atman which is akin to or even identical with Brahman.   The Gita, like all other formulations of the Perennial Philosophy, justifies God's ways to man by affirming —and the affirmation is based upon observation and immediate experience—that man can, if he so desires, die to his separate temporal selfness and so come to union with timeless Spirit. It affirms, too, that the Avatar becomes incarnate in order to assist human beings to achieve this union.   This he does in three ways—by teaching the true doctrine in a world blinded by voluntary ignorance; by inviting souls to a 'carnal love' of his humanity, not indeed as an end in itself, but as the means to spiritual love-knowledge of Spirit; and finally by serving as a channel of grace.

God who is Spirit can only be worshipped in spirit and for his own sake; but God in time is normally worshipped by material means with a view to achieving temporal ends. God in time is manifestly the destroyer as well as the creator; and because this is so, it has seemed proper to worship him by methods which are as terrible as the destructions he himself inflicts. Hence, in India, the blood sacrifices to Kali, in her aspect as Nature-the-Destroyer; hence those offerings of children to 'the Molochs,' denounced by the Hebrew prophets; hence the human sacrifices practised, for example, by the Phoenicians, the Carthaginians, the Druids, the Aztecs. In all such cases the divinity addressed was a god in time, or a personification of Nature, which is nothing else but Time itself, the devourer of its own offspring; and in all cases the purpose of the rite was to obtain a future benefit or to avoid one of the enormous evils which Time and Nature for ever hold in store. For this it was thought to be worth while to pay a high price in that currency of suffering, which the Destroyer so evidently valued. The importance of the temporal end justified the use of means that were intrinsically terrible, because intrinsically time-like. Sublimated traces of these ancient patterns of thought and behaviour are still to be found in certain theories of the Atonement, and in the conception of the Mass as a perpetually repeated sacrifice of the God-Man.

In the modern world the gods to whom human sacrifice is offered are personifications, not of Nature, but of man's own, home-made political ideals. These, of course, all refer to events in time—actual events in the past or the present, fancied events in the future. And here it should be noted that the philosophy which affirms the existence and the immediate realizableness of eternity is related to one kind of political theory and practice; the philosophy which affirms that what goes on in time is the only reality, results in a different kind of theory and justifies quite another kind of political practice. This has been clearly recognized by Marxist writers,* who point out that when Christianity is mainly preoccupied with events in time, it is a 'revolutionary religion,' and that when, under mystical influences, it stresses the Eternal Gospel, of which the historical or pseudo-historical facts recorded in Scripture are but symbols, it becomes politically 'static' and 'reactionary.'

This Marxian account of the matter is somewhat over-simplified. It is not quite true to say that all theologies and philosophies whose primary concern is with time, rather than eternity, are necessarily revolutionary. The aim of all revolutions is to make the future radically different from and better than the past. But some time-obsessed philosophies are primarily concerned with the past, not the future, and their politics are entirely a matter of preserving or restoring the *status quo* and getting back to the good old days. But the retrospective time-worshippers have one thing in common with the revolutionary devotees of the bigger and better future; they are prepared to use unlimited violence to achieve their ends. It is here that we discover the essential difference between the politics of eternity-philosophers and the politics of time-philosophers. For the latter, the ultimate good is to be found in the temporal world—in a future, where everyone will be happy because all are doing and thinking something either entirely new and unprecedented or, alternatively, something old, traditional and hallowed. And because the ultimate good lies in time, they feel justified in making use of any temporal means for achieving it. The Inquisition burns and tortures in order to perpetuate a creed, a ritual and an ecclesi-astico-politico-financial organization regarded as necessary to men's eternal salvation. Bible-worshipping Protestants fight long and savage wars, in order to make the world safe for what they fondly imagine to be the genuinely antique Christianity of apostolic times. Jacobins and Bolsheviks are ready to sacrifice millions of human lives for the sake of a political and economic future gorgeously unlike the present. And now all

* See, for example, Professor J. B. S. Haldane's *The Marxist Philosophy and the Sciences*.

Europe and most of Asia has had to be sacrificed to a crystal-gazer's vision of perpetual Co-Prosperity and the Thousand-Year Reich. From the records of history it seems to be abundantly clear that most of the religions and philosophies which take time too seriously are correlated with political theories that inculcate and justify the use of large-scale violence. The only exceptions are those simple Epicurean faiths, in which the reaction to an all too real time is 'Eat, drink and be merry, for tomorrow we die.' This is not a very noble, nor even a very realistic kind of morality. But it seems to make a good deal more sense than the revolutionary ethic: 'Die (and kill), for tomorrow someone else will eat, drink and be merry.' In practice, of course, the prospect even of somebody else's future merriment is extremely precarious. For the process of wholesale dying and killing creates material, social and psychological conditions that practically guarantee the revolution against the achievement of its beneficent ends.

For those whose philosophy does not compel them to take time with an excessive seriousness the ultimate good is to be sought neither in the revolutionary's progressive social apocalypse, nor in the reactionary's revived and perpetuated past, but in an eternal divine now which those who sufficiently desire this good can realize as a fact of immediate experience. The mere act of dying is not in itself a passport to eternity; nor can wholesale killing do anything to bring deliverance either to the slayers or the slain or their posterity. The peace that passes all understanding is the fruit of liberation into eternity; but in its ordinary everyday form peace is also the root of liberation. For where there are violent passions and compelling distractions, this ultimate good can never be realized. That is one of the reasons why the policy correlated with eternity-philosophies is tolerant and non-violent. The other reason is that the eternity, whose realization is the ultimate good, is a kingdom of heaven within. Thou art That; and though That is immortal and impassible, the killing and torturing of individual 'thous' is a matter of cosmic significance, inasmuch as it interferes with the normal and natural relationship between individual souls and the divine eternal Ground of all being. Every violence is, over and above everything else, a sacrilegious rebellion against the divine order.

Passing now from theory to historical fact, we find that the religions, whose theology has been least preoccupied with events in time and most concerned with eternity, have been consistently the least violent and the most humane in political practice. Unlike early Judaism, Christianity and Moham-medanism (all of them obsessed with time), Hinduism and Buddhism have never been persecuting faiths, have preached almost no holy wars and have refrained from that proselytizing religious imperialism, which has gone hand in hand with the political and economic oppression of the coloured peoples. For four hundred years, from the beginning of the sixteenth century to the beginning of the twentieth, most of the Chris-tian nations of Europe have spent a good part of their time and energy in attacking, conquering and exploiting their non-Christian neighbours in other continents. In the course of these centuries many individual churchmen did their best to mitigate the consequences of such iniquities; but none of the major Christian churches officially condemned them. The first collective protest against the slave system, introduced by the English and the Spaniards into the New World, was made in 1688 by the Quaker Meeting of Germantown. This fact is highly significant. Of all Christian sects in the seventeenth century, the Quakers were the least obsessed with history, the least addicted to the idolatry of things in time. They believed that the inner light was in all human beings and that salvation came to those who lived in conformity with that light and was not dependent on the profession of belief in historical or pseudo-historical events, nor on the performance of certain rites, nor on the support of a particular ecclesiastical organiza-tion. Moreover, their eternity-philosophy preserved them from the materialistic apocalypticism of that progress-worship which in recent times has justified every kind of iniquity from war and revolution to sweated labour, slavery and the exploitation of savages and children—has justified them on the ground that the supreme good is in future time and that any temporal means, however intrinsically horrible, may be used to achieve that good. Because Quaker theology was a form of eternity-philosophy, Quaker political theory rejected war and persecution as means to ideal ends, denounced slavery and proclaimed racial equality. Members of other denominations had done good work for the African victims of the white man's rapacity. One thinks, for example, of St. Peter Claver at Cartagena. But this heroically charitable 'slave of the slaves' never raised his voice against the institution of slavery or the criminal trade by which it was sustained; nor, so far as the extant documents reveal, did he ever, like John Woolman, attempt to persuade the slave-owners to free their human chattels. The reason, presumably, was that Claver was a Jesuit, vowed to perfect obedience and constrained by his theology to regard a certain political and ecclesiastical organization as being the mystical body of Christ. The heads of this organization had not pronounced against slavery or the slave trade. Who was he, Pedro Claver, to express a thought not officially approved by his superiors?

Another practical corollary of the great historical eternity-philosophies, such as Hinduism and Buddhism, is a morality inculcating kindness to animals. Judaism and orthodox Christianity taught that animals might be used as things, for the realization of man's temporal ends. Even St. Francis' attitude towards the brute creation was not entirely unequivocal. True, he converted a wolf and preached sermons to birds; but when Brother Juniper hacked the feet off a living pig in order to satisfy a sick man's craving for fried trotters, the saint merely blamed his disciple's intemperate zeal in damaging a valuable piece of private property. It was not until the nineteenth century, when orthodox Christianity had lost much of its power over European minds, that the idea that it might be a good thing to behave humanely towards animals began to make headway. This new morality was correlated with the new interest in Nature, which had been stimulated by the romantic poets and the men of science. Because it was not founded upon an eternity-philosophy, a doctrine of divinity dwelling in all living creatures, the modern movement in favour of kindness to animals was and is perfectly compatible with intolerance, persecution and systematic cruelty towards human beings. Young Nazis are taught to be gentle with dogs and cats, ruthless with Jews. That is because Nazism is a typical time-philosophy, which regards the ultimate good as existing, not in eternity, but in the future. Jews are, *ex hypothesi*, obstacles in the way of the realization of the supreme good; dogs and cats are not. The rest follows logically.

Selfishness and partiality are very inhuman and base qualities even in the things of this world; but in the doctrines of religion they are of a baser nature. Now, this is the greatest evil that the division of the church has brought forth; it raises in every communion a selfish, partial orthodoxy, which consists in courageously defending all that it has, and condemning all that it has not. And thus every champion is trained up in defence of their own truth, their own learning and their own church, and he has the most merit, the most honour, who likes everything, defends everything, among themselves, and leaves nothing uncensored in those that are of a different communion. Now, how can truth and goodness and union and religion be more struck at than by such defenders of it? If you ask why the great Bishop of Meaux wrote so many learned books against all parts of the Reformation, it is because he was born in France and bred up in the bosom of Mother Church. Had he been born in England, had Oxford or Cambridge been his *Alma Mater*, he might have rivalled our great Bishop Stillingfleet, and would have wrote as many learned folios against the Church of Rome as he has done. And yet I will venture to say that if each Church could produce but one man apiece that had the piety of an apostle and the impartial love of the first Christians in the first Church at Jerusalem, that a Protestant and a Papist of this stamp would not want half a sheet of paper to hold their articles of union, nor be half an hour before they were of one religion. If, therefore, it should be said that churches are divided, estranged and made unfriendly to one

P

another by a learning, a logic, a history, a criticism in the hands of
partiality, it would be saying that which each particular church
too much proves to be true. Ask why even the best amongst the
Catholics are very shy of owning the validity of the orders of our
Church; it is because they are afraid of removing any odium
from the Reformation. Ask why no Protestants anywhere touch
upon the benefit or necessity of celibacy in those who are separated from worldly business to preach the gospel; it is because
that would be seeming to lessen the Roman error of not suffering
marriage in her clergy. Ask why even the most worthy and pious
among the clergy of the Established Church are afraid to assert
the sufficiency of the Divine Light, the necessity of seeking only
the guidance and inspiration of the Holy Spirit; it is because the
Quakers, who have broke off from the church, have made this
doctrine their corner-stone. If we loved truth as such, if we
sought for it for its own sake, if we loved our neighbour as ourselves, if we desired nothing by our religion but to be acceptable
to God, if we equally desired the salvation of all men, if we were
afraid of error only because of its harmful nature to us and our
fellow-creatures, then nothing of this spirit could have any place
in us.

There is therefore a catholic spirit, a communion of saints in
the love of God and all goodness, which no one can learn from
that which is called orthodoxy in particular churches, but is only
to be had by a total dying to all worldly views, by a pure love of
God, and by such an unction from above as delivers the mind
from all selfishness and makes it love truth and goodness with an
equality of affection in every man, whether he is Christian, Jew
or Gentile. He that would obtain this divine and catholic spirit
in this disordered, divided state of things, and live in a divided
part of the church without partaking of its division, must have
these three truths deeply fixed in his mind. First, that universal
love, which gives the whole strength of the heart to God, and
makes us love every man as we love ourselves, is the noblest, the
most divine, the Godlike state of the soul, and is the utmost perfection to which the most perfect religion can raise us; and that
no religion does any man any good but so far as it brings this per-

fection of love into him. This truth will show us that true orthodoxy can nowhere be found but in a pure disinterested love of
God and our neighbour. Second, that in this present divided
state of the church, truth itself is torn and divided asunder; and
that, therefore, he can be the only true catholic who has more of
truth and less of error than is hedged in by any divided part. This
truth will enable us to live in a divided part unhurt by its division,
and keep us in a true liberty and fitness to be edified and assisted
by all the good that we hear or see in any other part of the church.
... Thirdly, he must always have in mind this great truth, that it
is the glory of the Divine Justice to have no respect of parties or
persons, but to stand equally disposed to that which is right and
wrong as well in the Jew as in the Gentile. He therefore that
would like as God likes, and condemn as God condemns, must
have neither the eyes of the Papist nor the Protestant; he must
like no truth the less because Ignatius Loyola or John Bunyan
were very zealous for it, nor have the less aversion to any error,
because Dr. Trapp or George Fox had brought it forth.

William Law

Dr. Trapp was the author of a religious tract entitled 'On the
Nature, Folly, Sin and Danger of Being Righteous Overmuch.'
One of Law's controversial pieces was an answer to this work.

Benares is to the East, Mecca to the West; but explore your own
heart, for there are both Rama and Allah.

Kabir

Like the bee gathering honey from different flowers, the wise
man accepts the essence of different Scriptures and sees only the
good in all religions.

From the Srimad Bhagavatam

His Sacred Majesty the King does reverence to men of all sects,
whether ascetics or householders, by gifts and various forms of
reverence. His Sacred Majesty, however, cares not so much for

gifts or external reverence as that there should be a growth in the essence of the matter in all sects. The growth of the essence of the matter assumes various forms, but the root of it is restraint of speech, to wit, a man must not do reverence to his own sect or disparage that of another without reason. Depreciation should be for specific reasons only; for the sects of other people all deserve reverence for one reason or another. . . . He who does reverence to his own sect, while disparaging the sects of others wholly from attachment to his own, with intent to enhance the glory of his own sect, in reality by such conduct inflicts the severest injury on his own sect. Concord therefore is meritorious, to wit, hearkening and hearkening willingly to the Law of Piety, as accepted by other people.

Edict of Asoka

It would be difficult, alas, to find any edict of a Christian king to match Asoka's. In the West the good old rule, the simple plan, was glorification of one's own sect, disparagement and even persecution of all others. Recently, however, governments have changed their policy. Proselytizing and persecuting zeal is reserved for the political pseudo-religions, such as Communism, Fascism and nationalism; and unless they are thought to stand in the way of advance towards the temporal ends professed by such pseudo-religions, the various manifestations of the Perennial Philosophy are treated with a contemptuously tolerant indifference.

The children of God are very dear but very queer, very nice but very narrow.

Sadhu Sundar Singh

Such was the conclusion to which the most celebrated of Indian converts was forced after some years of association with his fellow Christians. There are many honourable exceptions, of course; but the rule even among learned Protestants and Catholics is a certain blandly bumptious provincialism which, if it did not constitute such a grave offence against charity and truth, would be just uproariously funny. A hundred years ago, hardly anything was known of Sanskrit, Pali or Chinese. The ignorance of European scholars was sufficient reason for their provincialism. Today, when more or less adequate translations are available in plenty, there is not only no reason for it, there is no excuse. And yet most European and American authors of books about religion and metaphysics write as though nobody had ever thought about these subjects, except the Jews, the Greeks and the Christians of the Mediterranean basin and western Europe. This display of what, in the twentieth century, is an entirely voluntary and deliberate ignorance is not only absurd and discreditable; it is also socially dangerous. Like any other form of imperialism, theological imperialism is a menace to permanent world peace. The reign of violence will never come to an end until, first, most human beings accept the same, true philosophy of life; until, second, this Perennial Philosophy is recognized as the highest factor common to all the world religions; until, third, the adherents of every religion renounce the idolatrous time-philosophies, with which, in their own particular faith, the Perennial Philosophy of eternity has been overlaid; until, fourth, there is a world-wide rejection of all the political pseudo-religions, which place man's supreme good in future time and therefore justify and commend the commission of every sort of present iniquity as a means to that end. If these conditions are not fulfilled, no amount of political planning, no economic blue-prints however ingeniously drawn, can prevent the recrudescence of war and revolution.

Chapter 13

SALVATION, DELIVERANCE, ENLIGHTENMENT

SALVATION—but from what? Deliverance—out of which particular situation into what other situation? Men have given many answers to these questions, and because human temperaments are of such profoundly different kinds, because social situations are so various and fashions of thought and feeling so compelling while they last, the answers are many and mutually incompatible.

There is first of all material salvationism. In its simplest form this is merely the will to live expressing itself in a formulated desire to escape from circumstances that menace life. In practice, the effective fulfilment of such a wish depends on two things: the application of intelligence to particular economic and political problems, and the creation and maintenance of an atmosphere of goodwill, in which intelligence can do its work to the best advantage. But men are not content to be merely kind and clever within the limits of a concrete situation. They aspire to relate their actions, and the thoughts and feelings accompanying those actions, to general principles and a philosophy on the cosmic scale. When this directing and explanatory philosophy is not the Perennial Philosophy or one of the historical theologies more or less closely connected with the Perennial Philosophy, it takes the form of a pseudo-religion, a system of organized idolatry. Thus, the simple wish not to starve, the well-founded conviction that it is very difficult to be good or wise or happy when one is desperately hungry, comes to be elaborated, under the influence of the metaphysic of Inevitable Progress, into prophetic Utopianism; the desire to escape from oppression and exploitation comes to be explained and guided by a belief in apocalyptic revolutionism, combined, not always in theory, but invariably in practice, with the Moloch-worship of the nation as the highest of all goods. In all these cases salvation is regarded as a deliverance, by means of a variety of political and economic devices, out of the miseries and evils associated with bad material conditions into another set of future material conditions so much better than the present that, somehow or other, they will cause everybody to be perfectly happy, wise and virtuous. Officially promulgated in all the totalitarian countries, whether of the right or the left, this confession of faith is still only semi-official in the nominally Christian world of capitalistic democracy, where it is drummed into the popular mind, not by the representatives of state or church, but by those most influential of popular moralists and philosophers, the writers of advertising copy (the only authors in all the history of literature whose works are read every day by every member of the population).

In the theologies of the various religions, salvation is also regarded as a deliverance out of folly, evil and misery into happiness, goodness and wisdom. But political and economic means are held to be subsidiary to the cultivation of personal holiness, to the acquiring of personal merit and to the maintenance of personal faith in some divine principle or person having power, in one way or another, to forgive and sanctify the individual soul. Moreover, the end to be achieved is not regarded as existing in some Utopian future period, beginning, say, in the twenty-second century or perhaps even a little earlier, if our favourite politicians remain in power and make the right laws; the end exists 'in heaven.' This last phrase has two very different meanings. For what is probably the majority of those who profess the great historical religions, it signifies and has always signified a happy posthumous condition of indefinite personal survival, conceived of as a reward for good behaviour and correct belief and a compensation for the miseries inseparable from life in a body. But for those who, within the various religious traditions, have accepted the Perennial Philosophy as a theory and have done their best to live it out in practice, 'heaven' is something else. They aspire to be delivered out of separate selfhood in time and into eternity as realized in the unitive knowledge of the divine Ground. Since the Ground can and ought to be unitively known in the present life (whose ultimate end and purpose is nothing but this knowledge), 'heaven' is not an exclusively posthumous condition. He only is completely 'saved' who is delivered here and now. As to the means to salvation, these are simultaneously ethical, intellectual and spiritual and have been summed up with admirable clarity and economy in the Buddha's Eightfold Path. Complete deliverance is conditional on the following: first, Right Belief in the all too obvious truth that the cause of pain and evil is craving for separative, egocentred existence, with its corollary that there can be no deliverance from evil, whether personal or collective, except by getting rid of such craving and the obsession of 'I,' 'me,' 'mine'; second, Right Will, the will to deliver oneself and others; third, Right Speech, directed by compassion and charity towards all sentient beings; fourth, Right Action, with the aim of creating and maintaining peace and goodwill; fifth, Right Means of Livelihood, or the choice only of such professions as are not harmful, in their exercise, to any human being or, if possible, any living creature; sixth, Right Effort towards Self-control; seventh, Right Attention or Recollectedness, to be practised in all the circumstances of life, so that we may never do evil by mere thoughtlessness, because 'we know not what we do'; and, eighth, Right Contemplation, the unitive knowledge of the Ground, to which recollectedness and the ethical self-naughting prescribed in the first six branches of the Path give access. Such then are the means which it is within the power of the human being to employ in order to achieve man's final end and be 'saved.' Of the means which are employed by the divine Ground for helping human beings to reach their goal, the Buddha of the Pali scriptures (a teacher whose dislike of 'footless questions' is no less intense than that of the severest experimental physicist of the twentieth century) declines to speak. All he is prepared to talk about is 'sorrow and the ending of sorrow'—the huge brute fact of pain and evil and the other, no less empirical fact that there is a method by which the individual can free himself from evil and do something to diminish the sum of evil in the world around him. It is only in Mahayana Buddhism that the mysteries of grace are discussed with anything like the fullness of treatment accorded to the subject in the speculations of Hindu and especially Christian theology. The primitive, Hinayana teaching on deliverance is simply an elaboration of the Buddha's last recorded words: 'Decay is inherent in all component things. Work out your own salvation with diligence.' As in the well-known passage quoted below, all the stress is upon personal effort.

Therefore, Ananda, be ye lamps unto yourselves, be ye a refuge to yourselves. Betake yourselves to no external refuge. Hold fast to the Truth as a lamp; hold fast to the Truth as a refuge. Look not for a refuge in anyone beside yourselves. And those, Ananda, who either now or after I am dead shall be a lamp unto themselves, shall betake themselves to no external refuge, but holding fast to the Truth as their lamp, and holding fast to the Truth as their refuge, shall not look for refuge to anyone beside themselves—it is they who shall reach the very topmost Height. But they must be anxious to learn.

What follows is a passage freely translated from the Chandogya Upanishad. The truth which this little myth is meant to illustrate is that there are as many conceptions of salvation as there are degrees of spiritual knowledge and that the kind of liberation (or enslavement) actually achieved by any individual soul depends upon the extent to which that soul chooses to dissipate its essentially voluntary ignorance.

That Self who is free from impurities, from old age and death, from grief and thirst and hunger, whose desire is true and whose desires come true—that Self is to be sought after and enquired about, that Self is to be realized.

The Devas (gods or angels) and the Asuras (demons or titans) both heard of this Truth. They thought: 'Let us seek after and realize this Self, so that we can obtain all worlds and the fulfilment of all desires.'

Thereupon Indra from the Devas and Virochana from the Asuras approached Prajapati, the famous teacher. They lived with him as pupils for thirty-two years. Then Prajapati asked them: 'For what reason have you both lived here all this time?'

They replied: 'We have heard that one who realizes the Self obtains all the worlds and all his desires. We have lived here because we want to be taught the Self.'

Prajapati said to them: 'The person who is seen in the eye— that is the Self. That is immortal, that is fearless and that is Brahman.'

'Sir,' enquired the disciples, 'who is seen reflected in water or in a mirror?'

'He, the Atman,' was the reply. 'He indeed is seen in all these.' Then Prajapati added: 'Look at yourselves in the water, and whatever you do not understand, come and tell me.'

Indra and Virochana pored over their reflections in the water, and when they were asked what they had seen of the Self, they replied: 'Sir, we see the Self; we see even the hair and nails.'

Then Prajapati ordered them to put on their finest clothes and look again at their 'selves' in the water. This they did and when asked again what they had seen, they answered: 'We see the Self, exactly like ourselves, well adorned and in our finest clothes.'

Then said Prajapati: 'The Self is indeed seen in these. That Self is immortal and fearless, and that is Brahman.' And the pupils went away, pleased at heart.

But looking after them, Prajapati lamented thus: 'Both of them departed without analysing or discriminating, and without comprehending the true Self. Whoever follows this false doctrine of the Self must perish.'

Satisfied that he had found the Self, Virochana returned to the Asuras and began to teach them that the bodily self alone is to be worshipped, that the body alone is to be served, and that he who worships the ego and serves the body gains both worlds, this and the next. And this in effect is the doctrine of the Asuras.

But Indra, on his way back to the Devas, realized the uselessness of this knowledge. 'As this Self,' he reflected, 'seems to be well adorned when the body is well adorned, well dressed when the body is well dressed, so too will it be blind if the body is blind, lame if the body is lame, deformed if the body is deformed. Nay more, this same Self will die when the body dies. I see no good in such knowledge.' So Indra returned to Prajapati for further instruction. Prajapati compelled him to live with him for another span of thirty-two years; after which he began to instruct him, step by step, as it were.

Prajapati said: 'He who moves about in dreams, enjoying and glorified—he is the Self. That is immortal and fearless, and that is Brahman.'

Pleased at heart, Indra again departed. But before he had rejoined the other angelic beings, he realized the uselessness of that knowledge also. 'True it is,' he thought within himself, 'that this new Self is not blind if the body is blind, not lame, nor hurt, if the body is lame or hurt. But even in dreams the Self is conscious of many sufferings. So I see no good in this teaching.'

Accordingly he went back to Prajapati for more instruction, and Prajapati made him live with him for thirty-two years more. At the end of that time Prajapati taught him thus: 'When a person is asleep, resting in perfect tranquillity, dreaming no dreams, then he realizes the Self. That is immortal and fearless, and that is Brahman.'

Satisfied, Indra went away. But even before he had reached home, he felt the uselessness of this knowledge also. 'When one is asleep,' he thought, 'one does not know oneself as "This is I." One is not in fact conscious of any existence. That state is almost annihilation. I see no good in this knowledge either.'

So Indra went back once again to be taught. Prajapati made him stay with him for five years more. At the end of that time Prajapati taught him the highest truth of the Self.

'This body,' he said, 'is mortal, for ever in the clutch of death. But within it resides the Self, immortal, and without form. This

Self, when associated in consciousness with the body, is subject to pleasure and pain; and so long as this association continues, no man can find freedom from pains and pleasures. But when the association comes to an end, there is an end also of pain and pleasure. Rising above physical consciousness, knowing the Self as distinct from the sense-organs and the mind, knowing Him in his true light, one rejoices and one is free.'

From the Chandogya Upanishad

Having realized his own self as the Self, a man becomes selfless; and in virtue of selflessness he is to be conceived as unconditioned. This is the highest mystery, betokening emancipation; through selflessness he has no part in pleasure or pain, but attains absoluteness.

Maitrayana Upanishad

We should mark and know of a very truth that all manner of virtue and goodness, and even that Eternal Good, which is God Himself, can never make a man virtuous, good or happy so long as it is outside the soul, that is, so long as the man is holding converse with outward things through his senses and reason, and does not withdraw into himself and learn to understand his own life, who and what he is.

Theologia Germanica

Indeed, the saving truth has never been preached by the Buddha, seeing that one has to realize it within oneself.

Sutralamkara

In what does salvation consist? Not in any historic faith or knowledge of anything absent or distant, not in any variety of restraints, rules and methods of practising virtue, not in any formality of opinion about faith and works, repentance, forgiveness of sins, or justification and sanctification, not in any truth or righteousness that you can have from yourself, from the best of men and books, but solely and wholly from the life of God, or Christ of God,

quickened and born again in you, in other words in the restoration
and perfect union of the first twofold life in humanity.

William Law

Law is using here the phraseology of Boehme and those
other 'Spiritual Reformers,' whom the orthodox Protestants,
Lutheran, Calvinistic and Anglican, agreed (it was one of the
very few points they were able to agree on) either to ignore or
to persecute. But it is clear that what he and they call the new
birth of God within the soul is essentially the same fact of
experience as that which the Hindus, two thousand and more
years before, described as the realization of the Self as within
and yet transcendentally other than the individual ego.

Not by the slothful, nor the fool, the undiscerning, is that Nirvana to be reached, which is the untying of all knots.

Iti-vuttaka

This seems sufficiently self-evident. But most of us take
pleasure in being lazy, cannot be bothered to be constantly
recollected and yet passionately desire to be saved from the
results of sloth and unawareness. Consequently there has
been a widespread wish for and belief in Saviours who will step
into our lives, above all at the hour of their termination, and,
like Alexander, cut the Gordian knots which we have been too
lazy to untie. But God is not mocked. The nature of things
is such that the unitive knowledge of the Ground which is
contingent upon the achievement of a total selflessness cannot
possibly be realized, even with outside help, by those who are
not yet selfless. The salvation obtained by belief in the saving
power of Amida, say, or Jesus is not the total deliverance
described in the Upanishads, the Buddhist scriptures and the
writings of the Christian mystics. It is something different,
not merely in degree, but in kind.

Talk as much philosophy as you please, worship as many gods as
you like, observe all ceremonies, sing devoted praises to any

number of divine beings—liberation never comes, even at the end of a hundred aeons, without the realization of the Oneness of Self.

Shankara

This Self is not realizable by study nor even by intelligence and learning. The Self reveals its essence only to him who applies himself to the Self. He who has not given up the ways of vice, who cannot control himself, who is not at peace within, whose mind is distracted, can never realize the Self, though full of all the learning in the world.

Katha Upanishad

Nirvana is where there is no birth, no extinction; it is seeing into the state of Suchness, absolutely transcending all the categories constructed by mind; for it is the Tathagata's inner consciousness.

Lankavatara Sutra

The false or at best imperfect salvations described in the Chandogya Upanishad are of three kinds. There is first the pseudo-salvation associated with the belief that matter is the ultimate Reality. Virochana, the demonic being who is the apotheosis of power-loving, extraverted somatotonia, finds it perfectly natural to identify himself with his body, and he goes back to the other Titans to seek a purely material salvation. Incarnated in the present century, Virochana would have been an ardent Communist, Fascist or nationalist. Indra sees through material salvationism and is then offered dream-salvation, deliverance out of bodily existence into the intermediate world between matter and spirit—that fascinatingly odd and exciting psychic universe, out of which miracles and foreknowledge, 'spirit communications' and extra-sensory perceptions make their startling irruptions into ordinary life. But this freer kind of individualized existence is still all too personal and egocentric to satisfy a soul conscious of its own incompleteness and eager to be made whole. Indra accordingly goes further and is tempted to accept the undifferentiated consciousness of deep sleep, of false *samadhi* and quietistic trance, as the final deliverance. But he refuses, in Brahmananda's words, to mistake *tamas* for *sattvas*, sloth and sub-consciousness for poise and super-consciousness. And so, by discrimination, he comes to the realization of the Self, which is the enlightenment of the darkness that is ignorance and the deliverance from the mortal consequences of that ignorance.

The illusory salvations, against which we are warned in the other extracts, are of a different kind. The emphasis here is upon idolatry and superstition—above all the idolatrous worship of the analytical reason and its notions, and the superstitious belief in rites, dogmas and confessions of faith as being somehow magically efficacious in themselves. Many Christians, as Law implies, have been guilty of these idolatries and superstitions. For them, complete deliverance into union with the divine Ground is impossible, either in this world or posthumously. The best they can hope for is a meritorious but still egocentric life in the body and some sort of happy posthumous 'longevity,' as the Chinese call it, some form of survival, paradisal perhaps, but still involved in time, separateness and multiplicity.

The beatitude into which the enlightened soul is delivered is something quite different from pleasure. What, then, is its nature? The quotations which follow provide at least a partial answer. Blessedness depends on non-attachment and selflessness, therefore can be enjoyed without satiety and without revulsion; is a participation in eternity, and therefore remains itself without diminution or fluctuation.

Henceforth in the real Brahman, he (the liberated spirit) becomes perfected and another. His fruit is the untying of bonds. Without desires, he attains to bliss eternal and immeasurable, and therein abides.

Maitrayana Upanishad

God is to be enjoyed, creatures only used as means to That which is to be enjoyed.

St. Augustine

There is this difference between spiritual and corporal pleasures, that corporal ones beget a desire before we have obtained them and, after we have obtained them, a disgust; but spiritual pleasures, on the contrary, are not cared for when we have them not, but are desired when we have them.

St. Gregory the Great

When a man is in one of these two states (beatitude or dark night of the soul) all is right with him, and he is as safe in hell as in heaven. And so long as a man is on earth, it is possible for him to pass often-times from the one to the other—nay, even within the space of a day and night, and all without his own doing. But when a man is in neither of these two states, he holds converse with the creatures, and wavereth hither and thither and knoweth not what manner of man he is.

Theologia Germanica

Much of the literature of Sufism is poetical. Sometimes this poetry is rather strained and extravagant, sometimes beautiful with a luminous simplicity, sometimes darkly and almost disquietingly enigmatic. To this last class belong the utterances of that Moslem saint of the tenth century, Niffari the Egyptian. This is what he wrote on the subject of salvation.

God made me behold the sea, and I saw the ships sinking and the planks floating; then the planks too were submerged. And God said to me, 'Those who voyage are not saved.' And He said to me, 'Those who, instead of voyaging, cast themselves into the sea, take a risk.' And He said to me, 'Those who voyage and take no risk shall perish.' And He said to me, 'The surface of the sea is a gleam that cannot be reached. And the bottom is a darkness impenetrable. And between the two are great fishes, which are to be feared.'

The allegory is fairly clear. The ships that bear the individual voyagers across the sea of life are sects and churches, collections of dogmas and religious organizations. The planks which also sink at last are all good works falling short of total self-surrender and all faith less absolute than the unitive knowledge of God. Liberation into eternity is the result of 'throwing oneself into the sea'; in the language of the Gospels, one must lose one's life in order to save it. But throwing oneself into the sea is a risky business—not so risky, of course, as travelling in a vast *Queen Mary*, fitted up with the very latest in dogmatic conveniences and liturgical decorations, and bound either for Davy Jones's locker or at best, the wrong port, but still quite dangerous enough. For the surface of the sea—the divine Ground as it is manifested in the world of time and multiplicity—gleams with a reflected radiance that can no more be seized than the image of beauty in a mirror; while the bottom, the Ground as it is eternally in itself, seems merely darkness to the analytic mind, as it peers down into the depths; and when the analytic mind decides to join the will in the final necessary plunge into self-naughting it must run the gauntlet, as it sinks down, of those devouring pseudo-salvations described in the Chandogya Upanishad—dream-salvation into that fascinating psychic world, where the ego still survives, but with a happier and more untrammelled kind of life, or else the sleep-salvation of false *samadhi*, of unity in sub-consciousness instead of unity in super-consciousness.

Niffari's estimate of any individual's chances of achieving man's final end does not err on the side of excessive optimism. But then no saint or founder of a religion, no exponent of the Perennial Philosophy, has ever been optimistic. 'Many are called, but few are chosen.' Those who do not choose to be chosen cannot hope for anything better than some form of partial salvation under conditions that will permit them to advance towards complete deliverance.

Chapter 14

IMMORTALITY AND SURVIVAL

IMMORTALITY is participation in the eternal now of the divine Ground; survival is persistence in one of the forms of time. Immortality is the result of total deliverance. Survival is the lot of those who are partially delivered into some heaven, or who are not delivered at all, but find themselves, by the law of their own untranscended nature, compelled to choose some purgatorial or embodied servitude even more painful than the one they have just left.

Goodness and virtue make men know and love, believe and delight in their immortality. When the soul is purged and enlightened by true sanctity, it is more capable of those divine irradiations, whereby it feels itself in conjunction with God. It knows that almighty Love, by which it lives, is stronger than death. It knows that God will never forsake His own life, which He has quickened in the soul. Those breathings and gaspings after an eternal participation of Him are but the energy of His own breath within us.

John Smith, the Platonist

I have maintained ere this and I still maintain that I already possess all that is granted to me in eternity. For God in the fullness of his Godhead dwells eternally in his image—the soul.

Eckhart

Troubled or still, water is always water. What difference can embodiment or disembodiment make to the Liberated? Whether calm or in tempest, the sameness of the Ocean suffers no change.

Yogavasistha

To the question 'Where does the soul go, when the body dies?'

Jacob Boehme answered: 'There is no necessity for it to go anywhere.'

The word Tathagata (one of the names of the Buddha) signifies one who does not go to anywhere and does not come from anywhere; and therefore is he called Tathagata (Thus-gone), holy and fully enlightened.

Diamond Sutra

Seeing Him alone, one transcends death; there is no other way.

Svetasvatara Upanishad

God, in knowledge of whom standeth our eternal life. . . .

Book of Common Prayer

I died a mineral and became a plant.
I died a plant and rose an animal.
I died an animal and I was man.
Why should I fear? When was I less by dying?
Yet once more I shall die as man, to soar
With the blessed angels; but even from angelhood
I must pass on. All except God perishes.
When I have sacrificed my angel soul,
I shall become that which no mind ever conceived.
O, let me not exist! for Non-Existence proclaims,
'To Him we shall return.'

Jalal-uddin Rumi

There is a general agreement, East and West, that life in a body provides uniquely good opportunities for achieving salvation or deliverance. Catholic and Mahayana Buddhist doctrine is alike in insisting that the soul in its disembodied state after death cannot acquire merit, but merely suffers in purgatory the consequences of its past acts. But whereas Catholic orthodoxy declares that there is no possibility of progress in the next world, and that the degree of the soul's beatitude is determined solely by what it has done and thought in its earthly life, the eschatologists of the Orient affirm that there are certain posthumous conditions in which meritorious souls are capable of advancing from a heaven of happy personal survival to genuine immortality in union with the timeless, eternal Godhead. And, of course, there is also the possibility (indeed, for most individuals, the necessity) of returning to some form of embodied life, in which the advance towards complete beatification, or deliverance through enlightenment, can be continued. Meanwhile, the fact that one has been born in a human body is one of the things for which, says Shankara, one should daily give thanks to God.

The spiritual creature which we are has need of a body, without which it could nowise attain that knowledge which it obtains as the only approach to those things, by knowledge of which it is made blessed.

St. Bernard

Having achieved human birth, a rare and blessed incarnation, the wise man, leaving all vanity to those who are vain, should strive to know God, and Him only, before life passes into death.

Srimad Bhagavatam

Good men spiritualize their bodies; bad men incarnate their souls.

Benjamin Whichcote

More precisely, good men spiritualize their mind-bodies; bad men incarnate and mentalize their spirits. The completely spiritualized mind-body is a Tathagata, who doesn't go anywhere when he dies, for the good reason that he is already, actually and consciously, where everyone has always potentially been without knowing. The person who has not, in this life, gone into Thusness, into the eternal principle of all states of being, goes at death into some particular state, either purgatorial or paradisal. In the Hindu scriptures and their commentaries several different kinds of posthumous salvation are distinguished. The 'thus-gone' soul is completely delivered into complete union with the divine Ground; but it is also possible to achieve other kinds of *mukti*, or liberation, even while retaining a form of purified I-consciousness. The nature of any individual's deliverance after death depends upon three factors: the degree of holiness achieved by him while in the body, the particular aspect of the divine Reality to which he gave his primary allegiance, and the particular path he chose to follow. Similarly, in the *Divine Comedy*, Paradise has its various circles; but whereas in the oriental eschatologies the saved soul can go out of even sublimated individuality, out of survival even in some kind of celestial time, to a complete deliverance into the eternal, Dante's souls remain for ever where (after passing through the unmeritorious sufferings of purgatory) they find themselves as the result of their single incarnation in a body. Orthodox Christian doctrine does not admit the possibility, either in the posthumous state or in some other embodiment, of any further growth towards the ultimate perfection of a total union with the Godhead. But in the Hindu and Buddhist versions of the Perennial Philosophy the divine mercy is matched by the divine patience: both are infinite. For oriental theologians there is no eternal damnation; there are only purgatories and then an indefinite series of second chances to go forward towards not only man's, but the whole creation's final end—total reunion with the Ground of all being.

Preoccupation with posthumous deliverance is not one of the means to such deliverance, and may easily, indeed, become an obstacle in the way of advance towards it. There is not the slightest reason to suppose that ardent spiritualists are more likely to be saved than those who have never attended a séance or familiarized themselves with the literature, speculative or evidential. My intention here is not to add to that literature, but rather to give the baldest summary of what has been written about the subject of survival within the various religious traditions.

In oriental discussions of the subject, that which survives death is not the personality. Buddhism accepts the doctrine of reincarnation; but it is not a soul that passes on (Buddhism denies the existence of a soul); it is the character. What we choose to make of our mental and physical constitution in the course of our life on earth affects the psychic medium within which individual minds lead a part at least of their amphibious existence, and this modification of the medium results, after the body's death, in the initiation of a new existence either in a heaven, or a purgatory, or another body.

In the Vedanta cosmology there is, over and above the Atman or spiritual Self, identical with the divine Ground, something in the nature of a soul that reincarnates in a gross or subtle body, or manifests itself in some incorporeal state. This soul is not the personality of the defunct, but rather the particularized I-consciousness out of which a personality arises.

Either one of these conceptions of survival is logically self-consistent and can be made to 'save the appearances'—in other words, to fit the odd and obscure facts of psychical research. The only personalities with which we have any direct acquaintance are incarnate beings, compounds of a body and some unknown x. But if x plus a body equals a personality, then, obviously, it is impossible for x minus a body to equal the same thing. The apparently personal entities which psychical research sometimes seems to discover can only be regarded as temporary pseudo-personalities compounded of x and the medium's body.

These two conceptions are not mutually exclusive, and survival may be the joint product of a persistent consciousness and a modification of the psychic medium. If this is so, it is possible for a given human being to survive in more than one posthumous form. His 'soul'—the non-personal ground and principle of past and future personalities—may go marching on in one mode of being, while the traces left by his thoughts and volitions in the psychic medium may become the origin of new individualized existences, having quite other modes of being.

Chapter 15

SILENCE

The Father uttered one Word; that Word is His Son, and He utters Him for ever in everlasting silence; and in silence the soul has to hear it.

St. John of the Cross

The spiritual life is nothing else but the working of the Spirit of God within us, and therefore our own silence must be a great part of our preparation for it, and much speaking or delight in it will be often no small hindrance of that good which we can only have from hearing what the Spirit and voice of God speaketh within us. . . . Rhetoric and fine language about the things of the spirit is a vainer babble than in other matters; and he that thinks to grow in true goodness by hearing or speaking flaming words or striking expressions, as is now much the way of the world, may have a great deal of talk, but will have little of his conversation in heaven.

William Law

He who knows does not speak;
He who speaks does not know.

Lao Tzu

UNRESTRAINED and indiscriminate talk is morally evil and spiritually dangerous. 'But I say unto you, That every idle word that men shall speak, they shall give account thereof in the day of judgment.' This may seem a very hard saying. And yet if we pass in review the words we have given vent to in the course of the average day, we shall find that the greater number of them may be classified under three main heads: words inspired by malice and uncharitableness towards our neighbours; words inspired by greed, sensuality and self-love; words inspired by pure imbecility and uttered without rhyme or reason, but merely for the sake of making a distracting noise. These are idle words; and we shall find, if we look into the matter, that they tend to outnumber the words that are dictated by reason, charity or necessity. And if the unspoken words of our mind's endless, idiot monologue are counted, the majority for idleness becomes, for most of us, overwhelmingly large.

All these idle words, the silly no less than the self-regarding and the uncharitable, are impediments in the way of the unitive knowledge of the divine Ground, a dance of dust and flies obscuring the inward and the outward Light. The guard of the tongue (which is also, of course, a guard of the mind) is not only one of the most difficult and searching of all mortifications; it is also the most fruitful.

When the hen has laid, she must needs cackle. And what does she get by it? Straightway comes the chough and robs her of her eggs, and devours all that of which she should have brought forth her live birds. And just so that wicked chough, the devil, beareth away from the cackling anchoresses, and swalloweth up all the goods they have brought forth, and which ought, as birds, to bear them up towards heaven, if it had not been cackled.

Modernized from the Ancren Riwle

You cannot practise too rigid a fast from the charms of worldly talk.

Fénelon

What need of so much news from abroad, when all that concerns either life or death is all transacting and at work within us?

William Law

My dear Mother, heed well the precepts of the saints, who have all warned those who would become holy to speak little of themselves and their own affairs.

St. François de Sales
(in a letter to St. Jeanne de Chantal)

A dog is not considered a good dog because he is a good barker. A man is not considered a good man because he is a good talker.

Chuang Tzu

The dog barks; the Caravan passes.

Arabic Proverb

It was not from want of will that I have refrained from writing to you, for truly do I wish you all good; but because it seemed to me that enough has been said already to effect all that is needful, and that what is wanting (if indeed anything be wanting) is not writing or speaking—whereof ordinarily there is more than enough—but silence and work. For whereas speaking distracts, silence and work collect the thoughts and strengthen the spirit. As soon therefore as a person understands what has been said to him for his good, there is no further need to hear or to discuss; but to set himself in earnest to practise what he has learnt with silence and attention, in humility, charity and contempt of self.

St. John of the Cross

Molinos (and doubtless he was not the first to use this classification) distinguished three degrees of silence—silence of the mouth, silence of the mind and silence of the will. To refrain from idle talk is hard; to quiet the gibbering of memory and imagination is much harder; hardest of all is to still the voices of craving and aversion within the will.

The twentieth century is, among other things, the Age of Noise. Physical noise, mental noise and noise of desire—we hold history's record for all of them. And no wonder; for all the resources of our almost miraculous technology have been thrown into the current assault against silence. That most popular and influential of all recent inventions, the radio, is nothing but a conduit through which pre-fabricated din can flow into our homes. And this din goes far deeper, of course, than the ear-drums. It penetrates the mind, filling it with a babel of distractions—news items, mutually irrelevant bits of information, blasts of corybantic or sentimental music, continually repeated doses of drama that bring no catharsis, but merely create a craving for daily or even hourly emotional enemas. And where, as in most countries, the broadcasting stations support themselves by selling time to advertisers, the noise is carried from the ears, through the realms of phantasy, knowledge and feeling to the ego's central core of wish and desire. Spoken or printed, broadcast over the ether or on wood-pulp, all advertising copy has but one purpose—to prevent the will from ever achieving silence. Desirelessness is the condition of deliverance and illumination. The condition of an expanding and technologically progressive system of mass-production is universal craving. Advertising is the organized effort to extend and intensify craving—to extend and intensify, that is to say, the workings of that force, which (as all the saints and teachers of all the higher religions have always taught) is the principal cause of suffering and wrong-doing and the greatest obstacle between the human soul and its divine Ground.

Chapter 16

PRAYER

THE word 'prayer' is applied to at least four distinct procedures—petition, intercession, adoration, contemplation.
Petition is the asking of something for ourselves. Intercession
is the asking of something for other people. Adoration is the
use of intellect, feeling, will and imagination in making acts
of devotion directed towards God in his personal aspect or as
incarnated in human form. Contemplation is that condition
of alert passivity in which the soul lays itself open to the divine
Ground within and without, the immanent and transcendent
Godhead.

Psychologically, it is all but impossible for a human being
to practise contemplation without preparing for it by some
kind of adoration and without feeling the need to revert at
more or less frequent intervals to intercession and some form
at least of petition. On the other hand, it is both possible and
easy to practise petition apart not only from contemplation, but
also from adoration and, in rare cases of extreme and unmitigated egotism, even from intercession. Petitionary and inter-
cessory prayer may be used—and used, what is more, with
what would ordinarily be regarded as success—without any
but the most perfunctory and superficial reference to God in
any of his aspects. To acquire the knack of getting his petitions
answered, a man does not have to know or love God, or even
to know or love the image of God in his own mind. All that
he requires is a burning sense of the importance of his own
ego and its desires, coupled with a firm conviction that there
exists, out there in the universe, something not himself which
can be wheedled or dragooned into satisfying those desires. If
I repeat 'My will be done,' with the necessary degree of faith
and persistency, the chances are that, sooner or later and somehow or other, I shall get what I want. Whether my will coin-

cides with the will of God, and whether in getting what I want
I shall get what is spiritually, morally or even materially good
for me, are questions which I cannot answer in advance. Only
time and eternity will show. Meanwhile we shall be well advised to heed the warnings of folk-lore. Those anonymous
realists who wrote the world's fairy stories knew a great deal
about wishes and their fulfilment. They knew, first of all,
that in certain circumstances petitions actually get themselves
answered; but they also knew that God is not the only
answerer and that if one asks for something in the wrong
spirit, it may in effect be given—but given with a vengeance
and not by a divine Giver. Getting what one wants by means
of self-regarding petition is a form of *hubris*, which invites its
condign and appropriate *nemesis*. Thus, the folk-lore of the
North American Indian is full of stories about people who fast
and pray egotistically, in order to get more than a reasonable
man ought to have, and who, receiving what they ask for,
thereby bring about their own downfall. From the other side
of the world come all the tales of the men and women who
make use of some kind of magic to get their petitions answered
—always with farcical or catastrophic consequence. Hardly
ever do the Three Wishes of our traditional fairy lore lead to
anything but a bad end for the successful wisher.

> Picture God as saying to you, 'My son, why is it that day by day
> you rise and pray, and genuflect, and even strike the ground with
> your forehead, nay, sometimes even shed tears, while you say to
> Me: "My Father, my God, give me wealth!" If I were to give
> it to you, you would think yourself of some importance, you
> would fancy you had gained something very great. Because you
> asked for it, you have it. But take care to make good use of it.
> Before you had it you were humble; now that you have begun
> to be rich you despise the poor. What kind of a good is that
> which only makes you worse? For worse you are, since you
> were bad already. And that it would make you worse you knew
> not; hence you asked it of Me. I gave it you and I proved you;
> you have found—and you are found out! Ask of Me better

things than these, greater things than these. Ask of Me spiritual
things. Ask of Me Myself.'

St. Augustine

O Lord, I, a beggar, ask of Thee more than a thousand kings may
ask of Thee. Each one has something he needs to ask of Thee;
I have come to ask Thee to give me Thyself.

Ansari of Herat

In the words of Aquinas, it is legitimate for us to pray for anything which it is legitimate for us to desire. There are some
things that nobody has the right to desire—such as the fruits
of crime or wrong-doing. Other things may be legitimately
desired by people on one level of spiritual development, but
should not be desired (and indeed cease to be desired) by those
on another, higher level. Thus, St. François de Sales had
reached a point where he could say, 'I have hardly any desires,
but if I were to be born again I should have none at all. We
should ask nothing and refuse nothing, but leave ourselves in
the arms of divine Providence without wasting time in any
desire, except to will what God wills of us.' But meanwhile
the third clause of the Lord's Prayer is repeated daily by millions, who have not the slightest intention of letting any will
be done, except their own.

The savour of wandering in the ocean of deathless life has rid me
    of all my asking;
As the tree is in the seed, so all diseases are in this asking.

Kabir

Lord, I know not what to ask of thee. Thou only knowest what
I need. Thou lovest me better than I know how to love myself.
Father, give to thy child that which he himself knows not how to
ask. Smite or heal, depress me or raise me up: I adore all thy
purposes without knowing them. I am silent; I offer myself up
in a sacrifice; I yield myself to Thee; I would have no other

desire than to accomplish thy will.   Teach me to pray.   Pray
Thyself in me.

Fénelon

(A dervish was tempted by the devil to cease calling upon Allah,
on the ground that Allah never answered, 'Here am I.'   The
Prophet Khadir appeared to him in a vision with a message from
God.)
    Was it not I who summoned thee to my service?
    Was it not I who made thee busy with my name?
    Thy calling 'Allah!' *was* my 'Here am I.'

Jalal-uddin Rumi

I pray God the Omnipotent to place us in the ranks of his
chosen, among the number of those whom He directs to the path
of safety; in whom He inspires fervour lest they forget Him;
whom He cleanses from all defilement, that nothing may remain
in them except Himself; yea, of those whom He indwells completely, that they may adore none beside Him.

Al-Ghazzali

About intercession, as about so many other subjects, it is
William Law who writes most clearly, simply and to the point.

By considering yourself as an advocate with God for your neighbours and acquaintances, you would never find it hard to be at
peace with them yourself.   It would be easy for you to bear with
and forgive those, for whom you particularly implored the divine
mercy and forgiveness.

William Law

Intercession is the best arbitrator of all differences, the best pro-
moter of true friendship, the best cure and preservative against
all unkind tempers, all angry and haughty passions.

William Law

You cannot possibly have any ill-temper, or show any unkind

behaviour to a man for whose welfare you are so much concerned, as to be his advocate with God in private.   For you
cannot possibly despise and ridicule that man whom your private
prayers recommend to the love and favour of God.

William Law

Intercession, then, is at once the means to, and the expression
of, the love of one's neighbour.   And in the same way adoration is the means to, and the expression of, the love of God—a
love that finds its consummation in the unitive knowledge of
the Godhead which is the fruit of contemplation.   It is to these
higher forms of communion with God that the authors of the
following extracts refer whenever they use the word 'prayer.'

The aim and end of prayer is to revere, to recognize and to adore
the sovereign majesty of God, through what He is in Himself
rather than what He is in regard to us, and rather to love his
goodness by the love of that goodness itself than for what it
sends us.

Bourgoing

In prayer he (Charles de Condren) did not stop at the frontiers
of his knowledge and his reasoning.   He adored God and his
mysteries as they are in themselves and not as he understood
them.

Amelote

'What God is in Himself,' 'God and his mysteries as they are
in themselves'—the phrases have a Kantian ring.   But if Kant
was right and the Thing in itself is unknowable, Bourgoing,
De Condren and all the other masters of the spiritual life were
engaged in a wild-goose chase.   But Kant was right only as
regards minds that have not yet come to enlightenment and
deliverance.   To such minds Reality, whether material, psychic
or spiritual, presents itself as it is darkened, tinged and refracted
by the medium of their own individual natures.   But in those
who are pure in heart and poor in spirit there is no distortion

of Reality, because there is no separate selfhood to obscure or
refract, no painted lantern slide of intellectual beliefs and hallowed imagery to give a personal and historical colouring to
the 'white radiance of Eternity.' For such minds, as Olier says,
'even ideas of the saints, of the Blessed Virgin, and the sight of
Jesus Christ in his humanity are impediments in the way of the
sight of God in his purity.' The Thing in itself *can* be perceived—but only by one who, in himself, is no-thing.

By prayer I do not understand petition or supplication which,
according to the doctrines of the schools, is exercised principally
by the understanding, being a signification of what the person
desires to receive from God. But prayer here specially meant is
an offering and giving to God whatsoever He may justly require
from us.

Now prayer, in its general notion, may be defined to be an
elevation of the mind to God, or more largely and expressly thus:
prayer is an actuation of an intellective soul towards God, expressing, or at least implying, an entire dependence on Him as
the author and fountain of all good, a will and readiness to
give Him his due, which is no less than all love, all obedience,
adoration, glory and worship, by humbling and annihilating the
self and all creatures in his presence; and lastly, a desire and
intention to aspire to an union of spirit with Him.

Hence it appears that prayer is the most perfect and most
divine action that a rational soul is capable of. It is of all actions
and duties the most indispensably necessary.

Augustine Baker

Lord, teach me to seek Thee and reveal Thyself to me when I
seek Thee. For I cannot seek Thee except Thou teach me, nor
find Thee except Thou reveal Thyself. Let me seek Thee in
longing, let me long for Thee in seeking: let me find Thee in
love and love Thee in finding. Lord, I acknowledge and I
thank Thee that Thou hast created me in this Thine image, in
order that I may be mindful of Thee, may conceive of Thee and
love Thee: but that image has been so consumed and wasted away

by vices and obscured by the smoke of wrong-doing that it cannot achieve that for which it was made, except Thou renew it and create it anew. Is the eye of the soul darkened by its infirmity, or dazzled by Thy glory? Surely, it is both darkened in itself and dazzled by Thee. Lord, this is the unapproachable light in which Thou dwellest. Truly I see it not, because it is too bright for me; and yet whatever I see, I see through it, as the weak eye sees what it sees through the light of the sun, which in the sun itself it cannot look upon. Oh supreme and unapproachable light, oh holy and blessed truth, how far art Thou from me who am so near to Thee, how far art Thou removed from my vision, though I am so near to Thine! Everywhere Thou art wholly present, and I see Thee not. In Thee I move and in Thee I have my being, and cannot come to Thee, Thou art within me and about me, and I feel Thee not.

St. Anselm

Oh Lord, put no trust in me; for I shall surely fail if Thou uphold me not.

St. Philip Neri

To pretend to devotion without great humility and renunciation of all worldly tempers is to pretend to impossibilities. He that would be devout must first be humble, have a full sense of his own miseries and wants and the vanity of the world, and then his soul will be full of desire after God. A proud, or vain, or worldly-minded man may use a manual of prayers, but he cannot be devout, because devotion is the application of an humble heart to God as its only happiness.

William Law

The spirit, in order to work, must have all sensible images, both good and bad, removed. The beginner in a spiritual course commences with the use of good sensible images, and it is impossible to begin in a good spiritual course with the exercises of the spirit. . . . Those souls who have not a propensity to the interior must abide always in the exercises, in which sensible images are used,

R

and these souls will find the sensible exercises very profitable to themselves and to others, and pleasing to God. And this is the way of the active life. But others, who have the propensity to the interior, do not always remain in the exercises of the senses, but after a time these will give place to the exercises of the spirit, which are independent of the senses and the imagination and consist simply in the elevation of the will of the intellective soul to God.... The soul elevates her will towards God, apprehended by the understanding as a spirit, and not as an imaginary thing, the human spirit in this way aspiring to a union with the Divine Spirit.

Augustine Baker

You tell me you do nothing in prayer. But what do you want to do in prayer except what you are doing, which is, presenting and representing your nothingness and misery to God? When beggars expose their ulcers and their necessities to our sight, that is the best appeal they can make. But from what you tell me, you sometimes do nothing of this, but lie there like a shadow or a statue. They put statues in palaces simply to please the prince's eyes. Be content to be that in the presence of God: He will bring the statue to life when He pleases.

St. François de Sales

I have come to see that I do not limit my mind enough simply to prayer, that I always want to do something myself in it, wherein I do very wrong.... I wish most definitely to cut off and separate my mind from all that, and to hold it with all my strength, as much as I can, to the sole regard and simple unity. By allowing the fear of being ineffectual to enter into the state of prayer, and by wishing to accomplish something myself, I spoilt it all.

St. Jeanne Chantal

So long as you seek Buddhahood, specifically exercising yourself for it, there is no attainment for you.

Yung-chia Ta-shih

'How does a man set himself in harmony with the Tao?' 'I am already out of harmony.'

Shih-t'ou

How shall I grasp it? Do not grasp it. That which remains when there is no more grasping is the Self.

Panchadasi

I order you to remain simply either in God or close to God, without trying to do anything there, and without asking anything of Him, unless He urges it.

St. François de Sales

Adoration is an activity of the loving, but still separate, individuality. Contemplation is the state of union with the divine Ground of all being. The highest prayer is the most passive. Inevitably; for the less there is of self, the more there is of God. That is why the path to passive or infused contemplation is so hard and, for many, so painful—a passage through successive or simultaneous Dark Nights, in which the pilgrim must die to the life of sense as an end in itself, to the life of private and even of traditionally hallowed thinking and believing, and finally to the deep source of all ignorance and evil, the life of the separate, individualized will.

Chapter 17

SUFFERING

THE Godhead is impassible; for where there is perfection and unity, there can be no suffering. The capacity to suffer arises where there is imperfection, disunity and separation from an embracing totality; and the capacity is actualized to the extent that imperfection, disunity and separateness are accompanied by an urge towards the intensification of these creaturely conditions. For the individual who achieves unity within his own organism and union with the divine Ground, there is an end of suffering. The goal of creation is the return of all sentient beings out of separateness and that infatuating urge-to-separateness which results in suffering, through unitive knowledge, into the wholeness of eternal Reality.

> The elements which make up man produce a capacity for pain.
> The cause of pain is the craving for individual life.
> Deliverance from craving does away with pain.
> The way of deliverance is the Eightfold Path.
>
> *The Four Noble Truths of Buddhism*

The urge-to-separateness, or craving for independent and individualized existence, can manifest itself on all the levels of life, from the merely cellular and physiological, through the instinctive, to the fully conscious. It can be the craving of a whole organism for an intensification of its separateness from the environment and the divine Ground. Or it can be the urge of a part within an organism for an intensification of its own partial life as distinct from (and consequently at the expense of) the life of the organism as a whole. In the first case we speak of impulse, passion, desire, self-will, sin; in the second, we describe what is happening as illness, injury, functional or

260

organic disorder. In both cases the craving for separateness results in suffering, not only for the craver, but also for the craver's sentient environment—other organisms in the external world, or other organs within the same organism. In one way suffering is entirely private; in another, fatally contagious. No living creature is able to experience the suffering of another creature. But the craving for separateness which, sooner or later, directly or indirectly, results in some form of private and unshareable suffering for the craver, also results, sooner or later, directly or indirectly, in suffering (equally private and unshareable) for others. Suffering and moral evil have the same source—a craving for the intensification of the separateness which is the primary datum of all creatureliness.

It will be as well to illustrate these generalizations by a few examples. Let us consider first the suffering inflicted by living organisms on themselves and on other living organisms in the mere process of keeping alive. The cause of such suffering is the craving for individual existence, expressing itself specifically in the form of hunger. Hunger is entirely natural—a part of every creature's *dharma*. The suffering it causes alike to the hungry and to those who satisfy their hunger is inseparable from the existence of sentient creatures. The existence of sentient creatures has a goal and purpose which is ultimately the supreme good of every one of them. But meanwhile the suffering of creatures remains a fact and is a necessary part of creatureliness. In so far as this is the case, creation is the beginning of the Fall. The consummation of the Fall takes place when creatures seek to intensify their separateness beyond the limits prescribed by the law of their being. On the biological level the Fall would seem to have been consummated very frequently during the course of evolutionary history. Every species, except the human, chose immediate, short-range success by means of specialization. But specialization always leads into blind alleys. It is only by remaining precariously generalized that an organism can advance towards that rational intelligence which is its compensation for not having a body and instincts perfectly adapted to one particular kind of life in one particular kind of environment. Rational intelligence makes possible unparalleled worldly success on the one hand and, on the other, a further advance towards spirituality and a return, through unitive knowledge, to the divine Ground.

Because the human species refrained from consummating the Fall on the biological level, human individuals now possess the momentous power of choosing either selflessness and union with God, or the intensification of separate selfhood in ways and to a degree, which are entirely beyond the ken of the lower animals. Their capacity for good is infinite, since they can, if they so desire, make room within themselves for divine Reality. But at the same time their capacity for evil is, not indeed infinite (since evil is always ultimately self-destructive and therefore temporary), but uniquely great. Hell is total separation from God, and the devil is the will to that separation. Being rational and free, human beings are capable of being diabolic. This is a feat which no animal can duplicate, for no animal is sufficiently clever, sufficiently purposeful, sufficiently strong-willed or sufficiently moral to be a devil. (We should note that, to be diabolic on the grand scale, one must, like Milton's Satan, exhibit in a high degree all the moral virtues, except only charity and wisdom.)

Man's capacity to crave more violently than any animal for the intensification of his separateness results not only in moral evil and the sufferings which moral evil inflicts, in one way or another, upon the victims of evil and the perpetrators of it, but also in certain characteristically human derangements of the body. Animals suffer mainly from contagious diseases, which assume epidemic proportions whenever the urge to reproduction combines with exceptionally favourable circumstances to produce overcrowding, and from diseases due to infestation by parasites. (These last are simply a special case of the sufferings that must inevitably arise when many species of creatures co-exist and can only survive at one another's expense.) Civilized man has been fairly successful in protecting himself against these plagues, but in their place he has called up a formidable array of degenerative diseases hardly known among the lower animals. Most of these degenerative diseases are due to the fact that civilized human beings do not, on any level of their being, live in harmony with Tao, or the divine Nature of Things. They love to intensify their selfhood through gluttony, therefore eat the wrong food and too much of it; they inflict upon themselves chronic anxiety over money and, because they crave excitement, chronic over-stimulation; they suffer, during their working hours, from the chronic boredom and frustration imposed by the sort of jobs that have to be done in order to satisfy the artificially stimulated demand for the fruits of fully mechanized mass-production. Among the consequences of these wrong uses of the psycho-physical organism are degenerative changes in particular organs, such as the heart, kidneys, pancreas, intestines and arteries. Asserting their partial selfhood in a kind of declaration of independence from the organism as a whole, the degenerating organs cause suffering to themselves and their physiological environment. In exactly the same way the human individual asserts his own partial selfhood and his separateness from his neighbours, from Nature and from God—with disastrous consequences to himself, his family, his friends and society in general. And, reciprocally, a disordered society, professional group or family, living by a false philosophy, influences its members to assert their individual selfhood and separateness, just as the wrong-living and wrong-thinking individual influences his own organs to assert, by some excess or defect of function, their partial selfhood at the expense of the total organism.

The effects of suffering may be morally and spiritually bad, neutral or good, according to the way in which the suffering is endured and reacted to. In other words, it may stimulate in the sufferer a conscious or unconscious craving for the intensification of his separateness; or it may leave the craving such as it was before the suffering; or, finally, it may mitigate it and so become a means for advance towards self-abandonment and the love and knowledge of God. Which of these three alternatives shall be realized depends, in the last analysis, upon the sufferer's choice. This seems to be true even on the sub-human level. The higher animals, at any rate, often seem to resign themselves to pain, sickness and death with a kind of serene acceptance of what the divine Nature of Things has decreed for them. But in other cases there is panic fear and struggle, a frenzied resistance to those decrees. To some extent, at least, the embodied animal self appears to be free, in the face of suffering, to choose self-abandonment or self-assertion. For embodied human selves, this freedom of choice is unquestionable. The choice of self-abandonment in suffering makes possible the reception of grace—grace on the spiritual level, in the form of an accession of the love and knowledge of God, and grace in the mental and physiological levels, in the form of a diminution of fear, self-concern and even of pain.

When we conceive the love of suffering, we lose the sensibility of the senses and dead, dead we will live in that garden.

St. Catherine of Siena

He who suffers for love does not suffer, for all suffering is forgot.

Eckhart

In this life there is not purgatory, but only heaven or hell; for he who bears afflictions with patience has paradise, and he who does not has hell.

St. Philip Neri

Many sufferings are the immediate consequence of moral evil, and these cannot have any good effects upon the sufferer, so long as the causes of his distress are not eradicated.

Each sin begetteth a special spiritual suffering. A suffering of this kind is like unto that of hell, for the more you suffer, the worse you become. This happeneth to sinners; the more they suffer through their sins, the more wicked they become; and they fall continually more and more into their sins in order to get free from their suffering.

The Following of Christ

The idea of vicarious suffering has too often been formulated in crudely juridical and commercial terms. A has committed an offence for which the law decrees a certain punishment; B voluntarily undergoes the punishment; justice and the law-giver's honour are satisfied; consequently A may go free. Or else it is all a matter of debts and repayments. A owes C a sum which he cannot pay; B steps in with the cash and so prevents C from foreclosing on the mortgage. Applied to the facts of man's suffering and his relations to the divine Ground, these conceptions are neither enlightening nor edifying. The ortho-dox doctrine of the Atonement attributes to God character-istics that would be discreditable even to a human potentate, and its model of the universe is not the product of spiritual insight rationalized by philosophic reflection, but rather the projection of a lawyer's phantasy. But in spite of these deplor-able crudities in their formulation, the idea of vicarious suffer-ing and the other, closely related idea of the transferability of merit are based upon genuine facts of experience. The selfless and God-filled person can and does act as a channel through which grace is able to pass into the unfortunate being who has made himself impervious to the divine by the habitual craving for intensifications of his own separateness and selfhood. It is because of this that the saints are able to exercise authority, all the greater for being entirely non-compulsive, over their fellow-beings. They 'transfer merit' to those who are in need of it; but that which converts the victims of self-will and puts them on the path of liberation is not the merit of the saintly individual—a merit that consists in his having made himself capable of eternal Reality, as a pipe, by being cleaned out, is made capable of water; it is rather the divine charge he carries, the eternal Reality for which he has become the conduit. And similarly, in vicarious suffering, it is not the actual pains experi-enced by the saint which are redemptive—for to believe that God is angry at sin and that his anger cannot be propitiated except by the offer of a certain sum of pain is to blaspheme against the divine Nature. No, what saves is the gift from beyond the temporal order, brought to those imprisoned in selfhood by these selfless and God-filled persons, who have been ready to accept suffering, in order to help their fellows. The Bodhisattva's vow is a promise to forgo the immediate fruits of enlightenment and to accept rebirth and its inevitable concomitants, pain and death, again and again, until such time as, thanks to his labours and the graces of which, being selfless, he is the channel, all sentient beings shall have come to final and complete deliverance.

> I saw a mass of matter of a dull gloomy colour between the North and the East, and was informed that this mass was human beings, in as great misery as they could be, and live; and that I was mixed up with them and henceforth I must not consider myself as a distinct or separate being.
>
> *John Woolman*

Why must the righteous and the innocent endure undeserved suffering? For anyone who conceives of human individuals as Hume conceived of events and things, as 'loose and separate,' the question admits of no acceptable answer. But, in fact, human individuals are not loose and separate, and the only reason why we think they are is our own wrongly interpreted self-interest. We want to 'do what we damned well like,' to have 'a good time' and no responsibilities. Consequently, we find it convenient to be misled by the inadequacies of language and to believe (not always, of course, but just when it suits us) that things, persons and events are as completely distinct and separate one from another as the words by means of which we think about them. The truth is, of course, that we are all organically related to God, to Nature and to our fellow-men. If every human being were constantly and consciously in a proper relationship with his divine, natural and social environments there would be only so much suffering as Creation makes inevitable. But actually most human beings are chronically in an improper relation to God, Nature and some at least of their fellows. The results of these wrong relationships are manifest on the social level as wars, revolutions, exploitation and disorder; on the natural level, as waste and exhaustion of irreplaceable resources; on the biological level, as degenerative diseases and the deterioration of racial stocks; on the moral level, as an overweening bumptiousness; and on the spiritual level, as blindness to divine Reality and complete ignorance of the reason and purpose of human existence. In such circumstances it would be extraordinary if the innocent and righteous did not suffer—just as it would be extraordinary if the innocent kidneys and the righteous heart were not to suffer for the sins of a licorous palate and overloaded stomach, sins, we may add, imposed upon those organs by the will of the gluttonous individual to whom they belong, as he himself belongs to a society which other individuals, his contemporaries and predecessors, have built up into a vast and enduring incarnation of disorder, inflicting suffering upon its members and infecting them with its own ignorance and wickedness. The righteous man can escape suffering only by accepting it and passing beyond it; and he can accomplish this only by being converted from righteousness to total selflessness and God-centredness, by ceasing to be just a Pharisee, or good citizen, and becoming 'perfect as your Father which is in heaven is perfect.' The difficulties in the way of such a transfiguration are, obviously, enormous. But of those who 'speak with authority,' who has ever said that the road to complete deliverance was easy or the gate anything but 'strait and narrow'?

Chapter 18

FAITH

THE word 'faith' has a variety of meanings, which it is important to distinguish. In some contexts it is used as a synonym for 'trust,' as when we say that we have faith in Dr. X's diagnostic skill or in lawyer Y's integrity. Analogous to this is our 'faith' in authority—the belief that what certain persons say about certain subjects is likely, because of their special qualifications, to be true. On other occasions 'faith' stands for belief in propositions which we have not had occasion to verify for ourselves, but which we know that we could verify if we had the inclination, the opportunity and the necessary capacities. In this sense of the word we have 'faith,' even though we may never have been to Australia, that there is such a creature as a duck-billed platypus; we have 'faith' in the atomic theory, even though we may never have performed the experiments on which that theory rests, and be incapable of understanding the mathematics by which it is supported. And finally there is the 'faith,' which is a belief in propositions which we know we cannot verify, even if we should desire to do so—propositions such as those of the Athanasian Creed or those which constitute the doctrine of the Immaculate Conception. This kind of 'faith' is defined by the Scholastics as an act of the intellect moved to assent by the will.

Faith in the first three senses of the word plays a very important part, not only in the activities of everyday life, but even in those of pure and applied science. *Credo ut intelligam* —and also, we should add, *ut agam* and *ut vivam*. Faith is a pre-condition of all systematic knowing, all purposive doing and all decent living. Societies are held together, not primarily by the fear of the many for the coercive power of the few, but by a widespread faith in the other fellow's decency. Such a faith tends to create its own object, while the widespread mutual mistrust, due, for example, to war or domestic dissension, creates the object of mistrust. Passing now from the moral to the intellectual sphere, we find faith lying at the root of all organized thinking. Science and technology could not exist unless we had faith in the reliability of the universe—unless, in Clerk Maxwell's words, we implicitly believed that the book of Nature is really a book and not a magazine, a coherent work of art and not a hodge-podge of mutually irrelevant snippets. To this general faith in the reasonableness and trustworthiness of the world the searcher after truth must add two kinds of special faith—faith in the authority of qualified experts, sufficient to permit him to take their word for statements which he personally has not verified; and faith in his own working hypotheses, sufficient to induce him to test his provisional beliefs by means of appropriate action. This action may confirm the belief which inspired it. Alternatively it may bring proof that the original working hypothesis was ill founded, in which case it will have to be modified until it becomes conformable to the facts and so passes from the realm of faith to that of knowledge.

The fourth kind of faith is the thing which is commonly called 'religious faith.' The usage is justifiable, not because the other kinds of faith are not fundamental in religion just as they are in secular affairs, but because this willed assent to propositions which are known to be unverifiable occurs in religion, and only in religion, as a characteristic addition to faith as trust, faith in authority and faith in unverified but verifiable propositions. This is the kind of faith which, according to Christian theologians, justifies and saves. In its extreme and most uncompromising form, such a doctrine can be very dangerous. Here, for example, is a passage from one of Luther's letters. *Esto peccator, et pecca fortiter ; sed fortius crede et gaude in Christo, qui victor est peccati, mortis et mundi. Peccandum est quam diu sic sumus ; vita haec non est habitatio justitiae.* ('Be a sinner and sin strongly; but yet more strongly believe and rejoice in Christ, who is the conqueror of sin, death and the world. So long as we are as we are, there must

be sinning; this life is not the dwelling place of righteousness.') To the danger that faith in the doctrine of justification
by faith may serve as an excuse for and even an invitation to
sin must be added another danger, namely, that the faith which
is supposed to save may be faith in propositions not merely
unverifiable, but repugnant to reason and the moral sense, and
entirely at variance with the findings of those who have fulfilled the conditions of spiritual insight into the Nature of
Things. 'This is the acme of faith,' says Luther in his *De
Servo Arbitrio*, 'to believe that God who saves so few and
condemns so many, is merciful; that He is just who, at his
own pleasure, has made us necessarily doomed to damnation,
so that He seems to delight in the torture of the wretched and
to be more deserving of hate than of love. If by any effort of
reason I could conceive how God, who shows so much anger
and harshness, could be merciful and just, there would be no
need of faith.' Revelation (which, when it is genuine, is simply
the record of the immediate experience of those who are pure
enough in heart and poor enough in spirit to be able to see
God) says nothing at all of these hideous doctrines, to which
the will forces the quite naturally and rightly reluctant intellect to give assent. Such notions are the product, not of the
insight of saints, but of the busy phantasy of jurists, who were
so far from having transcended selfness and the prejudices of
education that they had the folly and presumption to interpret
the universe in terms of the Jewish and Roman law with which
they happened to be familiar. 'Woe unto you lawyers,' said
Christ. The denunciation was prophetic and for all time.

The core and spiritual heart of all the higher religions is the
Perennial Philosophy; and the Perennial Philosophy can be
assented to and acted upon without resort to the kind of faith
about which Luther was writing in the foregoing passages.
There must, of course, be faith as trust—for confidence in one's
fellows is the beginning of charity towards men, and confidence
not only in the material, but also the moral and spiritual reliability of the universe, is the beginning of charity or love-
knowledge in relation to God. There must also be faith in

authority—the authority of those whose selflessness has qualified them to know the spiritual Ground of all being by direct
acquaintance as well as by report. And finally there must be
faith in such propositions about Reality as are enunciated by
philosophers in the light of genuine revelation—propositions
which the believer knows that he can, if he is prepared to fulfil
the necessary conditions, verify for himself. But, so long as
the Perennial Philosophy is accepted in its essential simplicity,
there is no need of willed assent to propositions known in
advance to be unverifiable. Here it is necessary to add that
such unverifiable propositions may become verifiable to the
extent that intense faith affects the psychic substratum and so
creates an existence, whose derived objectivity can actually be
discovered 'out there.' Let us, however, remember that an
existence which derives its objectivity from the mental activity
of those who intensely believe in it cannot possibly be the
spiritual Ground of the world, and that a mind busily engaged
in the voluntary and intellectual activity, which is 'religious
faith,' cannot possibly be in the state of selflessness and alert
passivity which is the necessary condition of the unitive knowledge of the Ground. That is why the Buddhists affirm that
'loving faith leads to heaven; but obedience to the Dharma
leads to Nirvana.' Faith in the existence and power of any
supernatural entity which is less than ultimate spiritual Reality,
and in any form of worship that falls short of self-naughting,
will certainly, if the object of faith is intrinsically good, result
in improvement of character, and probably in posthumous survival of the improved personality under 'heavenly' conditions.
But this personal survival within what is still the temporal
order is not the eternal life of timeless union with the Spirit.
This eternal life 'stands in the knowledge' of the Godhead,
not in faith in anything less than the Godhead.

The immortality attained through the acquisition of any objective
condition (e.g., the condition—merited through good works,
which have been inspired by love of, and faith in, something less
than the supreme Godhead—of being united in act to what is

worshipped) is liable to end; for it is distinctly stated in the Scriptures that *karma* is never the cause of emancipation.

Shankara

Karma is the causal sequence in time, from which we are delivered solely by 'dying to' the temporal self and becoming united with the eternal, which is beyond time and cause. For 'as to the notion of a First Cause, or a *Causa Sui*' (to quote the words of an eminent theologian and philosopher, Dr. F. R. Tennant), 'we have, on the one hand, to bear in mind that we refute ourselves in trying to establish it by extension of the application of the causal category, for causality when universalized contains a contradiction; and, on the other, to remember that the ultimate Ground simply "is."' Only when the individual also 'simply is,' by reason of his union through love-knowledge with the Ground, can there be any question of complete and eternal liberation.

Chapter 19

GOD IS NOT MOCKED

Why hast thou said, 'I have sinned so much,
And God in His mercy has not punished my sins'?
How many times do I smite thee, and thou knowest not!
Thou art bound in my chains from head to foot.
On thy heart is rust on rust collected
So that thou art blind to divine mysteries.
When a man is stubborn and follows evil practices,
He casts dust in the eyes of his discernment.
Old shame for sin and calling on God quit him;
Dust five layers deep settles on his mirror,
Rust spots begin to gnaw his iron,
The colour of his jewel grows less and less.

Jalal-uddin Rumi

IF there is freedom (and even Determinists consistently act as if they were certain of it) and if (as everyone who has qualified himself to talk about the subject has always been convinced) there is a spiritual Reality, which it is the final end and purpose of consciousness to know; then all life is in the nature of an intelligence test, and the higher the level of awareness and the greater the potentialities of the creature, the more searchingly difficult will be the questions asked. For, in Bagehot's words, 'we could not be what we ought to be, if we lived in the sort of universe we should expect. . . . A latent Providence, a confused life, an odd material world, an existence broken short in the midst and on a sudden, are not real difficulties, but real helps; for they, or something like them, are essential conditions of a moral life in a subordinate being.' Because we are free, it is possible for us to answer life's questions either well or badly. If we answer them badly, we shall bring down upon ourselves self-stultification. Most often this self-

S

stultification will take subtle and not immediately detectable forms, as when our failure to answer properly makes it impossible for us to realize the higher potentialities of our being. Sometimes, on the contrary, the self-stultification is manifest on the physical level, and may involve not only individuals as individuals, but entire societies, which go down in catastrophe or sink more slowly into decay. The giving of correct answers is rewarded primarily by spiritual growth and progressive realization of latent potentialities, and secondarily (when circumstances make it possible) by the adding of all the rest to the realized kingdom of God. *Karma* exists; but its equivalence of act and award is not always obvious and material, as the earlier Buddhist and Hebrew writers ingenuously imagined that it should be. The bad man in prosperity may, all unknown to himself, be darkened and corroded with inward rust, while the good man under afflictions may be in the rewarding process of spiritual growth. No, God is not mocked; but also, let us always remember, He is not understood.

Però nella giustizia sempiterna
la vista che riceve vostro mondo,
com'occhio per lo mar, dentro s'interna,
chè, benchè dalla proda veggia il fondo,
in pelago nol vede, e non di meno
è lì, ma cela lui l'esser profondo.

('Wherefore, in the eternal justice, such sight as your earth receives is engulfed, like the eye in the sea; for though by the shore it can see the bottom, in the ocean it cannot see it; yet none the less the bottom is there, but the depth hides it.') Love is the plummet as well as the astrolabe of God's mysteries, and the pure in heart can see far down into the depths of the divine justice, to catch a glimpse, not indeed of the details of the cosmic process, but at least of its principle and nature. These insights permit them to say, with Juliana of Norwich, that all shall be well, that, in spite of time, all *is* well, and that the problem of evil has its solution in the eternity, which men can, if they so desire, experience, but can never describe.

But, you urge, if men sin from the necessity of their nature, they are excusable; you do not explain, however, what you would infer from this fact. Is it perhaps that God will be prevented from growing angry with them? Or is it rather that they have deserved that blessedness which consists in the knowledge and love of God? If you mean the former, I altogether agree that God does not grow angry and that all things happen by his decree. But I deny that, for this reason, all men ought to be happy. Surely men may be excusable and nevertheless miss happiness, and be tormented in many ways. A horse is excusable for being a horse and not a man; but nevertheless he must needs be a horse and not a man. One who goes mad from the bite of a dog is excusable; yet it is right that he should die of suffocation. So, too, he who cannot rule his passions, nor hold them in check out of respect for the law, while he may be excusable on the ground of weakness, is incapable of enjoying conformity of spirit and knowledge and love of God; and he is lost inevitably.

Spinoza

Horizontally and vertically, in physical and temperamental kind as well as in degree of inborn ability and native goodness, human beings differ profoundly one from another. Why? To what end and for what past causes? 'Master, who did sin, this man or his parents, that he was born blind?' Jesus answered, 'Neither hath this man sinned nor his parents, but that the works of God should be made manifest in him.' The man of science, on the contrary, would say that the responsibility rested with the parents who had caused the blindness of their child either by having the wrong kind of genes, or by contracting some avoidable disease. Hindu or Buddhist believers in reincarnation according to the laws of *karma* (the destiny which, by their actions, individuals and groups of individuals impose upon themselves, one another and their descendants) would give another answer and say that, owing to what he had done in previous existences, the blind man had predestined himself to choose the sort of parents from whom he would have to inherit blindness.

These three answers are not mutually incompatible. The parents are responsible for making the child what, by heredity and upbringing, he turns out to be. The soul or character incarnated in the child is of such a nature, owing to past behaviour, that it is forced to select those particular parents. And collaborating with the material and efficient causes is the final cause, the teleological pull from in front. This teleological pull is a pull from the divine Ground of things acting upon that part of the timeless now, which a finite mind must regard as the future. Men sin and their parents sin; but the works of God have to be manifested in every sentient being (either by exceptional ways, as in this case of supernormal healing, or in the ordinary course of events)—have to be manifested again and again, with the infinite patience of eternity, until at last the creature makes itself fit for the perfect and consummate manifestation of unitive knowledge, of the state of 'not I, but God in me.'

> '*Karma*,' according to the Hindus, 'never dispels ignorance, being under the same category with it. Knowledge alone dispels ignorance, just as light alone dispels darkness.'

In other words, the causal process takes place within time and cannot possibly result in deliverance from time. Such a deliverance can only be achieved as a consequence of the intervention of eternity in the temporal domain; and eternity cannot intervene unless the individual will makes a creative act of self-denial, thus producing, as it were, a vacuum into which eternity can flow. To suppose that the causal process in time can of itself result in deliverance from time is like supposing that water will rise into a space from which the air has not been previously exhausted.

The right relation between prayer and conduct is not that con-

duct is supremely important and prayer may help it, but that
prayer is supremely important and conduct tests it.

Archbishop Temple

The aim and purpose of human life is the unitive knowledge
of God. Among the indispensable means to that end is right
conduct, and by the degree and kind of virtue achieved, the
degree of liberating knowledge may be assessed and its quality
evaluated. In a word, the tree is known by its fruits; God is
not mocked.

Religious beliefs and practices are certainly not the only
factors determining the behaviour of a given society. But, no
less certainly, they are among the determining factors. At
least to some extent, the collective conduct of a nation is a test
of the religion prevailing within it, a criterion by which we
may legitimately judge the doctrinal validity of that religion
and its practical efficiency in helping individuals to advance
towards the goal of human existence.

In the past the nations of Christendom persecuted in the
name of their faith, fought religious wars and undertook crusades against infidels and heretics; today they have ceased to
be Christian in anything but name, and the only religion they
profess is some brand of local idolatry, such as nationalism,
state-worship, boss-worship and revolutionism. From these
fruits of (among other things) historic Christianity, what inferences can we draw as to the nature of the tree? The answer
has already been given in the section on 'Time and Eternity.'
If Christians used to be persecutors and are now no longer
Christians, the reason is that the Perennial Philosophy incor-
porated in their religion was overlaid by wrong beliefs that
led inevitably, since God is never mocked, to wrong actions.
These wrong beliefs had one element in common—namely, an
over-valuation of happenings in time and an under-valuation
of the everlasting, timeless fact of eternity. Thus, belief in the
supreme importance for salvation of remote historical events
resulted in bloody disputes over the interpretation of the not
very adequate and often conflicting records. And belief in the

sacredness, nay, the actual divinity, of the ecclesiastico-politico-financial organizations, which developed after the fall of the Roman Empire, not only added bitterness to the all too human struggles for their control, but served to rationalize and justify the worst excesses of those who fought for place, wealth and power within and through the Church.   But this is not the whole story.   The same over-valuation of events in time, which once caused Christians to persecute and fight religious wars, led at last to a widespread indifference to a religion that, in spite of everything, was still in part preoccupied with eternity.   But nature abhors a vacuum, and into the yawning void of this indifference there flowed the tide of political idolatry. The practical consequences of such idolatry, as we now see, are total war, revolution and tyranny.

Meanwhile, on the credit side of the balance sheet, we find such items as the following: an immense increase in technical and governmental efficiency and an immense increase in scientific knowledge—each of them a result of the general shift of Western man's attention from the eternal to the temporal order, first within the sphere of Christianity and then, inevitably, outside it.

Chapter 20

TANTUM RELIGIO POTUIT SUADERE MALORUM

Would you know whence it is that so many false spirits have appeared in the world, who have deceived themselves and others with false fire and false light, laying claim to information, illumination and openings of the divine Life, particularly to do wonders under extraordinary calls from God? It is this: they have turned to God without turning from themselves; would be alive to God before they are dead to their own nature. Now religion in the hands of self, or corrupt nature, serves only to discover vices of a worse kind than in nature left to itself. Hence are all the disorderly passions of religious men, which burn in a worse flame than passions only employed about worldly matters; pride, self-exaltation, hatred and persecution, under a cloak of religious zeal, will sanctify actions which nature, left to itself, would be ashamed to own.

William Law

'TURNING to God without turning from self'—the formula is absurdly simple; and yet, simple as it is, it explains all the follies and iniquities committed in the name of religion. Those who turn to God without turning from themselves are tempted to evil in several characteristic and easily recognizable ways. They are tempted, first of all, to practise magical rites, by means of which they hope to compel God to answer their petitions and, in general, to serve their private or collective ends. All the ugly business of sacrifice, incantation and what Jesus called 'vain repetition' is a product of this wish to treat God as a means to indefinite self-aggrandizement, rather than as an end to be reached through total self-denial. Next, they are tempted to use the name of God to justify what they do in pursuit of place, power and wealth. And because they believe themselves to have divine justification for their actions, they proceed, with a good conscience, to perpetrate abominations, 'which nature, left to itself, would be ashamed to own.' Throughout recorded history an incredible sum of mischief has been done by ambitious idealists, self-deluded by their own verbiage and a lust for power into a conviction that they were acting for the highest good of their fellow-men. In the past, the justification for such wickedness was 'God' or 'the Church,' or 'the True Faith'; today idealists kill and torture and exploit in the name of 'the Revolution,' 'the New Order,' 'the World of the Common Man,' or simply 'the Future.' Finally there are the temptations which arise when the falsely religious begin to acquire the powers which are the fruit of their pious and magical practices. For, let there be no mistake, sacrifice, incantation and 'vain repetition' actually do produce fruits, especially when practised in conjunction with physical austerities. Men who turn towards God without turning away from themselves do not, of course, reach God; but if they devote themselves energetically enough to their pseudo-religion, they will get results. Some of these results are doubtless the product of auto-suggestion. (It was through 'vain repetition' that Coué got his patients to cure themselves of their diseases.) Others are due, apparently, to that 'something not ourselves' in the psychic medium—that something which makes, not necessarily for righteousness, but always for power. Whether this something is a piece of second-hand objectivity, projected into the medium by the individual worshipper and his fellows and predecessors; whether it is a piece of first-hand objectivity, corresponding, on the psychic level, to the data of the material universe; or whether it is a combination of both these things, it is impossible to determine. All that need be said in this place is that people who turn towards God without turning from themselves often seem to acquire a knack of getting their petitions answered and sometimes develop considerable supernormal powers, such as those of psychic healing and extra-sensory perception. But, it may be asked: Is it necessarily a good thing to be able to get one's petitions answered in the way one wants them to be.? And how far is it spiritually profitable to be possessed of these 'miraculous' powers? These are questions which were considered in the chapter on 'Prayer' and will be further discussed in the chapter on 'The Miraculous.'

The Grand Augur, in his ceremonial robes, approached the shambles and thus addressed the pigs. 'How can you object to die? I shall fatten you for three months. I shall discipline myself for ten days and fast for three. I shall strew fine grass and place you bodily upon a carved sacrificial dish. Does not this satisfy you?'

Then, speaking from the pigs' point of view, he continued: 'It is better perhaps, after all, to live on bran and escape from the shambles.'

'But then,' he added, speaking from his own point of view, 'to enjoy honour when alive, one would readily die on a warshield or in the headsman's basket.'

So he rejected the pigs' point of view and adopted his own point of view. In what sense, then, was he different from the pigs?

Chuang Tzu

Anyone who sacrifices anything but his own person or his own interests is on exactly the same level as Chuang Tzu's pigs. The pigs seek their own advantage inasmuch as they prefer life and bran to honour and the shambles; the sacrificers seek their own advantage inasmuch as they prefer the magical, God-constraining death of pigs to the death of their own passions and self-will. And what applies to sacrifice, applies equally to incantations, rituals and vain repetitions, when these are used (as they all too frequently are, even in the higher religions) as a form of compulsive magic. Rites and vain repetitions have a legitimate place in religion as aids to recollectedness, reminders of truth momentarily forgotten in the turmoil of worldly distractions. When spoken or performed as a kind of magic, their use is either completely pointless; or else (and this is worse) it may have ego-enhancing results, which do not in any way contribute to the attainment of man's final end.

The vestments of Isis are variegated to represent the cosmos; that of Osiris is white, symbolizing the Intelligible Light beyond the cosmos.

Plutarch

So long as the symbol remains, in the worshipper's mind, firmly attached and instrumental to that which is symbolized, the use of such things as white and variegated vestments can do no harm. But if the symbol breaks loose, as it were, and becomes an end in itself, then we have, at the best, a futile aestheticism and sentimentality, at the worst a form of psychologically effective magic.

All externals must yield to love; for they are for the sake of love, and not love for them.

Hans Denk

Ceremonies in themselves are not sin; but whoever supposes that he can attain to life either by baptism or by partaking of bread is still in superstition.

Hans Denk

If you be always handling the letter of the Word, always licking the letter, always chewing upon that, what great thing do you? No marvel you are such starvelings.

John Everard

While the Right Law still prevailed, innumerable were the converts who fathomed the depths of the Dharma by merely listening to half a stanza or even to a single phrase of the Buddha's teaching. But as we come to the age of similitude and to these latter days of Buddhism, we are indeed far away from the Sage.

People find themselves drowning in a sea of letters; they do not know how to get at the one substance which alone is truth. This was what caused the appearance of the Fathers (of Zen Buddhism) who, pointing directly at the human mind, told us to see here the ultimate ground of all things and thereby to attain Buddhahood. This is known as a special transmission outside the scriptural teaching. If one is endowed with superior talents or a special sharpness of mind, a gesture or a word will suffice to give one an immediate knowledge of the truth. Hence, since they were advocates of 'special transmission,' Ummon treated the (historical) Buddha with the utmost irreverence and Yakusan forbade his followers even to read the sutras.

Zen is the name given to this branch of Buddhism, which keeps itself away from the Buddha. It is also called the mystical branch, because it does not adhere to the literal meaning of the sutras. It is for this reason that those who blindly follow the steps of Buddha are sure to deride Zen, while those who have no liking for the letter are naturally inclined towards the mystical approach. The followers of the two schools know how to shake the head at each other, but fail to realize that they are after all complementary. Is not Zen one of the six virtues of perfection? If so, how can it conflict with the teachings of the Buddha? In my view, Zen is the outcome of the Buddha's teaching, and the mystical issues from the letters. There is no reason why a man should shun Zen because of the Buddha's teaching; nor need we disregard the letters on account of the mystical teachings of Zen. . . . Students of scriptural Buddhism run the risk of becoming sticklers for the scriptures, the real meaning of which they fail to understand. By such men ultimate reality is never grasped, and for them Zen would mean salvation. Whereas those who study Zen are too apt to run into the habit of making empty talks and practising sophistry. They fail to understand the significance of letters. To save them, the study of Buddhist scriptures is recommended. It is only when these one-sided views are mutually corrected that there is a perfect appreciation of the Buddha's teaching.

Chiang Chih-chi

It would be hard to find a better summing up of the conclusions, to which any spiritually and psychologically realistic mind must sooner or later come, than the foregoing paragraphs written in the eleventh century by one of the masters of Zen Buddhism.

The extract that follows is a moving protest against the crimes and follies perpetrated in the name of religion by those sixteenth-century Reformers who had turned to God without turning away from themselves and who were therefore far more keenly interested in the temporal aspects of historic Christianity—the ecclesiastical organization, the logic-chopping, the letter of Scripture—than in the Spirit who must be worshipped in spirit, the eternal Reality in the selfless knowledge of whom stands man's eternal life. Its author was Sebastian Castellio, who was at one time Calvin's favourite disciple, but who parted company with his master when the latter burned Servetus for heresy against his own heresy. Fortunately Castellio was living in Basel when he made his plea for charity and common decency; penned in Geneva, it would have earned him torture and death.

If you, illustrious Prince (the words were addressed to the Duke of Würtemberg) had informed your subjects that you were coming to visit them at an unnamed time, and had requested them to be prepared in white garments to meet you at your coming, what would you do if on arrival you should find that, instead of robing themselves in white, they had spent their time in violent debate about your person—some insisting that you were in France, others that you were in Spain; some declaring that you would come on horseback, others that you would come by chariot; some holding that you would come with great pomp and others that you would come without any train or following? And what especially would you say if they debated not only with words, but with blows of fist and sword strokes, and if some succeeded in killing and destroying others who differed from them? 'He will come on horseback.' 'No, he will not; it will be by chariot.' 'You lie.' 'I do not; *you* are the liar.' 'Take that'—

a blow with the fist. 'Take *that*'—a sword-thrust through the body. Prince, what would you think of such citizens? Christ asked us to put on the white robes of a pure and holy life; but what occupies our thoughts? We dispute not only of the way to Christ, but of his relation to God the Father, of the Trinity, of predestination, of free will, of the nature of God, of the angels, of the condition of the soul after death—of a multitude of matters that are not essential to salvation; matters, moreover, which can never be known until our hearts are pure; for they are things which must be spiritually perceived.

Sebastian Castellio

People always get what they ask for; the only trouble is that they never know, until they get it, what it actually is that they have asked for. Thus, Protestants might, if they had so desired, have followed the lead of Castellio and Denk; but they preferred Calvin and Luther—preferred them because the doctrines of justification by faith and of predestination were more exciting than those of the Perennial Philosophy. And not only more exciting, but also less exacting; for if they were true, one could be saved without going through that distasteful process of self-naughting, which is the necessary pre-condition of deliverance into the knowledge of eternal Reality. And not only less exacting, but also more satisfying to the intellectual's appetite for clear-cut formulae and the syllogistic demonstrations of abstract truths. Waiting on God is a bore; but what fun to argue, to score off opponents, to lose one's temper and call it 'righteous indignation,' and at last to pass from controversy to blows, from words to what St. Augustine so deliciously described as the 'benignant asperity' of persecution and punishment!

Choosing Luther and Calvin instead of the spiritual reformers who were their contemporaries, Protestant Europe got the kind of theology it liked. But it also got, along with other unanticipated by-products, the Thirty Years War, capitalism and the first rudiments of modern Germany. 'If we wish,' Dean Inge has recently written, 'to find a scapegoat on whose shoulders we may lay the miseries which Germany has brought upon the world . . . I am more and more convinced that the worst evil genius of that country is not Hitler or Bismarck or Frederick the Great, but Martin Luther. . . . It (Lutheranism) worships a God who is neither just nor merciful. . . . The Law of Nature, which ought to be the court of appeal against unjust authority, is identified (by Luther) with the existing order of society, to which absolute obedience is due.' And so on. Right belief is the first branch of the Eightfold Path leading to deliverance; the root and primal cause of bondage is wrong belief, or ignorance—an ignorance, let us remember, which is never completely invincible, but always, in the last analysis, a matter of will. If we don't know, it is because we find it more convenient not to know. Original ignorance is the same thing as original sin.

Chapter 21

IDOLATRY

TO educated persons the more primitive kinds of idolatry have ceased to be attractive. They find it easy to resist the temptation to believe that particular natural objects are gods, or that certain symbols and images are the very forms of divine entities and as such must be worshipped and propitiated. True, much fetishistic superstition survives even today. But though it survives, it is not considered respectable. Like drinking and prostitution, the primitive forms of idolatry are tolerated, but not approved. Their place in the accredited hierarchy of values is among the lowest.

How different is the case with the developed and more modern forms of idolatry! These have achieved not merely survival, but the highest degree of respectability. They are recommended by men of science as an up-to-date substitute for genuine religion and by many professional religious teachers are equated with the worship of God. All this may be deplorable; but it is not in the least surprising. Our education disparages the more primitive forms of idolatry; but at the same time it disparages, or at the best it ignores, the Perennial Philosophy and the practice of spirituality. In place of mumbo-jumbo at the bottom and of the immanent and transcendent Godhead at the top, it sets up, as objects of admiration, faith and worship, a pantheon of strictly human ideas and ideals. In academic circles and among those who have been subjected to higher education, there are few fetishists and few devout contemplatives; but the enthusiastic devotees of some form of political or social idolatry are as common as blackberries. Significantly enough, I have observed, when making use of university libraries, that books on spiritual religion were taken out much less frequently than was the case in public libraries, patronized in the main by men and women who had not enjoyed the advantages, or suffered under the handicaps, of prolonged academic instruction.

The many varieties of higher idolatry may be classed under three main heads: technological, political and moral. Technological idolatry is the most ingenuous and primitive of the three; for its devotees, like those of the lower idolatry, believe that their redemption and liberation depend upon material objects—in this case gadgets. Technological idolatry is the religion whose doctrines are promulgated, explicitly or by implication, in the advertisement pages of our newspapers and magazines—the source, we may add parenthetically, from which millions of men, women and children in the capitalistic countries derive their working philosophy of life. In Soviet Russia too, technological idolatry was strenuously preached, becoming, during the years of that country's industrialization, a kind of state religion. So whole-hearted is the modern faith in technological idols that (despite all the lessons of mechanized warfare) it is impossible to discover in the popular thinking of our time any trace of the ancient and profoundly realistic doctrine of *hubris* and inevitable *nemesis*. There is a very general belief that, where gadgets are concerned, we can get something for nothing—can enjoy all the advantages of an elaborate, top-heavy and constantly advancing technology without having to pay for them by any compensating disadvantages.

Only a little less ingenuous are the political idolaters. For the worship of redemptive gadgets these have substituted the worship of redemptive social and economic organizations. Impose the right kind of organizations upon human beings, and all their problems, from sin and unhappiness to nationalism and war, will automatically disappear. Most political idolaters are also technological idolaters—and this in spite of the fact that the two pseudo-religions are finally incompatible, since technological progress at its present rate makes nonsense of any political blue-print, however ingeniously drawn, within a matter, not of generations, but of years and sometimes even of months. Further, the human being is, unfortunately, a creature endowed with free will; and if, for any reason, individuals do not choose to make it work, even the best organization will not produce the results it was intended to produce.

The moral idolaters are realists inasmuch as they see that gadgets and organizations are not enough to guarantee the triumph of virtue and the increase of happiness, and that the individuals who compose societies and use machines are the arbiters who finally determine whether there shall be decency in personal relationship, order or disorder in society. Material and organizational instruments are indispensable, and a good tool is preferable to a bad one. But in listless or malicious hands the finest instrument is either useless or a means to evil.

The moralists cease to be realistic and commit idolatry inasmuch as they worship, not God, but their own ethical ideals, inasmuch as they treat virtue as an end in itself and not as the necessary condition of the knowledge and love of God—a knowledge and love without which that virtue will never be made perfect or even socially effective.

What follows is an extract from a very remarkable letter written in 1836 by Thomas Arnold to his old pupil and future biographer, A. P. Stanley. 'Fanaticism is idolatry; and it has the moral evil of idolatry in it; that is, a fanatic worships something which is the creation of his own desire, and thus even his self-devotion in support of it is only an apparent self-devotion; for in fact it is making the parts of his nature or his mind, which he least values, offer sacrifice to that which he most values. The moral fault, as it appears to me, is the idolatry—the setting up of some idea which is most kindred to our own minds, and the putting it in the place of Christ, who alone cannot be made an idol and inspire idolatry, because He combines all ideas of perfection and exhibits them in their just harmony and combination. Now in my own mind, by its natural tendency—that is, taking my mind at its best—truth and justice would be the idols I should follow; and they would be idols, for they would not supply *all* the food which the mind wants, and whilst worshipping them, reverence and

T

humility and tenderness might very likely be forgotten. But Christ Himself includes at once truth and justice and all these other qualities too. . . . Narrow-mindedness tends to wickedness, because it does not extend its watchfulness to every part of our moral nature, and the neglect fosters wickedness in the parts so neglected.'

As a piece of psychological analysis this is admirable. Its only defect is one of omission; for it neglects to take into account those influxes from the eternal order into the temporal, which are called grace or inspiration. Grace and inspiration are given when, and to the extent to which, a human being gives up self-will and abandons himself, moment by moment, through constant recollectedness and non-attachment, to the will of God. As well as the animal and spiritual graces, whose source is the divine Nature of Things, there are human pseudo-graces—such as, for example, the accessions of strength and virtue that follow self-devotion to some form of political or moral idolatry. To distinguish the true grace from the false is often difficult; but as time and circumstances reveal the full extent of their consequences on the soul, discrimination becomes possible even to observers having no special gifts of insight. Where the grace is genuinely 'supernatural,' an amelioration in one aspect of the total personality is not paid for by atrophy or deterioration elsewhere. The virtue which is accompanied and perfected by the love and knowledge of God is something quite different from the 'righteousness of the scribes and Pharisees' which, for Christ, was among the worst of moral evils. Hardness, fanaticism, uncharitableness and spiritual pride—these are the ordinary by-products of a course of stoical self-improvement by means of personal effort, either unassisted or, if assisted, seconded only by the pseudo-graces which are given when the individual devotes himself to the achievement of an end which is not his true end, when the goal is not God, but merely a magnified projection of his own favourite ideas or moral excellences. The idolatrous worship of ethical values in and for themselves defeats its own object—

and defeats it not only because, as Arnold insists, there is a lack of all-round development, but also and above all because even the highest forms of moral idolatry are God-eclipsing and therefore guarantee the idolater against the enlightening and liberating knowledge of Reality.

Chapter 22

EMOTIONALISM

You have spent all your life in the belief that you are wholly devoted to others, and never self-seeking. Nothing so feeds self-conceit as this sort of internal testimony that one is quite free from self-love, and always generously devoted to one's neighbours. But all this devotion that seems to be for others is really for yourself. Your self-love reaches to the point of perpetual self-congratulation that you are free from it; all your sensitiveness is lest you might not be fully satisfied with self; this is at the root of all your scruples. It is the 'I' which makes you so keen and sensitive. You want God as well as man to be always satisfied with you, and you want to be satisfied with yourself in all your dealings with God.

Besides, you are not accustomed to be contented with a simple good will—your self-love wants a lively emotion, a reassuring pleasure, some kind of charm or excitement. You are too much used to be guided by imagination and to suppose that your mind and will are inactive, unless you are conscious of their workings. And thus you are dependent upon a kind of excitement similar to that which the passions arouse, or theatrical representations. By dint of refinement you fall into the opposite extreme—a real coarseness of imagination. Nothing is more opposed, not only to the life of faith, but also to true wisdom. There is no more dangerous illusion than the fancies by which people try to avoid illusion. It is imagination which leads us astray; and the certainty which we seek through imagination, feeling, and taste, is one of the most dangerous sources from which fanaticism springs. This is the gulf of vanity and corruption which God would make you discover in your heart; you must look upon it with the calm and simplicity belonging to true humility. It is mere self-love to be inconsolable at seeing one's own imperfections; but to stand face to face with them, neither flattering nor tolerating them, seeking to correct oneself without becoming pettish—this is to desire what is good for its own sake, and for God's.

Fénelon

A LETTER from the Archbishop of Cambrai—what an event, what a signal honour! And yet it must have been with a certain trepidation that one broke the emblazoned seal. To ask for advice and a frank opinion of oneself from a man who combines the character of a saint with the talents of a Marcel Proust, is to ask for the severest kind of shock to one's self-esteem. And duly, in the most exquisitely lucid prose, the shock would be administered—and, along with the shock, the spiritual antidote to its excruciating consequences. Fénelon never hesitated to disintegrate a correspondent's complacent ego; but the disintegration was always performed with a view to reintegration on a higher, non-egotistic level.

This particular letter is not only an admirable piece of character analysis; it also contains some very interesting remarks on the subject of emotional excitement in its relation to the life of the spirit.

The phrase, 'religion of experience,' has two distinct and mutually incompatible meanings. There is the 'experience' of which the Perennial Philosophy treats—the direct apprehension of the divine Ground in an act of intuition possible, in its fullness, only to the selflessly pure in heart. And there is the 'experience' induced by revivalist sermons, impressive ceremonials, or the deliberate efforts of one's own imagination. This 'experience' is a state of emotional excitement—an excitement which may be mild and enduring or brief and epileptically violent, which is sometimes exultant in tone and sometimes despairing, which expresses itself here in song and dance, there in uncontrollable weeping. But emotional excitement, whatever its cause and whatever its nature, is always excitement of that individualized self, which must be died to by anyone who aspires to live to divine Reality. 'Experience' as emotion about God (the highest form of this kind of excitement) is incompatible with 'experience' as immediate awareness of God by a pure heart which has mortified even its most exalted emotions. That is why Fénelon, in the foregoing extract, insists upon the need for 'calm and simplicity,' why St. François de Sales is never tired of preaching the serenity which he himself so consistently practised, why all the Buddhist scriptures harp on tranquillity of mind as a necessary condition of deliverance. The peace that passes all understanding is one of the fruits of the spirit. But there is also the peace that does not pass understanding, the humbler peace of emotional self-control and self-denial; this is not a fruit of the spirit, but rather one of its indispensable roots.

The imperfect destroy true devotion, because they seek sensible sweetness in prayer.

St. John of the Cross

The fly that touches honey cannot use its wings; so the soul that clings to spiritual sweetness ruins its freedom and hinders contemplation.

St. John of the Cross

What is true of the sweet emotions is equally true of the bitter. For as some people enjoy bad health, so others enjoy a bad conscience. Repentance is *metanoia*, or 'change of mind'; and without it there cannot be even a beginning of the spiritual life—for the life of the spirit is incompatible with the life of that 'old man,' whose acts, whose thoughts, whose very existence are the obstructing evils which have to be repented. This necessary change of mind is normally accompanied by sorrow and self-loathing. But these emotions are not to be persisted in and must never be allowed to become a settled habit of remorse. In Middle English 'remorse' is rendered, with a literalness which to modern readers is at once startling and stimulating, as 'again-bite.' In this cannibalistic encounter, who bites whom? Observation and self-analysis provide the answer: the creditable aspects of the self bite the discreditable and are themselves bitten, receiving wounds that fester with incurable shame and despair. But, in Fénelon's words, 'it is mere self-love to be inconsolable at seeing one's own imperfections.' Self-reproach is painful; but the very pain is a reassuring proof that the self is still intact; so long as attention is fixed on the delinquent ego, it cannot be fixed upon God and the ego (which lives upon attention and dies only when that sustenance is withheld) cannot be dissolved in the divine Light.

Eschew as though it were a hell the consideration of yourself and your offences. No one should ever think of these things except to humiliate himself and love Our Lord. It is enough to regard yourself *in general* as a sinner, even as there are many saints in heaven who were such.

Charles de Condren

Faults will turn to good, provided we use them to our own humiliation, without slackening in the effort to correct ourselves. Discouragement serves no possible purpose; it is simply the despair of wounded self-love. The real way of profiting by the humiliation of one's own faults is to face them in their true hideousness, without ceasing to hope in God, while hoping nothing from self.

Fénelon

Came she (Mary Magdalene) down from the height of her desire for God into the depth of her sinful life, and searched in the foul stinking fen and dunghill of her soul? Nay, surely she did not do so. And why? Because God let her know by His grace in her soul that she should never so bring it about. For so might she sooner have raised in herself an ableness to have often sinned than have purchased by that work any plain forgiveness of all her sins.

The Cloud of Unknowing

In the light of what has been said above, we can understand the peculiar spiritual dangers by which every kind of predominantly emotional religion is always menaced. A hell-fire faith that uses the theatrical techniques of revivalism in order to stimulate remorse and induce the crisis of sudden conversion; a saviour cult that is for ever stirring up what St. Bernard calls the *amor carnalis* or fleshly love of the Avatar and personal God; a ritualistic mystery-religion that generates high feelings of awe and reverence and aesthetic ecstasy by means of its sacraments and ceremonials, its music and its incense, its numinous darknesses and sacred lights—in its own special way, each one of these runs the risk of becoming a form of psychological idolatry, in which God is identified with the ego's affective attitude towards God and finally the emotion becomes an end in itself, to be eagerly sought after and worshipped, as the addicts of a drug spend life in the pursuit of their artificial paradise. All this is obvious enough. But it is no less obvious that religions that make no appeal to the emotions have very few adherents. Moreover, when pseudo-religions with a strong emotional appeal make their appearance, they immediately win millions of enthusiastic devotees from among the masses to whom the real religions have ceased to have a meaning or to be a comfort. But whereas no adherent of a pseudo-religion (such as one of our current political idolatries, compounded of nationalism and revolutionism) can possibly go forward into the way of genuine spirituality, such a way always remains open to the adherents of even the most highly emotionalized varieties of genuine religion. Those who have actually followed this way to its end in the unitive knowledge of the divine Ground constitute a very small minority of the total. Many are called; but, since few choose to be chosen, few are chosen. The rest, say the oriental exponents of the Perennial Philosophy, earn themselves another chance, in circumstances more or less propitious according to their deserts, to take the cosmic intelligence test. If they are 'saved,' their incomplete and undefinitive deliverance is into some paradisal state of freer personal existence, from which (directly or through further incarnations) they may go on to the final release into eternity. If they are 'lost,' their 'hell' is a temporal

and temporary condition of thicker darkness and more oppres-
sive bondage to self-will, the root and principle of all evil.

We see, then, that if it is persisted in, the way of emotional
religion may lead, indeed, to a great good, but not to the
greatest. But the emotional way opens into the way of unitive
knowledge, and those who care to go on in this other way are
well prepared for their task if they have used the emotional
approach without succumbing to the temptations which have
beset them on the way. Only the perfectly selfless and enlightened can do good that does not, in some way or other, have to
be paid for by actual or potential evils. The religious systems
of the world have been built up, in the main, by men and
women who were not completely selfless or enlightened.
Hence all religions have had their dark and even frightful
aspects, while the good they do is rarely gratuitous, but must,
in most cases, be paid for, either on the nail or by instalments.
The emotion-rousing doctrines and practices, which play so
important a part in all the world's organized religions, are no
exception to this rule. They do good, but not gratuitously.
The price paid varies according to the nature of the individual
worshippers. Some of these choose to wallow in emotionalism
and, becoming idolaters of feeling, pay for the good of their
religion by a spiritual evil that may actually outweigh that
good. Others resist the temptation to self-enhancement and
go forward to the mortification of self, including the self's
emotional side, and to the worship of God rather than of their
own feelings and fancies about God. The further they go in
this direction, the less they have to pay for the good which
emotionalism brought them and which, but for emotionalism,
most of them might never have had.

Chapter 23

THE MIRACULOUS

Revelations are the aberration of faith; they are an amusement that spoils simplicity in relation to God, that embarrasses the soul and makes it swerve from its directness in relation to God. They distract the soul and occupy it with other things than God. Special illuminations, auditions, prophecies and the rest are marks of weakness in a soul that cannot support the assaults of temptation or of anxiety about the future and God's judgment upon it. Prophecies are also marks of creaturely curiosity in a soul to whom God is indulgent and to whom, as a father to his importunate child, he gives a few trifling sweetmeats to satisfy its appetite.

J. J. Olier

The slightest degree of sanctifying grace is superior to a miracle, which is supernatural only by reason of its cause, by its mode of production (*quoad modum*), not by its intimate reality; the life restored to a corpse is only the natural life, low indeed in comparison with that of grace.

R. Garrigou-Lagrange

Can you walk on water? You have done no better than a straw. Can you fly in the air? You have done no better than a bluebottle. Conquer your heart; then you may become somebody.

Ansari of Herat

THE abnormal bodily states, by which the immediate awareness of the divine Ground is often accompanied, are not, of course, essential parts of that experience. Many mystics, indeed, deplored such things as being signs, not of divine grace, but of the body's weakness. To levitate, to go into trance, to lose the use of one's senses—in De Condren's words, this is 'to receive the effects of God and his holy communications in a very animal and carnal way.'

'One ounce of sanctifying grace,' he (St. François de Sales) used to say, 'is worth more than a hundredweight of those graces which theologians call "gratuitous," among which is the gift of miracles. It is possible to receive such gifts and yet to be in mortal sin; nor are they necessary to salvation.'

Jean Pierre Camus

The Sufis regard miracles as 'veils' intervening between the soul and God. The masters of Hindu spirituality urge their disciples to pay no attention to the *siddhis*, or psychic powers, which may come to them unsought, as a by-product of one-pointed contemplation. The cultivation of these powers, they warn, distracts the soul from Reality and sets up insurmountable obstacles in the way of enlightenment and deliverance. A similar attitude is taken by the best Buddhist teachers, and in one of the Pali scriptures there is an anecdote recording the Buddha's own characteristically dry comment on a prodigious feat of levitation performed by one of his disciples. 'This,' he said, 'will not conduce to the conversion of the unconverted, nor to the advantage of the converted.' Then he went back to talking about deliverance.

Because they know nothing of spirituality and regard the material world and their hypotheses about it as supremely significant, rationalists are anxious to convince themselves and others that miracles do not and cannot happen. Because they have had experience of the spiritual life and its by-products, the exponents of the Perennial Philosophy are convinced that miracles do happen, but regard them as things of little importance, and that mainly negative and anti-spiritual.

The miracles which at present are in greatest demand, and of which there is the steadiest supply, are those of psychic healing. In what circumstances and to what extent the power of psychic healing should be used has been clearly indicated in the Gospel: 'Whether is it easier to say to the sick of the palsy, Thy sins be forgiven thee; or to say, Arise, and take up thy bed and walk?' If one can 'forgive sins,' one can safely use the gift of healing. But the forgiving of sins is possible, in its fullness, only to those who 'speak with authority,' in virtue of being selfless channels of the divine Spirit. To these theocentric saints the ordinary, unregenerate human being reacts with a mixture of love and awe—longing to be close to them and yet constrained by their very holiness to say, 'Depart from me, for I am a sinful man.' Such holiness makes holy to the extent that the sins of those who approach it are forgiven and they are enabled to make a new start, to face the consequences of their past wrong-doings (for of course the consequences remain) in a new spirit that makes it possible for them to neutralize the evil or turn it into positive good. A less perfect kind of forgiveness can be bestowed by those who are not themselves outstandingly holy, but who speak with the delegated authority of an institution which the sinner believes to be in some way a channel of supernatural grace. In this case the contact between unregenerate soul and divine Spirit is not direct, but is mediated through the sinner's imagination.

Those who are holy in virtue of being selfless channels of the Spirit may practise psychic healing with perfect safety; for they will know which of the sick are ready to accept forgiveness along with the mere miracle of a bodily cure. Those who are not holy, but who can forgive sins in virtue of belonging to an institution which is believed to be a channel of grace, may also practise healing with a fair confidence that they will not do more harm than good. But unfortunately the knack of psychic healing seems in some persons to be inborn, while others can acquire it without acquiring the smallest degree of holiness. ('It is possible to receive such graces and yet be in mortal sin.') Such persons will use their knack indiscriminately, either to show off or for profit. Often they produce spectacular cures—but, lacking the power to forgive sins or even to understand the psychological correlates, conditions or causes of the symptoms they have so miraculously dispelled, they leave a soul empty, swept and garnished against the coming of seven other devils worse than the first.

Chapter 24

RITUAL, SYMBOL, SACRAMENT

Aswala: Yajnavalkya, since everything connected with the sacrifice is pervaded by death and is subject to death, by what means can the sacrificer overcome death?

Yajnavalkya: By the knowledge of the identity between the sacrificer, the fire and the ritual word. For the ritual word is indeed the sacrificer, and the ritual word is the fire, and the fire, which is one with Brahman, is the sacrificer. This knowledge leads to liberation. This knowledge leads one beyond death.

Brihad Aranyaka Upanishad

IN other words, rites, sacraments, and ceremonials are valuable to the extent that they remind those who take part in them of the true Nature of Things, remind them of what ought to be and (if only they would be docile to the immanent and transcendent Spirit) of what actually might be their own relation to the world and its divine Ground. Theoretically any ritual or sacrament is as good as any other ritual or sacrament, provided always that the object symbolized be in fact some aspect of divine Reality and that the relation between symbol and fact be clearly defined and constant. In the same way, one language is theoretically as good as another. Human experience can be thought about as effectively in Chinese as in English or French. But in practice Chinese is the best language for those brought up in China, English for those brought up in England and French for those brought up in France. It is, of course, much easier to learn the order of a rite and to understand its doctrinal significance than to master the intricacies of a foreign language. Nevertheless what has been said of language is true, in large measure, of religious ritual. For persons who have been brought up to think of God by means of one set of symbols, it is very hard to think of Him in terms of other and, in their eyes, unhallowed sets of words, ceremonies and images.

> The Lord Buddha then warned Subhuti, saying, 'Subhuti, do not think that the Tathagata ever considers in his own mind: I ought to enunciate a system of teaching for the elucidation of the Dharma. You should never cherish such a thought. And why? Because if any disciple harboured such a thought he would not only be misunderstanding the Tathagata's teaching, but he would be slandering him as well. Moreover, the expression "a system of teaching" has no meaning; for Truth (in the sense of Reality) cannot be cut up into pieces and arranged into a system. The words can only be used as a figure of speech.'
>
> *Diamond Sutra*

But for all their inadequacy and their radical unlikeness to the facts to which they refer, words remain the most reliable and accurate of our symbols. Whenever we want to have a precise report of facts or ideas, we must resort to words. A ceremony, a carved or painted image, may convey more meanings and overtones of meaning in a smaller compass and with greater vividness than can a verbal formula; but it is liable to convey them in a form that is much more vague and indefinite. One often meets, in modern literature, with the notion that mediaeval churches were the architectural, sculptural and pictorial equivalents of a theological *summa*, and that mediaeval worshippers who admired the works of art around them were thereby enlightened on the subject of doctrine. This view was evidently not shared by the more earnest churchmen of the Middle Ages. Coulton cites the utterances of preachers who complained that congregations were getting entirely false ideas of Catholicism by looking at the pictures in the churches instead of listening to sermons. (Similarly, in our own day the Catholic Indians of Central America have evolved the wildest heresies by brooding on the carved and painted symbols with which the Conquistadors filled their churches.) St. Bernard's objection to the richness of Cluniac architecture, sculpture and ceremonial was motivated by intellectual as well as strictly moral considerations. 'So great and marvellous a variety of divers forms meets the eye that one is tempted to read in the marbles rather than in the books, to pass the whole day looking at these carvings one after another rather than in meditating on the law of God.' It is in imageless contemplation that the soul comes to the unitive knowledge of Reality; consequently, for those who, like St. Bernard and his Cistercians, are really concerned to achieve man's final end, the fewer distracting symbols the better.

Most men worship the gods because they want success in their worldly undertakings. This kind of material success can be gained very quickly (by such worship), here on earth.

Bhagavad-Gita

Among those who are purified by their good deeds there are four kinds of men who worship Me: the world-weary, the seeker for knowledge, the seeker for happiness and the man of spiritual discrimination. The man of discrimination is the highest of these. He is continually united with Me. He devotes himself to Me always, and to no other. For I am very dear to that man, and he to Me.

Certainly, all these are noble;
But the man of discrimination
I see as my very Self.
For he alone loves Me
Because I am Myself,
The last and only goal
Of his devoted heart.

Through many a long life
His discrimination ripens;
He makes Me his refuge,
Knows that Brahman is all.
How rare are such great ones!

Men whose discrimination has been blunted by worldly desires, establish this or that ritual or cult and resort to various deities, according to the impulse of their inborn nature. But no matter what deity a devotee chooses to worship, if he has faith, I make his faith unwavering. Endowed with the faith I give him, he worships that deity and gets from it everything he prays for. In reality, I alone am the giver.

But these men of small understanding pray only for what is transient and perishable. The worshippers of the devas will go to the devas. Those who worship Me will come to Me.

Bhagavad-Gita

If sacramental rites are constantly repeated in a spirit of faith and devotion, a more or less enduring effect is produced in the psychic medium, in which individual minds bathe and from which they have, so to speak, been crystallized out into personalities more or less fully developed, according to the more or less perfect development of the bodies with which they are associated. (Of this psychic medium an eminent contemporary philosopher, Dr. C. D. Broad, has written, in an essay on telepathy contributed to the *Proceedings of the Society for Psychical Research*, as follows : 'We must therefore consider seriously the possibility that a person's experience initiates more or less permanent modifications of structure or process in something which is neither his mind nor his brain. There is no reason to suppose that this substratum would be anything to which possessive adjectives, such as "mine" and "yours" and "his," could properly be applied, as they can be to minds and animated bodies.... Modifications which have been produced in the substratum by certain of M's past experiences are activated by N's present experiences or interests, and they become cause factors in producing or modifying N's later experiences.') Within this psychic medium or non-personal substratum of individual minds, something which we may think of metaphorically as a vortex persists as an independent existence, possessing its own derived and secondary objectivity, so that, wherever the rites are performed, those whose faith and

devotion are sufficiently intense actually discover something
'out there,' as distinct from the subjective something in their
own imaginations. And so long as this projected psychic
entity is nourished by the faith and love of its worshippers, it
will possess, not merely objectivity, but power to get people's
prayers answered. Ultimately, of course, 'I alone am the
giver,' in the sense that all this happens in accordance with the
divine laws governing the universe in its psychic and spiritual,
no less than in its material, aspects. Nevertheless, the devas
(those imperfect forms under which, because of their own
voluntary ignorance, men worship the divine Ground) may be
thought of as relatively independent powers. The primitive
notion that the gods feed on the sacrifices made to them is
simply the crude expression of a profound truth. When their
worship falls off, when faith and devotion lose their intensity,
the devas sicken and finally die. Europe is full of old shrines,
whose saints and Virgins and relics have lost the power and
the second-hand psychic objectivity which they once possessed.
Thus, when Chaucer lived and wrote, the deva called Thomas
Becket was giving to any Canterbury pilgrim, who had sufficient faith, all the boons he could ask for. This once-powerful
deity is now stone-dead; but there are still certain churches in
the West, certain mosques and temples in the East, where even
the most irreligious and un-psychic tourist cannot fail to be
aware of some intensely 'numinous' presence. It would, of
course, be a mistake to imagine that this presence is the presence
of that God who is a Spirit and must be worshipped in spirit;
it is rather the psychic presence of men's thoughts and feelings
about the particular, limited form of God, to which they have
resorted 'according to the impulse of their inborn nature'—
thoughts and feelings projected into objectivity and haunting
the sacred place in the same way as thoughts and feelings of
another kind, but of equal intensity, haunt the scenes of some
past suffering or crime. The presence in these consecrated
buildings, the presence evoked by the performance of traditional rites, the presence inherent in a sacramental object, name
or formula—all these are real presences, but real presences, not

U

of God or the Avatar, but of something which, though it may reflect the divine Reality, is yet less and other than it.

> *Dulcis Jesu memoria*
> *dans vera cordi gaudia :*
> *sed super mel et omnia*
> *ejus dulcis praesentia.*

'Sweet is the memory of Jesus, giving true joys to the heart; but sweeter beyond honey and all else is his presence.' This opening stanza of the famous twelfth-century hymn summarizes in fifteen words the relations subsisting between ritual and real presence and the character of the worshipper's reaction to each. Systematically cultivated *memoria* (a thing in itself full of sweetness) first contributes to the evocation, then results, for certain souls, in the immediate apprehension of *praesentia*, which brings with it joys of a totally different and higher kind. This presence (whose projected objectivity is occasionally so complete as to be apprehensible not merely by the devout worshipper, but by more or less indifferent outsiders) is always that of the divine being who has been previously remembered, Jesus here, Krishna or Amitabha Buddha there.

The value of this practice (repetition of the name of Amitabha Buddha) is this. So long as one person practises his method (of spirituality) and another practises a different method, they counterbalance one another and their meeting is just the same as their not meeting. Whereas if two persons practise the same method, their mindfulness tends to become deeper and deeper, and they tend to remember each other and to develop affinities for each other, life after life. Moreover, whoever recites the name of Amitabha Buddha, whether in the present time or in future time, will surely see the Buddha Amitabha and never become separated from him. By reason of that association, just as one associating with a maker of perfumes becomes permeated with the same perfumes, so he will become perfumed by Amitabha's compassion, and will become enlightened without resort to any other expedient means.

Surangama Sutra

We see then that intense faith and devotion, coupled with perseverance by many persons in the same forms of worship or spiritual exercise, have a tendency to objectify the idea or memory which is their content and so to create, in some sort, a numinous real presence, which worshippers actually find 'out there' no less, and in quite another way, than 'in here.' In so far as this is the case, the ritualist is perfectly correct in attributing to his hallowed acts and words a power which, in another context, would be called magical. The *mantram* works, the sacrifice really does something, the sacrament confers grace *ex opere operato*: these are, or rather may be, matters of direct experience, facts which anyone who chooses to fulfil the necessary conditions can verify empirically for himself. But the grace conferred *ex opere operato* is not always spiritual grace and the hallowed acts and formulae have a power which is not necessarily from God. Worshippers can, and very often do, get grace and power from one another and from the faith and devotion of their predecessors, projected into independent psychic existences that are hauntingly associated with certain places, words and acts. A great deal of ritualistic religion is not spirituality, but occultism, a refined and well-meaning kind of white magic. Now, just as there is no harm in art, say, or science, but a great deal of good, provided always that these activities are not regarded as ends, but simply as means to the final end of all life, so too there is no harm in white magic, but the possibilities of much good, so long as it is treated, not as true religion, but as one of the roads to true religion—an effective way of reminding people with a certain kind of psycho-physical make-up that there is a God, 'in knowledge of whom standeth their eternal life.' If ritualistic white magic is regarded as being in itself true religion; if the real presences it evokes are taken to be God in Himself and not the projections of human thoughts and feelings about God or even about something less than God; and if the sacramental rites are performed and attended for the sake of the 'spiritual sweetness' experienced and the powers and advantages conferred—then there is idolatry. This idolatry is, at its best, a very lofty and, in many ways, beneficent kind of religion. But the consequences of worshipping God as anything but Spirit and in any way except in spirit and in truth are necessarily undesirable in this sense—that they lead only to a partial salvation and delay the soul's ultimate reunion with the eternal Ground.

That very large numbers of men and women have an ineradicable desire for rites and ceremonies is clearly demonstrated by the history of religion. Almost all the Hebrew prophets were opposed to ritualism. 'Rend your hearts and not your garments.' 'I desire mercy and not sacrifice.' 'I hate, I despise your feasts; I take no delight in your solemn assemblies.' And yet, in spite of the fact that what the prophets wrote was regarded as divinely inspired, the Temple at Jerusalem continued to be, for hundreds of years after their time, the centre of a religion of rites, ceremonials and blood sacrifice. (It may be remarked in passing that the shedding of blood, one's own or that of animals or other human beings, seems to be a peculiarly efficacious way of constraining the 'occult' or psychic world to answer petitions and confer supernormal powers. If this is a fact, as from the anthropological and antiquarian evidence it appears to be, it would supply yet another cogent reason for avoiding animal sacrifices, savage bodily austerities and even, since thought is a form of action, that imaginative gloating over spilled blood which is so common in certain Christian circles.) What the Jews did in spite of their prophets, Christians have done in spite of Christ. The Christ of the Gospels is a preacher and not a dispenser of sacraments or performer of rites; he speaks against vain repetitions; he insists on the supreme importance of private worship; he has no use for sacrifices and not much use for the Temple. But this did not prevent historic Christianity from going its own, all too human, way. A precisely similar development took place in Buddhism. For the Buddha of the Pali scriptures, ritual was one of the fetters holding back the soul from enlightenment and liberation. Nevertheless, the religion he founded has made full use of ceremonies, vain repetitions and sacramental rites.

There would seem to be two main reasons for the observed developments of the historical religions. First, most people do not want spirituality or deliverance, but rather a religion that gives them emotional satisfactions, answers to prayer, super-normal powers and partial salvation in some sort of posthumous heaven. Second, some of those few who do desire spirituality and deliverance find that, for them, the most effective means to those ends are ceremonies, 'vain repetitions' and sacramental rites. It is by participating in these acts and uttering these formulae that they are most powerfully reminded of the eternal Ground of all being; it is by immersing themselves in the symbols that they can most easily come through to that which is symbolized. Every thing, event or thought is a point of intersection between creature and Creator, between a more or less distant manifestation of God and a ray, so to speak, of the unmanifest Godhead; every thing, event or thought can therefore be made the doorway through which a soul may pass out of time into eternity. That is why ritualistic and sacramental religion can lead to deliverance. But at the same time every human being loves power and self-enhancement, and every hallowed ceremony, form of words or sacramental rite is a channel through which power can flow out of the fascinating psychic universe into the universe of embodied selves. That is why ritualistic and sacramental religion can also lead away from deliverance.

There is another disadvantage inherent in any system of organized sacramentalism, and that is that it gives to the priestly caste a power which it is all too natural for them to abuse. In a society which has been taught that salvation is exclusively or mainly through certain sacraments, and that these sacraments can be administered effectively only by a professional priesthood, that professional priesthood will possess an enormous coercive power. The possession of such power is a standing temptation to use it for individual satisfaction and corporate aggrandizement. To a temptation of this kind, if repeated often enough, most human beings who are not saints almost inevitably succumb. That is why Christ taught his disciples to pray that they should not be led into temptation. This is, or should be, the guiding principle of all social reform —to organize the economic, political and social relationships between human beings in such a way that there shall be, for any given individual or group within the society, a minimum of temptations to covetousness, pride, cruelty and lust for power. Men and women being what they are, it is only by reducing the number and intensity of temptations that human societies can be, in some measure at least, delivered from evil. Now, the sort of temptations to which a priestly caste is exposed in a society that accepts a predominantly sacramental religion are such that none but the most saintly persons can be expected consistently to resist them. What happens when ministers of religion are led into these temptations is clearly illustrated by the history of the Roman Church. Because Catholic Christianity taught a version of the Perennial Philosophy, it produced a succession of great saints. But because the Perennial Philosophy was overlaid with an excessive amount of sacramentalism and with an idolatrous preoccupation with things in time, the less saintly members of its hierarchy were exposed to enormous and quite unnecessary temptations and, duly succumbing to them, launched out into persecution, simony, power politics, secret diplomacy, high finance and collaboration with despots.

> I very much doubt whether, since the Lord by his grace brought me into the faith of his dear Son, I have ever broken bread or drunk wine, even in the ordinary course of life, without remembrance of, and some devout feeling regarding, the broken body and the blood-shedding of my dear Lord and Saviour.
>
> *Stephen Grellet*

We have seen that, when they are promoted to be the central

core of organized religious worship, ritualism and sacramental-ism are by no means unmixed blessings. But that the whole of a man's workaday life should be transformed by him into a kind of continuous ritual, that every object in the world around him should be regarded as a symbol of the world's eternal Ground, that all his actions should be performed sacramentally —this would seem to be wholly desirable. All the masters of the spiritual life, from the authors of the Upanishads to Socrates, from Buddha to St. Bernard, are agreed that without self-knowledge there cannot be adequate knowledge of God, that without a constant recollectedness there can be no complete deliverance. The man who has learnt to regard things as symbols, persons as temples of the Holy Spirit and actions as sacraments, is a man who has learned constantly to remind himself who he is, where he stands in relation to the universe and its Ground, how he should behave towards his fellows and what he must do to come to his final end.

'Because of this indwelling of the Logos,' writes Mr. Kenneth Saunders in his valuable study of the Fourth Gospel, the Gita and the Lotus Sutra, 'all things have a reality. They are sacra-ments, not illusions like the phenomenal word of the Vedanta.' That the Logos is in things, lives and conscious minds, and they in the Logos, was taught much more emphatically and explicitly by the Vedantists than by the author of the Fourth Gospel; and the same idea is, of course, basic in the theology of Taoism. But though all things in fact exist at the inter-section between a divine manifestation and a ray of the unmani-fest Godhead, it by no means follows that everyone always knows that this is so. On the contrary, the vast majority of human beings believe that their own selfness and the objects around them possess a reality in themselves, wholly independ-ent of the Logos. This belief leads them to identify their being with their sensations, cravings and private notions, and in its turn this self-identification with what they are not effectively walls them off from divine influence and the very possibility of deliverance. To most of us on most occasions things are not symbols and actions are not sacramental; and we have to teach ourselves, consciously and deliberately, to remember that they are.

> The world is imprisoned in its own activity, except when actions are performed as worship of God. Therefore you must perform every action sacramentally (as if it were *yajna*, the sacrifice that, in its divine Logos-essence, is identical with the Godhead to whom it is offered), and be free from all attachment to results.
>
> *Bhagavad-Gita*

Precisely similar teachings are found in Christian writers, who recommend that persons and even things should be regarded as temples of the Holy Ghost and that everything done or suffered should be constantly 'offered to God.'

It is hardly necessary to add that this process of conscious sacramentalization can be applied only to such actions as are not intrinsically evil. Somewhat unfortunately, the Gita was not originally published as an independent work, but as a theological digression within an epic poem; and since, like most epics, the Mahabharata is largely concerned with the exploits of warriors, it is primarily in relation to warfare that the Gita's advice to act with non-attachment and for God's sake only is given. Now, war is accompanied and followed, among other things, by a widespread dissemination of anger and hatred, pride, cruelty and fear. But, it may be asked, is it possible (the Nature of Things being what it is) to sacramentalize actions whose psychological by-products are so completely God-eclipsing as are these passions? The Buddha of the Pali scriptures would certainly have answered this question in the negative. So would the Lao Tzu of the Tao Teh King. So would the Christ of the Synoptic Gospels. The Krishna of the Gita (who is also, by a kind of literary accident, the Krishna of the Mahabharata) gives an affirmative answer. But this affirmative answer, it should be remembered, is hedged around with limiting conditions. Non-attached slaughter is recommended only to those who are warriors by caste, and to whom warfare is a duty and vocation. But what is duty or *dharma* for the

Kshatriya is *adharma* and forbidden to the Brahman; nor is it any part of the normal vocation or caste duty of the mercantile and labouring classes. Any confusion of castes, any assumption by one man of another man's vocation and duties of state, is always, say the Hindus, a moral evil and a menace to social stability. Thus, it is the business of the Brahmans to fit themselves to be seers, so that they may be able to explain to their fellow-men the nature of the universe, of man's last end and of the way to liberation. When soldiers or administrators, or usurers, or manufacturers or workers usurp the functions of the Brahmans and formulate a philosophy of life in accordance with their variously distorted notions of the universe, then society is thrown into confusion. Similarly, confusion reigns when the Brahman, the man of non-coercive spiritual authority, assumes the coercive power of the Kshatriya, or when the Kshatriya's job of ruling is usurped by bankers and stock-jobbers, or finally when the warrior caste's *dharma* of fighting is imposed, by conscription, on Brahman, Vaisya and Sudra alike. The history of Europe during the later Middle Ages and Renaissance is largely a history of the social confusions that arise when large numbers of those who should be seers abandon spiritual authority in favour of money and political power. And contemporary history is the hideous record of what happens when political bosses, business men or class-conscious proletarians assume the Brahman's function of formulating a philosophy of life; when usurers dictate policy and debate the issues of war and peace; and when the warrior's caste duty is imposed on all and sundry, regardless of psycho-physical make-up and vocation.

Chapter 25

SPIRITUAL EXERCISES

RITES, sacraments, ceremonies, liturgies—all these belong to public worship. They are devices, by means of which the individual members of a congregation are reminded of the true Nature of Things and of their proper relations to one another, the universe and God. What ritual is to public worship, spiritual exercises are to private devotion. They are devices to be used by the solitary individual when he enters into his closet, shuts the door and prays to his Father which is in secret. Like all other devices, from psalm-singing to Swedish exercises and from logic to internal-combustion engines, spiritual exercises can be used either well or badly. Some of those who use spiritual exercises make progress in the life of the spirit; others, using the same exercises, make no progress. To believe that their use either constitutes enlightenment or guarantees it, is mere idolatry and superstition. To neglect them altogether, to refuse to find out whether and in what way they can help in the achievement of our final end, is nothing but self-opinionatedness and stubborn obscurantism.

St. François de Sales used to say, 'I hear of nothing but perfection on every side, so far as talk goes; but I see very few people who really practise it. Everybody has his own notion of perfection. One man thinks it lies in the cut of his clothes, another in fasting, a third in almsgiving, or in frequenting the Sacraments, in meditation, in some special gift of contemplation, or in extraordinary gifts or graces—but they are all mistaken, as it seems to me, because they confuse the means, or the results, with the end and cause.

'For my part, the only perfection I know of is a hearty love of God, and to love one's neighbour as oneself. Charity is the only virtue which rightly unites us to God and man. Such union is our final aim and end, and all the rest is mere delusion.'

Jean Pierre Camus

St. François himself recommended the use of spiritual exercises as a means to the love of God and one's neighbours, and affirmed that such exercises deserved to be greatly cherished; but this affection for the set forms and hours of mental prayer must never, he warned, be allowed to become excessive. To neglect any urgent call to charity or obedience for the sake of practising one's spiritual exercises would be to neglect the end and the proximate means for the sake of means which are not proximate, but at several removes from the ultimate goal.

Spiritual exercises constitute a special class of ascetic practices, whose purpose is, primarily, to prepare the intellect and emotions for those higher forms of prayer in which the soul is essentially passive in relation to divine Reality, and secondarily, by means of this self-exposure to the Light and of the increased self-knowledge and self-loathing resulting from it, to modify character.

In the Orient the systematization of mental prayer was carried out at some unknown but certainly very early date. Both in India and China spiritual exercises (accompanied or preceded by more or less elaborate physical exercises, especially breathing exercises) are known to have been used several centuries before the birth of Christ. In the West, the monks of the Thebaïd spent a good part of each day in meditation as a means to contemplation or the unitive knowledge of God; and at all periods of Christian history, more or less methodical mental prayer has been largely used to supplement the vocal praying of public and private worship. But the systematization of mental prayer into elaborate spiritual exercises was not undertaken, it would seem, until near the end of the Middle Ages, when reformers within the Church popularized this new form of spirituality in an effort to revivify a decaying monasticism and to reinforce the religious life of a laity that had been bewildered by the Great Schism and profoundly shocked by the corruption of the clergy. Among these early systematizers the most effective and influential were the canons of Windesheim, who were in close touch with the Brethren of the Common Life. During the later sixteenth and early seventeenth centuries spiritual exercises became, one might almost say, positively fashionable. The early Jesuits had shown what extraordinary transformations of character, what intensities of will and devotion, could be achieved by men systematically trained on the intellectual and imaginative exercises of St. Ignatius Loyola, and as the prestige of the Jesuits stood very high, at this time, in Catholic Europe, the prestige of spiritual exercises also stood high. Throughout the first century of the Counter-Reformation numerous systems of mental prayer (many of them, unlike the Ignatian exercises, specifically mystical) were composed, published and eagerly bought. After the Quietist controversy mysticism fell into disrepute and, along with mysticism, many of the once popular systems, which their authors had designed to assist the soul on the path towards contemplation. For more detailed information on this interesting and important subject the reader should consult Pourrat's *Christian Spirituality*, Bede Frost's *The Art of Mental Prayer*, Edward Leen's *Progress through Mental Prayer* and Aelfrida Tillyard's *Spiritual Exercises*. Here it is only possible to give a few characteristic specimens from the various religious traditions.

> Know that when you learn to lose yourself, you will reach the Beloved. There is no other secret to be learnt, and more than this is not known to me.
>
> *Ansari of Herat*

Six hundred years later, as we have seen, St. François de Sales was saying very much the same thing to young Camus and all the others who came to him in the ingenuous hope that he could reveal some easy and infallible trick for achieving the unitive knowledge of God. But to lose self in the Beloved—there is no other secret. And yet the Sufis, like their Christian counterparts, made ample use of spiritual exercises—not, of course, as ends in themselves, not even as proximate means, but as means to the proximate means of union with God, namely selfless and loving contemplation.

> For twelve years I was the smith of my soul. I put it in the furnace of austerity and burned it in the fire of combat, I laid it on the anvil of reproach and smote it with the hammer of blame until I made of my soul a mirror. Five years I was the mirror of myself and was ever polishing that mirror with divers acts of worship and piety. Then for a year I gazed in contemplation. On my waist I saw a girdle of pride and vanity and self-conceit and reliance on devotion and approbation of my works. I laboured for five years more until that girdle became worn out and I professed Islam anew. I looked and saw that all created things were dead. I pronounced four *akbirs* over them and returned from the funeral of them all, and without intrusion of creatures, through God's help alone, I attained unto God.
>
> *Bayazid of Bistun*

The simplest and most widely practised form of spiritual exercise is repetition of the divine name, or of some phrase affirming God's existence and the soul's dependence upon Him.

> And therefore, when thou purposest thee to this work (of contemplation), and feelest by grace that thou art called by God, lift up thine heart unto God with a meek stirring of love. And mean God that made thee, and bought thee, and graciously called thee to thy degree, and receive none other thought of God. And yet not all these, except thou desirest; for a naked intent directed unto God, without any other cause than Himself, sufficeth wholly.
>
> And if thou desirest to have this intent lapped and folden in one word, so that thou mayest have better hold thereupon, take thee but a little word of one syllable, for so it is better than of two; for the shorter the word, the better it accordeth with the work of the spirit. And such a word is this word GOD or this word LOVE. Choose whichever thou wilt, or another; whatever

word thou likest best of one syllable. And fasten this word to thy heart that so it may never go thence for anything that befalleth.

The word shall be thy shield and thy spear, whether thou ridest on peace or on war. With this word thou shalt beat on this cloud and this darkness above thee. With this word thou shalt smite down all manner of thought under the *cloud of forgetting*. Insomuch that, if any thought press upon thee to ask what thou wouldst have, answer with no more words than with this one word (GOD or LOVE). And if he offer of his great learning to expound to thee that word, say to him that thou wilt have it all whole, and not broken nor undone. And if thou wilt hold fast to this purpose, be sure that that thought will no while bide.

The Cloud of Unknowing

In another chapter the author of the *Cloud* suggests that the word symbolizing our final end should sometimes be alternated with a word denoting our present position in relation to that end. The words to be repeated in this exercise are SIN and GOD.

Not breaking or expounding these words with curiosity of wit, considering the qualities of these words, as if thou wouldst by that consideration increase thy devotion. I believe it should never be so in this case and in this work. But hold them all whole, these words; and mean by SIN a *lump*, thou knowest never what, none other thing but thyself. . . . And because ever the whiles thou livest in this wretched life, thou must always feel in some part this foul stinking lump of sin, as it were oned and congealed with the substance of thy being, therefore shalt thou alternately mean these two words—SIN and GOD. With this general understanding that, if thou hadst God, then shouldst thou lack sin; and mightest thou lack sin, then shouldst thou have God.

The Cloud of Unknowing

The shaykh took my hand and led me into the convent. I sat

down in the portico, and the shaykh picked up a book and began to read. As is the way of scholars, I could not help wondering what the book was.

The shaykh perceived my thoughts. 'Abu Sa'id,' he said, 'all the hundred and twenty-four thousand prophets were sent to preach one word. They bade the people say, "Allah," and devote themselves to Him. Those who heard this word by the ear alone let it go out by the other ear; but those who heard it with their souls imprinted it on their souls and repeated it until it penetrated their hearts and souls, and their whole beings became this word. They were made independent of the pronunciation of the word; they were released from the sound of the letters. Having understood the spiritual meaning of this word, they became so absorbed in it that they were no more conscious of their own non-existence.'

Abu Sa'id

Take a short verse of a psalm, and it shall be shield and buckler to you against all your foes.

Cassian, quoting Abbot Isaac

In India the repetition of the divine name or the *mantram* (a short devotional or doctrinal affirmation) is called *japam* and is a favourite spiritual exercise among all the sects of Hinduism and Buddhism. The shortest *mantram* is OM—a spoken symbol that concentrates within itself the whole Vedanta philosophy. To this and other *mantrams* Hindus attribute a kind of magical power. The repetition of them is a sacramental act, conferring grace *ex opere operato*. A similar efficacity was and indeed still is attributed to sacred words and formulae by Buddhists, Moslems, Jews and Christians. And, of course, just as traditional religious rites seem to possess the power to evoke the real presence of existents projected into psychic objectivity by the faith and devotion of generations of worshippers, so too long-hallowed words and phrases may become channels for conveying powers other and greater than those belonging to the individual who happens at the moment to be pronouncing them. And meanwhile the constant repetition of 'this word GOD or this word LOVE' may, in favourable circumstances, have a profound effect upon the subconscious mind, inducing that selfless one-pointedness of will and thought and feeling, without which the unitive knowledge of God is impossible. Furthermore, it may happen that, if the word is simply repeated 'all whole, and not broken up or undone' by discursive analysis, the Fact for which the word stands will end by presenting itself to the soul in the form of an integral intuition. When this happens, 'the doors of the letters of this word are opened' (to use the language of the Sufis) and the soul passes through into Reality. But though all this *may* happen, it need not necessarily happen. For there is no spiritual patent medicine, no pleasant and infallible panacea for souls suffering from separateness and the deprivation of God. No, there is no guaranteed cure; and, if used improperly, the medicine of spiritual exercises may start a new disease or aggravate the old. For example, a mere mechanical repetition of the divine name can result in a kind of numbed stupefaction that is as much below analytical thought as intellectual vision is above it. And because the sacred word constitutes a kind of prejudgment of the experience induced by its repetition, this stupefaction, or some other abnormal state, is taken to be the immediate awareness of Reality and is idolatrously cultivated and hunted after, with a turning of the will towards what is supposed to be God before there has been a turning of it away from the self.

The dangers which beset the practiser of *japam*, who is insufficiently mortified and insufficiently recollected and aware, are encountered in the same or different forms by those who make use of more elaborate spiritual exercises. Intense concentration on an image or idea, such as is recommended by many teachers, both Eastern and Western, may be very helpful for certain persons in certain circumstances, very harmful in other cases. It is helpful when the concentration results in such mental stillness, such a silence of intellect, will and feeling, that the divine Word can be uttered within the soul. It is harmful when the image concentrated upon becomes so hallucinatingly real that it is taken for objective Reality and idolatrously worshipped; harmful, too, when the exercise of concentration produces unusual psycho-physical results, in which the person experiencing them takes a personal pride, as being special graces and divine communications. Of these unusual psycho-physical occurrences the most ordinary are visions and auditions, foreknowledge, telepathy and other psychic powers, and the curious bodily phenomenon of intense heat. Many persons who practise concentration exercises experience this heat occasionally. A number of Christian saints, of whom the best known are St. Philip Neri and St. Catherine of Siena, have experienced it continuously. In the East techniques have been developed whereby the accession of heat resulting from intense concentration can be regulated, controlled and put to do useful work, such as keeping the contemplative warm in freezing weather. In Europe, where the phenomenon is not well understood, many would-be contemplatives have experienced this heat, and have imagined it to be some special divine favour, or even the experience of union, and being insufficiently mortified and humble, have fallen into idolatry and a God-eclipsing spiritual pride.

The following passage from one of the great Mahayana scriptures contains a searching criticism of the kind of spiritual exercises prescribed by Hinayanist teachers—concentration on symbolic objects, meditations on transience and decay (to wean the soul away from attachment to earthly things), on the different virtues which must be cultivated, on the fundamental doctrines of Buddhism. (Many of these exercises are described at length in *The Path of Purity*, a book which has been translated in full and published by the Pali Text Society. Mahayanist exercises are described in the Surangama Sutra, translated by Dwight Goddard, and in the volume on *Tibetan Yoga*, edited by Dr. Evans-Wentz.)

In his exercise the Yogin sees (imaginatively) the form of the sun or moon, or something looking like a lotus, or the underworld, or various forms, such as sky, fire and the like. All these appearances lead him in the way of the philosophers; they throw him down into the state of Sravakahood, into the realm of the Pratyekabuddhas. When all these are put aside and there is a state of imagelessness, then a condition in conformity with Suchness presents itself, and the Buddhas will come together from all their countries and with their shining hands will touch the head of this benefactor.

Lankavatara Sutra

In other words intense concentration on any image (even if the image be a sacred symbol, like the lotus) or on any idea, from the idea of hell to the idea of some desirable virtue or its apotheosis in one of the divine attributes, is always concentration on something produced by one's own mind. Sometimes, in mortified and recollected persons, the art of concentration merges into the state of openness and alert passivity, in which true contemplation becomes possible. But sometimes the fact that the concentration is on a product of the concentrator's own mind results in some kind of false or incomplete contemplation. Suchness, or the divine Ground of all being, reveals itself to those in whom there is no ego-centredness (nor even any alter-ego-centredness) either of will, imagination, feeling or intellect.

I say, then, that introversion must be rejected, because extraversion must never be admitted; but one must live continuously in the abyss of the divine Essence and in the nothingness of things; and if at times a man finds himself separated from them (the divine Essence and created nothingness) he must return to them, not by introversion, but by annihilation.

Benet of Canfield

Introversion is the process condemned in the Lankavatara Sutra as the way of the Yogin, the way that leads at worst to idolatry, at best to a partial knowledge of God in the heights within, never to complete knowledge in the fullness without as well as within, Annihilation (of which Father Benet distinguishes two kinds, passive and active) is for the Mahayanist the 'state of imagelessness' in contemplation and, in active life, the state of total non-attachment, in which eternity can be apprehended within time, and *samsara* is known to be one with *nirvana*.

> And therefore, if thou wilt stand and not fall, cease never in thine intent, but beat evermore on this cloud of unknowing that is betwixt thee and thy God, with a sharp dart of longing love. And loathe to think of aught under God. And go not thence for anything that befalleth. For this only is that work that destroyeth the ground and the root of sin. . . .
>
> Yea, and what more? Weep thou never so much for sorrow of thy sins, or of the passion of Christ, or have thou never so much thought of the joys of heaven, what may it do to thee? Surely much good, much help, much profit, much grace will it get thee. But in comparison of this blind stirring of love, it is but little that It doth, or may do, without this. This by itself is the *best part* of Mary, without these other. They without it profit but little or nought. It destroyeth not only the ground and the root of sin, as it may be here, but also it getteth virtues. For if it be truly conceived, all virtues shall be subtly and perfectly conceived, felt and comprehended in it, without any mingling of thine intent. And have a man never so many virtues without it, all they be mingled with some crooked intent, for the which they be imperfect. For virtue is nought else but an ordered and measured affection, plainly directed unto God for Himself.
>
> *The Cloud of Unknowing*

If exercises in concentration, repetitions of the divine name, or meditations on God's attributes or on imagined scenes in the life of saint or Avatar help those who make use of them to come to selflessness, openness and (to use Augustine Baker's phrase) that 'love of the pure divinity,' which makes possible the soul's union with the Godhead, then such spiritual exercises are wholly good and desirable. If they have other results—well, the tree is known by its fruits.

Benet of Canfield, the English Capuchin who wrote *The Rule of Perfection* and was the spiritual guide of Mme Acarie and Cardinal Bérulle, hints in his treatise at a method by which concentration on an image may be made to lead up to imageless contemplation, 'blind beholding,' 'love of the pure divinity.' The period of mental prayer is to begin with intense concentration on a scene of Christ's passion; then the mind is, as it were, to abolish this imagination of the sacred humanity and to pass from it to the formless and attributeless Godhead which that humanity incarnates. A strikingly similar exercise is described in the *Bardo Thödol* or Tibetan Book of the Dead (a work of quite extraordinary profundity and beauty, now fortunately available in translation with a valuable introduction and notes by Dr. Evans-Wentz).

Whosoever thy tutelary deity may be, meditate upon the form for much time—as being apparent, yet non-existent in reality, like a form produced by a magician. . . . Then let the visualization of the tutelary deity melt away from the extremities, till nothing at all remaineth visible of it; and put thyself in the state of the Clearness and the Voidness—which thou canst not conceive as something—and abide in that state for a little while. Again meditate upon the tutelary deity; again meditate upon the Clear Light; do this alternately. Afterwards allow thine own intellect to melt away gradually, beginning from the extremities.

The Tibetan Book of the Dead

As a final summing up of the whole matter we may cite a sentence of Eckhart's. 'He who seeks God under settled form lays hold of the form, while missing the God concealed in it.' Here, the key word is 'settled.' It is permissible to seek God provisionally under a form which is from the first recognized as merely a symbol of Reality, and a symbol which must sooner or later be discarded in favour of what it stands for. To seek Him under a settled form—settled because regarded as the very shape of Reality—is to commit oneself to illusion and a kind of idolatry.

The chief impediments in the way of taking up the practice of some form of mental prayer are ignorance of the Nature of Things (which has never, of course, been more abysmal than in this age of free compulsory education) and the absorption in self-interest, in positive and negative emotions connected with the passions and with what is technically known as a 'good time.' And when the practice has been taken up, the chief impediments in the way of advance towards the goal of mental prayer are distractions.

Probably all persons, even the most saintly, suffer to some extent from distractions. But it is obvious that a person who, in the intervals of mental prayer, leads a dispersed, unrecollected, self-centred life will have more and worse distractions to contend with than one who lives one-pointedly, never forgetting who he is and how related to the universe and its divine Ground. Some of the most profitable spiritual exercises actually make use of distractions, in such a way that these impediments to self-abandonment, mental silence and passivity in relation to God are transformed into means of progress.

But first, by way of preface to the description of these exercises, it should be remarked that all teachers of the art of mental prayer concur in advising their pupils never to use violent efforts of the surface will against the distractions which arise in the mind during periods of recollection. The reason for this has been succinctly stated by Benet of Canfield in his *Rule of Perfection*. 'The more a man operates, the more he is and exists. And the more he is and exists, the less of God is and exists within him.' Every enhancement of the separate personal self produces a corresponding diminution of that self's awareness of divine Reality. But any violent reaction of the surface will against distractions automatically enhances the separate, personal self and therefore reduces the individual's chances of coming to the knowledge and love of God. In the process of trying forcibly to abolish our God-eclipsing day-dreams, we merely deepen the darkness of our native ignorance. This being so, we must give up the attempt to fight distrac-

tions and find ways either of circumventing them, or of somehow making use of them. For example, if we have already
achieved a certain degree of alert passivity in relation to Reality
and distractions intervene, we can simply 'look over the
shoulder' of the malicious and concupiscent imbecile who
stands between us and the object of our 'simple regard.' The
distractions now appear in the foreground of consciousness;
we take notice of their presence, then, lightly and gently,
without any straining of the will, we shift the focus of attention to Reality which we glimpse, or divine, or (by past
experience or an act of faith) merely know about, in the background. In many cases, this effortless shift of attention will
cause the distractions to lose their obsessive 'thereness' and,
for a time at least, to disappear.

> If the heart wanders or is distracted, bring it back to the point
> quite gently and replace it tenderly in its Master's presence. And
> even if you did nothing during the whole of your hour but bring
> your heart back and place it again in Our Lord's presence, though
> it went away every time you brought it back, your hour would
> be very well employed.
>
> *St François de Sales*

In this case the circumvention of distractions constitutes a
valuable lesson in patience and perseverance. Another and
more direct method of making use of the monkey in our heart
is described in *The Cloud of Unknowing*.

> When thou feelest that thou mayest in no wise put them (dis-
> tractions) down, cower then down under them as a caitiff and a
> coward overcome in battle, and think it is but folly to strive any
> longer with them, and therefore thou yieldest thyself to God in
> the hands of thine enemies. . . . And surely, I think, if this device
> be truly conceived, it is nought else but a true knowing and a feel-
> ing of thyself as thou art, a wretch and a filthy thing, far worse
> than nought; the which knowing and feeling is meekness (humil-
> ity). And this meekness meriteth to have God mightily descend-

ing to venge thee on thine enemies, so as to take thee up and
cherishingly dry thy ghostly eyes, as the father doth to the child
that is at the point to perish under the mouths of wild swine and
mad biting bears.

The Cloud of Unknowing

Finally, there is the exercise, much employed in India, which
consists in dispassionately examining the distractions as they
arise and in tracing them back, through the memory of particular thoughts, feelings and actions, to their origins in
temperament and character, constitution and acquired habit.
This procedure reveals to the soul the true reasons for its
separation from the divine Ground of its being. It comes to
realize that its spiritual ignorance is due to the inert recalcitrance or positive rebelliousness of its selfhood, and it dis-
covers, specifically, the points where that eclipsing selfhood
congeals, as it were, into the hardest, densest clots. Then,
having made the resolution to do what it can, in the course of
daily living, to rid itself of these impediments to Light, it
quietly puts aside the thought of them and, empty, purged and
silent, passively exposes itself to whatever it may be that lies
beyond and within.

'*Noverim me, noverim Te,*' St. Francis of Assisi used to
repeat. Self-knowledge, leading to self-hatred and humility,
is the condition of the love and knowledge of God. Spiritual
exercises that make use of distractions have this great merit,
that they increase self-knowledge. Every soul that approaches
God must be aware of who and what it is. To practise a form
of mental or vocal prayer that is, so to speak, above one's
moral station is to act a lie: and the consequences of such
lying are wrong notions about God, idolatrous worship of
private and unrealistic phantasies and (for lack of the humility
of self-knowledge) spiritual pride.

It is hardly necessary to add that this method has, like every
other, its dangers as well as its advantages. For those who
employ it there is a standing temptation to forget the end in
the all too squalidly personal means—to become absorbed in

a whitewashing or remorseful essay in autobiography to the exclusion of the pure Divinity, before whom the 'angry ape' played all the fantastic tricks which he now so relishingly remembers.

We come now to what may be called the spiritual exercises of daily life. The problem, here, is simple enough—how to keep oneself reminded, during the hours of work and recreation, that there is a good deal more to the universe than that which meets the eye of one absorbed in business or pleasure? There is no single solution to this problem. Some kinds of work and recreation are so simple and unexactive that they permit of continuous repetition of sacred name or phrase, unbroken thought about divine Reality, or, what is still better, uninterrupted mental silence and alert passivity. Such occupations as were the daily task of Brother Lawrence (whose 'practice of the presence of God' has enjoyed a kind of celebrity in circles otherwise completely uninterested in mental prayer or spiritual exercises) were almost all of this simple and unexacting kind. But there are other tasks too complex to admit of this constant recollectedness. Thus, to quote Eckhart, 'a celebrant of the mass who is over-intent on recollection is liable to make mistakes. The best way is to try to concentrate the mind before and afterwards, but, when saying it, to do so quite straightforwardly.' This advice applies to any occupation demanding undivided attention. But undivided attention is seldom demanded and is with difficulty sustained for long periods at a stretch. There are always intervals of relaxation. Everyone is free to choose whether these intervals shall be filled with day-dreaming or with something better.

Whoever has God in mind, simply and solely God, in all things, such a man carries God with him into all his works and into all places, and God alone does all his works. He seeks nothing but God, nothing seems good to him but God. He becomes one with God in every thought. Just as no multiplicity can dissipate God, so nothing can dissipate this man or make him multiple.

Eckhart

I do not mean that we ought voluntarily to put ourselves in the way of dissipating influences; God forbid! That would be tempting God and seeking danger. But such distractions as come in any way providentially, if met with due precaution and carefully guarded hours of prayer and reading, will turn to good. Often those things which make you sigh for solitude are more profitable to your humiliation and self-denial than the most utter solitude itself would be. . . . Sometimes a stimulating book of devotion, a fervent meditation, a striking conversation, may flatter your tastes and make you feel self-satisfied and complacent, imagining yourself far advanced towards perfection; and by filling you with unreal notions, be all the time swelling your pride and making you come from your religious exercises less tolerant of whatever crosses your will. I would have you hold fast to this simple rule: seek nothing dissipating, but bear quietly with whatever God sends without your seeking it, whether of dissipation or interruption. It is a great delusion to seek God afar off in matters perhaps quite unattainable, ignoring that He is beside us in our daily annoyances, so long as we bear humbly and bravely all those which arise from the manifold imperfections of our neighbours and ourselves.

Fénelon

Consider that your life is a perpetual perishing, and lift up your mind to God above all whenever the clock strikes, saying, 'God, I adore your eternal being; I am happy that my being should perish every moment, so that at every moment it may render homage to your eternity.'

J. J. Olier

When you are walking alone, or elsewhere, glance at the general will of God, by which He wills all the works of his mercy and justice in heaven, on earth, under the earth, and approve, praise and then love that sovereign will, all holy, all just, all beautiful. Glance next at the special will of God, by which He loves his own, and works in them in divers ways, by consolation and tribulation. And then you should ponder a little, considering the variety of consolations, but especially of tribulations, that the good suffer; and then with great humility approve, praise and love all this will. Consider that will in your own person, in all the good or ill that happens to you and may happen to you, except sin; then approve, praise and love all that, protesting that you will ever cherish, honour and adore that sovereign will, and submitting to God's pleasure and giving Him all who are yours, amongst whom am I. End in a great confidence in that will, that it will work all good for us and our happiness. I add that, when you have performed this exercise two or three times in this way, you can shorten it, vary it and arrange it, as you find best, for it should often be thrust into your heart as an aspiration.

St. François de Sales

Dwelling in the light, there is no occasion at all for stumbling, for all things are discovered in the light. When thou art walking abroad it is present with thee in thy bosom, thou needest not to say, Lo here, or Lo there; and as thou lyest in thy bed, it is present to teach thee and judge thy wandering mind, which wanders abroad, and thy high thoughts and imaginations, and makes them subject. For following thy thoughts, thou art quickly lost. By dwelling in this light, it will discover to thee the body of sin and thy corruptions and fallen estate, where thou art. In that light which shows thee all this, stand; go neither to the right nor to the left.

George Fox

The extract which follows is taken from the translation by Waitao and Goddard of the Chinese text of *The Awakening of Faith*, by Ashvaghosha—a work originally composed in Sanskrit during the first century of our era, but of which the original has been lost. Ashvaghosha devotes a section of his treatise to the 'expedient means,' as they are called in Buddhist terminology, whereby unitive knowledge of Thusness may be achieved. The list of these indispensable means includes charity and compassion towards all sentient beings, sub-human as well as human, self-naughting or mortification,

personal devotion to the incarnations of the Absolute Buddha-
nature, and spiritual exercises designed to free the mind from
its infatuating desires for separateness and independent selfhood and so make it capable of realizing the identity of its
own essence with the universal Essence of Mind. Of these
various 'expedient means' I will cite only the last two—the
Way of Tranquillity, and the Way of Wisdom.

The Way of Tranquillity. The purpose of this discipline is twofold: to bring to a standstill all disturbing thoughts (and all discriminating thoughts are disturbing), to quiet all engrossing
moods and emotions, so that it will be possible to concentrate
the mind for the purpose of meditation and realization. Secondly,
when the mind is tranquillized by stopping all discursive thinking, to practise 'reflection' or meditation, not in a discriminating,
analytical way, but in a more intellectual way (cp. the scholastic
distinction between reason and intellect), by realizing the meaning and significances of one's thoughts and experiences. By this
twofold practice of 'stopping and realizing' one's faith, which has
already been awakened, will be developed, and gradually the two
aspects of this practice will merge into one another—the mind
perfectly tranquil, but most active in realization. In the past one
naturally had confidence in one's faculty of discrimination
(analytical thinking), but this is now to be eradicated and ended.

Those who are practising 'stopping' should retire to some
quiet place and there, sitting erect, earnestly seek to tranquillize
and concentrate the mind. While one may at first think of one's
breathing, it is not wise to continue this practice very long, nor
to let the mind rest on any particular appearances, or sights, or
conceptions, arising from the senses, such as the primal elements
of earth, water, fire and ether (objects on which Hinayanists were
wont to concentrate at one stage of their spiritual training), nor
to let it rest on any of the mind's perceptions, particularizations,
discriminations, moods or emotions. All kinds of ideation are to
be discarded as fast as they arise; even the notions of controlling
and discarding are to be got rid of. One's mind should become
like a mirror, reflecting things, but not judging them or retaining

them. Conceptions of themselves have no substance; let them arise and pass away unheeded. Conceptions arising from the senses and lower mind will not take form of themselves, unless they are grasped by the attention; if they are ignored, there will be no appearing and no disappearing. The same is true of conditions outside the mind; they should not be allowed to engross one's attention and so to hinder one's practice. The mind cannot be absolutely vacant, and as the thoughts arising from the senses and the lower mind are discarded and ignored, one must supply their place by right mentation. The question then arises: what is right mentation? The reply is: right mentation is the realization of mind itself, of its pure undifferentiated Essence. When the mind is fixed on its pure Essence, there should be no lingering notions of the self, even of the self in the act of realizing, nor of realization as a phenomenon. . . .

The Way of Wisdom. The purpose of this discipline is to bring a man into the habit of applying the insight that has come to him as the result of the preceding disciplines. When one is rising, standing, walking, doing something, stopping, one should constantly concentrate one's mind on the act and the doing of it, not on one's relation to the act, or its character or value. One should think: there is walking, there is stopping, there is realizing; not, I am walking, I am doing this, it is a good thing, it is disagreeable, I am gaining merit, it is I who am realizing how wonderful it is. Thence come vagrant thoughts, feelings of elation or of failure and unhappiness. Instead of all this, one should simply practise concentration of the mind on the act itself, understanding it to be an expedient means for attaining tranquillity of mind, realization, insight and Wisdom; and one should follow the practice in faith, willingness and gladness. After long practice the bondage of old habits becomes weakened and disappears, and in its place appear confidence, satisfaction, awareness and tranquillity.

What is this Way of Wisdom designed to accomplish? There are three classes of conditions that hinder one from advancing along the path to Enlightenment. First, there are the allurements arising from the senses, from external conditions and from the discriminating mind.   Second, there are the internal conditions of the mind, its thoughts, desires and mood.   All these the earlier practices (ethical and mortificatory) are designed to eliminate.   In the third class of impediments are placed the individual's instinctive and fundamental (and therefore most insidious and persistent) urges—the will to live and to enjoy, the will to cherish one's personality, the will to propagate, which give rise to greed and lust, fear and anger, infatuation, pride and egotism.   The practice of the Wisdom Paramita is designed to control and eliminate these fundamental and instinctive hindrances.   By means of it the mind gradually grows clearer, more luminous, more peaceful. Insight becomes more penetrating, faith deepens and broadens, until they merge into the inconceivable Samadhi of the Mind's Pure Essence.   As one continues the practice of the Way of Wisdom, one yields less and less to thoughts of comfort or desolation; faith becomes surer, more pervasive, beneficent and joyous; and fear of retrogression vanishes.   But do not think that the consummation is to be attained easily or quickly; many rebirths may be necessary, many aeons may have to elapse.   So long as doubts, unbelief, slanders, evil conduct, hindrances of karma, weakness of faith, pride, sloth and mental agitation persist, so long as even their shadows linger, there can be no attainment of the Samadhi of the Buddhas.   But he who has attained to the radiance of highest Samadhi, or unitive Knowledge, will be able to realize, with all the Buddhas, the perfect unity of all sentient beings with Buddhahood's Dharmakaya.   In the pure Dharmakaya there is no dualism, neither shadow of differentiation.   All sentient beings, if only they were able to realize it, are already in Nirvana.   The Mind's pure Essence is Highest Samadhi, is *Anuttara-samyak-sambodhi*, is *Prajna Paramita*, is Highest Perfect Wisdom.

Ashvaghosha

Chapter 26

PERSEVERANCE AND REGULARITY

He who interrupts the course of his spiritual exercises and prayer
is like a man who allows a bird to escape from his hand; he can
hardly catch it again.

St. John of the Cross

Si volumus non redire, currendum est. (If we wish not to go backwards, we must run.)

Pelagius

If thou shouldst say, 'It is enough, I have reached perfection,'
all is lost. For it is the function of perfection to make one know
one's imperfection.

St. Augustine

THE Buddhists have a similar saying to the effect that, if an
arhat thinks to himself that he is an arhat, that is proof
that he is not an arhat.

I tell you that no one can experience this birth (of God realized
in the soul) without a mighty effort. No one can attain this birth
unless he can withdraw his mind entirely from things.

Eckhart

If a sharp penance had been laid upon me, I know of none that I
would not very often have willingly undertaken, rather than prepare myself for prayer by self-recollection. And certainly the
violence with which Satan assailed me was so irresistible, or my
evil habits were so strong, that I did not betake myself to prayer;
and the sadness I felt on entering the oratory was so great that

334

it required all the courage I had to force myself in. They say of me that my courage is not slight, and it is known that God has given me a courage beyond that of a woman; but I have made a bad use of it. In the end Our Lord came to my relief, and when I had done this violence to myself, I found greater peace and joy than I sometimes had when I had a desire to pray.

St. Teresa

To one of his spiritual children our dear father (St. François de Sales) said, 'Be patient with everyone, but above all with yourself. I mean, do not be disheartened by your imperfections, but always rise up with fresh courage. I am glad you make a fresh beginning daily; there is no better means of attaining to the spiritual life than by continually beginning again, and never thinking that we have done enough. How are we to be patient in bearing with our neighbour's faults, if we are impatient in bearing with our own? He who is fretted by his own failings will not correct them; all profitable correction comes from a calm, peaceful mind.'

Jean Pierre Camus

There are scarce any souls that give themselves to internal prayer but some time or other do find themselves in great indisposition thereto, having great obscurities in the mind and great insensibility in their affections, so that if imperfect souls be not well instructed and prepared, they will be in danger, in case that such contradictions of inferior nature continue long, to be dejected, yea, and perhaps deterred from pursuing prayer, for they will be apt to think that their recollections are to no purpose at all, since, for as much as seems to them, whatsoever they think or actuate towards God is a mere loss of time and of no worth at all; and therefore that it would be more profitable for them to employ their time some other way.

Yea, some souls there are conducted by Almighty God by no other way, but only by such prayer of aridity, finding no sensible contentment in any recollection, but, on the contrary, continual

pain and contradiction, and yet, by a privy grace and courage
imprinted deeply in the spirit, cease not for all that, but resolutely
break through all difficulties and continue, the best way they can,
their internal exercises to the great advancement of their spirit.

Augustine Baker

Chapter 27

CONTEMPLATION, ACTION AND
SOCIAL UTILITY

IN all the historic formulations of the Perennial Philosophy it is axiomatic that the end of human life is contemplation, or the direct and intuitive awareness of God; that action is the means to that end; that a society is good to the extent that it renders contemplation possible for its members; and that the existence of at least a minority of contemplatives is necessary for the well-being of any society. In the popular philosophy of our own time it goes without saying that the end of human life is action; that contemplation (above all in its lower forms of discursive thought) is the means to that end; that a society is good to the extent that the actions of its members make for progress in technology and organization (a progress which is assumed to be causally related to ethical and cultural advance); and that a minority of contemplatives is perfectly useless and perhaps even harmful to the community which tolerates it. To expatiate further on the modern *Weltanschauung* is unnecessary; explicitly or by implication it is set forth on every page of the advertising sections of every newspaper and magazine. The extracts that follow have been chosen in order to illustrate the older, truer, less familiar theses of the Perennial Philosophy.

Work is for the purification of the mind, not for the perception of Reality. The realization of Truth is brought about by discrimination, and not in the least by ten millions of acts.

Shankara

Now, the last end of each thing is that which is intended by the first author or mover of that thing; and the first author and mover of the universe is an intellect. Consequently, the last end of the universe must be the good of the intellect; and this is truth. Therefore truth must be the last end of the whole universe, and the consideration thereof must be the chief occupation of wisdom. And for this reason divine Wisdom, clothed in flesh, declares that He came into the world to make known the truth. ... Moreover Aristotle defines the First Philosophy as being the knowledge of truth, not of any truth, but of that truth which is the source of all truth, of that, namely, which refers to the first principle of being of all things; wherefore its truth is the principle of all truth, since the disposition of things is the same in truth as in being.

St. Thomas Aquinas

A thing may belong to the contemplative life in two ways, essentially or as a predisposition. ... The moral virtues belong to the contemplative life as a predisposition. For the act of contemplation, in which the contemplative life essentially consists, is hindered both by the impetuosity of the passions and by outward disturbances. Now the moral virtues curb the impetuosity of the passions and quell the disturbance of outward occupations. Hence moral virtues belong to the contemplative life as a predisposition.

St. Thomas Aquinas

These works (of mercy), though they be but active, yet they help very much, and dispose a man in the beginning to attain afterwards to contemplation.

Walter Hilton

In Buddhism, as in Vedanta and in all but the most recent forms of Christianity, right action is the means by which the mind is prepared for contemplation. The first seven branches of the Eightfold Path are the active, ethical preparation for unitive knowledge of Suchness. Only those who consistently practise the Four Virtuous Acts, in which all other virtues are included —namely, the requital of hatred by love, resignation, 'holy indifference' or desirelessness, obedience to the *dharma* or

Nature of Things—can hope to achieve the liberating realization that *samsara* and *nirvana* are one, that the soul and all other beings have as their living principle the Intelligible Light or Buddha-womb.

A question now, quite naturally, presents itself: Who is called to that highest form of prayer which is contemplation? The answer is unequivocally plain. All are called to contemplation, because all are called to achieve deliverance, which is nothing else but the knowledge that unites the knower with what is known, namely the eternal Ground or Godhead. The oriental exponents of the Perennial Philosophy would probably deny that everyone is called here and now; in this particular life, they would say, it may be to all intents and purposes impossible for a given individual to achieve more than a partial deliverance, such as personal survival in some kind of 'heaven,' from which there may be either an advance towards total liberation or else a return to those material conditions which, as all the masters of the spiritual life agree, are so uniquely propitious for taking the cosmic intelligence test that results in enlightenment. In orthodox Christianity it is denied that the individual soul can have more than one incarnation, or that it can make any progress in its posthumous existence. If it goes to hell, it stays there. If it goes to purgatory, it merely expiates past evil doing, so as to become capable of the beatific vision. And when it gets to heaven, it has just so much of the beatific vision as its conduct during its one brief life on earth made it capable of, and everlastingly no more. Granted these postulates, it follows that, if all are called to contemplation, they are called to it from that particular position in the hierarchy of being, to which nature, nurture, free will and grace have conspired to assign them. In the words of an eminent contemporary theologian, Father Garrigou-Lagrange, 'all souls receive a general remote call to the mystical life, and if all were faithful in avoiding, as they should, not only mortal but venial sins, if they were, each according to his condition, generally docile to the Holy Ghost, and if they lived long enough, a day would come when they would receive the proximate and efficacious vocation to a high perfection and to the mystical life properly so called.' This view—that the life of mystical contemplation is the proper and normal development of the 'interior life' of recollectedness and devotion to God— is then justified by the following considerations. First, the principle of the two lives is the same. Second, it is only in the life of mystical contemplation that the interior life finds its consummation. Third, their end, which is eternal life, is the same; moreover, only the life of mystical contemplation prepares immediately and perfectly for that end.

There are few contemplatives, because few souls are perfectly humble.

The Imitation of Christ

God does not reserve such a lofty vocation (that of mystical contemplation) to certain souls only; on the contrary, He is willing that all should embrace it. But He finds few who permit Him to work such sublime things for them. There are many who, when He sends them trials, shrink from the labour and refuse to bear with the dryness and mortification, instead of submitting, as they must, with perfect patience.

St. John of the Cross

This assertion that all are called to contemplation seems to conflict with what we know about the inborn varieties of temperament and with the doctrine that there are at least three principal roads to liberation—the ways of works and devotion as well as the way of knowledge. But the conflict is more apparent than real. If the ways of devotion and works lead to liberation, it is because they lead into the way of knowledge. For total deliverance comes only through unitive knowledge. A soul which does not go on from the ways of devotion and works into the way of knowledge is not totally delivered, but achieves at the best the incomplete salvation of 'heaven.' Coming now to the question of temperament, we find that, in effect, certain individuals are naturally drawn to lay the main doctrinal and practical emphasis in one place, certain others elsewhere. But though there may be born devotees, born workers, born contemplatives, it is nevertheless true that even those at the extreme limits of temperamental eccentricity are capable of making use of other ways than that to which they are naturally drawn. Given the requisite degree of obedience to the leadings of the Light, the born contemplative can learn to purify his heart by work and direct his mind by one-pointed adoration; the born devotee and the born worker can learn to 'be still and know that I am God.' Nobody need be the victim of his peculiar talents. Few or many, of this stamp or of that, they are given us to be used for the gaining of one great end. We have the power to choose whether to use them well or badly—in the easier, worse way or the harder and better.

Those who are more adapted to the active life can prepare themselves for contemplation in the practice of the active life, while those who are more adapted to the contemplative life can take upon themselves the works of the active life so as to become yet more apt for contemplation.

St. Thomas Aquinas

He who is strong in faith, weak in understanding, will generally place his confidence in good-for-nothing people and believe in the wrong object. He who is strong in understanding, weak in faith, leans towards dishonesty and is difficult to cure, like a disease caused by medicine. One in whom both are equal believes in the right object.

He who is strong in concentration, weak in energy, is overcome by idleness, since concentration partakes of the nature of idleness. He who is strong in energy, weak in concentration, is overcome by distractions, since energy partakes of the nature of distraction. Therefore they should be made equal to one another, since from equality in both comes contemplation and ecstasy. . . .

Mindfulness should be strong everywhere, for mindfulness keeps the mind away from distraction, into which it might fall, since faith, energy and understanding partake of the nature of distraction: and away from idleness, into which it might fall, since concentration partakes of the nature of idleness.

Buddhaghosha

At this point it is worth remarking parenthetically that God is by no means the only possible object of contemplation. There have been and still are many philosophic, aesthetic and scientific contemplatives. One-pointed concentration on that which is not the highest may become a dangerous form of idolatry. In a letter to Hooker, Darwin wrote that 'it is a cursed evil to any man to become so absorbed in any subject as I am in mine.' It is an evil because such one-pointedness may result in the more or less total atrophy of all but one side of the mind. Darwin himself records that in later life he was unable to take the smallest interest in poetry, art or religion. Professionally, in relation to his chosen specialty, a man may be completely mature. Spiritually and sometimes even ethically, in relation to God and his neighbours, he may be hardly more than a foetus.

In cases where the one-pointed contemplation is of God there is also a risk that the mind's unemployed capacities may atrophy. The hermits of Tibet and the Thebaïd were certainly one-pointed, but with a one-pointedness of exclusion and mutilation. It may be, however, that if they had been more truly 'docile to the Holy Ghost,' they would have come to understand that the one-pointedness of exclusion is at best a preparation for the one-pointedness of inclusion—the realization of God in the fullness of cosmic being as well as in the interior height of the individual soul. Like the Taoist sage, they would at last have turned back into the world riding on their tamed and regenerate individuality; they would have 'come eating and drinking,' would have associated with 'publicans and sinners' or their Buddhist equivalents, 'wine-bibbers and butchers.' For the fully enlightened, totally liberated person, *samsara* and *nirvana*, time and eternity, the phenomenal and the Real, are essentially one. His whole life is an unsleeping and one-pointed contemplation of the Godhead in and through the things, lives, minds and events of the world of becoming. There is here no mutilation of the soul, no atrophy of any of its powers and capacities. Rather, there is a general enhancement and intensification of consciousness, and at the same time an extension and transfiguration. No saint has ever complained that absorption in God was a 'cursed evil.'

In the beginning was the Word; behold Him to whom Mary listened. And the Word was made flesh; behold Him whom Martha served.

St. Augustine

God aspires us into Himself in contemplation, and then we must be wholly His; but afterwards the Spirit of God expires us without, for the practice of love and good works.

Ruysbroeck

Action, says Aquinas, should be something added to the life of prayer, not something taken away from it. One of the reasons for this recommendation is strictly utilitarian; action that is 'taken away from the life of prayer' is action unenlightened by contact with Reality, uninspired and unguided; consequently it is apt to be ineffective and even harmful. 'The sages of old,' says Chuang Tzu, 'first got Tao for themselves, then got it for others.' There can be no taking of motes out of other people's eyes so long as the beam in our own eye prevents us from seeing the divine Sun and working by its light. Speaking of those who prefer immediate action to acquiring, through contemplation, the power to act well, St. John of the Cross asks, 'What do they accomplish?' And he answers, *Poco mas que nada, y a veces nada, y aun a veces dano* ('Little more than nothing, and sometimes nothing at all, and sometimes even harm'). Income must balance expenditure. This is necessary not merely on the economic level, but also on the physiological, the intellectual, the ethical and the spiritual. We cannot put forth physical energy unless we stoke our body

with fuel in the form of food. We cannot hope to utter anything worth saying, unless we read and inwardly digest the
utterances of our betters. We cannot act rightly and effectively
unless we are in the habit of laying ourselves open to leadings
of the divine Nature of Things. We must draw in the goods
of eternity in order to be able to give out the goods of time.
But the goods of eternity cannot be had except by giving up
at least a little of our time to silently waiting for them. This
means that the life in which ethical expenditure is balanced by
spiritual income must be a life in which action alternates with repose, speech with alertly passive silence. *Otium sanctum quaerit
caritas veritatis ; negotium justum suscipit necessitas caritatis*
('The love of Truth seeks holy leisure; the necessity of love
undertakes righteous action'). The bodies of men and animals
are reciprocating engines, in which tension is always succeeded
by relaxation. Even the unsleeping heart rests between beat
and beat. There is nothing in living Nature that even distantly
resembles man's greatest technical invention, the continuously
revolving wheel. (It is this fact, no doubt, which accounts for
the boredom, weariness and apathy of those who, in modern
factories, are forced to adapt their bodily and mental movements to circular motions of mechanically uniform velocity.)
'What a man takes in by contemplation,' says Eckhart, 'that
he pours out in love.' The well-meaning humanist and the
merely muscular Christian, who imagines that he can obey the
second of the great commandments without taking time even
to think how best he may love God with all his heart, soul and
mind, are people engaged in the impossible task of pouring
unceasingly from a container that is never replenished.

Daughters of Charity ought to love prayer as the body loves the
soul. And just as the body cannot live without the soul, so the
soul cannot live without prayer. And in so far as a daughter
prays as she ought to pray, she will do well. She will not walk,
she will run in the ways of the Lord, and will be raised to a high
degree of the love of God.

St. Vincent de Paul

Households, cities, countries and nations have enjoyed great happiness, when a single individual has taken heed of the Good and Beautiful. . . . Such men not only liberate themselves; they fill those they meet with a free mind.

Philo

Similar views are expressed by Al-Ghazzali, who regards the mystics not only as the ultimate source of our knowledge of the soul and its capacities and defects, but as the salt which preserves human societies from decay. 'In the time of the philosophers,' he writes, 'as at every other period, there existed some of these fervent mystics. God does not deprive this world of them, for they are its sustainers.' It is they who, dying to themselves, become capable of perpetual inspiration and so are made the instruments through which divine grace is mediated to those whose unregenerate nature is impervious to the delicate touches of the Spirit.

A LIST OF RECOMMENDED BOOKS

AL-GHAZZALI. *Confessions.* Translated by Claud Field (London, 1909).

ANSARI OF HERAT. *The Invocations of Sheikh Abdullah Ansari of Herat.* Translated by Sardar Sir Jogendra Singh (London, 1939).

ATTAR. *Selections.* Translated by Margaret Smith (London, 1932).

AUGUSTINE, ST. *Confessions* (numerous editions).

AUROBINDO, SRI. *The Life Divine,* 3 vols. (Calcutta, 1939).

BAKER, AUGUSTINE. *Holy Wisdom* (London, 1876).

BEAUSOBRE, JULIA DE. *The Woman Who Could Not Die* (London and New York, 1938).

BERNARD OF CLAIRVAUX, ST. *The Steps of Humility* (Cambridge, Mass., 1940).
On the Love of God (New York, 1937).
Selected Letters (London, 1904). An admirably lucid account of St. Bernard's thought may be found in *The Mystical Doctrine of Saint Bernard,* by Professor Étienne Gilson (London and New York, 1940).

BERTOCCI, PETER A. *The Empirical Argument for God in Late British Philosophy* (Cambridge, Mass., 1938).

Bhagavad-Gita. Among many translations of this Hindu scripture the best, from a literary point of view, is that of Swami Prabhavananda and Christopher Isherwood (Los Angeles, 1944). Valuable notes, based upon the commentaries of Shankara, are to be found in Swami Nikhilananda's edition (New York, 1944), and Professor Franklin Edgerton's literal translation (Cambridge, Mass., 1944) is preceded by a long and scholarly introduction.

BINYON, L. *The Flight of the Dragon* (London, 1911).

BOEHME, JAKOB. Some good introduction is needed to the work of this important but difficult mystic. On the theological and devotional side the Danish Bishop H. L. Martensen's *Jacob Boehme* (trans., London, 1885) is recommended; or from a more philosophical viewpoint A. Koyré's splendid volume *La Philosophie de Jacob Boehme* (not yet translated, Paris, 1929) or H. H. Brinton's *The Mystic Will* (New York, 1930).

BRAHMANANDA, SWAMI. Records of his teaching and a biography by Swami Prabhavananda are contained in *The Eternal Companion* (Los Angeles, 1944).

CAMUS, JEAN PIERRE. *The Spirit of St. François de Sales* (London, n.d.).

CAUSSADE, J. P. DE. *Abandonment* (New York, 1887).
Spiritual Letters, 3 vols. (London, 1937).

CHANTAL, ST. JEANNE FRANÇOISE. *Selected Letters* (London and New York, 1918).

CHAPMAN, ABBOT JOHN. *Spiritual Letters* (London, 1935).

CHUANG TZU. *Chuang Tzu, Mystic, Moralist and Social Reformer*. Translated by Herbert Giles (Shanghai, 1936).
Musings of a Chinese Mystic (London, 1920).
Chinese Philosophy in Classical Times. Translated by E. R. Hughes (London, 1943).

The Cloud of Unknowing (with commentary by Augustine Baker). Edited with an introduction by Justice McCann (London, 1924).

COOMARASWAMY, ANANDA K. *Buddha and the Gospel of Buddhism* (New York, 1916).
The Transformation of Nature in Art (Cambridge, Mass., 1935).
Hinduism and Buddhism (New York, n.d.).

CURTIS, A. M. *The Way of Silence* (Burton Bradstock, Dorset, 1937).

DEUSSEN, PAUL. *The Philosophy of the Upanishads* (London, 1906).

DIONYSIUS THE AREOPAGITE. *On the Divine Names and the Mystical Theology*. Translated with an introduction by C. E. Rolt (London, 1920).

ECKHART, MEISTER. *Works*, translated by C. B. Evans (London, 1924).
Meister Eckhart, A Modern Translation. By R. B. Blakney (New York, 1941).

EVANS-WENTZ, W. Y. *The Tibetan Book of the Dead* (New York, 1927).
Tibet's Great Yogi, Milarepa (New York, 1928).
Tibetan Yoga and Secret Doctrines (New York, 1935).

The Following of Christ. Unknown author, but mistakenly attributed to Tauler in the first English edition (London, 1886).

FOX, GEORGE. *Journal* (London, 1911).

FROST, BEDE. *The Art of Mental Prayer* (London, 1940).
Saint John of the Cross (London, 1937).

GARRIGOU-LAGRANGE, R. *Christian Perfection and Contemplation* (London and St. Louis, 1937).

GODDARD, DWIGHT. *A Buddhist Bible* (published by the editor, Thetford, Maine, 1938). This volume contains translations of several Mahayana texts not to be found, or to be found only with much difficulty, elsewhere. Among these are 'The Diamond Sutra,' 'The Surangama Sutra,' 'The Lankavatara Sutra,' 'The Awakening of Faith' and 'The Sutra of the Sixth Patriarch.'

GUÉNON, RENÉ. *Man and His Becoming according to the Vedanta* (London, n.d.).
East and West (London, 1941).
The Crisis of the Modern World (London, 1942).

HEARD, GERALD. *The Creed of Christ* (New York, 1940).
The Code of Christ (New York, 1941).
Preface to Prayer (New York, 1944).

HILTON, WALTER. *The Scale of Perfection* (London, 1927).

HUEGEL, FRIEDRICH VON. *The Mystical Element in Religion as Studied in Saint Catherine of Genoa and Her Friends* (London, 1923).

IBN TUFAIL. *The Awakening of the Soul.* Translated by Paul Bronnle (London, 1910).

The Imitation of Christ. Whitford's translation, edited by E. J. Klein (New York, 1941).

INGE, W. R. *Christian Mysticism* (London, 1899).
Studies of English Mystics—including William Law (London, 1906).

JOHN OF THE CROSS, ST. *Works,* 3 vols. (London, 1934-1935).

JONES, RUFUS. *Studies in Mystical Religion.*
The Spiritual Reformers in the 16th and 17th Centuries (New York, 1914).
The Flowering of Mysticism (New York, 1939).

JORGENSEN, JOHANNES. *Saint Catherine of Siena* (London, 1938).

JULIANA OF NORWICH. *Revelations of Divine Love* (London, 1917).

LAO TZU. There are many translations of the Tao Teh King. Consult and compare those of Arthur Waley in *The Way and Its Power* (London, 1933), of F. R. Hughes in *Chinese Philosophy in Classical Times* (Everyman's Library) and of Ch'u Ta-Kao (London, 1927) reprinted in *The Bible of the World* (New York, 1939).

LAW, WILLIAM. Several modern editions of his *Serious Call* are available. But none of Law's still finer and much more distinctly mystical works, such as *The Spirit of Prayer* and *The Spirit of Love,* have been reprinted in full in recent years. Long extracts from them may however be found in Stephen Hobhouse's *Selected Mystical Writings of William Law* (London, 1939) (a work which also contains some useful 'Notes and Studies in the mystical theology of William Law and Jacob Boehme') and in the same writer's *William Law and Eighteenth Century Quakerism* (London, 1927). Alexander Whyte also compiled a fine anthology, *Characters and Characteristics of William Law* (4th ed. London, 1907); while for the student there is Christopher Walton's extraordinary encyclopaedic collection of *Notes and Materials for an adequate biography of William Law* (London, 1856).

Leen, Edward. *Progress through Mental Prayer* (London, 1940).

McKeon, Richard. Selections from Medieval Philosophers, 2 vols. (New York, 1929).

The Mirror of Simple Souls. Author unknown (London, 1927).

Nicholas of Cusa. *The Idiot* (San Francisco, 1940).
The Vision of God (London and New York, 1928).

Nicholson, R. *The Mystics of Islam* (London, 1914).

Oman, John. *The Natural and the Supernatural* (London, 1938).

Otto, Rudolf. *India's Religion of Grace* (London, 1930).
Mysticism East and West (London, 1932).

Patanjali. *Yoga Aphorisms.* Translated with a commentary by Swami Vivekananda (New York, 1899).

Plotinus. *The Essence of Plotinus* (G. H. Turnbull, New York, 1934). A good anthology of this very important and voluminous mystic.

Ponnelle, L. and L. Bordet. *St. Philip Neri and the Roman Society of His Time* (London, 1932).

Poulain, A. *The Graces of Interior Prayer* (London, 1910).

Pourrat, P. *Christian Spirituality*, 3 vols. (London, 1922).

Pratt, J. B. *The Pilgrimage of Buddhism* (New York, 1928).

Quakers. *The Beginnings of Quakerism*, by W. P. Braithwaite (London, 1912). See also George Fox, p. 348.

Radhakrishnan, S. *The Hindu View of Life* (London and New York, 1927).
Indian Philosophy (London and New York, 1923-1927).
Eastern Religions and Western Thought (New York, 1939).

Ramakrishna, Sri. *The Gospel of Sri Ramakrishna.* Translated from the Bengali narrative of 'M' by Swami Nikhilananda (New York, 1942).

Rumi, Jalal-uddin. *Masnavi.* Translated by E. H. Whinfield (London, 1898).

RUYSBROECK, JAN VAN. *The Adornment of the Spiritual Marriage* (London, 1916). Consult also the studies by Evelyn Underhill (London, 1915) and Wautier d'Aygalliers (London, 1925).

SALES, ST. FRANÇOIS DE. *Introduction to the Devout Life* (numerous editions).
　Treatise on the Love of God (new edition, Westminster, Md., 1942).
　Spiritual Conferences (London, 1868).
　See also J. P. Camus.

The Secret of the Golden Flower. Translated from the Chinese by Richard Wilhelm. Commentary by Dr. C. G. Jung (London and New York, 1931).

SPURGEON, CAROLINE. *Mysticism in English Literature* (Cambridge, 1913).

STOCKS, J. L. *Time, Cause and Eternity* (London, 1938).

STOUT, G. F. *Mind and Matter* (London, 1931).

Sutra Spoken by the Sixth Patriarch, Hui Neng. Translated by Wung Mou-lam (Shanghai, 1930). Reprinted in *A Buddhist Bible* (Thetford, 1938).

SUZUKI, B. L. *Mahayana Buddhism* (London, 1938).

SUZUKI, D. T. *Studies in Zen Buddhism* (London, 1927).
　Studies in the Lankavatara Sutra (Kyoto and London, 1935).
　Manual of Zen Buddhism (Kyoto, 1935).

TAGORE, RABINDRANATH. *One Hundred Poems of Kabir* (London, 1915).

TAULER, JOHANN. *Life and Sermons* (London, 1907).
　The Inner Way (London, 1909).
　Consult Inge's *Christian Mysticism*, Rufus Jones's *Studies in Mystical Religion* and Pourrat's *Christian Spirituality*.

TENNANT, F. R. *Philosophical Theology* (Cambridge, 1923).

Theologia Germanica. Winkworth's translation (new edition, London, 1937).

TILLYARD, AELFRIDA. *Spiritual Exercises* (London, 1927).

TRAHERNE, THOMAS. *Centuries of Meditation* (London, 1908).
Consult *Thomas Traherne, A Critical Biography*, by Gladys I.
Wade (Princeton, 1944).

UNDERHILL, EVELYN. *Mysticism* (London, 1924).
The Mystics of the Church (London, 1925).

Upanishads. *The Thirteen Principal Upanishads.* Translated by
R. E. Hume (New York, 1931).
The Ten Principal Upanishads. Translated by Shree Purohit
and W. B. Yeats (London, 1937).
The Himalayas of the Soul. Translated by J. Mascaro (London,
1938).

WATTS, ALAN W. *The Spirit of Zen* (London, 1936).

WHITNEY, JANET. *John Woolman, American Quaker* (Boston,
1942).
Elizabeth Fry, Quaker Heroine (Boston, 1936).

INDEX

Printed in Great Britain
at Hopetoun Street, Edinburgh,
by T. and A. CONSTABLE LTD.
Printers to the University of Edinburgh